JOHN SANDFORD

THREE COMPLETE NOVELS

ALSO BY JOHN SANDFORD

JOHN SANDFORD

THREE COMPLETE NOVELS

MIND PREY

———

SUDDEN PREY

———

SECRET PREY

G. P. PUTNAM'S SONS

New York

Mind Prey copyright © 1995 by John Sandford
Sudden Prey copyright © 1996 by John Sandford
Secret Prey copyright © 1998 by John Sandford
All rights reserved. This book, or parts thereof, may not
be reproduced in any form without permission.
Published simultaneously in Canada

G. P. PUTNAM'S SONS
Publishers Since 1838
a member of
Penguin Putnam Inc.
375 Hudson Street
New York, NY 10014

Library of Congress Cataloging-in-Publication Data

Sandford, John, date.
[Novels. Selections]
Three complete novels : Mind prey, Sudden prey, Secret prey / John Sandford.
p.   cm.
ISBN 0-399-14651-2
1. Davenport, Lucas (Fictitious character)—Fiction.
2. Private investigators—Minnesota—Minneapolis—Fiction.
3. Detective and mystery stories, American.
4. Minneapolis (Minn.)—Fiction.   I. Title.
PS3569.A516 A6   2000   00-044562
813'.54—dc21

Printed in the United States of America

1   3   5   7   9   10   8   6   4   2

Book design by Julie Duquet

CONTENTS

MIND PREY

1

T HE STORM BLEW up late in the afternoon, tight, gray clouds
hustling over the lake like dirty, balled-up sweat socks spilling from a basket.
A chilly wind knocked leaves from the elms, oaks, and maples at the water's
edge. The white phlox and black-eyed Susans bowed their heads before it.

The end of summer; too soon.

John Mail walked down the floating dock at Irv's Boat Works, through the
scents of premix gasoline, dead, drying minnows and moss, the old man trailing
behind with his hands in the pockets of his worn gabardines. John Mail didn't
know about old-style machinery—chokes, priming bulbs, carburetors, all that.
He knew diodes and resistors, the strengths of one chip and the weaknesses of
another. But in Minnesota, boat lore is considered part of the genetic pattern:
he had no trouble renting a fourteen-foot Lund with a 9.9 Johnson outboard.
A driver's license and a twenty-dollar deposit were all he needed at Irv's.

Mail stepped down into the boat, and with an open hand wiped a film of
water from the bench seat and sat down. Irv squatted beside the boat and
showed him how to start the motor and kill it, how to steer it and accelerate.
The lesson took thirty seconds. Then John Mail, with his cheap Zebco rod and
reel and empty, red-plastic tackle box, put out on Lake Minnetonka.

"Back before dark," Irv hollered after him. The white-haired man stood on
the dock and watched John Mail putter away.

When Mail left Irv's dock, the sky was clear, the air limpid and summery,
if a little nervous in the west. Something was coming, he thought. Something
was hiding below the treeline. But no matter. This was just a look, just a taste.

He followed the shoreline east and north for three miles. Big houses were
elbow to elbow, millions of dollars' worth of stone and brick with manicured
lawns running down to the water. Professionally tended flower beds were stuck
on the lawns like postage stamps, with faux-cobblestone walks snaking between
them. Stone swans and plaster ducks paddled across the grass.

Everything looked different from the water side. Mail thought he'd gone too
far, but he still hadn't picked out the house. He stopped and went back, then
circled. Finally, much further north than he thought it would be, he spotted
the weird-looking tower house, a local landmark. And down the shore, one-
two-three, yes, there it was, stone, glass and cedar, red shingles, and, barely
visible on the far side of the roof, the tips of the huge blue spruces that lined

the street. A bed of petunias, large swirls of red, white, and blue, glowed patriotically from the top of a flagstone wall set into the slope of the lawn. An open cruiser crouched on a boat lift next to the floating dock.

Mail killed the outboard, and let the boat drift to a stop. The storm was still below the trees, the wind was dying down. He picked up the fishing rod, pulled line off the reel and threaded it through the guides and out the tip. Then he took a handful of line and threw it overboard, hookless and weightless. The rat's-nest of monofilament drifted on the surface, but that was good enough. He *looked* like he was fishing.

Settling on the hard bench seat, Mail hunched his shoulders and watched the house. Nothing moved. After a few minutes, he began to manufacture fantasies.

He was good at this: a specialist, in a way. There were times when he'd been locked up as punishment, was allowed no books, no games, no TV. A claustrophobic—and they knew he was claustrophobic, that was part of the punishment—he'd escaped into fantasy to preserve his mind, sat on his bunk and turned to the blank facing wall and played his own mind-films, dancing dreams of sex and fire.

Andi Manette starred in the early mind-films; fewer later on, almost none in the past two years. He'd almost forgotten her. Then the calls came, and she was back.

Andi Manette. Her perfume could arouse the dead. She had a long, slender body, with a small waist and large, pale breasts, a graceful neckline, when seen from the back with her dark hair up over her small ears.

Mail stared at the water, eyes open, fishing rod drooping over the gunwales, and watched, in his mind, as she walked across a dark chamber toward him, peeling off a silken robe. He smiled. When he touched her, her flesh was warm, and smooth, unblemished. He could feel her on his fingertips. "Do this," he'd say, out loud; and then he'd giggle. "Down here," he'd say . . .

He sat for an hour, for two, talking occasionally, then he sighed and shivered, and woke from the daydream. The world had changed.

The sky was gray, angry, the low clouds rolling in. A wind whipped around the boat, blowing the rat's-nest of monofilament across the water like a tumbleweed. Across the fattest part of the lake, he could see the breaking curl of a whitecap.

Time to go.

He reached back to crank the outboard and saw her. She stood in the bay window, wearing a white dress—though she was three hundred yards away, he knew the figure, and the unique, attentive stillness. He could feel the eye contact. Andi Manette was psychic. She could look right into your brain and say the words you were trying to hide.

John Mail looked away, to protect himself.

So she wouldn't know he was coming.

————

ANDI MANETTE STOOD in the bay window and watched the rain sweep across the water toward the house, and the darkness coming behind. At the concave drop of the lawn, at the water's edge, the tall heads of the white phlox bobbed in the wind. They'd be gone by the weekend. Beyond them, a lone fisherman sat in one of the orange-tipped rental boats from Irv's. He'd been out there since five o'clock and, as far as she could tell, hadn't caught a thing. She could've told him that the bottom was mostly sterile muck, that she'd never caught a fish from the dock.

As she watched, he turned to start the outboard. Andi had been around boats all of her life, and something about the way the man moved suggested that he didn't know about outboards—how to sit down and crank at the same time.

When he turned toward her, she felt his eyes—and thought, ridiculously, that she might know him. He was so far away that she couldn't even make out the shape of his face. But still, the total package—head, eyes, shoulders, movement—seemed familiar . . .

Then he yanked the starter cord again, and a few seconds later he was on his way down the shoreline, one hand holding his hat on his head, the other hand on the outboard tiller. He'd never seen her, she thought. The rain swept in behind him.

And she thought: the clouds come in, the leaves falling down.

The end of summer.

Too soon.

ANDI STEPPED AWAY from the window and moved through the living room, turning on the lamps. The room was furnished with warmth and a sure touch: heavy country couches and chairs, craftsman tables, lamps and rugs. A hint of Shaker there in the corner, lots of natural wood and fabric, subdued, but with a subtle, occasionally bold, touch of color—a flash of red in the rug that went with the antique maple table, a streak of blue that hinted of the sky outside the bay windows.

The house, always warm in the past, felt cold with George gone.

With what George had done.

George was movement and intensity and argument, and even a sense of protection, with his burliness and aggression, his tough face, intelligent eyes. Now . . . this.

Andi was a slender woman, tall, dark-haired, unconsciously dignified. She often seemed posed, although she was unaware of it. Her limbs simply fell into arrangements, her head cocked for a portrait. Her hair-do and pearl earrings said horses and sailboats and vacations in Greece.

She couldn't help it. She wouldn't change it if she could.

With the living room lights cutting the growing gloom, Andi climbed the stairs, to get the girls organized: first day of school, clothes to choose, early to bed.

At the top of the stairs, she started right, toward the girls' room—then heard the tinny music of a bad movie coming from the opposite direction.

They were watching television in the master bedroom suite. As she walked down the hall, she heard the sudden disconnect of a channel change. By the time she got to the bedroom, the girls were engrossed in a CNN newscast, with a couple of talking heads rambling on about the Consumer Price Index.

"Hi, Mom," Genevieve said cheerfully. And Grace looked up and smiled, a bit too pleased to see her.

"Hi," Andi said. She looked around. "Where's the remote?"

Grace said, unconcernedly, "Over on the bed."

The remote was a long way from either of the girls, halfway across the room in the middle of the bedspread. Hastily thrown, Andi thought. She picked it up, said, "Excuse me," and backtracked through the channels. On one of the premiums, she found a clinch scene, fully nude, still in progress.

"You guys," she said, reproachfully.

"It's good for us," the younger one protested, not bothering with denials. "We gotta find things out."

"This is not the way to do it," Andi said, punching out the channel. "Come talk to me." She looked at Grace, but her older daughter was looking away— a little angry, maybe, and embarrassed. "Come on," Andi said. "Let's everybody organize our school stuff and take our baths."

"We're talking like a doctor again, Mom," Grace said.

"Sorry."

On the way down to the girls' bedrooms, Genevieve blurted, "God, that guy was really hung."

After a second of shocked silence, Grace started to giggle, and two seconds later Andi started, and five seconds after that all three of them sprawled on the carpet in the hallway, laughing until the tears ran down their faces.

THE RAIN FELL steadily through the night, stopped for a few hours in the morning, then started again.

Andi got the girls on the bus, arrived at work ten minutes early, and worked efficiently through her patient list, listening carefully, smiling encouragement, occasionally talking with some intensity. To a woman who could not escape thoughts of suicide; to another who felt she was male, trapped in a female body; to a man who was obsessed by a need to control the smallest details of his family's life—he knew he was wrong but couldn't stop.

At noon, she walked two blocks out to a deli and brought a bag lunch back for herself and her partner. They spent the lunch hour talking about Social Security and worker compensation taxes with the bookkeeper.

In the afternoon, a bright spot: a police officer, deeply bound by the million threads of chronic depression, seemed to be responding to new medication. He was a dour, pasty-faced man who reeked of nicotine, but today he smiled shyly at her and said, "My God, this was my best week in five years: I was looking at women."

ANDI LEFT THE office early, and drove through an annoying, mud-producing drizzle to the west side of the loop, to the rambling, white New England cottages and green playing fields of the Birches School. Hard maples boxed the school parking lot; flames of red autumn color were stitched through their lush crowns. Toward the school entrance, a grove of namesake birch had gone a sunny gold, a brilliant greeting on a dismal day.

Andi left the car in the parking lot and hurried inside, the warm smell of a soaking rain hanging like a fog over the wet asphalt.

The teacher-parent conferences were routine—Andi went to them every year, the first day of school: meet the teachers, smile at everyone, agree to work on the Thanksgiving pageant, write a check to the strings program. *So looking forward to working with Grace, she's a very bright child, active, school leader, blah blah blah.*

She was happy to go to them. Always happy when they were over.

WHEN THEY WERE done, she and the girls walked back outside and found the rain had intensified, hissing down from the crazy sky. "I'll tell you what, Mom," Grace said, as they stood in the school's covered entry, watching a woman with a broken umbrella scurry down the sidewalk. Grace was often very serious when talking with adults. "I'm in a very good dress, and it's barely wrinkled, so I could wear it again. Why don't you get the car and pick me up here?"

"All right." No point in all of them getting wet.

"I'm not afraid of the rain," Genevieve said, pugnaciously. "Let's go."

"Why don't you wait with Grace?" Andi asked.

"Nah. Grace is just afraid to get wet 'cause she'll melt, the old witch," Genevieve said.

Grace caught her sister's eye and made a pinching sign with her thumb and forefinger.

"Mom," Genevieve wailed.

"Grace," Andi said, reprovingly.

"Tonight, when you're almost asleep," Grace muttered. She knew how to deal with her sister.

At twelve, Grace was the older and by far the taller of the two, gawky, but beginning to show the curves of adolescence. She was a serious girl, almost solemn, as though expecting imminent unhappiness. Someday a doctor.

Genevieve, on the other hand, was competitive, frivolous, loud. Almost too pretty. Even at nine, everyone said, it was obvious that she'd be a trial to the boys. To whole flocks of boys. But that was years away. Now she was sitting on the concrete, messing with the sole of her tennis shoe, peeling the bottom layer off.

"Gen," Andi said.

"It's gonna come off anyway," Genevieve said, not looking up. "I told you I needed new shoes."

A man in a raincoat hurried up the walk, hatless, head bowed in the rain. David Girdler, who called himself a psychotherapist and who was active in the Parent-Teacher Cooperative. He was a boring man, given to pronunciations about *proper roles in life,* and *hard-wired behavior.* There were rumors that he used tarot cards in his work. He fawned on Andi. "Dr. Manette," he said, nodding, slowing. "Nasty day."

"Yes," Andi said. But her breeding wouldn't let her stop so curtly, even with a man she disliked. "It's supposed to rain all night again."

"That's what I hear," Girdler said. "Say, did you see this month's *Therapodist?* There's an article on the structure of recovered memory . . ."

He rambled on for a moment, Andi smiling automatically, then Genevieve interrupted, loudly, "Mom, we're super-late," and Andi said, "We've really got to go, David," and then, because of the breeding, "But I'll be sure to look it up."

"Sure, nice talking to you," Girdler said.

When he'd gone inside, Genevieve said, looking after him, from the corner of her mouth like Bogart, "What do we say, Mom?"

"Thank you, Gen," Andi said, smiling.

"You're welcome, Mom."

"OKAY," ANDI SAID. "I'll run for it." She looked down the parking lot. A red van had parked on the driver's side of her car and she'd have to run around the back of it.

"I'm coming, too," Genevieve said.

"I get the front," Grace said.

"I get the front . . ."

"You got the front on the way over, beetle," Grace said.

"Mom, she called me . . ."

Grace made the pinching sign again, and Andi said, "You get in the back, Gen. You had the front on the way over."

"Or I'll pinch you," Grace added.

They half-ran through the rain, Andi in her low heels, Genevieve with her still-short legs, holding hands. Andi released Gen's hand as they crossed behind the Econoline van. She pointed her key at the car and pushed the electronic lock button, heard the locks pop up over the hissing of the rain.

Head bent, she hurried down between the van and the car, Gen a step behind her, and reached for the door handles.

ANDI HEARD THE doors slide on the van behind her; felt the presence of the man, the motion. Automatically began to smile, turning.

Heard Genevieve grunt, turned and saw the strange round head coming for her, the mop of dirty blond hair.

Saw the road-map lines buried in a face much too young for them.

Saw the teeth, and the spit, and the hands like clubs.

Andi screamed, "Run."

And the man hit her in the face.

She saw the blow coming but was unable to turn away. The impact smashed her against her car door, and she slid down it, her knees going out.

She didn't feel the blow as pain, only as impact, the fist on her face, the car on her back. She felt the man turning, felt blood on her skin, smelled the worms of the pavement as she hit it, the rough, wet blacktop on the palms of her hand, thought crazily—for just the torn half of an instant—about ruining her suit, felt the man step away.

She tried to scream "Run" again, but the word came out as a groan, and she felt—maybe saw, maybe not—the man moving on Genevieve, and she tried to scream again, to say something, anything, and blood bubbled out of her nose and the pain hit her, a blinding, wrenching pain like fire on her face.

And in the distance, she heard Genevieve scream, and she tried to push up. A hand pulled at her coat, lifting her, and she flew through the air, to crash against a sheet of metal. She rolled again, facedown, tried to get her knees beneath her, and heard a car door slam.

Half-sensible, Andi rolled, eyes wild, saw Genevieve in a heap, and bloody from head to toe. She reach out to her daughter, who sat up, eyes bright. Andi tried to stop her, then realized that it wasn't blood that stained her red, it was something else: and Genevieve, inches away, screamed, "Momma, you're bleeding . . ."

Van, she thought.

They were in the van. She figured that out, pulled herself to her knees, and was thrown back down as the van screeched out of the parking place.

Grace will see us, she thought.

She struggled up again, and again was knocked down, this time as the van swung left and braked. The driver's door opened and light flooded in, and she heard a shout, and the doors opened on the side of the truck, and Grace came headlong through the opening, landing on Genevieve, her white dress stained the same rusty red as the truck.

The doors slammed again; and the van roared out of the parking lot.

Andi got to her knees, arms flailing, trying to make sense of it: Grace screaming, Genevieve wailing, the red stuff all over them.

And she knew from the smell and taste of it that she *was* bleeding. She turned and saw the bulk of the man in the driver's seat behind a chain-link mesh. She shouted at him, "Stop, stop it. Stop it," but the driver paid no attention, took a corner, took another.

"Momma, I'm hurt," Genevieve said. Andi turned back to her daughters, who were on their hands and knees. Grace had a sad, hound-dog look on her face; she'd known this man would come for her someday.

Andi looked at the van doors, for a way out, but metal plates had been screwed over the spot where the handles must've been. She rolled back and kicked at the door with all her strength, but the door wouldn't budge. She kicked again, and again, her long legs lashing out. Then Grace kicked and Genevieve kicked and nothing moved, and Genevieve began screeching, screeching. Andi kicked until she felt faint from the effort, and she said to Grace, panting, three or four times, "We've got to get out, we've got to get out, get out, get out . . ."

And the man in the front seat began to laugh, a loud, carnival-ride laughter that rolled over Genevieve's screams; the laughter eventually silenced them and they saw his eyes in the rearview mirror and he said, "You won't get out. I made sure of that. I know all about doors without handles."

That was the first time they'd heard his voice, and the girls shrank back from it. Andi swayed to her feet, crouched under the low roof, realized that she'd lost her shoes—and her purse. Her purse was there on the passenger seat, in front. How had it gotten there? She tried to steady herself by clinging to the mesh screen, and kicked at the side window. Her heel connected and the glass cracked.

The van swerved to the side, braking, and the man in front turned, violent anger in his voice, and held up a black .45 and said, "You break my fuckin' window and I'll kill the fuckin' kids."

She could only see the side of his face, but suddenly thought: I know him. But he looks different. From where? Where? Andi sank back to the floor of the van and the man in front turned back to the wheel and then pulled away from the curb, muttering, "Break my fuckin' window? Break my fuckin' window?"

"Who are you?" Andi asked.

That seemed to make him even angrier. *Who was he?* "John," he said harshly.

"John *who?* What do you want?"

John Who? John the Fuck Who? "You know John the Fuck Who."

Grace was bleeding from her nose, her eyes wild; Genevieve was huddled in the corner, and Andi said again, helplessly, "John who?"

He looked over his shoulder, a spark of hate in his eyes, reached up and pulled a blond wig off his head.

Andi, a half-second later, said, "Oh, no. No. Not John Mail."

2

THE RAIN WAS cold, but more of an irritant than a hazard. If it had come two months later, it would've been a killer blizzard, and they'd be wading shin-deep in snow and ice. Marcy Sherrill had done that often enough and didn't like it: you got weird, ugly phenomena like blood-bergs, or worse. Rain, no matter how cold, tended to clean things up. Sherrill looked up at the night sky and thought, *small blessings.*

Sherrill stood in the headlights of the crime-scene truck, her hands in her raincoat pockets, looking at the feet of the man on the ground. The feet were sticking out from under the rear door of a creme-colored Lexus with real leather seats. Every few seconds, the feet gave a convulsive jerk.

"What're you doing, Hendrix?" she asked.

The man under the car said something unintelligible.

Sherrill's partner bent over so the man under the car could hear him. "I think he said, 'Chokin' the chicken.'" The rain dribbled off his hat, just past the tip of a perfectly dry cigarette. He waited for a reaction from the guy on the ground—a born-again Christian—but got none. "Fuckin' dweeb," he muttered, straightening up.

"I wish this shit'd stop," Sherrill said. She looked up at the sky again. The *National Enquirer* would like it, she thought. This was a sky that might produce an image of Satan. The ragged storm clouds churned through the lights from the loop, picking up the ugly scarlet flicker from the cop cars.

Down the street, past the line of cop cars, TV trucks squatted patiently in the rain, and reporters stood in the street around them, looking down at Sherrill and the cops by the Lexus. Those would be the cameramen and the pencil press. The talent would be sitting in the trucks, keeping their makeup straight.

Sherrill shivered and turned her head down and wiped the water from her eyebrows. She'd had a rain cap, once, but she'd lost it at some other crime scene with drizzle or sleet or snow or hail or . . . Everything dripped on her sooner or later.

"Shoulda brought a hat," her partner said. His name was Tom Black, and he was not quite openly gay. "Or an umbrella."

They'd once had an umbrella, too, but they'd lost it. Or, more likely, it had been stolen by another cop who knew a nice umbrella when he saw it. So now Sherrill had the icy rain dripping down her neck, and she was pissed because it was six-thirty and she was still working while her goddamn husband was down at Applebee's entertaining the barmaid with his rapierlike wit.

And more pissed because Black was dry and snug, and she was wet, and he hadn't offered her the hat, even though she was a woman.

And even more pissed knowing that if he had offered, she'd have had to turn it down, because she was one of only two women in the Homicide Unit and she still felt like she had to prove that she could handle herself, even though she'd been handling herself for a dozen years now, in uniform and plainclothes, doing decoy work, undercover drugs, sex, and now Homicide.

"Hendrix," she said, "I wanna get out of this fuckin' rain, man . . ."

From the street, a car decelerated with a deepening groan, and Sherrill looked over Black's shoulder and said, "Uh-oh." A black Porsche 911 paused at the curb, where the uniforms had set up their line. Two of the TV cameras lit up to film the car, and one of the cops pointed at the crime van. The Porsche snapped down the drive toward the parking lot, quick, like a weasel or a rubber band.

"Davenport," Black said, turning to look. Black was short, slightly round, and carried a bulbous nose over a brush mustache. He was exceedingly calm at all times, except when he was talking about the President of the United States, whom he referred to as *that socialist shithead,* or, occasionally, *that fascist motherfucker,* depending on his mood.

"Bad news," Sherrill said. A little stream of water ran off her hair and unerringly down her spine. She straightened and shivered. She was a tall, slender woman with a long nose, kinky black hair, soft breasts, and a secret, satisfying knowledge of her high desirability rating around the department.

"Mmmm," Black said. Then, "You ever get in his shorts? Davenport's?"

"Of course not," Sherrill said. Black had an exaggerated idea of her sexual history. "I never tried."

"If you're gonna try, you better do it," Black said laconically. "He's getting married."

"Yeah?"

The Porsche parked sideways on some clearly painted parking-space lines and the door popped open as its lights died.

"That's what I heard," Black said. He flicked the butt of his cigarette into the grass bank just off the parking lot.

"He'd be nine miles of bad road," Sherrill said.

"Mike's a fuckin' freeway, huh?" Mike was Sherrill's husband.

"I can handle Mike," Sherrill said. "I wonder what Davenport . . ."

There was a sudden brilliant flash of light, and the feet sticking out from under the car convulsed. Hendrix said, "Goldarnit."

Sherrill looked down. "What? Hendrix?"

"I almost electrocuted myself," said the man under the car. "This rain is a . . . pain in the behind."

"Yeah, well, watch your language," Black said. "There's a lady present."

"I'm sorry." The voice was sincere, in a muffled way.

"Get out of there, and give us the fuckin' shoe," Sherrill said. She kicked a foot.

"Darn it. Don't do that. I'm trying to get a picture."

Sherrill looked back across the parking lot. Davenport was walking down toward them, long smooth strides, like a professional jock, his hands in his coat pockets, the coat flapping around his legs. He looked like a big broad-shouldered mobster, a Mafia guy with an expensive mohair suit and bullet scars, she thought, like in a New York movie.

Or maybe he was an Indian or a Spaniard. Then you saw those pale blue eyes and the mean smile. She shivered again. "He does give off a certain"—Sherrill groped for a word—"pulse."

"You got that," Black said calmly.

Sherrill had a sudden image of Black and Davenport in bed together, lots of shoulder hair and rude parts. She smiled, just a crinkle. Black, who could read her mind, said, "Fuck you, honey."

DEPUTY CHIEF LUCAS Davenport's trench coat had a roll-out hood like a parka, and he'd rolled it out, and as he crossed the lot, he pulled it over his head like a monk; he was as dry and snug as Black. Sherrill was about to say something when he handed her a khaki tennis hat. "Put this on," he said gruffly.

"What're we doing?"

"There's a shoe under the car," Sherrill said as she pulled the cap on. With the rain out of her face, she instantly felt better. "There was another one in the lot. She must've got hit pretty hard to get knocked out of her shoes."

"Real hard," Black agreed.

Lucas was a tall man with heavy shoulders and a boxer's hands, large, square, and battered. His face reflected his hands: a fighter's face, with those startling blue eyes. A white scar, thin like a razor rip, slashed down his forehead and across his right eye socket, showing up against his dark complexion. Another scar, round, puckered, hung on his throat like a flattened wad of bubble gum—a bullet hole and jack-knife tracheotomy scar, just now going white. He crouched next to the feet under the car and said, "Get out of there, Hendrix."

"Yes, yes, another minute. You can't have the shoe, though. There's blood on it."

"Well, hurry it up," Lucas said. He stood up.

"You talk to Girdler?" Sherrill asked.

"Who's that?"

"A witness," she said. She was wearing the good perfume, the Obsession, and suddenly thought of it with a tinkle of pleasure.

Lucas shook his head. "I was out in Stillwater. At dinner. People called me every five minutes on the way in, to tell me about the politics. That's all I know—I don't know anything about what you guys got."

Black said, "The woman . . ."

". . . Manette," said Lucas.

"Yeah, Manette and her daughters, Grace and Genevieve, were leaving the school after a parent-teacher conference. The mother and one kid were picked up in a red van. We don't know exactly how—if they were tear-gassed, or strong-armed, or shot. We just don't know. However it was done, it must have been a few seconds before the second daughter was taken off the porch over there." Black pointed back toward the school. "We think what happened was, the mother and Genevieve ran out to the car in the rain, were grabbed. The older daughter was waiting to get picked up, and then she was snatched."

"Why didn't she run?" Lucas asked.

"We don't know," Sherrill said. "Maybe it was somebody she knew."

"Where were the witnesses?"

"Inside the school. One of them is an adult, a shrink of some kind, one was a kid. A student. They only saw the last part of it, when Grace Manette was grabbed. But they say the mother was still alive, on her hands and knees in the van, but she had blood on her face. The younger daughter was facedown on the floor of the van, and there was apparently a lot of blood on her, too. Nobody heard any gun shots. Nobody saw a gun. Only one guy was seen, but there might have been another one in the van. We don't see how one guy could have roped all three of them in, by himself. Unless he really messed them up."

"Huh. What else?"

"White guy," Sherrill said. "Van had a nose on it—it was an engine front, not a cab-over. We think it was probably an Econoline or a Chevy G10 or Dodge B150, like that. Nobody saw a tag."

"How long before we heard?" Lucas asked.

"There was a 911 call," Sherrill said. "There was some confusion, and it was probably three or four minutes after the snatch, before the call was made. Then the car took three or four more minutes to get here. The call was sort of unsure, like maybe nothing happened. Then it was maybe five more minutes before we put the truck on the air."

"So the guy was ten miles away before anybody started looking," Lucas said.

"That's about it. Broad daylight and he's gone," Black said. They all stood around, thinking about that for a moment, listening to the hiss of rain on their hats, then Sherrill said, "What're you doing here, anyway?"

Lucas's right hand came out of his pocket, and he made an odd gesture with it. Sherrill realized he was twisting something between his fingers. "This could be . . . difficult," Lucas said. He looked at the school. "Where're the witnesses?"

"The shrink is over there, in the cafeteria," Sherrill said. "I don't know where the kid is. Greave is talking to them. Why is it difficult?"

"Because everybody's rich," Lucas said, looking at her. "The Manette woman is Tower Manette's daughter."

"I'd heard that," Sherrill said. She looked up at Lucas, her forehead wrinkled. "Black and I are gonna lead on this one, and we really don't need the attention. We've still got that assisted-suicide bullshit going on . . ."

"You might as well give up on that," Lucas said. "You're never gonna get him."

"Pisses me off," Sherrill said. "He never thought his old lady needed to kill herself until he ran into his little tootsie. I know he fuckin' talked her into it . . ."

"Tootsie?" Lucas asked. He grinned and looked at Black.

"She's a wordsmith," Black said.

"Pisses me off," Sherrill said. Then: "So what's Tower Manette doing? Pulling all the political switches?"

"Exactly," Lucas said. "And Manette's husband and the kids' father, it turns out, is George Dunn. I didn't know that. North Light Development. The Republican Party. Lotsa bucks."

"And Manette's the Democrats," Black said gloomily. "Jesus Christ, they got us surrounded."

"I bet the chief is peeing her political underwear," Sherrill said.

Lucas nodded. "Yeah, exactly," he said. "Can this shrink give us a picture of the guy?"

Sherrill shook her head doubtfully. "Greave told me the guy didn't see much. Just the end of it. I didn't talk to him much, but he seems a little . . . hinky."

"Great. And Greave's doing the interview?"

"Yeah." There was a moment of silence. Nobody said it, but Greave's interrogations weren't the best. They weren't even very good. Lucas took a step toward the school, and Sherrill said to his back, "Dunn did it."

Ninety percent of the time, she'd be right. But Lucas stopped, turned, shook his head at her. "Don't say that, Marcy—'cause maybe he did." His fingers were still playing with whatever-it-was, turning it, twisting it. "I don't want people thinking we went after him without some evidence."

"Do we have any?" Black asked.

Lucas said, "Nobody's said anything about it, but Dunn and Andi Manette just separated. There's another woman, I guess. Still . . ."

Sherrill said, "Be polite."

"Yeah. With everybody. Stay on their asses, but be nice about it," Lucas said. "And . . . I don't know. If it's Dunn, he'd have to have somebody working with him."

Sherrill nodded. "Somebody to take care of them, while he was talking to the cops."

"Unless he just took them out and wasted them," Black suggested.

Nobody wanted to think about that. They all looked up at the same moment and got their faces rained on. Then Hendrix slid out from under the Lexus, with a ratcheting of metal wheels, and they all looked down at him. Hendrix was riding a lowboy, wore a white mechanic's jumpsuit and spectacles with lenses the size of nickels: he looked like an albino mole.

"There's a bloodstain on the shoe—*I think* it's blood. Don't disturb it," he said to Sherrill, passing her a transparent plastic bag.

Sherrill looked at the black high-heeled shoe, said, "She's got good taste."

Lucas flipped whatever-it-was between his middle and ring fingers, fumbled it, and then unconsciously slipped it over the end of his index finger. "Maybe the blood's from the asshole."

"Fat chance," Black said.

He pulled the mole to his feet and Lucas frowned and said, "What's that shit?"

He pointed at the leg of the mole's jumpsuit. In the headlights of the crime-scene truck, one of his pant legs was stained pink, as though he were bleeding from a calf wound.

"Jesus," Black said. He pulled on the seams of his own legs, lifting the cuffs above the shoes. "It's blood."

The mole dropped to his knees, pulled a paper napkin from a pocket, and laid it flat on the wet blacktop. When it was wet, he picked it up and held it in the truck lights. The handkerchief showed a pinkish tinge.

"They must've emptied her out," Sherrill said.

The mole shook his head. "Not blood," he said. He held the towel between himself and the truck lights and looked through it.

"Then what is it?"

The tech shrugged. "Paint. Maybe lawn chemicals. It's not blood, though."

"That's something," Sherrill said, her face pale in the headlights. She looked down at her shoes. "I hate wading around in it. If you don't clean it up right away, it stinks."

"But it's blood on the shoe," Lucas said.

"I believe it is," said the mole.

Sherrill had been watching Lucas fumble with the whatever-it-was and finally figured it out. A ring. "Is that a ring?" she asked.

Lucas quickly pushed his hand in his coat pocket; he might have blushed. "Yeah. I guess."

"You guess? Don't you know?" She handed the shoe bag to Black. "Engagement?"

"Yeah."

"Can I see it?" She stepped closer and consciously batted her eyes.

"What for?" He stepped back; there was no place to hide.

"So I can fuckin' steal the stone," Sherrill said impatiently. Then, wheedling again: " 'Cause I want to look at it, why do you think?"

"Better show it to her," Black said. "If you don't, she'll be whining about it the rest of the night . . ."

"Shut up," Sherrill snapped at Black. Black shut up and the mole stepped back. To Lucas, "Come on, let me see it. Please?"

Lucas reluctantly took his hand out of his pocket and dropped the ring into Sherrill's open palm. She half-turned, so she could see the stone in the headlights. "Holy cow," she said reverently. She looked at Black. "The diamond is bigger'n your dick."

"But not nearly as hard," Black said.

The mole sadly shook his head. This kind of talk between unmarried men and women was another sign that the world was going to heck in a handbasket; that the final days were here.

They all started through the drizzle toward the school, the mole looking into the sky, for signs of God or Lucifer; Black, carrying the bloody shoe; Lucas with his head down; and Sherrill marvelling at the three-carat, tear-shaped diamond sparkling in all the brilliant flashing cop lights.

THE SCHOOL CAFETERIA was decorated with hand-painted Looney Tunes characters, and was gloomy despite it: the place had the feel of a bunker, all concrete block and small windows too high to see out of.

Bob Greave sat at a too-short cafeteria table in a too-short chair, drinking a Diet Coke, taking notes on a secretarial pad. He wore a rust-colored Italian-cut suit and a lightweight, beige micro-fiber raincoat. A thin man in a trench coat sat next to him, in another too-short chair, his bony knees sticking up like Ichabod Crane's. He looked as though he might twitch.

Lucas walked through the double doors with Black, Sherrill, and the mole trailing like wet ducklings. "Hey, Bob," Lucas said.

"Is that the shoe?" Greave asked, looking at the bag Black was carrying.

"No, it's Tom's," Lucas said, a half-second before he remembered about Black and had to smother a nervous laugh. Black apparently didn't notice. The man with the incipient twitch said, "Are you Chief Davenport?"

Lucas nodded. "Yeah."

"Mr. Greave"—the man nodded at the detective—"said I had to stay until you got here. But I don't have anything else to say. So can I go?"

"I want to hear the story," Lucas said.

Girdler ran through it quickly. He had come to the school to talk to the chairperson about the year's PTA agenda, and had encountered Mrs. Manette and her daughters just outside the door, in the shelter of the overhang. Mrs. Manette had asked his advice about a particular problem—he was a therapist, as was she—and they chatted for a few moments, and he went inside.

Halfway down the hall and around a corner, he recalled a magazine citation she'd asked for, and that he couldn't remember when she'd first asked. He started back, and when he turned the corner, fifty or sixty feet from the door, he saw a man struggling with Manette's daughter.

"He pushed her into the van and went around it and drove away," Girdler said.

"And you saw the kids in the van?"

"Mmmm, yes . . ." he said, his eyes sliding away, and Lucas thought, *He's lying.* "They were both on the floor. Mrs. Manette was sitting up, but she had blood on her face."

"What were you doing?" Lucas asked.

"I was running down the hall toward the doors. I thought maybe I could stop them," Girdler said, and again his eyes slid away. "I got there too late. He was already going out the drive. I'm sure he had a Minnesota license plate, though. Red truck, sliding doors. A younger man, big. Not fat, but muscular. He was wearing a t-shirt and jeans."

"You didn't see his face."

"Not at all. But he was blond and had long hair, like a rock 'n' roll person. Hair down to his shoulders."

"Huh. And that's it?"

Girdler was offended: "I thought it was quite a bit. I mean, I chased after him, but he was gone. Then I ran back and got the women in the office to dial 911. If you didn't catch him, it's not my fault."

Lucas smiled and said, "I understand there was a kid here. A girl, who saw some of it."

Girdler shrugged. "I doubt she saw much. She seemed confused. Maybe not too bright."

Lucas turned to Greave, who said, "I got what I could from her. It's about the same as Mr. Girdler. The kid's mother was pretty upset."

"Great," Lucas said.

He hung around for another ten minutes, finishing with Girdler, talking to Greave and the other cops. "Not much, is there?"

"Just the blood," Sherrill said. "I guess we already knew there was blood, from Girdler and the kid."

"And the red stuff in the parking lot," said the mole, looking at the napkin he'd used to soak it up. "I bet it's some kind of semi-water-soluble paint, and he painted the van to disguise it."

"Think so?"

"Everybody says it was red, and this is red. I think it's a possibility. But I just don't see . . ."

"What?"

The mole scratched his head. "Why did he do it this way? Why right in the middle of the day, and three-to-one? I wonder if it could be a mistake or some spur-of-the-moment thing by a guy on drugs? But if it was spur-of-the-moment, how would he know to take Mrs. Manette? He must've known who she was . . . unless he just came here because it's a rich kid's school and he'd take anybody, and he saw the Lexus."

"Then why not just snatch a kid? You don't want the folks if you're looking for ransom. You want the parents getting the money for you," Black said.

"Sounds goofier'n shit," Sherrill said, and they all nodded.

"That could be an answer—she's a shrink, and maybe the guy used to be a patient. A nut," Black said.

"Whatever, I hope it was planned and done for the money," Lucas said.

"Yeah?" The mole looked at him with interest. "Why?"

" 'Cause if it was some doper or a goddamn gang-banger doing a spur-of-the-moment thing, and they haven't dropped them off by now . . ."

"Then they're dead," Sherrill finished.

"Yeah." Lucas looked around the little circle of cops. "If it wasn't planned, Andi Manette and her kids are outa here."

3
——

THE CHIEF LIVED in a 1920's brown-brick bungalow in a wooded neighborhood east of Lake Harriet in Minneapolis, cheek-by-jowl with half the other smart politicians in the city; a house you had to be the right age to buy in 1978.

The gabble of a televised football game was audible through the front door, and a moment after Lucas pushed the doorbell, the chief's husband opened it and peered out nearsightedly; his glasses were up on his forehead. "Come on in," he said, pushing open the door. "Rose Marie's in the study."

"How is she?" Lucas asked.

"Unhappy." He was a tall, balding lawyer, who wore a button vest and smelled vaguely of pipe tobacco. He reminded Lucas of Adlai Stevenson. Lucas followed him down through the house, a comfortable accumulation of over-stuffed couches and chairs, mixed with turn-of-the-century oak, furnishings they might have inherited from prosperous farmer-parents.

Rose Marie Roux, the Minneapolis Chief of Police, was sitting in the den, in a La-Z-Boy, with her feet up. She was wearing a sober blue business suit with white sweat socks. She was smoking.

"Tell me you found them," she said, curling her toes at Lucas.

"Yeah, they were shopping at the Mall of America," Lucas said. He dropped into the La-Z-Boy facing the chief. "They're all okay, and Tower Manette's talking about running you for the U.S. Senate."

"Yeah, yeah," Roux said sourly. Her husband shook his head. "Tell me," she said.

"She was hit so hard she was knocked out of her shoes and there's blood on one of them," Lucas said. "We've got some eyewitness who says that Andi Manette and the younger of the daughters were covered with blood, although there's a possibility it was something else, like paint. And we've got a description of the guy who did it . . ."

"The perp," said Roux's husband.

They both looked at him. He hadn't seen the inside of a courtroom since he was twenty-five. He got his cop talk from the television. "Yeah, the perp," Lucas said. And to Rose Marie, "The description is pretty general: big, tough, dirty-blond."

"Damnit." Roux took a drag on her cigarette, blew it at the ceiling, then said, "The FBI will be in tomorrow . . ."

"I know. The Minneapolis AIC is talking to Lester," Lucas said. "He wanted to know if we were going to declare it as a kidnapping. Lester said we probably would. We're covering the phone lines at Tower Manette's office and house. The same for Dunn and Andi Manette, offices and houses."

"Gotta be a kidnapping," Roux's husband said, getting comfortable with the conversation. "What else could it be?"

Lucas looked at him and said, "Could be a nut—Manette's a shrink. Could be murder. Marital murder or something in the family. There's lots of money around. Lots of motive."

"I don't want to think about that," Roux said. Then, "What about Dunn?"

"Shaffer talked to him. He's got no alibi, not really. But we do know it wasn't him in the van. He says he was in his car—he's got a phone in his car, but he didn't use it within a half-hour of the kidnapping."

"Huh."

"You don't know him? Dunn?" Rose Marie Roux asked.

"No. I'll get to him tonight."

"He's a tough guy," she said. "But he's not crazy. Not unless something happened since the last time I saw him."

"Marital problems," Lucas suggested again.

"He's the type who'd have some," Roux said. "He'd manage them. He wouldn't flip out." She grunted as she pushed herself out of the La-Z-Boy. "Come on, we've got an appointment."

Lucas looked at his watch. Eight o'clock. "Where? I was gonna see Dunn."

"We've got to talk to Tower Manette first. At his place, Lake of the Isles."

"You need me?"

"Yeah. He called and asked if I'd put you on the case. I said I already had. He wants to meet you."

THE CHIEF TRADED her sweat socks for panty hose and short heels and they took the Porsche five minutes north to Lake of the Isles.

"Your husband said *perp*," Lucas said in the car.

"I love him anyway," she said.

Manette's house was a Prairie-style landmark posed on the west rim of the lake, above a serpentine driveway. The drive was edged with a flagstone wall, and Lucas caught the color of a late-summer perennial garden in the flash of the headlights. The house, of the same brown brick used in Roux's, was built in three offset levels, and every level was brilliantly lit; peals of light sliced across the evergreens under the windows and dappled the driveway. "Everybody's up," Lucas said.

"She's his only child," Roux said.

"How old is he now?"

"Seventy, I guess," Roux said. "He's not been well."

"Heart?"

"He had an aneurysm, mmm, last spring, I think. A couple of days after they fixed it, he had a mild stroke. He supposedly made a complete recovery, but he's not been the same. He got . . . frail, or something."

"You know him pretty well," Lucas said.

"I've known him for years. He and Humphrey ran the Party in the sixties and seventies."

Lucas parked next to a green Mazda Miata; Roux struggled out of the passenger seat, found her purse, slammed the door, and said, "I need a larger car."

"Porsches are a bad habit," Lucas agreed as they crossed the porch.

A man in a gray business suit, with the professionally concerned face of an undertaker, was standing behind the glass in the front door. He opened it when he saw Roux reach for the doorbell. "Ralph Enright, chief," he said, in a hushed voice. "We talked at the Sponsor's Ball."

"Sure, how are you?" Roux said. "I didn't know you and Tower were friends."

"Um, he asked me to take a consultive role," Enright said. He looked as though he were waxed in the morning.

"Good," said Roux, nodding dismissively. "Is Tower around?"

"In here," Enright said. He looked at Lucas. "And you're . . ."

"Lucas Davenport."

"Of course. This way."

"Lawyer," Roux muttered, as Enright started into the depths of the house. Lucas could see the light glittering from his hair. "Gofer."

THE HOUSE WAS high-style Prairie, with deep Oriental carpets setting off the arts-and-crafts furniture. A touch of deco added glamour, and a definite deco taste was reflected in the thirties art prints. Lucas knew nothing of decoration or art, but the smell of money seeped from the walls. *That* he recognized.

Enright led them to a sprawling center room, with two interlocking groups of couches and chairs. Three men in suits were standing, talking. Two well-dressed women sat on chairs facing each other. They all had the expectant air of a group waiting for their picture to be taken.

"Rose Marie . . ." Tower Manette walked toward them. He was a tall man with fine, high cheekbones and a trademark shock of white hair falling over wooly-bear white eyebrows. Another man, tanned, solid, tight-jawed, Lucas knew as a senior agent with the Minneapolis office of the FBI. He nodded and Lucas nodded back. The third man was Danny Kupicek, an intelligence cop who had worked for Lucas on special investigations. He raised a hand and said, "Chiefs."

The two women were unfamiliar.

"Thanks for coming," Manette said. He was thinner than Lucas remembered from seeing him on television, and paler, but there was a quick aggressive flash in his eyes. His suit was French-cut but conservative, showing his narrow waist, and his tie might have been chosen by a French president: the look of a ladies' man.

But the corner of his mouth trembled when he reached out to Roux, and when he shook hands with Lucas, his hand felt cool and delicate; the skin was loose and heavily veined. "And Lucas Davenport, I've heard about you for years. Is there any more news? Why don't we step into the library; I'll be right back, folks."

The library was a small rectangular room stuffed with leather-bound books, tan, oxblood, green covers stamped with gold. They all came in sets: great works, great thoughts, great ideas, great battles, great men.

"Great library," Lucas said.

"Thank you," Tower said. "Is there anything new?"

"There have been some further . . . disturbing developments," Roux said.

Tower turned his head away, as though his face were about to be slapped. "That is . . . ?"

Roux nodded at Lucas, and Lucas said, "I just got back from the school. We found one of your daughter's shoes in the parking lot, under her car, out of the rain. There was blood on it. We've got her blood type from medical school, so we should be able to tell fairly quickly if it's her blood. If it *is* hers, she was probably bleeding fairly heavily—but that could be from a blow to the nose or a cut lip, or even a small scalp wound. They all bleed profusely . . . But there was some blood. Witnesses also suggest that your daughter and her younger daughter, Genevieve . . ."

"Yes, Gen," Manette said weakly.

". . . apparently were bleeding after the assault, when they were seen in the back of the kidnapper's van. But we've also found that the kidnapper may have tried to disguise his van by painting it with some kind of red water-soluble paint, so that may be what was seen on your daughter. We don't know about that."

"Oh, God." Manette's voice came out as a croak: the emotion was real.

"This could turn out badly," Roux said. "We're hoping it won't, but you've got to be ready."

"There must be something I can do," Manette said. "Do you think a reward? An appeal?"

"We could talk about a reward," Roux said. "But we should wait awhile, see if anyone calls asking for ransom."

"Do you have any ideas—anything at all—about what might be going on?" Lucas asked. "Anybody who might want to get at you, or at Miz Manette?"

"No . . ." But he said it slowly, as if he had to think about it. "Why?"

"She may have been stalked. This doesn't look like a spontaneous attack," Lucas said. "But there's an element of craziness about it, too. All kinds of things could've gone wrong. I mean, he kidnapped three people in broad daylight and got away with it."

"I'll tell you what, Mr. Davenport," Manette said. He took three shaky steps to an overstuffed library chair and sat down. "I've got more enemies than most men. There must be several dozen people in this state who genuinely detest me—people who blame me for destroying their careers, their prospects, and probably their families. That's politics. It's unfortunate, but that's what happens when your side loses in a political contest. You lose. So there are people out there . . ."

"It doesn't feel political," Roux said. Lucas noticed that she'd taken a cigarette out of a pocket and was rolling it, unlit, in her left hand.

Manette nodded. "I agree. As crazy as some of those people may be, I don't think this kind of thing would ever occur to them."

Lucas said, "There's always the possibility . . ."

Roux looked at him. "Political people always leave themselves escape hatches. With this, there's no escape hatch. Even if he just dropped them off on the corner, he'd be looking at years in prison for the kidnapping. A political mind wouldn't do that."

"Unless he was nuts," Lucas said.

Roux nodded, and looked at Manette and said, "There is that possibility."

"Which brings us to your daughter's psychiatric practice," Lucas said to Manette. "We need access to her records."

"The woman on the couch"—Manette tipped his head toward the living room—"the younger one, is Andi's partner, Nancy Wolfe. I'll talk to her."

"We'd like to start as soon as we can," Lucas said. "Tomorrow morning."

"I hope it's a kidnapping," Manette said. "I hope it's for profit—I don't like to think of some nut taking them."

"How about George Dunn?" Lucas asked. "He says he was in his car during the attack. No witnesses."

"That sonofabitch," Manette said. He pushed himself out of the chair and took a quick turn around the room and made a sound like a dog's growl. "He's a goddamn psycho. I didn't think before tonight that he'd do anything to hurt Andi or the girls, but now . . . I don't know."

"You think he might?"

"He's a cold-hearted sonofabitch," Manette said. "He could do anything."

They talked about the case for a few more minutes, then the two women came to the door and looked inside. "Tower? Are you okay?"

"I'm fine," he said.

The women stepped inside. The younger of the two, Nancy Wolfe, was a slender, well-tanned woman. She wore a soft woollen dress, but no jewelry or makeup, and her auburn hair showed a few threads of gray. Speaking to Manette, she said, "You need some quiet. I'm telling you that as an M.D., not as a psychiatrist."

The other woman was paler, older, with a loose, jowly face touched expertly with rouge. She nodded, stepped closer to Manette, and took his arm. "Just come on upstairs, Tower. Even if you can't sleep, you could lie down . . ."

"I don't go to bed until two o'clock in the morning," Manette said irritably. "There's no point in going up now."

"But it's been exhausting," the woman said. She seemed to be talking about herself, and Lucas realized that she must be Manette's wife. She spoke to Roux: "Tower's under a lot of stress, and he's had health problems."

"We wanted him to know that we're doing everything we can," Roux said. She looked back at Manette. "I've assigned Lucas to oversee the investigation."

"Thank you," Manette said. And to Lucas: "Anything you need, anybody that I know, that you want to talk to, just call. And let me know about that reward, if it would be useful."

"George Dunn," Lucas said.

"Get him on the phone, will you, Helen?" Manette said to his wife. "I'll talk to him."

"And after that, Tower, I want you to kick back and close your eyes, even if it's just for half an hour," Wolfe said. She reached out and touched his hand. "Take some time to think."

LUCAS DROPPED THE chief at her house, promising to call back at midnight, or when anything broke.

"Lester's running the routine," Roux said as the car idled in her driveway. "I need you to pluck this thing out of the sky, so to speak."

"Doesn't have a plucking feel about it," Lucas said. "Something complicated is going on."

"If you don't, *we're* gonna get plucked," Roux said. Then: "You want fifteen seconds of politics?"

"Sure."

"This is one of those cases that people will talk about for a generation," Roux said. "If we find Manette and her kids, we're gold. We'll be untouchable. But if we fuck it up . . ." She let her voice trail away.

"Let me go pluck," Lucas said.

GEORGE DUNN'S HOUSE was a modest white ranch, tucked away on a big tree-filled lot on a dead-end street in Edina. Lucas left the Porsche in the driveway and climbed the stone walk to the front door, pushed the doorbell. A thick-faced cop, usually in uniform, now in slacks and a golf shirt, pushed open the door.

"Chief Davenport . . ."

"Hey, Rick," Lucas said. "They've got you watching the phones?"

"Yeah." In a lower voice. "And Dunn."

"Where is he?"

"Back in his office—the light back there." The cop nodded to the left.

The house was stacked with brown cardboard moving boxes, a dozen of them in the front room, more visible in the kitchen and breakfast area. There was little furniture—a couch and chair in the living room, a round oak table in the breakfast nook. Lucas followed a hall back to the light and found Dunn sitting at a rectangular dining table in what had been meant as a family room. A large-screen TV sat against one wall, the picture on, the sound off. A stereo system was stacked on a pile of three cardboard boxes.

Dunn was huddled over a pile of paper, with a crooked-neck lamp pulled close to them, his face half-in and half-out of the light. To his left, a half-dozen two-drawer file cabinets were pushed against a wall. Half of them had open drawers. Another stack of cardboard boxes sat on the floor beside the file cabinets. On the far side of the room, three chairs faced each other across a glass coffee table.

Lucas stepped inside the room and said, "Mr. Dunn."

Dunn looked up. "Davenport," he said. He dropped his pen, pushed back from the table, and stood to shake hands.

Dunn was a fullback ten years off the playing field: broad shoulders, bullet head, beat-up face. His front teeth were so even, so white and perfect, that they had to be a bridge. He wore a gray cashmere sweater, with the sleeves pushed up, showing a gold Rolex; jeans, and loafers without socks. He shook hands, held the grip for a second, nodded, pointed at a chair, sat down, and said, "Ask."

"You want a lawyer?" Lucas asked.

"I had one. It was a waste of money," Dunn said.

Lucas sat down, leaned forward, an elbow on his thigh. "You say you were in your car when your wife was taken. But you don't have any witnesses and you made no calls that would confirm it."

"I made one call to her, while she was on her way over to the school. I told that to the other guys . . ."

"But that was an hour before she was taken. A prosecutor might say that the call tipped you off to exactly where she'd be, so you'd have time to get there. Or send somebody," Lucas said. "And after that call, you were out of your office, and out of everybody's sight."

"I know it. If I'd done . . . this thing . . . I'd have a better alibi," Dunn said. He made a sliding gesture with one hand. "I'd have been someplace besides my car. But the fact is, I spend maybe a quarter of my business day in my car. I've got a half-dozen developments going around the Cities, from west of Minnetonka to the St. Croix. I hit every one every day."

"And you use your car phone all the time," Lucas pointed out.

"Not after business hours," Dunn said, shaking his head. "I called the office from Yorkville—that's the job over in Woodbury—and after that, and after I talked to Andi, I just headed back in. When I got here, the cops were waiting for me."

"Who do you think took her?" Lucas asked.

Dunn shook his head. "It's gotta be one of the nuts she handles," he said. "She gets the worst. Sex criminals, pyromaniacs, killers. Nobody's too crazy for her."

Lucas gazed at him for a moment. The gooseneck lamp made a pool of light around his hands, but his pug's face was half in shadow; in an old black-and-white movie, he might have been the devil. "How much do you dislike her?" Lucas asked. "Your wife?"

"I don't dislike her," Dunn said, bouncing once in the chair. "I love her."

"That's not the word around town."

"Yeah, yeah, yeah." He put his fingers to his forehead, scrubbed at it. "I screwed a woman from the office. Once." Lucas let the silence grow, and Dunn finally launched himself from his chair, walked to a box, opened it, took out a bottle of scotch. "Whiskey?"

"No, thanks." And he let the silence go.

"We're talking about a major-league cookie, this chick, in my face five days a week," Dunn said. He made a Coke-bottle tits-and-ass figure with his hands. "Andi and I had a few disagreements—not big ones, but we've got a lot going on. Careers, busy all the time, we don't see each other enough . . . like that. So this chick is there, in the office—she was my traffic manager—and finally I jump her. Right there on her desk, pencils and pens all over the place, Post-it notes stuck to her butt. The next thing I know, she gets her little handbag and her business suit and shows up at Andi's office to announce that she loves me and I love her." He ran his hands through his hair, then laughed, a short, half-humorous bark. "Christ, what a nightmare that must've been."

"Doesn't sound like one of your better days," Lucas admitted. He remembered days like that.

"Man, I wish I hadn't done it," Dunn said. He lipped the bottle of whiskey in his hand, caught it. "I lost my wife and a pretty goddamn good traffic manager on the same day."

Lucas watched him for a long beat. He wasn't acting.

"Is there any reason you might've killed your wife for her money?"

Dunn looked up, vaguely surprised: "Christ, you don't fuck around, do you?"

Lucas shook his head. "Could you have done that? Does it make sense?"

"No. Just between you and me—there isn't that much money."

"Um . . ."

"I know, Tower Manette and his millions, the Manette Trust, the Manette Foundation, all that shit," Dunn said. He flicked a hand as if batting away a cobweb, then walked across the room, stepped through a doorway and flicked on a light. He opened a refrigerator door, dropped a couple of ice cubes in his glass, and came back. "Andi gets a hundred thousand a year, more or less, from her share of the Manette Trust. When the kids turn eighteen, they'll get a piece of it. And they'll get bigger pieces when they turn twenty-five and forty. If they were . . . to die . . . I wouldn't see any of that. What I'd get is the house, and the stuff in it. Frankly, I don't need it."

"So what about Manette? You said . . ."

"Tower had maybe ten million back in the fifties, plus the income from the trust, and a board seat at the Foundation. But he was running all over the world, buying yachts, buying a house in Palm Beach, screwing everything in a skirt. And he was putting the good stuff up his nose—he was heavy into cocaine back in the Seventies. Anyway, after a few years, the interest on the ten mil wasn't cutting it. He started dipping into the principal. Then he got into politics—bought his way in, really—and he dipped a little deeper. It must've seemed like taking water out of the ocean with a teacup. But it added up. Then, in the late seventies and eighties, he did everything wrong—he was stuck in bonds during the big inflation, finally unloaded them at a terrific loss. Then sometime in there, he met Helen . . ."

"Helen's his second wife, right?" Lucas said. "She's quite a bit younger than he is?"

Dunn said, "I guess she's . . . what? Fifty-three, fifty-four? She's not that young. His first wife, Bernie—that's Andi's mother—died about ten years ago. He was already seeing Helen by that time. She was a good-looking woman. She had the face and real star-quality tits. Tower always liked tits. Anyway, Helen was in real estate and she got him deep into REITs as a way to recoup his bond losses . . ."

"What's a *reet?*" Lucas asked.

"Sorry; real-estate investment trust. Anyway, that was just before real estate fell out of bed, and he got hammered again. And the crash of eighty-seven . . . Hell, the guy was the kiss of death. You didn't want to stand next to him."

"So he's broke?"

Dunn looked up at the ceiling as if he were running a calculator in his head. After a moment, he said, "Right now, if Tower hunted around, he might come up with . . . a million? Of course, the house is paid for, that's better'n a mil, but he can't really get at it. He has to live somewhere and it has to be up to his standards . . . So figure that he gets sixty thousand from the million that's his, and another hundred thousand from the trust. And he's still got that seat on the Foundation board, but that probably doesn't pay more than twenty or thirty. So what's that? Less than two hundred?"

"Jesus, he's eating dog food," Lucas said, with just a rime of sarcasm in his voice.

Dunn pointed a finger at Lucas: "But that's *exactly* what he feels like. *Exactly*. He was spending a half-million a year when a Cadillac cost six thousand bucks and a million was really something. Now he's scraping along on maybe a quarter mil and a Caddy costs forty thousand."

"Poor sonofabitch."

"Listen, a million ain't that much any more," Dunn said wryly. "A guy who owns two good Exxon stations—he's worth at least a mil, probably more. Two gas stations. We're not talking about yachts and polo."

"So if you took your wife off, you wouldn't have done it for the money," Lucas said.

"Hell, if anybody got taken off, it should've been me. I'm worth fifteen or twenty times what Tower is. Of course, it ain't as good as Tower's money," he said ruefully.

"Why's that?"

" 'Cause I earned it," Dunn said. "Just like you did, with your computer company. I read about you in *Cities' Biz*. They said you're worth probably five million, and growing. You must feel it—that your money's got a taint."

"I've never seen any of it, the money," Lucas said. "It's all paper, at this point." Then: "What about insurance? Is there insurance on Andi?"

"Well, yeah." Dunn's forehead wrinkled and he scratched his chin. "Actually, quite a bit."

"Who'd get it?"

Dunn shrugged. "The kids . . . unless . . . Ah, Christ. If the kids died, I'd get it."

"Sole beneficiary?"

"Yeah . . . except, you know, Nancy Wolfe would get a half-million. They do pretty well in that partnership, and they both have key-man—key-woman— insurance to help cover their mortgage and so on, if somebody died."

"Is a half-million a lot for Nancy Wolfe?"

Dunn thought again, and then said, "It'd be quite a bit. She pulls down something between $150,000 and $175,000 a year, and she can't protect any of it—taxes eat her alive—so another half mil would be nice."

"Will you sign a release saying that we can look at your wife's records?" Lucas asked.

"Sure. Why wouldn't I?"

"Because a lot of medical people think psychiatric records should be privileged," Lucas said. "That people need treatment, not cops."

"Fuck that. I'll sign," Dunn said. "You got a paper with you?"

"I'll have one sent over tonight," Lucas said.

Dunn was watching Lucas's hand and asked, "What're you playing with?"

Lucas looked down at his hand and saw the ring. "Ring."

"Uh-oh. Coming or going?" Dunn asked.

"Thinking about it," Lucas said.

"Marriage is wonderful," Dunn said. He spread his arms. "Look around. A box for everything and everything in its box."

"You seem . . . sort of *lighthearted* about this whole thing."

Dunn suddenly leaned forward, his face like a stone. "Davenport, I'm so fuckin' scared I can't spit. I honest-to-God never knew what it meant, being scared spitless. I thought it was just a phrase, but it's not . . . You gotta get my guys back."

Lucas grunted and stood up. "You'll stick around." It wasn't a question.

"Yeah." Dunn stood up, facing him. "You're a tough guy, right?"

"Maybe," Lucas said.

"Football, I bet."

"Hockey."

"Yeah, you got the cuts . . . Think you could take me?" Dunn had relaxed again, and a faintly amused look crossed his face.

Lucas nodded. "Yeah."

Dunn said, "Huh," like he didn't necessarily agree, and then, losing the smile, "What d'you think—you gonna find my wife and kids?"

"I'll find them," Lucas said.

"But you won't guarantee their condition," Dunn said.

Lucas looked away, into the dark house: he felt like something was pushing his face. "No," he said to the darkness.

4

THE HOMICIDE OFFICE resembled the city room of a slightly seedy small-town daily. Individual cubicles for the detectives were separated by shoulder-high partitions; some desks were neat, others were a swamp of paper and souvenirs. Three different kinds of gray or putty-colored metal file cabinets were stuck wherever there was space. Old fliers and notes and cartoons and bureaucratic missives were tacked or taped on walls and bulletin boards. A brown plastic radio the size of a toaster, the kind last made in the sixties with a big, round tuning dial, sat on top of a file cabinet, a bent steel clothes hanger jammed into the back as an antenna. An adenoidal voice squeaked from the primitive speaker.

". . . is one of the most historical of crimes, from the Rape of the Sabine women to the Lindbergh kidnapping of our own era . . ."

Lucas was drinking chicken noodle Soup-in-a-Cup, and paused just inside the door with the cup two inches from his lips. The voice was familiar, but he couldn't place it until the DJ interrupted:

> *You're listening to Blackjack Billy Walker, go ahead, Edina, with a question for Dr. David Girdler . . .*
> *Dr. Girdler, you said a minute ago that kidnapping victims identify with their kidnappers. All I can say is, that's a perfect example of what happens when the liberal school system shoves this politically correct garbage down the kids' throats, teaching them things the kids know are wrong but they gotta believe because somebody in authority says so, like these union hacks that call themselves teachers . . .*

Girdler's voice was consciously mellow, hushed, artificially and dramatically deepened. He said:

> *I understand your feelings—heh heh—about this, although I don't entirely agree with your sentiments: there are many good teachers. That aside, yes, that identification often takes place and begins within hours of the kidnapping; the victims may actually suggest ways that the police can be more effectively foiled in their efforts . . .*

Lucas stared at the radio, not believing it. Greave was sitting at his desk, eating a Mr. Goodbar. "Sounds like a fuckin' politician, doesn't he? He couldn't wait to get on the radio. He walked out of the school and drove right down to the station."

"How long has he been on?" Lucas finished the Soup-in-a-Cup and dropped the cup in a wastebasket.

"Hour," Greave said. "Lotta newsies have been looking for you, by the way."

"Fuck 'em," Lucas said. "For now, anyway."

A dozen detectives were milling around the office—everybody from Homicide/Violent Crimes, more from Vice, Sex, and Intelligence. Some were at desks, others were parked on swivel chairs, some were leaning against file cabinets. A very tall man and a very short one were talking golf swings. A guy from Sex elbowed past with a cafeteria tray full of cups of coffee and Coke. Almost everybody was eating or drinking. The office smelled like coffee, microwave popcorn, and Tombstone pizza.

Harmon Anderson wandered over to Greave's desk, eating a chicken-salad sandwich. A glob of mayonnaise was stuck to his upper lip. "Anything for a buck," he said between chews. Anderson was a hillbilly and a computer expert. "Girdler is *not* a doctor. He has a B.A. in psychology from some redneck college in North Carolina."

Sherrill, still damp, strolled in, pulled off the tennis hat, slapped it against her coat, then took off her coat and hung it up. She nodded at Lucas, tipped her head at the radio, and said, "Have you been listening?"

Lucas said, "Just now," and to Greave, "Did you ask him not to?"

Greave nodded. "The standard line. I said we should keep it to ourselves so the perpetrators don't know exactly what we have, and so we can present a better image if we get to court."

"Did you say perpetrator?" Lucas asked.

"Yeah. So shoot me."

"I'd say he didn't give a fuck," Sherrill said, fluffing her hair. "I was listening on the way over. He's remembering stuff he didn't give to us . . ."

"Making it up," Lucas said.

"Everybody's gotta be a movie star," Greave said. And they paused for a moment to listen:

Dr. Girdler, you know, the police don't stop crime; they simply record it, and sometimes they catch the people who do it. But by then, it's too late. This kid-napping is a perfect example. If Mrs. Manette had been carrying even a simple handgun, or if you had been carrying a handgun, you could've stopped this thug in his tracks. Instead, you were left standing there in the hallway and you couldn't do anything. I'll tell you, the criminals have guns; it's time we honest citizens took advantage of our Second Amendment rights . . .

"Damnit," Sherrill said. "It's gonna turn into a circus."

"Already has." They all turned toward the door. Frank Lester, deputy chief for investigation, stepped inside with a handful of papers. He was tired, his face drawn. Too many years. "Anything more?"

Lucas shook his head. "I talked to Dunn. He seems pretty straight."

"He's a candidate, though," Greave said.

"Yeah, he's a candidate," Lucas said. To Lester: "Have the Feds come in yet?"

"They're about to," Lester said. "They can't avoid it much longer."

Lucas twisted the engagement ring around the end of his forefinger, saw Lester looking at it, and pushed it down in his pocket. Lester continued, "Even if the Feds come in, Manette wants us working it, too. The chief agrees."

"Jesus, I wish this shit would stop," Greave said, rubbing his forehead.

"Been doing it since Cain and Abel," said Anderson.

Greave stopped rubbing: "I didn't mean crime. I meant politics. If crime stopped, I'd have to get a job."

"You could probably get on the fuckin' radio with that suit," Sherrill said.

Lester waved them silent, held up a yellow legal pad on which he'd scribbled notes. "Listen up, everybody."

The talk died as the cops arranged themselves around Lester. "Harmon Anderson will be passing out assignments, but I want to outline what we're looking at and get ideas on anything we're missing."

"What's the overtime situation?" somebody called from the back.

"We're clear for whatever it takes," Lester said. He looked at one of the papers in his hand. "Okay. Most of you guys are gonna be doing house-to-house . . ."

Lester dipped his head into a chorus of groans—it was still raining outside—and then said, "And there's a lot of small stuff we've got to get quick. We need to know about the paint in the parking lot, by morning. And we need to check the school, for that color or type of paint. Jim Hill here"—he nodded at one of the detectives—"points out that you hardly ever see poster paint outside a school, so maybe the school is somehow involved."

"Her old man did it," somebody said.

"We're checking that," Lester said. "In the meantime, we got the blood on that shoe, and we need somebody to walk the blood tests around, 'cause we need to know quick if the blood's Manette's or one of the kids'. If it's not—if it's somebody else's—we'll run it through the state's DNA offender bank. And we need to talk to the University medical school, get Manette's blood type. I'm told she occasionally volunteered for medical studies, so they may even have a DNA on her, and if the blood on the shoe belongs to one of the kids, a DNA might tell us that . . ."

"DNA takes a while," said a short, pink cop who wore a snap-brim hat with a feather in the hatband.

"Not this one," Lester said. He looked at the paper again. "We need Ford Econolines checked against all her patients, against the school staff, all relatives, and against whatever data base we can find on felony convictions, Minnesota and however much of Wisconsin we can get. We need to see if any Manette- or Dunn-related companies own Econolines. Go to Ford, see if we can get a list of Econolines from their warranty program—they said it was an older one, so go back as far as you can. We need to run the registration lists for Econolines against her patient list, which we're trying to get . . ."

Anderson broke in. "I'm setting up a data base of patient names. Any name that pops up in the investigation, we can run against the list—so get all the names you can. All the teachers at the school, her phone records, anything."

Lester nodded and continued. "We need to check Manette's and Dunn's credit ratings, see if anybody's got money problems. Check insurance policies. What else?"

"Manette's putting together an enemies list," Lucas said.

"Run that, too," Lester told Anderson. "What are we missing?"

"Public appeals," said a black cop in a pearl-gray suit. "Pictures of Manette and the kids."

"All the news outlets already have some kind of pictures, but we're putting out some high-quality stuff in the next couple of hours," Lester said. "There's some talk of a reward for information. We'll get back to you on that. And I want to say now, all the news contacts should go through the Public Affairs

Department. I don't want anybody talking to the press. Everybody clear on that?"

Everybody was. Lester turned to Sherrill. "How's the house-to-house going?"

"We've hit all the houses where the residents could see the school, except for two, where there's nobody home, and we're looking for those people in case they were there during the kidnapping," Sherrill said. "The only thing we have so far is one woman who saw the van, and she picked out Econoline taillights as the lights she saw. So we think that ID is solid. Now we're going back for a second round, to talk about what people might've seen in the past couple of days—and we're doing the same thing in Manette's neighborhood. If this was planned out, he must've been scouting her. So, that's about it."

"Okay," Lester said. He looked around the room. "You all know the general picture. Get your assignments from Anderson and let's get it on the road. I want everybody breaking their balls on this one. This one's gonna be tough, and we need to look good."

As the other detectives gathered around Anderson, Lucas leaned toward Greave and asked, "Did the kid, the witness kid, did she see anything different from what Girdler gave us?"

Greave scratched the back of his head, and his eyes defocused. "Ah, the kid, I don't know, I didn't get much from her. She was fairly freaked out. Didn't seem like much."

"You got her phone number?" Lucas asked.

"Sure. You want it?"

"Doesn't she live over in St. Paul? Highland Park?"

"Someplace around there . . ."

LESTER CAUGHT LUCAS outside his office as Lucas was locking the door.

"Any ideas?" he asked.

"What everybody else says—money or a nut," Lucas said. "If we don't get a ransom call, we'll find him in her files or in her family."

"There could be a problem with the files," Lester said. "Manette talked to the Wolfe woman and she hit the roof. I guess there was a hell of an argument. Medical privilege."

"Doesn't exist, Frank," Lucas said. "Subpoena the records. Don't talk about it. If you talk about it, it'll turn into a big deal and the media will be wringing their wrists. Get a judge out of bed, get the subpoena. I'll take it over myself, if you want."

"That'd be good, but not tonight," Lester said. "We've got too much going on already. I'll have it here at seven o'clock tomorrow morning."

Lucas nodded. "I'll pick it up as early as I can drag my ass out of bed," he said. He didn't get up early. "I'm gonna stop and see the kid, too. Tonight."

"Bob talked to her," Lester said, uncomfortably.

"Yeah, he did," Lucas said. And after a moment, "That's your problem."

"Bob's a nice guy," Lester said.

"He couldn't catch the clap in a whorehouse, Frank."

"Yeah, yeah . . . did you talk to the kid's folks?"

"Two minutes ago," Lucas said. "I told them I was on the way."

CLARICE BERNET WORE a suit and tie. Her husband, Thomas, wore a cash-mere sweater and a tie. "We don't want her frightened any more than she is," Clarice Bernet said. She hissed it, like a snake. She was a bony woman with tight blonde hair and a thin nose. Her front teeth were angled like a rodent's, and she was in Lucas's face.

"I'm not here to frighten her," Lucas said.

"You better not," Bernet said. She shook a finger at him: "There's been enough trouble from this already. The first officer questioned her without allowing us time to get there."

"We were hoping to stop the kidnapper's van," Lucas said mildly, but he was getting angry.

Thomas Bernet waggled his jowls: "We appreciate that, but you have to understand that this has been a trauma."

They were standing in the quarry-tiled entry of the Bernets' house, a closet to one side, a framed poster on the opposite wall, a souvenir from a Rembrandt show at the Rijksmuseum Amsterdam in 1992. A sad, middle-aged Rembrandt peered out at Lucas. "*You* have to understand that this is a kidnapping investigation and it could become a murder investigation," Lucas snapped, his voice developing an edge. "One way or another, we'll talk to your daughter and get answers from her. We can do it pleasantly, here, or unpleasantly down at Homicide, with a court order." He paused for a half-beat. "I'd rather not get the court order."

"*We* don't need threats," Thomas Bernet said. He was a division manager at General Mills and knew a threat when he heard one.

"I'm not threatening you; I'm laying out the legal realities," Lucas said. "Three people's lives are in jeopardy and if your daughter has a bad night's sleep over it, or two bad nights, that's tough. I've got to think about the victims and what they're going through. Now, do I talk to, uh, Mercedes, or do I get the court order?"

MERCEDES BERNET WAS a small girl with a pointed chin, a hundred-dollar haircut, and eyes that were five years too old. She wore a pink silk kimono and sat on the living room couch, next to a Yamaha grand piano, with her ankles crossed. She had recently developed breasts, Lucas thought, and sat with her back coyly arched, making the best of what was not yet too much. With her mother sitting beside her, and her father hovering behind the chair, she told Lucas what she'd seen.

"Grace was standing there, looking back and forth, like she didn't know what was going on. She even walked back toward the door for a minute, then she went back out. Then this van pulled around in front, going that way." She pointed to her left. "And this guy jumps out, and he runs up to her and she started to back up and the guy just grabbed her by her blouse and by her hair and he jerked her right off the porch-thing . . ."

"The portico," Clarice Bernet said.

"Yeah, whatever," said Mercedes, rolling her eyes. "Anyway, he pulled her toward the van and slid the door back and threw her inside. I mean, he was this *huge* dude. He just threw her. And before he closed the door, I saw two other people in there. Mrs. Dunn . . ."

"Mrs. Manette," her mother said.

"Yeah, whatever, and she had blood on her face. She was, like, *crawling.* Then there was another kid in there that I thought was Genevieve, but I couldn't see her face. She was, like, lying down on the floor, and then the guy closed the door."

"Where was Mr. Girdler during all of this?"

"I didn't see him until afterwards. He was behind me somewhere. I told him to call 911, but he was like, *Duh.*" She rolled her eyes again and Lucas smiled.

Then: "Think about this," Lucas said. "Tell me exactly what the kidnapper looked like."

Mercedes leaned back, closed her eyes, and a minute later, eyes still closed, said, "Big. Yellow hair, but it looked kinda weird, like it was peroxided or something. 'Cause his skin looked dark, not like a black dude, but you know . . . dark." She opened her eyes, and studied Lucas's face. "Like you, kinda. His face didn't look like yours—he had, like, a real narrow face—but he was about your color and big like you."

"What was he wearing? Anything special?"

She closed her eyes again and lived through the scene, then opened her eyes, looking surprised, and said, "Oh, shit."

"Young lady!" Clarice Bernet was shocked.

Lucas wagged his head once and asked, "What?"

"He was wearing a GenCon shirt. I *knew* there was something . . ."

He said, "GenCon? Are you sure? Did you see what year?"

"You know what it is?" A skeptical eyebrow went up.

"Sure. I write role-playing games . . ."

"Really? My boyfriend . . ."

"Mercedes!" Her mother's voice took a warning tone and Mercedes swerved into safer territory.

"A friend at school has one. I recognized it right away—the shirt isn't the same as my friend's, but it was a GenCon. Great big GenCon right on the front, and one of those weird dice. Everything black and white, kinda cheap . . ."

"What's a GenCon?" asked Thomas Bernet, looking suspiciously from his daughter to Lucas, as though GenCon might somehow be linked to ConDom.

"It's a gamer's convention, over in Lake Geneva," Lucas said. To Mercedes: "Why didn't you tell the other officer?"

"I could barely get his attention," she said. "And that asshole Girdler . . ."

"Mercedes!" Her mother was on the word like a wolf on a lamb.

"Well, he is," she said, barely defensive. "He kept talking all over me—I don't think he saw hardly any of it. He was mostly hiding down the hall."

"Okay," Lucas said. "What about the truck? Anything unusual about it?"

She nodded. "Yeah, there was, and I told the other cop. They'd painted over the sign on the truck. I don't know what it said, but there were letters on the door and they were painted right over."

"What letters?"

She shrugged. "I don't know. It was just something I sorta noticed when I went up closer to the windows and he was driving away. It wasn't a good paint job, you know? They just slopped right over the old letters."

LUCAS USED THE Bernets' phone to call back to the office, and dropped the t-shirt and truck information with Anderson.

"Heading home?" Anderson asked.

"Not much more to do tonight, unless we get a call. Are we still doing the door-to-door?"

"Yeah, up in Manette's neighborhood now. Asking for suspicious activities. Haven't heard anything back."

"Let me know."

"Yeah, I'll be putting together a book on it . . . Have you asked Weather yet?"

"Jesus Christ . . ." Lucas laughed.

"Hey, it's primo gossip."

"I'll let you know," Lucas said. He could feel the engagement ring in his pants pocket. Maybe ask her, he thought.

"I got a feeling about this," Anderson said.

"About Weather?"

"No. About the Manettes. There's something going on here. So they're not dead yet. They're out there waiting for us."

WEATHER KARKINNEN MADE a bump on the left side of the bed, near the window. The window was open an inch or two, so she could get the fresh cold air.

"Bad?" she asked, sleepily.

"Yes." He slipped in beside her, rolled close, kissed her on the neck behind the ear.

"Tell me," she said. She rolled onto her back.

"It's late," he said. She was a surgeon. She operated almost every day, usually starting at seven o'clock.

"I'm okay; I've got a late starting time tomorrow."

"It's Tower Manette's daughter and her two children, her daughters." He outlined the kidnapping, told her about the blood on the shoe.

"I hate it when there are kids involved," she said.

"I know."

Weather was a surgeon, but she looked like a jock—a fighter, actually, somebody who'd gone a few rounds too many. She had wide shoulders and she tended to carry her hands in front of her, fists clenched, like a punch-drunk boxer. Her nose was a little too large and bent slightly to the left; her hair was cut short, a soft brown touched with white. She had the high Slavic cheekbones of a full-blooded Finn, and dark blue eyes. For all of her jockiness, she was a small woman. Lucas could pick her up like a parcel and carry her around the house. Which he had done, on occasion; but never fully clothed.

Weather was not pretty, but she reached him with a power he hadn't experienced before: His attraction had grown so strong that it scared him at times. He'd lie awake at night, watching her sleep, inventing nightmares in which she left him.

They'd met in northern Wisconsin, where Weather had been working as a surgeon in a local hospital. Lucas had run down a child-sex ring, and the killer at the heart of it. In the final moments of a chase through the woods, he'd been shot in the throat by a young girl, and Weather had saved his life, opening his throat with a jack knife.

Hell of a way to get together . . .

Lucas put his hands on her waist. "Just how late can you go in?" he whispered.

"Men are animals," she said, moving closer.

WHEN SHE WENT to sleep, Lucas, relaxed, warm, moved against her. She snuggled deeper into her pillow, and pushed her butt out against him. The best time to ask her to marry him, he thought, would be now: he was awake, articulate, feeling romantic . . . and she was sleeping like a baby. He smiled to himself and patted her on the hip, and let his head fall on his pillow.

He kept the ring in the bottom of his sock drawer, waiting for the right moment. He could feel it there and wondered if it made black sparkles in the dark.

5

THE ROOM WAS a concrete-and-stone hole that smelled like rotten potatoes. Four fist-sized openings pierced the top of one wall, too high to see through. The openings reminded Andi of the holes that a child would punch in the top of a Ball jar, to give air to his insect collection.

A stained double-bed mattress lay in one corner, and the girls slept on it. John Mail had been gone for three hours, by Andi's watch. When he'd left, the steel door banging behind him, they'd all crouched on the mattress, waiting wide-eyed for his return.

He hadn't come back. The fear burning them out, the girls eventually curled up and fell asleep like kittens in a cat box, too exhausted to stay awake. Grace slept badly, groaning and whimpering, Genevieve slept heavily, her mouth open, even snoring at times.

Andi sat on the cold floor, with her back to the gritty wall, taking inventory for the fiftieth time, trying to find something, anything, that would get them out.

There was a light socket overhead, with a single sixty-watt bulb and a pull-chain. She hadn't yet had the courage to turn the light off. A Porta-Potti sat in a corner, smelling faintly of chemical rinse. The portable toilet was meant for small sailboats and campers, and was made of plastic. She could think of no way to use it as a weapon, or as anything other than a toilet. A Coleman cooler sat next to the door, half-full of melting ice and generic strawberry soda. And beside her, on a low plastic table, a game console and a monitor. The console and monitor were plugged into a four-socket power bar, which was plugged into an outlet above the light bulb.

And that was all.

A weapon? Perhaps one of the cans could be used as a club . . . somehow? Could the cord could be used to strangle him?

No. That was all absurd. Mail was too big, too violent.

Could you wire the door, somehow? Strip the wire out of the cord to the computer, connect it to the door handle?

Andi knew nothing about electricity—and if all Mail got was a shock, he'd simply turn off the power, and then come down, and . . . what?

That was what she couldn't deal with: what did he want? What would he do?

He'd obviously planned for this.

Their cell had once been a root cellar in a farm house, a deep hole, well below the frost line, with walls of granite fieldstone and concrete. Mail had knocked out part of an interior wall and had rebuilt it with concrete block to accommodate a steel fire door. The wiring was all new, nothing more than a cord run in from the outside.

Although the walls were old, except for the part Mail had redone, they were solid: Andi had pushed or kicked at every stone, had probed the interstices with her fingernails. Her hands were raw from it, and she'd found no weaknesses.

Overhead, between two-by-ten joists, was a plank ceiling. They could reach it by standing on the Porta-Potti, but when they beat on it, the sound was frighteningly dead: Andi feared that if they somehow pulled out a board, they'd find themselves buried underground.

The door itself was impossible, all steel with a simple slide latch on the outside. No amount of patience with a hairpin would pick the lock—if she'd known how to pick a lock in the first place, which she didn't.

She did the inventory again, straining to think of ways out. The chemical in the toilet? If it were harsh enough, perhaps she could throw it in his eyes and slip past him up the stairs?

He would kill them . . .

ANDI CLOSED HER eyes and relived the trip out of the Cities.

They'd rattled around the back of the van like dice in a cup—the cargo space had been stripped and was no more than a steel box, without handholds or comfort. Mail had apparently rigged the steel screen and removed the door handles for the kidnapping.

When they'd left the school, Mail had dodged from street to street, watching the rearview mirror, then took the van onto I-35, heading south, Andi thought. They were on I-35 for several minutes, then exited to an unfamiliar two-lane highway, out through the whiskey billboards and into the pastel suburbs south of the Cities, as the kids screamed and beat at the sides of the truck and then fell into an alternating, spasmodic weeping.

Andi was still bleeding inside her mouth, where her teeth had cut into her lip. The taste of blood and the smell of exhaust nauseated her; fighting to get to her hands and knees as Mail dodged through the side streets, she eventually crawled into a corner and vomited. The stench set Genevieve off; she began to retch, and Grace began to weep and shudder, shaking uncontrollably. Andi took all of it in but was unable to focus on it, unable to sort it out and react, until finally, dumbly, she simply took the children in her arms and held them and let them scream.

Mail paid no attention.

After a while, they all got to their knees and looked out the windows as the suburbs dwindled, and the truck entered the great green sea of corn, beans, and alfalfa outside the Cities.

Up front, Mail punched buttons on the radio, seemingly without purpose:

he went from Aerosmith to Toad the Wet Sprocket to Haydn to George Strait to three, four, five talk shows.

Listen, most of these criminals are weaklings; the only thing that makes them anything is that we give them a gun. Take the gun away, and they'll crawl back to the gutters where they came from . . .

They spent five minutes on a rural highway, bumping over long, snaky tar joints in the cracked concrete; then Mail took them off the highway onto a gravel road, and they left a spiraling cloud of gray dust in their wake. Red barns and white farmhouses flicked past the windows, and a black rural mailbox in a cluster of orange day lilies, dusty from the gravel.

Grace staggered to her feet and grabbed the chain-link fence separating them from Mail, and screamed, "Let me out of here, you fuck, let me out of here let me out . . ."

Genevieve panicked when her sister began to scream and wailed, a high, sirenlike keening, and her eyes rolled up into her head. She fell back and Andi thought for a moment that she'd had a stroke and crawled toward her, but Genevieve's eyes rolled and got straight and she started again, the keening, and Andi put her hands over her ears and Grace shouted, *Let me out of here* . . .

Mail put a hand over the ear closest to Grace, and, without looking back at her, shouted, *shut up shut up shut up,* and spit sprayed down the length of the windshield.

Andi grabbed her daughter and pulled her down, shook her head, held her daughter's face close and said, "Don't make him mad," then gathered up Genevieve and held her, squeezed her until the keening died away.

Then came a moment, just a moment, when Andi thought something different could happen, a streak of possibility rolling through her bloodied mind. They'd turned off the gravel road and started up a dirt lane.

Ragweed and black-eyed Susans grew in the middle of the track, and along both sides; farther away to the right, ancient, gray-barked apple trees stood with branches crabbed like scarecrow fingers.

An old farmhouse waited at the end of the lane: a dying house, shot through with rot, the paint peeling off the clapboard siding, a front porch falling off to one side. Behind it, down the far side of the hill, a barn's foundation crouched in a hollow. The barn itself was gone, but the lower level remained, covered by what had been the floor of the old structure, and by a blue plastic tarp tied at the corners with yellow polypropylene rope. An open doorway poked into the dark interior, like the entrance to a cave. Around the barn foundation, two or three other crumbling outbuildings subsided into the soil.

When they stopped, Andi thought in the recesses of her mind there would be three of them, only one of him. She could take him on, hold him while the girls ran. A cornfield bordered the farmhouse plot. There was no fence. Grace was fast and smart, and once in the cornfield, which was as dense as a rain forest, she could escape . . .

John Mail stopped the truck and they all rocked back and forth once, and Grace got to her knees and looked out the dirty window. Mail turned in his seat. He had an oddly high-pitched voice, almost childlike, and said to Andi: "If you try to run, I'll shoot the little kid first, then the next one, then you."

And the streak of possibility died.

GENETICS HAD MADE John Mail a psychopath. His parents had made him a sociopath.

He was a crazy killer and he didn't care about labels.

Andi had met him as part of her post-doc routine at the University of Minnesota, a new psychiatrist looking at the strange cases locked in the Hennepin County jails. She'd recognized a hard, quick intelligence in the cave of Mail's mind. He was smart enough—and large enough—to dominate his peers, and to avoid the cops for a while, but he was no match for a trained psychiatrist.

Andi had peeled him like an orange.

Mail's father had never married his mother, had never lived with them; last heard of, he was with the Air Force in Panama. Mail had never seen him.

When he was a baby, his mother would leave him for hours, sometimes all day and overnight, stuck in a bassinet, alone in a barren room. She married a man when he was three—three and still unable to talk—who didn't care much about her and less about Mail, except as an annoyance. When he was annoyed, when he was drunk, he'd use his leather belt on the kid; later, he moved to switches and finally to broom sticks and dowel rods.

As a child, Mail found intense pleasure in torturing animals, skinning cats and burning dogs. He moved up to attacking other children, both boys and girls—the class bully. In fourth grade, the attacks on girls had taken a sexual turn. He liked to get their pants off, penetrate them with his fingers. He didn't know yet what he wanted, but he was getting close.

In fifth grade, big for his age, he started riding out to the malls, Rosedale, Ridgedale, catching suburban kids outside the game rooms, mugging them.

He carried a t-ball bat, then a knife. In sixth grade, a science teacher, who also coached football, pushed him against a wall when he called a girl a cunt in the teacher's hearing. The teacher's house burned down a week later.

The fire was a trip: five more houses went down, all owned by parents of children who'd crossed him.

In June, after sixth grade, he torched the home of an elderly couple, who ran the last of the mom-and-pop groceries on St. Paul's east side. The old couple were asleep when the smoke rolled under the door. They died together near the head of the stairs, of smoke inhalation.

A smart arson cop finally found the pattern, and he was caught.

He denied it all—never stopped denying it—but they knew he'd done it. They brought Andi in, to see exactly what they'd caught, and Mail had talked about his life in a flat lizard's voice, casually, his young eyes crawling around her body, over her breasts, down to her hips. He scared her, and she didn't like it. He was too young to scare her . . .

Mail, at twelve, had already shown the size he'd be. And he had tension-built muscles in his body and face, and eyes like hard-boiled eggs. He talked about his stepfather.

"When you say he beat you, you mean with his fists?" Andi asked.

Mail grunted, and smiled at her naivete. "Shit, fists. The fucker had this dowel he took out of a closet, you know, a clothes rod? He whipped me with that. He beat my old lady, too. He'd catch her in the kitchen and beat the shit out of her and she'd be screaming and yelling and he'd just beat her until he got tired. Christ, there'd be blood all over the place like catsup."

"Nobody ever called the police?"

"Oh, yeah, but they never did anything. My old lady used to say that it was none of the neighbors' business."

"When he died, it got better?"

"I don't know, I wasn't living there any more; not much."

"Where'd you live?"

He shrugged: "Oh, you know: under the interstate, in the summer. There's some caves over in St. Paul, by the tracks, lots of guys over there . . ."

"You never went back?"

"Yeah, I went back. I got really hungry and fucked up and thought she maybe had some money, but she called the cops on me. If I hadn't gone back, I'd still be out. She said, 'Eat some Cheerios, I'll go get some cake,' and she went out in the front room and called the cops. Learned me a lesson, all right. Kill the bitch when I get out. If I can find her."

"Where is she now?"

"Took off with some guy."

After two months of therapy, Andi had recommended that John Mail be sent to a state hospital. He was more than a bad kid. He was more than unbalanced. He was insane. A kid with the devil inside.

THE GIRLS HAD stopped weeping when Mail opened the van door. He took them out, single file, through the side door of the old farm house and straight into the basement. The basement smelled wet, smelled of fresh dirt and disinfectant. Mail had cleaned it not long ago, she thought. A small spark of hope: he wasn't going to kill them. Not right away. If they had a little time, just a little time, she could work on him.

Then he locked them away. They listened for him, fearful, expecting him back at any moment, Genevieve asking, over and over, "Mom, what's he going to do? Mom, what's he going to do?"

A minute became ten minutes, and ten minutes an hour, and the girls finally slept while Andi put her back to the wall and tried to think . . .

————

MAIL CAME FOR her at three in the morning, drunk, excited.

"Get out here," he growled at her. He had a beer can in his left hand. The girls woke at the sound of the latch, and they crawled across the mattress until they had their backs to the wall, but curled, like small animals in a den.

"What do you want?" Andi said. She kept looking at her watch, as if this were a normal conversation and she was on her way somewhere else. But the fear made her voice tremble, as much as she tried to control it. "You can't keep us here, John. It's not right."

"Fuck that," Mail said. "Now get out here, goddamnit."

He took a step toward her, his eyes dark and angry, and she could smell the beer.

"All right. Don't hurt us, just don't hurt us. Come on, girls . . ."

"Not them," Mail said. "Just you."

"Just me?" Her stomach clutched.

"That's right." He smiled at her and put his free hand on the doorsill, as though he needed help staying upright. Or maybe he was being cool. He'd teased his hair into bangs, and now she realized that in addition to the beer, she could smell aftershave or cologne.

Andi glanced at the girls, then at Mail, and at the girls again. "I'll be right back," she said. "John won't hurt me."

Neither of the girls said a word. Neither of them believed her.

Andi walked around him, as far away as she could. In the outer basement, the air was cooler and fresher, but the first thing she noticed was that he'd dragged another mattress down the stairs. She stepped toward the stairs as the steel door clanged shut behind her and Mail said, "Don't move."

She stopped, afraid to move, and he walked around her, until he was between her and the door. He stared at her for a moment, a little out of balance, she thought. He was seriously drunk, and his eyes looked closed in, heavy-lidded, and his lips curled in an ugly, contemptuous smile.

"They don't have any idea where you're at or who took you," he said. He nearly laughed, but somewhere, under there, he was a bit unsure of himself, she thought. "They been talking about it on the radio all night. They're running around like chickens with their heads cut off."

"John, they'll come sooner or later," Andi said. "Your best option, I believe . . ." She automatically fell into her academic voice, the slightly dry observational tone that she used when dealing with patients on a sensitive point. A tone that seemed educated and aristocratic at the same time, and often sold her viewpoint on its own.

Not this time.

Mail moved very quickly, shockingly quickly, like a middleweight boxer, and slapped her face hard, nearly knocking her down. An instant before, she'd been a Ph.D. applying psychology; now she was a wounded animal, trying to find its balance before it became simply meat.

Mail stepped close to her, close enough to smell, close enough to see the texture in his jeans, and he snarled, "Don't you ever talk that way. And they're never gonna find us. Never in this world. Now stand up straight. Stand the fuck up."

She had her hand to her face, nothing coherent in her head: her thoughts were like Scrabble pieces on a dropped board. There was a crunching sound and she looked toward Mail, who was watching her, still angry. He'd crushed the beer can in his hand, and now he threw it into a corner, where it clattered off the wall and then bounced back toward them.

"Let's see 'em," he said.

"What?" She had no idea.

"Let's see 'em," he said.

"What?" Stupidly, shaking her head.

"Your tits, let's see your tits."

She tried to back away, one step, two, but there was no place to go. Behind her, an old coal-burning furnace stood like an old, close-cropped oak, the coal door open and leaning to the left; and behind it, a dark space, a place she really didn't want to go. "John, you don't want to hurt me. John," she said. "I took care of you."

He thrust a finger at her. "You don't want to talk about that. You don't want to talk about that. You took care of me, all right, you sent me down to the fuckin' hospital. You took care of me, all right." He looked around wildly, then saw the beer can on the floor. He'd forgotten that he'd finished it. He came back at her. "Come on, let's see 'em."

She crossed her arms over her chest. "John, I can't . . ."

And as quickly as he had before, he hit her again, open-handed, not quite as hard. When she put her hands up, he hit her again, and then again. She couldn't block the blows, she couldn't stop, she couldn't even see them coming.

Then he was on her, slamming her back against the stone wall, ripping at her jacket, at her blouse. She screamed at him, "No, don't, John . . ."

And he swatted her again, knocked her down, pulling her hair, guiding her to the mattress, and landed on top of her, straddling her waist. She struck at him, flailed uselessly. He caught her hands, brought them together, took them in one of his, held them. She couldn't see him very well, realized that she was bleeding, that she had blood in one eye.

"John . . ." She began to weep, not believing that he could go on.

But he did.

WHEN HE WAS done, he was angrier than when he had started.

He made her dress, as best she could—her blouse was ripped nearly in half, and he took her bra away from her—and then thrust her back in the cell.

Both of the girls, even the small Genevieve, knew what had happened. When Andi dropped onto the mattress, they automatically curled around her and held her head, while the steel door clanged shut.

Andi couldn't cry.

Her eyes had dried, or something. When she thought of Mail—not his face, not his voice, but the smell of him—she wanted to gag, and sometimes did, a reflexive clutching of her throat and stomach.

But she couldn't cry.

She hurt, though. She was bruised, and felt small muscle pulls and tears, when she'd struggled and twisted against his strength. There wasn't any blood: she checked herself, and though she felt raw, he hadn't ripped anything.

She was dry-eyed, stunned, when Mail came back.

They felt something, a muffled part of the sound, vibrations from the floor above, and knew he was coming. They were all facing the door, sitting on the mattress, when the door opened. Andi tucked her skirt beneath her.

Mail was wearing jeans, a plaid shirt, and wrap-around sunglasses, and held a pistol. He stood in the open door for a moment, then said, "I can't keep all of you." He pointed at Genevieve. "Come on, I'm taking you out."

"No, no," Andi blurted. She caught Genevieve's arm, and the girl pulled into her side. "No, John, please, no, don't take her, I'll take care of her here, she won't be a problem, John . . ."

Mail looked away. "I'll take her out to the Wal-mart and drop her off. She's smart enough to call the cops and get back home."

Andi stood up, pleading. "John, I'll take care of her, honest to God, she won't be a problem."

"She is a problem. Just thinking about her in my head, she's a problem." He pointed the pistol at Grace, who flinched away. "I gotta keep her, because she's too old and she could bring the cops back. But the kid, here—I'll put a bag on her head and take her out to the van and drop her at Wal-Mart."

"John, please," Andi begged.

Mail snarled at Genevieve, "Get out of here, kid, or I'll beat the shit out of you and drag your ass out."

Andi got to her knees and then to her feet, reached toward him. "John . . ."

He stepped back and his hand came up and caught her throat, and for a half-instant she thought she was dead: he squeezed for a second, then threw her back. "Get the fuck away." And to Genevieve: "Get out of here, kid, out the door."

"Wait, wait," Andi said. "Gen, take your coat, it's cold . . ." Genevieve had rolled her coat into a pillow, and Andi got it off the mattress, unrolled it, and fitted it around the child and buttoned it, kneeling, looking into Gen's eyes.

"Just be good," she said. "John won't hurt you . . ."

Genevieve went like her feet were stuck in glue, and Andi called, "Genevieve, honey, ask for a policeman. When you get to the mall, ask for a policeman and tell them who you are. They'll take you home to Daddy."

The door slammed in her face. Faintly, faintly, she could hear footsteps outside in the basement, but nothing else behind the muffled steel door.

"She'll be okay," Grace said. But she was beginning to cry, and the words came hard through the tears: "She's been in lots of malls. She'll just find a policeman and she'll go home. Dad'll take care of her."

"Yes." Andi dropped to the mattress, her hands covering her face: "Oh my God, Grace. Oh my God."

6

"I HATE RICH PEOPLE," Sherrill muttered. She was wearing the same coat as the night before, but she'd added her own hat, a green baseball cap with a pale blue bill. Her hair was tucked underneath. She finished the outfit with pale blue sneaks, a tom-boy-with-great-breasts look. With her rosy cheeks and easy smile, Black thought she looked good enough to eat.

They'd dumped the city car in the parking lot outside Andi Manette's office building. The building, Sherrill thought, had been designed by a seriously snotty architect: black windows, red bricks, and copper flashing, snuggled into the side of a cattail-ringed pond, with a twisted chunk of rusty Corten steel out front. Black paused by the sculpture: the plaque said, *Ray-Tracing Wrigley*.

"You know what that's supposed to be?" he asked, looking up at it.

"Looks like a big stick of rusty steel chewing gum that somebody twisted," Sherrill said.

Black said, "Jesus, you're an art critic. That's what it must be."

Sherrill led the way across a bridge over a moatlike finger from the pond. Somebody had thrown a half-bucket of corn into the water, and a cluster of mallards and two Canada geese rooted through the shallow water weeds for the kernels. A half-dozen koi circled slowly among the ducks, their golden bodies just under the surface. The rain had stopped, and a thin sunshine, broken up by the yellow branches of weeping willows, dappled the pond.

"There's Davenport," Black said, and Sherrill looked back at the parking lot. Lucas was just getting out of his Porsche. The lot around him was sprinkled with 700-series BMWs and S-Class Mercedeses, a few Lexuses and Cadillacs, and the odd Jaguar, among the usual Chevys and Fords. Lucas circled a black Acura NSX that had been carefully parked away from other cars, stopped to look in the driver's side window.

"Speaking of rich," Sherrill said.

They waited and, after a second, Lucas broke away from the NSX and came up the walk, nodded at Black, grinned at Sherrill, and she felt a little *thump*. "If I was gonna steal cars, this would be the place," he said. "Gotta have money to get your head shrunk."

"Or get the county to pay for it," Black said.

"Did you ask her?" Sherrill asked.

"Not yet," Lucas said.

They checked the building directory, an arty rectangle decorated with a blue bird. Manette's office was at the back of the building, a multiroom suite with quiet, gray carpets and Scandinavian furnishings. A matronly Scandinavian receptionist sat behind a blonde oak desk, writing into a computer. She looked up when Lucas, Black, and Sherrill walked in, turned away from the computer. "Can I . . . ?"

"We're Minneapolis police officers. I'm Deputy Chief Lucas Davenport and we have a subpoena for Dr. Manette's records and a search warrant for her office," Lucas said. "Could you show us her office?"

"I'll get Mrs. Carney and Dr. Wolfe . . ."

"No. Show us the office, then get whomever you wish," Lucas said politely. "Who is Mrs. Carney?"

"The office manager," the woman said. "I'll get . . ."

"No. Show us Dr. Manette's office."

Manette's office was large, informal, with a comfortable couch and a loveseat at right angles to each other, and a glass coffee table in the angle. Two Kirk Lyttle ceramic sculptures stood in the middle of the table; they looked like crippled birds, straining for the sky.

"Where are her files?"

"In, um, there." The receptionist was ready to panic, but she poked a finger at a line of wood folding doors. Sherrill crossed to the doors and pulled them back. A half-dozen four-drawer file cabinets were lined up in an alcove, along with a short table that held an automatic espresso maker and a small refrigerator.

"Thank you," Lucas said, nodding at the receptionist. The woman stepped backwards through the door, then turned and ran. "Gonna be some noise," he said.

"Tough shit," said Sherrill.

Lucas took off his coat, tossed it on a chair, went to the first of the file cabinets, and pulled open a drawer.

"Get out of there," Nancy Wolfe shouted at him. She steamed through the door, her hands out to grab him, push him, or hit him. Lucas set his feet, and when she grabbed him and pushed, he didn't move. Wolfe went backward with a little hop.

"If you push me again, I'll arrest you and send you downtown in handcuffs," Lucas said quietly. "Assault on a police officer has a mandatory jail sentence."

Wolfe's black eyes were blazing with anger: "You're in my files, you've got no right . . ."

"I've got a subpoena, a search warrant, and the written approval of Dr. Manette's next of kin," Lucas said. "We're gonna look at the files."

She stepped toward him again, her hands moving, and Lucas turned just a half an inch and tucked his chin even less, but he saw the flinch in her eyes. She believed he'd hit her back, and she stopped, stepped sideways, and crossed her arms. "You're referring to George Dunn?"

"Yes."

"George Dunn is hardly close to Andi, not any more," Wolfe said. Her face had been white with anger, but now it was reddening, with heat. She was an attractive woman, in a professorial way—slender, salt-and-pepper hair, just a boarding-school touch of makeup. But her red face clashed with her cool, mint-green suit and the Hermès scarf at her neck. "I don't believe . . ."

"Mr. Dunn is her husband," Sherrill said. "Andi Manette and her children have been kidnapped, and even though nobody has said it, they may already be dead somewhere."

"If they're not, they may be, soon," Lucas added. "If you try to fuck us around on the records, you'll lose. But the delay could kill your partner and her daughters."

Lucas said *fuck* deliberately, to harden the statement, to shock, to keep her on the defensive. Wolfe talked right through it: "I want to call my attorney."

"Call him," Lucas said.

Wolfe looked at him, then spun on a heel and stormed out.

When Wolfe was gone, Black asked, "How solid are we?"

"Solid, but they might find a friendly judge and slow us down," Lucas said. Sherrill nodded and pulled open another file cabinet. "Skim everything, get all the names and addresses—read them into your tape recorders, transcribe later. We need speed. If there's a problem, we'll have that much, anyway. And if there is a problem, refer it to Tyler down at the County Attorney's office and just keep working. When you get all the names on the recorder, go back through the records and look for anything likely. References to violence, to threats. Sexual deviation. Males only, to start."

"Where're you going?" Sherrill asked.

"To see some guys about some games," Lucas said.

Nancy Wolfe met him in the hallway as he was going out. "My attorney is on the way. He said for you to leave the files alone until he gets here."

"Yeah, well, as soon as your attorney is elevated to the district court, I'll follow his instructions," Lucas said. Then he let some air into his voice: "Look, we're not gonna persecute your patients—we won't even look at most of them. But we've got to move fast. We've got to."

"You'll set us back years with some of these people. You'll destroy the trust they've built up with us—the only people they can trust, for most of them. And the people who need treatment for sexual deviation, or other possibly criminal behavior, they won't be back at all. Not after they hear what you've done."

"Why do they have to hear?" Lucas asked. "If you don't make a big deal out of it, nobody'll know except the few people we actually talk to. And with them, we can make it seem like we got the information from someplace else—not deal with the records."

She was shaking her head. "If you go through those records, I'll feel it incumbent upon me to inform the patients."

Lucas tightened up and his voice dropped, got a little gravel. "You don't tell them before we look at them. If you do, by God, and one of them turns out to be the kidnapper, I'll charge you as an accomplice to the kidnapping."

Wolfe's hand went to the Hermès scarf at her throat: "That's ludicrous."

"Is it true that you'll get a half-million dollars if Andi Manette is dead?"

Wolfe's mouth tightened in a line that might have indicated disgust. "Get away from me," she said. She brushed at him with one hand and started down the hall toward Manette's office. "Just get away."

But as he was going out the door, she shouted down the hall, "Who told you that? George? Did George tell you that?"

LUCAS HIT A game store in Dinkytown, near the campus of the University of Minnesota, another on Snelling Avenue in St. Paul, then dropped down to South Minneapolis.

Erewhon was run by Marcus Paloma, a refugee from the days of LSD and peyote tea. The shop was just off Chicago, a few blocks below Lake, surrounded by small stucco houses painted in postwar pastels, all crumbling into their crab-grass lawns.

Lucas parked and ambled toward the shop. The cool, rain-washed air felt alive around him, the streets clear of their usual dust, the leaves of the trees burning like neon.

The shop was exactly the opposite: dim, musty, a little dusty. Bins of comics in plastic sleeves pressed against boxes of used role-playing and war games. Lucite racks of metallic miniatures—trolls, wizards, thieves, fighters, clerics, and goblins—guarded the cash register counter.

Marcus Paloma was gaunt, with a goatee and heavy glasses. His thinning gray hair was worn bouffant; he was dressed in a gray sweatsuit with Nike cross-training shoes. He'd once finished eighth in the St. Paul Marathon. "I got a concept," he shouted down the store, past the bins of comics, when he saw Lucas. "I'm gonna make a million bucks."

John Mail was sitting in a folding chair, looking through a cardboard box of used D&D modules. He glanced down the store at Lucas, and then looked back into the box. Two other gamers, one of each sex, looked up when Paloma shouted at Lucas.

"A feminist role-playing game, modelled on Dungeons and Dragons," Paloma said, gradually moderating his voice as he walked toward Lucas. "Set in prehistoric times, but dealing with problems like heterosexual mating and child birth in an essentially lesbian-oriented setting. I'm calling it The Nest."

Lucas laughed. "Marcus, everything you know about feminism, you could write on the back of a fuckin' postage stamp with a laundry pen," he said.

The female gamer said, "Profanity is a sign of ignorance," and faced him, waiting to be challenged.

Marcus, coming up the store, said, "That was an obscenity, sweetheart, not a profanity. Get your shit straight. That's a vulgarity, by the way—shit is." To Lucas, he said, "How you been? Shoot anybody lately?"

"Not for several days," Lucas said. They shook, and Lucas added, "You're looking good."

"Thanks." Marcus's face was its usual dusty gray. "I'm watching my diet. I've eliminated all fats except a tablespoon of extra virgin olive oil, on salad, at noon."

"Yeah?"

"Yeah. Could you sign some stock since you're here?"

"Sure."

"Hey, are you Davenport?" the female gamer asked. She was a dark-haired high school senior, quivering with caffeine.

"Yes."

"I've got *Blades* at home, I'd love you to sign it."

"You still got the book on that?" Marcus asked the girl.

"Sure," the girl said.

"I'll get him to sign a book on a used one, and you bring yours in, and we'll trade," Marcus said.

"Dude," said the girl.

"Marcus, we gotta go in the back," Lucas said. "I need to talk for a minute."

"All right, let me get those games." He stepped over to the cash register stand, took a half-dozen boxes off a rack, walked to the used bin and picked up two more, and led Lucas down the length of the store into the back. Just before ducking through a gray curtain into his office, he called back to the girl, "Keep an eye on the desk, will you, Carol?"

The office was filled with cardboard shipping boxes. A roll-top desk was shoved into a corner, buried under ten pounds of unopened junk mail. There were three chairs, one overstuffed and comfortable, two folding, covered with green vinyl. The room smelled of old newsprint and slightly stale cat food. A fat red tabby was lying on the back ledge of the rolltop. The cat looked at Lucas, and Lucas's gray silk suit, and seemed to think about it.

"Sit down," Paloma said, waving one hand expansively. "Damn cat is sitting on my orders. Get off of there, Bennie."

They talked the games business for a minute or two—who was winning, who was losing, the sales wars. "Listen, Marcus, something's up," Lucas said. He leaned forward and tapped Paloma on the knee.

"Sure. Cop business?" Paloma had done a little snitching for Lucas.

"Yeah. You heard about that shrink getting snatched? And her kids? Big news in the *Strib* this morning?"

"Yeah, I saw that," Paloma said, amazed. "Took her right out of the parking lot."

"The guy who did it might be a gamer," Lucas said.

"A gamer?" Paloma asked doubtfully. Another cat came out of the back, a gray one, a solemn female. Marcus picked her up and scratched her ears, and she stared at Lucas with her yellow eyes.

"Yeah. Big guy, wearing a GenCon t-shirt, middle twenties. Probably strong, like a body builder. Has a violent streak. Blond, shoulder-length hair."

"Nice Dexie," Paloma said to the cat. Then he shook his head, slowly, thinking. "Not really. Big and tough, huh? That doesn't sound like too many gamers." He scratched his nose, thinking. "Except . . ."

"Who?"

"The guy out there now—he's a big guy." Paloma nodded toward the door to the front. "Pretty tough-looking. And I think I've seen him in a GenCon shirt."

"Where? Sitting down? He was kinda short." Lucas looked toward the curtain that separated the office from the sales floor.

"He was sitting in an old folding chair. He's probably six-four, maybe two-twenty. Strong as a bull," Paloma said.

Lucas stepped toward the door. "What's his name?"

"I don't know. I've seen him two or three times before. Never said much to me."

"Have you ever seen his car?"

"No. Not that I know of," Paloma said.

"Huh," Lucas said. He went back through the door in a hurry, but the dark-haired man was no longer sitting in the chair. To the girl he said, "Where did that guy go? The guy who was sitting over there . . ."

She shook her head. "He left. You gonna sign a book for me?"

"Who is he? You know him?" Lucas hurried toward the street door.

"Nope. Never saw him before," she said. "Why?"

"How about you?" he called back to the male gamer. "You know him?"

"Nope. I'm with her."

Out on the sidewalk, Lucas went to the corner and looked all four ways down the intersecting streets. No van in sight. Nothing but a green Mazda, driven by a redheaded woman in a green dress, who seemed to be lost.

How long had they been talking in the back? Four or five minutes, no more. And the guy had gone, disappeared, in that time.

Lucas stood on the street corner, wondering.

THE PARKING GARAGE that had once faced the back entrance to City Hall had been razed, and Lucas left the Porsche on the street. Paloma, who'd been following in a Studebaker Golden Hawk, found another space a half-block further on. As they walked back toward City Hall, they could hear the City Hall bell ringer playing "You Are My Sunshine," the tune clanging out above police headquarters.

A thin man fell in step with them. As Lucas turned to him, Sloan said, looking up at the bell tower, "Hope there are no fuckin' acid-heads around right now."

Lucas grinned: "That would be hard to explain to yourself—'You Are My Sunshine' banging around your brain."

"Makes me want to jump off the tower. And I'm not even high," Paloma said.

SHERRILL CAUGHT THEM in the hallway outside Lucas's office. She was carrying a manila file: "We've got a problem." She glanced at Paloma, then turned back to Lucas. "We need to talk. Now."

"What? They got a court order?" Lucas asked.

"No. But you're not gonna like it."

Lucas turned to Sloan: "Marcus is here to look at the composite on the Manette kidnapper. He might want to add some stuff. Could you get him down there?"

"Sure," Sloan said. And to Marcus: "Let's go."

Lucas opened his office, nodded Sherrill into a chair, and hung his coat and jacket on an old-fashioned oak coat rack. "Tell me," he said. And he decided that he liked the tomboy-with-great-breasts look. He'd never hit on Sherrill, and now couldn't think how he'd missed her.

"There's a guy named Darrell Aldhus, a senior vice president at Jodrell National," Sherrill said. "He's been diddling little boys in his Scout troop."

Lucas frowned. "Does this have anything . . ."

"No. Nothing to do with Andi Manette, except that she hasn't reported the guy. And that's a felony. What's happening is, is what everybody was afraid was gonna happen. Aldhus admits in here—" Sherrill slapped the file—"that he's had several sexual contacts with boys, and he's trying to get himself cured. If we go after him, a defense attorney is gonna tell him to get the hell out of therapy and don't say shit to anybody. Since all we've got is her notes, nothing on tape, we really don't have that strong a case—not without her to back them up. We could put the Sex guys on it, have them start talking to kids . . ."

"Do we have any of the kids' names?" Lucas asked.

"No, but if we went in hard, I'm sure we could find some," she said.

"Goddamnit." Lucas opened a desk drawer and put his feet on it. "I didn't want this."

"The press is gonna be on us like a hot sweat," Sherrill said. "This guy is big enough that if we bust him, it'll be front-page stuff."

"In that case, we oughta do the right thing."

"Yeah? And what's that?" Sherrill asked.

"Beats the shit out of me," Lucas said.

"You figure it out," she said. She handed him the file. "I'm gonna go back and look at the rest of it. I wouldn't be surprised if Black hasn't already found more of these things . . . this was like the fourth file I looked at."

"But nothing on Manette?"

"So far, no—but Nancy Wolfe . . ."

"Yeah?"

"She says you're a bully," Sherrill said.

LUCAS UNLOADED THE Aldhus file on the chief, who treated it like a live rattlesnake.

"Give me a couple of suggestions," Roux said.

"Sit on it."

"While this guy is diddling little boys?"

"He hasn't done any diddling lately. And I don't want to start a fuckin' pie fight right in the middle of the Manette thing."

"All right." She looked at the file, half-closed her eyes. "I'll confer with Frank Lester and he can assign it to an appropriate officer for preliminary assessments of the veracity of the material."

"Exactly," Lucas said. "Under the rug, at least for now. How are the politics shaking out?"

"I briefed the family again, me and Lester, on the overnights. Manette looked like death had kissed him on the lips."

SLOAN CAUGHT LUCAS in the corridor.

"Your friend the doper looked at the composite: he says it could be our guy."

"Sonofabitch," Lucas said. He put his hands over his eyes, as if shielding them from a bright light. "He was right there. I didn't even see his face."

GREAVE HAD ON a fresh, bluish suit; Lester's eyes were red-rimmed from lack of sleep.

"They giving you shit?" Lucas asked, stepping into Homicide.

"Yeah," Lester said, straightening up. "Whataya got?"

Lucas gave him a one-minute run-down: "It coulda been him."

"And it coulda been Lawrence of Iowa," Greave said.

Lester handed over the composite sketch based on information from Girdler and the girl. "Had a hell of a time getting them to agree on anything," Lester said. "I have a feeling that our eyewitnesses . . . Mmmm, what's the word I'm looking for?"

"*Suck,*" said Greave.

"That's it," Lester said. "Our eyewitnesses suck."

"Maybe my guy can add something," Lucas said. The face in the composite was tough, and carried a blankness that might have reflected a lack of infor-mation, or a stone-craziness. "Did Anderson tell you about the GenCon shirt?"

"Yeah," Lester nodded. He stretched, yawned, and said, "We're trying to get a list of people who registered for the convention the past couple of years, hotel registrations . . . did you see the *Star-Tribune* this morning?"

"Yeah, but I missed the television last night," Lucas said. "I understand they got a little exercised."

Lester snorted. "They were hysterical."

Lucas shrugged. "She's a white, professional, upper-middle-class woman from a moneyed family. That's the hysteria button. If it was a black woman, there'd be one scratch-ass guy with a pencil."

A phone rang in the empty lieutenant's office, and Greave got up and wandered over, picked it up on the fourth ring, looked back toward Lucas.

"Hey, Lucas—you've got a call. The guy says it's an emergency. A Doctor Morton."

Lucas, puzzled, shook his head and said, "Never heard of him."

Greave shrugged, waved the phone. "Well?"

Lucas said, "Jesus, Weather?" He took the phone from Greave. "Davenport."

"Lucas Davenport?" A man's voice, young, but with back gravel in it, like a pot smoker's rasp.

"Yes?" There was silence, and Lucas said, "Dr. Morton?"

"No, not really. I just told them that so you'd answer the phone." The man stopped talking, waiting for a question.

Lucas felt a small tingle at the back of his throat. "Well?"

"Well, I got those people, Andi Manette and her kids, and I saw in the paper that you're investigating, and I thought I ought to call you 'cause I'm one of your fans. Like, I play your games."

"You took them? Mrs. Manette and her daughters? Who the hell is this?" Lucas dosed his voice with impatience, while frantically waving at the other two. Lester grabbed a phone; Greave looked this way and that, not sure of what to do, then hurried to his cubicle and a second later came back with a tape recorder with a suction-cup pickup. Lucas nodded, and while Mail talked, Greave licked the suction cup, stuck it on the earpiece of the phone, and started the recorder.

"I'm sorta the Dungeon Master in this little game," John Mail was saying. "I thought maybe you'd like to roll the dice and get started."

"This is bullshit," Lucas said, stretching for time. Lester was talking urgently into his telephone. "We run into you assholes every time something like this gets in the paper. So listen to this, pal: you want to get your face on TV, you're gonna have to do it on your own. I'm not gonna help."

"You don't believe me?" Mail was perplexed.

Lucas said, "I'll believe you if you can tell me one thing about the Manettes that's not in the newspaper or on television."

"Andi's got a scar like a rocket ship," Mail said.

"A rocket ship?"

"That's what I said. An old German V-2 with a flame coming out of the ass-end. You can ask her old man where it is."

Lucas closed his eyes. "Are they all right?"

"We've had a casualty," John Mail said, off-handedly. "Anyway, I gotta go before you trace this and send a cop car. But I'll call back, to see how you're doing. Do you have a cellular phone?"

"Yes."

"Give me the number."

Lucas recited the number, and Mail repeated it. "You better carry it with you," he said. Then, "This really turns my crank, Davenport. OK, so roll a D20."

"What?"

"On your Zen dice."

"Uh, okay . . . just a minute." In the office, Lester was bent over the desk, talking urgently into the phone. Lucas said, "I'm rolling . . . I get a four."

"Ah, that's a good roll: Here's the clue: Go ye to the Nethinims and check 'em out. Got that?"

"No."

"Well, then, tough shit," Mail said. "Doesn't look like you're gonna do too well."

"We're already doing well. We knew you were a gamer," Lucas said. "We've been on your ass since last night."

Mail exhaled impatiently, then said, "You got lucky, that's all . . ."

"Not luck: you're fuckin' up on the details, pal. You'd be a hell of a lot better off . . ."

"Don't tell me how I'd be better off. Not one fuckin' guy in a million would've recognized that shirt. Blind fuckin' luck."

And he was gone. Lucas turned to Lester, who was working two phones at once. After a moment, he put one down, then the other, looked up at Lucas, shook his head. "Not enough time."

"Jesus, half the people in town have Caller ID. And we're still calling up the company for traces?" Lucas said. "Why don't we get a goddamn Caller ID like half the civilians in the state?"

"Well," Lester said. He shrugged: he didn't know why. "Was it him?"

"I'd bet on it," Lucas said. He told Lester about the scar like a rocket ship.

"What—you think it's on her ass or something?"

"That's what I think," Lucas said. "We better check with Dunn. But the way he said it, that's what I think . . . And he said they'd had a casualty. I think somebody's dead."

"Aw, shit," Lester said.

THEY WENT OVER Greave's tape together, three or four other cops gathering around to listen. They played it through once without interruption, then went back and listened to pieces. They could hear cars in the background. "Pay phone at a busy intersection. Big fuckin' help," Lester said. "And what's a D20? And who are the Nethinims?"

"D20s are twenty-sided dice. Gamers use them," Lucas said. "I don't know about the Netha-whachamacallits."

"Sounds like some kind of street gang, but I never heard of them," Greave said. "Play it again."

As they rewound the tape, Lucas said, "He knew about the shirt. Who'd we tell?"

"Nobody. I mean, the family, maybe. And the kid knows . . ."

"And probably that fuckin' Girdler. We better see if we can get a tape of that radio show, see if what all he talked about . . ."

"And maybe that goddamn kid is talking to the press—everybody else is blabbing."

Greave punched the tape, and they listened to it again and Greave said, "Yeah, he said Nethinims. N-E-T-H-I-N-I-M-S or N-E-T-H-A-N-I-M-S."

Lucas looked in the phone book, Lester tried directory assistance. "Nothing."

Lucas, walking around, staring at the ceiling, came back to Lester. "Was I on the news? In the paper, about being on the case?"

Lester showed a thin grin: Lucas attracted a lot of publicity over the years. Sometimes it chafed. "No."

"This guy said he knew I was investigating, because he'd seen it in the paper . . ."

"Well, we got the *Pioneer Press* around here somewhere, and all kinds of *Star-Tribune*s, you could look—but I don't think so. I read the stories."

"TV or radio?"

He shrugged. "I don't know. Maybe. They know you by sight—they know your car. There were all kinds of reporters around that school. Or maybe somebody interviewed Manette or Dunn and they mentioned something. Or that guy on the radio last night . . ."

"Huh." And he thought about the kid he'd seen in the game store that morning, sitting down. The kid who'd left so quickly, who looked like the right guy.

"You want me to check out these Nethinims dudes?" Greave asked.

Lucas turned to him, nodded. Greave was okay with books. "Yeah. If you ask around, and nobody knows, check a couple of game stores and see if it's a new game character or set. Then check like, uh, Tolkien's Ring cycle—*Lord of the Rings,* all that. There're a couple of science fiction stores in town—call and talk to a clerk, see if anybody recognizes the name from a book series . . . a fantasy series probably."

"The guy sounds like a smart little wiseass," Lester said.

"Yeah." Lucas nodded. "And he can't help proving it. He'll last five days or a week—I just hope somebody's left alive when we get him."

7

THE RAPE HAD done something to her, beyond the obvious. Had damaged her.

When Mail had finished with her, she was panicked, injured, in pain—but generally coherent. When Mail had taken Genevieve, she'd argued with him, pleaded.

An hour after that, she began to drift.

She curled on the mattress, stopped talking to Grace, closed her eyes, trembled, shuddered, tightened into a ball. She lost the most elemental sense of what was going on—how much time was passing, where sounds came from, who was in the cell with her.

Grace came to her several times, gave her strawberry soda, tried to get her to eat, took off her own coat and gave it to her mother. This last, the coat, Andi found useful: she huddled under it, away from the naked lightbulb, the Porta-Potti, the stark gray walls. With the coat over her head, she could almost believe she was at home, dreaming . . .

She seemed to wake a few times and she spoke with both Grace and Genevieve, and once with George. Sometimes she felt her mind drifting above herself, like a cloud: she watched her body huddled on the mattress, and wondered, *why?*

But sometimes she felt needle-sharp: she opened her eyes and looked at her knees, pulled up tight to her chin, and felt herself clever not to come out from under the coat.

Beneath it all, she knew her mind simply wasn't functioning correctly. This, she thought during a passing moment of rationality, was insanity. She'd been outside of it for years: this was the first time she'd been inside.

Once she had a dream, or a vision: several men, friendly but hurried, wearing technicians' or scientists' coats, lowered her into a steel cylinder with an interior the size of a phone booth. When she was inside, a steel cap with interlocking flanges was lowered on top of the cylinder, to seal it off. One of the technicians, an intelligent, soft-spoken man with blond hair, glasses, and an easy German accent, said, "You'll only have to last through the heat. If you make it through the heat, you'll be all right . . ."

Some kind of protection dream, she thought, during one of the lucid moments. The blond man, she thought, she'd seen in a Mercedes-Benz commercial, or a BMW ad. But the man wasn't the thing. The cylinder was: nobody, nothing could get at her in the cylinder.

AFTER A VERY long time of wandering in and out of consciousness, she closed in on herself. Found a ray of rationality, followed it to a kind of spark, and sat up. Grace was sitting on the concrete floor, facing the computer monitor. The screen was blank.

"Grace, are you all right?"

Andi was whispering. Grace reflexively looked up at the ceiling, as though the whisper might have come from the outside, from God. Then she looked over her shoulder at Andi: "Mom?"

"Yes." Andi rolled up to a sitting position.

"Mom, are you . . ."

"I'm getting better," Andi said, shaking.

Grace crawled toward her. Her slender daughter looked even thinner, like a winter-hungry fox: "Jeez, Mom, you were arguing with Daddy for a while . . ."

"John Mail beat me up; he raped me," Andi said. She simply let the word out. Grace had to know what was happening, had to help.

"I know." Grace looked away, tears trickling down her cheek. "But you're better?"

"I think so." Andi pushed herself up to her knees, then stepped off the mattress, shakily, one hand on the wall. Her legs felt like cheese, thick, soft, unreliable, until the blood began to flow again. She pulled her skirt up, pulled her blouse together. He'd taken her bra: she remembered that. The assault was coming back.

She turned her back to her daughter, pulled up her skirt, pulled down her underpants, looked inside: just a spot of blood. She wasn't badly torn.

"Are you okay?" Grace whispered.

"I think so."

"What are we going to do?" Grace asked. "What about Genevieve?"

"Genevieve?" *My God. Genevieve.* "We've got to think," Andi said, turning around to look at her daughter again. She knelt on the mattress, pulled Grace's head close to her lips and whispered, "The first thing we've got to do is find out if he's listening to us, or if we can talk. We have to keep talking, but I want you to get on my shoulders, and I'm going to try to stand up. Then I want you to look at the ceiling, see if there is anything that might be, you know, a microphone. It probably won't be very sophisticated—he'd just stick a tape recorder microphone in one of the airholes, or something."

Grace nodded, and Andi said, out loud, "I don't think I'm too hurt, but I need some sleep."

"So just lie down for a while," Grace said. Andi squatted, and Grace stepped over her shoulders. She probably weighed eighty pounds, Andi thought. She had to push herself up with help from the wall, but she got straight, and they walked back and forth through the room, Grace's head almost at the ceiling, the girl dragging her fingers across the dark wooden boards, probing into corners, poking her fingers into the airholes in the concrete walls. Finally she whispered, "Okay," and Andi squatted again and Grace got off, shook her head. She'd found nothing.

Andi put her lips close to Grace's ear again. "I'm going to say some things about John Mail. We want to see if he refers to what I say, when he comes down next time. Ask me a question about him. Ask me why he's doing this."

Grace nodded. "Mom, why is Mr. Mail doing this? Why is he hurting you?" The question sounded phony, artificial, but maybe on a crude tape it'd be okay.

Andi counted out a long, thoughtful pause. "I believe he's compensating for sexual problems he had when he was a child. His parents made it worse—he had a stepfather who'd beat him with a club . . ."

"You mean, he's a sex pervert."

Andi shook her in a warning: *don't push it too far . . .*

"There's always the possibility that he has a straight-forward medical problem, a hormone imbalance that we simply don't understand. We did tests, and he seemed normal enough, but we didn't have the tools back then that we do now."

Grace nodded and said, "I hope he doesn't hurt us any more."

Andi said, "So do I. Now try to sleep."

THEY FELT HIM coming, a sense of impact, a heavy body moving around. Then they heard him on the cellar steps, the footfalls muffled and far away. Grace huddled into her, and Andi felt her mind beginning to slip. No. She had to hold on.

Then the door opened: the scraping of the slide lock, the screak of the hinge. Grace said, "Don't let him take me alone, like Genevieve."

Mail's eye appeared at the crack of the door, took them in. Then he closed the door again, and she heard another rattle. A chain. She hadn't heard that before, hadn't seen that when she was outside: he had two locks, so they couldn't rush the door.

"Don't move," he said. He was wearing jeans and an olive-colored shirt with a collar, the first time they'd seen him in anything but a t-shirt. He had two microwave meals on plastic plates, with plastic spoons. He left them on the floor and backed away.

"Where's Genevieve?" Andi asked, pushing herself up. She gripped her blouse button-line with her left hand. She did it unthinkingly and only noticed when she saw Mail pick it up.

"Dropped her at the Hudson Mall," Mail said. "Told her to find a cop."

"I don't believe you," Andi said.

"Well, I did," Mail said, but his eyes shifted and a black dread grew in Andi's heart. Then: "They've got Davenport looking for us."

"Davenport?"

"He's a big cop in Minneapolis," Mail said. He seemed impressed. "He writes games."

"Games?" She was confused.

"Yeah, you know. War games and role-playing games, and some computer games. He's like this rich dude now. And he's a cop."

"Oh." She put her finger tips to her lips. "I *have* heard of him . . . Do you know him?"

"I called him," Mail said. "I talked to him."

"You mean . . . today?"

"About two hours ago." He was proud of himself.

"Did you tell him about Genevieve?"

Again he looked away: "Nah. I called him from this Wal-Mart right after I dropped her off. He probably didn't know about her yet."

Andi hadn't fully recovered from the attack and felt less than completely sharp, but she pushed herself to understand the man, what he was saying. And she thought she saw fear or, possibly, uncertainty.

"This Davenport . . . are you afraid of him?"

"Fuck no. I'll kick his ass," Mail said. "He's not gonna find us."

"Isn't he supposed to be mean? Wasn't he fired for brutality or something? Beating up a suspect?"

"Pimp," Mail said. "He beat up a pimp because the guy cut one of his stoolies."

"Doesn't sound like somebody you'd want to challenge," Andi suggested. "I wouldn't think you'd want to play with him—if that's what you're doing."

"That's sorta what I'm doing," Mail said. He laughed, seemed lifted by the thought. Then, "I'll see you later. Eat the food, it's good."

And he was gone.

After a moment, Grace crawled over to one of the plates, poked the food, tasted it. "It's not very warm."

Andi said, "But we need it. We'll eat it all."

"What if he poisoned it?"

"He doesn't have to poison it," Andi said, coolly.

Grace looked at her, then nodded. They carried the plates back to the mattress, and in a second, they were gobbling it down. Grace stopped long enough to get two cans of strawberry soda, passed one to her mother, glanced at the Porta-Potti. "God, I'm gonna hate . . . going."

Andi stopped eating, looked at the pot, then at her daughter. A daughter of privilege: she'd had a private bathroom since she was old enough to sleep in her own room. "Grace," she said, "we are in a desperately bad situation. We're trying to stay alive until the police find us. So we eat his food and we aren't embarrassed by each other. We just try to hang on the best we can."

"Right," Grace said. "But I wish Genevieve was here . . ."

Andi choked, forced herself to hold it down. Genevieve, she thought, might be dead. But Grace couldn't be told that. She had to protect Grace: "Listen, honey . . ."

"She could be dead," Grace said, her eyes wide, like an owl's. "God, I hope she's not . . ." She put down her spoon and began to cry and Andi started to comfort her, but then dropped her plate and she began to cry as well. A few seconds later, Grace crawled next to her and they huddled together, weeping; and Andi's mind flashed back to the night when they'd all sprawled on the upstairs rug, laughing, after Genevieve's *"God, that guy was really hung . . ."*

Much later, Grace said, "He didn't say anything about being a sex pervert . . ."

"He's not listening," Andi said. "He hadn't heard it."

"So what are we going to do?"

"We have to judge him," Andi said. "If we think he's going to kill us, we have to attack him. We have to think about the best ways to do that."

"He's too strong."

"But we have to try . . . and maybe . . . I don't know. Listen: John Mail is a very smart boy. But maybe we can manipulate him."

"How?"

"I've been thinking about that. If he's talking to this Davenport person, maybe we can send a message."

"How?"

Andi sighed. "I don't know. Not yet."

JOHN MAIL CAME back an hour later. Again they felt him coming before they heard him, the vibration of a body on the stairs. He opened the door as he had before, carefully. Andi and Grace were on the mattress. He looked at them both, his gaze lingering on Grace until she looked away, and then he said to Andi, "Come out."

8

LUCAS SPENT THE early afternoon reading the papers, then tripping around to the television stations. After his last stop, he called in to Homicide and asked that Sloan be sent to meet him at Nancy Wolfe's office.

When Lucas arrived at Wolfe's, Sloan was examining the same NSX that Lucas had cruised in the morning.

"Heavy metal," he said, as he slouched over to Lucas. "Makes the Porsche look like a fuckin' Packard."

Sloan was a thin man, a man who looked at the world sideways, with a skeptical grin. He liked brown suits and had several of varied intensity: in the summer he leaned toward off-tans and not-quite-beiges, and striped neckties, and straw hats; in the winter, he went for darker tones and felt hats. He'd just shifted to winter wear, and was a dark spot in the parking lot.

"The NSX could bite you on the ass," Lucas said, looking at the car. He flipped the engagement ring in the air, caught it, and slipped it over the end of his thumb. The stone sparkled like high-rent fire.

"What're we doing?" Sloan asked.

"Good guy–bad guy with Nancy Wolfe, Manette's partner. You're the good guy."

"What has she got to do with it?"

"You know about the call from the asshole?" Lucas asked.

"Yeah, Lester played the tape for me."

"I've been running around asking questions," Lucas said. "Nobody—none of the papers, none of the stations—carried anything about the shirt. Nobody had anything about me working the case. The only people who knew, outside the department, were the family and a few people close to the family. Wolfe. A lawyer."

"Christ." Sloan scratched his head. "You think somebody's talking to him? The asshole?"

"Maybe. I can explain him knowing about me," Lucas said. "I can't explain the shirt, unless he made a pretty big intuitive leap."

"Huh." They passed the chewing-gum sculpture. Sloan looked up at it and asked, "How about Miranda?"

"Yep. We do the whole thing . . . And she asks for an attorney, we say *fine*. I'm going after her pretty hard. We want to shake her up. Same thing for the rest of the family, when we get to them."

"LUCAS. HEY, LUCAS." They'd started across the bridge, stopped for just a second to look at the koi, heard the woman's voice, turned and saw Jan Reed hurrying across the street. A TV van was making an illegal U-turn that would take it into the parking lot.

"*This* one makes my dick hard," Sloan muttered.

Reed had large dark eyes, auburn hair that fell to her shoulders, and long, tanned legs. She wore a plum suit and matching shoes, and carried a Gucci shoulder bag. She had a slight overbite; a tiny lisp added to her charm.

"Are you working this?" Lucas asked as Reed came up. "This is . . ."

"Detective Sloan, of course," Reed said. She took Sloan's hand, gave him a two-hundred-watt smile. Then to Lucas: "I'm trying for an interview with Nancy Wolfe. I understand her records were subpoenaed this morning by the local Nazis."

"That was me," Lucas said.

Reed's smile widened slightly: she'd known. "Really? Well, why'd you do that?"

Lucas glanced toward the truck and then said to Reed, "Jan, Jan, Jan. You've got a sleazy unethical microphone in the truck, don't you? I mean, my golly, that's very slimy, a really tacky, disgusting, snakelike invasion of my privacy. In fact, it's very close to criminal. It may even be criminal."

Reed sighed. "Lucas . . ."

Lucas leaned close to her ear and whispered, "Go fuck yourself."

She leaned close to his ear and said, "I like the basic concept, but I hate flying solo."

Lucas, backing away, felt the ring in his pocket and said, "C'mon, Sloan, let's see if we can get to Mrs. Wolfe before the media does . . ."

"Goddamnit, Lucas," Reed said, and she stamped her foot.

INSIDE, SLOAN ASKED, "Do you really think they had a mike?"

"I'm sure they did," Lucas said.

"Do you think they heard what I said? About Reed making my dick hard?"

"No question about it," Lucas said, biting back a grin. "And they'll use it, too, the treacherous assholes."

"You're giving me shit, man. Don't give me shit, I need to know."

The receptionist looked like she wanted to hide when she saw Lucas and Sloan coming down the hall. Lucas asked to see Wolfe, and she said, "Dr. Wolfe is with a patient. She should be finished"—she looked at a desk clock—"in five minutes or so. I hate to interrupt . . ."

"When she's done," Lucas said. "We'll be in Dr. Manette's office."

Sherrill and Black were sitting on the floor, working through a pile of manila folders.

"Anything new?" Lucas asked.

"Hey, Sloan," said Sherrill.

"These people are nuts," Black said, patting a small stack of folders. "These are neurotic"—he pointed toward another, larger stack—"and the big stack are just fucked up," he said, pointing at a third pile. "Some of the nuts are in jail or in hospitals; some of them we don't know about. When we get one, we call it downtown."

"What are we doing about the bank guy?" Sherrill asked.

"I unloaded it on the chief," Lucas said. "Did you find any more of those?"

"Maybe. There are a couple where it seems like she's getting cute . . . cryptic notes. References to other files, which we haven't found. There are computer files somewhere, but we haven't found the disks. Anderson's gonna come down and take a crack at her system." She nodded at an IBM computer on a credenza behind Manette's desk.

Wolfe walked in then, her face grim, her anger barely suppressed, and faced Lucas. Her arms were straight to her sides, her fists clenched. "What do you want?"

"We need to ask you some questions," Lucas said.

"Should I get my attorney?"

Lucas shrugged. "It's up to you. I do have to warn you: you have a right to an attorney."

Wolfe went pale as Lucas recited the Miranda warning. "You're serious."

Lucas nodded. "Yes. We're very serious, Dr. Wolfe."

Sloan broke in, his voice cheerful, placating. "We really are just asking basic stuff. I mean, you have to make the decision, but we're not gonna sweat you, Miz Wolfe, I mean, we're not gonna pull a light down over your head. We're just trying to figure out a few angles. If this wasn't done by one of her patients, why was it done? It was obviously planned, so it wasn't just some maniac picking people at random. We need to know who would benefit . . ."

"This man"—Wolfe, talking to Sloan, jabbed a finger at Lucas—"suggested this morning that I would benefit from Andi's death. I resent that. Andi's my dearest friend, a life-long friend. She's been my best friend since college, and if something should happen to her, it would be a personal disaster, not a benefit. And I bitterly . . ."

Sloan glanced at Lucas, shook his head, looked back at Wolfe and said, "Sometimes Lucas and I don't see eye-to-eye on these things . . ."

"Sloan," Lucas said, in a warning tone. But Sloan held up a hand.

"He's not a bad guy," Sloan said to Wolfe. "But he's a street guy. I'm sure he didn't mean to offend you, but sometimes he sort of . . . overstates things."

Lucas let the irritation show. "Hey, Sloan . . ."

But Sloan put up a warning hand. "We're really just looking for facts. Not trying to put pressure on you. We're trying to find out if anyone would benefit from Andi Manette's death or disappearance, and we don't mean you. At least, I don't."

Wolfe was shaking her head. "I don't see how anybody would benefit. I would get some key-person insurance if Andi died, but that wouldn't make up for the loss, financially or emotionally. I would imagine that George Dunn would get quite a bit—you know, she started out with all the money in her family. George would be a carpenter some place if he hadn't married Andi."

"Can we do this down in your office? We should be someplace a little more private, huh?" Sloan asked winningly.

On the way to Wolfe's office, with Wolfe several steps ahead, Sloan leaned to Lucas and muttered: "You know that Sherrill? She makes my dick hard, too. I think something's going on with my dick."

"That's not what you'd call a *big* change," Lucas said. He flipped the ring in the air and caught it. Sherrill. Sherrill was nice; so was Jan Reed, and he most certainly would have bundled Reed off to his cabin if it hadn't been for Weather. Lucas liked women, liked them a lot. Maybe too much. And that was another item on the long list of mental questions he had about marriage.

He was always shocked when a married friend went after another woman. That never seemed right. If you hadn't made the commitment, all right—do anything you wanted. But now, with the possibility of marriage looming . . . would he miss the hunt? Would he miss it enough to betray Weather? Would he even be considering this question if he should ask her to marry him? On the other hand, he really didn't want Reed. He didn't want Sherrill. He only wanted Weather.

"What's wrong?" Sloan asked quietly.

"Huh?" Lucas started.

"You looked like you'd had a stroke or something," Sloan said. They were just outside Wolfe's office, and Sloan was staring at him curiously.

"Ah, nothing. Lot of stuff going on," Lucas said.

Sloan grinned. "Yeah."

WOLFE'S OFFICE WAS a mirror of Manette's, with furniture of the same style, and the same files-and-coffee niche in one wall. Sloan was charming and got Wolfe talking.

She did not like George Dunn. Dunn was facing imminent divorce, Wolfe said. If Andi died, not only would he inherit and collect any life insurance, he would also save half of his own fortune. "That's what she'd get—when they got married, he had the shirt on his back, and that was all. He made all of his money since they were married, and you know Minnesota divorce law."

Tower Manette wouldn't get anything from his daughter's death, Wolfe said, except at the end of a long string of unlikely circumstances. Andi and both the children would have to die, and George Dunn would have to be convicted of the crime.

"All you would get is the key-man insurance?" Lucas asked.

"That's right."

"Who'd take Dr. Manette's patients?"

Wolfe looked exasperated. "I would, Mr. Davenport. And I would make a little money on them. And as quickly as I could, I would bring somebody else in to handle them. I have a full slate right now. I simply couldn't handle her patient load, not by myself."

"So there's the insurance and the patients . . ."

"Goddamnit," Wolfe said. "I hate these insinuations."

"They're not insinuations. We're talking serious money and you're not being very forthcoming," Lucas rasped.

"All right, all right," said Sloan. "Take it easy, Lucas."

They talked for half an hour, but got very little more. As they were leaving, Wolfe said to Lucas, "I'm sure you've heard about the lawsuit."

"No."

"We've gone to court to repossess our records," she said.

Lucas shrugged: "That's not my problem. The lawyers can sort it out."

"What you're doing is shameful," she said.

"Tell that to Andi Manette and her kids—if we get them back."

"I'm sure Andi would agree with our position," Wolfe said. *"We'd* review the records and pass on anything that might be significant."

"You aren't cops," Lucas snapped. "What's significant to cops might not be significant to shrinks."

"You aren't doing much good," Wolfe snapped back. "As far as I know, you haven't detected a thing."

Lucas took the composite drawing from his pocket: the accumulated memories of two eyewitnesses and Marcus Paloma, the game store owner. "Do you know this man?"

Wolfe took the picture, frowned, shook her head. "No, I don't think so. But he does look sort of . . . generic. Who is he?"

"The kidnapper," Lucas said. "That's what we've detected so far."

"THERE'S A WOMAN who doesn't think the sun shines out of your ass," Sloan said as they walked down the hall.

"Yeah, that's what?" Lucas didn't mind being disliked, but sometimes the taste was sour. "Six thousand that we know of?"

"I think it's eight thousand," Sloan said.

"Does *she* make your dick hard?" Lucas asked.

"No-no," Sloan said. He pushed through the door outside. "She's the one with the hard-on, and it ain't for me." After a moment, Sloan said, "Where now? Manette's?"

"Yeah. Jesus, I can feel the time passing." Lucas stopped to look at the koi, hovering in the pond, their gill flaps slowly opening and closing. Mellow, the koi: and he felt like somebody had stacked another brick on his chest. "Manette and the kids . . . Jesus."

TOWER MANETTE AGAIN said that Dunn would get everything unless he was convicted of a part in the crime.

"Do you think he could do it?" Sloan asked.

"I don't know about the kids," Tower said. He took a turn around the carpet, nibbling at a thumbnail. "He always acted like he loved the kids, but basically, George Dunn could do anything. Suppose he hired some cretin who was supposed to . . . take Andi. And instead, the guy takes all of them because they're witnesses in this screwed-up kidnapping. George would hardly be in a position to tell you about it."

"I don't think so," said Helen Manette. Her face was lined with worry, her eyes confused. "I always liked George. More than Tower did, anyway. I think if he was in on this, he'd make sure that the kids weren't hurt."

Manette stopped, turned on a heel, poked a finger at Lucas. "I really think you're barking up the wrong tree—you should be out looking for crazy people, not trying to figure out who'd benefit."

"We're working every angle we can find," Lucas said. "We're working everything."

"Are you getting anything? Anything at all?"

"Some things: we've got a picture of the kidnapper," Lucas said.

"What? Can I see it?"

Lucas took the picture out of his pocket. The Manettes looked at it, and both shook their heads at the same time. "Don't know him," Tower said.

"And nobody benefits from her death, except George Dunn . . ."

"Well," Helen Manette said hesitantly. "I hate to . . ."

"What?" Sloan asked. "We'll take anything."

"Well . . . Nancy Wolfe. The key-man insurance isn't the only thing she'd get. They have a partnership and six associates. If Andi disappeared, she'd get the business, along with the insurance money."

"That's ridiculous," Tower Manette said. "Nancy's an old friend of the family. She's Andi's oldest friend . . ."

"Who dated George Dunn before Andi took him away," Helen said. "And their business—they've done very well."

"But Dr. Wolfe says that if Andi was gone, she'd just have to hire another associate," Sloan said.

"Sure, she would," Helen said. "But instead of a partnership, she'd be a sole owner and she'd get a piece of everybody's action." The word *action* tripped easily from Helen Manette's mouth, out-of-place for a woman in this house; too close to the street. "Nancy Wolfe would . . . make out."

"ANOTHER HAPPY COUPLE," Sloan said on the way to the car. "Helen is a tarantula disguised as Betty Crocker. And Tower looked like somebody was pulling a trotline out of his ass."

"Yeah—but that partnership business. Wolfe didn't exactly tell us everything, did she?"

GEORGE DUNN HAD two offices.

One was furnished in contemporary cherry furniture, with leather chairs, a deep wine carpet, and original duck-stamp art on the walls. The desk was clear of everything but an appointment pad and a large dark wooden box for cigars.

The other office, in the back of the building, had a commercial carpet on the floor, fluorescent lighting, a dozen desks and drafting tables with computer terminals, and two women and two men working in shirtsleeves. Dunn sat at a U-shaped desk littered with paper, a telephone to his ear. When he saw Lucas and Sloan, he said a few last words into the phone and dropped it on the hook.

"Okay, everybody, everybody knows what to do? Tom will run things, Clarice will handle traffic; I'll be back as soon as we find Andi and the kids."

He took Lucas and Sloan down to the green-leather office, where they could talk. "I've turned everything over to the guys until this is done with," he said. "Have you heard anything at all?"

"We've had a couple of odd incidents. We think we have a picture of the kidnapper, but we don't know his name."

Lucas showed the picture to Dunn, who studied it, scratched his forehead. "There was a guy, a carpenter. Goddamn, he looks something like this. He's got those lips."

"What's his name? Any reason to think . . . ?"

"Dick, Dick, Dick . . ." Dunn scratched his forehead again. "Saddle? Seddle. Dick Seddle. He thought he ought to be a foreman, and when he didn't get a job that opened up, he got pissed and quit. He was mad—but that was last winter. He went around saying he was gonna clean my clock, but nothing ever came of it."

"You know where we could find him?"

"Payroll would have an address. He's married, he lives over in South St. Paul somewhere. But I don't know. He's an older guy than what you were talking about. He's maybe thirty-five, forty."

"Where's payroll?" Sloan asked.

"Down the hall on your left . . ."

"I'll get it," Sloan said to Lucas.

As Sloan left, Dunn picked up his phone, poked a button, and said, "A cop is on his way down. Give him whatever he needs on Dick Seddle. He's a carpenter, worked on the Woodbury project until last winter, January, I think. Yeah. Yeah."

When he hung up, Lucas said, "We're talking to everybody, all over again. We're asking who'd win if Andi Manette's dead. Your name keeps coming up."

"Fuck those people," Dunn snarled. He banged a large fist in the middle of the leather appointment pad. "Fuck 'em."

Lucas said, "They say that Andi was going after a divorce . . ."

"That's bullshit. We'd have worked it out."

". . . and if you were divorced, you'd lose at least half of everything. They say you started this company with some of her money, and having to pay out half could be pretty troublesome."

"Yeah, it would," Dunn said, nodding. "But there's not a dime of her money in this place. Not a goddamn dime. That was part of the deal when I married her: I wasn't gonna owe her. And it would take a fucking lunatic to suggest I'd do anything to Andi and the kids. A fuckin' lunatic."

"Then we got a bunch of fuckin' lunatics, 'cause everybody we talked to suggested it," Lucas said.

"Yeah, well . . ."

"I know, fuck 'em," Lucas said. "So: who else would benefit?"

"Nobody else," Dunn said.

"Helen Manette suggested that Nancy Wolfe would pick up a pretty thriving business."

Dunn thought for a moment, then said, "I suppose she would, but she's never been that interested in business . . . or money. Andi's always been the leader and the businesswoman. Nancy was the intellectual. She publishes papers and that. She's still connected to the university and she's a bigwig in the psychiatric society. That's why they're good partners—Andi takes care of business, Nancy builds their reputation in the field."

"You don't think Wolfe's a candidate?"

"No, I don't."

"I understand you dated her."

"Jesus, they really did dump it on you, didn't they," Dunn said, his voice softening. "I took Nancy out twice. Neither one of us was much interested in a third try. So when we were saying good-bye that second time, the last time, she said, 'You know, I've got somebody who'd be perfect for you.' And she was right. I called up Andi and we got married a year later."

Lucas hesitated, then said, "Does your wife have any distinguishing marks on her body? Scars?"

Dunn froze: "You've got a body somewhere?"

"No, no. But if we should contact the people who have her, if there's a question . . ."

Dunn wasn't buying it. "What's going on?"

"We got a call from a guy," Lucas said.

"He said she's got a scar?"

"Yeah."

"What kind of scar?"

Lucas said, "He said it looked like a rocketship . . ."

"Oh, no," Dunn groaned. "Oh no . . ."

Sloan came in, looked at the two men facing each other. "What's going on?"

Lucas told Dunn, "We'll get back."

Dunn swung a large workman's hand across the cherry desk, and the cigar safe flew across the room, the fat Cuban cigars spraying out like so much shrapnel. "Well, fuckin' find something," Dunn shouted. "You're supposed to be the fuckin' Sherlock Holmes. Quit hanging around my ass and get out and do something."

Outside the office, Sloan said, "What was all that?"

"I asked him about the rocketship."

"Oh-oh."

"Whoever it is, he's raping her," Lucas said.

AS THEY STOOD talking in the parking lot, Greave called from the Minneapolis Public Library. "It's the Bible," he said. "The Nethinims are mentioned a bunch of times, but they don't seem to amount to much."

"Xerox the references and bring them back to the office. I'll be there in ten minutes," Lucas said. He punched Greave out and called Andi Manette's office, and got Black: "Can you bring a batch of the best files downtown?"

"Yeah. On the way. And we got another problem case. A guy who runs a chain of video-game arcades."

"SO WHAT'RE WE doing?" Sloan asked.

"You want to work this?" Lucas asked.

Sloan shrugged. "I ain't got much else. I got that Turkey case, but we're having trouble getting anybody who can speak good Turk, so it's not going anywhere."

"I've never met any Turks who didn't speak pretty good English," Lucas said.

"Yeah, well, you oughta try investigating a Turk murder sometime," Sloan said. "They're yellin' no-speaka-da-English when I'm walking down the street. The guy who was killed was outa Detroit, he was sharkin', he probably had thirty grand on the street and nobody was sorry to see him go."

"Talk with Lester," Lucas said. "We need somebody to keep digging around the Manettes, Wolfe, Dunn, and anybody else who might make something out of Andi Manette dying . . ." He flipped the engagement ring up in the air and caught it, rolled it between his palms.

Sloan said, "You're gonna lose that fuckin' stone. You're gonna drop it and the ring is gonna bounce right down a sewer."

Lucas looked in his hand and saw the ring: he hadn't been conscious of it. "I gotta do something about this, with Weather."

"There's pretty general agreement on that," Sloan said. "My old lady is peeing her pants, waiting for you to ask. She wants all the details. If I don't get her the details, I'm a dead man."

GREAVE WAS WAITING with a sheaf of computer printer-paper and handed it to Lucas. "There's not much. The Nethinims were mostly just mentioned in passing—if there's anything, it's probably in Nehemiah. Here, 3:26."

Lucas looked at the passage. *Moreover the Nethinims dwelt in Ophel unto the place over against the water gate toward the east, and the tower that lieth out.*

"Huh." He passed the paper to Sloan and walked down the office to a wall map of the Metro area, traced the Mississippi with his finger. "One thing you can see from the river is all those green water towers," he said. "They're like mushrooms along the tops of all the tallest hills. The water gate could be any of the dams."

"Want me to check?"

Lucas grinned. "Take you two days. Just call all the towns along here." He snapped his finger at the map. "Hastings, Cottage Grove, St. Paul Park, Newport, Inver Grove, South St. Paul, like that. Tell them you're working Manette and ask them to swing a patrol car by the water towers; see if there's anything to see."

BLACK SHOWED UP ten minutes later, morose, handed Lucas a file and a tape. "Guy's messing with kids. Somebody ought to cut his fuckin' nuts off."

"Pretty explicit?"

"It's all there, and I don't give a shit what the shrinks say. This guy *likes* doing it. And he likes talking about it—he likes the attention he's getting from Manette. He'll never stop."

"Yeah, he will," Lucas said, flipping through the file. "For several years . . . I'll take it to the chief. We want to hold off until Manette's out of the way."

Black nodded. "We got some doozies in the files." He sat down opposite Lucas, spread five files on the desk like a poker hand, pushed one toward Lucas. "Look at this guy. I think he may have raped a half-dozen women, but he talks them out of doing anything about it. He brags about it: breaks down for them, weeps. Then he laughs about it. He says he's addicted to sex, and he's coming on to Manette . . . right here, see, she mentions it, and how she might have to redirect his therapy."

THEY WERE READING files an hour later when Greave hurried in. "They've got something in Cottage Grove."

Lucas stood up. "What is it?"

"They said it's like an oil drum under one of the water towers."

"How do they know?"

"It's got your name spray-painted on it," Greave said.

"*My* name?"

Greave shrugged. "That's what they said—and they are freaked out. They want your ass down there."

ON THE WAY down to Cottage Grove, the cellular buzzed and Lucas flipped it open. "Yeah?"

Mail cooed, "Hey, Davenport, got it figured out?"

Lucas knew the voice before the third word was out. "Listen, I . . ."

But he was gone.

9

SIX BLOCKS FROM the water tower, Lucas ran into a police blockade, two squad cars V-ed across the street. The civilian traffic was turning around, jamming up the street. He put the Porsche on the yellow line and accelerated past the frustrated drivers, until two cops ran toward him waving him off.

A red-faced patrolman, one hand on his pistol, leaned up to the window. "Hey, what the hell . . ."

Lucas held up his ID and said, "Davenport, Minneapolis PD. Get me through."

The cop ran back to one of the squads, yelled something through an open window, and the cop inside backed it up. Lucas accelerated through the gap and up toward the water tower. Along the way, he saw cops in the streets, two different sets of uniforms. They were evacuating houses along the way, and women with kids in station wagons hurried down the streets away from the tower.

A bomb? Chemicals? What?

The water tower looked like an aqua-green alien from *War of the Worlds,* its big egg-shaped body supported by fat, squat legs. Three fire trucks, a cluster of squad cars, a bomb squad truck, two ambulances, and a wrecker were parked a hundred yards away. Lucas pulled into the cluster.

"Davenport?" A stout, red-faced man in a too-tight cop's uniform waved him over. "Don Carpenter, Cottage Grove." He wiped his face on his sleeve. He was sweating heavily, though the day was cool. "We might have a big problem."

"Bomb?"

Carpenter looked toward the top of the hill. "We don't know. But it's an oil barrel, and it's full of something heavy. We haven't tried to move it, but it's substantial."

"Somebody said my name is on it."

"That's right: *Lucas Davenport, Minneapolis Police.* Standard bullshit graffiti-artist spray paint. We were gonna open it, but then someone said, 'Jesus, if this guy's fuckin' with Davenport, what's to keep him from putting a few pounds of dynamite or some shit in there? Or a gas bomb or something?' So we're standing back."

"Huh." Lucas looked up toward the tower. Two men were there, talking. "Who are those guys?"

"Bomb squad. We were all over the place before somebody thought it might be a bomb, so we don't think it's dangerous to get near. A time bomb doesn't make sense, because he didn't know when we'd find it."

"Let's take a look," Lucas said.

The bottom of the tower was enclosed by the hurricane fence, with a truck-sized gate on one end. "Cut the chain on the gate and drove right in," Carpenter said. They were at the crest of the hill, and below them a steady stream of cars was leaving the neighborhood.

"But nobody saw it."

"We don't know—we were talking about a door-to-door, but then the bomb idea came up, and we never got to it."

"Maybe later," Lucas said.

The two bomb squad cops walked over and Lucas recognized one of them. He said, "How are you? You were on that case out in Lake Elmo." The guy said, "Yeah, Bill Path, and this is Jesus Martinez." He threw a thumb at his partner, and Lucas said, "What've we got?"

"Maybe nothing," Path said, looking back at the tower. Lucas could see the black oil drum through the hurricane fence. It sat directly under the bulb of the four-legged water tower. "But we don't want to try to move it. We're gonna pull the lid from a distance and see what happens."

"We've drained the tower," Carpenter said. He wiped his sweating face on his sleeve again. "Just in case."

"Can I?" Lucas said, nodding at the oil barrel.

"Sure," said Path. "Just don't kick it."

The barrel sat in the shade of the tower, and Lucas walked over to look at it, and then around it: a standard oil barrel, with a little rust, and a lid that looked professionally tight.

"One of the first guys knocked on it, and nothing happened; so we knocked on it when we got here," Martinez said, grinning at Lucas. He stepped up to the barrel and knocked on it. "It's full of something."

"Could be water," said Path. "If it's full, and it's water, it'd weigh about four-fifty."

"How'd he move it?" Lucas asked. "He couldn't use a fork lift."

"I think he rolled it," Path said. "Look . . ."

He walked away from the barrel, peered around, then pointed. There was a deep edge-cut in the soft earth, then a series of interlocking rings along with a wavy line. "I think he rolled it to here, then tipped it up, then rim-rolled it to the middle."

Lucas nodded: he could see the pattern in the dirt.

"Hey, look at this, Bill," Martinez said to Path. He pointed at a lower corner of the barrel. "Is that just condensation, or is there a pinhole?"

A drop of liquid seemed to be squeezing out of the barrel. Path got to his knees, peered at it, then grunted, "Looks like a pinhole." He picked up a dandelion leaf, caught the drop on the leaf, smelled it, and passed it to Martinez.

"What?" Lucas asked.

Martinez said, "Nothing—probably water."

"So let's jerk the lid."

Path fixed a block to an access ladder on the water tower, while Martinez fitted a harness around the lid. Then he tied a rock climber's rope to the harness, ran it up through the block and down to the tow truck. The truck let out all of its cable, and when they finished, they were a hundred and fifty yards from the barrel.

"You ready for a big noise?" Path asked Carpenter.

The chief said, "Don't talk like that. Do you mean that? Do you think?"

They all squatted behind cars, the wrecker rolled forward, and the lid flipped off like a beer cap. Nothing happened. Lucas could hear a plane droning down the river.

"Well, shit," Martinez said after a moment. He stood up. "Let's go look."

They walked slowly back to the barrel. From thirty feet away, Lucas could see that it was filled with water. When they got next to it, they looked carefully inside. A small body was at the bottom of the barrel, a pale oval face turned to look up at them. The water was cloudy with a sediment of some kind, and the body shimmered, out of focus, a white dress floating around it like gauze, black hair drifting around the head.

Martinez looked in the barrel and said, "No. I don't do this." And he walked away.

"Oh, shit. Who is it?" Carpenter asked, peering open-mouthed into the barrel.

The body was small. "Probably Genevieve Dunn," Lucas said. "Are we sure this is water?"

Path, looking in, put his face close to the surface and said, "Yeah. It's water. He could have a big chunk of white phosphorus in there, waiting for us to get rid of the water."

Lucas shook his head: "Nah. This is what he wanted me to see. A jack-in-the-box. The motherfucker is playing games . . . Is that the Medical Examiner down there?"

Carpenter nodded. "Yeah. I'll get him."

Lucas stepped away and looked down the hill, waiting. There should be something else—or Mail would call again, to gloat. Carpenter, standing beside him, said, "I'd pull the trigger on this guy. How can you kill a kid?"

Lucas said, "Yeah?" He remembered the line from a Vietnam vet, a street guy. How can you kill a kid? Just lead them a little less . . .

The Medical Examiner was a young man with a thin face, thin spectacles, and a large Adam's apple. He walked up, glanced in the barrel, and said, "What's the shit in the water?"

Nobody knew.

"Well, give me something I can fish around with, huh?" He was unselfconsciously cheerful, even for a Medical Examiner. "Give me one of those fire axes. I don't want to put my hand in there if we don't know what it is."

"Take it easy with the ax," Carpenter said.

"Don't worry about it," the examiner said. He looked in the barrel again. "That's not a kid."

"What?" Lucas walked back.

"Not unless she had deformed hands and too big a head," he said confidently.

Lucas looked in the water again—it still looked like a child's body. "I think it's some kind of big plastic doll," the examiner said. A fireman came up with a long curved tool that looked like an oversized poker. "Here."

The Medical Examiner took it, grabbed the body, but it slipped away. "Anchored with something," he grunted. "Look, if this is just water, why don't we dump it?"

They did; the water spilled out on the grass, and the ME reached inside and pulled out a four-foot doll, plastic flesh, black hair, and paint-flaking baby blue eyes. Its feet were folded beneath it and tied to a brick to keep the doll from floating.

"Got the big sense of humor, huh?" said the examiner. A white plastic tag floated from the doll's neck. The examiner turned it. It said, in black grease pencil, "CLUE."

"I don't think he has a sense of humor," Lucas said. "I really don't think he does."

"Then what is this shit?"

"I don't know," Lucas said.

LUCAS CALLED IN, then headed back toward Minneapolis. As he passed the refinery off Highway 61, Mail called again.

"Goddamn, you were fast, Lucas. Can I call you Lucas? How'd you like all those fire trucks? I drove by while you guys were up there. What were you doing? Somebody said they thought it was a bomb or something. Is that right? Did you have the bomb squad up there?"

"Listen, we think you might have some trouble, you know, making the world work right. And we think you might know it. We can get you help . . ."

"You mean I'm fuckin' nuts? Is that what you mean?"

"Listen, I personally had a bad episode of depression a few years back, and I know what it's like. The shit in your head is wrong, and it's not your fault . . ."

"Fuck that, Davenport, there's nothing wrong with my fuckin' head. There's something wrong with the fuckin' world. Turn on your TV sometime, asshole. There's nothing wrong with me."

And he was gone again.

THE PHONE COMPANY was automatically tracing all calls to Lucas's cellular phone and alerting the Dispatch Department at the same time. Dispatch would start cars toward the phone. But when Lester called, two minutes after Mail hung up, he said, "He was too quick. He was on the strip near the airport. We had cars there in two minutes forty-five seconds after he rang you, but he was gone. We stopped seven vans, nothing going there."

"Damnit. He won't talk for more than ten seconds or so."

"He knows what he's doing."

"All right. I'm heading back."

"Sherrill came up with another problem case, a guy fooling around with children—he's been screwing ten-year-old girls at a playground. I don't know what's gonna happen, but if we get Manette back, she might wind up doing some time."

Lucas shook his head and looked at the phone, then said, "Frank, we're not secure here. This phone is a fuckin' radio."

LESTER WAS WAITING when Lucas got back.

"This Manette thing, the sex things," he said.

"Yeah?"

"An awful lot of people know. They know down in Sex, and they're pissed that they can't move. It's gonna get out, and it won't be long."

"Are we running the names of all these guys?"

"All of them."

"How about people they've abused? Could somebody be trying to get revenge on Manette?"

Lester shrugged. "So we plug in all the victims. We got more goddamned names, and nothing coming up. What do you make of that thing out at the water tower?"

"I don't know," Lucas said. "He says it's a clue, but what kind of a clue? Why was it full of water? Watery grave? Was it the barrel?"

Anderson came through, handed each of them a fat plastic binder with perhaps three hundred pages inside. "Everything we've got, except what might come out of the lab on the doll. And we're not getting anything from the feebs."

"Big surprise." Lucas flipped through the text.

"Any ideas?" Lester asked.

"Watery grave," Lucas said. "That's about it."

NOTHING MOVED. NOBODY called.

Lucas finally phoned Anderson: "There's an interview in your book with one of Manette's neighbors."

"Yeah?"

"She said there was somebody hanging around in a boat, in a spot where there aren't any fish. Maybe we ought to run boat licenses against the other lists."

"Jesus, Lucas, we got hundreds of names already."

Later, Lucas called St. Anne's College and asked for the psychology department. "Sister Mary Joseph, please."

"Is this Lucas?" The voice on the other end was breathless.

"Yes."

"We were wondering if you'd call," the receptionist said. "I'll go get her."

Elle Kruger—Sister Mary Joseph—picked up the phone a moment later, her voice dry: "Well, they're all in a tizzy around here. Sister Marple goes off to solve another one. And this one's a gamer, I hear."

"Yeah. And it's ugly," Lucas said. "I think one of the kids is dead."

"Oh, no." The wry quality disappeared from her voice. "How sure?"

"The guy who took them left a clue: a doll in an oil barrel filled with water. I think the doll was supposed to represent one of the kids."

"I see. Do you want to come over and talk?"

"Weather should be home around six. If you'd like to walk over, I'll cook some steaks."

"Six-thirty," she said. "See you then."

ON HIS WAY home, Lucas took University Avenue toward St. Paul and stopped just short of the St. Paul city line. Davenport Simulations occupied a suite of offices on the first floor of a faceless but well-kept office building. Most of the offices in the building were closed. Davenport Simulations was completely lit up: most of the programmers started work in the early afternoon, and ran until midnight, or later.

Lucas smiled at the receptionist as he went by; she smiled and waved and kept talking on her phone. Barry Hunt was in his office with one of the techies, poring over a printout. When Lucas knocked, he gave a friendly, "Hey, come on in," while his face struggled to find an appropriate expression.

Hunt had been finishing his MBA at St. Thomas when Lucas started looking for somebody to take over the company. For ten years, Lucas had run it out of his study, writing war and role-playing games, selling the games to three different companies. Almost against his will, he got involved in the shift to computer gaming. At the same time, he'd been forced out of the department;

he wound up working full-time, writing emergency scenarios for what became a line of police-training software. The software sold, and everything began to move too quickly: he didn't know about payroll, taxes, social security, royalties, worker's comp, operator training.

Elle had met Hunt in one of her psych classes and recommended him. Hunt took over the company operations and had done well, for both of them. But Hunt and Lucas were not especially compatible, and Lucas was no longer certain that Hunt was happy to see him drop by.

"Barry, I need to talk to the software guys for a minute," Lucas said. "I've got a problem. It's this Manette thing."

Hunt shrugged. "Sure. Go ahead. I think everybody's here."

"I swear, just a minute."

"Great . . ."

The back two-thirds of the office suite was a single bay, cut up into small cubicles by shoulder-high dividers, exactly the kind used in the Homicide office. Seven men and two women, all young, were at work: six at individual monitors, three clustered around a large screen, running a search-trainer simulation. Another man and a heavy-set young woman, both with Coke-bottle glasses, were drinking coffee by a window. When Lucas walked in with Hunt, the room went quiet.

"Hey, everybody," Lucas said.

"Lucas," somebody said. Faces turned toward him.

"You've all probably heard about the Manette kidnapping case. The guy who took her is a gamer. I've got a composite sketch, and I'd like you all to look at it, see if you recognize him. And I'd appreciate it if you'd fax it or ship it to everybody you can think of, here in the Cities. We really need the help."

He passed out copies of the composite: nobody knew the face.

"He's a big guy?" asked one of the programmers, a woman named Ice.

"Yeah. Tall, muscular, thin," Lucas said. "Crazy, apparently. Maybe medically crazy."

"Sounds like my last date," Ice said.

"Will you put it on the 'Net?" Lucas asked.

"No problem," Ice said. She was a throwback to the days of punk, with short-cropped hair, bright red lipstick that somewhat flowed out of the lines of her lips, and nose rings. Hunt said she wrote more code than anyone in the place. An idea began to tickle the back of Lucas's head, but he pushed it away for the moment.

"Good," he said. "Let's do it."

On the way out, Hunt said, "Lucas, we need to get together."

"Trouble?" Lucas feared the day that the IRS would knock on the door and ask for his records. *Records? We don't got no steenking records.*

"We need a loan," Hunt said. "I've talked to Norwest, and there won't be any problem getting it. You'd have to approve."

"A loan? I thought we were . . ."

"We need to buy Probleco," Hunt said. "They've got a half-dozen hardware products that would fit with ours like the last pieces in a puzzle. And they're for sale. Jim Duncan wants to go back to engineering."

"How much do you want to borrow? Maybe I could . . ."

"Eight mil," Hunt said.

Lucas was startled. "Jesus, Barry, eight million dollars?"

"Eight million would buy us dominance in the field, Lucas. Nobody else would be close. Nobody else could get close."

"But, my God, that's a lot of money," Lucas said, flustered. "What if we fall on our butts?"

"You hired me to keep us off our butts, and we are," Hunt said. "We'll stay that way. But that's why we've got to meet, so I can explain it all."

"All right; but we'll have to wait until after this Manette thing. And I'd like you maybe to come up with a couple of other options."

"I can think of one big one, right off the top of my head."

"What?"

"Take the company public. It's a little early for that, but if you wanted out, well . . . we could take the company public and probably get you, I don't know, something between eight and ten mil."

"Holy cats," Lucas said.

He'd never said that before, in public or private, but now it bleated out and Hunt jerked out a quick smile. "If we borrow the eight mil, and hang on for another five years, it'll be thirty mil. I promise."

"All right, all right, we'll talk," Lucas said, starting down the hall. "Give me a week. Thirty mil. Holy cats."

"Say hello to Weather," Hunt said. He seemed about to say something else but stopped. Lucas was halfway out the door before he realized what it was, and walked back. Hunt had just sat down in his office, and Lucas stuck his head in. "This Manette thing can't last for more than a couple of weeks, so set a meeting with the bank. And lay out the stock thing we talked about——the share plan."

Hunt nodded. "I've been meaning to bring it up."

Lucas said, "Now's the time. I told you if it worked, you'd get a piece of it. It seems to be working."

WEATHER.

Lucas toyed with the engagement ring: he should ask her. He could feel her waiting. But the advice was rolling in, unsolicited, from everywhere, and somehow, it slowed him down.

Women suggested a romantic proposal: a short preface, declaring that he loved her, with a more or less elaborate description of what their life together would be like, and then a suggestion that they marry; most of the men suggested a plain, straight-forward question: Hey babe, how about it? A few thought he was crazy for tying up with a woman at all. A park cop suggested that golf would be a complete replacement for any woman, and cheaper.

"Fuck golf," Lucas said. "I like women."

"Well, that's the other half of the equation," the guy admitted. "Women are also a complete replacement for golf."

"ANYTHING?" WEATHER ASKED as soon as he came in the door. He could feel the ring in his pocket, against his thigh. "With the Manettes?"

"Bizarre bullshit," he said, and he told her about the oil barrel. "Elle's coming over at six-thirty; I promised her steak."

"Excellent," Weather said. "I'll do the salad."

Lucas went to start the charcoal and touched the ring in his pocket. What if she said *no, not yet . . . ?* Would that change everything? Would she feel like she had to move out?

Weather was bustling around the kitchen, bumping into him as he got the barbecue sauce out of the refrigerator. She asked with elaborate, chatty unconcern, "Do you think you and Elle would have gotten married, if . . ."

"If she'd hadn't become a nun?" Lucas laughed. "No. We grew up together. We were too close, too young. Romancing her just wouldn't have seemed . . . right. Too much like incest."

"Does she think the same way?"

Lucas shrugged. "I don't know. I never know what women think."

"You wouldn't rule it out, though."

"Weather?"

"What?"

"Shut the fuck up."

SISTER MARY JOSEPH—Elle Kruger—still wore the traditional black habit with a long rosary swaying by her side. Lucas had asked her about it, and she'd said, "I like it. The other dress . . . it looks dowdy. I don't feel dowdy."

"Do you feel like a penguin?"

"Not in the slightest."

Elle had been a beautiful child, and still ran through Lucas's dreams, an eleven-year-old blonde touched by grace and merriment: and later scarred by acne so foul that she'd retreated from life, to emerge ten years later as Sister Joseph. She'd told him that her choice was not brought by her face, that she had a vocation. He wasn't certain; he never quite bought it.

Elle arrived in a black Chevrolet as Lucas was putting the first of the steaks on the grill. Weather gave her a beer.

"What's the status?" Elle asked.

"One's dead, maybe; the others aren't yet," Lucas said. "But the guy is cracking open and all the gunk is oozing out of his head. He's gonna kill them soon."

"I know her—Andi Manette. She's not the most powerful mind, but she's got an ability to . . . touch people," Elle said, sipping the beer. The smell of steak floated in from the porch. "She reaches out and you talk to her. I think it's something that aristocrats develop. It's a touch."

"Can she stay alive?"

Elle nodded. "For a while—for longer than another woman could. She'll try to manipulate him. If he's had therapy, it's hard to tell which way he'll jump. He'll recognize the manipulation, but some people become so habituated to therapy that they need it, like a drug. She could keep him going."

"Like Scheherazade," Weather said.

"Like that," Elle agreed.

"I need to keep him talking," Lucas said. "He calls me on the telephone, and we try to track him."

"Do you think he was in therapy with her? A patient?"

"We don't know. We're looking, but we haven't found much."

"If he is, then you should go to his problem. Not accuse him of being ill."

"I did that this afternoon," Lucas said ruefully. "He got pissed . . . sorry."

"Ask him how he's taking care of them," Elle suggested. "See if you can make him feel some responsibility, or that you think he's shirking a responsibility. Ask him if there's anything you can do that would allow them to go free. Something he would trade. Ask him not to answer right away, but to consider it. What would he like? You need questions on that order."

Later, over the steaks, Lucas said, "We've got another problem. We're going through Manette's records. She was treating people for child abuse—and she hadn't notified anybody."

Elle put down her fork. "Oh, no. You're not going to prosecute."

"That's up in the air," Lucas said.

Now Elle was angry. "That's the most primitive law this state has ever passed. We know that people are ill, but we insist on putting them into positions where they can't get help, and they'll just go on . . ."

". . . Unless we slap their asses in jail . . ."

"What about the ones you never find out about? The ones who'd like to get treatment but can't because the minute they open their mouths, the cops'll be on them like wolves?"

"I know you've got a point-of-view," Lucas said, trying to back out of the argument.

"What?" Weather asked. "What happens?"

Elle turned to her. "If a person abuses a child in this state, and realizes he's sick, and tries to get treatment, the therapist is required to report him. If she does that, her records get seized by the state and are used as evidence against the patient. So as soon as the state acts, the patient, of course, gets a lawyer, who tells him to get out of treatment and keep his mouth shut. And if the man's acquitted—they frequently are, since he's admitted that he's mentally ill and that casts doubt on the records, and the therapists are very reluctant witnesses—well, then he's turned loose and all he knows for sure is that he can't ever go back to treatment, because he might wind up in prison."

Weather stared at her for a moment, then said to Lucas, "That can't be right."

"Sort of a Catch-22," Lucas admitted.

"Sort of barbaric is what it is," Weather said sharply.

"Child abuse is barbaric," Lucas snapped back.

"But if a person is trying to get help, what do you want? Throw him in a hole somewhere?"

"Listen, I really don't want to argue about it," Lucas said. "You either believe or you don't."

"Lucas . . ."

"Listen, will you guys let me chicken out of this thing and eat my steak? For . . . gosh sakes."

"Makes me really unhappy," Elle growled. "Really unhappy."

LATE THAT NIGHT, Weather rolled up on a shoulder and said, "Barbaric."

"I didn't want to argue about it with Elle right there," Lucas said. "But you know what I really think? Therapy doesn't work with child abusers. The shrinks are flattering themselves. What you do with child abusers is you put their asses in jail. Each and every one of them, wherever you find them."

"And you call yourself a liberal," Weather said in the dark.

"Libertine. Not liberal," Lucas said, easing toward her.

"Stay on your side of the bed," she said.

"How about if I put just one finger over?"

"No." And a moment later, "*That's* not a finger . . ."

10

JOHN MAIL WATCHED the late news with a sense of well-being. He was alone except for the wide-screen television and his computers. He had a dial-up Internet link, and monitored twenty-four news groups dealing with sex or computers or both. He had two phone lines and three computers going at once. As he watched the news, he punched through *alt.sex.blondes* on the 'Net, and now and then pulled out a piece and shipped it to a second computer.

Mail was a little sleepy, a little burned out, with a pleasant ache in his lower belly and a burn on his knees. Andi Manette was a package, all right: he'd known that when he'd first laid eyes on her ten years earlier. She was everything he'd expected: nice body, and she fought him. He enjoyed the fight, and enjoyed smothering it. Every time he rode her, he finished with a sense of victory.

And now here he was, on television, dominating the news. Everybody was looking for him—and they might find him, he thought, given a few weeks, or months. He'd have to do something about that, eventually.

He pushed the thought away and went back to his favorite: Davenport. Davenport was in hiding. Nothing was said about him. Nothing.

Mail ran through the Internet news groups as he watched TV, sorting the messages by subject. He was tempted to post something about Manette and what he was doing with her. He might do that, if he could get to a machine at the university. Some people on the *alt.sex* groups who would appreciate what he had to say . . .

Maybe just a quick note now, just a hint? No. There was always a path they could get back on, a way to trace him—his Internet link had his real phone number.

Though not his real name.

On the Internet, he was Tab Post and Pete Rate, names he got off his computer keyboard. Down at the store, and with the store van, he was Larry F. Roses. The real Larry F. Roses was down south somewhere, Florida, Louisiana. He'd sold the van and its papers for cash, to avoid having to split the money with his ex-wife. To the mortgage company, he was Martin LaDoux. He had Marty's papers—driver's license, with his own photo on it now, a Social Security card, even a passport. He paid Marty's income taxes.

He wasn't John Mail anywhere. John Mail was dead . . .

Mail sat up and pushed away the TV tray with the aluminum foil chicken-pot-pie tin. Chicken-pot-pie and a Coke; just about his favorite. And he thought about Grace. Got up, went to the kitchen, got another can of Coke, and thought about her some more.

Grace might be good. Fresh. Her body was just starting to turn, and she'd fight, all right. He dropped on the couch and closed his eyes. Still, when he looked at her, he didn't feel the hunger he felt for the mother. That still surprised him. The first time he'd taken Andi Manette to the mattress, he'd almost blacked out with the joy of it. Maybe, Grace. Sometime. As an experiment. Bet she'd freak out when she saw it coming . . .

He'd just finished the Coke when the phone rang on the corner table behind his head. He groped for it, found it. "Hello?"

"Yes, Mr. LaDoux." Mail sat up: *this* voice he paid attention to.

"They are looking for your boat. The police know you were watching her from the lake." Click. Mail stared at the phone. Shit. He wished he knew who it was: a face-to-face talk would be interesting.

But the boat. He frowned. When he'd rented the boat, he'd had to show an ID, the LaDoux driver's license, his home name. The old guy at the rental place had stamped it on the back of a duplicate form. Where he put the form, Mail didn't know. Hadn't paid attention. Damnit. That's how Davenport would get him: when he didn't pay attention.

Mail stood up, got a jacket and a flashlight, and went outside. Chilly. But the clouds had vanished with the sun, and overhead, the Milky Way stretched across the sky like God's own Rolex. Drive up? Nah. Good night for a stroll. Maybe some pussy at the end of it, although his testicles were beginning to ache.

With the flashlight picking out the bumps and holes, Mail took the driveway down to the gravel frontage road, checked the rural mailbox out of habit. Nothing; the mailman always came before ten o'clock, and Mail had picked up the day's delivery when he'd got up. He shut the mailbox and went down the gravel road.

To the north, the lights of the Cities were visible as a thin orange glow above the roadside trees. But when he turned south, up the track to the shack where he kept the women, it was as dark as the inside of a bone; and it all smelled of corn leaves.

Mail lived on what once had been a small farm. A neighbor had bought it when the farm could no longer support itself, had shorn a hundred and fifty acres of crop land from the original plot, and had sold the remaining ten acres containing the original farmhouse and a few crumbling outbuildings. The new owner, an alcoholic slaughter-house worker, had allowed the house to fall apart before he killed himself. The next owner built a small house closer to the road, and a two-horse stable out back. When his children had grown, he'd moved to Florida. The next owner converted the stable to a garage, got lonely in the country winter, and moved back to the city. The next owner was Mail.

By the time Mail took the place, the old house was a ruin, a shack. A caved-in chicken coop squatted behind the shack, with the remains of what might have been a machine shed, now reduced to a pile of rotting boards. A still-recognizable two-seater outhouse was out to one side, nearly buried in the corn. Further to the back was the foundation of a barn.

If the farmhouse was a ruin, the basement and root cellar were solid. Mail had run a new electrical cable out to the place from his own house, a job that had taken him two hours.

He had worried, for a while, about keeping the women in the house. A trespassing antique hunter might accidentally stumble over them. Antique hunters were everywhere, stripping old farmhouses of their antique brass doorknobs and doorstops and forced-air register fittings, old pickle crocks—those were getting hard to find—and even nails, if they were hand-forged and in good shape.

But antique scavengers were a nervous lot. Judges treated them like burglars, which is what they were, so Mail had put in two Radio Shack battery-operated motion alarms and felt fairly safe. Any antique hunter tripping an alarm would be out of the house in an instant; and if it was anybody else, the cops, for instance, the jig would be up anyway.

The only other danger was Hecht, the neighboring farmer. Hecht was a phlegmatic German, a member of some weird religious sect. He had no television, there was no newspaper box on his mailbox post. He had never shown much interest in anything beyond his tractor and his land. Mail had never seen him near the old house, except at planting and harvest time, when he was working in the adjacent fields. By then, the women would be long gone.

Mail walked in the thin oval of illumination from the flashlight, smelling the corn and the dust; and when he crossed the crest of the hill and turned the light toward it, the old farmhouse came up like a witch-house in a Gothic novel, glowing with a faint, ghostly luminescence often found in old clapboard houses that had once been painted white.

As Mail passed the porch, on the way around back, a nervous chill trickled down his spine: a finger of graveyard fear as he passed the cistern. Scratching sounds? No.

He clumped inside.

GRACE HEARD HIM coming and pushed herself against the wall. She wasn't sure that her mother had heard: Andi had been lying on the mattress for hours, one arm crooked over her eyes, not asleep, but not conscious. She had drifted away again, after the last attack. Grace had tried to rouse her, but Andi wouldn't respond.

Grace had decided to go after Mail.

Mail had attacked her mother four times now, battering her each time, raping her after the beating. She could hear the crack of his hand through the steel door, and thinner, weaker sounds that must have been her mother's voice, pleading. He slapped, Andi had told her. Hit her with an open hand, but it was like being hit with a board. This last time, something had broken, and Andi was out of it, Grace thought.

She'd have to go after Mail, even if she had nothing but her fingernails. He was killing her mother, and when he'd done it, she'd go too.

"No." Andi pushed herself up. Blood ringed her nostrils, a dark reddish-black crust. Her eyes were like holes, her lips swollen. But she'd heard the footsteps, and roused herself, half-turning to croak the single warning word.

"I have to do something," Grace whispered. He was coming.

"No." Andi shook her head. "I don't think . . . I don't think he'll do anything when I'm like this."

"He's killing you. I thought you were dying already," Grace whispered. She was crouched on the back corner of the mattress, like a cowering dog at the pound, Andi thought. The girl's eyes were too bright, her lips pale, her skin stretched thin like tracing paper.

"He might be, but we can't fight him yet. He's too big. We need . . .

something." She pushed herself up, feeling the impact of Mail's footsteps on the stairs. "We need something we can kill him with."

"What?" Grace looked wildly around the cell. There was nothing.

"We have to think . . . but I can't think. I can't think." Andi put her hands to her head, at the temples, as though trying to hold her skull together.

He was close, on the stairs. "You have to lie down, just like you were," Grace said fiercely. "With your hands over your eyes. Don't say anything, no matter what."

She pushed her mother down, and they heard the slide-lock pulled back. Andi, too weak to argue, and without the time, nodded and put her arm up and closed her eyes. Grace pulled back in the corner, her feet pulled tight to her thighs, her arms around her legs, looking up at the door.

Mail peered through the crack, saw them, undid the chain, opened the door. "Get up," he said to Andi.

Grace, frightened, said, "You did something to her. She hasn't moved since you left."

That pushed him back.

Mail's forehead wrinkled and he said, harshly, "Get up," and he pushed Andi's foot with his own.

Andi rolled half over, then pulled herself away from him, toward the wall, like a cartoon woman dying of thirst in a desert. She inched away, pathetic.

"You really hurt her, this time," Grace said, and she began to bawl.

"Shut up," Mail snarled. "Shut up, goddamnit, little fuckin' whiner . . ."

He took a step toward her, as though to hit her, and Grace choked off the sobs and tried to pull herself tighter to the wall. Mail hesitated, then pushed Andi again. "Get up."

Andi rolled some more, and began to inch away again. Mail caught her feet and twisted them, and she flipped onto her back. "Water," she whimpered.

"What?"

Her eyes closed and she lay limp as a rag. Grace began bawling again, and Mail shouted, "Shut up, I said," and backed away, uncertain now.

"You hurt her," Grace said.

"She wasn't like this when I put her back in," Mail said. "She was walking."

"I think you did something to her . . . mind. She talks to Genevieve and Daddy. Where's Gen? What did you do with her? Is she with Daddy?"

"Ah, fuck," Mail said, exasperated. He probed Andi again, pushing her left foot with his own. "You'd best get better, 'cause I'm not done with you yet," he said. "We're not done, at-all."

He backed out of the room, and said to Grace, "Give her some water."

"I do," Grace sobbed. "But then she . . . wets on the floor."

"Ah, for Christ sakes," Mail said. The door slammed, but the bolt didn't slide shut. Grace held her breath. Had he forgotten? No. The door opened again, and Mail threw in a towel.

Grace had seen it, when he'd taken her mother out of the cell, lying on the floor beside the mattress he used when he raped her. "Clean her up," Mail said. "I'll be back in the morning."

The door closed again, and they heard his footsteps on the stairs. They waited, unmoving, but he didn't return.

"That was great," Andi whispered. She pushed herself up and felt the tears running down her face and she actually smiled through her cracked lips. "Grace, that was wonderful."

"That's once we beat him," Grace whispered back.

"We can do it again," Andi said. She propped herself up and tilted her head back. "But we've got to find something."

"Find what?"

"A weapon. Something we can kill him with."

"In here?" Grace looked around the barren cell, her eyes wide but not quite hopeless. "Where?"

"We'll find something," Andi said. "We have to."

MAIL TOOK THE VAN—the van was blue now, and the sign on the side doors was clear: "Computer Roses"—and rode it down to Highway Three and I-494, filled the tank, and put a little more than four gallons in the red, five-gallon plastic gas can in the back. Inside the convenience store, he bought two quarts of motor oil and paid for it all with a twenty.

He took forty minutes riding out to Minnetonka, thinking it over. Mail thought a lot about crime, about the way things worked. If he were in a movie, he'd break into the boat works, use a flashlight, go through the files, and then play a breathless game of hide-and-seek with a security guard.

But this wasn't a movie, and his best protection was simply timing and invisibility.

Irv's Boat Works was tucked into a curve in the road just off the lake, along with a shabby gas station, a grocery store, and an ice cream parlor, all closed. He drove by once, looking for movement, looking for cops. He saw two moving cars, one in front and one behind, and no cops. Nobody walking. The only light in the buildings was in an ice cream freezer.

He drove a half-mile down the road to an intersection, did a U-turn, and went back the same way. Another car passed; a house a quarter mile past the station was fully lit, although he didn't see anybody around. He drove out to a SuperAmerica store, parked, walked around to the back of the van, and let himself inside. He took just a minute to mix the motor oil with the gas, the fumes giving him a small mental charge: he hadn't done this since he got out of the hospital—he didn't need it anymore—but it still held something for him.

When he finished mixing, he went into the Tom Thumb and bought a cheap plastic cigarette lighter and a Coke. He already had a role of duct tape in the glove compartment. Back in the truck, he put the tape on the lighter so it'd be ready, opened the Coke and put it in the van's can-holder, and drove back toward Irv's.

The place was little more than a wooden shack, with a dock, gas pump, and launching ramp out back. Twenty aluminum fishing boats bobbed off the dock. Inside, he remembered a counter with a cash register, a half-dozen tanks for minnows and shiners, a few pieces of cheap fishing gear in wall racks, and a big, loose pile of green flotation cushions and orange round-the-neck life preservers. The whole place smelled of gas and oil, waterweed and rot.

Mail drove by once more, did his U-turn, looked for cars coming up behind, waited until one passed, and then followed it back to Irv's. Nothing out ahead. He swerved into the parking lot, stopped just outside the dusty picture-window where the fading red stick-up letters said, IRV'S BOAT WORK with a missing final "s."

He left the engine running, walked quickly around to the back of the van, took a jackknife out of his pocket, and cut a grapefruit-size hole in the top of the plastic gas can. The smell of gas was thick. He picked the can up, ready to ease it out the door, when headlights came up. He stopped, listening, but the car purred past.

He climbed out, got the lighter off the passenger seat, turned it up full, taped the sparking-lever down so he had a miniature torch, then picked up the five-gallon jug and heaved it through the window.

The window shattered with the sound of a load of dishes dropped in a diner: but nobody yelled, nobody came running. He tossed the lighter after the gas, and the building went up with a hollow *whoom*. By the time he was out of the parking lot, the fire was all over the inside of the building.

Damn. Wished he could stay.

He watched the building in the rearview mirror, until it disappeared behind a curve. When he was a kid, he'd torched a house in North St. Paul and had come back to sit on an elementary school embankment to watch the action. He liked the flames. Even more, he'd liked the excitement and companionship of the crowd, gathered to watch the fire. He felt like an entertainer, a movie star: he'd done this.

And listening, back then, he realized that everybody could find a little joy in watching one of their neighbors get burned out.

On the way back home, under the night sky, he thought about Andi Manette. Maybe this break was for the better. He'd been fucking her a lot, he could use the rest.

Tomorrow, though, he'd need her—need one of them, anyway.

He could feel that already.

11

LUCAS GOT UP a few minutes after Weather, struggling with the early hour, the morning light pale in the east windows. Weather put breakfast together while Lucas cleaned up. When he was dressed, Lucas got the ring from his sock drawer, fiddled with it, then dropped it in his pants pocket as he had almost every day for a month.

In the kitchen, Weather was standing at the sink, humming to herself as she sliced the orange heart out of a cantaloupe. Lucas still felt like he'd been hit in the forehead with a gavel.

"Anything good today?" he asked. His morning voice sounded like a rusty gate, but she was used to it.

"Not especially interesting," she said. "The first one is a woman with facial scarring from an electrical shock." She touched her cheek in front of her ear, to indicate where the scarring was. "I'm going to take out as much of the scar as I can—all of it, I hope."

"Sounds like she needs a plastic surgeon," Lucas said. He pushed two slices of bread into the toaster and started looking for the cinnamon.

"Sometimes I am a plastic surgeon," Weather said. "We do have that child coming up; that will be interesting. Six operations, probably. We're going to have to rotate her skull backwards . . ."

He liked watching her talk, her enthusiasm for the work, even when he had no idea of what she was talking about. He'd seen a half-dozen operations now, gowning up and learning where to stand, how to stay out of the way. The precision of it astonished him as did her easy way of command, and he found himself thinking that he could have done the work and been happy with it.

Although there was an odd, steely ego that went with surgeons, Weather had it—she ran the operating room like a sergeant major might—and so did George Howell, Weather's mentor. Howell was a fiftyish reconstructive surgeon who often stopped by when Weather was working, and Lucas usually felt a small, controllable urge to stuff the guy in a sewer somewhere, though Howell was a good enough guy.

"Are you listening?" Weather asked.

"Sure," Lucas said, peering down into the toaster. "It's just that I'm near death."

"There's something wrong with your metabolism," she said. "How can you be doing six things at three o'clock in the morning, but you can't add two and two at six o'clock in the morning? You should have a physical. How long has it been?"

Lucas rolled his eyes. "Having some guy shine his flashlight up my asshole isn't gonna improve my addition," he said. He looked glumly out the kitchen window. A robin hopped in the yard, peering this way and that for worms. "Christ, where's my .45 when I need it?"

Weather, up from the table, stopped to look outside, saw the robin and said, "I'd turn you in to Friends of Animals. You'd have bird lovers over here at five in the morning, making dove calls on the front porch."

"More fodder for the .45," he said. They ate together, talking about the daily routine, then Lucas kissed her good-bye, patted her on the ass, and went to lie facedown on the couch.

SHERRILL AND BLACK were finishing at Manette's office. Lucas stopped by at eight o'clock, still feeling that he was out of his time zone. Black was the same way, grumping at his partner, shaking his head at Lucas. "Six guys. No women. Anderson has the rundown on all of them. They'll all be in today's book. We're looking at all of them, and the FBI's going through its records. Now we're going back and looking at the second choices . . . the not-so-looney tunes."

"How about the six?"

"Severe goofs," Black said.

"Severe," Sherrill repeated. Like Weather, she was fairly chipper; in fact, seemed to soak up chipperness from Lucas and her partner. "I'd still like to know what we're doing about the sex cases."

"We'll get to them," Lucas promised. "We just don't want the media up in smoke. Not any more than they already are."

"I think Channel Three set new records in stupidity last night," Sherrill said. "The stuff they were saying was so stupid it made my teeth hurt."

"I don't understand what those guys are about," Black said. "I really don't."

"Making money," Lucas said. "That's all they're about."

As Lucas was leaving Manette's office, the receptionist, who'd been so flustered the first day, held up a hand, then looked both ways into the inner offices, a furtive look that Lucas recognized instantly. He continued out into the hall, looked back, caught her eye, and turned left. At the end of the hall was an alcove with Coke, coffee, and candy machines. A second later, she found him there, sipping a Diet Coke.

"I feel not so good, talking to you," the woman said. She wore a name tag that said "Marcella," and her voice was tentative, as though she hadn't made up her mind.

"Anything might help," Lucas said. "Anything. There are two kids out there."

She nodded. "It's just that with all the arguments and lawyers, it makes me feel . . . disloyal. Nancy doesn't have to know?"

Lucas shook his head. "Nobody will know."

The woman glanced nervously back at her office again. "Well: Andi's files are complete, but only for here."

Lucas frowned, gestured with the cup of Coke. "Only for here? I was told that this is the only place that she worked."

"On her own. But when she was doing her post-doc work, at the U, she did lots of people in the Hennepin County jail. You know, court-ordered evaluations. Most of them were juveniles, but that was so long ago that lots of them would be adults by now."

"Did she ever mention anyone in particular?"

"No, she really couldn't, because, you know . . . confidentiality. But they scared her—she'd talk about that sometimes—about how a guy'd get her up against a door, or he'd hiss at her like a cat, and she could feel them getting ready to come at her. The sex ones scared her, especially. She said you could feel the hunger coming across the room. She said some of them would have attacked her right there, in the jail interview rooms, if they hadn't been restrained. I think the people she saw there . . . those are the worst ones."

"Well, Jesus, why didn't somebody say something?" Lucas asked.

The woman looked down at the floor. "You know why, Mr. Davenport. Everybody hates you getting these records. I'm not even sure you should. You might be undoing a lot of work. But then there's Andi, and I keep thinking about the girls."

"Okay. You've been a help, Marcella," Lucas said. "I'm serious. This is all between you and me, but if something comes out of it, and you approve, I'll let Miz Manette know you helped."

Lucas let her get back into the office while he finished the Diet Coke, then returned himself.

"What?" Sherrill asked, when she saw him coming back.

"I think we've been euchred—there's a whole other set of records. Criminal stuff. C'mon, we're way behind."

THE UNIVERSITY MIGHT have objected on grounds of patient privacy, but the chief called the governor, the governor called three of the Regents, and the Regents called down to the university president, who issued a statement that said, "Given the circumstances—that we may have a monster preying on innocent women and girls, and helping oppress all genders and races by making the streets unsafe—we have agreed to provide the City of Minneapolis limited access to limited numbers of psychological records."

"How limited?" Lucas asked the records section supervisor at the university. He'd gone with Black and Sherrill because his title added weight.

"Limited to what you ask for," the supervisor said wryly.

"These guys will do the asking," Lucas said, tipping his head at Black and Sherrill. "We really appreciate anything you can do."

LUCAS LEARNED ABOUT the fire at Irv's Boat Works while he ate a late breakfast at his desk. The fire was reported in a routine, four-inch filler in the *Star-Tribune:* FIRE STRIKES MINNETONKA BOAT RENTAL. The article quoted a fire marshal: "It was arson, but there was no attempt to hide it, and we don't have a motive as yet. We're asking the public . . ."

Lucas called the marshal, whom he'd known vaguely from the neighborhood.

"It was a bomb, essentially, a Molotov cocktail, gas and motor oil," the fire marshall said. "Not a pro job, but a pro couldn't have done it any better. Burned that thing right down to the foundation. Old Irv didn't have but six thousand dollars in insurance, so he didn't do it. Not unless I'm missing something."

AT THE UNIVERSITY, Sherrill sat gloomily at a microfilm reader, operating the antiquated equipment by hand, eyes red from staring at the scratchy images of ten-year-old records. "Jesus Christ."

"What?" Black was on the next chair, three empty root beer cans next to his foot. He was wearing tan socks with blue clocks.

"This guy went around fucking exhaust pipes," Sherrill said.

Black looked at her: "You mean on cars?"

"Honest to God." She missed the double entendre and giggled, her finger trailing down the screen, over the projected image. "You know how they caught him?"

"He got stuck," Black suggested.

"No."

Black thought for a second. "His lawnmower sued for sexual harassment?"

"He tried to fuck a hot one," Sherrill said. "He had to go to the hospital with third-degree burns."

"Aw, man," Black groaned. He reached into his crotch and rearranged himself, then scribbled a note on the pad next to his hand.

"Anything good?" Sherrill asked as he made the note.

"Kid who was into sex and fire," Black said. "I think he scared her bad." He rolled through to the next page. "She says he shows signs of 'substantial sexual maladjustment manifested in improper, aggressive sexual behavior and identification with fire.' "

"Guys are so fucked up," Sherrill said as Black pushed the printout button. "You never see women doing this stuff."

"Have you heard the 'best friend' joke's been going around?"

"Oh, no. Don't tell me." She shook her head unconvincingly.

"See, there was this guy goes to work, gets there late, and the boss jumps him . . ."

"C'mon, don't tell me," Sherrill said.

"All right. If you really don't want to hear it," he said. "Let me get this printout."

He came back a minute later with the printout and she said, "All right, let's hear it. The joke."

Black dropped the printout next to the microfilm reader and went on, ". . . so the boss says, 'Get the fuck out of here. You're fired. I don't want to see your ass again.' So the guy drags out the door, really upset, gets in his car, and halfway home he's t-boned at an intersection by a teenager. Trashes his car, and the kid's got no insurance. Jesus. This is turning into the worst day of his life. So his car is towed, and the guy has to take the bus home—and when he gets there, eleven o'clock in the morning, he hears sounds coming from the bedroom. Like sex. Moaning, groaning, sheets being scratched. And he sneaks back there, and there's his wife, having sex with his best friend."

"No shit," said Sherrill.

"And the guy freaks out," Black said. "He yells at his wife, 'Get out of here, you slut. Get your clothes, get dressed, and get out. Don't ever come back or I'll beat your ass into the floor.' And he turns to his best friend and says, 'As for you—Bad dog! Bad dog!' "

"That's really fuckin' funny," Sherrill said; she turned away to smile.

"So don't laugh," Black said, knowing she liked it. And on the top of the printout he wrote "John Mail."

IRV WAS A broad-shouldered old man with a crown of fine white hair, with a pink spot in the middle of it. His nose was pitted and red, as though he might like his whiskey too much. He wore a faded flannel shirt and canvas trousers, and sat on a park bench next to his dock. A cash box sat on the bench beside him. "What can I do you for?" he asked when Lucas rolled up.

"Are you Irv?" Off to the left, there was a scorched stone foundation with raw dirt inside, and nothing else.

"Yeah." Irv squinted up at him. "You a cop?"

"Yeah, Minneapolis," Lucas said. "What do you think? Will you get it back together?"

"I suppose." Irv rubbed his large nose with the back of one hand. "Don't have much else to do, and the insurance'll probably get me halfway there."

Lucas walked over to the foundation. There wasn't much evidence of fire, except for soot on the stones. "Got it cleaned up in a hurry."

The old man shrugged. "Wasn't anything in it but wood and glass, and a few minnie tanks. It burned like a torch. What didn't burn, they took out with a front-end loader. The whole kit and caboodle was out of here in five minutes." He took off his glasses and cleaned the lenses on his flannel shirt. "Goddamnit."

Lucas turned away, inspected the foundation some more, and, when Irv got his glasses straight, walked back and handed him the flier. "Did you see this guy in here last week?"

Irv tipped his head back so he could look at the flier with his bifocals. Then he looked up and said, "Is this the sonofabitch that burned me out?"

"Was he in here?"

Irv nodded. "I believe he was. He doesn't look quite like this—the mouth is wrong—but he looks something like it, and I wondered what he was doing when he came in here. He wasn't any fisherman; he didn't know how to start the kicker. And it was cold that day."

"When was this?" Lucas asked.

"Two days ago—the day the rain came in. He came back in the rain."

"You remember his name?"

Irv scratched his chin. "No, no, I don't. I'd have his name off his driver's license, in my receipt box. If I had a receipt box anymore." He looked up at Lucas, the sun glittering off his glasses. "This is the one that took the Manette girl and her daughters, isn't it?"

"Could be," Lucas said. And he thought: *Yes, it is.*

JOHN MAIL CALLED Lucas at one o'clock in the afternoon. "Here I am, figuring the cops are coming down on me at any minute. I mean, I'm buying my food a day at a time, so I don't waste any. Where are you guys?"

"We're coming," Lucas growled. The voice was beginning to get to him: he was looking at his watch as he talked, counting the seconds. "We're taking bets on how long you last. Nobody's out as far as a week. We can't give that bet away."

"That's interesting," Mail said cheerfully. "I mean, that's very interesting. I best do as much fuckin' as I can, then, because I might not get any more for a while. Have to do with those hairy old assholes out at Stillwater."

"Be your asshole," Lucas snarled.

Mail's voice went cold: "Oh, I don't think so. I don't think so, Lucas."

"What?" Lucas asked. "You got a magic spell?"

"Nothing like that," Mail said. "But after people get to know me, they don't fuck with me; and that's the truth. But hey, gotta go."

"Wait a minute," Lucas said. "Are you taking care of those people? You've got them for now, and that puts some responsibility on you."

Mail hesitated, then said, "I don't have time to talk. But yeah, I'm taking care of them. Sometimes she makes me angry, but I don't know: subconsciously, she likes me. She always did, but she repressed it. She has a guilt complex about our doctor-patient relationship, but she used to sit there . . ."

He paused again, then said, "I've got to go."

Given a different context, he might have sounded almost human, Lucas thought, as the phone went *click.* As it was, he simply sounded insane.

"FIRE," LUCAS SAID to Black and Sherrill. "Sex. Probably he's been institutionalized—he talks about Stillwater like . . . I don't know. He doesn't really know about it, but he's heard a lot about it."

Lester came in. "He called from out in Woodbury somewhere."

"Woodbury. That's 494," Lucas said. "The guy's riding up and down the 494 strip, so he's someplace south."

"Yeah. We've whittled it down to one-point-two million people."

"The fire and sex thing," Sherrill said. "We got one just like that."

"Yeah." Black thumbed through a stack of paper. "This guy. John Mail. Let me see, he was fourteen when she saw him . . . Huh. He'd be about twenty-five right now."

Lucas looked at Lester. "That'd be pretty good. That'd be about prime time for a psycho."

Lester tapped the file. "Let's isolate that one and get on it."

LUCAS LOOKED AT his watch: almost two o'clock. Nearly forty-eight hours since the kidnapping. He locked the door to his office, closed the blinds, pulled the curtains, put his feet back on his desk, and thought about it. And the more he thought about it, the more the telephone link seemed the best immediate possibility.

He closed his eyes and visualized a map of the metro area. All right: if they coordinated cops from all over the metro area—if they set everything up in advance—how far down could they push the reaction time? A minute? Forty-five seconds? Even less than that, if they got lucky. And if they caught him in a shopping center, some place with restricted access, only a couple of exits—if they did that, they should be able to seal the place before he could get the car out. They could process every plate in the lot, check every ID . . .

Lucas was putting the idea together when another thought occurred: what had Dunn said? That he talked to Andi in her car? So Andi Manette had a cellular phone? What kind? A purse phone, or a dedicated car phone?

He sat up, turned on the desk light, rang Black's desk, got no answer, tried Sherrill, no answer. Got Anderson's daily book, flipped through it, found Dunn's phone number and dialed.

A cop answered. "He's probably on his car phone, chief."

Lucas got the number and called, and Dunn answered.

"Does your wife have a cellular?"

"Sure."

"A car phone, or a personal phone?"

"She carries it in her purse," Dunn said.

12

THE FBI'S AGENT-IN-CHARGE had a cleft chin and blond hair; his name was T. Conrad Haward, and he thought he looked like a Yale footballer, just now easing into his prime. But he had large, fuzzy ears and behind his back was called Dumbo.

Lucas, Lester, and an anonymous FBI tech sat in Haward's office underlooking the Minneapolis skyline. Haward interlaced his fingers in the middle of his leatherette desk pad and said, "It's all on the way, with the techs to operate it. The Chicago flight lands in an hour; the LA flight is still three hours out. The Dallas stuff, I don't know if we'll get that tonight. We'll go ahead in any case. Time is too much of a problem. In sixty-five percent of the cases, the victims have been terminated at this point on the time line."

"I just hope he's got that fucking phone," Lester said.

"He plays computer games—he won't throw out a piece of technology like a new flip phone," Lucas said.

The FBI tech, an older man with a silvery crewcut and striped clip-on tie, said, "The big question is, how do we hold him on the phone, if he answers it?"

"We're working on it," Lucas said, leaning forward in his chair. "We talked to one of the local rock-radio stations—the general manager is a friend of mine, and the only people who'd know about this would be him, one DJ, and an engineer. We're gonna have the DJ call, with a contest they've been running. It's a real contest, real prizes, and it'll really go out over the air. The only difference being that we'll feed them the phone number. If he doesn't answer the first time, we'll try again in a few hours. If he answers—whenever he answers—we'll have the DJ ready to go. The typical air time, for one of these contest things, is only about a minute or a little more. We're working out credible ways to stretch it."

"Unless we're lucky, we'll need at least two or three minutes to get a really good fix," the tech said. "You gotta hold him on there."

"He's a gamer—we're gonna appeal to his vanity," Lucas said. "He'll stay on long enough to deal with the question. And when he answers, if he's right, the DJ's gonna say, 'Hang on while I do an intro to the next song.' Then he'll do it—take his time, maybe do a little ad—and then come back for a mailing address."

"We'll never get an address," Lester said. He grinned. "But wouldn't that be something?"

Lucas shook his head. "He'd just give us some bullshit. But if we can hold him on that long, we ought to get the fix."

"When you say, 'Really good fix,' what does that mean?" Lester asked the tech. Dumbo frowned. The conversation seemed to be flowing around him. "A half-mile, a block, six inches, what?"

"If we could risk riding the signal in, we could get it right down to the house," the tech said. "As it is, we'll be able to put you on the right block."

"Why not go closer?" Dumbo asked.

"Because if he's really nuts, he might slit their throats and run for it," the tech said, turning to his boss. "He'd hear the choppers coming when they were six blocks away."

Lucas said, "You get us to the block, we'll have him out of there in an hour, guaranteed."

"If you can get us the air time, we'll put you on the block," the tech said.

On the way out of the building, Lester said, "Do you believe them?"

Lucas nodded. "Yeah. This is what the feebs are good at—technology. If he answers the phone, and we can keep him on, they'll track him."

"Dumbo was right about one thing—it's getting long," Lester said. He glanced at his watch as if to check the date. "The asshole won't keep them much more than four or five days at the outside. The pressure'll get to him."

"How about the full-court-press idea?" Lucas asked.

"Anderson's trying to set it up, but it'll be tomorrow before we're ready. It's a goddamned administrative nightmare. Even then . . . I don't know. There are too many people involved. Somebody will fuck it up."

"It's a shot," Lucas said. "What about that guy Black and Sherrill were tracking? The kid who liked sex and fire?"

"John Mail," Lester said. "That's a definite washout. I don't know why, but Black left a note for me. They're looking into three other possibilities."

"Shit," Lucas said. "The guy sounded good."

WITH TWO SETS of cellular tracking equipment, they would need six helicopters, one flying high and two flying low in each of two groups. The gear from Chicago arrived first, along with three techs, and they busied themselves fixing odd-looking globe antennas to the support struts on the choppers. The gear from Los Angeles arrived two hours later, and the other group was put together. When the choppers were ready, and the equipment checked, they assembled on a landing pad at the airport.

"All you have to do," one of the techs told the assembled pilots, "is generally face in the direction we tell you, and hold it there. The instruments will do the fine tuning. And keep track of what you're doing: I don't want to get hit by a goddamned jumbo jet because you get interested in what *we're* doing, and I don't want anybody running into anybody else."

"Glad he said that," Lucas muttered to Sloan, who was riding with the second group.

"You ready?" Sloan asked. Lucas feared airplanes in a way that amused other cops. Sloan no longer thought it was very funny.

"Yeah."

"They're pretty safe . . ."

"Helicopters don't bother me the way planes do," Lucas said. He grinned briefly and looked up at the chopper. "I don't know why, but I can ride a chopper."

AT EIGHT FORTY-FIVE they were in the air, lifting out of the airport landing zone, Lucas's group of choppers fixing themselves over I-494 south of Minneapolis, while Sloan's group hovered south of St. Paul. Below them, the lights in the cars on I-494 went by like streams of luminescent salmon, and the street and house lights stretched into the distance in a psychedelic chessboard. At nine-twenty, the techs were happy: "Let's do it," said the tech in Lucas's chopper.

And at the radio station, the DJ picked up a phone, said, "OK," looked through the glass of the broadcast booth at the engineer and the general manager behind him, and nodded.

> . . . *wrapping up with "Bohemian Rhapsody" from Queen. Tell you what, sports fans, it's time to play a little squeeze. Here, I'll stick my hand in the fifty-five-gallon drum . . . (There was a deep thumping, a man trapped inside an oil drum) . . . and pull out one of these telephone numbers. We'll give it ten rings. If we don't get it in ten, then we push the prize up by ninety-three dollars and try again. So . . .*

John Mail listened with half an ear: he was playing one of Davenport's fantasy games on a Gateway P5-90. He was in trouble: all of Davenport's games were full of traps and reversals. When you were killed, you could restart the game, carefully edge up to the point when you were killed—and get killed by something that passed you through the first time. A back-trail trap, a switchback ambush; must be some kind of circular counting mechanism in the program, Mail thought. He felt he was learning something about the opposition.

On the tuner, the DJ's voice followed a nice set of Queen. His phony bubblegum rap was a subliminal annoyance, but not worth changing. Mail heard the *beep-beep-boop* of the phone dialing. And when the phone rang on the radio—at that very instant—the phone rang in Andi Manette's purse.

Mail sat up, pushed away from the game with a spasm of fear. *What was that? Something outside? The cops?*

When he'd finished with Andi Manette the first night, he'd gone to the store for groceries and beer. Andi's purse was on the front seat of the van, where he'd thrown it after the attack. He opened it as he drove and pawed through it. He found her billfold, took out almost six hundred dollars, a pleasant surprise. He found her appointment book, a calculator, miscellaneous makeup, and the two pounds of junk that women seem to accumulate. He'd pushed it all back in the purse.

Later, a little drunk, and preoccupied with the question of Genevieve—the presence of the too-young girl bothered him; a kind of psychological thorn, for no reason that he understood—he dropped the purse on the floor near the kitchen door, intending to get rid of it later.

Now he stood, tense, up on the balls of his feet. *Gun,* he thought. The .45 was on a bookcase, and in two steps, he had it. Lights? No, if he turned them off, they'd know he'd heard them.

The buzzing continued. Nothing furtive about it. The fear recoiled a notch, but he kept the gun. Somebody outside? Or the stove clock? A broken smoke alarm? He moved quickly toward the kitchen, looked around—and saw the purse. In the background, the phone was ringing on the radio, the DJ said, "That's four . . ." and Mail's ear picked up the synchronized ringing between the radio and the purse.

He dumped the purse on the table. No phone, but the purse still rang at him, and was too heavy in his hand. He pulled open the front pocket and found it, a portable phone. As he looked at it, the DJ was saying, "That's six . . . and that's seven. George Dunn, if you're on the pot you better get off, 'cause . . . that's eight . . ."

Mail turned the phone in his hands, flipped it open, saw the phone switch. He looked out the window—nothing. If it was the cops calling, they didn't know where he was.

"HE'S NOT GONNA answer," the tech said. "That's nine."

Mail answered on the tenth ring. "Hello?" And Lucas jabbed a finger at the tech: "That's him."

At the radio station, the DJ leaned into it. "George Dunn? Damn, boy, you almost missed the call of your life, of the week, anyway."

And Mail could hear it all on the radio.

"This is Milo Weet at K-LIK with a We-Squeeze-It, You-Suck-It-Up; one thousand, two hundred and nine dollars on the line. You know how we play— we squeeze out a classic rock song in five seconds, the whole song, and you have ten seconds to tell us what it is. Are you ready?"

Mail knew the game. They thought his name was George Dunn, that was Manette's husband, but Weet was asking again, "Uh, George, excuse me, this is where you're supposed to say, 'Go ahead, dude,' unless you been into the vegetable matter again, in which case, give me your address and I'll be right out."

"Uh, go ahead, dude," Mail said. He'd never been on the radio. He could hear himself with his other ear, a strange, electronic echo.

"Here it comes, then, Georgie." There was a second of dead air, and then a nearly incomprehensible packet of noise with a vague rhythm to it, almost recognizable. *What was it?* Da-duh-da-Duh-da-Duh . . . *Let's see.*

THE TECH WAS working what looked like a television set, shouting at the pilot, "Hold it there, hold it, hold it . . ." while yellow numbers scrambled across the screen, and then, "Go 160, go, go . . ." and they took off, southeast.

"GEORGE? YOU THERE, boy? You got it? Tell you what, buddy, this is getting old. I'll give you another five seconds, another song by the same group. Not the same song, the same group . . ."

THE TECH WAS saying, "We've got him on, goddamn, he's right between us." He clicked on his microphone. "Frank, you got him?"

From the radio: "We got him, we're heading out at 195, but we're getting some shake in the reception . . ."

THE SECOND SQUIRT of sound ended, and Mail said to Weet, " 'All Night Long, by AC/DC'."

He added, on the air, "Davenport, you cocksucker."

And he was gone.

13

MAIL PUNCHED THE Off button and with the phone still in his hand, ran outside. Overhead, a jetliner passed in-bound for Minneapolis–St. Paul. *That's how they'd come,* he thought, looking into the sky for lights, red or white, blinking, swooping, focusing on him. Choppers. An envelopment.

He ran down to the drive and piled into the van, fumbled the keys out of his jeans pocket, roared backwards out of the driveway onto the gravel road. If they were coming, and if he could get just a little bit north, maybe he could lose himself in the suburban traffic . . .

Mail wasn't frightened as much as he was excited. And angry. They'd played him for a sucker. He'd bet a hundred-to-one that Davenport was behind the call. Hell, he'd go a thousand-to-one. It was all very slick. So slick that he found himself grinning in the night, then sliding into an angry sulk, then grinning again, despite himself. Slick.

But not quite slick enough, he thought.

From a mile away, atop a hill, Mail looked back at his house. He couldn't really see it, but he could see the lighted kitchen door, which he'd left open, a thin candlestick against the dark fields. There was nothing near him—nothing coming. He shifted into park, and let the engine idle. Nothing at all.

After a moment, he turned off the engine and got out to listen: nothing but a thin breeze blowing through the goldenrod in his headlights . . .

ANDI AND GRACE had nearly given up on the weapon idea. The only thing they could find, that might be anything at all, was a large nail that had bent over when it was being driven into the rafters above them. If they could pull it free, Andi thought, they might be able to hone it on the granite fieldstone in the walls.

"It'd be like a short ice pick, I guess," Andi said. They had nothing to work with, except the aluminum cans that the strawberry soda came in. While they were trying to figure out how to use the cans to pull the nail free, they began experimenting with the cans themselves. They could pull the tops and bottoms off without too much trouble—Andi wrapped her fingers in her shirt, and literally tore the aluminum free. They then had a thin, flexible sheet of aluminum. They tried folding it and flattening it, with the idea of sharpening the point and using it like a knife blade.

They could get a point, but not with enough stiffness to penetrate skin and muscle deeply enough to do damage. They might get an eye.

They tried twisting the stuff into spirals, but that wasn't as good as folding it. Grace suggested that since the edges of the aluminum were quite sharp when freshly torn, if they could somehow mount an edge between folded pieces, they might be able to use it like a razor. Again, it seemed that it might cut, but not enough to do mortal damage.

"If he was . . . on you, and I tried to cut his throat . . ." Grace suggested, her face pale.

Andi shook her head and pressed a strip of aluminum ingot into the back of her arm. "It takes too much force," she said. "Look."

She pressed hard, and got a long red line with just a hint of blood at one end. "It's harder to cut really deeply than you'd think. I remember from med school: the bodies cut like clay." She looked at the ceiling, and the bent nail. "The nail would do it, though. If we could get it out . . ."

"We'll just have to work on it," Grace said.

And they did, Grace sitting on Andi's shoulders, digging at the wood with small pieces of the torn aluminum. The nail head was free, but stubbornly unmoving, when they heard him coming.

Grace took her arm, and Andi was struck at how old her daughter had become. "Don't fight him," Grace said. "Please, don't fight."

BUT SHE WOULD.

She had to. If she didn't, he might start losing interest, and look at Grace, or . . . just get rid of them. Mail wanted her to fight. Wanted to conquer her, she'd figured that much.

Mail took her out of the cell, locked it, and then spun her toward the mattress. She let herself spin, stumbled, and went down hard. Better to go down than be knocked down.

And he liked the fear in her voice. He'd beat her to inspire it, if he had to, so she'd learned to beg: "Please, John," she said. "Please, you don't have to hurt me."

"Get out of the clothes," Mail said. Andi started pulling off her blouse. But now she looked around, carefully, the fearful look pasted on her face. Was there anything in the basement that might be used in a brawl?

"Come on, hurry up, goddamnit," Mail said. He was nude, erect, coming across the basement at her.

"John . . ."

He was standing over her. "We're gonna move on, try something new. If I get bit—I really don't wanna get bit—if I get bit, I'll beat the shit out of you, then I'll take Grace down to the house and put her hands in the garbage disposal, then bring her back here so you can look at her. You got that?"

She nodded dumbly, and he said, "Okay, then . . ."

AFTERWARDS, LYING ON the mattress, he said, "You know what that fuckin' Davenport did?" And he told her about the radio. "I saw it, though," he bragged. "They took me for a minute, but I saw right through it and I said it right on the air, 'Davenport, you cocksucker,' I said." He was animated as he talked, and they might have been teenage lovers lying on a mattress in a cold-water flat, talking about dreams. "He thinks he's pretty fuckin' smart. But what he don't know is hurtin' him."

"I . . . what?" She was responding automatically, keeping the talk going as she inventoried the basement. Mail hadn't beaten her this time, and the sex had become inconsequential; there just wasn't much more that he could do to her, and she could handle it . . . she thought.

The inventory: a stack of old terra-cotta pots in the corner—they could be thrown, or used as a club. And over there, was that a beer bottle? God, if she could get that bottle, they could break off an end of it, maybe get some glass splinters. Those would be real weapons.

Mail said, "I've got a spy watching his every move."

Andi, doing her reconnaissance, had lost track of the conversation. A spy? "A spy?" she asked. A delusion?

"Somebody you know," Mail said to her, turning to watch her reaction. "A friend of yours; put me on you in the first place."

"Who?" His voice suggested this was more than a delusion—he was too matter-of-fact.

"Can't tell you," Mail said.

"Why?"

" 'Cause I want you thinking about it. Maybe it's your husband, trying to get rid of you and the daughters. Maybe it's your mother . . ."

"My mother's dead."

"Yeah? How'd she die?"

"She drowned."

"Huh." Mail seemed about to say something else, but then he rolled to his knees, looming over her again. "Well, then, maybe it's your partner. Maybe it's your father."

She took the risk. "John, I think you're making it up."

For a moment, she thought he might strike her—his eyes widened in instant, unreflective anger, and he seemed to pull within himself, as when he beat her. But then he smiled, slightly, and said, "Yeah, I'm bullshitting you. There really is a spy. But I don't know who it is."

She shook her head.

"Called me up out of the blue," he said. "Said, 'Remember Andi Manette who sent you away? She talks about you all the time . . .' "

"Somebody said that?" She believed him now—and she was appalled.

"Yeah. Said you thought I was some kind of devil. Pretty soon I couldn't get you out of my head. I never forgot you, but you were in the back of my mind some place. I didn't have to deal with you. But the spy called . . ."

"Yes?" A psychiatrist's prompt, and she felt a little thrill of power.

"I can remember sitting in that detention room, and you always sat there in these . . . dresses . . . you had these tits, you wore this perfume, I could see up your legs sometimes, I used to think I could see your pussy in there; I'd lay up at night and think about it. Could I see it? Or maybe not . . ."

"I didn't realize . . ." Another prompt.

"You never knew what made me work, and I couldn't explain it," Mail said. "After a while I'd just sit there and look at your tits and burn."

"Somebody kept calling you?"

"I don't wanna talk any more," he said, the anger suddenly back. And his eyes turned inward, jelled over. "I want to fuck . . ." He swatted at her and hit her on a shoulder. She quailed away, and he said, "Get over here, or I'll really fuckin' beat your ass."

————

LATER SHE SAID, "Can I call somebody? My husband, or somebody, to tell them that we're alive?"

He was irritated. "Fuck no."

"John, pretty soon they'll think we're dead. Pretty soon all this activity will die down, and it'll just be one long grinding hunt, and they'll get you and lock you up forever. If they know I'm alive, you might be able to . . . move better. There might be a deal somewhere, something you can work."

Again, talking almost like lovers: she concerned for his future. He shook it off. "There won't be any deal. Not with me."

"It gives you more power," she said. "If they convince themselves that I'm dead, they can do anything they want. If they know I'm alive, things'll be more awkward for them. As a gamer, I'm sure you can see that. And I just want people to know that I'm still out here. I don't want them to forget me."

Mail stood up, began to dress, kicked her clothes at her. "Put them on." And when she was dressed, he said, "I'll think about it. You can't call direct, but maybe we could tape something. I could call the tape in from somewhere else."

"John, that would be . . ." She almost laughed. "That would be great."

He reacted to that: he puffed up, she thought. He liked the flattery, especially from her. "I'll think about it."

BACK INSIDE THE cell, after the door had closed and his feet had thumped away, she said to Grace, "We've got to think of a message to tape—he might tape a message for us. We have to figure out a code, or something."

She was excited, and Grace watched her, her young face solemn, withdrawn, and Andi finally said, "What? What?"

And Grace said, "You've got blood all over your face, Mom. It's all over."

Grace pointed to the right side of Andi's face and suddenly her hand began to shake with fear, and she began to cry, backing away from Andi, and Andi scrubbed at the side of her face and the blood from her nose that had dried there, after Mail, excited, had begun slapping her during the last sexual frenzy.

She hadn't noticed the blood, she thought, as Grace huddled in the corner. She was becoming used to it; a condition of her servitude.

But things had changed this time. Things had changed.

14

Rose Marie Roux, looking too tired to be a chief of police, her purse dangling from her hand, struggled up the stairs and through the open door.

Lucas followed the chief and T. Conrad Haward—Dumbo—into Manette's house, to a gathering in the ornate living room. Dunn was there, tense, unhappy, hair in disarray, eyes heavy; he had his back to a cold fireplace, a heavy crystal liquor glass in his hand. He looked past Roux and Dumbo to nod at Lucas.

Helen Manette perched on an antique chair, mouth too wide and too tight, and Lucas thought she might be drunk, although she wasn't drinking anything. Nancy Wolfe, in a soft, moss-colored suit, glared at him from across the room. When he looked steadily back, she bounced her hair and looked away. She was sipping from a small cognac glass, and posed in front of a nineteenth-century oil painting of a woman with cold, dark eyes, a coal-black dress, and a surprisingly sensual lower lip.

The gofer attorney was getting drinks; a Minneapolis Intelligence cop in a plaid sportcoat and t-shirt, with a bump on his hip that was probably a large automatic, leaned in a doorway and gobbled popcorn from a plastic sack. He was waiting for the phone call that had never come, and looked bored.

Manette stood in the center of the circle, wearing a gray suit with an Italian necktie, the knot tight at his throat. He was worn and older than he'd looked only the day before. But somehow, down in his soul, Lucas thought, watching him, Manette also enjoyed being at the center of a tragedy.

"No-go," the chief said to Manette, shaking her head. "I'm sorry."

"Shit." Dunn turned away from them, and Lucas thought he might chunk the bourbon glass into the fireplace. Instead, he leaned against the rock-facing, head down.

"Not a complete loss," Dumbo said. A fine patina of sweat covered his forehead. He hated dealing with the rich, people who knew U.S. Senators by their nicknames and toilet habits. "We had him on, but we couldn't hold him long enough. We had him for twenty seconds and he figured it out. We've got an idea where he is: south of the rivers, down in Eagan or Apple Valley."

"You've got projects down there," Manette said to Dunn.

Dunn turned around, his face sullen, a little heat lightning in his eyes. "Yeah, but I wasn't answering any telephones down there tonight," he growled.

"That's not what I meant," Manette said, squaring off to Dunn. "I meant, you know the area."

Nancy Wolfe caught Tower's jacket sleeve and pulled him back an inch, and Dunn said, "Yeah, and I know there're three hundred thousand people in the fuckin' area . . ."

"Watch your mouth," Manette snapped. "There are women here."

Lucas, now watching Wolfe, behind Manette, her hand on his sleeve, thought: *Huh.*

"He, uh, mentioned Davenport," Dumbo said, looking at Lucas. "He apparently, uh, feels Chief Davenport is"—he groped for a word, finally found one—*"responsible* for the"—he groped for another one—"radio procedure."

"Well, he is," Dunn said to Dumbo. "He's the only cop I've talked to so far doesn't have his head up his ass."

"George . . ." Manette said, his face still red under his shock of white hair. Dunn ignored him and stepped closer to Lucas. "I want to put up a reward. I don't care how much. A million."

"Not that much," Lucas said. "We'd have freaks coming out of the woodwork. Start at fifty thousand."

"Good. I'm gonna announce it right now," Dunn said. He looked at Manette, but Manette said nothing, just shook his head with a sour, skeptical smile and turned away from them all.

ON THE WAY out, the chief said, "Happy little family."

"Nancy Wolfe, Tower Manette, what do you think?"

Nothing surprised Rose Marie Roux: she'd been in politics too long. After a moment of silence, she said, in a voice that was almost pleased, "It's possible. When we briefed them last night, she touched the back of his hand."

"And tonight, she tried to stop him from fighting Dunn . . . or made a move that way. Protective."

"Huh," the chief said. Then, "You know, Lucas, you have a strong feminine side."

"What?"

"Never mind," she said.

"No, what'd you mean?" Lucas was amused.

The chief said, "You're more willing than most men to rely on intuition. I mean, you suspect that Nancy Wolfe and Tower Manette are having an affair."

"There's no question about it," he said. "Now that I think about it."

"Because she caught his sleeve." Now Roux was amused. "That's a pretty good leap."

"It was *how* she touched his sleeve," Lucas said. "If that's feminine, I accept the label."

"What'd you think I meant?" Roux asked.

"I don't know," he said vaguely. "Maybe, you know—I had nice tits."

Roux started to laugh: "Christ, I'm running a fuckin' zoo, the people I've got."

THE MIDDLE OF the night, all foul-mouthed, their shirts seeming to pull willfully out of their pants and rumple on their own, they stood around a six-by-five Metro wall map and looked at the red-crayoned box southeast of the airport.

"It's something," Lester insisted. "He was smarter than we gave him credit for. Christ, another minute. One more minute and we've got him."

Lucas threw a paper coffee cup at a waste basket, the old coffee like acid in his mouth. "We gotta go for the full-court press. He'll be calling back. I'm surprised he hasn't already."

"We can do it with the next shift," Anderson says. "Right now, we'd be eighty percent. By tomorrow morning, we'll be at full strength."

"We gotta be ready to do it now," Lucas said.

"We are—just not a hundred percent. It's a matter of getting people through the shifts," Anderson said.

"We should flood the 494 strip, and extra people down I-35 all the way through Apple Valley," Lucas said.

"Smart little fuck," Lester said, staring moodily at the map.

WEATHER WAS ASLEEP and moaned softly when he slipped into bed. He needed to wake her up to talk, but she would be cutting on someone in the morning, and he didn't dare do it. Instead, he lay awake for an hour, plotting the twists and turns of the day, feeling the warmth from Weather seeping over him. He finally slept, one arm at her waist, the smell of Chanel around him.

WEATHER WAS GONE, and Lucas was just out of the shower when the cellular phone rang. He stopped, listening, then hurried into the living room, trailing streams of water. He'd left the phone on the dining room table, and now he picked it up and clicked it on.

"Lucas, how they hanging?" Mail sounded unnaturally cheerful.

"Are they still alive?" The squad cars should be rolling. Thirty seconds.

"Are you trying to trace me?"

Lucas hesitated, then repeated his original question: "Are they alive, or not?" Lucas asked.

"Yeah, they're alive," Mail said grudgingly. "In fact, I've got a message for you from Andi Manette."

"Let me get a pencil," Lucas said.

"Oh, horseshit, this is all recorded," Mail said impatiently. "Not that it's gonna do you any good. I'm using the cellular, but this time I'm riding around, a long way from anywhere."

Shit. "Go ahead: I've got a pencil."

"Here it is. I don't know how clear it'll be . . ."

George, Daddy, Genevieve, Aunt Lisa, this is Andi. We're okay, Grace and me, and we hope Genevieve is back and everything is fine with her. The man with us won't let us say anything about him, but he was good enough to let us send this. I hope we can talk to you again, and this man with us, please give him whatever he wants so we can come back safely. That's all I can say . . .

Andi Manette's voice was plaintive, fearful, trembling with hope; cut off with a click of a recorder button.

"That's all for now, sports fans," Mail said cheerfully. "I have to say, though, I liked the disk-jockey thing. It really woke me up. Tell the guy I'm gonna stop by his house and visit his family some day while he's gone. I'm gonna bring a pair of wire cutters with me. We're gonna have a lot of fun."

WHEN MAIL HUNG up, Lucas turned the phone off, laid it on the table, and stared at it like an ebony cockroach; fifteen seconds later, Martha Gresham called from the communications center and said, "We got it all."

"Excellent. Is Lester there?"

"No, but Donna's talking to him now, so he knows."

Lucas hurried back to the bedroom and dressed, waiting for the phone to ring. It rang as he was knotting the tie: "Yeah, Frank. Was it her?"

"It's her. And she's trying to tell us something, but we don't know what," Lester said.

"How do you know?"

"Because she said hello to her aunt Lisa."

"Yeah?"

"I talked to Tower Manette one minute ago," Lester said. "Her aunt Lisa's been dead for ten years."

"Get somebody going: we need everything we can get on the aunt."

"We're going, but I want you looking at it," Lester said. "Goddamnit, Lucas, we need somebody to pull a rabbit out of a hat."

Lucas said, "You gotta cover Milo, over at the station. And his family. He's got two kids himself."

"We're on the way. But what about Genevieve?"

"Genevieve's dead," Lucas said. "We know that, but Andi Manette doesn't."

THEY DID A group therapy with Manette and Dunn, in Roux's office: why Aunt Lisa?

"Lisa Farmer was my first wife's sister," Manette said. "She had this big place out in the country, with horses, and when Andi was a kid she'd go out and ride. Maybe she's telling us that the guy's a farmer—or that he's a horse guy, or something. It's gotta be something like that."

"Unless she's just lost it," Dunn said quietly.

"My daughter . . ." Manette started.

"Hey." Dunn pointed a finger at Manette, his voice cold. "I know you love your daughter, Tower, but I do too, and frankly, I know her better. She is fucked up. Her voice has changed, her manner's changed, she is desperate and she's hurt. I want to think that she's sending a message, but I don't want to cut off everything and just concentrate on that one thing. Because it's possible that she's lost it."

Manette looked away, sideways at nothing, down at the floor. Dunn, uncomfortable, patted him on the back, then looked across Manette at Lucas. "Genevieve's dead, isn't she?"

"You better be ready," Lucas said.

THEY WOULD DO a fast scan of farms and horses, running the Dakota County agricultural assessment rolls against sex crime records and other lists. Lucas got Anderson's running case log and carried it back to his office and read for a while. Nothing occurred to him. Restless, he wandered down to Homicide, and ran into Black and Sherrill.

"What's happening at the U?" he asked.

"We've got five more possibles, including one with fire and sex. We're looking for him now," Sherrill said. She held up a stack of files. "You want Xeroxes?"

"Yeah. Anderson said something about the one guy—Mail?—that he was a washout?"

"Yeah," Black said. "Really washed out. He washed out of the river. He's dead."

"Shit," Lucas said. "He sounded good."

Sherrill nodded. "They let him out of St. Peter and two months later he went off the Lake Street Bridge, middle of the night. They found him down by Fort Snelling. He'd been in the water for a week."

"How'd they ID him?" Lucas asked.

"They found a state ID card on the body," Sherrill said. "The ME went ahead and did a dental on him; it was him."

"All right," Lucas nodded. "Who's this other guy, the fire and sex guy?"

"Francis Xavier Peter, age—now—thirty-four. He set sixteen fires in ten days out in St. Louis Park, nobody hurt, several houses damaged. We talked to his parents, and they say he's out on the West Coast being an actor. They haven't heard from him lately, and he doesn't have a phone. Andi Manette treated him; he was a patient for two years. She didn't like him much. He came on to her during a couple of therapy sessions."

"An actor?"

"That's what they say," Sherrill said.

"This guy we're dealing with," Lucas said, "he could be an actor. He likes games . . ."

"One thing," Black said. "Francis Xavier Peter is a blond and wore his hair long."

"Jesus: could be the guy. Does he look anything like the composite?" Lucas asked.

"He has a round face, sort of German-country boy," Sherrill said.

"What you mean is, *No,*" Lucas said. "He doesn't look like the composite."

"Not too much," she conceded.

"Well, push it," Lucas said.

15

THE VOICE WAS tense: "They're getting close to you. You've got to move on."

Mail, standing in the litter of two decapitated mini-tower systems—he was switching out hard drives—sneered at the phone, and the distant personality at the end of it. "Say what you mean. You don't mean, *move on.* You mean, kill them and dump them."

"I mean, get yourself out," the voice said. "I didn't think anything like this was going to happen . . ."

"Bullshit," Mail said. "You thought you were manipulating me. You were pushing my buttons."

He could hear the breathing on the other end—exasperation, desperation, anticipation? Mail would have enjoyed knowing. Someday, he thought, he'd figure the voice out. Then . . . "Besides, they're nowhere near as close as you think. You just want me to get rid of them."

"Did you know that Andi Manette sent a message with that tape recording you let her make? Her aunt is dead—she's been dead a long time. Her name was Lisa Farmer, and she lived on a farm. And they're looking in Dakota County, at farm houses, because that's where they put you with that little cellular phone trick. You don't have much time now."

Click.

Mail looked at the phone, then dropped it back on the hook and wandered around the living room, whistling, stepping over computer parts. The tune he whistled came from the bad old days at the hospital, when they piped Minnesota Public Radio into the cells. Simple Mozart: he'd probably heard it a hundred times. Mail had no time for Mozart. He wanted rhythm, not melody. He wanted sticks hammering out a blood-beat; he wanted drums, tambourines, maracas. He wanted timpani. He didn't want tinkly music.

But now he whistled it, a little Mozart two-finger melody, because he didn't want to think about Andi Manette tricking him, because he didn't want to kill her yet.

Had she done this? She had——he knew it in his heart. And it made him so *angry*. Because he'd trusted her. He'd given her an opportunity, and she'd betrayed him. This *always* happened. He should have *known* it was going to happen again. He put his hands to his temples, he could feel the blood beating through them, the pain that was going to come. Christ, this was the story of his life: when he tried to do something, somebody *always* spoiled it.

He took several laps around the living room and the kitchen, opened the refrigerator door, looked blindly inside, slammed it; the whistling began a humming noise deep in his throat, and the humming became a growl——still two-finger Mozart——and then he walked out the back door and cut across the lawn toward the pasture beyond, and the old house in the back.

He jumped the fallen-down fence, passed an antique iron disker half-buried in the bluestem and asters; halfway up the hill, he was running, his fists clenched, his eyes like frosted marbles.

THEY THOUGHT THEY were making progress, working on Mail: he hadn't become gentle, but Andi felt a relationship forming. If she didn't exactly have power, she had influence.

And they were still working on the nail. They couldn't move it, but a full inch of it was exposed. A few more hours, she thought, and they might pull it free.

Then Mail came.

They heard him running across the floor above them, *pounding* down the stairs. She and Grace looked at each other. Something was happening, and Grace, who'd been squatting in front of the game monitor, rocked uneasily.

Then the door opened, and Mail's face was a boiled-egg mask with the turned-in, frosted-marble eyes, his hair bushed like a frightened cat's. He said, "Get the fuck out here."

GRACE COULD HEAR the beating.

She could feel it, even through the steel door. She stretched herself up the door and pounded on it and cried, "Mom, mama, mother. Mom . . ."

And after a while, she stopped and went back to the mattress and put her hands on her ears so she couldn't hear. A few minutes later, weeping, she closed her eyes and put her hands on her mouth like the speak-no-evil monkey and felt herself a traitor. She wanted the beating to stop, but she wouldn't cry out. She didn't want Mail to come for *her*.

AN HOUR AFTER he'd taken Andi, Mail brought her back. Always, in the past, her mother had been clothed when Mail put her back in the room: this time, she was nude, as was Mail himself.

Grace huddled back against the wall as he stood in the doorway, facing her, the hostile frontality frightening as nothing else ever had been. Finally, she bowed her head between her knees and closed her eyes and began to sing to herself, to close out the world. Mail listened to her for a moment, then a tiny, bitter smile crossed his face, and he shut the door with a *clang.*

ANDI DIDN'T MOVE.

When the door closed, Grace was afraid to look up—afraid that Mail might be inside the room with her. But after a few seconds, when nothing moved, she peeked. He was gone.

Grace whispered, "Mother? Mom?"

Andi moaned and turned to look at her daughter, and blood ran out of her mouth.

16

LUCAS PUT DOWN the file and picked up the phone. "Lucas Davenport."

"Yeah, um, I'm a game player?" The woman's voice was tentative, slightly unplugged. Her statements came as questions. "I was told I should talk to you?"

"Yes?"

He was impatient; he was waiting for the LA cops to get back with information on Francis Xavier Peter, the fire-starting actor.

"I think, um, I've seen the guy in the picture," the woman said. "I played D&D with him a couple of months ago, in this girl's house? In Dinkytown?"

Lucas sat up. "Do you know his name, or where he lives?"

"No, but he was with this girl, and we were at her house, so she knows him."

"How sure are you?"

"I wouldn't be sure except for his eyes? The eyes are the same. The mouth's different? But the eyes are right? And he was really a gamer, he was a good dungeon master, he knew everything. But he was scary? Really wired? And something this girl said made me think he'd been in treatment?"

Lucas looked at his watch. "Where are you? I'd like to come over and talk." He wrote it down.

"Sloan, c'mon," Lucas said.

The narrow man got his jacket, a new one, a new shade of brown. "Where're we going?"

Lucas explained as they walked out. "She had a sound about her," Lucas said. "I don't think it's bullshit."

The woman lived in a student apartment complex across I-494 from the university. Lucas put the gray city Plymouth in a fire zone and they went inside, following a blonde co-ed in a short skirt and bowling jacket. They all stopped at the elevator, Sloan and Lucas looking at the girl from the corners of their eyes; she was very pretty, with round blue eyes and a *retroussé* nose that might have been natural. The girl studied the numbers at the top of the elevator doors with rapt attention. Nobody said anything. The elevator came, they all got on, and all three watched the numbers at the top of the door.

The woman got off at three, turned, smiled, and walked away. The doors closed and Sloan said, "I think she smiled at me."

"I beg your pardon," Lucas said. "I believe it was *me* she smiled at."

"Bullshit. You stepped in front of it, that's all."

CINDY MCPHERSON, THE gamer, was a confused Wisconsin milkmaid. She was a large girl with a perfect complexion and a sweet country smile, who dressed in black from head to foot, and wore a seven-pointed star around her neck on a leather shoestring.

"The more I looked at the picture, the more I was sure it was him," she said. She sat on the edge of the Salvation Army couch, using her hands to talk: Lucas had the impression that under the black dress was a former high school basketball jock. "There's something about his face," she said. "It's like a coyote's——he's got those narrow eyes and the cheekbones. He could've been pretty sexy, but it was like there was something . . . missing. He just didn't connect. I think he connected with Gloria, though. She was pawing him."

"This Gloria——what's her last name?"

She shrugged. "I don't know. I've seen her around with people, we hang out over there, but she's not a good friend of mine. A couple of years ago, there were some raves over, like, in the industrial park up 280? That's where I met her. Then I'd see her over in Dinkytown, and a couple of months ago I saw her and she said they were starting a game. So I went up and he was the dungeon master."

"Can you show us the place?" Sloan asked.

"Sure. And Gloria's name is on the mailbox. She checked her mailbox when we were going up the stairs and I saw that it said Gloria something."

DINKYTOWN IS AN island of well-worn commerce off the campus at the University of Minnesota, two- and three-story buildings selling clothes and fast food and compact discs and pharmaceuticals and Xerox copies. They were backing into a parking space when McPherson pointed across the street and said, "There she is. That's Gloria. And that's her building."

Gloria was a thin, hunch-shouldered woman, dressed, like McPherson, in head-to-toe black; like McPherson, she wore an amulet. But while McPherson had that perfect, open face and peaches-and-cream complexion, Gloria was dark, saturnine, her face closed and wary like a fox's.

"Wait here, or go get a sandwich or something," Lucas said to McPherson. "We might have some more questions for you."

He and Sloan scrambled through the traffic and hurried through the apartment house door. Gloria was just locking her mailbox and held a green electric-bill envelope in her teeth.

"Gloria?" Lucas was out front.

She took the envelope out and looked at them. "Yes?"

"We're police officers, we'd . . ."

"Like your help," Sloan finished.

GLORIA CROSBY MIGHT have been pretty, but she wasn't: she was unkempt, a little dirty, her face was formed in a frown. She reluctantly took them to her apartment on the top floor. "Been working on a thesis, haven't had much time to clean," she said. When she opened her door, the apartment smelled of tomato soup and feathers, with an overlay of tobacco and marijuana.

"Do a little grass from time to time?" Sloan asked cheerfully.

"I don't, no," she said. She seemed almost slow. "Marijuana makes you more stupid than you already are. Some people choose that, and I say, 'Okay.' But I don't choose it."

"Smells sort of grassy up here," Sloan said.

"A couple of people were visiting last night, and they smoked," she said offhandedly. "I didn't."

"You don't think that's wrong?" Lucas asked.

"No, do you?"

Lucas shrugged and Sloan laughed. Sloan said, "About two months ago, you played D&D up here with a group of five people. The dungeon master was this man. We need his name." He handed her a copy of the composite.

Crosby took the flier, looked at it for a long time. Then her forehead wrinkled and she said, "Well—this isn't the guy, but I know who you're talking about. He looks sort of like this, but the eyes are wrong. His name is . . . David." She dropped her hand to her side and went to a window and looked down at the street and pulled on her lower lip.

Lucas said, "What . . ."

She put up a hand to silence him, continued to look down at the street. After a moment, "David . . . Ellers. E-L-L-E-R-S. God, I almost forgot. Tells you about my relationships, huh?"

"Do you know . . ."

"How'd you know about the game?" she asked, turning to look at them. She was interested, but totally unflustered: so unflustered that Lucas wondered if she was on medication.

"I'm in the gaming net, besides being a cop," Lucas said.

She pointed a finger at him and said, with the first flicker of animation, "Davenport."

"Yeah."

"You did some wicked games, before you went to computers," she said. "Your computer games suck."

"Thanks," Lucas said, dryly. "Do you know where this guy lives?"

"He's the guy who took the Manette chick?"

"Well, we're looking into that . . ."

"I think you're barking up the wrong tree," she said. "David was from Connecticut and he was on his way to California."

"I got the impression that you knew him pretty well," Lucas said.

She sighed, dropped into a chair. "Well, he stayed here for a week and fucked me every day, but he was just here that one week."

"What kind of a car did he have?" Lucas asked.

She snorted and showed what might have been either a smile or a grimace. "A traveling gamer, on his way to California? What do you think?"

Lucas thought a minute, and then said, "A Harley."

"Absolutely," Gloria said. "A Harley-Davidson sportster. He tried to scam me: he said he'd love to take me with him, but he needed the money to trade up to a softtail. I told him to pick me up when he got it."

She had few details about David Ellers: she'd met him at a McDonald's, where he was arguing with some people about the MYST game. He didn't have a place to stay, and he looked nice, so she asked if he wanted to stay over. He did, for a week.

"I hated to see him go," she said. "He was *intense*."

He was from Connecticut, she said. "I think his parents had money, like insurance or something. He was from Hartford, maybe."

"WHAT DO YOU think?" Lucas asked Sloan when they were back on the street. McPherson was walking back toward them, eating a cheeseburger, carrying a McDonald's bag.

"I don't know," Sloan said. "If she was lying, she was good at it. But it didn't sound like the truth, either. Goddamn dopers, it's hard to tell. They don't have that edge of fear."

They got to the car just as McPherson did; she offered some fries to Lucas and Sloan, and seemed slightly chagrined when Sloan took some. "What happened?" she asked.

"She said he was passing through," Lucas said, briefly. "She said his name is David Ellers, he's from Connecticut, and he was on his way to the West Coast."

McPherson had taken a large bite out of the cheeseburger, but she stopped chewing for a moment, then looked sideways out the car window, shook her head at Lucas, finished chewing, swallowed, licked her lips, and said, "God: when you said that, Connecticut, it popped into my head. I asked this guy if he knew my friend David, because they both came from the same town. Wayzata. But he said he went to a private school and didn't know him."

"Wayzata?" Sloan asked.

"I'm pretty sure," she said.

"Gloria said *his* name was David," Lucas said.

McPherson shook her head. "It wasn't. I would have remembered that—I mean, two Davids from the same town and the same age and all."

Sloan sighed and looked at Lucas. "God, it's a shame the way young people lie to us nowadays."

"And the old people," Lucas said. "And the middle-aged." To McPherson he said, "C'mon. Let's go see if she remembers you, and if that helps her remember the guy's name."

"Jeez, I kinda hate to be seen with cops," McPherson said.

"Is that what they taught you in Wisconsin?" Sloan asked as they got back out of the car.

"Nope. They taught me that if I get lost, ask a cop. So I got over here at the U, and I got lost, and I asked a cop. He wanted to take me home. With him, I mean."

"Must've been a St. Paul cop," Lucas said. "C'mon, let's go."

THEY CLIMBED THE stairs again, but when they knocked on Gloria's door, there was no answer. "Could be visiting another apartment," Sloan said. But it didn't feel that way. The building was silent, nothing moving.

Lucas walked down to the end of the hall and looked out a window: "Fire escape," he said. An old iron drop-ladder fire escape hung on the side of the building. He checked the window above it, and the window slid open easily. "The window's unlocked from inside. Goes down the back."

He leaned out: nothing moved.

Sloan said, "She's running."

Lucas said, "And she knows him—you go that way."

Sloan ran for the stairs, while Lucas went out the window and ran down the fire escape. At the top of the lowest flight, he had to wait for a counter-weight to drop the stairs to a narrow walkway between the apartment and the next building. The walkway was filled with debris, blown paper, a few boards, a bent and rusting real-estate sign, and wine bottles. Lucas looked one way toward the street, and the other toward an alley that ran along the back of the buildings.

If she'd gone out to the street, they should have seen her. He ran the other way, toward the alley, high-stepping over dried dog shit and a knee-high pile of what looked like cat litter. Just down the alley was the rear door of a pizza shop, with a window. Behind the window, a kid was hosing down dishes in a stainless-steel sink. Lucas went to the door and pushed through: and a woman leaned against a counter, smoking a cigarette, and the kid looked up. "Hey," she said, straightening up. "You're not supposed to . . ."

"I'm a cop," Lucas said. "Did either of you guys see a woman come down the fire escape in back of the building across the alley? Five, six minutes ago?"

The woman and the dishwasher looked at each other and then the dishwasher said, "I guess. Skinny, dressed in black?"

"That's her," Lucas said. "Did you see where she went?"

"She walked up that way . . ." The dishwasher pointed.

"Was she in a hurry?"

"Yeah. She sort of skipped, and she was carrying like a laundry bag. She went around the corner. What'd she do?"

Lucas left without answering, ran down to the corner. There was a bus stop, with nobody waiting. He ran across a street, into a bakery, flashed his badge and asked to use a phone: a flour-dusted fat man led him into the back and pointed at a wall phone. Lucas called Dispatch: "She might be on a bus, or she might be walking someplace. But flood it: we're looking for a tall, pale woman in her middle twenties, dressed all in black, probably in a hurry, probably carrying a bag of some kind. Maybe a sack. Check for a car registration and get that out."

Back on the street, he looked both ways: he could see three or four women dressed in black. One might have been Crosby, but when she turned to cross a street, Lucas, running up from behind, saw it wasn't her. A cop flashed by: two guys looking out the windows. Lucas turned back: there were students everywhere.

Too many of them in black.

LUCAS WALKED BACK to the apartment's front door. Sloan turned the corner and walked toward him from the other end of the street. Sloan shook his head, took off his hat, smoothed his hair, and said, "Didn't see a thing."

"Goddamnit, this is just like the fuckin' game store. We were this close," Lucas said, showing an inch between his thumb and forefinger. He looked up at the building. "Let's see if there's a manager."

A glassed-over building directory showed a manager in 3A; his wife sent them down the basement, where they found him building a box kite.

Lucas explained the problem, and asked, "Have you got a key?"

"Sure." The manager had a thick German accent. He gave the box kite a final tweak, tightened a balsa-wood joint with a c-clamp, and said, "Gum dis vay." He didn't mention a warrant.

McPHERSON WAS WAITING in the hall outside Gloria's room. "Could you take a cab?" Lucas asked.

"Well . . ."

"Here's twenty bucks; that's to cover the cab and buy you dinner," he said, handing her the bill. "And thanks. If you think of anything . . ."

"I've got your number," she nodded.

The manager let them into Gloria's apartment. They did a quick walk-through: something was bothering Lucas—he'd seen something, but he didn't know what. Something his eye had picked up. But when? During the talk with Crosby? No. It was just now . . . he looked around, couldn't think of it. *Getting old,* he thought.

"Do you know any of her friends?" Lucas asked the manager, with little hope.

The German went through an elaborate, Frenchlike shrug, and said, "Not me."

THEY KNOCKED ON every door in the building, with the manager trailing behind them. Few people were in their apartments, and nobody had seen her. Two patrol cops showed up and Lucas said, "Go with the manager. He has legal access, so you don't need a search warrant. Check every single apartment. Don't mess with anything, just check for the girl." As they were walking away, he called, "Look under the beds," and one of the cops said, with an edge, "Right, chief."

Lucas, scowling, turned and said to Sloan, "Find the best picture you can, get it back to the office, and get it out. Tell Rose Marie to hand it out to the press."

"What're you doing?" Sloan asked.

Lucas looked around. "I'm gonna tear the place to pieces, see what I can see. Oh. Get somebody to check the phone company, see if she just made a call."

"All right. And maybe I ought to get a search warrant."

"Yeah, yeah, yeah."

Sloan started looking, while Lucas did another walk-through. The apartment had only three rooms—a living room with a kitchenette at one end, a tiny bath, and a small bedroom.

A battered bureau, probably from the Salvation Army store, was pushed against one wall of the bedroom. Several drawers stood open. He'd glanced in the bedroom during the original interview, and he didn't remember the drawers being open: so she'd taken some clothes. He lifted her mattress, looked under it. Nothing. He tossed the bureau drawers onto the mattress. Nothing. Rolled her shoes out of a closet, patted down her clothes. Nothing.

He walked back out to the kitchenette, looked in the refrigerator, pulled out the ice trays. He checked every scrap of paper within reach of the telephone. In ten minutes he had a dozen phone numbers, mostly scrawled on the backs of junk-mail envelopes, a few more on a phone book. He checked the exchanges: none was in Eagan, or Apple Valley, or down that way. He stacked the phone book on the counter with the envelopes, mentioned them to Sloan.

He went to the bathroom next and peered into the medicine cabinet. There were a dozen brown pill bottles on the top shelf, lined up like chessmen. "She's got some weird meds," Lucas called to Sloan. "Let's find out where she gets them and what they're for. Get somebody to check the local pharmacies and maybe the U clinic. This looks like serious shit, so she might need some more."

"Okay," Sloan called back. Lucas opened the door to a small linen closet— women hid things in linen closets, refrigerators, and bureau drawers. He found nothing useful.

Sloan stuck his head in. "She didn't like cameras," he said. He showed Lucas a handful of Polaroids and a couple of prints. She was always in black, almost always alone, standing against something. The few other people in the prints were women.

"So get them all out," Lucas said briefly. He slammed a drawer shut, and they heard glass breaking inside.

"All right," Sloan said. Then: "Chill out, man. We'll get her, sooner or later. You're freaking out."

"She knows him, goddamnit," Lucas said. He turned and kicked the bathroom wall, the toe of his shoe breaking through the drywall. They both stood and looked at the hole for a second. Then Lucas said, "She knows who the motherfucker is, and where the motherfucker is, and we let her go."

17

ANDERSON TRACKED GLORIA Crosby through the state records, starting with a driver's license to get her exact age, then into the national crime computers—she'd been twice convicted of shoplifting from Walgreen's drug stores—and through the court records into the mental health system. Crosby had been in and out of treatment programs and hospitals since she was a young teenager; her home address was listed as North Oaks, a suburban bedroom north of St. Paul.

"We oughta get some people up there," Anderson said, leaning in the office door.

"I'm not doing anything except reading the book," Lucas said, taking his feet out of his desk drawer. "Is Sloan still wandering around?"

"He was drinking coffee down in Homicide."

THEY TOOK LUCAS'S Porsche, Sloan driving it hard. Lucas said, "I hope Gloria doesn't set our guy off. If he gets the feeling that people *know* . . ."

Sloan, grunting as he shifted up and hammered the Porsche through the North Oaks entry, said, "If I was Gloria, I'd be very fucking careful. Very careful." The address came up, a small redwood rambler that looked out of place among the larger homes. The house was set into a low rise, with a split-rail fence defining the yard. Sloan asked, "Put it right in the driveway?"

"Yeah. I'll take the back."

"Sure."

Sloan squealed into the driveway, hit the brakes, and they were out, Lucas heading around the side of the house. The grass on the open parts of the yard had been thoroughly burned off, though the summer hadn't been especially hot or dry. In the shadier spots, it was long and ragged, untended.

Sloan walked up to the front door, passed a picture window with drawn curtains, stopped, peered through a crack in the curtains, saw nobody, and rang the doorbell.

MARILYN CROSBY WAS a slight, gray-haired woman, stooped, suspicious, her face lined with worry. She stood in the doorway, one hand clutching her housecoat at the throat. "I haven't seen her or heard from her since last spring, some time. She wanted money. I gave her seventy-five dollars; but we're not close any more."

"We need to talk," Sloan said, low-keyed, relaxing. "She may be involved with the man who did the Manette kidnapping. We need to know as much about her as we can—who her friends are."

"Well . . ." She was reluctant, but finally pushed the door open and stepped back. Sloan followed her in.

"She's not here, is she?" Sloan asked.

"No. Of course not." Crosby frowned. "I wouldn't lie to the police."

Sloan looked at her, nodded. "All right. Where's your back door?"

"Through there, through the kitchen . . . What?"

Sloan walked through the kitchen with its odor of old coffee grounds and rancid potatoes and pushed open the back door.

"Lucas . . . yeah, c'mon."

"You had me surrounded?" Crosby seemed offended.

"We really need to find your daughter," Sloan said. Lucas came inside, and Sloan said, "So let's talk. Is your husband home?"

"He's dead," Crosby said. She turned and walked back into the house, Sloan and Lucas trailing behind. She led them to a darkened living room, with a shag carpet and drawn curtains. The television was tuned to *Wheel of Fortune*. A green wine bottle sat next to a lamp on a corner table. Crosby dropped into an overstuffed chair and pulled up her feet.

"He was out cutting a limb off an apple tree, got dizzy, and went like that." She snapped her fingers. "He had seventy thousand in insurance. That was it. I can't get at his pension until I'm fifty-seven."

"That's a tragedy," Sloan said.

"Three years ago last month, it was," she said, looking up at Sloan with rheumy eyes. "You know what his last words to me were? He said, 'Boy, I feel like shit.' How's that for last words?"

"Honest," Lucas muttered.

"What?" She looked at him, the suspicion right at the surface. Sloan turned so Crosby couldn't see his face, and rolled his eyes. Lucas was stepping on his act.

"Have you seen this man? He might have been younger when he came around," Sloan said, turning back to Marilyn Crosby. He handed her the composite drawing. She studied it for a moment and then said, "Maybe. Oh, last winter, maybe, he might have come around once. But his hair was different."

"Were they with anyone else?"

"No, just the two of them," she said, passing the composite back. "They were only here for a minute. He was a big guy, though. Sort of mean-looking, like he could fight. Not the kind Gloria usually came back with."

"What type was that?"

"Bums, mostly," Crosby said flatly. "No-goods who never did anything." Then, confidentially, to Sloan: "You know, Gloria's crazy. She got it from her father's side of the family. Several crazy people there—though, of course, I didn't know it until it was too late."

"We need the names of all her friends," Lucas said. "Friends or relatives that she might turn to. Anybody. Doctors."

"I don't know anything like that. Well, I know a doctor."

"There's a reward for information leading to an arrest," Lucas said. "Fifty thousand."

"Oh, really?" Marilyn Crosby brightened. "Well, I could go get the things she left here. Or maybe you'd like to come up and look in her room. You'd know better than I do what you're looking for."

"That'd be good," Sloan said.

GLORIA CROSBY'S BEDROOM was an eleven-foot-square cubicle with a window in one wall, a bed, and a small pine desk and matching dresser. The dresser was empty, but the desk was stuffed with school papers, music tapes, rubber bands, broken pencils, crayons, rock 'n' roll concert badges, drawings, calendars, pushpins.

"Usual stuff," Sloan said. He went through it all. Lucas helped for a few minutes, then found Marilyn Crosby in the kitchen, drinking from the wine bottle, and got the name of Gloria's last doctor. He looked the name up in the phone book, noted the address, and called Sherrill, who was doing phone work on the patients they'd uncovered at the university. "Anything you can get," Lucas said.

When he got back to the bedroom, he lay down on Gloria Crosby's bed, a narrow, sagging single-width that was too short by six inches. A Mr. Happy Tooth poster hung on the wall opposite the bed. "Hi! I'm Gloria!" was written in careful block letters on the cartoon molar. The molar was doing a root dance on a red line that might have been an infected gum.

"Three names so far," Sloan said, nodding at the pile of junk on the desk. He was halfway through it. "From high school."

"We've got a better shot at the pharmacy. She'll have to go in there sooner or later," Lucas said. He sat up. "We should check the places she was hospitalized and get the names of patients who overlapped with her, and run them against Manette's patient list."

"Anderson's already doing that," Sloan said.

"Yeah?" Lucas dropped back on the bed and closed his eyes.

After a minute, Sloan asked, "Taking a nap?"

"Thinking," Lucas said.

"What do you think?"

"I think we're wasting our time, Sloan."

"What else is there to do?"

"I don't know."

As they were leaving, Marilyn Crosby leaned in the kitchen doorway. She held a twelve-ounce tumbler of what looked like water, but she sipped like wine. "Find anything?"

"No."

"If, uh, my daughter got in touch—you know, if she wanted more money or something—and if I put you in touch with her, who'd get the reward?"

"If you put us in touch and we got the information from her, you'd get it," Lucas said. "We know she knows who it is. All we have to do is ask her."

"Leave a number where I can get you quick," Marilyn Crosby said. She took a sip from the glass. "If she calls, I'll get in touch. For her own good."

"Right," Lucas said.

Sloan took the wheel again, and Lucas slumped in the passenger seat and stared out the window as they dropped past the wooded lawns and headed toward the gate.

"Listen," he said finally, "have you met the new PR chick? I only talked to her a couple of times."

"Yeah. I met her," Sloan said.

"Is she decent?"

Sloan shrugged. "She's okay. Why?"

"I'd like to get a story written about my company, but I don't want to go around and ask somebody to do it. I'd like to get the PR chick to talk the idea around, and have the TV people come to me."

Sloan said doubtfully, "I don't know, it's a private business and all. What're you thinking?"

"This guy, whoever he is, is fairly intelligent, right?"

"Right."

"And he plays computer games. I'd be willing to bet that he's a computer freak. Ninety percent of male gamers are," Lucas said. He was staring sightlessly out the window, thinking of Ice, the programmer. "His girlfriend knows my computer games, 'cause she said they suck. So I'm wondering, if there were stories on TV and in the papers about how my computer guys were counter-gaming this asshole, I wonder if he'd take a look? You know, cruise the building. How about if we had a really . . . progressive-looking woman talking to him?"

"Sounds a little thin," Sloan said. "He'll be suspicious after that radio gag. But he might."

"I'll talk to the PR chick," Lucas said. "See if we can get something going."

"Don't call her a chick, huh? You make me nervous when you talk that way. She carries a can opener in her purse," Sloan said.

"Okay."

Sloan was driving too fast through traffic, and when Lucas tilted his head back, he punched the radio up, a country station, and they listened to Hank Williams, Jr., until Lucas said, "I feel like my head's stuffed with cotton."

"What?"

"Nothing's going through it at all." He was fumbling with his hand and looked down and saw the ring on his thumb at the same moment that Sloan saw it.

"You gonna ask her, or what?"

"Every time I go home, she's asleep," Lucas said. "When I get up, she's gone."

"You're a cop; that's the way it goes. She's smart enough to know that," Sloan said. "At least you're not doing shift work."

"Yeah, it's just this fuckin' case," Lucas said, holding the ring up to the windshield, peering through the rock. "After this case, we can get back on some kind of schedule."

LUCAS CLEARED THE idea with the chief, then talked to Anita Segundo, the press liaison.

"I don't know whether we should tell them it's bullshit, and that they're helping catch the kidnapper, or just feed them the story," Lucas said.

"It wouldn't be honest to just feed them the story—but that's the way I'd do it," Segundo said. She was dark-haired, with a smooth, olive complexion and large black eyes. She spoke with a slight West Texas accent, biting off her words like a TV cowgirl.

"How fast could we get it done?" Lucas asked.

"I could tip the TV stations to what might make a good story—and they'd jump all over it. Anything to do with Manette is hot stuff. Of course, the papers'll bite if TV does."

"Give me an hour," Lucas said. "Then put it through."

LUCAS FOUND BARRY Hunt in a huddle with salesmen, pulled him out, and outlined the story idea. Hunt thought about it for fifteen seconds, then nodded. "I don't see a downside, as long as we have enough cops around for protection."

"You'll have the cops. But the downside is, it might not work," Lucas said.

"That's not what I meant," Hunt said. "I meant, there's no downside for *us*. Whether or not we catch the guy, we can use the stories—video and print— in our PR. You know, tracking a vicious nut kidnapper blah blah blah."

"Oh." Lucas scratched his head. He'd hired the guy to think like this. "Yeah. Listen, then, I'd like Ice to make the presentation to the TV people."

Hunt studied him for a moment and then said, "You're going a little deeper than I expected. But you're right—if we have the protection."

THE PROGRAMMERS THOUGHT the idea was great: Ice almost hopped up and down when Hunt said she'd lead the presentation of the story. The idea fit with her sense of humor.

"Listen, you guys," Lucas said anxiously, "if you pull their weenies too hard, they're gonna *know*. Then they're gonna screw us, because the press don't like to get their weenies pulled. Worse than that, this guy, this asshole, *he* might know. He's no dummy. We gotta play this straight: or mostly straight. We gotta look good. So let's, like, you know, try not to . . ." He trailed off.

"What?" somebody asked.

"Geek out," Lucas said.

"One thing we could do," said Ice, "is we could take that composite you've been passing around, and make up a hundred different variations of what he looks like. We could do that in an hour with one of the landscape programs. Then we could call them up for the TV people. It'd be very visual . . ."

"Do that," Lucas said, jabbing a finger at her. "Now, I was thinking—when we tried to grab him by tracing the phone call . . ." He explained the FBI's cellular phone direction-finding gear. "That's really high tech. I thought there might be something in it."

"All right, how about this," said another programmer, a short redhead with a yellow pencil behind each ear. "We scan in a map of Dakota County, do some lift-up 3-D shit, then program where the helicopters were and do some graphic overlays on the signal strengths, like we're trying to refine where on the map the signals came from . . ."

"Can you do that?" Lucas asked. "I mean, really?"

The programmer shrugged: "Beats the shit outa me. Maybe, if we had the data. But I was thinking more like, you know, making a cartoon for the TV people."

"Jesus, I can see it. We'd do the whole screen in blood red," Ice said. She looked at Lucas. "It'd look great: they'd eat the whole thing."

"That's what we want," Lucas said. "It's only gotta hold water for a couple of days."

The receptionist stepped into the doorway of the work room, looked around for Hunt, saw him perched on the end of a work bench. "Barry? We've got Channel Three on the phone. They want to do a story."

Hunt hopped off the bench. "How long do you guys need?"

Ice looked around the room, said, "We'll need a few hours to set up, get everything together."

"Could you do it tomorrow morning?"

"No problem," Ice said.

"Excellent," said Lucas.

18

GLORIA WAS WALKING up to Mail's front porch when the sheriff's car pulled into the driveway. She turned, smiling, and waited. The cop wrote something on a clipboard on the passenger seat, then got out of the car, smiled, nodded politely.

"Ma'am? Are you the owner?"

"Yes? Is there a problem?"

"Well, we're just checking ownership records of houses down here," the police officer said. "You're . . ." He looked at his clipboard and waited.

"Gloria LaDoux," Gloria said. "My husband is Martin, but he's not home yet."

"He works up in the Cities?"

"Yup." She thought quickly, picking out the most boring job she could think of. "He's at the Mall of America? At Brothers Shoes?"

The cop nodded, made a mark on the board. "Have you seen anything that would be, like, unusual along the road here? We're looking for a man in a van . . ."

MAIL WAS A half-mile from the house, the passenger seat full of groceries, when he saw the car in the driveway.

He stopped on the side of the road and closed his eyes for a moment. He knew the car, a rusty brown Chevy Cavalier. It belonged to a guy named Bob Something, who had a ponytail and a nose ring and bit his fingernails down to the quick. Bob didn't know where he lived, but Gloria did—and Gloria drove Bob's car when she needed one.

Gloria.

She'd been a good contact at the hospital. She worked in the clinic. She could steal cigarettes, small change, candy, and sometimes a few painkillers. Outside, she'd been trouble. She'd helped him with the Marty LaDoux thing, she'd switched the dental records, she'd collected John Mail's life insurance when the body was found in the river. Then she started going on about their *relationship.* And though she'd never made any direct threats, she'd hinted that her knowledge of Martin LaDoux made her special.

He'd worried about that. He hadn't done anything, because she was as implicated as he was, and she was smart enough to know it. On the other hand, she had *liked* it inside. She'd told him that when she was inside, she felt secure.

And she loved to talk.

If she'd figured out the Manette kidnapping, she wouldn't leave it alone. Eventually she'd tell someone. Gloria was always in therapy. She'd never get enough of talking about her problems, of hearing someone else analyze them.

Shit. *Gloria . . .*

Mail pulled the van off the shoulder and went down the road to the house.

GLORIA CROSBY FELT *expansive.* For weeks, she'd felt as though she were living in a box. One day was much like the next as she waited for something to happen, for a direction to emerge. Now it was happening. John had Andi Manette and the kids, she was sure of that: and he must have a plan to get at the Manette money. When they had it, they'd have to leave. Go south, maybe. He was smart, he had ideas, but he wasn't good at details. She could do the detail work, just like she had with Martin LaDoux.

Martin LaDoux had been a robo-geek, the worst of the worst, frightened by everybody, allergic to everything, crowded by Others who'd keep him up all night, talking to him. Her mental picture of Martin was of a tall, thin, pimply teenager with a handkerchief, rubbing his Rudolph-red nose while his eyes watered, trying to smile . . .

He was useless until the state swept them all out of the hospital and gave them, in a ludicrous gesture at their presumed normalcy, both medical and life insurance, along with their places in a halfway house. The life insurance had doomed Martin LaDoux.

Gloria was sitting on Mail's front porch, waiting, not at all impatient. The house was locked, but John was around—through the front window, she could see the pieces of a microwave meal sitting on a TV tray in the living room.

The question was, where was he keeping Manette and the kids? The house felt empty. There was nothing living inside. A feather of unease touched Gloria's heart. Could he have gotten rid of them already?

No. She knew about John and Manette. He'd keep her for a while, she was sure of that.

Gloria was sitting on the front steps, chewing on a grass stem. When Mail pulled the van into the yard, she stood up—dressed all in black, she looked like the wicked witch's apprentice—and sauntered down to meet him.

"John," she said. Her face was pallid, soft, an indoor face, an institutional face. "How are you?"

"Okay," he said, shortly. "What's going on?"

"I came out to see how you're doing? Got a beer?"

He looked at her for a moment, and her face shone with knowledge and expectation. *She knew*. He nodded to the question. "Yeah, sure. Come on in."

She followed him inside, looked around. "Same old place," she said. She plunked down on his computer chair and looked at the blind eyes of the computer monitors. "Got some new ones," she said. "Any new games?"

"I've been off games," he said.

He got two beers from the refrigerator and handed one to the woman, and she twisted the top off, watching him.

"You've got a Davenport game," she said, picking up a software box. There was a pamphlet inside, and three loose discs.

"Yeah." He took a hit of the beer. "How's your head?" he asked.

"Been okay." She thumbed through the game pamphlet.

"Still on your meds?"

"Ehh, sometimes." She frowned. "But I left them back at my apartment."

"Yeah?"

"Yeah. I don't think I can go back there." She said it as a teaser. She wanted him to ask why not. She tossed the pamphlet back in the software box and looked up at him.

"Why not?"

"The cops were there," she said. She took a drink from the bottle, eyes fixed on him. "Looking for you."

"For me?"

"Yup. They had a picture. I don't know who told them that I know you, but they knew. I managed to put them off and slid out of there."

"Jesus, are you sure? That they didn't follow . . ." He looked at the front window, half-expecting squad cars.

"Yeah. They were stupid; it was easy. Hey, you know who one of them was?"

"Davenport."

She nodded. "Yeah."

"Goddamnit, Gloria."

"I jumped a bus, rode it eight blocks, hopped off, walked through Janis's apartment building, and took the walkway to Bob's, borrowed the car key from Bob . . ."

"Did you tell him you were coming to see me?"

"Nope." She was proud of herself. "I told him I had to bring some school stuff home. Anyway, I got the key, went down into the parking garage, and got his car. There was nobody around when I left."

He watched her as she talked, and when she finished, he nodded. "All right. I've been having some trouble with the cops."

"I know," she said. And she popped it out, a surprise: "They were here, too."

"Here?" Now he *was* worried.

"A cop pulled in just after I got here—they're checking all the farmhouses. I don't think he was too interested after I told him I was your wife, and we lived here together."

Mail looked at her for a moment, and then said, "You did."

"I did," she said. "And he left."

"All right," he said, his voice flat.

She caught the hems of her dress and did a mock curtsey, oddly crowlike in its bobbing dip. "You took the Manette lady and her kids."

He was dumbstruck by the baldness of it. He tried to recover: "What?"

"Come on, John," she said. "This is Gloria. You can't lie to me. Where've you got them?"

"Gloria . . ."

But she was shaking her head. "We took down fifteen thousand, remember?"

"Yeah."

"That was sweet," she said. "I'd like to help you collect on Manette . . . if you'll let me."

"Jesus." He looked at her and scratched his head.

"Can I see them? I mean, you know, put a stocking over my head or something? I assume they haven't seen your face or anything."

"Gloria, this isn't about money," Mail said. "This is about what she did to me in the old days."

That stopped her. She said, "Oh." Then: "What're you doing to her?"

Mail thought about it for ten seconds, then said, "Whatever I want."

"God," Gloria said. "That's so"—she wiggled in the chair—"neat."

Mail smiled now and said, "C'mon. I'll show you."

ON THE WAY out the back, Gloria said, "You told me you'd stopped thinking about her."

"I started again," Mail said.

"How come?"

Mail thought about not answering, but Gloria had been inside with him. As dreary and unlikable as she was, she was one of the few people who really might know how his mind worked, how he *felt*.

"A woman started calling me," he said. "Somebody who doesn't like Andi Manette. I don't know who—just that it's a woman. She said Manette still talks about me, about what I was like. She said Manette said I was interested in her sexually, and that she could feel the sex coming out of me. She must have called fifteen times."

"God, that's a little weird," Gloria said.

"Yeah." Mail scratched his chin, thinking about it. "The really strange thing is, she called me here. She knows who I am, but she won't tell me who she is. I can't figure that out. But she doesn't like Andi, that's for sure. She kept pushing, and I kept thinking, and pretty soon . . . you know how it gets. It's like you can't get a song out of your head."

"Yeah. Like when I was counting to a thousand." Gloria had once spent a year counting to one thousand, over and over. Then, one day, the counting stopped. She didn't feel like she'd had much to do with it, either starting or stopping it, but she was grateful for the silence in her brain.

Mail grinned: "Drives you nuts . . ."

On the way down the stairs, into the musty basement, Gloria realized who the woman was—who was calling John Mail. She opened her mouth to tell him, but then decided, *Later*. That would be something to tease him with, not something simply to blurt out. John had to be controlled, to some extent; you had to fight to maintain your equality.

"I built a room," Mail said, gesturing at a steel door in the basement wall. "Used to be a root cellar. Damn near killed me, working in that hole. I'd have to stop every ten minutes and run outside."

Gloria nodded: she knew about his claustrophobia. "Open it," she said.

ANDI AND GRACE had used the snap tab from Grace's bra to work on the nail in the overhead joist but could work only a half-hour or so before the skin on their fingers grew too painful to continue. They were making progress—a half-inch of the nail was in the clear—but Andi thought it might take another week to extract it.

She didn't think they had a week: Mail was becoming more animated, and darker, at the same time. She could feel the devils driving him, she could see them in his eyes. He was losing control.

"Never get it out," Grace said. She was standing on the Porta-Potti. "Mom, we're never gonna get it." She dropped the snap tab and sat down on the Potti cover and put her face in her hands. She didn't cry: both of them had gone dry-eyed, as though they'd run out of tears.

Andi squatted next to her, took her daughter's hand, and rolled it: the skin where she'd been holding the too-small tab was pinched and scarlet, overlying a deeper, dark-blue bruise. "You'll have to stop. Don't do any more until the red goes away." She looked up at the joist, rubbing her thumb against the shredded skin of her own forefinger. "I'll try to do a little more."

"No good anyway," Grace said. "He's too big for us. He's a monster."

"We've got to try," Andi said. "If we can only get a weapon, we can . . ."

They heard the thumps of feet overhead. "He's coming," Grace said. She shrank back to the mattress, to the corner.

Andi closed her eyes for a moment, opened them, said, "Remember: no eye contact."

She spit into her hand, dabbed a finger into a dusty corner, reached up and rubbed the combination of dirt and saliva on the raw wood where Grace had been digging around the nail. The moisture darkened the wood and made the rawness less noticeable. When she was satisfied—when the footsteps were on the stairs, and she could wait no longer—she stepped down, pushed the Porta-Potti against a wall, and sat on it.

"Don't talk unless he talks to you, and keep your head down. I'll start talking as soon as he comes in. Okay? Grace, okay?"

"Okay." Grace rolled onto the mattress, facing the wall, pulled her tattered dress around her legs.

Mail was at the door.

"John," Andi said, her voice dull, her face slack. She was desperately trying to project an image of weariness, of lifelessness. She wanted to do nothing that would provoke him.

"Come on, up, we've got a visitor." Andi's head snapped up despite herself, and from the corner of her eye, she saw Grace roll over. Mail stepped down into the cell, and as Andi got to her feet, he took her arm, and she shuffled to the door.

"Can I come?" Grace squeaked. Andi's heart sank.

"No," Mail said. He never looked at the girl, and Andi said, quickly, so he wouldn't have a chance to think of her, "Who is it, John?"

"An old nuthouse friend of mine," Mail said. He thrust her through the door, stepped out behind her, and closed the door and bolted it. A woman, all dressed in black, was standing at the bottom of the dusty basement stairs. She had a long, thin stick in her hand; a tree branch. In her other hand, she held a bottle of beer by the neck.

Witch, Andi thought. And then, Executioner.

"God, John," the woman breathed. She came closer and walked around Andi, looking her up and down, as though she were a mannequin. "Do you hit her a lot?"

"Not a lot; I mostly fuck her."

"Does she let you, or do you make her?" The woman was only inches away, and Andi could smell her breath, the sourness of the beer.

"Mostly, I just go ahead and do it," Mail said. "When she gives me any trouble, I pound her a little." Andi stood dumbly, not knowing what to do. And Mail said, "I try not to break anything. Mostly I just use my open hand. Like this."

He swatted Andi's face, hard, and she went down, but her head was clear. Mail hit her almost every time he took her out of the room, and she had learned to anticipate the motion. By moving with it, just a bit, the blow was softened. By falling, she assuaged whatever it was that made him hit her.

Sometimes he helped her pick herself up. Not this time. This time he stood over her, with the woman in black.

"Brought some rope," he said to Andi. He showed her several four-foot lengths of yellow plastic water-ski rope. "Put your hands up—no, don't stand up. Just put your hands up."

Andi did what he told her, and he tied her hands at the wrist. The rope was stiff and cut into her skin.

"John, don't hurt me," she said as calmly as she could.

"I'm not going to," Mail said.

He tied a second length of the rope to the bindings at her wrist, led it over a joist-mounted rack in the ceiling, and pulled on the end until Andi's hands and arms were above her head, then tied it off.

"There you go," Mail said to Gloria. "Just the way you wanted her."

"God," Gloria said. She walked around Andi, and Andi turned with her, watching. "Don't turn, or you'll really get it," Gloria snapped.

Andi stopped, closed her eyes. A second later, she heard a thin, quick whistle and then the tree branch hit her in the back. Most of the impact was soaked up by her dress, but it hurt, and she screeched, "Ahhhh," and arced away from the other woman.

Gloria's voice was hot, excited. "God. Can we get her dress off? I want to hit her on the tits."

"Go ahead," Mail said. "She can't do anything to you."

Gloria walked straight up to Andi, and, as she reached for her blouse, said, "You should have taken her clothes away from her, anyway. We oughta cut them off with a knife. Same with the kid, we oughta . . ."

Mail had come up directly behind her, a third length of the rope held between his hands. He flipped it over Gloria's neck and twisted: the rope cut into the woman's throat, and she tried to turn, tried to grab the rope. Her face, eyes bulging, was inches from Andi's. Andi tried to swing away, to turn, but Mail shouted, "No, watch this. Watch."

She turned back. The woman's tongue was out now, and she did a little dance, her feet tapping on the floor, her arms windmilling for a moment, then her fingers would pluck at the rope, then she'd windmill again.

The muscles stood out in Mail's arms and face as he twisted the rope and controlled the woman at the same time; eventually, he held her slack body like a puppet, held her, held her, until her bladder relaxed and the smell of urine floated through the room. He held her for another ten seconds, but now he was watching Andi's face.

Andi was watching, but without much feeling: her capacity for horror had dried out as thoroughly as her tears. She'd imagined John Mail killing herself, or Grace, much in this way. And she'd dreamed of Genevieve, not at home, but in a grave somewhere, in her first-day-of-school dress. The murder of Gloria seemed almost insignificant.

Mail let go of the rope, and Gloria fell face-first to the floor, wide-eyed, and never flinched when it came up to meet her. Mail put a knee in her back, tightened the rope again, held it for another minute, threw a quick sailor's knot into it, then stood up and made a hand-dusting gesture.

"She was a pain in the ass," he said, looking down at the body. Then he smiled at Andi. "You see? I take care of you. She would've beat the shit out of you."

Andi's hands were still over her head, and she said, "This is hurting my shoulders . . ."

"Really? Tough shit." He walked behind her, put his hands around her waist, pressed his teeth against the back of her shoulder, and looked down at the body. "This is kind of"—he looked for a word and remembered Gloria's—"kind of *neat,*" he said.

19

Lucas's cellular phone buzzed, and he looked down at his pocket. "I told all my friends to stay off, unless it was an emergency," he said. Lester picked up another phone and dialed, and Lucas let the phone ring once more before he snapped it open and said, "Yeah?"

"Ah, Lucas." Mail's voice. Traffic was busy in the background. "Is your ass getting tired of chasing me? I'm thinking of going on vacation, tell you the truth."

"Are you driving around?" Lucas asked. He flapped his hand at Lester, nodding, and Lester whispered urgently into his phone, then dropped it and sprinted out of the room. "Feel pretty safe?"

"Yeah, I'm driving," Mail said. "Are you trying to track me?"

"I don't know. Probably," Lucas said. "I need to talk to you and I need to finish what I've got to say, with no bullshit."

"Well, spit it out, man. But don't take too long. I've got a clue for you. And this is a good one."

"Why don't you give me that, first?" Lucas said. "Just in case I piss you off."

Mail laughed, and then said, "You're a funny guy. But listen, this is a real clue. Not sort of remote, like the first one."

"Tell me about the first one?"

"Fuck no." Mail was amused. "But I'll tell you—if you figure this one out, you'll get me fair and square. You ever watch Monty Python? It'd be like"— he lapsed into a bad British accent—"a fair cop."

"So what is it?"

"Just a minute, I got it written down. I've got to read it to you, to get it right. Okay, here it is . . ." He paused, then said, in a reading voice: "A little blank verse, one-twelve-ten, four-four, one-forty-seven-nine, and a long line; twenty-three-two, thirty-two-nine, sixty-nine-twenty-two."

"That's it?" Lucas asked.

"That's it. This is a very simple code, but I don't think you'll crack it. If you do, I'm done. Mrs. Manette bet me that you'd break it. And I'll tell you, I have to be honest about this, you sure don't want her to lose the bet, Lucas. Hey, did you say it was all right for me to call you Lucas?"

Lucas said, "Mrs. Manette's still okay? Can I talk to her?"

"After the stunt she pulled last time? Bullshit. We had a hard little talk about that. What do you cops call it? Tough love?"

"She's still alive?"

"Yeah. But I'm gonna have to go. I feel like a whole cloud of cops are closing in on me."

"No, no—listen to me," Lucas said urgently. "You don't feel it, but you're ill. I mean, you're gonna die from it. If you come in, I swear to God nothing will happen to you, except we'll try to fix things . . ."

Mail's voice turned to a growl. "Hey, I've been fixed. Best and the brightest tried to fix me, Davenport. They used to strap me to a table and fix the shit out of me. Sometimes I remember whole months that I'd forgotten because they fixed me so good. So don't give me any of that fixed shit. I been fixed. I'm what you get, when they fix somebody." His voice changed again, went Hollywood. "But, hey, dude, I gotta run. Got a little pussy lined up after dinner, know what I mean? Catch you later."

And he was gone.

Lucas ran down the hall and through the security doors on the 911 center. Lester was already there, with a man Lucas recognized as an FBI agent. They were looking over the shoulder of one of the operators, who was speaking into a microphone: "Dark Econoline van or like that, probably no further west than Rice Street . . ."

Lester said to Lucas, "Probably 694, east to west. We're flooding it right now. We're taking every van off the road."

THEY HUNG AROUND Dispatch for fifteen minutes, listening as vans were pulled off the highway wholesale. After a while, they walked back to the Homicide Office together and found Sloan with his feet on his desk, looking at a printout.

"Da clue," he said, waving the printout at them.

"Already?" Lucas said. "What do you think?"

"Could be Bible verses," Sloan said. "They got that kind of numbers and he used the Bible last time."

"Unless he's cooked up something clever and he's fucking with us," Lester said. "Maybe it's got something to do with the numbers."

"Maybe it's his address," Sloan said. "And his driver's license number."

"And maybe it's the Bible," Lucas said. "I've got somebody who can look into that possibility."

"Elle," Sloan said, looking up from the list of clues. "Does a nunnery got a fax machine?"

"Yeah," Lucas said, vaguely. He read through a transcript of the tape. "Shit."

"What?"

"Don't go away," Lucas said. "Let me fax this to Elle."

WHEN HE CAME back, five minutes later, he glanced around the Homicide Office. A half-dozen detectives were sitting at desks, talking, looking at maps, eating. Two of them had found a Bible and were paging through it with some perplexity.

Lucas stepped close to Sloan's desk and crooked a finger at Lester. Lester stepped over and Lucas said, in a low voice, "There were two things he said. He was fixed—so our guy has been in a state hospital. We've gotta be sure that every state hospital employee and every long-term resident has seen the composite."

Lester nodded. "Why are we whispering?"

" 'Cause of the other thing," Lucas said. "Remember how he knew that we'd spotted his gamer's shirt? Now he knows that Andi Manette tried to send a message to us. He *knows*. He's gotta be getting information. He's gotta."

"From here?" Lester breathed, looking around.

"Probably not, but I don't know. I'd bet it comes out of the family briefings. Somebody out there has a motive to get rid of Manette. Whoever it is, is talking to this guy."

Lester scratched his nose, nervous, his Adam's apple bobbing up and down. "The chief is gonna be delighted," he said.

"Maybe we shouldn't tell her," Lucas said. "I mean, for her own good."

"What're you thinking about?" Lester said.

"I'm thinking that we ought to come up with a bunch of little nuggets, different nuggets, bullshit, that we feed through all the different family members—and then we wait to see if anything comes out the other side. Stuff that our guy would react to. If we can find who's feeding him, we can crack him. Or her."

"Christ." Lester scratched his nose, then his head. Then, "We gotta tell Roux. That's what she's paid for."

Roux said, "I wish you hadn't told me."

"That's what you're paid for," Lucas said, straight-faced.

Roux sighed and said, "Right. So. Anything critical, we keep to ourselves, though I don't see how we could keep Manette's message to ourselves. We wouldn't have known what it meant."

Lester explained Lucas's idea about feeding false information through the family: Roux grudgingly approved but rolled her eyes to the ceiling and said, "Please, God, don't let it be Tower."

"One other thing," Lucas said. "We've got recorders on everybody's listed numbers, because we were only looking for incoming calls from a stranger. We should start looking at the private phones, too, the unlisted numbers, the outgoing calls. And we need to be quiet about it."

Roux looked at Lester, who nodded and said, "I agree," and then closed her eyes and said, "They'll be pissed when they find out."

"When they find out, we can explain it," Lucas said. "But we need to get on this right now. I mean, *right now*. We're running out of time."

"But I really don't think whoever it is would call from his own phone."

"They might, if they think they know what's being monitored," Lucas said. "And when the asshole needs to get in touch with them, *he's* got to call. We need to know about anything anomalous—odd rings, cryptic phone calls, funny-sounding wrong numbers, anything."

Roux sighed, spread her hands on her desk, looked at them. "I knew there'd be days like this," she said.

"You gotta do it," Lucas said.

"All right," Roux said. "I'll call Larry Baxter—he'd sign a warrant on the Little Old Lady Who Lived in a Shoe."

"Tonight," Lucas said. "Get Anderson to call the phone company and get a list of all their numbers, on every single one of the family members. Then get a guy over to the phone company and have him sit there and listen."

"We're running out of guys," Lester said.

"Pull some uniforms," Lucas said. "We don't need Einstein over there."

One hundred and forty-four vans were stopped along I-694 after Mail's call to Lucas. Two men were held briefly while checks were run on them, and then they were released.

"You know what he was doing?" Lucas said, looking up at a wall map in the Homicide Office. He pointed at the top of the map, at the belt highway. "I bet he's on a secondary road driving parallel to the highway. I bet he was on County Road C, knowing that if we're tracking him, we'd be looking on 694."

"So . . . that's gonna be tough," Lester said, looking at the map. "We'll have to try to flood a whole area, instead of just a road, or a street."

"We won't get him that way," Lucas said. "He'll keep changing up on us."

Lucas was just ready to leave again when Elle called back. "I'm pushing the button on my fax. You should have a fax coming in."

A second later, Lucas heard the fax phone ring once, and then the fax machine started buzzing at the other end of the office: "It's coming now."

"Okay," she said. "Now. If it's the Bible, it's Psalms, of course."

"How do you know that?"

"Psalms is the only book that has chapter numbers as high as the ones he cited," she said. "If they're not from Psalms, then it's just a bunch of gibberish. It could be anything."

"But what if they're all from Psalms?" Lucas asked.

"This is what he said," Elle intoned. "He said, 'A little blank verse' and then the numbers. And here are the first three verses. These are from the King James Version, by the way—I think he'd probably be using one, since I doubt that he's religious, and if he's not, he's probably got a James."

"All right. But the pope'll be pissed." There was silence on the other end and Lucas said, "Sorry."

She said, "Why don't you go get that fax?"

"Just a minute." He put the phone down, got the fax, and walked back. "Ready."

"Psalm 112:10," she said. Lucas followed along on the fax as she read, *"The wicked shall see it, and be grieved; he shall gnash with his teeth, and melt away: the desire of the wicked shall perish.*

"Psalm 4:4: *Stand in awe and sin not: commune with your own heart upon your bed, and be still. Selah.*

"Psalm 147:9: *He giveth to the beast his food, and to the young ravens which cry."*

There was a rustling of paper and Elle said, "Got that?"

"Yeah. But what is it?" He studied the Psalms but found no pattern at all.

"I couldn't see *anything* at first. I kept thinking that the verses must relate to his condition, or the condition of the women. I thought he must've made a psychotic connection between them. These are powerful images—gnashing teeth, ravens and beasts, the wicked and the grieved. The problem is, I couldn't relate them to anything. There was no thread."

"Elle? What are you leading up to?" Lucas asked.

"A silly question," the nun said. "It's so silly that I don't want to explain it unless the answer is yes."

"So ask."

"Is there anybody named Crosby involved with this whole thing?"

After a moment of silence, Lucas said, "Elle, we're getting ready to plaster the papers and the TV newscasts with pictures of a woman named Gloria Crosby. She knows our man. How did you know?"

Elle laughed softly and said, "I thought it was so stupid."

"What?"

"The sequence of single words in the first three verses, with that 'blank verse' coming first."

"Elle, damnit . . ."

"Each verse has one of these words, in order: Blank, Gnash, still, young."

Lucas closed his eyes and then grinned. "God, I like this kid. It's the group: Crosby, Nash, Stills and Young. I think the order is wrong, but . . ."

"I think that's it."

Lucas's smile faded. "Then he's got her. Crosby."

"That would be my interpretation. After that verse, he says, 'long line.' That breaks the meaning of the top three verses from the next three. For the first two of those three, I have no clue. Well, I have some clue, but it's pretty general."

Lucas read the two verses, under the long line she'd drawn across the paper. The first was Psalm 23:2: *He maketh me to lie down in green pastures; he leadeth me beside the still waters.*

"She's dead," Lucas said. "That's the verse you read at a funeral."

"Unless he's hinting that he's taken her to Stillwater."

"Yeah." He scanned the fifth verse, Psalm 32:9: *Be ye not as the horse, or as the mule, which have no understanding: whose mouth must be held in with bit and bridle, lest they come near unto thee.*"

After a long moment of silence, Lucas said, "Doesn't mean anything to me."

"Me either. But I'll think about it."

"How about the last one?"

"That's the one that worries me: 69:22: *Let their table become a snare before them: and that which should have been for their welfare, let it become a trap.*"

"Huh," Lucas said.

"Be careful," Elle said. "He's warning you."

"I will. And Elle: thanks."

"I'm praying for Dr. Manette and the children," Elle said. "But you've got to hurry, Lucas."

BEFORE LUCAS LEFT, he called Anderson and said, "Check and see if there are any horse farms—or mule farms, for that matter—out near Stillwater."

"There are," Anderson said. "Lots of them. It's sorta St. Paul's horsey country."

"Better start running the owners," Lucas said. "Make a list."

20

WEATHER WAS SLEEPING soundly when Lucas finally got home. He slipped out of his clothes to the light from the hall, coming through a crack in the door, and dropped his jacket, pants, and shirt over a chair. After tiptoeing to the bathroom, and then back out, he took off his watch, put it on the bed table, and slipped in beside her.

She was warm, comfortable, but Lucas was unable to sleep. After a few minutes, he got up and tiptoed out to the study, sat in the old leather chair, and tried to think.

There were too many things going on at once. Too much to think about. And he was messing around with facts, rather than looking for patterns, or for revealing holes. He put his feet up, steepled his fingers, closed his eyes, and let his mind roam.

And in ten minutes concluded that the case would break when they identified the probable killer through hospital records, or when they cracked the kidnapper's source of information. Two solid angles, but not enough pressure on them.

So: Dunn, Tower and Helen Manette, Wolfe.

Of course, there was a small chance that the leak was not from the family. It could be an investigation insider—a cop. But Lucas thought not. The kidnapper was clearly crazy. A cop would be unlikely to stick his neck out for a nut, even a family nut. They were simply too unreliable.

No. Somebody had to benefit.

Wolfe. Wolfe was sleeping with Manette. Manette didn't have much left, in the way of money. Dog food . . .

Lucas frowned, glanced at his watch. Dunn was up late every night. Lucas got Anderson's daily log, looked up Dunn's home phone, and dialed. Dunn picked it up, a little breathless, on the second ring: "Hello?"

"Mr. Dunn, Lucas Davenport."

"Davenport—you scared me. I thought it might be the guy, this time of night." In an aside to somebody, he said, *Lucas Davenport.* Then: "What can I do for you?"

Lucas said, "When I talked to you the night of the kidnapping, you told me that Tower and Andi Manette shared money from a trust."

"That's right."

"If your wife was gone, and the kids were gone, what would happen to the trust?"

After a long moment of silence, Dunn said, "I don't know. That would be up to the terms of the trust, and the trustees. The only beneficiaries are Tower and his descendants. If he didn't have any descendants . . . I suppose it'd go to Tower."

"If Tower croaked . . . excuse me . . ."

"Yeah, yeah, if Tower croaked, what?"

"Would his wife get it?"

"No. I mean, not if Andi and the kids were still around. Jesus, listen to the way I'm talking, for christ sakes." And the phone went dead. Lucas looked at the receiver, unsure about what had happened. He redialed.

A cop picked up on the first ring, and without preamble said, "Chief Davenport?"

"Yeah, I was talking to Dunn."

"Well, Jesus, sir, I don't know what you said, but he cracked up. He's back in his bedroom."

"Ah."

"Do you want me to get him?"

"No, no, let him go. Tell him I'm sorry, okay?"

"Sure, I will . . ."

"And after he's got back together, ask him if I could get a copy of the Manette Trust document. They must have one around."

LUCAS, STILL WIDE awake, crawled back into bed and lay looking at the ceiling for a moment, then rolled over and gripped Weather's shoulder and whispered in her ear, "Can you wake up?"

"Hmmm?" she asked sleepily.

"Are you operating in the morning?"

"At ten," she said.

"Oh . . ."

"What?" She rolled more on her back and reached up and touched his face.

"I need to talk to you about the case. I need an opinion from a woman. But if you're working . . ."

"I'm fine," she said, more awake now. "Tell me."

He told her, and finished with, "Tower could die anytime. If Andi and the kids are gone, his wife is gonna get a load. Whatever he's got, plus—maybe—whatever's in the trust. Probably four million, plus a million-dollar house. So the question is, could Nancy Wolfe do that? How about Helen?"

Weather had been listening intently. "I can't say—it could be either one. Normally, I'd say no to Wolfe. Even if she's having an affair with Tower, she can't be so sure that he'll marry her, that she'd already be maneuvering for the money. Not to the extent of killing three people. Helen, well, Helen doesn't have anything invested in Andi and the children. She was having an affair with Tower before Andi's mother was gone—so she and Andi probably dislike each other. And if Helen knows about the affair with Nancy Wolfe, maybe . . ."

"Yeah. If Andi and the kids are gone, she gets more from a divorce, if there is one. If Andi and the kids are gone, and Manette croaked from the stress, or from the stress before a divorce, or both . . . well, all the better. So Helen looks good."

"Except."

"Except," Lucas repeated.

"Except that we don't know much about Wolfe's relationship with Andi Manette. They are partners and old friends, we're told—but that's exactly where you'll find some really deep, rich, suppressed hatreds. Things that go back decades. My best friend in high school got married when she was nineteen, had a bunch of kids, and wound up flipping burgers in a motel. The last time I saw her, I realized . . . I think she hates me. Andi was always rich, Wolfe didn't have money; Andi married a man who Wolfe met first, and who went on to become a multimillionaire. Andi has good-looking kids, Wolfe is at the time of life when she's got to face the possibility that she won't get married and have children at all. And maybe Andi would interfere with this affair. I wonder if she knows about it. Anyway—that's all pretty emotional stuff and pretty tangled up."

"Yeah. And there's something else," Lucas said. "If somebody sicced a fruit-cake killer on Andi Manette, who'd know more about picking a fruitcake killer than Wolfe?"

"Maybe you're looking at the wrong files," Weather said. "Maybe you should be looking at Nancy Wolfe's." After a moment, "And there's always George Dunn."

"He doesn't feel right to me, anymore," Lucas said. "He'd have to be a great liar, a great actor."

"In other words, a sociopath," Weather said.

"Glad you said that," Lucas said.

"A lot of very successful businessmen are—at least, that's what I've heard anecdotally. Like surgeons . . ."

"Nancy Wolfe once called him a sociopath," Lucas said.

". . . and if he were facing a divorce that would cut his business in half . . . How much did you say he was worth?" Weather asked.

"If he wasn't lying, could be anything up to thirty million."

"So Andi Manette's death could be worth fifteen million dollars to him," Weather said. "I'll tell you something. Rich people get very attached to their money. It's like one of their organs, or more than that. If you asked most people who have two million dollars whether they'd rather lose one million, or lose a foot, I think most of them would rather lose the foot."

"But that only holds if Andi Manette really wants a divorce," Lucas said. "Dunn says he was trying to put it back together."

"What else *would* he say? That he hates her and he's glad they were kid-napped?"

"Yeah." The problem wasn't a lack of motive. The problem was picking one.

"Don't forget the last possibility," Weather said. "Tower. Her father."

"You've got a sick mind, Karkinnen."

"It wouldn't be the first time that a father went after his daughter. If he's desperate . . ."

Lucas lay flat on his back, his fingers laced across his stomach, and he said, "When I had my little bout of depression, whenever that was, one of the worst things was lying awake at night with everything running through my head, in circles, and not being able to stop it. This isn't quite the same, but it's related. Jesus. I keep going around and around: Dunn, Wolfe, the Manettes; Dunn, Wolfe, the Manettes. The answer is there."

Weather patted his leg. "You'll figure it out."

"Something else is bothering me. I saw something in Gloria Crosby's apartment, but I can't remember what it was. But it's important."

She pushed herself up: "You *forgot?*"

"Not exactly forgot. It was there, but it's like I never really recognized it. It's like when you see a face in the street, and an hour later you realize it was an old classmate. Like that. I saw something . . ."

"Sleep on it," she said. "Maybe your subconscious will kick it out."

After a while in the dark, after Weather had rolled back to her own pillow, he said, "You know, those two Bible verses have me whipped, too. Must be Stillwater. That would be too much of a coincidence—or a trick, or something—not to be right. But what's he talking about?"

And Weather said something that sounded like "ZZZzzttug."

WHEN HE WOKE, before he opened his eyes, he thought of the Bible verses. Maybe the *not* was the key. *Be ye* not *as the horse, or as the mule, which have no understanding; whose mouth must be held in with bit and bridle, lest they come near unto thee.* But even if the *not* was the key word, he thought wryly, ye had no understanding. And who was coming near unto whom?

He thought about it through shaving, through the shower, and came up with nothing brilliant, and began dressing. The day was gorgeous: sunlight slanted in through the wooden blinds in the living room, and the whole feel was that of a perfect fall day. As he put on a shirt and tie, he watched the *Openers* morning show. The weatherman said that the low pressure system responsible for all the rain had rambled off to the east and was presently peeing on Ohio; additional micturatory activity could be expected in New York by evening, if you were going there. The weatherman said neither *peeing* nor *micturatory,* but should have, Lucas thought. He found himself whistling, stopped to wonder why, and decided a nice day was a nice day. The kidnapping wasn't the day's fault, but he stopped whistling.

"SO WE'RE STUCK?" Roux asked. She lit a cigarette, forgetting the one already burning in an ashtray behind her. Her office stank of nicotine, and would need new curtains every year. "All we can do is grind along?"

"I had those Bible verses sent out to Stillwater," Lucas said. "Maybe the local cops will figure something out."

"And maybe the fairy godmother will kiss me on the sweet patootie," Lester said.

"Nasty thought," Roux said. "Nasty."

"I think we ought to start pushing the big four: the Manettes, Dunn, Wolfe. Start taking them apart. Somebody is talking."

Roux shook her head. "I haven't entirely bought that. We've got the wiretaps going, but I don't think I'm ready for a full-scale assault."

"Who's listening to the wires?" Lucas asked.

Lester made a sound like he was clearing his throat.

"What?"

"Larry Carter, from uniform, then tonight, uh, Bob. Greave."

"Ah, shit," Lucas groaned.

"He can do that," Lester said defensively. "He's not stupid, he's just . . ." He groped for a phrase.

"Investigatively challenged," Roux suggested.

"That's it," Lester said.

Lucas stood up. "I've gotten everything I can out of the raw paper on Dunn, Wolfe, and the Manettes, and I want to look at all the stuff from the hospitals and the possible candidates from Andi Manette's files," he said. "That's where it'll break—unless we get a piece of luck."

"Good luck; there's a lot of it," Lester said. "And you better pick up a new copy of Anderson's book. There's more new stuff in there. We got lists coming out the wazoo."

LUCAS SPENT THE day like a medieval monk, bent over the paper. Anything useful, he xeroxed and stuck in a smaller file. By the end of the day, he had fifty pieces of paper for additional review, plus a foot-tall stack of files to take home. He left at six, enjoying the lingering daylight, regretting the great day missed, and gone forever. This would have been a day to go up north with Weather, to learn a little more about sailing from her. They were talking about buying an S2 and racing it. Maybe next year . . .

They spent a quiet evening: a quick mile run, a small, easy dinner with a lot of carrots. Afterwards, Lucas dipped into the homework files, while Weather read a Larry Rivers autobiography called *What Did I Do?* Occasionally she'd read him a paragraph, and they'd laugh or groan together. As she sat in the red chair, with the yellow light illuminating half of her face, he thought she looked like a painting he'd seen in New York. Vermeer, that was it. Or Van Gogh—but Van Gogh was the crazy guy, so it must have been Vermeer. Anyway, he remembered the light in the painting.

And she looked like that, he thought, in the light.

"Gotta go to bed," she said, regretfully, a little after nine o'clock. "Gotta be up at five-thirty. We oughta do this more often."

"What?"

"Nothing, together."

When she'd gone, Lucas started through the stack of files again; came to the one marked JOHN MAIL; after the name, somebody had scrawled [*deceased.*]

This one had looked good, Lucas thought. He opened it and started reading. The phone rang and he picked it up.

"Yeah?"

Greave: "Lucas, I'm peeing my pants. The asshole is talking to Dunn."

21

GREAVE MET LUCAS at the elevator doors. He was in shirt-sleeves, his tie hanging around his shoulders, his hair sticking up in clumps. "Christ, lit me up like a fuckin' Christmas tree," he said. "I couldn't believe what I was hearing."

He led Lucas down a bare but brightly lit hallway toward an open office door, their heels echoing on the tile floor.

"You call the feebs?" Lucas asked.

"No. Should I?"

"Not yet." The office was furnished with a cafeteria-style folding table, three office chairs, and a television. A group of beige push-button telephones and a tape recorder sat on the table with a plate of donut crumbs; the TV was on but the sound was off, Jane Fonda hustling a treadmill. A pile of magazines sat on the floor beside the table.

"Got it cued up," Greave said. He pushed a button on the recorder, and the tape began to roll with the sound of a phone ringing, then being picked up.

"*George Dunn.*"

"*George?*" Mail's voice was cheerful, insouciant. "*I'm calling for your wife, Andi.*"

"*What? What'd you say?*" Dunn seemed stunned.

"*I'm calling for your wife. Is this call being monitored? And you better tell the truth, for Andi's sake.*"

"*No, for christ sakes. I'm in the car. Who is this?*"

"*An old friend of Andi's . . . Now listen: I want a hundred thousand for the package. For the three of them.*"

"*How do I know this isn't a con?*" Dunn asked.

"*I'm gonna play a recording.*" There was some apparent fumbling, then Andi

Manette's voice, tinny, recorded: *"George, this is Andi. Do what this man tells you. Um, he said to tell you what we talked about the last time we talked . . . You called me from the club and you wanted to come over, but I said that the kids were already in bed and I wasn't ready to . . ."*

The recording ended in mid-sentence and Mail said, *"She gets a little sloppy after that, George. You wouldn't want to hear it. Anyway, you got any more questions about whether this is real?"*

Dunn's voice sounded like a rock. *"No."*

"So. I don't want you to go to the bank and get a bunch of money with the numbers recorded and dusted with UV powder and all that FBI shit. If you do it, I'll know, and I'll kill them all."

"I gotta get the money."

"George, you've got almost sixty thousand in case money, mostly kruggerrands, that nobody knows about, in a safety deposit box in Prescott, Wisconsin. Okay? You've got a Rolex worth $8,000 that you never wear anyway. Andi has $25,000 in diamond jewelry and a ruby from her mother, all in your joint safety deposit box at First Bank. And you've got several thousand dollars in cash hidden in the two houses . . . get that."

"You sonofabitch."

"Hey. Let's try to keep this businesslike, okay?" Mail's voice was wry, but not quite taunting.

"How do I get it to you? I've got cops staying with me, waiting for you to call."

"Take I-94 east all the way to the St. Croix, get off on Highway 95, get back on going west, and pull off at the Minnesota Welcome station. You know where that is?"

"Yeah."

"There's a phone by the Coke machine. Get on it just before seven o'clock, but keep your finger on the hook. I'll call right at seven o'clock. If it's busy, I'll try again at five after seven. If it's still busy, I'll try at ten after, but that's it: after that, I'm gone. Don't even think about telling the cops. I'll be driving around, and they can't track me when I'm moving. They've been trying. When I get you on the phone, I'll give you some instructions."

"Okay."

"If I see any cops, I'm gone."

THE PHONE WENT dead.

"That's it," Greave said.

"Jesus." Lucas walked in a quick circle, stopped to look out the window at the lights of the city, then said, "We talk to Lester and the chief. Nobody else. Nobody. We've got to get a team going."

Roux brought the FBI in. Lucas argued against it, but she insisted: "For christ sakes, Lucas, this is the thing they do. This is their big specialty. We can't leave them out—if we do, and if we blow it, it'll be all our asses. And it should be."

"We can handle it."

"I'm sure we can, if it's real. But if it's anything else, we'd be in deep shit, my friend. No, they've got to come in."

Lucas looked at Lester, who nodded, agreeing with Roux.

"So. I'll call them, and you two can brief them. We'll want representatives on the team that tracks Dunn. You, Lucas, somebody else."

"Sloan or Capslock."

"Whichever, or both," Roux said. She turned away from them, flicked her lighter, and touched off another cigarette. "Christ, I hope this is the end of it."

LUCAS, UP ALL night, arguing with Roux or briefing the feebs, stopped home at five-thirty and ate breakfast with Weather.

"Do you think it's real?" she asked. She was running a seminar for post-docs that morning, and was dressed in a pale linen suit with a silk scarf.

"It sure sounded good," Lucas said. "Dunn was absolutely spontaneous. We didn't have that phone monitored until yesterday, and we didn't tell him about it . . . so, yeah, I believe the call. I don't think this asshole is gonna hand over his wife and kids, though."

"Then the call was good for one thing," Weather said.

Lucas nodded. "If it's real, it eliminates Dunn from the list."

"Unless . . ." Weather said.

"What?"

"Unless he's talking to somebody in his office, and that person is passing the word along."

Lucas waved her off. "That's too complicated to think about. Possible, but we'd never get to them."

They heard the *Pioneer-Press* paper-delivery car slow outside the house, and the paper hit the walk. Lucas ran out to get it, and as he did, the *Star-Tribune* car came by, and he got that, too. Both papers had photos of Crosby above the fold.

"For all the good it does us," Lucas said, scanning the stories. "He's got her."

"Aren't you planning to talk to the papers today?"

Lucas slapped his forehead. "Yes. Damnit. Noon."

"Get some sleep," she said.

"Yeah." He glanced at his watch. Almost six. "A few hours, anyway."

Weather took her coffee cup and the plate on which she'd had her toast, carried them to the sink, then laughed as she walked back to the table and ruffled his hair.

"What?" he asked.

"You look like you're fifteen and going on your first date. You always do when you get something going. And the more awful it is, and the more tired you get, the happier you look. This whole thing is terrible: and you're getting high on it."

"It's interesting," Lucas admitted. "This kid we're talking to, he's an inter-

144 ——— J O H N   S A N D F O R D

esting kid." He looked out the window, where the neighbor from across the street was walking his elderly cocker spaniel, and the day was beginning as quietly as a mouse. "I mean, you know, for a nightmare."

REPORTERS FROM FIVE television stations and both major papers showed up at the company headquarters at noon. Lucas talked for five minutes about police tactical simulation software and gaming programs, then passed the reporters to Ice.

Ice said, with the camera rolling, "We're gonna show you how we're gonna catch this sucker and nail his butt to the wall."

Lucas saw the quick smiles from the cameramen and the reporters: he had a hit on his hands. Barry Hunt caught his eye and they nodded at each other.

"The first thing is, we know what he looks like."

Ice ran the art program that manipulated the facial characteristics of the composite drawing of the suspect, adding and deleting hair, mustaches, beards, glasses, and collar styles. The other techies set up a camera to take pictures of the on-air reporters and manipulate their faces through the various styles. Then they put up a show that involved rotating three-dimensional maps of the Twin Cities, supposedly showing general locations of the kidnapper's hideout.

"It's going fuckin' great, as long as nobody asks what it means and how it'll help catch the guy," Ice muttered to Lucas just before he left.

Lucas looked back at the crowd of laughing reporters standing around the computer displays: "Don't worry about it," he said. "This is great video. Nobody'll be stupid enough to ask anything that'd spoil it."

AT THREE O'CLOCK the Dunn task force met at the federal building, with Roux, Lucas, and Sloan representing the city. Roux and Sloan were just walking in when Lucas arrived, and Roux said, "Dunn's picking up the money. The feds are all over him."

"Excellent," Lucas said.

Dumbo and twenty FBI agents were packed in a conference room, with space left for the three city reps. Lucas sat down next to a girl whom he thought must be an intern of some sort, though she hardly seemed old enough. Fifteen, he thought, or sixteen. She looked at him, a level, speculating glance that struck him as too old for her body and face. He felt uncomfortable with her sitting behind him as he faced Dumbo.

Dumbo laid out the procedure: fourteen agents on the ground in seven cars, plus a chopper with a spotter in the air. "We've already marked his car with an infra-red flasher wired into the taillight. I understand that Minneapolis uses the same technique," Dumbo said, his ears flapping.

"Something like it," Sloan said. "I like the taillight deal. That's a nice touch. We oughta talk."

Dumbo looked pleased: "So. You guys want to ride in the chopper or go on the ground?"

"I'm ground," Lucas said.

"I'll go with Lucas," Sloan said. "We've got to coordinate on the radio codes."

"Sure." Dumbo pointed at one of the FBI technical people.

"Who's going into the rest stop?" Lucas asked. "It's gotta look good."

"Marie," Dumbo said, and nodded at the woman behind Lucas. Lucas glanced back at her and she grinned. "We'll put her in a high school letter jacket and a pleated skirt, give her some bubble gum. She'll go in right behind Dunn and head for the phones. There are four of them in a pod. We're monitoring all four. If Dunn has to wait, so will she. If they don't, she'll get on one and start talking to her boyfriend. She'll be looking for anything and anybody."

Roux, peering at the woman from across the table, said, "You're either precocious or older than you look."

"I'm thirty-two," the woman said, in a sweet young soprano.

"And Danny McGreff"—Dumbo nodded at a man with a large square face and two-day beard—"will get there a half-hour before Dunn is scheduled to, will get Dunn's phone and stay on it until he sees Dunn come in the door. Then he'll say good-bye, and drop it on the hook and leave. We don't think anyone should be waiting—there's never been a time when all four of them have been tied up, in the time we've been monitoring them."

"So you'll have one agent in the place and at least one outside . . ."

"We'll have three in the place," Dumbo said. "There's a storage room, lockable, and we'll put two men in there a couple of hours ahead of time. They simply won't come out, and there won't be any way to check inside without a key."

As the meeting was breaking up, Dumbo said, "Let's try to keep the radio communications clean, huh? Washington has asked us to allow a cameraman to ride with us tonight, for a documentary being made, uh, anyway for a documentary. I've agreed."

On the way out the door, an FBI technician muttered at Lucas, "Keep your box on Fox."

SLOAN SAID, "WE could be in a world of hurt."

"How?" Roux asked. They pushed through the brass revolving doors onto the street.

"They've got everything figured out," Sloan said. He started peeling a Dentine pack. "Everything's on a schedule. But this can't be as easy as it looks—there's a joker in the deck somewhere."

Lucas looked up and down the street, and saw a one-time pimp named Robert Lika, whom the local wits called Leica because of his fondness for flashing preteen girls. Lika was peeing into a doorway, one hand braced on the door jamb as though the doorway were an ordinary urinal. "Will you look at this?"

"Rather not," said Roux, and her face colored.

"You're a little pink," Lucas said.

"You know, you didn't see much of that until the last two or three years,"

Roux said, looking down at Lika. "Now you see it all the time. It's such a weird . . . turn."

THE FEDERAL OPERATION was already moving, but Lucas and Sloan wouldn't be involved until Dunn started toward the rest stop. The feds were monitoring him: after making a morning round of the banks, he'd gone to his office and was still there.

Sloan's wife had had a bunion removed, and her foot was still tender, and Sloan snuck off to do some grocery shopping on city time. Lucas, restless, caught lunch at a cop bar, put twenty dollars on the Vikes over Chicago, eating the eight-point spread—the Bears sucked—walked the skyways for a while, looking at women and clothes, and played with the ring in his pocket.

He was gonna do it, he decided. Something simple—no juvenile tricks, no sophomoric misdirection or declarations. He'd just ask. What could she say, other than no? But she wouldn't say no. She had to know what he was thinking—she could read his mind, she'd proved that. Hell, she was probably getting impatient; maybe she saw all this delay as some kind of insult. But the main thing was, she wouldn't say no. Well, technically, you know, she *could* say no. What if she started out to be really nice about it . . . Fuckin' women.

Wonder what Dunn's doing?

AT FOUR-THIRTY, HE went back to the office, got the files out, and started reading through again. The file on the dead kid, where was he? Let's see, subject reported to have jumped from the Lake Street Bridge, reporting officers called boat . . .

The PR woman stuck her head in the door. "Lucas, they're talking about you on TV, on the promos, so you'll be up in the next couple of minutes if you want to watch."

"Yeah, I want . . ." Lucas had just turned the page on the report and looked up at the PR lady, but an after-image stuck in his eye and the after-image was Gloria. He looked back down at the page, trying to find it.

"Lucas?"

"Yeah, I'll be along . . ." Where was it? He found it at the bottom of the page:

". . . witness Gloria Crosby said he'd been depressed since getting out of the state hospital and had stopped taking his prescription medication. Crosby said he may have been taking street drugs and had been acting irrational and that on 8/9 she had him admitted to Hennepin General for apparent drug overdose. Crosby said subject called her and asked to meet him at the Stanley Grill on Lake Street and that when she got there he was already walking toward the bridge. She walked after him, but when she got to the bridge the subject was standing on the railing and stepped off before she could approach him. Crosby said she ran back to Stanley Grill to call for assistance . . ."

Damnit. Gloria Crosby. Crouched over the desk, he thumbed through the rest of the papers, trying to figure out what had happened. The phone rang and he snatched it off the desk:

"What?"

"Lucas, you're on . . ."

"Yeah, yeah." He banged down the receiver, went back to the papers, and then picked up the phone again, punched in Anderson's number.

"This is Lucas . . ."

"Lucas, you're on . . ."

"Yeah, yeah, fuck that, listen, you gotta get everything you can find on a guy named John Mail, DOB 7/7/68. Did time in the state hospital. We need the most recent photo we can find. Check the DMV and find his parents . . . wait, wait, I've got this . . ." Lucas shuffled through the papers. "His folks lived at 28 Sharf Lane in Wayzata. Goddamnit, that's where McPherson said he was from."

"Who?"

"Just get that shit, man. This is something."

Off the phone again, he went through the file on Mail and found the reference to the dental records. Damnit. He got his book, looked up the Medical Examiner's number.

"Sharon, this is Lucas Davenport . . . yeah, fine, it's all healed up, yeah, listen, I need you to pull something for me. You should have some records on a guy named John Mail went off the Lake Street Bridge a few years back, I can get you the date if you need it. John Mail. Yeah, I'll wait."

Ten seconds later, she was back. Mail was on the computer. "Just hold it there," Lucas said. "I'm gonna run over right now."

Lucas was out the door and down the street, a fast five-minute walk to the Medical Examiner's. An ME's investigator named Brunswick was peering at a computer.

"Something hot?" he asked.

"You say a guy is dead," Lucas said. "I think he might still be alive."

"Well, the guy we saw was dead," Brunswick said. "I've been looking at the pictures." He passed a group of eight-by-ten color photographs to Lucas. The remains of the body. Still partly wrapped in the remains of a pair of Levi blue jeans, was spread on a stainless steel table. Most of it was bone, although the torso looked like a gray ball of string or grass. The face was gone, but the dark hair was still there. Both hands were missing, as was one leg.

"Bad shape. Were the hands—is that natural? Is there any possibility they were taken off?"

Brunswick shook his head. "No way to tell. The body was falling apart. The one unusual thing is that there was evidence of a ligature around the torso—wire, or something. God knows, in that part of the Mississippi, it could have been anything."

"Could somebody have anchored the body somewhere? Until it was ready to be found?"

"You've got a nasty turn of mind, Davenport."

"But you already thought of that," Lucas said.

"Yeah. And it's possible. Whatever it was tied him down, had him for a while. Nearly cut the body through, in the end. There was no sign of any ligature when the body was found, though."

"What about the dental records?"

"It's the right guy, by the records. Here are the X rays on the body, and you can see the dental X rays."

Lucas bent over them and looked: they were patently identical. In the corner of the dental records was a response phone number at the state hospital. Lucas picked up Brunswick's phone and punched the number in.

"Can't be right," Lucas said.

A woman answered. Lucas identified himself and said, "I need to talk to Dr. L. D. Rehder, does he still work there? I'm sorry, she? Yeah, it really is important. Yeah."

To Brunswick, he said, "I'm on hold."

Brunswick said, "Is this the Manette case?"

"Part of it," Lucas said.

"My wife went on a march last night to protest violence against women," Brunswick said.

"Hope it works," Lucas said.

On the phone, a woman said, "This is Dr. Rehder."

"Yeah, Dr. Rehder, some time ago one of your patients apparently committed suicide. The body ID was confirmed by dental records from your office," Lucas said. "A kid named John Mail."

"I remember John." Her voice was pleasantly clipped. "He was with us for quite a while."

"Is there any way he could've gotten to the records to switch them with somebody else's? I mean, before he got out of the hospital?"

"Oh, I don't think so. He was confined in a completely different area. He would have had to escape over there, break in here without being detected, then get out of here and break back in over there. It would have been very difficult."

"Damnit," Lucas said.

"Is there some question about whether it was John who jumped off the bridge?" Rehder asked.

"Yes. Have you by any chance seen the police composite pictures of the man who kidnapped Mrs. Manette and her daughters?"

Rehder said, "Yes, I have. John had dark hair."

"He may have changed the hair color . . ."

"Just a minute, let me get my paper."

"Getting her paper," Lucas said to Brunswick. He shuffled through the pictures of the body while they waited. Then Rehder came back on and said, "If the hair was changed, if the hair was black, I've just colored it in with my felt-tip pen. It could be John. There's something not quite right about the chin line."

Lucas nodded. He knew he was right. "Okay. Does the name Gloria Crosby mean anything to you?"

"Gloria?" Rehder said. "Gloria was an aide—Gloria worked for us."

Lucas closed his eyes. *Gotcha*.

22

ANDERSON, HARRIED, HIS hands full of paper, his sharecropper's face pickled in a permanent squint, said, "Sloan said to tell you he's bringing the car. Dunn's moving: you gotta get out of here."

"Stay on the Mail thing," Lucas said, pulling on his jacket.

Anderson ticked it off on his fingers. "We're tracking his friends, to see if anybody's run into him since the bridge, if anybody has a name. We're trying to figure out who the body really was, but that will be a problem. It has to be somebody at the hospital who had dental care, who was close to Mail's size and age, and who was out at the same time, but there are hundreds of people who fit, all of them are mentally ill, and a lot of them are impossible to find. We're trying to find Mail's parents—his mother and stepfather. We think they might have split up. We know they moved to the Seattle area, but one of the step-father's friends heard they split out there, and the mother might have remarried."

"What about decent photos of the guy?"

"We've got photos coming from the hospital and the DMV, but they're all years old," Anderson said.

"Yeah, but with something real to work from, we can age him. Get them over to the company, if you need to. They were doing some good stuff this morning."

"Okay. But you need to talk with the chief about whether to release them to the press. If he's as close to the edge as you say he is . . ."

"Yeah. I'll be back. Don't do anything until we talk about it. And if anything breaks—*anything*—call me. I'll be on the phone."

WHEN LUCAS RAN out, Sloan was walking up to the building, carrying a baseball cap.

"Where is he? Dunn?"

"He's coming through town right now," Sloan said over his shoulder as he turned and headed back into the street. He had a gray, four-year-old Chevy Caprice sitting in traffic with its engine running. "We've got to motivate."

The radios they'd gotten from the feds were standard: Lucas called in, checking the identification protocols, and was told that *zebra is underway; the subject has been acquired.*

"That means they can see the car from the chopper," Lucas said.

"Fuckin' wonderful," Sloan said.

"It's better than the ten-four bullshit," Lucas said. "I never did understand that."

"Did you bring the maps?"

"Yeah, and I got one for the Hudson area, just in case." Lucas took the maps out of his pocket. The radio burped:

Approaching White Bear Avenue Interchange.

"This is really fucked, you know?" Lucas said. "I'm sitting here thinking that it's a little too strange."

As they paced Dunn's car through the city and into the 'burbs, Lucas told Sloan about the identification of John Mail. "Haven't pinned him yet," Lucas said.

"If he's the guy, we will," Sloan said confidently. "Once we get a face . . ."

"I hope," Lucas said.

They were in the countryside now, and white puffy clouds cast long shadows on new-cut hay, the last cut of the year. The beans and corn, as far as Lucas could tell, were about as good as they ever got in Minnesota, the corn showing stripes of gold along the edge of the leaves, the beans already brown and drying. A few miles out of St. Paul, an ultra-light aircraft circled over the highway, the pilot plainly visible in his leathers and black helmet. Further on, toward the St. Croix River, a half-dozen brightly colored hot-air balloons drifted east toward Wisconsin.

And the radio said, *He's off at 95 . . . he's back on, heading east.*

This is five; we got him coming in.

Dumbo: *Everybody in position,* now.

"Get off at Highway 15," Lucas said, pointing at an exit sign. "Go north, find a place to turn around and start back. We don't want to sit anywhere. If Mail is out roaming around, and sees us, he'd recognize me."

Sloan took the off-ramp, paused at the top, and started north on the black-topped road. "Van coming up from behind," Sloan said.

Lucas slid down in his seat and Sloan took the first left. The van stayed on the main road. Sloan, looking in the rearview mirror, said, "Blonde. Woman." He did a U-turn and started back.

He's inside. We've got him covered.

"They're doing okay," Lucas said nervously.

"Give them time," Sloan said. "The feebs could fuck up a wet dream."

Lucas and Sloan both looked at their watches simultaneously. Sloan said, "Five minutes," and Lucas grunted.

They were headed back toward the interstate, no other cars in sight. The landscape was littered with new suburban houses with plastic siding in pastel tints ranging from sunset to sage; here and there a farm field came up to the edge of the road. A flock of sheep grazed over a pasture.

Lucas said, "Green pastures."

"Say what?" Sloan looked at him.

Lucas said, "These are the green pastures, from Psalms. Elle was right. I'll bet my ass that he's about to lead us into Stillwater. How far are we from Stillwater? Ten miles?"

"About that."

"Let's head that way," Lucas said urgently. "We're pretty useless anyway."

"If he's leading us, then this might not be what it looks like . . ."

"Yeah, yeah," Lucas said. "Exactly right."

And the radio said, *We've got a confirmed hit, confirmed hit. He's off, he's gone, Jimmy get me . . . what? We've got cellular confirmed but no cell designation, it was too quick. Can we run that, Jimmy? Jimmy? Subject is out of the rest stop on his way to the car, can we get the intercept up . . .*

"What the fuck did he say?" Lucas asked. "What'd Mail say?"

And the radio said, *Subject was told to go to a picnic table and pull a note off the bottom side and follow instructions . . . subject is at the picnic table, subject is walking back to the car, he's reading a paper, he has the instructions . . .*

"Come on, goddamnit, we gotta move," Lucas said. "It's Stillwater."

Subject is in car proceeding west on I-94.

"Wrong way," Sloan grunted.

"He's got no choice from there," Lucas said. He slapped his own forehead. "And think about it, think about it: the guy makes the initial contact on Dunn's cellular phone, and routes him to a public phone? Why'd he do that? Why didn't he call him on the cellular again? Then he wouldn't have to fuck around with the possibility that somebody else was using the pay phone. Why'd he do that, Sloan?"

"I don't know." Sloan frowned as he thought about it. "Maybe . . . no. If he doesn't trust the cellular now, why'd he trust it yesterday?"

"He didn't. Maybe he figured we'd be monitoring it," Lucas said. "Maybe he did it so we'd be close by, but he'd know where we were at. I'll bet that sonofabitch is in Stillwater right now. Goddamnit, what's he doing?"

Three minutes later the radio burped, *Subject exiting at Highway 15 . . . crossing Interstate, reentering Interstate . . .*

"What's he doing?" Sloan asked. "Why didn't he go this way?"

"He's going down to 95 and he'll take 95 north to Stillwater," Lucas said. "It's simpler, if you don't have a map. How fast can we get there?"

"We'll be there in six or seven minutes. He'll be ten minutes behind us. If you're right."

"I'm right."

"Yeah, I know." Sloan had the Chevy up to ninety, sloughed past the Lake Elmo airport with its pole-barn hangars, and onto Highway 5 east toward Stillwater.

"Goddamnit, I wish we were set up with the Stillwater cops. Just a few guys to sit and watch. We could've shipped a picture of Mail out here."

They listened to the parade moving east on the interstate, then Lucas got on the radio to Dumbo. "We're headed to Stillwater, we think he's playing out the Bible verses he sent us. You probably ought to have your lead cars get off at Highway 95 and start north. And take it easy: we've got two more verses to go, but the last one talks about a trap."

"Got it covered, Minneapolis," Dumbo said. "Keep your heads down. We don't want a crowd."

"Thanks for the technical advice," Sloan muttered.

As DUNN AND the federal parade turned off the interstate, Sloan blew past a Dodge pickup on the Highway 36 entrance ramp. The truck swerved onto the shoulder as they passed, and the driver, a young, long-haired man, leaned on his horn and then came after them as they weaved through the traffic, down a long passage of convenience stores and fast-food joints.

"Asshole," Sloan said, grinning into his rearview mirror.

"Better hope he doesn't kill any kids," Lucas said.

"Yeah. The fuckin' paperwork alone. We gotta light coming up, you wanna hop out and chat with him?"

"Unless you want to run the light."

"All right."

The truck loomed behind them as they slowed for the light, closed to eight inches from their bumper, and the kid was back on the horn.

Lucas turned to look over the backseat. The trucker had one hand on the wheel and the other on the horn; a young woman, next to him in the passenger seat, seemed to be yelling—he could see the points of her canine teeth—but Lucas couldn't tell whether she was yelling at the driver or at him. Then she gave him the finger and Lucas decided that he was definitely the target. The trucker dropped the transmission into park, popped his door, and started to climb out, and Sloan went through the red light.

"Goddamn, he's coming through the red," Sloan said, peering in the mirror.

The radio: *Two miles out of Bayport, slow and steady.*

"We gotta do something about this guy," Sloan said as they took the long sweeping curve toward the St. Croix River. They'd cut the corner off Dunn's route and were approaching Highway 95 ahead of him. "Dunn's not five miles away. Going through Bayport'll slow him down, but this asshole . . ." He looked in the mirror, and the truck was coming after them.

"All right," Lucas said. "There's a marina up ahead. Pull in there. He'll come in behind us and I'll take him in the parking lot." Lucas pulled his .45 out of the shoulder rig, popped the magazine, jacked the shell out of the chamber, slapped the magazine back in the butt, and dropped the extra shell in his coat pocket. "What a pain in the ass."

"Ready?" Sloan asked.

"Yeah. You got cuffs? If we need them?"

"Glove compartment."

Sloan kept the speed up until he was on top of the marina entrance, then stood on the brakes and took them off the highway. The trucker almost rammed them, swerved out at the last minute, then cranked the truck down the road behind them. Sloan kept moving until they hit the parking lot, then pulled around in a circle. The trucker cut inside them, and they stopped, nearly nose-to-nose.

Lucas popped the door and climbed out, the pistol back in its holster. The trucker was already on the ground, running around the back of his truck, reaching into the open truck bed for something. Lucas ran toward him and the trucker pulled out a length of two-by-four and Lucas screamed, "Police," showed his badge in his left hand, and pulled the pistol in his right. "On the ground. On the ground, asshole."

The trucker looked at the two-by-four, his eyes puzzled, as though it had gotten into his hand by mistake, then chunked it back into the truck. "You cut me off," he said.

"Get on the fuckin' ground," Lucas shouted.

The woman started out of the passenger side, but when she saw the gun, she got back in and punched down the door locks. Sloan got out and held up a badge where she could see it.

The trucker was flat on the blacktop, looking up, and Lucas said, "We're on an emergency run, we're in a big goddamn hurry or I'd kick your ass into fuckin' strawberry jam. As it is, I'm gonna take your truck license number. I want you to sit here, out of the way, for a half-hour. You can sit in the truck, but you sit for a half-hour, and then you can leave. If you leave before then, I'll be all over your ass. I'll put your ass in jail on fifteen fuckin' traffic counts and a couple of felonies, like interfering with officers. You understand that?"

"I understand, sir." The trucker had grown calm.

"All right. Get in the truck and sit. Half an hour."

Lucas hurried back to the car and Sloan pulled it around in a circle and they were halfway out of the parking lot before they started laughing.

"Funny, but Christ, I wished that hadn't happened just then," Lucas said as he reloaded the .45. "They say anything more on the radio?"

"Yeah, they said . . ." Before Sloan could get it out, the radio said, *He's into Bayport, still proceeding north. We got him.*

"We've got five minutes," Sloan said.

"Main Street's only about ten blocks long. Let's run down it and see what we can see," Lucas said.

STILLWATER WAS AN old lumber mill town, with most of the turn-of-the-century mercantile buildings still in place, crowding Main Street. The buildings had been renovated with tourists in mind, and were now filed with bricks-and-copper-pot restaurants, fern bars, and butter-churn antique stores; the long row of brick store fronts was inflected by the white plastic of a Fina station.

Lucas slumped in his seat, Sloan's baseball cap on his head, only his eyes above the window sill. He hoped he looked like a child but wouldn't have bet on it. "Two million vans," he said. "Everywhere you look, there's a van, if the sonofabitch is dumb enough to still be driving that van around."

The chopper: *Subject proceeding through Bayport.*

Sloan idled the length of the town, and they saw nothing of interest: storefronts full of tourists, teenagers idling along the walks, one kid who might've been Mail but wasn't. In the light of a pizza place, his face was five years too young.

At the north end of town, Lucas said, "We've got three or four minutes to set up. Let's go back to the other end and find a spot where we can watch the street. If he turns off right away, we should be able to see him. If he goes on past, we can fall in behind."

"Piss off the feds," Sloan said.

"Fuck 'em. Something's happening."

Sloan made a U-turn in the parking lot of a run-down building with a line of dancing cowboy boots painted on the bare, corrugated metal in flaking house paint. They waited for a break in traffic and then drove back to the south end of town, pulled into a parking lot, and found an empty handicapped parking space facing the street. A line of pine trees separated the lot from the street. "Probably get a ticket," Sloan said as he pulled into the handicapped space.

"I don't know," Lucas said. "I've always thought of you as handicapped."

Radio: *The subject has exited Bayport and is proceeding north.*

"Why's he talking like that?" Sloan asked.

"He's got that camera with him. He'll say *perpetrator* in a minute."

From their vantage in the parking lot, they could look through the line of trees and see the cars coming into town on Highway 95. Dunn drove a silver Mercedes 500 S, and as the chopper radio said *Subject is entering Stillwater,* Lucas picked it out in the traffic stream.

"See him?"

"I've got him."

"Let him get past."

Sloan backed the car out of the handicapped slot. "I wonder where the feds are?"

"Probably not real close."

They waited behind the trees until the Mercedes went past, and then Sloan pulled out of the lot and back onto Main Street. There were two cars between them and Dunn. Lucas, slumped in his seat, couldn't see him.

"What's he doing?" he asked, when they all stopped for a red light.

Sloan had edged a bit to the left, and said, "Nothing. Looking straight ahead."

"What do you think? Is Dunn legit?"

Sloan looked at him. "If he's not, they had to set it up ahead of time."

"Well, he's a smart guy."

"I don't know," Sloan said. The traffic started moving again. "That'd be awful tricky."

"Yeah."

After a moment, Sloan said, "It looks like he's going all the way through town. Unless he's going to that old train station. Or one of the antique places."

"Shit: I hope he doesn't take a boat somewhere. Did the feds think of a boat? Boy, if the sonofabitch goes out on the water . . ."

"We could grab a boat from somebody," Sloan said.

"I'd give ten bucks to see that note he got from the picnic table."

"With your money, you could do better," Sloan said. "Hey. He's slowing down. Goddamn, he's turning around right where we did."

"Go on past," Lucas said. He sat up a bit and saw the silver Benz turning in the gravel parking lot outside the building painted with the cowboy boots. Sloan pulled into the next parking lot, a marina, and found a space with two cars between them and Dunn.

"Goddamnit," Lucas said. He put his hand to his forehead.

Subject has stopped. Subject has stopped. Five, are you on him?

We see him, we're proceeding into parking lot down the street.

"The whole fuckin' lot's gonna be full of cops," Sloan said. "That must be them." A dark Ford bumped into the lot, and Lucas could see that it was full of adult-sized heads.

"Can you see the name of that place?" Lucas asked. "Where he's at?"

"No light," Sloan said. Across the street, Dunn was getting out of his car. He looked up at the boot store and started toward it, ponderously. He carried a briefcase and slumped with it, as though it weighed a hundred pounds.

Lucas picked up the federal radio. "This is Davenport. We're in the same parking lot with your guys. If he tries to go into that building, I'm going to stop him. We need you to spread your people out on the street, set up a net and look at faces, see if you can spot Mail. He's around here."

Dumbo was sputtering. "Davenport, you stay the heck out of here. You stay out of here, we've got it under control."

Sloan was looking at him curiously, and said, "Lucas, I don't think . . ."

"Fuck me, fuck me," Lucas said. He pushed open the door.

"Lucas!" Sloan was whispering, though Dunn was a long way away.

A concrete loading dock ran along the front of the cowboy building, and Dunn was climbing heavily up the steps at one end. The building was dark, with no sign of movement. Dunn went to the door, and Lucas climbed out of the car, radio in his hand.

Sloan said, "Lucas . . ."

And Lucas put the radio to his mouth and said, "I gotta stop him. Get your men out." He tossed the radio back into the car and started running, yelling at Dunn: "Dunn, Dunn! Wait. George Dunn . . ."

Dunn stopped, his hand on the door of the store. Lucas waved, and, glancing back, saw Sloan coming after him. "Take the back of the building," Lucas shouted. Sloan yelled something and broke off, and Lucas ran toward Dunn, who simply stood.

"Get down off of there," Lucas shouted as he came up.

"You sonofabitch," Dunn shouted back. "You've killed my kids . . ."

"Get out of there," Lucas yelled. He ran up the steps—saw in the dark window the barely discernible words, "Bit & Bridle"—and reached for his gun.

"What the fuck are you doing here?" Dunn asked. His face was stretched with tension and anger.

"There's something wrong," Lucas said. "This whole thing is a set-up."

"Set-up," Dunn shouted. "Set-up? You just fuckin' . . ." And before Lucas could stop him, Dunn turned the door knob and shoved the door open. Lucas flinched. Nothing happened. ". . . fuckin' killed my kids . . ."

Lucas pulled his .45 and stepped past Dunn into the building, groped for a light switch, found it, flicked the switch up. To his surprise, the lights came on. The store was empty, and apparently had been for some time. He was facing a long bare counter top, with vacant shelves behind it. All of it was covered with a patina of dust.

A fed ran up the steps. "What the hell are you doing?" he shouted at Lucas. Lucas waved him away, then said, "You oughta get out on the street and watch for Mail. He's watching this from somewhere."

"Watching what?"

"Whatever he's got going here," Lucas said. "This used to be a place called the Bit and Bridle. One of those Bible verses said something about a bit and bridle. It was all too fuckin' easy."

The fed looked around the empty room, then reached back under his jacket and pulled out a Smith & Wesson automatic. "You want to try that door? Or you think we should wait for the bomb squad?"

"Let's take a look," Lucas suggested. To Dunn, he said, "You wait outside."

"Yeah, bullshit."

"Wait the fuck outside," Lucas said.

Dunn dropped the briefcase and said, "You wanna find out right now if you can take me?"

"Ah, Jesus," Lucas said. He turned away from Dunn and went to a doorway that led into the back of the building. The doorway was open just an inch, and Lucas, standing well off to the back side of it, pushed it open another inch. Nothing happened. The fed moved in from the opening side, reached around the corner, groped for a minute, found the light switch, and turned it on.

The place was deadly silent until Dunn said, "There's nothing here. He's gone."

Lucas looked through the two-inch opening, saw nothing, then pushed the door open a foot, then all the way. The door opened into what looked like a storage room. A stack of shelves, covered with dust, sat against one wall. A handful of blank receipt forms was scattered over the wooden floor. A 1991 Snap-On Tool calendar still hung on a wall.

"Somebody's been here," the fed said. He pointed his Smith at the floor, at a tangled line of footprints in the dust. The prints came through another door further back. The door was open several inches. Lucas stood next to it and called out, "Mail? John Mail?"

"Who's that?" Dunn asked. "Is that the guy?"

"Yeah."

"There's a light switch," the fed said. "I'm gonna get it, watch it."

He hit the switch, and three light bulbs, scattered around the central shaft of the building, popped on. The building had been remodelled since it had last been used to store grain, and the grain storage shaft had been partitioned into storage rooms and a receiving dock. The rooms had no ceilings, but looked straight to the top of the shaft. The light inside the shaft was weak—the volume was too big for the three operable bulbs.

But in the gloom above them, something moved. They all saw it at once, and Lucas and the fed pressed back against the walls, their guns up.

"What is it?"

"Aw, Jesus," Dunn shouted, turning in his own footprints, head craned up. "It's Andi, Jesus . . ."

Then Lucas could see it, the body in black, the feet below it, twisting from a yellow rope at the top of the shaft. The door they had not yet tried went into the receiving dock and the main part of the shaft itself. Dunn broke toward it, hands out to stiff-arm the door . . .

"Wait, wait," Lucas screamed. He launched himself cross the room in a body block, caught Dunn just behind the knees, and cut him down. The fed stood frozen as they thrashed on the floor for a moment, and Lucas, gun still in one hand, trying to control it, sputtered at the fed, "Hold him, for christ sakes."

"That's Andi," Dunn groaned as the fed put away his pistol and grabbed Dunn's coat. "Let me up."

"That's not your wife," Lucas said. "That's a woman named Crosby."

"Crosby? Who's Crosby?"

"A friend of Mail's," Lucas said shortly. "We've been trying to track her, but he got to her first."

Lucas, back on his feet, holstered his pistol and went to the partially open door to the shaft. There was a slight draft through the doorway, but nothing else. Lucas reached through, found another light switch, hesitated, then flipped it on. Again, the lights worked. He looked through the crack in the door, saw nothing. No wires, nothing that might be a bomb. He gave the door a push and was ready to step through.

But the door seemed to resist for a split second, just a hair-trigger hold, and then a break, almost imperceptible, but enough that Lucas jumped back.

"What?" The FBI man was grinning at him.

"I thought I felt . . ." Lucas started. He put his hand out toward the door and took a step.

And was nearly knocked off his feet as the door seemed to explode a foot from his face.

CAN SEE, HE thought, his hands up in front of his face. *Nothing hurts . . .*

"WHAT?" THE FED was shouting, his gun out again, pointing at the shattered wooden door. "What? What? What was that?"

Dust filtered down on them and rolled out of the back room like smoke. Lucas could taste dirt in his mouth, feel the grit in his eyes. Dunn had reflexively turned away, but now turned back, his hair and shoulders covered with grime.

"What was that?"

Lucas stepped back to the door, pushed it, pushed it again, pushed hard. It opened a foot and he looked through. On the other side, the floor was littered with river rocks, granite cobblestones the size of pumpkins, fifteen or twenty of them.

"Trap," Lucas said. He pushed the door again and a rock rolled away from it. Lucas stepped through and saw the rope from the top of the door leading up into the darkness. "They fell a long way. If one of them hit you, it'd be like getting hit by a cannonball."

"But that's not Andi?" Dunn said, following him through, looking up at the body. In the stronger light, they could now see the soles of the woman's feet, like dancing footprints above their heads.

"No. That's just bait," Lucas said. "That was to get us to run through the door without thinking about it."

"Asshole," said the fed. He was dusting himself off. "Somebody could have got hurt."

23

MAIL'S TRAP HAD snapped, but it had come up empty. Still, it had excited him: figuring it out, setting it up. He hadn't planned to put Gloria's body in the loft section, but it had worked so well in his mind—the cheese to pull them, unthinking, into the trap.

And it must've been close, because they'd tripped it. He could tell by the way they were acting.

"WE KNEW THERE'D be a booby trap, that there'd be *something,*" Davenport said. He seemed to find the situation almost funny, in a grim way. He stood with his back to the Bit & Bridle, his hard face made even harder by the television lights; his suit seemed unwrinkled, his tie went with his cool blue eyes. "We were hoping that by flooding the area with unmarked cars, we'd spot him. We're still processing license numbers."

"You're lying, asshole," Mail shouted at the television screen. Then he laughed, pointed at the screen with a beer bottle. "You got lucky, motherfucker."

Davenport looked out at him, unblinking. Behind Davenport, cops swarmed over the Bit & Bridle storefront. He missed some of what Davenport had said, and picked up on, ". . . we'll have to wait for the Medical Examiner's report on Gloria Crosby. She may have been up there for quite a while. We don't think he'd risk confronting us."

"You're fuckin' lying," Mail shouted. He jumped out of the chair and punched the TV off, sat down, bounced twice, picked up the remote, and punched it back on.

This was not right: he'd pulled them into Stillwater with the phony verses—he'd known that they'd look at Stillwater, but they wouldn't have gone into the city when Dunn was just outside it. They would've stayed with Dunn. Mail had been in Stillwater in the early morning hours, just after his first call to Dunn, and there'd been no cops anywhere. Unmarked cars, bullshit. He would have noticed.

But he worried about his plates: *were* they on a list somewhere?

The talking head had moved on: Davenport was gone, and the news program had gone to a room full of computer cubicles, and a group of young people gathered around a monitor. There was an air of urgency among them, like a war room.

The reporter was saying, ". . . is also the owner of a company that makes police and security-oriented computer training software. He has placed those resources at the command of the department, for the duration of the hunt for Andi Manette and her children. A working group of gaming and software experts anticipated the kidnapper's moves, including the possibility of a booby trap . . ."

What?

". . . believe they are closing in on the kidnapper or kidnappers . . ."

"That's bullshit," Mail said. But as he watched the video of the group crouched over their screens, he envied them. Good equipment, good group. They were all dressed informally, and two of the men were holding oversized coffee mugs. They probably all went out at night for pizza and beer and laughed.

The reporter was saying, ". . . but everybody just calls her by her last name, Ice." A startlingly attractive young woman with a punk haircut and a nose ring grinned out at Mail and said, "We've almost had him twice. Almost. And it's really a rush. I never worked with the cops before—I mean, except for Lucas— and it's pretty interesting. Totally better'n programming some pinball game or something. Totally."

"Do you think you'll get him?" the reporter asked.

Ice nodded. "Oh, yeah, if the cops don't get him first 'cause of some routine f—— mistake." She'd been about to say fuck-up, Mail thought. And he liked her. "Right now, over there"—she pointed at two women huddled over key- boards—"we're keying in everything we know about the guy, and we know quite a bit. We include a list of all the possible suspects, you know, like profiles of previous offenders from the police department, Andi Manette's patients, and so on. Not too long from now, we'll push a button and some names'll come out, cross-referenced by the other things we know. I'd bet my [beep] that our guy's name's like totally on the list."

When the story ended, Mail went into the kitchen and pulled out a phone book, looked up Davenport's company. He found it on University Avenue, in Minneapolis, down in the old warehouse and rail yard district west of Highway 280. Huh. Probably cops all over the place.

Back in the front room, a different talking head was going on about a troop movement in the Middle East, and Mail picked up the remote and surfed.

Ice came up again—Channel Three. "The guy has shown a certain crude intelligence, so we think it's possible that he wore a wig or colored his hair during the actual attack. One of the witnesses mentioned that his hair didn't look quite right. If he's really dark-haired, he'd look more like this . . ."

The TV went to a composite. Mail was riveted: the computer composite didn't look exactly like him, but it was close enough. And they knew about the van, and about the gaming.

He nibbled nervously on a thumbnail. Maybe these people really did amount to something.

This Ice chick: she was as good as Andi Manette. He'd like to try her sometime.

But Davenport and this computer operation . . . something should be done.

ANDI AND GRACE had lost their grip on passing time: Andi tried to keep them alert but found that more and more they were sleeping between Mail's visits, huddled on the mattress, curled like discarded fetuses.

Andi had lost count of the assaults. Mail was becoming increasingly violent and increasingly angry. After the episode with the witch-woman, Mail had beaten her with her arms overhead, and she'd been unable to protect herself; that night, she'd found blood in her urine.

She was disappointing him, now, but she didn't know what he had expected and so couldn't do anything about it. He had begun talking to Grace—a word or two, a sentence—when he took Andi out and put her back in. Andi could feel his interest shifting.

So could Grace, who hid from it, in sleep. And sometimes, in nightmares, she'd groan or whimper. Andi first held her, then tried to cover her own ears, then got angry at the girl for her fear, then was washed at guilt because of her anger, and held the girl, and then she got angry again . . .

When they talked, Andi had little to suggest. "If he takes you, wet yourself. Just . . . pee. That's supposed to turn off a lot of people like this."

"God, mom . . ." Grace's eyes pleaded with her to do something: a nightmare of Andi's own, but she couldn't wake from it.

THE NAIL IN the overhead beam was perhaps half-exposed, and was as unmovable as before. They'd given up working on it, but when Andi rolled onto her back, she could see the nail head glowing faintly in the dark wood. A reproach . . .

She and Grace hadn't spoken for two hours when Grace, exhausted but unable to sleep, rolled from her left side to her right, and a spring-tensioner broke in the mattress. The spring pushed up into the pad that covered it, and thrust a small, uncomfortable bump into Grace's cheek.

"God," was all Grace said.

Andi: "What?" She rolled onto her back and looked up at the light bulb. Sooner or later, it'd burn out, she thought, and they'd be in the dark. Would that be better? She tried to think.

"Something broke in the mattress," Grace said. She pushed herself up with one hand and punched the bump with the other hand. "It makes a bump."

Andi turned her head to look: the bump looked like somebody were gently trying to push a thumb through the pad. "Just move over . . ." Then, suddenly, she sat up. "Grace—there's a spring in there."

Grace said, "So?"

"So a spring is as good as a nail."

Grace looked at her, then at the mattress, and some of the dullness seemed to lift from her face. "Can we get one out?"

"I'm sure."

They crawled off the mattress, flipped it over, and tried to scratch through the fabric. The fabric was as tough as leather; Andi broke a nail without even damaging it.

"We're trying to go too fast," Grace said. "We've got to go slow, like with the nail. Let me chew on it."

Grace chewed on it forever—for five minutes—then Andi chewed on it for another two, and finally cut through. The hole was small, but with a little worrying, they opened it enough that Grace could get a finger through. Tugging on the hole, she started to split the fabric, and then Andi could get fingers from both hands through at once, and she ripped a two-foot hole in the bottom of the mattress.

The springs were coiled steel, both tied and sewn in. They took another twenty minutes working one free, using their teeth.

"Got it," Andi said, lifting it out of the hole. Grace took it, turned it in her hands. The spring had a sharp, nipped-off tip. She used it to pick at the stitching around another spring, and in a minute had the second one free.

"I bet we could get the nail out with these," Grace said, looking up at the overhead. Her face was grimy, with dirt grimed into wrinkles around her eyes.

"We could try—but let's see what happens when we stretch these things out. Maybe we won't need it." Andi rubbed the end of the spring on an exposed granite rock in the wall, the concrete floor: after a moment she looked at it, and then at Grace. "It works," she said. "We can sharpen them."

A moment later, they heard the feet on the floor above. "Back in the mattress," Andi snapped. They put the springs back in the hole, flipped the mattress over, shoved it against the wall, curled up on it.

Grace's back was to Andi, so she whispered to the wall, "Be nice to him. Maybe he won't hurt you."

"I . . . can't be," Andi whispered. "When he takes me out there, something turns off."

"Try," Grace pleaded. "If he keeps beating you, you'll die."

"I'll try," Andi said. As the steps got closer, she whispered, "Head down. No eye contact."

24

ROUX HAD HER feet up in the half-dark of her office. She was looking pensively out at the night street, the glow of her cigarette like a firefly.

"I made nice with Stillwater," she said without turning her head.

"Thanks." Lucas popped the top on a Diet Coke and sat down. "What about Dunn? Are the feds gonna charge him with anything?"

"They're making noises, but they won't. Dunn's already talking with Washington," she said. She blew a smoke ring toward her curtains.

"We should have known that it was too easy—that Mail was jerking us around," Lucas said. "By the way, I don't know if Lester told you, but Crosby was killed before she ever got to the loft. We didn't kill her."

"He told me. You looked great on the tube, by the way. You almost might've been telling the truth, about figuring out the trap business," Roux said.

"The feds are going along," Lucas said.

"Not much choice. If they don't, they look like fools." Roux turned to tamp the cigarette out in an ashtray, fumbled another one out of the pack, and lit it with a plastic lighter. "Are you sure we're looking for this Mail guy?"

"Yeah. Pretty sure," Lucas said.

"But you don't want to go out with it."

"I'm afraid it might trigger him. If we put his actual face on the air, he'd have to run for it. He wouldn't leave anybody behind."

"Huh." Roux tapped ashes off the cigarette. "I could use something that would look like progress."

"I don't have anything like that."

"Mail's name is gonna get out," she said.

"Yeah, but maybe not for a day or two. I don't see it going much longer than that."

"I wonder if she's still alive? Manette."

"I think so," Lucas said. "When he kills her, we won't hear from him any more. There wouldn't be any point. As long as he's fucking with us, as long as he's calling me, she's alive. And I think one of the girls."

"Christ, I'm tired," she said.

"Tell me," Lucas said. He yawned. "I'm sleeping at the company tonight. On a cot."

"Who's with you?"

"Intelligence guys. And Sloan is over there tonight."

"You still think he'll come in?"

"If he's watching TV, he might. He'll be curious. And in the meantime, we're trying to nail down his friends."

A FEW CLOUDS had come through in the late evening and dropped just enough rain to clear the air. Now they'd gone, and the brighter stars were visible through the ground lights. Lucas got the car and cut across town to University Avenue. He noticed a van in his rearview mirror and thought about it: there were tens of thousands of vans in the Twin Cities. If Mail showed up at the company during the day, and they flooded the area with squads, as they were planning, how many vans would be in the net? A hundred? A hundred might be manageable. But what if it were five hundred, or a thousand?

Maybe the techies at the office had some kind of statistics software that would tell him how many vans he could expect in, say, a ten-minute period in a square mile of the city. Would the density of vans be higher in an industrial area than in a suburb?

He was still mulling it over when he pulled into a Subway shop off University. He could see two young sandwich makers through the front window, both red-haired, maybe twins. Nobody else was in the shop. He yawned, went inside. The place smelled of pickles and relish; the clean, watery odor of lettuce mingled with the yeast smell of bread.

"Give me a foot-long BMT on white, everything but the jalapeos," he said.

One of the redheads had disappeared into the back. The other started working on the sandwich. Lucas leaned on the counter and yawned again and turned his head. A van was parked across the street. As Lucas turned his head, the taillight flickered. Somebody inside the dark vehicle had stepped on the brake pedal. The van looked like the one he'd seen in his rearview mirror.

"Hey, kid," Lucas said, turning back to the sandwich man. "I'm a cop and I've got to make a cop call. I don't want you to look up while I'm talking. Just keep working on the sandwich, huh?"

The kid didn't look up. "What's going on?"

"There's a van across the street, and it might be trouble. I'm gonna call in a squad car to check. Hand me one of those large root beer cups and keep working on the sandwich."

"I'm almost done," the kid said, glancing up at Lucas.

"Make another one. Same thing. Don't look out the window."

Lucas carried the root beer cup to the soda machine, where he was out of sight, took the cellular phone out of his pocket, and called in. "This is Davenport. I've got a van tailing me out to a Subway on University Avenue, I need a couple of cars here quick." He gave the dispatcher the address and asked that the cars come in at the corners on either side of the van. "Get one guy out of each car to walk to the corner on foot. Let me know when they're in position, and I'll come out."

"Hang on." The dispatcher was back fifteen seconds later. "Two cars on the way, Lucas. They'll be there in a minute or a little more. Stay on, and we'll let you know."

"Do they know what they're supposed to do?"

"Yes. They'll wait until they see you moving out of the Subway."

The kid was finishing the second sandwich when Lucas moved back to the counter with the cup full of cellular telephone.

"We gonna get robbed?" the kid asked, keeping his head down.

"I don't think so," Lucas said. "I think this is something else."

"Been robbed twice, this place has," the kid said. "I wasn't here. My brother was."

"Just give them the money," Lucas said, handing the kid a ten-dollar bill.

"That's what everybody says." The kid handed him some change, and the cellular scratched from the cup. Lucas put it to his face and said, "Say that again?"

"We're all set."

"I'm on my way out."

A HELL OF A WAY TO END IT, Lucas thought as he walked toward the entrance. He was tight: something was wrong at the van. Something was about to happen. Anyone who had been on the streets would have seen it, would have felt it coming.

At the door, the sandwich bag in one hand and the cup and cellular phone in the other, he paused, put his hand in his pocket as though fumbling for car keys, and checked the van. It was older, with rusted-out holes on the fenders, side panels, and around the taillights. The cup said something to him, and he put it to his mouth. "What?"

"Two men just got out of the other side of the vehicle where you can't see them. They may be armed."

"Okay." Two men?

Lucas pushed through the door and started toward the Porsche. He was halfway to the car when the two men came around the back of the car and started toward him. One was tall and thin, with a thin goatee; the other short and muscular, with long, heavy arms. The tall one wore a thin cotton jacket; the short one wore a high school letter jacket without a letter. They were pointing toward him, and he thought: *A mugging? Maybe nothing to do with Mail?*

They were twenty yards away and walking fast, hands in their pockets, looking at him, cutting him off from the car. Lucas stopped suddenly, and they changed direction toward him, and he stooped and put the sandwiches on the blacktop and drew his pistol in the same motion, pointed it at them.

"Police. Stop right there. Get your hands in the air, get your hands up."

And two uniformed cops came running in from behind, guns drawn, and one shouted, "Police."

The van tried to leave—the driver, unseen behind the dark glass, cranked the engine, gunned it forward, and a squad popped out of the street halfway down the block, and paused. The van driver stopped, then pulled to the side of the street. The two men in the street were looking around, uncertainly, and one pulled his hands from his pockets slowly and said, "What? What do you want?" The other slowly lifted his hands.

"On the ground," Lucas shouted. "C'mon, you know the routine: on the ground."

And they knew. They dropped to their knees, then lay on the ground with their hands behind their heads.

Lucas moved in close and asked, "Is that Mail in the van?"

"Don't got no mail," the taller of the two men said. "What're you doing to us?"

"You know what the fuck I'm talking about," Lucas said harshly. "You've got Andi Manette and her daughters, and if we don't find out real fuckin' quick where they're at, we're gonna turn you over to the feds. The federal penalty for kidnapping is the electric chair, my fine friends."

The shorter man now turned his eyes up. He was scared and puzzled. "What? What're you talking about?"

The two cops on foot had arrived, while the two squads boxed the van. "Cuff 'em," Lucas said.

He walked down to the van, where the driver was slowly climbing out, keeping his hands in sight. He was black. Lucas said, "Shit," and walked back to the two men on the ground. The uniforms had frisked them and had come up with a Davis .32 and a can of pepper gas.

"So what are we doing?" asked one of the uniforms, a sergeant named Harper Coos.

"Aw, they were gonna mug me," Lucas said. "Probably picked up on the car. I thought it might be the other thing."

The cops at the van called, "We got a gun."

"Run 'em, and if you can do a gun charge, do it," Lucas said. "Otherwise, you're gonna have to cut them loose. I never gave them a chance to actually start mugging me."

"Too bad," Coos said.

"Yeah," Lucas said. "Fuckheads had me excited."

THERE WERE A half-dozen cars in the parking lot outside the company, and almost every light in the building was turned on.

"Bring me a sandwich?" The voice floated down out of the sky.

"Who's that?" Lucas looked up, but with the brightly lit windows couldn't see anything in the dark along the roof line.

"Haywood."

"I got an extra sub."

"I'd pay a hundred bucks for a sub."

"I'll run it right up."

"How about, uh, three bucks? Which is what I got."

"You can owe the ninety-seven," Lucas said.

Sloan and three young programmers were staring at a single screen, when one of the programmers saw Lucas come in. He prodded the guy working the keyboard, who turned and said, "Ah. Hi." The screen in front of him went blank.

"Hey. I'm gonna run this sub up on the roof. What you got going?"

"Um, just messing around."

"Show him," said Sloan. "He'll probably make another million with it."

"Yeah, show me," said Lucas, walking over to the group.

The programmers were all grinning at the guy in the chair, who shrugged and started tapping on keys. "You know those screen-savers? The flying toasters, and the tropical fish that swim around the screen, and all that?"

"Yeah."

"And you know how some of the magazines put out, uh, pinups as screen-savers?"

"Yeah."

"Well . . ." A pinup appeared on the screen, one leg lifted coyly, but her almost impossibly perky breasts in full view.

"Yeah?" Lucas waited. The woman was pretty but nothing special.

Until her breasts took off and began flying around the screen on their own, like the flying toasters.

"Flying hooters—Davenport Simulations' answer to the Flying Toasters," the kid said.

"If Davenport Simulations' name appears anywhere on this product, I'll be forced to take out my gun and kill you all," Lucas said.

"Some people might feel it's in poor taste," the kid in the chair conceded.

"Does this mean you wouldn't be interested in the swimming pussys?" asked Sloan.

"I'll pass," Lucas said.

He started away and then turned. "What does Ice think about these things?"

The programmer in the chair shuddered: "She doesn't know. If she knew, she'd hunt us down and kill us like vermin."

"Which reminds me," said one of the others. "She called and asked if you were around. She said she'd try you at the police department."

"When was this?"

The other man shrugged. "Ten, fifteen minutes ago. She's at home—I got her number." He handed Lucas a slip of paper.

"Okay." Lucas stuck the paper in his pocket and walked through the back to the stairs, took them to the second floor, then on up a shorter flight to the roof.

HAYWOOD WAS PACING the perimeter of the building when Lucas came through the roof door.

"Anything?"

"A bunch of juvie skaters coming and going, that's about it," the cop said. He was wearing a black, long-sleeved shirt and blue jeans, with a black-and-green Treebark camo face mask. He'd be invisible from the street. "There's a little coke getting served outside the Bottle Cap, down on the next block."

"Nothing new there," Lucas said.

THE NIGHT WAS pleasant, cool, with the stars brighter away from the heavy lights of the loop. Lucas handed him a sandwich and they sat on the wall along the edge of the roof and unwrapped them. Haywood alternately chewed and scanned the streets with a pair of Night Mariner glasses, not saying much.

Lucas finished his sub, then took the cellular phone and the note from Ice out of his pocket and punched the number in. She answered on the second ring.

"Ms. Ice, this is Lucas Davenport."

"Mr. Davenport, Lucas." She sounded a little out of breath. "I think somebody is here. Looking at me. At my house."

25

ICE LIVED IN a brick two-story in St. Paul's Desnoyer Park, a few blocks from the Mississippi. Only the upper floor was lit: when Del touched the doorbell, he said, without looking back, "Nothing."

Lucas was in the back of Del's van, invisible behind the tinted glass, a radio in one hand, a phone in the other. His .45 was on the floor; he could see almost nothing in the dark. Behind them was a hurricane fence, and on the other side, the Town and Country Club golf course. "The guy on the porch can't see anything," he said into the phone.

"Should I go down?" Ice asked.

"No, no, just wait. He'll be up, if the door's open."

"It should be . . ."

"Hang on," Lucas said to Ice. And to Del, on the radio, "Go on in. Straight ahead to the white door, through it, then a hard right up the stairs."

"Jesus, I love this shit," Del said. He was wearing a Derby hat, a white shirt pulled out at the waist, pants that were too large and too short, and a cotton jacket. A guitar case was slung over his shoulder. In the dark, from a distance, he might pass for a musician in his twenties. "I'm going in."

Del pushed through the front door, his right hand crooked awkwardly in front of his belly. He was holding a Ruger .357, trying to keep it out of sight from the street.

When he disappeared into the house, Lucas crawled to the other side of the van and looked out, then quickly checked the street through the front and rear windows. There were only a few lights on. Nothing moved on the street. Lights went on, then off, in Ice's house. Then Del's voice burped from the radio. "I'm at the stairs. Not a sound. I'm on my way up."

Lucas said into the phone, "He's coming up," and to himself, *He's gone . . .*

MAIL HADN'T DECIDED what to do about Ice. Actually, he thought, he'd like to date her. They'd go well together. But that didn't seem possible, not anymore. He was beginning to feel the pressure, to feel the sides of the bubble collapsing upon him. He was beginning to think beyond Andi Manette and her body.

When he became aware of it—became aware of the barely conscious planning for "afterwards"—a kind of depression settled on him. He and Andi were working something out: a relationship.

If he moved on, something would have to be done about her and the kid. He'd started working through it in his mind. The best way to do it, he thought, would be to take Andi out, and upstairs, and out in the yard, and shoot her. There'd be no evidence in the house, and he could throw the body in the cistern. Then the kid: just go down, open the door, and do it. And after a while, he could dump some junk into the cistern—there was an old disker he could drag over, and other metal junk that nobody would want to take out. Then, when somebody else rented the place, even if they looked in the cistern, there'd be no attempt to clean it out. Just fill it up with dirt and rebuild.

Getting close to the time, he thought.

But it depressed him. The last few days had been the most fulfilling he'd known. But then, he was young: he could fall in love again.

With somebody like Ice.

Mail was parked a block from Ice's house, in the driveway of a house with a For Sale sign in the front yard. He'd been driving by when a saleswoman pulled the drapes on the picture window so she could show the view to a young couple from Cedar Rapids. Mail looked in: there was no furniture in the place. Nobody living there. When the saleswoman left, he pulled into the driveway, all the way to the garage, and simply sat and watched the lights in Ice's house. He knew the layout of the neighborhood from fifteen minutes circling the golf course. If he wanted, he could probably get down the alley and come up from the back of the house, and maybe force the back door.

But he wasn't sure he wanted that. He just wasn't sure what he was doing—but Ice's image was in his mind.

He was still waiting when the guitar player arrived in a blue minivan. And he was waiting when the guitar player left with Ice. An odd time to leave, he thought.

He followed them, staying well back.

ICE AND DEL came down the sidewalk together, Ice wearing a Korean War–era Army field jacket and tights, smoking a cigarette. She flicked the cigarette into the street, blew smoke, and climbed in the passenger side of the van.

As they headed across the interstate back toward the company offices, she half-turned to talk to Lucas. And he thought how young she was: her unmarked face, the way she bounced in the front seat, out of excitement, engagement.

She was emphatic. "Three people saw him, two of them out front, one of them around by the alley; he was going through in a van, and Mr. Turner, who's the guy behind me, saw his face up close. When I showed him the composites we made, he picked out the one where we aged Mail's face. He was sure. He said Mail was the guy in the alley."

"He saw you on television," Lucas said. "I thought he'd go after the company. I didn't think he'd come after you in person."

"Why me?"

" 'Cause of the way you look," Del said bluntly, after a couple seconds of silence. "We've got an idea of the kind of kid he is. We thought he might go for you."

"That's why the TV people were all over you," Lucas said. "You sorta stand out in a crowd of techies."

She looked Lucas full in the face. "Is that why you were so happy to have me involved?"

Lucas started to say no, but then nodded and said, "Yeah."

"All right," she said, turning back to the front. He saw her eyes in the rearview mirror. "Is this a good time to ask for a raise?"

Lucas grinned and said, "We can talk about it."

"How come you didn't come in with Del?" Ice asked.

"He knows who I am, that I write games," Lucas said. "And he probably knows me by sight. I think I actually ran into the sonofabitch the day after the kidnapping."

"At least he's sniffing around," Del said.

"Yeah," Lucas nodded, looking out the back windows. Another van was back there—and yet another was waiting at a cross street. "He's out there."

"Good thing I had a gun," Ice said.

Lucas turned back to her and said, "What?"

Ice dug into her waistband and came up with a blued .380 automatic, turned it in the dome light, worked the safety.

"Gimme that," Lucas said, irritated, putting his hand out.

"Fuck you, pal," she said. She pushed it back in her waistband. "I'm keeping it."

"You're asking for trouble," Lucas said. "Tell her, Del."

Del shrugged: "I just bought one for my old lady. Not a piece of shit like that, though." He looked at Ice. "If you're gonna have one, get something bigger."

Ice shook her head: "I like this one. It's cute."

"You gotta shell in the chamber?"

"Nope."

"Good. You don't have to worry about blowing your nuts off, carrying it in your pants like that."

MAIL STAYED A full two blocks back, following them up St. Anthony to Cretin, across the interstate to University. When they turned left, he let them go.

Davenport's, he thought. *She's going back to work.*

He wondered who the musician was—a full-time relationship, or just a ride?

He'd like to take a look at Davenport's, but it simply smelled wrong. Of course, maybe he was simply being paranoid. Mail laughed at himself. He *was* paranoid; everybody said so. Still, if he had to look at Davenport's, it might be a good idea to make a test run. To send in a dummy.

He thought, *I wonder where Ricky Brennan is . . .*

26

HAYWOOD CALLED FROM the roof. "We got somebody coming in."

Lucas had been on the cot for an hour, half-wrapped in an unzipped sleeping bag, his mind moving too restlessly for sleep. He kicked the bag off, groped for the radio. "Coming in? What do you mean?"

"I mean there's this asshole down there along the tracks, coming straight in, kind of dodging in and out like he's in fuckin' Vietnam. But he's coming here. I can see his face, he's looking at the building."

"Stay on him," Lucas said. He stood up, flipped on the storeroom lights, and pulled on his pants. The radio burped again. Sloan asked, "We moving?"

"Maybe." Lucas called Dispatch. "You're up on the flood plan?"

"Yes." A little tension popped into the dispatcher's voice.

"I might call it," Lucas said. "On my address. Put out a preliminary call right now, get people to their staging points, but don't bring anybody in yet."

"Got it."

They'd been sleeping in a conference room, Sloan on an air mattress under the conference table, Lucas next to the door. Sloan fumbled into his pants and shirt, in the dark. "What's going on?"

Lucas had slept in his clothes, except for his jacket. He pulled on his pistol rig and said, "Got somebody coming in. Hay's watching him."

Haywood called. "He's coming up to the back of the building, boys. He's like sneaking up on the place. I think he's heading for that old loading dock . . . that's padlocked, right?"

"Yeah. He'll probably come around the dark side, going for the windows," Lucas said. "Stay on him, call him for us. We're going to plug in."

"Hate these fuckin' things," Sloan grumbled, pushing the flesh-colored radio plug into his ear. Lucas had trouble with his, finally got it in as they started down the stairs. Lucas said, "You go around the building to the left, I'll go around to the right."

"Take it easy," Sloan said. He had his piece out, pointing down his leg.

"Yeah." Lucas jacked a round into the chamber of the .45, a harsh, ratcheting noise in the tiled hallway.

"He's headed for the windows," Haywood said. His voice seemed to come from the middle of Lucas's skull. "This guy is something else. He's like tiptoeing. He looks like Sylvester the Cat sneaking up on Tweety Bird."

Lucas shook his head: his mental picture of Mail was neither funny nor stupid. "We're out," he muttered into his microphone. "We'll take him."

Sloan ran around to the left, while Lucas moved slowly to the right, the pistol up and ready. At the corner, he waited, listening. Too many cars, and a voice floating down from the doper bar: *You see that? Did you see what she did? Do that again . . .*

"He's trying the windows. I'm right over his head." Haywood spoke softly into Lucas's ear. Sloan should be ready.

Lucas stepped around the corner of the building. A man was just breaking out a corner of a window, just swinging a piece of rerod, when Lucas stepped around and shouted, "Freeze."

Sloan, coming from the other side, shouted "Police," a second later, and they both moved out from the building a step, two steps, the guy pinned between them at the point of a widening triangle. The trapped man had blond, shoulder-length hair, and Lucas thought of the first descriptions of the kidnapper. He was muscular, too—but short. His head snapped first at Lucas, and then at Sloan, then back to Lucas.

And then without a word he rushed at Sloan, lifting the rerod.

"Stop, stop . . ." Sloan and Lucas were both screaming, but the man rushed in. Lucas brought up his weapon, but the man was closing on Sloan too quickly. Sloan shot him.

There was a quick, flat muzzle flash and the man screamed, staggered, and went down, and Sloan said, "Ah, shit, ah, shit."

Lucas said to Haywood, "Get Dispatch. Tell them we got a guy down. Tell them to get an ambulance over here."

"Calling," Haywood said.

"Got it, Lucas. Ambulance on the way."

The man on the ground was rolling, holding his leg, and Lucas put his pistol away and walked over, knelt on the man's back, cuffed him, patted him, found a cheap chrome .38 and handed it to Sloan, who put it in his pocket. Then Lucas rolled the wounded man: he groaned, swore. He had a fat, round face and pale blue eyes. This was not John Mail. "Can you talk?"

"Fuckin' leg, man." The wounded man's eyes glittered with tears. "My leg's broken. I can feel the fuckin' bone."

"Ah, Jesus," Sloan said. "What a fuckin' day."

Lucas checked in the bad light and saw the spreading wet patch on the man's right thigh. "Where're the Manettes?" he asked.

"Who?" The man was frightened and seemed genuinely confused.

"Who are you? What's your name?" Lucas asked.

"Ricky Brennan."

"Why'd you come here, Ricky? Why'd you pick this place?"

"Well, man . . ." Ricky's eyes slid away from Lucas, and Lucas thought he might lose him.

"Come on, asshole," Lucas said.

"Well, this dude said I could pick up a little toot from the computer freaks. Said they had a bag of toot in the back room, like a couple ounces to keep them going all night. My fuckin' leg, man, my fuckin' leg is killing me."

"Shit," Sloan said, and he looked like he was going into shock.

Lucas got on the radio: "Janet? Flood it. I'm calling the flood."

"You got it."

Sloan sat down beside the wounded man. "Got an ambulance coming," he said.

"I'm really hurting, man."

Haywood ran up and Lucas said, "You got a flash?"

"Yeah."

Lucas pulled a folded pad of paper from his pocket, unfolded it, sorted through the composites, and found the one of Mail with dark hair.

"Is this the dude?" Lucas turned the flashlight on the paper.

Ricky was slipping away again, but the light brought him back and he focused on the paper. "Yeah. That's the dude."

"Where is he?"

"He was gonna wait in the parking ramp." He flopped an arm out. The ramp was out of sight, on the far side of the building. Lucas got back on the radio. "Janet, goddamnit, this is the real thing, he's here, somewhere. Keep them coming."

"They oughta be there, Lucas. They're already out on the perimeter with the dogs."

And then Lucas heard the sirens: fifteen or twenty of them, coming from every direction. More would be arriving later. The patrol people had decided to use the sirens in an effort to pin Mail down, to frighten him. "Tell them to look in the information packets they got tonight, and look at composite C as in Cat. That's our guy."

"C as in Cat."

Lucas bent over Ricky again. "The guy's name is John Mail, right?"

"Oh, man, my fuckin' leg."

"John Mail?"

"Yeah, man. John. I see him around. You know. I see him around and I say, 'Hey, John.' And he says 'Hey, Ricky.' And that's all. Said there was some toot over here. He seen it. My fuckin' leg, man, you got something? You got any, like, Percodan?"

"You know where he lives?"

"Oh, man, I don't even know the dude, you know, I used to see him when we were inside, he'd just be, 'Hi, Ricky.' That's all." Ricky groaned. "How about the Percodan, man?"

"Sent in a decoy, to see what we'd do," Lucas said to Sloan. Then: "You stay here. They're gonna want a statement and your gun."

To Haywood: "C'mon. You got those glasses?"

"Yeah."

And to Sloan, "You okay?"

Sloan swallowed and nodded. "First time," he said. "I don't think I like it."

"Just get him in the ambulance and don't worry about it." Lucas grinned at him and slapped him on the back. "I can't believe you shot low, you dumb shit," he said. "If you'd missed him, he'd of sunk that rerod about six inches into your skull."

"Yeah, yeah." Sloan swallowed. "Actually, I was aiming at the middle of his chest."

Lucas grinned and said, "I know how that goes. C'mon, Hay."

Lucas and Haywood ran around to the front of the building, Lucas glancing back once. Sloan was standing over Ricky, and Lucas thought he might be apologizing. He'd have to watch his friend: Sloan seemed unbalanced by the shooting. And that was in character, Lucas thought. Sloan liked the relationships that came out with cop work, the tussle. He even enjoyed an occasional fight. But he never really wanted to hurt anybody.

Then Lucas turned back toward the parking ramp and he and Haywood ran up the sidewalk together, weapons out. Far up University, they could see the roadblocks going in, and everywhere, in every direction, the red flashing lights.

"Looks like a fuckin' light-rack convention," Haywood panted.

Lucas heard him but had no time to answer: they'd rounded the office building on University and were coming up on the ramp. Lucas said, "Let's go up. Ready?"

"Outa fuckin' shape," Haywood said. "Let's go."

Lucas took the first set of steps: there were a half-dozen cars parked in the first floor, and they checked them quickly. Then up the next set of steps, and Lucas, looking over the low, concrete deck wall, saw taillights flicker to the north, headed toward the railroad tracks.

"Did you see that?"

"What?"

The lights flickered again. "There."

"Yeah. Somebody crawling along in the dark, no headlights," Haywood said.

"Sonofabitch, that's him." Lucas put the radio to his face: "I need a car at the . . . what the fuck is the name of this building? I need a car by the Hansen dairy place, first road west of the Hansen dairy trucks. We've got the suspect in sight, going down toward the elevators."

Haywood was already running across the slab and down the stairs, Lucas a few steps behind. The blacked-out vehicle was almost two blocks away, and once they were on the ground, they could no longer see it. They were running awkwardly over the uneven ground toward the grain elevator when one set of headlights caught them in the back, then another. They turned and saw two squads coming down toward them; Lucas waved them on and kept running.

When the cars caught up, Lucas pointed up ahead. "He was going under the elevator."

The driver in the lead car was a sergeant. "No way out of there," he grunted. "That's all dead end back there."

"Could he just bump it across the tracks?"

The cop shrugged. "Maybe. But we'd see him. He might be able to snake his way out alongside of them." He picked up his radio and said, "We need a car on the 280 overpass across the tracks. Put some light down onto the tracks. Where's the chopper?"

"Chopper's just leaving the airport, he'll be five minutes. We're confirming the car on the tracks."

"Get some K9 down here," Lucas said.

The sergeant said, "We called them; they're on the way." And the car pulled ahead of them, the second car close behind him. The sergeant spoke into the radio: "We need some guys north of the tracks."

"GONNA BE DARK in there," Haywood grunted as they jogged up toward the elevators.

"But once we got him, even if we only get his van, we get the VIN even if he's pulled the plates . . . then we get a name and an address."

"You're counting your chickens," Haywood said.

"First goddamn chicken we've had to count, and I'm counting the sonofabitch," Lucas said.

27

THE COP SLIPPED down the side of the building, his right hand cocked away from his body.

Carrying a gun, Mail thought. The night air was thick, cool, and moist, and the night seemed particularly dark; he couldn't see that well, but the cop was too small to be Davenport.

Still, it *had* been a trap, a rudimentary one. Mail smiled and turned to go, then slowed, turned back, lingered. Davenport's building was a block away and he felt remote from it, as though he were watching a movie. The movie was just getting good.

He'd found Ricky on a Hennepin Avenue street corner, half-drunk, his face sullen, his hair stuck together like cotton candy. He'd whispered *cocaine,* and *just a bunch of computer pussies in there,* and Ricky'd started slavering. He couldn't wait to get started.

Ricky needed drugs to function: without cocaine, speed, acid, grass, peyote, alcohol, even two or three of them at a time, the world was not right. He'd spent years on the inside and barely remembered a time where he didn't have a drug flowing through his veins—and what he remembered about that drugless state, he didn't like. He needed more dentists, he thought, people who'd say, "Here—I'll numb that up for you."

Even inside, with very strange people around—people who spoke to God, and got personal letters back—Ricky had been considered mad as a hatter.

But he could function in society, the shrinks said, so they had let him out and seemed proud of themselves when they did it. Now Ricky ate from trashcans and shit in doorways and carried a piece-of-crap revolver in his waistband. He gobbled up any pill he could beg, buy, or steal.

NOW RICKY WAS out of sight, trying the windows on the far side of the building. The cop was running along the back of the building, to the side where

Ricky was; he looked like an inmate in a prison movie, caught in a spotlight as he ran along a wall. The cop stopped at the corner, did a quick peek, pulled his head back, peeked again, ran out from the building, pointing his gun, and the shouting began, the words indistinguishable in the distance.

Again, Mail turned to go. Then he heard the gunshot, and turned back: "Sonofabitch."

He smiled again, amused; he almost laughed. What a joke. They'd shot Ricky, or Ricky had shot one of them. The cop he could see had dropped his pistol to his side and moved forward. So it *had* been Ricky.

Time to move.

He ran across the parking ramp, down a short flight of stairs, to the street. The van was already pointed into University Avenue. He'd be a mile away in a minute and a half. He unlocked the door, hopped in—he'd leave the lights blacked out for a few hundred feet—pulled up to the corner, looked right, looked left. And heard the sirens, saw the lights.

A cop car, far down the street to the left, coming in a hurry: but that was the way he wanted to go. If he turned right, he'd have to drive past Davenport's building. He didn't want to do that.

He hesitated. The cop was probably on the way to the shooting. He could wait until he passed.

Mail shifted into reverse and started to back up—but then the cop car, still six or eight blocks away, unexpectedly slewed sideways across the street. And then he saw more lights far down to his right, and then another car joining the squad blocking the street to his left.

"Motherfuckers."

He felt as though a hand had grabbed his heart and squeezed it. He'd underestimated Davenport. The building wasn't the trap. The whole goddamn area was the trap.

Headlights still off, he did a quick U-turn and rolled down the street toward a grain elevator at the end. He hadn't been down there, didn't know what to expect, but once out of the immediate neighborhood, he could work his way through back streets until he was completely clear.

A cold sweat broke on his face, and his hands held the steering wheel so tightly that they hurt. He had to break out of this.

But he couldn't see much without the lights. Strange, odd shapes, wheelless tractor trailers, loomed off to the left. Here and there, a machine with claws, like mutated, earth-moving equipment. He drove between two elevator buildings, slowed. The van dropped into a pothole seven inches deep and half as long as the van itself, then climbed out the other side. Two trailers were parked against a loading dock. Another van was tucked in between them, facing out.

Mail leaned toward the windshield, trying to see better, then rolled down the side window, trying to hear. The area smelled of milled grain, corn, maybe. He bumped along through the dark, then into a lighter patch, the light thrown from a naked bulb over an office door.

No lights on in the office, though . . .

The road ended at a gate, a gate closed and locked, with dark buildings behind it. A dead end? There'd been no dead-end sign. He backed up, found a gravel track that went east along the side of the grain elevator. Ahead, he could see the lights of a busy street, a little higher than he was, maybe up a hill? If he could work his way over there . . . But what was that?

A cop car, lights flashing, stopped on the hill, and Mail realized it was not a hill at all but an overpass. No way up, no way to the street. The track he was on went from gravel to dirt. To the left, there was nothing but darkness, like an unlit farm field. To the right, there was a line of the boxes that looked like the wheelless tractor trailers he'd seen back in the lot.

He slowed, thought about going back, looked over his shoulders, and saw the cop lights at the elevator. Had they seen him? He had to go forward.

Suddenly, a huge dark shape slid past to his left, almost soundlessly, and he jerked the van to the right.

"What?" he shouted. Frightened now, gripping the wheel, peering out into the dark. The shape made no noise, but he could feel the rumble of it: the thing had materialized from the dark, like some creature from a Japanese horror flick, like Rodan . . . and he realized it was a string of freight cars, ghosting by in the night. There was no engine attached to them. They simply glided by.

And he realized that off to his left, in the darkness that looked like a farm field, were multiple lines of railroad tracks. He could see some of them now, in the dim, ambient light, thin, steely reflections against the field of black. He couldn't see how many there were, but there were several.

The cop car on the overpass suddenly lit up, and a searchlight swung across the tracks, left to right. If it had come the other way, right to left, it might have caught him, though he was still a half-mile away. As it was, he had time to drive into a hole in a wall of the boxes that lined the track.

In between the boxes, he couldn't see at all—he had to risk the parking lights. The cop searchlight swept the field behind him, and he edged forward again, and found another row of boxes parallel to the boxes he was crossing through. Another dirt track ran between the rows of boxes, and he turned onto it. His parking lights caught a sign that said "Burlington Northern Container Yard—Trespassers Will Be Prosecuted."

Containers. Huh. The track ended when the containers did: nothing ahead but dirt and grass and the certainty of being seen. A second cop car had joined the first on the overpass, and a second searchlight popped out and probed the tracks. He could see the cops, like tiny action figures, standing along the overpass railing.

"Goddamn. Goddamn." He was caught, stuck. He reached under the seat, got his .45. The gun was not comforting: it was a big, cold lump in his hand. If he had to use it, he was dead.

He put the gun between his thighs, backed the van up until he was out of sight of the overpass, turned it off, started to get out—but the overhead light flickered and he quickly pulled the door closed. Shit. How to do this? He finally reached back, scratched the dome off the overhead light, and twisted out the bulb. Then he got out, put the gun in his pocket, and slipped down to the end of the line of boxes.

There were sirens everywhere, like nothing he'd ever heard before, not even when he was starting fires, all those years ago. The sirens didn't seem especially close, but they came from every possible direction.

"Fucked," he said, half out loud. "I'm fucked." And he kicked one of the containers. "Fucked."

He ran his hands through his hair. Had to get out. He ran back to the van, stopped for a second, then ran further down the line of containers. The container boxes were stacked two by two, end to end, in two long rows, with the track between them. In places, a container had been pulled. In a few, both containers had been pulled—like the hole he'd driven through.

In those spots, he could see out, either across the tracks, or into the neighborhood on the other side of the elevators. He found one of the double breaks and walked carefully down it, trailing his hand along the edge of the container, feeling the clumped weeds underfoot. The neighborhood on the other side of the elevator was coming awake. Lights were on all up and down the street, and he heard a man shouting. The reflections of red flashing lights bounced off the side windows of the houses. Cops all over the place.

Damnit, damnit.

They had him, or they would have him. The van, anyway.

He walked back toward it, and it occurred to him that if he backed it into one of the spaces left where a single container had been pulled, then nobody could see it unless they walked down the center track and looked into each space. If a cop simply looked down the track, the track would appear to be empty.

That might give him some time.

Mail hurried down to the truck, backed it up fifty feet, then maneuvered it into a single container space. He doubted that he'd see it again. He'd have to abandon the Roses name along with the van, and probably all his computers.

What about fingerprints? If they found the Roses name, that would be fine—but if they found his fingerprints, he'd never have any peace.

He stripped off his jacket, shirt, and t-shirt, put the shirt and jacket back on, and used the t-shirt to wipe everything he might have touched in the van. His mind was working furiously: *get the door handles, the wheel, of course, the ash tray, the seats, the glove compartment, the dashboard . . . get rid of all the paper crap on the floor.*

But then he thought: *the computers. Damn. Everything at the self-storage would have his prints. If they found the van, they'd find the storage place, and get his prints there.*

He continued wiping, working the problem in his mind. He finished inside, got out, pushed the door shut with his elbow, and started wiping outside. *The goddamn computers.*

He did the outside handles, plates, took a swipe at the wipers. He never messed with the engine, had never lifted the hood in his life, so that wasn't a problem.

And he thought: *Fire.*

If he could get back to the store, there could be a fire. A fire would do it. Ten gallons of gas, a little oil, and the computers would burn like kindling.

Even so, he couldn't take any chances. He might not get everything—they might find a print, or two. So he'd have to get lost for a while, and that meant he'd have to settle Andi Manette and the girl. He could dump them in the cistern; that'd only take a second. He felt a small, dark tug at the thought—but he'd known it was coming.

Okay. Done. He took a last swipe at the door handles, stuffed the t-shirt in his jacket pocket, and walked through the dark shadows of the containers to an opening that looked across the tracks.

With the dark jacket and the jeans, he was almost invisible in the rail yard. He started walking through the dark, one hand in front of him for balance, his feet picking the way over the rough ground. Behind him, back toward the elevator, a dog barked; then another.

A PATROL CAPTAIN arrived as Lucas was punching the driver's side window out of the van. He used a piece of paving stone to break out the glass, then reached through the broken window and popped the lock. Haywood was beside him, trying to peer through the dirty windows.

"Paper," Lucas grunted when they got the door open. A clipboard lay on the floor of the passenger side, and he picked it up. A pad of pink paper was clipped into it, with a letterhead that said "Carmody Foods."

"Got him?" the captain asked, coming up.

Lucas frowned, shook his head. "I think this belongs here . . . we oughta check it out, but we better look for another van. It's here, we saw it coming back here."

The captain walked around to the front of the van, fished around for a moment, then said, "Engine's cold."

"Then this ain't it," Lucas said. He tossed the clipboard back in the truck. "C'mon, Hay, let's go down the tracks."

"How do you want to work this, chief?" the captain asked. "It's your call."

"You run it," Lucas said. "You know how to do this shit better than I do. Just tell your people that Haywood and I'll be out there, wandering around."

Captain nodded. "You got it." He jogged away, yelling for somebody, and they heard a K9 car arrive, and a moment later, the helicopter buzzed overhead on its first pass. The elevator yard had been dark, forbidding, when Lucas and

Haywood first ran down into it. Now there were headlights everywhere, and the chopper lit up a searchlight. There were still dark areas, but there was less and less room to hide.

"That was an elevator down in Stillwater, wasn't it? Where you found the hanged girl?" Haywood asked, craning his neck to look at the elevator above them. "I wonder if there's a connection?"

"That doesn't seem . . . reasonable. That's got to be a coincidence," Lucas said.

"You don't believe in coincidences," Haywood said.

"Except when they happen," Lucas said. They were walking behind a canine officer with a leashed German shepherd. When the cop and his dog went to examine the back of the elevator, Haywood said, "What do you think?"

Lucas looked around: there were a number of buildings, ranging from small switch shacks to the huge elevators, on the near side of the tracks, and more on the far side. Another set of elevators loomed back to the west. "I doubt that he's hiding. Given the chance, he'd run. And there's no van, and all these little side tracks tend to go east. He probably picked one out and rode it as long as he could."

"There were squads up on 280 before he could've gotten through there."

"Yeah. So he's between here and there." They heard the beat and then the lights of the chopper coming in, and then a searchlight lit up the tracks beyond them and the chopper roared overhead. "Let's go down that way . . . follow the lights."

MAIL DECIDED TO cross the tracks: there was less activity on the other side, and in the growing illumination provided by the cop cars, he could see the rows of dark houses and small yards on the other side. Once in there, he could sneak away.

He started across, nearly got caught by a searchlight: they came more quickly than he'd expected, and he had to drop to his face, his hands beneath himself, to hide the flesh.

The light didn't pause but swept on, and he got to a crouch and started running again, and the light swept back and he went down again. He didn't bother to stand up the next time but simply scuttled on his hands and knees, over the rails, down the other side of the roadbed, then up the next, and across the rails. The rocks bit into his hands, but he felt more scuffed up than injured.

He was halfway across the yard when the helicopter showed up: the light tracking beneath it was fifty feet across. He watched it coming and realized that if he were caught in the chopper's light, he'd be done.

Mail got to his feet and ran, fell down, got up and ran, head down. The cop search light from the bridge flicked over and past him and he kept going, the helicopter light tracking more or less toward him, but sliding back and forth across the tracks as it came. A small shack loomed dead ahead, and he dove into the grass beside it and rolled hard against it as the searchlight burned overhead.

Even with his face turned down, the powerful light cut through the grass, dazzling him. And the light passed on.

He looked up, saw the zigzagging chopper chattering slowly toward the overpass. He got to his feet and began running again.

A cop car, lights flickering, ran through the neighborhood on the other side of the tracks, but a street or two west of him. He was running toward some kind of commercial building with trees around it. He swerved toward it; he could hide in the brush. The cops on the bridge swept him with the searchlight and he went down. A second later, the light came back, swept overhead, picking away at him. When it drifted back toward the tracks, he made it the last few feet to the trees.

And found his way blocked by water.

"No-no," he said, out loud. He couldn't catch a break.

He was in a small neighborhood park, with a pond in the middle of it. The light came back, and he dropped to his hands and knees and crawled toward the water. His hands slipped on the grass and a stench reached up to him. What? Whatever he was crawling through was slick; then a small thing moved to his right, and he realized it was a duck. He was crawling through duck shit. The light came back and he dropped into the stuff, then slithered down the bank into the chill water. And heard the shouting behind him.

THE NIGHT GLASSES were useless. They were fine in steady, low light, but the sweeping searchlights were screwing up the sensors, and Haywood put them away.

"That way," Lucas said. "Up in those containers."

They ran along the track and were quickly pinned and dazzled by the searchlights from the overpass. Lucas got on the radio, waved the lights off.

"Can't see a fuckin' thing," Haywood said. "I never been on the other end of those lights."

Lucas stepped into a hole in the line of containers, found a second row of containers with a track between them, all dark as pitch.

"If he's down there and he's got a gun, it'd be suicide to go in," Haywood said.

"Yeah." Lucas got on the radio, got the chopper. "Can you come back toward the elevator? There's a double line of containers; we want the light right down the middle."

The pilot took a minute to get lined up, then hung above them, the downwash from the rotors battering down at them as they walked up the line. A hundred feet from the end, Lucas caught an edge of chrome in a hole in the wall. He shouted "Whoa" into the radio and caught Haywood's arm, shouted, "There's the van, there's the van."

Haywood went right while Lucas went left, and the chopper moved up, found the hole, and dropped the light on it.

THE COPS WERE walking through the neighborhood, and lights were coming on. Mail could hear their voices, far away, but distinct enough: a woman yelling to a neighbor, "Is it the gas? Is it the gas?"

And the answer, "They're looking for a crazy guy."

Mail dog-paddled across the pond to a muddy point, where a weeping willow tree hung over the water. A half-dozen ducks woke and started inquisitively quacking. "Get the fuck . . ." he hissed and started out of the water. The ducks took off in a rush of wings, quacking.

Christ, if anybody heard that . . .

He crawled up on the bank, shivering—very cold now—and had started through the trees when he heard the cops coming, marked by a line of bobbing flashlights. He looked around, then back at the water, and reluctantly slipped in, his head below the cutbank under the willow.

The chill water was only about three feet deep but wanted to float him. Groping along the bank, his hand caught a willow root, and he used it to push himself down and stabilize. He turned his face to the bank and pulled the dark jacket over his head.

"Probably breathing through a straw," a cop said, the voice young and far away.

"Yeah, like you're talking through your ass," said another, equally young. "Jesus, there's goose shit all over the place."

"Duck shit," the first voice said. Farm boy. "Goose shit's bigger; looks like stogies."

A third voice: "Hey, we got a shit expert."

"Somebody ought to kick through those bushes . . ."

"I'll get it . . . ?"

Mail bowed his head as the footsteps got closer. Then the cop began kicking through the brush overhead. The cop came all the way down to the willow tree: Mail could have reached out of the water and grabbed his leg. But the cop just shined his light out over the water and then headed back for the others, calling, "Nothing here."

Mail was on the same side of the pond as the cops. When they'd moved on, he dog-paddled across the pond and crawled out, picking up more duck shit. Now he began shivering uncontrollably. Cold; he'd never been this cold. He crawled straight ahead, toward the corner of the commercial building, the rubble on the ground cutting into his hands. He pushed into a clump of brush, where he stopped, and pulled his legs beneath him, trying to control the shivering. His hair hung across his forehead, and he pushed it back with one hand; he smelled like duck shit.

Across the tracks, the helicopter was hovering in one spot, and three cop cars were bumping along the line of containers.

"Found it," he said out loud. They'd already found the goddamn van. The barking started again: were they tracking him with dogs? Jesus.

More dogs were barking through the neighborhood, aroused by all the cops walking through. He had to move. Had to get out of here. He crawled back through the bushes, finally stood up and looked around. The cops seemed to have set up a perimeter, with more cops sweeping the area inside of it. He'd have to cross it, sooner or later.

He thought: *Sewer.*

And dismissed it. He didn't know anything about sewers. If he crawled down a sewer, he'd probably die down there. And the idea of the sewer walls closing in . . .

He'd always been claustrophobic, one reason he'd never go back to the hospital. The hospital didn't fuck around with beatings; they knew how to really punish you. His claustrophobia had come out early in his stay, and they'd introduced him to the Quiet Room . . .

Half-crouching, Mail crossed a driveway and climbed a short fence into the first yard. He crossed the yard, ran behind a house with several lights on, and down a line of bridal-wreath bushes, where he crawled over a wire fence, crossed the next yard, and climbed the fence again. He crossed the next yard, came to another fence, and heard the dog. Large dog, woofing along in the night at the other end of the yard. Take a chance? The dog smelled him at the same time he heard it, turned, and rushed the fence where he was hiding, snarling, slavering for him. Big black-and-tan body, white teeth like a tiger's. No way.

Mail went back, crawled over a fence, and turned left, looking for another way.

A cop car flashed past, light rack spinning; dogs were barking everywhere, now, a mad chorus of mutts.

This could take a while . . .

LUCAS CALLED IN the plate number on the van, and the VIN.

Thirty seconds later, on the radio: "Lucas: we've got an address down in Eagan."

28

THE BEDSPRINGS WERE too flexible to make decent weapons. They'd hoped for something like an icepick, but the springs would not fully uncurl. When pressed against anything resistant, they flexed.

But if they couldn't get icepicks from the springs, they got two fat, three-inch-long needles, honed on the granite rocks in the fieldstone walls.

Grace stood on the Porta-Potti and began picking at the nail: "Lots better," she told Andi. "This works great."

She picked for ten minutes and Andi picked for ten minutes more, then Grace started again. Grace was working on it when it finally came free. She thought it moved under the spring-needle, and grabbed it between a thumb and forefinger. It turned in her fingers, and she held tighter and put weight on it, felt it twist again.

Grace said, breathlessly, "Mom, it's coming. It's coming out." And she pulled it free, like a tooth.

Andi put a finger to her lips. "Listen."

Grace froze, and they listened. But there were no thumps, no footsteps, and Andi said, "I thought I heard something."

"I wonder where he is?" Grace looked nervously at the door. Mail had been gone a long time.

"I don't know. We just need a little more time." Andi took the nail, sat on the mattress, and began to hone it on a granite pebble. The nail left behind what looked like tiny scratches in the rock, but were actually whisper-thin metal scrapings. "Next time he comes, we have to do it," she said. "He'll kill me, soon, if we don't. And when he kills me, he'll kill you."

"Yes." Grace nodded. She'd thought about it.

Andi stopped honing the nail to look at her daughter. Grace had lost ten pounds. Her hair was stuck together in strings and ropes; the skin of her face was waxy, almost transparent, and her arms trembled when she stood up. Her dress was tattered, soiling, torn. She looked, Andi thought, like an old photograph of a Nazi prison-camp inmate.

"So: we do it." She went back to scraping the nail, then turned it in her hand. The rust was gone from the tip, and the wedge-shaped nail point was fining down to a needletip.

"What we have to do is figure out a . . . scenario for attacking him," she said. Grace was sitting at the end of the mattress, her knees pulled up under her chin. She had a bruise on her forearm. Where'd she gotten that? Mail hadn't touched her, yet, though the last two times he'd assaulted Andi, he hadn't bothered to dress before he pushed her back in the cell. He was displaying for Grace. Sooner or later, he'd take her . . .

She put a finger to her lips. "Listen."

There was nothing. Grace whispered, "What?"

"I thought I heard him."

Grace said, "I don't hear anything."

They listened for a long time, tense, the fear holding them silent; but nobody came. Finally, Andi went back to honing the nail, the ragged *zzzt zzzt zzzt* the only sound in the hole.

She had Mail in her mind as she honed it. They'd been in the hole for almost five days. He had attacked her . . . she didn't know how many times, but probably twenty. Twenty? Could it be that many?

She thought so.

She honed the nail, thinking, with each stroke, *For John Mail. For John Mail . . .*

29

LUCAS AND HAYWOOD went past Lucas's building at seventy— Sloan still standing in the lot, now in the center of a circle of plainclothes cops; an ambulance had hauled Ricky away—slipped onto Highway 280 and then I-94, east to I-35E, south through St. Paul, Haywood hanging on the safety belt, three cars trailing, all with lights.

A dispatcher came back. "Eagan's in. They're pulling a search warrant right now and they ought to have it by the time you're there."

"Patch me through—get them to pull us in there."

The directions from Eagan burped out over the radio and they crossed the Mississippi like a flock of big-assed birds, jumped off on Yankee Doodle Road, killed the flashers, and headed east.

"That's them," Haywood said. He was holding on to the safety belt with one hand and had the other braced on the dashboard. Below them, in a shallow valley, two squad cars and a gray sedan were lined up at the curb. Lucas pulled over next to the sedan and hopped out. A man in a suit hustled around the nose of the car.

"Chief Davenport?"

"Danny Carlton. I'm the chief out here." Carlton was young, with curly red hair and a pink face. "We got your search warrant, but I don't think you're gonna be happy."

"Yeah?"

Carlton pointed down the road, where it rose along the opposite wall of the valley. "The place you're looking for is right up there. But it's one of them self-storage places. You know, like two hundred rental garages."

"Damnit." Lucas shook his head: this sounded unlikely. "We have to check it, we can't fuck around."

THE SELF-STORAGE WAREHOUSE was a complex of long, one-story, concrete-block buildings, the long sides of the buildings each faced with twenty white garage doors. The whole place was surrounded by an eight-foot chain-link fence topped with barbed wire. A small blue gatehouse stood next to the only gate through the fence. An elderly man, pale, worried, met them at the gate. He carried a .38 that looked older than he was.

"No problem," he said when they gave him the warrant. "Roses, that'd be fifty-seven."

"Have you seen him?" Lucas asked.

"Hasn't come through here, not tonight."

Lucas showed him a copy of the computer-aged Mail photo. "Is that him?"

The guard held it under a light, tipping his head back the better to use his bifocals, stuck out a lip, raised his eyebrows, then handed it back. "That's him. Got him to a T," he said.

THE GARAGE DOOR was padlocked, but one of the Eagan cops had a pair of cutters and chopped the hasp. Lucas knocked it away, and with another cop, raised the door.

"Computers," Haywood said.

He found the light and flipped it on. The room was lined with tables, and the computers were stacked on them, dozens of beige cases and sullen, gray-screen monitors. Under the tables were plastic clothes baskets full of parts—disk drives, modems, sound and color cards, a mouse with its cord wrapped around it, miscellaneous electronic junk.

Nothing human.

A desk and an old cash register sat off to the left. Lucas walked over to the desk, pulled open a drawer. Scrap paper, a single ball-point. He pulled open another, and found stick-on labels, an indelible pen missing its cap, a dusty yellow legal pad. The middle drawer had another pencil and three X-Men comics in plastic sleeves.

"Tear it apart," Lucas said to the Minneapolis cops crowding up behind them. "Any piece of paper—anything that might point at the guy. Checks, receipts, credit card numbers, bills, anything."

The Eagan chief lit a cigarette, looked around, and said, "This is him, huh?"

"Yeah. This is him."

"I wonder where *they* are?"

"So do I," Lucas said.

He stepped outside and tipped his head back, and the Eagan chief thought for a moment that he was sniffing the wind. "I bet they're close—I bet this is the closest self-storage to his house. Goddamnit. Goddamnit, we're close."

The guard had come along out of curiosity, but when not much happened, started tottering back to the gatehouse. Lucas walked after him. "Hey, wait a minute."

The guard turned. "Huh?"

"You see this guy come and go? You ever see him spend any time here?"

The guard looked slowly left and right, as if checking for eavesdroppers. "He runs a store here on weekends. All kinds of long-haired kids running around."

"A store?"

The Eagan chief had come up behind him. "It's illegal, but you see it quite a bit, now," he said. "Part-time shops, nobody talks to the IRS, no sales tax. They call them flea markets, or garage sales, but you know—they're not."

"Does he have any employees? Any regulars?"

The guard touched his lips with his middle and index fingers, thinking, scratched his ass with the other hand, and finally shook his head. "Not that one. The guy in the next, uh, spot, sells lawnmowers 'n' hedgetrimmers and stuff. He might know."

"Where's he?"

"I got a list."

Lucas followed him back to the gate shack, where the guard fumbled under a counter top and finally produced a list of names and telephone numbers.

"What's under Roses' name? What number?"

The old man ran a shaky index finger down the list, came to ROSE, and followed it across to a blank space. "Ain't got one. Supposed to."

"Gimme the other guy's name, the lawnmower guy."

THE COP WASN'T going to leave.

Mail lay behind a bush thirty feet away and watched him. The cop checked his shotgun, then checked it again—playing with it, flipping a shell out, catching it in mid-air, shoving it back in—hummed to himself, spoke into a radio a couple of times, paced back and forth, and once, looking quickly around first, moved up close to a maple tree and took a leak.

But he wasn't going anywhere. He idled back and forth, watching the cars come and go at the end of the block, turned the shotgun like a baton. Whistled a snatch of a Paul Simon song . . .

The cop was at the thinnest spot along the line, a place where the street made an odd little curve before straightening again, as though it had been built around a stump. The curve had the effect of changing the angles, pushing out toward the next set of lawns.

If he could just get across. He thought about using the .45, but if the cop tried to fight him for it, or went for his gun, and he had to shoot—that'd be the end. If he was going to take the cop out, he had to be quick and silent and sure.

Mail pushed himself back, a foot at a time, until he reached the back edge of the house, where he got to his hands and knees. He couldn't see much, but he could see the dark shape of some kind of yard shed. He scurried over to it, looked around quickly, pulled open the door, and slid inside.

And felt instantly safe with the roof over his head. Nobody could see in, no light would catch him. The shed was full of yard tools and smelled of dead autumn leaves and old premix-gasoline. Groping in the dark, he found a couple of rakes, a hoe, a shovel. He could try the shovel, but it was awkward, and he groped along the floor for something else. He found a short piece of two-by-four, thought about it, decided he liked the shovel better. Moved on, found two snow shovels, a pair of hedge clippers; he touched a gas can, smelled the gas on his fingers; and then, in the corner, a spade handle.

The handle had broken off just above where the blade had been. He hefted it, made a short chopping motion. Okay. This would work.

He didn't want to go back outside, but he had to. He slipped outside, scrambled back to the corner, and eased down the side of the house to the bush where he'd watched the cop. The cop was still there, hat off, rubbing his head. Then he put the cap back on, said something to his radio, got something back, and whistled the snatch of Paul Simon again.

Like he had the song on his mind, Mail thought.

The cop turned, looking away from Mail, drifted toward the maple tree where he'd taken the leak. Mail tensed, and when the cop's head was behind the tree, stood up and padded toward the tree, slowly at first, but more quickly as the cop came out from behind it, his back still turned.

The cop heard him coming, though.

When Mail was ten feet away, he flinched and turned his head, his mouth open. But even a slow man can cross ten feet in a small fraction of a second, and Mail hit him with the spade handle, the steel grip burying itself in the cop's forehead with a wet crunch.

The cop dropped, his shotgun flying out to the side and clattering down the sidewalk. Mail dropped the spade handle, caught the cop under the armpits, and dragged him back between the houses. In a few seconds, he'd pulled off the cop's jacket, hat, and gunbelt. His own dark jeans would do well enough for uniform pants. The gunbelt was heavy and awkward, and he struggled to get it on.

The cop said a word, and Mail looked down at him, prodded him with a foot. The cop's head rolled to the other side, limp, loose.

"Die, motherfucker," Mail said. And he walked away, out to the sidewalk, pulling on the hat. It was too small, and perched on top of his head. But it would do. He picked up the shotgun, crossed the street, walked between a dark house and a lit one, and started running again.

A MAN IN the dark house, standing in the kitchen drinking coffee, saw him pass. Watched him go across the fence; couldn't see the police uniform, only the movement of the running man. He walked quickly back through his house, to tell the cop out front. But the cop out front was missing.

Huh. The man, cold in his undershirt, went out on his stoop, picked up the newspaper. In the very thin predawn light, he could see what looked like a shotgun lying on the sidewalk . . . and something else, further down the walk. Where was the cop?

The man looked around, then hurried across the street. What he thought was a shotgun turned out to be a spade handle. He turned, shaking his head, to go back to his house. Then he noticed the other object again. He stepped toward it, picked it up. A police radio.

And the cop on the grass groaned, and the man in the t-shirt said, "What? Who is that?"

THEY'D FOUND A thick wad of computer printout, and Lucas and Haywood were taking it apart a page at a time, looking for anything. They heard the running footsteps before they saw anyone coming and looked up. The Eagan chief spun in the door, grabbing the edge of the doorframe to stop himself.

"Lucas, you better call in. They got a big problem up there."

Lucas said, "Keep reading," to Haywood and started back toward the car. "What happened?"

"I think your guy killed a cop. And he might have gotten through your perimeter."

"Sonofabitch."

As they hurried back to the car, Lucas said, "Have your guys talked to MacElroy yet?" MacElroy ran the lawnmower shop.

"Talking to him now."

Lucas got the radio, called in. The dispatcher said the cop was still alive. "It's Larry White, Bob White's kid. He's really messed up, the guy hit him with a pipe or something. They're taking him to Ramsey."

"Jesus. What about Mail? Is he gone?"

"Maybe not. A guy who lives down there called us on 911 within a couple of minutes of White getting hit. They backed the perimeter off, making the house the middle of it. He should still be inside."

"All right. I'm coming back up there. Call Roux and Lester, tell them we need to talk."

"They're headed over to Ramsey. Both of them, along with Clemmons."
Clemmons ran the Uniform Division.

"Are they on the air?"

"Yeah."

"Tell them to wait for me."

MAIL MADE IT through the new perimeter, but not by much. Once outside
the original lines, he stayed out of sight for two blocks, then simply ran down
a long dark alley, stumbling now and then as he raced over the uneven ground.
He'd been running for a minute or perhaps a minute and a half, when he heard
the sirens screaming behind him. Christ, they'd found the cop. He ran faster.

Another minute, and a cop car flashed down a cross street in front of him
but continued past the alley. Mail slowed just a bit. He was breathing hard
now, still carrying the shotgun, the hat perched on his head.

At the end of the alley, he edged cautiously out toward the street. The cop
car was a block away, dropping off two foot patrolmen. They were crouched
over the car window, intent on what the man inside was saying, or the radio.
Mail took a breath, took two quick steps across that put him behind a car, then
another behind a maple tree. The cops were still talking. Mail took another
breath and walked quickly across the street to a maple on the other side.

And waited—but the cops had missed him.

Watching them, trying to keep the tree between himself and the mouth of
the alley, he walked backwards until he was into the alley, then turned and
broke into a run. A dog barked at him, and Mail ran faster, and the dog barked
a few more times. But there were still dogs barking everywhere. Nobody came
after him.

Mail stayed in the alley until it ended, then walked down a block to another
alley, and ran down that. The sirens were getting fainter, and he could no
longer see lights. But he *could* see houses against the sky. Dawn was getting
close—and the traffic would be picking up.

He would be more visible, now, and there'd be more people around.

He needed wheels.

30

A SURGEON IN A scrub suit was wandering aimlessly outside the emergency room exit, a mask hanging down on his chest, paper operating hat askew. He was smoking a cigarette, head down, shoulders humped against the cool air.

"Did you do the White kid?" Lucas asked as he hustled up the drive to the door.

The surgeon shook his head. "They're still working on him."

Inside the door, Lester was talking to two Minneapolis cops, while Roux was facing Bob White, the cop's father, and his mother, whose name Lucas couldn't remember. But he remembered that she liked hats, although this morning she was bareheaded, and holding on to a white handkerchief like it was a lifeline. Lucas walked up, nodded, said, "Bob, Mrs. White . . . how is he?"

"His head is real bad," White said. "But he's a fighter."

Lucas didn't know the son, but had the impression that he was somewhat dull; not a bad kid, though. "Yeah, he is. And this is the best trauma place in the country. He's gonna do good."

Mrs. White pushed the handkerchief into her face and started to shake and her husband turned toward her. Lucas looked at Roux and tilted his head toward the door. She gave him an almost imperceptible nod and lifted a hand at a priest who was talking with a St. Paul cop. The priest broke away and Roux stepped toward him and whispered, "I think Mrs. White could use a hand . . ."

Lester joined them, and Roux lit up as soon as they were outside. The surgeon was starting a new cigarette and stamped his feet and said, "Cold."

Roux and Lester and Lucas walked to the end of the driveway as Roux puffed on the cigarette and Lucas filled them in on Mail's computer shop. When he finished, he said, "We couldn't put his picture out before, because it might touch him off. Now he knows we're close, and that'll do it—he's gonna kill them. We've got to get that picture on the air, everywhere."

"How do you know he'll kill them?" Roux asked.

"I know. He's had them a long time. The pressure must be terrific. With this chase, he'll have cracked like a big fuckin' egg. And he's smart. He'll know we've got the van, and he'll know that we'll get the computer store, that we'll get his prints, that we'll identify him as John Mail. He'll figure all that out—

or he already has." Lucas nodded toward the hospital. "A cop has a shotgun, and Mail took him on with a club. He's freaking out."

Roux nodded. "All right. We can have the photo out in twenty minutes. He'll make all the morning news shows."

"Ask the TV guys to show the pictures at the beginning of the broadcasts, and to tell everybody to get their friends and come and watch, and show them again a couple of minutes later. As many times as they can. Flatter 'em: tell 'em if TV can't find the guy, Andi Manette's gonna die, and the kids, too. That'll keep them pushing the picture out there."

"How long have we got?"

"No time," Lucas said. "No time at all. If we don't find Manette in the next couple of hours, they're gone."

"Unless he's still in the perimeter," Lester said. "They think he might be, the guys up there."

"Yeah. We've gotta keep the perimeter tight. I'm gonna go over there, see if I can figure the odds that he's inside."

"Is there anything else?" Roux asked. "Any goddamn thing?"

Lucas hesitated, then said, "Two things. The first one is, I'd be willing to bet that wherever he's got them, it's within a few miles of that computer shop. That's where the phone calls were coming from, when we were trying to pinpoint the cellular phone. I think we oughta get everybody with a gun— highway patrol, local cops, everybody—and send them down there. We oughta filter every goddamn road. We don't have to stop everybody, but we ought to slow everything down, look in every backseat, see if we can spot somebody trying to elude the blockade."

"We can do that," Roux said.

Lucas looked at Lester, grinned slightly, and said, "Frank, could you call in? Could you get the picture thing going?"

Lester looked from Lucas to Roux and back, and then said, "What? I don't want to hear this?"

Lucas said, "You really don't."

Lester nodded. "All right," he said. "Back in a minute," and he went inside.

"What?" Roux asked when Lester was gone.

"I might call you later in the morning and suggest that you . . . I don't know, what?" He looked around, and then said, ". . . that you come over here and visit White. Spontaneously, without telling anybody exactly where you're going. You won't have to be out of touch long. Maybe half an hour."

She narrowed her eyes. "What're you going to do?"

"Are you willing to perjure yourself and say you didn't know?" Lucas asked. "Because you might want to say that."

Roux's vision seemed to turn inward, although she was gazing at Lucas's face. Then she said, "If it's that way . . ."

"It's that way, if you want to get them back—and keep your job."

"I'd do any fucking thing to get them back," she said. "But I hope you don't call."

"So do I," Lucas said. "If I do call, it'll mean that everything's gone in the toilet."

MAIL PICKED OUT a house with lights on in the back. From the alley, he could see an older woman working in what must be the kitchen. He crossed a chain-link fence into the yard, wary of dogs, saw nothing. As he passed the garage, he stopped to look in the window. There was a car inside, a Chevy, he thought, not new, but not too old, either. That would work.

He went on to the house, to the back door, leaned the shotgun against the stoop, took out the pistol, looked around for other eyes, other windows, and knocked on the door.

The woman, curious, came to look. She was sixty or so, he thought, her gray hair pulled back in a bun, her thin face just touched with makeup. She was wearing a jacket over a silky shirt. A saleswoman, maybe, or a secretary. She saw the police hat and the uniform jacket and opened the inner door, pushed out the storm door, and said, "Yes?"

Mail grabbed the handle on the storm door, jerked it open, and before she could make another sound, shoved her as hard as he could, his open hand hitting her in the middle of the chest. She went down, and he was inside, and she said, "What?" She tried to crawl away, slowly, and he straddled her and gripped the back of her neck and asked, "Where are your car keys?"

"Don't hurt me," she whimpered. Mail could hear a television working in the other room and turned his head to look at it. Was somebody else out there?

"Where're the fuckin' car keys?" he asked, keeping his voice down.

"My purse, my purse." She tried to crawl out from under him, her thin hands working on the vinyl floor, and he tightened his grip on her neck.

"Where's your purse?"

"There. On the kitchen table."

He turned his head, saw the purse. "Good."

He stood up to get a better swing, and hammered her on the side of the head with the butt of the shotgun. She went down, hard, groaned, kicked a couple of times, and was still. Mail looked at her for a moment, then made a quick check of the small house. A weatherman with what looked like false teeth was pointing at a satellite loop of the Twin Cities area: ". . . a lake advisory with these winds, which could kick up into the thirty-mile-per-hour category by this afternoon . . ."

The bedroom had only one bed, a double, already made up. A black-and-white photograph of a man in a Korean War Army uniform sat on the night-stand, under a crucifix. Nobody else to worry about.

He started back to the kitchen, and was stopped by his own image peering out of the television.

A woman was saying, ". . . John Mail, a former inmate at the state hospital. If you know this man, if you have seen him, contact the Minneapolis police at the number on your screen."

Mail was stunned. They knew him. Everything was gone. Everything. But they didn't know where he was. And they didn't say anything about the LaDoux name, they didn't say anything about finding Andi and the kid. And the TV would have that. So he was okay, for a while, anyway. But he had to get out, and get out now.

That fuckin' Davenport. Davenport was the one who'd done this. And it made him angry. That fuckin' Davenport, he wasn't fair. He had too much help.

The woman hadn't moved, and he dumped her purse on the kitchen table: car keys and a billfold. He opened the billfold, found twelve dollars.

"Shit."

He went back to the door, pausing to kick the woman in the side: twelve fuckin' dollars. You can't do anything with twelve fuckin' dollars. Her body moved sideways under the blow, leaving a trail of blood on the vinyl; she was bleeding from her ear.

Mail went on, through the door, picked up the shotgun at the stoop, and walked back to the garage. The side door was locked, and none of the keys fit it. He walked around to the alley side, tried the overhead door. That wouldn't budge, either. He walked back to the side door, used an elbow to put pressure on a window pane in the door, and pushed it in. Then he reached through, unlocked the door, and went inside.

A doorbell button was fixed to a block of wood beside the door. Mail pushed it, and the overhead door started up. He climbed in the car, started it, checked the gas. Damnit. Empty, or close enough. He'd have to risk a stop, or find another car. But there was enough to get him out of the neighborhood, anyway.

AFTER MAIL HAD gone, a neighbor woman looked out the back of her house and said, "That's odd."

"What?" Her husband was eating toast while he read the *Wizard of Id* in the comics.

"Mary left her garage door up."

"Getting old," her husband said. "I'll get it on the way to work."

"Don't forget," the woman said.

"How can I?" he asked, irritated. "I'm right across the alley."

"*You* could forget," his wife said. "That's why you've been shaving with soap for what, four days now?"

"Yeah, yeah, well, I'm not supposed to do the shopping for this family."

They argued. They always argued. In the heat of the argument, the woman's odd feeling evaporated—when her husband left, she went to get dressed herself, without waiting to see if he closed Mary's garage door.

THE MAN WHO found White's body showed Lucas the window. "I saw the guy running, and I went right out front."

"So let's walk through it," Lucas said. He looked at his watch. "You're back here, you walk to the door."

They walked through it, out the front, down to the walk, all the way to the point where the man found White's body.

"Did you hear the cop cars moving out before or after the ambulance got here?" Lucas asked.

"Uh, about the same time. There was sirens everywhere. I remember hearing all the sirens, and then the ambulance got here. There was already four cops here, and they sent everybody running around after the guy."

Sloan walked up as Lucas looked at his watch again. "So it was probably five minutes."

The man said, "It didn't seem like it was that long. The cops, they was here in a couple seconds, it seemed like."

"Listen, thanks a lot," Lucas said. He slapped the man on the shoulder.

"That's fine, I hope I helped."

As they walked away from him, Sloan said, "I go on administrative duty starting with the next shift, until the shooting's okayed."

"Yeah."

"Makes me nervous," Sloan said.

"Don't worry about it," Lucas said. "You got witnesses up to your eyeballs."

"Yeah." Sloan was still unhappy. "What's happening here?"

"I'm not sure," Lucas said. "They probably didn't have the new perimeter up for six or seven minutes. The new perimeter is a half-mile out there. He *could* have run through it—we haven't found any sign of him. If it was *me,* I would have run through it."

"Sonofabitch could be in somebody's home," Sloan said, looking at the rows of neat, anonymous little houses. "Laying up."

"Yeah. Or he could be out."

MAIL FOUND A cut-rate gas station with no customers and no visible television. He pulled in—the shotgun, the hat and cop jacket in the backseat—and pumped ten dollars' worth of gas into the car. A bored kid sat behind the counter eating a packet of beer nuts, and Mail passed him the old woman's ten-dollar bill. Another customer pulled in as he paid for the gas. Mail walked back out, head averted, got in the car, and left. The other customer filled his tank, walked inside, and said, "That guy who just left—he looked like the guy they've got on TV."

"Don't got no TV. Asshole owner won't let me," the kid said dully. He did the credit card, and the other man said, "Sure looked like him, though," and went off to work, where he talked about it most of the morning.

Mail went on down the block, stopped for a red light, turned on the radio. They were talking about him. ". . . apparently a long-time mental patient who faked his own death. Police have not yet identified the body found in the river."

Good. A break.

But they could be lying. Davenport could be mousetrapping him.

Another voice said, *No big difference. There's no way out anyway.* Anger cut through him, and he thought: *no way out.*

Another voice: *sure you can . . .*

He was smart. He could get down to the house, pick up what cash he had, take care of Manette and the kid, make it out to the countryside, knock off some rich farmer, somebody whose death wouldn't be noticed right away. If he could get a car for forty-eight hours, he could drive to the West Coast. And from the West Coast . . . he could go anywhere.

Anywhere. He smiled, visualized himself driving across the west, red buttes on the horizon, cowboys. Hollywood.

As the light changed to green, Mail saw the free-standing phone booth at the side of an Amoco station. He hesitated, but he wanted to talk. And shit, they *knew* who he was—they just didn't have the LaDoux name. He pulled into the station, dropped a quarter, and dialed Davenport.

THE PHONE RANG and Sloan looked at Lucas, and said, "If it's him, give me the high-sign, and I'll tell the Cap."

Lucas took the phone out, flipped it open. "Davenport."

Mail's voice was dark but controlled. "This was not fair. You had a lot more resources on your side."

"John, we're all done," Lucas said, jabbing a finger at Sloan. Sloan ran off to where the uniform captain was talking by radio with the cars on the perimeter. "Come on in. Give us Manette and the kids, huh?"

"Well, I just can't do that. That'd just be losing all the way around, you know? I mean, if they go away, then you've lost, too. You know? You've really lost, completely, in fact, because that's all you really want."

"John, I'm not worried about winning or losing . . ."

"I gotta go," Mail said, interrupting. "You've got those assholes tracing this."

"Are you trying to protect your friend? The one who's feeding you information on us?"

There was a moment of silence, then Mail laughed. "My friend? Fuck my friend. Fuck her."

And he hung up.

Lucas ran to the uniform captain's car, and the captain was saying, "Are you sure that's it? All right, I'm on the way."

To Lucas, he said, "It's an Amoco station not five miles from here. We didn't have anybody close. He's out."

Lucas said, "Shit," walked in a circle.

The uniform cop screeched out, leaving them, and Sloan said, "What'd he say?"

"He's gonna kill them."

"Aw, shit."

"But it's gonna take him a while to get there," Lucas said. "Patch through to Dispatch. Call Del, get him in. Get Loring from Intelligence and that rape guy, Franklin. Get him. Get them out of bed, anything you have to do, but tell them to meet me downtown in fifteen minutes. Tell them don't shave, don't clean up, just get there. Fifteen minutes."

"What're you gonna do?"

"You know somebody's feeding information to Mail?"

"I know you think that," Sloan said.

"I'm gonna arrest her," Lucas said.

Sloan's eyebrows went up. "Her? Who is it?"

"I don't know," Lucas said. "Get going."

Sloan, puzzled, hurried away. Lucas went back to the telephone, dialed. When the phone at the other end was picked up, he said, "Time to make your humanitarian visit to White."

"Lucas . . ." Roux was worried.

"Leave there in fifteen minutes."

"Lucas . . ."

"I just got a call from Mail. He's out, and he's going home to kill them. So go see White and keep your head down. Better keep it down for an hour."

"You gonna get him?"

"Yeah. I'm gonna get him."

31

WE HAVE TO be very fast," Andi said. "If we don't kill him, if we don't blind him, I'll try to hold his legs while you run. Run out and hide in the corn field. He won't find you there. Just run out by the road and hide until you see cars. Wait until you see more than one, in case he's in one, then run out."

Andi rambled along, hoping that she was making sense. Sometimes, now, she wasn't sure. She'd see Grace looking at her oddly, and she'd say, "What?"

and Grace would say, "You're calling me Gen," or "You were talking to Dad just now."

For a very long time, the sound of Andi scraping the nail had been the only noise in the cell, and then Grace sighed and said, "I think I could get the sole off my shoe. You know, with a piece of the bedspring."

Andi stopped scraping. "What for?"

"We could put the nail through it. We could use it like a push-handle."

When they were trying to work with the mattress springs, they'd found that the small pieces of metal were impossible to grip. Mail had given Andi some Band-Aids to patch a cut on her forehead, and Andi tried wrapping the wire with a bit of rag and the sticky-tape parts of the Band-Aids, but without much success.

Andi said, "Grace, that's a great idea. Let's see . . ."

Grace slipped her shoe off and handed it to her mother. The heel was capped by a thin slice of hard plastic. "We could break the plastic in half and make a hole in one half and put the nail through, and then put the other half over the nail head and tape it all together," Grace said. "When you stick him, you could have the nail coming out between your fingers with the heel in your hand."

Andi stared at her daughter: Grace had been thinking about this, how to kill him. Had visualized it, right down to the fatal punch. And it should work.

"Do it," she said. "I've got to keep scraping."

Another two hours, and they were done. The broken heel-cap and tape made a knob at the end of the nail, and held in her closed fist, with the nail protruding between her ring and middle finger, Andi could strike—and strike hard. The nail was five inches long. Nearly four were exposed beyond her fingers, and the last inch glittered with raw steel, like the tip of a new hypodermic needle.

"Now," Andi said, hefting the nail. "Let's go over it. When he comes, you're in the corner, playing with the computer. I'm lying on the mattress. I start to cry, but I don't get up. He comes to get me, just like he did the last couple of times. When he pulls me up, I put my left arm around his neck and pull up close, and my right hand hits him right below the breast bone, pointing up toward his heart. I do it a whole bunch of times, and try to turn him toward the wall . . ."

"And I come up from behind him and hit him in the eye with the spring," Grace said. She held up one of the thin needles she'd used to free the nail.

"So we should have room."

They danced it out, in the small cubicle: Grace was Mail, and bent over her mother, pulling her up. Andy struck at her mid-section, pulled back, did it again.

Then Andi was Mail, her back turned, standing on the Porta-Potti, and Grace came from behind, striking a roundhouse blow at the left eye with the wire. The wire wasn't stiff enough to penetrate muscle, but it would blind him.

When they'd gone through it a half-dozen times, they sat down, and Grace said, "He's been gone a long time. What if something happened? What if he doesn't come?"

"He'll come," Andi said. She looked around the hole and touched her temples. "I can feel him out there, thinking about us."

32

D EL LOOKED LIKE he'd been stuffed in a gunny sack and beaten with a pool cue. A patch of his blue jacket was discolored and stiff with something—ketchup? beer? His face was cut with stress lines, his hair was spiked from a pillow.

Franklin was not much better. He was a large black man, who wore a partial plate where his front teeth had been knocked out in a fight. He had the habit of dislodging the plate and rolling it with his tongue when he was thinking. Worse, a wandering eye gave him the appearance of a medieval insanity. He'd put on a suit, but he wore white gym shoes and a discolored t-shirt that said "Logan Septic Service: Satisfaction Guaranteed or Double Your Shit Back."

Loring was the prize. He was very large—fat—with a head the size and shape of a pumpkin, and eyes set so deep they were almost invisible. He hadn't shaved, and his beard was as thick and dangerous as a blackberry bramble. Sitting on top of the fat of his face, the beard shook like a bowl of cactus jelly. With his pale lavender suit and piss-yellow shirt, he looked crazier than Franklin.

Sloan simply looked worn out.

And all four were worried.

"You're talking about our ass," Franklin said. They were all standing, jammed into Lucas's office, the desk dwarfed by the bulk of the five large bodies.

"I can cover it," Lucas insisted. "You're just taking orders and there's no time to argue about it. You argue about it, those two are gonna be dead."

Del nodded. "I'll do it."

Franklin growled, "Yeah, you're Lucas's pal. But shit . . ." He looked at Loring. "What do you think?"

Loring shrugged, then sighed. "Fuck, what can they do to us?"

"Fire us, take our pensions away, put us in jail, and these chicks could sue us for every dime we got."

After a moment of silence, Loring said, "What else?"

Franklin and Del started laughing, and Lucas knew he had them.

LESTER STUCK HIS head in the office. "I just saw a gang of your buddies running across the street. What's going on?"

Shit. "What're you doing here, Frank?" Lucas asked.

Lester straightened, frowned. "What do you mean?"

"Frank, you don't want to be here. Not for an hour or so."

"Why not?"

"You just don't."

Lester stepped inside, pushed the door shut with his foot. "Cut the bullshit, Lucas. Tell me what's happening."

"On your head," Lucas said.

"I'm willing to lie about it," Lester said. "I was never here."

Lucas said, "Somebody is feeding information to Mail. I'm sure of it."

"Who?"

"I don't know—but I'm fairly sure it's either Nancy Wolfe or Helen Manette. None of the other people were around for both the sessions that Mail got information from."

"But which?"

"I don't know," Lucas said. "There just isn't any way to tell. They've both got motives—money, emotional problems, or both. In fact, it could have been Tower Manette or Dunn, but they didn't feel right, and when I talked to Mail, he said it was a she. So now I think it's got to be either Manette or Wolfe."

"So what're you going to do?"

"I'm arresting both of them," Lucas said. "I'm gonna have them dragged down here, searched, I'm gonna give them jail smocks and have them stuck in separate rooms, and I'm gonna have Franklin and Loring and Del and Sloan yell at them, until one of them cracks."

"Jesus Christ." Lester stared at him. "What about the innocent one?"

"I'm gonna apologize," Lucas said.

"You're fuckin' crazy," Lester said.

"Mail's on his way to kill those people. You heard the tapes. But he was a long way out, up north, and we've got cars tangling up traffic all over the south side of the Metro area. It'll take him a while to get there—but he *will* get there, and when he does, he's gonna kill them. That's how much time we've got."

"Does Roux know about this?" Lester asked.

"She's outa touch . . ."

"So am I," Lester said. He pulled open the door. "I never talked to you."

And he was gone. Lucas felt peculiarly alone, standing in his empty office. Nothing to do now except wait for the women to arrive. Then he heard footsteps outside, and Lester was back.

"How are you gonna cover it?" Lester demanded. "You got anything?"

Lucas shook his head. "Moral appeals. We were doing the only thing we could to save Manette's life, and the kid, if she's still alive."

Lester turned in a circle and said, "Christ, twenty-four years on the force." He ran a hand through his hair and said, "I gotta go do some paperwork."

Lucas said, "Frank: could you get us a helicopter in here? Across the street on the government center plaza?"

Lester thought for a second, then gave a quick nod. "Yeah, I can do that." And he was gone again.

NANCY WOLFE CAME in screaming. Helen Manette came in weeping.

Helen Manette arrived first, wrapped in a nightgown, with Tower Manette six feet behind her. They were moving fast, a tight clutch of cops, the fat Franklin and the frightening Loring and the middle-aged suspect, Tower Manette trotting a few feet behind, his white hair standing up in peaks. He spotted Lucas and ran at him, his thin face white with anger, his thin-man's wattles shaking with rage.

"What in the hell is going on?" He turned to point at the cops with his wife. "I'm told you're behind this . . . this fucking travesty of justice."

"Your wife has been arrested in the course of our investigation," Lucas said coldly. "I'd suggest you shut up."

"We've got a lawyer coming," Manette shouted. The cops were almost out of sight and Manette turned to run after them, shaking his finger at Lucas. "It's all over for you, you . . ."

"HE SOUNDED PLEASED," Lester said, stepping into the hallway.

Lucas couldn't suppress a cop-smile, an unhappy rictus that appeared when the world had turned to shit and there was no way out. "Yeah . . . how about the helicopter?"

"It's coming; it'll be across the street on the plaza."

"Excellent."

NANCY WOLFE, DRESSED in pajamas, a housecoat, and slippers, was frightened and angry, a towering rage that expressed itself in tears and nearly incoherent screaming: "I will sue, goddamn you, goddamn you all."

She saw Lucas and wrenched away from Del. "You will never again," she said, but couldn't finish. Del had cuffed her and when he tried to lead her past Lucas, she jerked her arm away and Lucas thought she was going to come after him with her teeth. "You are, you are . . ." she said. Again, she failed to find the word, but a thin line of saliva dribbled out the left side of her mouth.

"Take her down," Lucas said to Del. "Send the pajamas to the lab."

"My pajamas," she said. "My pajamas . . ."

Lucas waited until they were down the stairs, and out of sight, then hurried after them. Del, Sloan, Franklin, and Loring were gathered outside the processing room. Helen Manette had already been searched, photographed, and isolated, and her clothes had been packaged for a lab inspection. She'd been given a jail smock to replace them.

Wolfe was being photographed, and would be searched and her clothes taken away.

And Franklin said, "Ah, man, this scares the shit outa me. This scares the shit outa me, man. Christ, I think we oughta let up."

"Too late," Lucas said. "We're already in it. If we break one of them, we're out the other side. Now, when you get in there with them, I want them scared. We need all the pressure you can put on them: nobody gets hit, but you get your face right down in theirs, you . . ."

Loring said, "Behind you . . ."

Lucas turned around. Tower Manette was coming through the glass doors, an attorney in tow.

"I want to see my wife."

"When we're finished with the processing," Lucas said.

"We want to see her right fucking now," Manette shouted, jostling past Sloan toward Lucas.

"Touch another fuckin' cop and we'll put *your* ass in jail," Lucas snapped.

The attorney pulled Manette's sleeve, said, "Tower, cool off." And to Lucas: "We want to see Mrs. Manette, and we want to see her immediately. We have reason to believe that her civil rights have been grossly violated."

"Get a court order," Lucas said.

"We will," the attorney said. "We'll have one here in fifteen minutes." To Manette, he said, "C'mon, Tower: this is the way to do it."

"You motherfucker," Manette said to Lucas. "I met you in my house, I treated you like . . . like . . . quality, and you do this, you fuckin' . . ."

"What?" Lucas asked, genuinely curious. "Fuckin' what?"

"Trash," Manette said. And he was gone.

Franklin, who had been turning the partial plate in his mouth so his large front teeth rotated through his lips, clicked the plate back in place with his tongue, chuckled, and said, "You WASPs, he didn't know what to call you. Wanted to call you a nigger or a spic, but you're as white as he is."

"He's gonna be black and blue if something don't happen," Loring said, looking back at the processing rooms. "You think they'll get that court order?"

"Yes, I do," Lucas said. "That's why you get to be like Tower Manette. So you can wake up a judge and get a pal out of jail. Now: when you get in those rooms . . ."

WOLFE SAT IN the bare interview room, small with the bodies around her, her hair wild, her eyes large and frightened. The three men pressed in around her, Loring smoking, the smoke gathering around her head; she tried to stand up, once, but Del pushed her back into the chair. Lucas had never seen anything quite like it, an interrogation from a bad movie.

"How did you talk to him?" Loring asked. "That's all we want to know. How did you get in touch with him? Was he a patient? Were you treating him?"

"I don't know him, I don't . . ."

"Bullshit, bullshit, bullshit, we know he was a patient. Were you fucking him? Was that it? Is that why you're protecting him?"

"I'm not protecting anybody," she wailed.

"Aw, c'mon, for christ sakes, he's gonna go out there and kill your partner, and I'll tell you what, honey, you're gonna go into the women's prison and the dykes out there are gonna make a meal outa you. You don't wanna spent the rest of your life snuffin' up strange pussy, you better start talking right now."

Del, standing behind her, put his hands over his eyes: Loring was over the edge. Del waved him off, and, playing the soft guy, said, "Listen, darling, I know what it's like to be attached to somebody. I mean, you get involved with a guy like Mail . . ."

"I wasn't involved," she shrieked, her head twisting. "I didn't do anything, Christ, I want a lawyer, I want a lawyer now, you can't do this."

"You'll get a lawyer when we fuckin' well say you can," Loring said, his voice a slap in the face. "Now, what I want to know is how we can reach him. All we want is a phone number, or somebody who can tell us where we can get a phone number."

Del's voice, softer: "We can get you a deal. You'll do five years. Now, we know one of the girls is dead, and that's thirty years inside. No parole. You'd be an old . . . what's the word?"

"Crone," Lucas said.

". . . crone when you get out," Del said, his voice still soft, still reasonable.

"I WANT MY husband, I want him in here," Helen Manette wailed. She spent much of the time weeping uncontrollably, and questions were difficult to press.

Franklin finally got down on his knees, thrust his face to within an inch of hers, and said, "Listen, bitch, if you don't shut up, I'm gonna slap the shit out of you. You got that? You shut the fuck up, or I'm gonna stomp a mudhole in your white ass, and I'll fuckin' enjoy doing it. Your pal is gonna slice Miz Manette and her daughter into fuckin' dog food, and I want to know how to stop him, and you're gonna tell me."

"I want my husband . . ."

"Your husband doesn't give a shit about you," Franklin shouted. "He wants his daughter. He wants his granddaughters. But he's not gonna get his granddaughters, he's not gonna get both of them anyway, 'cause you and your pal killed one of them, didn't you?"

"Hey, c'mon, take it easy, take it easy," Sloan said, gently shoving Franklin out of the way. "You're gonna have a heart attack, man. Let me talk to her."

Sloan was sweating, though the room was cool. "Now listen, Miz Manette, we know there are all kinds of stresses in a person's life, and sometimes we do things we regret. Now we know that your husband is sleeping with Nancy Wolfe, and we know that you know. And we know that if Tower Manette left you, there just wouldn't be that much to share, would there? Now . . ."

Franklin looked at Lucas and shook his head, and Lucas made a *keep rolling* sign with his hands.

Franklin nodded and pushed and said to Sloan, "Hey, cut the psychological bullshit, Sloan; you know the bitch did it. Give me two minutes alone with her, and I'll get it out." He squatted, his face close to Helen Manette's, and he turned the partial plate with his tongue. "Two minutes would do it," he said.

He chuckled, a long gravelly roll, and Lucas winced.

WOLFE LOOKED AT Lucas and pleaded: "Get me out of here, just get me out of here. Please, get me out."

"I could help you, but you've got to help us," Lucas said. "We could use anything. A phone number would be great. An address. How did you get to know him? A little history . . ."

"I don't know him," she said hoarsely.

"Let me explain," Loring said, circling her. Del stood behind her, very close, so she could feel his pants leg near the back of her head. "We know that you're fucking Tower Manette. We know that Tower Manette's money is going to his daughter. Now, if you shoot Tower's old lady out of the saddle, and you were getting close, and if there was no daughter around, you'd get a bundle, right?"

"That's crazy," she blurted.

"And even if you don't get Tower, you'd get the key-man insurance from the shrink business, right? That's a bundle all by itself. You could buy a fleet of Porsches with that money alone."

"That . . ." she started, but Loring stuck a warning finger in her face.

"Shut the fuck up. I'm not done," he said. "Now we know that you were going out with George Dunn before Andi Manette took him away, and we've been having this argument: could that have triggered this off? Is it all because of George Dunn? Are you fucking Andi Manette's father to get back at Andi Manette because you can't fuck her husband? There's a pretty big kettle of psychological stew right there, huh? What'd old Desmond Freud have to say about that, huh?"

She went cool: "I want a lawyer. I promise you, if you don't get me a lawyer, none of you will ever again work as police officers. I'm willing to overlook . . ."

The door opened behind them, and Sloan stuck his head in: "Lucas. You better come in here." And to Loring and Del, he said, "Go easy."

HELEN MANETTE WAS slumped in the plastic chair; she'd stopped weeping and was chewing on a fingernail. She had snapped: she had a foxy look on her face, a dealer's look.

Lucas said, "What?" and Sloan said, "Miz Manette, tell Chief Davenport what you just told us."

"I don't know anybody like this Mail person," Helen Manette said. "But I know a boy, a renter in one of my apartments."

"Oh, shit," Lucas said. He turned away, put a hand to his face.

Sloan said, "Lucas? What?"

"The goddamn building directory card in Crosby's building. We both looked at it, and it had that blue bird on it, just like in Andi Manette's office building." He looked at Manette. "That's your management company, isn't it?"

"That's our logo, a royal blue bird, yes," she nodded brightly.

"Remember that? We saw it the first day. I didn't put it together, but I knew there was something . . ."

He squatted, looked into Helen Manette's watery eyes. "So you knew Mail from the apartment building."

"I didn't know who he was. He seemed like a nice boy."

"Then why did you call him?" Sloan asked.

"I didn't—he called me," she said. "He said he heard what was going on, and he wanted to say he was sorry and we . . . talked."

Lucas knew she was lying, but right now didn't care. "You have his phone number?"

Still bright: "Why, yes, I believe I do. Somewhere. If it's the same boy. He looks the same."

"Can you get it for us?"

"I believe I could, if I could go back home . . ."

Lucas said, "We'll get you back." He looked at Franklin. "Take Loring, put her in a squad, get her down there, full lights and sirens. I want it in six fuckin' minutes."

"You got it," Franklin said.

Lucas took his arm, pulled him to the side: "And you and Loring stay on top of her. Anything it takes."

On the way down to the room where Wolfe was being questioned, Lucas said to Sloan, "You're not supposed to be out with a gun. Stay here with Wolfe. Help her out. Be nice to her. Apologize. Explain what we were doing, and why. Get her home. If she wants a lawyer, help her out. But suggest that she talk with me before she does anything."

"What're you gonna tell her?"

"I'm gonna beg her to let it go," Lucas said, grinning.

"I don't think it's gonna work, man," Sloan said.

He stuck his head in the interview room, where Del and Loring were leaning against a wall, Loring smoking again. Wolfe was sitting straight in her chair, dry-eyed, expectant. Lucas said, "You two guys—let's go." And to Wolfe: "You're okay. You're free to go. Detective Sloan will help you."

SHERRILL WAS COMING in the door as Del and Lucas ran up the stairs to the front of the building: "I heard on the radio," she said. She was wearing jeans, boots, a plaid shirt, and her ball cap.

"Gotta go," Lucas called back as they passed her.

"I'm coming," she said, and she followed them out the door.

"I don't think . . ." Lucas said.

Sherrill interrupted: "Bullshit. I'm going." Then: "Where're we going?"

They ran together across the street to the plaza in front of the Hennepin County Government Center. A helicopter sat in the middle of the plaza, blades turning, and a TV crew was shooting film of it. When the cameraman saw the three running cops, he turned, and the camera followed them to the chopper.

"Let's go," Lucas said to the pilot.

"Where?"

"Down toward Eagan. Fast as you can."

33

THE CHOPPER TOOK off head-down, Lucas's stomach clutching as the black-visored pilot poured on the power and threw the machine out of the loop. They crossed I-94, rising over the tumult of the early rush hour, then projected out over the Mississippi and down the valley, past a tow with a barge, past a solitary powerboat running full-out on twin outboards, and past Lucas's house on Mississippi River Drive. Del tapped him on the shoulder and pointed down, past the pilot, and Lucas pushed up against the safety belt and saw his house, in strobelike flashes between the brilliant autumn maples, and Weather's car slowly backing out of the driveway. He felt the cut in the palm of his hand, looked down, and found the ring. Weather: Jesus. He strained to see her, but the car was out of sight, lost in the trees.

"I'll take us right down to the I-35 intersection with Highway 55. We'll orbit there until we get better directions," the pilot said. "I got maps."

She handed Lucas a spiral-bound book of Metro area maps, and Lucas held it between his legs. Del, in back, said, "What if this is some kind of dead-drop, like the computer shop?"

Lucas shook his head. "Then they're gone, Manette and the kids." He looked at his watch. "We may be too late now. We're an hour and fifteen minutes from when he called me. He could make it down there in forty-five minutes, except for the traffic tangles. We gotta hope that he takes her on one last time."

The pilot looked at him. "You gotta hope he takes her on . . . you mean, rapes her?"

"Yeah, that's what he's been doing," Lucas said. "It's better than death."

"Ah, my God," the pilot said. She turned away from him, and sent the chopper in a sickening swoop toward a twisted intersection below. "That's it, there. Look at that mess. Jeez, what happened?"

Below them, traffic was tied up in all directions, and blue lights winked through the worst jam Lucas had ever seen. "They're doing it, they're tying it up," he said, and he had to laugh, once, a short bark. "They'll be two hours getting that loose again. Maybe we got a chance. Maybe we got a chance."

Lucas found the map for the intersection as they orbited, once, twice, then again, like a bee in a bottle; and Del explained the interrogation scene to Sherrill.

"So where in the heck is Franklin?" Sherrill asked.

"Five minutes to the Manettes' house," Lucas said. "He oughta be calling."

"What's gonna happen to this guy?" the pilot asked.

"Gonna chain him in the basement of the state hospital," Lucas said. "Throw him a cheeseburger once a week."

"Better to shoot him," she said.

Lucas said, "Shhh," and they went around again.

Sherrill, huddled in the back, was greener than Lucas. "If Franklin doesn't call quick, I'm gonna blow a corn dog all over our pilot."

"Don't do that," the pilot said. Then: "I'll try to smooth things out."

Sherrill said, "C'mon, Franklin, you asshole, call."

And Franklin came then, patched through from Dispatch: "Lucas, we got it. His name is LaDoux. He's just north of Farmington, about a mile off Pilot Knob Road on Native American Trail. I got the address here."

Lucas found the map as Franklin read out the address, and the pilot poured it on, heading south.

And Franklin asked, "What about Miz Manette? I mean, this one?"

"Take her back downtown, get her a lawyer," Lucas said.

Del, from the backseat, shouted, "And read her rights to her."

Sherrill, marginally more cheerful, also shouting: "Yeah, we want it to be on the up-and-up."

Lucas, ignoring them, was talking to Dispatch. "Can you get us closer? These street numbers don't mean anything up here."

"Yeah, we're looking for the mailman on that route, and we've alerted Dakota County, but they don't have a lot of assets down there."

"I know, I can see them all from here," Lucas said. Down below, roof racks were lighting up the major intersections for miles, and he could see cops on the streets, peering into southbound cars. "But get some going south, if you can."

"Strangest thing I ever saw," Del said from the back as Lucas signed off the radio. Del, who liked high places, had his face pressed against his window. "A man-made traffic jam. God, look at those guys. I'd hate to be down there, though."

"Is that Pilot Knob there?" the pilot asked, pointing at a street with a gloved hand. "Or is that Cedar?"

"I don't know," Lucas said, turning the map. He hated flying, didn't like the exposed front on the helicopter: he would have preferred something solid, like sheet steel. "Where's due south?" The pilot pointed and he turned the map. "Okay, there should be a golf course."

"There's a golf course," the pilot said, pointing to her right. "But . . . there's another one."

"There should be a lake, a crescent-shaped lake," Lucas said.

"Okay, there's a lake."

"Okay, yeah, that's it—there's the little lake by the big one. So that's gotta be Pilot Knob right there."

They churned south, following the road, past another golf course, out into the countryside, corn going brown, a green-and-yellow John Deere rolling through a half-cut field of alfalfa.

Dispatch called back. "Lucas, we got the mailman, here he is . . ." There was a pause, and then a man's distant voice. "Hello?"

Lucas identified himself. "Did the dispatcher tell you what we need?"

The mailman said, "Yes. You want the fifth house from the corner, on the south side of the road. It's about three-quarters of a mile from the corner, sits up on a slope with a gravel driveway. White house—needs paint, though—and it's got a porch and a screen door and a couple old tumble-down buildings out back. There's a shutter off on the front; one window's only got one shutter. The mailbox is silver and there's an orange *Pioneer Press* delivery box on the same post under the mailbox."

"Got that," Lucas said. A swamp flicked past, a thousand feet down. "Thanks."

"Listen, you still there?"

"Yeah."

"One of the guys here has a TV going, and I just saw the picture. You got the right guy. That's him, all right. He's not around there much, but I saw him a couple times."

"Got that," Lucas said.

In the backseat, Del said, "Hot dog," and slipped his pistol out from under his jacket and punched out the clip.

Sherrill said, "Don't say that."

"What?"

"The dog thing," Sherrill said, and she swallowed, and started fumbling for her gun.

"Hold on, I'll have you on the ground in two minutes," the pilot said. She'd been looking at the map, where Lucas's fingers pinched the road. "So we're looking for a loop, like a suburb or something, and then it's three miles on."

"There's the loop coming up," Lucas said, pointing at a cluster of houses, with tiny trees sprouting in the expansive front yards. They all looked the same, variations of beige with simple, peaked roofs, like properties on a Monopoly board.

"Okay. Then that must be the road, right there," the pilot said. Up ahead, Native American Trail was a beige thread in a blanket of green. "There's somebody heading down there . . ."

A RED CAR was throwing up a cloud of gravel dust as they closed on the road. "One-two-three-four-five, Jesus, I think he's heading in there, he's slowing down, he's turning," Lucas said.

"Wrong drive, wrong drive. The fifth house is over there, down further," the pilot said, pointing.

"I don't know," Lucas said. "Look, he's in a hurry, he's moving."

The pilot groped at her feet and handed Lucas a pair of battered 8 × 50 marine binoculars. "You call it: whatever you want to do."

They were coming in fast, but they were still a half-mile out; Lucas put the heavy binoculars on the house, picked out the mailbox and the brilliant orange paperbox on the post below it. To the right, the red car had topped a hill, and as Lucas watched, a man got out of the car, turned his pale face toward them: black hair, tall; the white face, at the distance, a featureless wedge. But a wedge that felt right.

The man darted into the ramshackle house in the cornfield; he carried something—a shotgun? He was too far away to be certain. "That's him," Lucas said, half-shouting. "Put us on him, put us on him."

"What are we doing?" Sherrill shouted from the back. She had a revolver out, and a speed loader in her other hand. Below them to the front and right, three Dakota County sheriff's cars were pounding up Pilot Knob Road from the south. Lucas waved Sherrill off and got on the radio: "Tell the sheriff's guys it's the first road west of the house. Not the house, it's a track, goes across a ditch just west of the house . . . tell them to look for the chopper, where we're going in. We've got him in the house, we see him in the house."

"What're we doing?" Sherrill yelled again. "Are we going in? Are we going in?"

"Gotta try," Lucas said over his shoulder. "He's goofier than shit, and he might have some kind of long gun with him. Didn't he take a shotgun off White?"

"Shotgun," Del said.

"Yeah, so take it easy. But Christ, if he kills them now, we're thirty seconds late; and he's goofier'n shit, man, goofier'n shit."

The pilot said, "Hold on," and then, smiling beneath the black visor, dropped them out of the sky.

34

MAIL DROVE NORTH, cut I-694, the outer beltline around the Cities, took it east and then south, across I-94, where the highway changed numbers and became I-494. He was driving the old woman's car on remote control, his head thumping with the call to Davenport, the treachery of the cops, the humiliation of the duck shit, the nose-ring blonde at Davenport's computer company.

Had Davenport used the blonde to suck him in? Had he figured him that well? He relived the attack on the cop, the satisfying whack of the spade; the hit on the old lady, last seen crumpled on her kitchen floor, one leg under a chair, a broken plate on the floor by her head, a piece of buttered toast in the middle of her back; Gloria floated through his mind, her neck crooked with the nylon rope around her, her feet swinging like a pendulum overhead as he laid the river rocks into the booby trap.

And the parts of Andi Manette: tits, legs, face, ass, back. The way she talked, the way she curled away from him, fearing him.

He almost ran into the truck ahead. He cut left and saw the traffic jam. Cars, trucks, backed up a half-mile away from the river bridge. Blue cop-lights flashing along the road.

He sat in the traffic jam for five minutes, steaming, the bright movies in his brain now reduced to shadows. Up ahead, a Jeep cut onto the shoulder of the road. Mail edged over to watch: the Jeep rolled slowly along the shoulder, then cut across to an exit heading north on Highway 61. Mail followed. He didn't want to go back north, but he could make a U-turn, head back south. Must be a hell of an accident; there were cops all over the place.

He slid off the exit, running north; made an illegal U, and started south again. Everything around the bridge was blocked, but there was another bridge, little used, down in Newport.

More cops. He turned out east of the oil refinery, continued on Highway 61. The radio . . .

WCCO was full-time on the story, the announcer wearing his Tornado Alert Voice: ". . . the entire south end of the Metro area is tangled up as the police search for John Mail, identified as the kidnapper of Mrs. Andi Manette and her daughters Grace and Genevieve. There are checks at many of the major intersections in Dakota County, and all bridges across the Mississippi. All we can do is ask for patience as police check cars as quickly as possible, but delays are now running up to an hour on outbound lanes of I-35E and I-35W, all outbound bridges in downtown St. Paul. That would include the High Bridge, the Wabasha and Robert Street Bridges, and Highway 3, plus the Mendota Bridge, both I-694 bridges."

Christ, he couldn't get back home.

He was heading down to Hastings, straight into a checkpoint. The announcer hadn't said anything about Prescott, the St. Croix Bridge into Wisconsin.

If they were stopping cars on all those bridges, they hadn't found the house, hadn't found the women, still didn't have the LaDoux name.

He left Highway 61 just north of Hastings, crossed the St. Croix into Wisconsin, struck out in a wide southern swing through Wisconsin, and crossed the Mississippi back into Minnesota on the unguarded bridge at Red Wing. From Red Wing, he took Highway 61 north, and finally turned cross-country to Farmington.

There were no cops on the highway, none in town. None. It was almost eerie. Even the highway north seemed thinly traveled. At Native Americans Trail, he turned east, taking it slow, looking for lights, for cars, for movement. For anything.

There was nothing.

He shoved the gas pedal to the floor, moving now, breathing again, heart pounding, everything coming to a close. He flashed on Andi Manette, all those parts—and turned left off the road.

He stopped. He felt a beat, but couldn't identify it, listened for a second, then reached in the backseat, got the shotgun, and climbed out of the car.

The chopper was just coming in. He looked up, to the north, and saw the machine dropping out of the sky, screaming in on him.

He ran to Andi . . . .

THEY HEARD HIM running across the floor, pounding down the stairs. He'd never run before. Andi sat up, looked at her daughter. "Something's happening."

"Should we . . . ?" Grace was terrified.

"We've got to," Andi said.

Grace nodded, dropped to her knees, lifted the edge of the mattress. She took the needle and handed the nail to her mother.

Andi fitted it to her hand, kissed her daughter on the forehead. "Don't feel anything. Don't think, just do it," she said. "Just like we practiced; you get back there . . ."

The first day Mail had put them in the cell, she remembered the smell of old potatoes. She hadn't noticed the odor since—it had simply become part of the background—but she smelled it now. Potatoes, dust, urine, body sweat . . . The hole.

"Kill him," Grace rasped at her. Grace's eyes were too large, sunken. Her skin was like paper, her lips dry. "Kill him. Kill him."

Mail was rattling at the door, fumbling at it. When he opened it, he was carrying a shotgun, and for just an instant, Andi thought he was going to kill them without a word, open fire before they had a chance.

"Out," he screamed. "Both of you, out." His young-old face was dead white; he had a white bead of spittle at the corner of his mouth. He gestured with the gun, not pointing it at them, a sweep of his arm. "Get out here, both of you."

Andi had the nail by her side, and went first; she felt Grace reach out and grab the top of her tattered skirt, and pulled along behind.

"What?" Andi started.

"Get," Mail snarled, looking up the stairs. He grabbed her by the skin of her throat and pulled her, stepping back, still looking over his shoulder, expecting someone to burst in, the shotgun barrel straight up.

And she stepped straight into him and struck.

She rammed the nail into the space below his breastbone, trying to angle it into his heart, looking at his eyes as she struck.

And she screamed, "Grace, Grace . . ."

THE SHACK'S OUTSIDE door was half-open; Lucas kicked it the rest of the way, Del flattened against the outer wall, sweeping the fallen-down mudroom just inside.

Sherrill was on the other side of the house, watching the back. Lucas went through first, through the mudroom, following the sights of the .45, his thumb-knuckle white in the lower rim of his circle of vision.

The shack smelled of wood rot, and dim light shifted in through dirty windows. A broken-legged table crouched in the kitchen beyond the mudroom, and tracks were etched in the dirt of the floor, heading into the interior. There was an open door to the left, hung with cobwebs; another on the other side, showing a down-slanting wall: and from there, a light, and a man's voice shouting.

Del, just behind, slapping him on the shoulder: "Go."

Lucas went straight ahead, scrabbling along in a half-crouch, while Del covered the doorway. Lucas did a peek at the door, looking down the stairs, and a woman screamed, "Grace, Grace . . ."

WHEN ANDI MANETTE struck with the nail, Mail's eyes widened and his mouth opened in surprise and pain, and he jerked forward, turning away. Grace struck at his right eye and missed as he turned his head, the point of the needle skidding across the bridge of his nose, burying itself an inch deep in his left eye.

He screamed, pulled back, and Andi shouted, "Grace, run."

Grace ran, and Mail flailed at her and the girl was batted off her feet, lurching into the pile of tumble-down shelving on the back wall of the tiny cellar. She scrambled to her feet and tried for the stairs, and Andi saw the shotgun coming around and she pulled the nail out and struck again, felt it skid along his ribs.

The shotgun stopped in its track and Mail hit her in the face with an elbow and she fell, and saw her daughter's legs flying up the stairs. Mail fired the shotgun, a flash and a blast like thunder, straight up, into the ceiling, either by accident or simply to startle, to slow down whoever was up the stairs. He turned, and Andi saw his good eye fix on her—the other eye was a blotch of blood and she felt a thrill of satisfaction—and the barrel of the gun came around and opened at her face. They stood just for a second that way, Mail's face contorting. She could see his hand working on the trigger, but nothing was happening, and she rolled out of the line of fire.

LUCAS STARTED DOWN the stairs in a crouch, heard the man scream and a girl, a scarecrow, hair on end, blood on her face, ran to the stairs and started up, stopped when she saw Lucas. A shotgun went off, the blast like a physical blow; plaster sprayed around them, and Lucas fell sideways, tried to catch himself.

THERE WASN'T MUCH pain when Andi Manette stuck him, but Mail knew he'd been hurt. He pulled back, tried to get some space, but Manette clung to him and then the girl was there. He saw the hand coming up, the thin, steel glitter between her fingers, and turned his head. The needle slashed at him, hurt more than Manette's knife, or whatever it was. There was a black flash—was that possible?—in his left eye, and he wrenched away, spasmodically pulling at the trigger. The shotgun went off, the barrel not more than a foot from his ear, deafening him.

As dust and plaster rained on them from the ceiling, Manette struck again; she was screaming and he saw the girl running for the stairs. He swung at her; he felt no impact, but saw the girl go down. Everything was moving at a berserker's speed, like a movie cut too often, clips of this and that too fast for his brain to process . . . but he looked for Manette, his betrayer, found her at his feet.

Her mouth was open, she was screaming, and he pointed the barrel at her mouth and pulled the trigger. The trigger pulled back slackly, without tension. Nothing happened. He pulled it again, and again, saw the girl screaming on the stairs, Davenport falling, a gun in his hand.

Mail ran.

He ran behind the furnace, into the old rat's nest coal bin, up the coal chute to the rotten wooden door at the top. He knocked the door open with the stock of the gun and a shaft of light hit him full in the face.

DEL WAS AT the top of the stairs, frozen by the blast, his gun pointing down past Lucas. Lucas twisted, falling, struck the scarecrow girl, knocking her sideways, and staggering, caught himself on the post at the bottom of the stairs, his gun sweeping the room, looking for the face, the target.

"GRACE," ANDI SCREAMED, and screaming again, "Run, Grace . . ."

Then a man was there with a gun, a large man in a suit, shouting at her, then another man, a man who looked like a tramp, with another gun, maneuvering toward the cell. She shrank away, but heard, through the pain and fear, the single word, "Where?"

She pointed toward the furnace; and as she pointed, a shaft of sunlight broke into the room, from behind the furnace. Del was at another door, looking down, then back at him, and Lucas took three leaping steps across the room, past the furnace into a small wooden-sided room. Light poured through a hatch-like door in the foundation.

Andi heard the gunshots, the quick bite of a pistol, the deeper boom of the twelve-gauge . . .

ON THE GRASS, outside, on his knees, Mail looked left and brought the gun up. This time, he pumped the slide, saw an empty shell flip out to the right. That's why it hadn't fired. In the chaos in the basement, he'd forgotten to pump it.

But there were more cops here: he heard a man's voice, screaming, and more shouting in the basement. A chopper roar picked up, and the chopper slipped from behind the house, six feet off the ground, hovering.

Sherrill ran around the side of the house.

They saw each other at the same instant. Sherrill's pistol was up and a single shot plucked at Mail's coat. Mail returned the shot, firing once, and Sherrill went down, her legs knocked from beneath her. The helicopter came in like a giant locust, and he pointed the shotgun at the black-visored pilot behind the glass, pulled the trigger; again, nothing happened. Cursing, he pumped the gun, and as the chopper pilot roared two feet over head, he ran beneath the machine, past Sherrill, to the corner of the house.

Cops coming up the track. Three cars at least.

He turned and sprinted thirty yards across the yard toward the corn field, vaulted the fence, and submerged in the deep green leaves.

SHERRILL WAS ON the ground, screaming, the chopper thirty yards away, the pilot gesturing frantically, when Lucas crawled up the coal chute. Lucas turned and saw Mail vault a barbed-wire fence into the corn field; he vanished in an instant.

A sheriff's car slewed sideways in the yard as Lucas ran to Sherrill, put his hand on her back: "Hit?"

"My legs, man, my legs, it hurts so fuckin' bad, it just fuckin' burns . . ."

Del was out now, and Lucas waved at the pilot, pulling her down, then ran to the uniformed deputy, who stood by the fender of his car, a shotgun on his hip.

"He's in the cornfield—he's right in there," Lucas shouted over the blast of the chopper blades. Grass and bits of weed whipped past them as the chopper settled. "Get a couple guys on the road, and get in those hayfields. Cut him off, cut him off . . ."

The deputy nodded and ran back to the other cars. Lucas went back to Sherrill. Del was kneeling over her, had ripped open her pants leg. Sherrill had taken a solid hit on the inside of her left leg between her knee and her hip; bright red arterial blood was pulsing into the wound.

"Bleeding bad," Del said; his voice was cool, distant. He pulled off his jacket, ripped off a sleeve, and pressed it into the wound.

"Hold it there," Lucas said to Del. "I'll carry her."

"How bad? How bad is it?" Sherrill asked, her face a waxy white. "I hurt . . ."

"Just your leg, you'll be okay," Del said, and he grinned at Sherrill with his green teeth.

Lucas picked her up, cradling her, and carried her groaning with pain to the chopper, where the pilot had shoved open the passenger-side door. "Bleeding bad, hit an artery," Lucas shouted over the prop blast. "Got to get her to Ramsey."

The pilot nodded, gave him a thumbs-up. Lucas shouted at Del, "You go— keep the hole packed up."

"You're gonna need help . . ."

"Gonna have a lot of help in one minute," Lucas shouted back. "This is just gonna be a dog hunt now."

Del nodded, and they fitted Sherrill into the passenger seat with Del straddling her; and the chopper lifted off.

Lucas turned and saw Andi Manette at the door of the old farm house. She had her daughter under one arm, and with her hand, tried to hold together the pieces of what once had been a suit.

"You're Davenport," she said. She looked bad: she looked like she was dying.

"Yes," Lucas nodded. "Please sit down, both of you. You're okay . . ."

"He's afraid of you," Andi said. "John's afraid of you."

Lucas looked from Andi Manette and Grace toward the cornfield. "He should be," he said.

THE DAKOTA DEPUTIES had pursued people into cornfields before; they knew how to isolate a runner. The field itself covered a half-section, a mile long by a half-mile wide. The road ran along one edge, and recently cut alfalfa fields along two more. A bean field, still standing, stretched along the fourth side. Cop cars were stationed at three of the corners of the field, and cops climbed on top, with binoculars, so they had clear views down the road and the surrounding alfalfa and soybean fields.

Mail might try to crawl out through the beans, but that was on the far side of the corn, a long run; and within a couple of minutes, a cop car bumped down into the beans and quickly ripped a three-car-wide path along the edge of the corn, then retired to the highest point along the path. A deputy with a semiautomatic rifle set up behind the car.

For now, that would hold; in five minutes, there would be twenty cops around the field. In ten minutes, there would be fifty.

Lucas stood with Andi Manette, on the handset. "I've got Mrs. Manette and Grace. We need to lift them out of here, we need a medevac now."

"Lucas, the chief is here."

Roux came on. "They say you got them."

"Yeah, but we need to get them out, we need to get a chopper down here."

"Are they hurt bad?"

"Not critical," Lucas said, looking at the two women. "But they're pretty beat up. And Sherrill's hurt bad."

"I was listening to Capslock on the radio. They'll be at Ramsey in three or four minutes. We've got another chopper on the way. Dunn's being notified."

Andi Manette, now with both arms wrapped around her sobbing daughter, said, "Genevieve. Do you have Genevieve?"

Lucas shook his head, and her face contorted and she choked out, "Do you know . . . ?"

"We hoped she was with you," Lucas said.

"He said he would drop her off in a mall. I gave her a quarter to call with."

"I'm sorry . . ."

A caravan of police cars, now including city cars, barrelled up the track: two more jammed into the driveway at Mail's house, and all around them, cops with rifles and shotguns were posting around the cornfield. The ranking sheriff's deputy hurried toward them.

"Davenport?"

"Yeah. Who're you?"

"Dale Peterson. Are you sure he's in the corn?"

"Ninety-five percent. We saw him go in and there wasn't any place to get out."

"He's hurt bad," Andi Manette said. Peterson reached a hand out to her, but she edged away and Lucas backed him off with a quick shake of the head. "I stabbed him," she said. "Just before he ran."

She lifted her hand; she still held the spike, and her fingers were smeared with blood. Grace turned her head in her mother's arms and said, "I did, too. I stabbed him in the eye." And she showed them the bedspring needle.

"He was going to kill us," Andi said numbly.

Lucas said, "You did right." And he laughed, and said, "Goddamn, I'm proud of you." And he lifted his hand to pat her shoulder, and remembered, and turned instead toward Peterson. "You gonna handle this?"

The deputy nodded: "We can."

"Do it, then," Lucas said. "I'd like to help out. He just shot a friend of mine."

Peterson nodded. "We heard. But, you know . . . take care." He meant, *Don't murder him.*

"I'm fine," Lucas said, and Peterson nodded. To Andi: "Miz Manette, if you guys would like to ride down to the road, a helicopter will be picking you up."

"Got media coming," a deputy called from the last car down.

"Keep them out," Lucas said.

"Block them out at the corner," Peterson called. "And get Hank to call the FAA, keep the TV choppers out of here."

"Thank you," Andi Manette said to Peterson. And to her daughter, "Come on, Grace."

Grace said, "Genevieve?"

"We'll look for her," Andi promised.

Lucas walked with them toward the last of the sheriff's cars. "I'm sorry it took so long," he said. "He isn't stupid."

"No, he isn't," Andi said. A deputy opened the back door of his car. Andi helped Grace into the backseat, then turned to say something else to Lucas. Her eyes reached up toward his face, then stopped, looking past his shoulder. Lucas turned to see what she was looking at, his hand dropped toward his pistol. Had she seen Mail? Then she brushed past him, took three quick steps, and suddenly was running toward the house.

Lucas looked at the deputy, said, "Watch the kid," and started after her, walking quickly, and then, when he saw where she was going, broke into a run, shouting, "Mrs. Manette, wait, please wait, wait . . ."

Peterson was on the radio, but he dropped the microphone when he saw Andi Manette running toward the house, and he hurried after her.

She was running toward a six-foot square of weathered wood set on a six-inch-high concrete platform. Lucas, forty feet behind her, shouted, one last time, "Don't, wait," but she was already there. She stooped, caught the edges of the old cistern cover, and heaved.

Lucas had to stop her, because he'd realized what Andi Manette knew by instinct: this was where Genevieve was. The doll in the oil barrel was the girl in the cistern; a watery grave.

When Lucas had still been in uniform, he'd worked a kidnapping case where the child had been shot and thrown in a creek. The body had washed up on the bank, and he'd been with the group of searchers that had found it. He'd seen so much death in his years on the force that it no longer affected him, much. But that child, early in his career, with the white, pudding flesh, the absent eyes . . . he still saw them sometimes, in nightmares.

THE COVER ON the cistern was too heavy for Andi Manette. There was no way that she could lift it. But she got it up a foot, staggered, and as Lucas reached her, slipped it sideways and heaved, opening the hole.

Lucas grabbed her, wrenched her away as she screamed, "No," and Lucas, turning, looked down and saw . . . What?

Nothing, at first, just a bundle of junk on the side of the hole, above the black water at the bottom.

Then the bundle moved, and he saw a flash of white.

Peterson had wrapped his arms around Andi Manette, pulling her away, when Lucas, eyes wild, waved at him, shouted, "Jesus Christ, she's alive."

The cistern was perhaps fifteen feet deep, and the bundle hung just above the water. It moved again, and a face turned up.

"Get something," Lucas screamed back at the cars. "Get a goddamn rope."

A uniformed cop was pulling Andi Manette away; Andi was fighting him, crazy. Another cop popped the truck on a patrol car, and a second later was running toward them with a tow rope. Lucas peeled off his shoes and jacket.

"Just belay the end, get a couple of guys," Lucas yelled. There were cops running at them from all over the yard.

Andi Manette was pleading with the cop who held her; Peterson shouted into the swarm of men now around the cistern, "Let her come up, but hold her, hold her."

Lucas took the end of the rope and went over the side, feet against the rough fieldstone-and-concrete wall. The cistern smelled like new, wet earth, like early spring, like moss. He went down, passed the bundle on the wall, lowered himself into the water.

The water was three feet deep, coming up just to his hip joint; and it was cold.

"Genevieve," he breathed.

"Help me," she croaked. He could barely make out her voice.

Some kind of mechanism—a secondary pulley, perhaps—had once been mounted about three feet above what was now the water line. Whatever it was, was gone: but there were two metal support fixtures on either side of the cistern, and Genevieve had managed to crawl high enough up the rocks to spear the bottom of her raincoat over one of the fixtures.

With the coat buttoned, she had created a sturdy cloth sack hanging on the side of the cistern, above the water, like a cocoon. She'd crawled inside and hung there, legs in the sleeves, for nearly a hundred hours.

"Got you, honey," Lucas said, taking her weight.

"He threw me in . . . he threw me in," she said.

Peterson shouted down, "What do you want us to do? You need somebody else down there?"

"No. I'm gonna leave her in the coat, I'm gonna hook the rope through this hole. Take her up easy."

He hooked it up, and Genevieve groaned, and Lucas shouted, "Easy."

And Genevieve went up into the light.

35

HALF-BLIND, HIS EARS ringing with the blast of the shotgun, Mail crawled down the rows of corn, the field as dense as a rain forest. He couldn't see very well; he didn't really understand why, he just knew that one eye didn't seem to work. And every time his weight came down on his hand, pain shot through his abdomen.

But part of his mind still worked: fifty feet into the field, he went hard to his right, got to his feet, and running in a crablike crouch, one hand carrying the shotgun, the other pressed flat against his stomach, he headed downhill toward the road. Any other direction would lead to an open field, but if he could somehow get across the road, there was another mile-long cornfield, coming up to a farmhouse. The farmhouse would have a car.

And a culvert crossed under the road.

It wasn't large—maybe not even big enough to take his shoulders—but he remembered seeing the rust-stained end of it sticking out into a small cattail swamp in the ditch. If he could make it that far.

He was breathing hard, and the pain was growing, beating at him with every step. He fell, caught at the cornstalks with his free hand, went down. He lay there for a moment, then turned, rocked up on his butt, looked down at his stomach, and saw the blood. Lifting his shirt, he found a hole two inches below his breast bone, and a cut; blood was bubbling out of the hole.

The whole sequence, from the time he'd opened the door of the cell, through the shooting in the yard, was a shattered pane of memories, flashes of this and that. But now he remembered Andi Manette coming into him, and the bite of pain as she stabbed him with something.

Jesus. She'd stabbed him.

Mail's face contorted, and his shoulders lifted and he shuddered, and he began to sob. The cops would kill him if they found him; Manette had stabbed him. He had nowhere to go.

He sat, weeping, for fifteen seconds, then forced it all back. If he could get out of the field, if he could get through the culvert, if he could get a car and just get *away* from these people, just for a while; if he could *rest,* if he could just close his eyes—he could come back for Manette.

He *would* come back for her: she owed him a life.

Mail put his head down and began to crawl. Somewhere, he lost the shotgun, but he couldn't go back for it; and the pistol still rode in his belt. He looked back, once; there was nobody behind him, but he could see a thin trail of blood, winding down through the corn to where he lay.

LUCAS LAY ON his back on the long grass next to the cistern, catching his breath. The cops who'd pulled him out were walking away, coiling the tow rope. Peterson hurried up. "Another chopper's coming. Be here in a minute."

Lucas sat up. He was soaked to the waist, and cold. "How's the kid?"

Peterson shook his head. "I don't know. She's not good, but I've seen worse that made it. Are you all right?"

"I'm tired," Lucas said. A chopper was coming in, and cops were down at the road, waving it in. He could see two other cops, walking along the road, and more were forming around the edges of the field.

Lucas pulled on his shoes and jacket, and said to Peterson, "Tell your people I'm going into the field. I'm only going in a few feet."

"He's got a shotgun," Peterson objected.

"Tell them," Lucas said.

"Look, there's no point . . ."

"He's not waiting for us to do something," Lucas said, looking out over the field. "I know how his head works, and he's running. He won't set up an ambush and go down shooting. He'll always try to get out."

"We'll have a couple more choppers here in a few minutes, knock down that field . . ."

"I just want a peek," Lucas said, walking away from the house, toward the fence where Mail had gone over. "Tell your guys."

Lucas crossed the fence line, his city shoes filling with plant debris. Sand burr hung from his damp socks, cutting at his ankles. Just inside the field, the sweet smell of maturing corn caught him; the fat ears hung off the stalks, dried silk like brown stains at the top of the ears. He worked slowly along the weedy margin until he saw the fresh foot-cuts in the soft gray dirt.

He slipped his pistol out, stooped, turned, and duckwalked into the field. And here was a flash of blood, more scuffs in the dirt, more blood. Mail was hurt. Lucas stopped, listened, heard a few leaves rustling in the light wind, the sound of car engines, distant sirens, the beat of a chopper. A ladybug crawled up a corn leaf, and he duckwalked a little further into the field, following the sights of his .45.

At knee-level, the cornfield was incredibly dense, and Lucas could see almost nothing, except straight up. Mail's track went straight into the field; Lucas followed it for two minutes, and then the trail turned sharply to the right and disappeared down a corn row. Lucas couldn't see anything at all up ahead. Mail was apparently shifting between rows; following him would be suicidal.

Lucas stood up and looked in the new direction the trail had taken. From where he was, he could see the phone poles along the road. Moving slowly, carefully, he worked his way back to the edge of the field, and recrossed the fence.

Peterson was waiting. When he saw Lucas coming back, he put a handset to his face, said something, and then, to Lucas: "See anything?"

"Not much," Lucas said. "He might be tending down toward the road."

"We'll have ten guys there in five minutes, but there's no way he could get across," Peterson said. "I'm more worried about that damn bean field. We don't have enough people down there—if he could get into one of those rows, he could crawl a good way."

"He's hurt," Lucas said. "There's quite a bit of blood. Manette and the kid both stabbed him, and it could be bad."

"We can always hope the sonofabitch dies," Peterson said. "That'd be some kind of justice, anyway."

MAIL REACHED THE end of the field. The nearest cops were standing on top of a squad car three hundred yards away, but he could hear sirens, all the sirens in the world. In a few minutes, they'd be elbow-to-elbow.

The pain in his stomach was growing, but tolerable. He crawled sideways through the corn, careful not to disturb the stalks, then low-crawled to the fence. The cattails were now between him and the deputy, and he could see the open end of the culvert. A thin, keening excitement gripped him: it wasn't big, but he thought it would do. This just might be possible. Just barely. He'd slip these cocksuckers after all, Davenport and his thugs.

He lay on his back and edged under the lowest strand of barbed wire, then slid down the side of the ditch into the swampy patch. The cop turned his head, looking the other way, and Mail gained three feet, into the cattails, and stopped. If anybody walked down the shoulder of the road now, they'd look right down at him. But looking from down the road—from where the deputy stood, scanning the field with binoculars—he was covered. He found himself holding his breath, watching the deputy through a half-inch opening between blades of the cattails, and when the deputy turned his head again, he made another two feet, the water now almost covering him, like an alligator in wait.

The culvert was only ten feet away.

CHOPPERS COMING IN—the medevac one and a federal one. "They say they've got some plate in the floor, they can get right down on the deck with it," Peterson said.

Lucas nodded; "I'm gonna walk out along the road."

"Okay," Peterson nodded. "We'll flush him."

Lucas watched as Andi Manette, Grace, and Genevieve were loaded into the medical helicopter, Genevieve as an unrecognizable bundle of blankets. Andi

Manette stared blank-faced at him as the chopper lifted off. In a few seconds, it was a speck in the northern sky. At the same time, another machine, larger, powered in from the north. The feds, Lucas thought.

He walked down the road, slowly, a step or two at a time. There were only three deputies along the whole length of the road: the visibility was so good that Peterson was routing newcomers to the other edges. But Mail had come this way.

The corn waved in the light breeze, ripples running through it like wind fronts on a lake. Nothing jerky, nothing too quick. Lucas came up to the first deputy, a chunky blond with mirrored sunglasses and a shotgun on his hip.

"Was that the kid there in the well?" he asked as Lucas came up.

"In the cistern, yeah," Lucas said. "She's gonna make it. See anything at all?"

"Nothing. There's just enough wind that the corn's moving, and you can't see much." He pointed his nose into the wind and sniffed, like a hunting dog, and Lucas continued down the road, studying the field.

Two-thirds of the way to the next deputy, he saw the culvert poking through under the road. It wasn't more than eighteen inches in diameter, he thought, maybe too small.

But this was where Mail was headed.

In fact . . .

A thin vein of water led from the fence to the shallow puddle near the end of the culvert pipe. Could he already be inside?

Lucas stepped carefully down the embankment.

And saw the grooves in the mud heading to the culvert. Thighs and shoe tips. And there . . . a speck of blood, almost black on the green grass. The culvert was small, and he risked a quick peek inside. He could see only a tiny crescent of green on the other side. As he watched, the crescent vanished. Mail was pulling himself through. The space was tight, but he was moving.

Lucas climbed the bank, walked to the other side, and looked over the edge. The pipe emptied into another cattail swamp on the opposite side, with a little mud delta leading away from the pipe itself. The delta was undisturbed and Lucas again let himself down the bank. He could hear Mail, possibly halfway through, scraping along, struggling.

And what did Mail's file say? That he was a frantic claustrophobic?

MAIL HAD GONE headfirst into the pipe, his shoulders tight against the corrugated sides. There was mud in the bottom of the pipe, and halfway through, the pipe itself was more than half-blocked by a rotten wooden board and a clump of dead weeds. But on the other side of the blockage, he could see a disk of light. If he could get that far . . .

He pulled the board and the weeds away with his hands, passing them down the length of his body, then kicking them back with his feet. He had barely enough room to maneuver his arms, and his breath came harder. He kicked, found one foot held tight; he kicked again, and still was stuck.

Now the claustrophobia seized him, and he began tearing frantically at the mud, whimpering, spitting, grunting, his breath coming harder and harder . . . and he broke free. Twenty feet from the end, fifteen feet. Pain burned through his stomach, and he had to stop. Goddamn; he touched his shirt, pulled his hand away; he couldn't see it, but he could smell it. He was bleeding worse. When he tried to move, he found he was stuck again, and he kicked frantically at whatever held him; splashed water, where part of the pipe had corroded away. Heard a noise. A rat?

Was there a rat in here with him?

Close to panic, he bucked down the pipe, the pain tearing at him. But could see green at the end of the pipe.

Okay. Okay. He pushed the panic back: he'd have to be careful now. He'd have to make himself move slowly, even with the impulse to dash into the cornfield. If he could get in undetected, he could do this. He'd never really thought there was a chance, but now . . .

A heavy clump of something—dirt, sod—dropped into the circle of light at the end of the pipe, half-blocking it. Then another clump.

Mail, shocked, froze.

And a familiar voice said, "Is it wet down there, John?"

THE EMBANKMENT HAD been seeded with some kind of heavy, thick-bladed grass. The recent rain had softened it, and by grabbing clumps of the grass by the base, Lucas found he could pull up a foot-square clump of sod. He pulled out a half-dozen clumps, then sat down on the embankment above the pipe. When Mail was close enough, he dropped the first of the clumps into the mouth of the culvert.

"Is it wet down there, John?"

There was no answer for a moment, then Mail's voice, low, desperate. "Let me out of here."

"Nah," Lucas said. "We found the little girl in the cistern. She was alive, but not by much. How in the fuck could you do that, John? Throw the kid in the hole?" He dropped another clump of grass into the entrance of the culvert.

"Let me out of here, I'm hurt," Mail screamed.

"Not for long," Lucas said. "The water's draining through from the other end. I'll block this up, the pipe'll fill up . . . it won't take long. Nobody will know. They'll think you got away. It'll almost be like you won—except you'll be dead. And I'll have a good laugh."

Mail screamed, "Help . . . help me," and Lucas could hear his hands and feet beating on the inside of the pipe. He was apparently trying to move backwards.

MAIL PUSHED HIMSELF away from the sound of the voice, aware now that the water under him was moving with him. Must be downhill. Maybe the pipe would fill up . . . must get out. Must get out . . .

He backed away, frantically, until his feet hit the muck he'd passed behind himself coming in: and he remembered. He kicked at it, couldn't see it, couldn't move. He was stuck. Ahead, there was only a small square of light at the mouth of the culvert. He crawled forward again, stopped, twisted around enough that he could free the pistol, and pushed it out ahead of him.

"Let me out," he screamed. He fired the pistol. The muzzle blast and flash stunned and deafened him. He inched forward like a mole, in the water, fired again.

He couldn't see much at all, just a thin rim of light. Davenport said something, but Mail couldn't make it out. He simply lay in the deepening water, in the dark, with the pain in his stomach, the strange blindness in his eye, the world closing in on him. Davenport would bury him alive, he could feel the water rising. He thrashed and couldn't move, couldn't move; he had the gun, and without thinking, pushed it under his chin.

LUCAS HEARD THE muffled shot, and waited.

"John?"

He listened, heard nothing. The frantic beating had stopped. He looked back up the road, where the cops were still standing on the tops of their cars, looking the wrong way, into the cornfield. The shots from inside the culvert had been almost inaudible on the outside. Lucas started pulling the clumps of muck out of the pipe.

A little flow of water came out.

And then some blood.

And a clump of bloody, pulped flesh, floating like a child's leaf-ship, on the thin stream of muddy water.

Lucas stood up, and with the toe of one ruined shoe, pushed the clumps of grass out of the mouth of the culvert, and climbed to the road.

"Hey." He yelled at the cop on the closest car. When the cop turned, he pointed into the ditch and people began to run toward him.

36

SLOAN DROVE DOWN to the farm, gunless, suspended, afraid he was missing the action. He found a dozen cops on their hands and knees next to a culvert, and Lucas sitting on the steps of the tumble-down farmhouse.

"Need a ride, sweetheart?"

"I need a cigarette," Lucas said. "I don't know why I ever quit."

Sloan told him about it as they headed back to town:

"Wolfe wouldn't have anything to do with me, so I went with Franklin and Helen Manette. I sort of bullshitted her, being nice, and Helen opened her mouth and everything came out."

"Won't do much good," Lucas said. "A court won't take anything after the first time she asked for a lawyer, and we didn't get one."

"I wasn't thinking about that," Sloan said. "I just wanted to know why she did it."

"Money," Lucas said. "Some way or another."

Sloan nodded. "She knew all about Tower and Wolfe. Tower is in a lot worse financial shape than anybody knows. Almost everything is gone. His salary at the foundation has been cut, and they took a big equity loan on the house five years ago, and they've had a hard time making payments. The only thing they had going for them was the money from the trust—and there's a provision in the deed of trust that if the trustees decided that there was no possibility of the last benefactor having children, then the trust would be dissolved and the last benefactor would get the whole thing. A lump sum. Right now, thirteen million dollars."

"Jesus," Lucas said. "That much?"

"Yep. The trust was in bonds. The trust company had to put aside enough income every year to cover inflation, and the rest of the income was divided up among the eligible people—Tower, Andi, and her two daughters. They were all getting about a hundred grand a year. If Andi and the two daughters were dead, and Tower pushed for it, the trust would be dissolved and he'd get the lump. And that's what Helen Manette was looking for. She figured Tower was about to dump her. She figured she'd get half."

"And she met Mail at the apartment?"

"Yeah. He asked about her name, said he'd had a doctor named Manette. He said some things that made her realize that he was the guy Andi had talked about a few times—the guy so crazy that he scared the life out of her. He gave her a name, Martin LaDoux. She found his phone number and started calling him."

"We could have seen it," Lucas said.

"We would have," Sloan said. "But man, it's only been five days. Not a whole five days, yet."

"Seems like a century," Lucas said.

A moment later, Sloan said, "You know what she asked me?"

"What?"

"If her helping us would qualify for Dunn's reward money . . ."

Halfway back, they got a call from the chief's secretary, saying Roux was on the way to the hospital. She wanted Lucas and Sloan to stop by. When they arrived, the hospital's turnout was clogged with cars.

Sloan looked him over. "Maybe I oughta drop you at emergency," he said. "You look like shit."

"I'm all right," Lucas said, getting out of the car. His shoes were ruined, his suit pants, still wet, clung to his legs. His underwear and shirt, both soaked, felt like they were full of sand. His tie was a wet, twisted wreck; he hadn't shaved.

Sloan looked him over. "Your suit coat looks nice," he said.

ROUX SAW HIM first, hurried down the tile hallway, and caught him in her arms with a powerful hug. "Jesus, you got them back. I never would have believed it."

Dunn was there, pounding him on the back. "Jesus Christ, all of them." His face was luminous.

"Easy," Lucas said. "How's Genevieve?"

"Exposure," Dunn said, his face going dark. "She wouldn't have lasted the rest of the day. And she may have nerve damage in her legs. Maybe not too serious, it's too soon to tell. But the way she was caught up in the coat, the nerves were all pinched up . . ."

"Andi and Grace?"

Dunn looked at the floor, and then away. "Physically, they'll be okay; psychologically, they're in terrible shape. Andi is just . . . just rambling. God, I don't know . . ." And he turned and walked away without another word, back toward a cluster of doctors.

"You heard about Helen Manette?" Lucas asked Roux.

"From Franklin," she said. She shook her head. "I don't know what's gonna happen. We gotta talk with everybody from the state's attorney's office. We're gonna arrest her, but if we ever get her in court, I just don't know. But she's not our biggest problem."

Lucas nodded. "Wolfe?"

"Yeah. We're meeting with her and her lawyer." Roux looked at her watch. "In about forty-five minutes. You better be around, in case I need you."

"I'd hoped she'd go away, on her own," Lucas said.

"She hasn't," Roux said grimly.

There was a buzz of noise at the hospital, and Lucas looked down the hall. The mayor pushed through, and Roux said, "I gotta go. Stick close to your office."

"Sure," Lucas said.

ROUX CALLED AN hour later, as Lucas sat in his office, talking with Sloan and Del. "You better come down."

The chief's secretary waved him through, saying, "They're waiting," and "God, that was great this morning. You're my hero."

"Yeah, but for how long?" Lucas asked.

"Rest of the week," she promised.

Nancy Wolfe, a loose-fleshed man with freckles and shiny red hair, Lester, and Rose Marie Roux faced each other in a tense rectangle around Roux's desk. The red-haired man's hands were steepled, and he wore a careful gray suit with a gold lapel pin. A lawyer, Lucas thought.

Roux pointed at an empty chair next to Lester. "Sit down. We're trying to work out what happened this morning."

"You know what happened," Wolfe snapped. She looked across the desk at Lucas, her eyes on fire. "The question is, what are you going to do about it?"

"What do you want?" Lucas asked.

"I want you out," she said. "I'll reserve the right to go to court no matter what happens, but I want you out now."

"We saved your partner's life," Lucas said.

"You should have found another way to do it . . ."

"There was no time."

". . . without . . . *violating me.*"

Lucas shook his head. "No time."

"You should have made some," Wolfe said.

Rose Marie cleared her throat. "Lucas will be staying. I won't fire him. In fact, I'm putting him in for a commendation. I'm sorry that you were inconvenienced."

"Inconvenienced?" Wolfe shrilled. "I was strip-searched and given these prison clothes and they made me sit there while they shouted at me"—her lip trembled—"and they wouldn't let me call anybody, a lawyer, or anybody."

"Rose Marie, we're talking about a lot of money," the lawyer said, dryly. "Guys have done a lot less than Davenport, to people who deserved it a lot more, and they've been hammered. People are tired of this department, the way it handles people. You lose a million, two million, five million—and that's possible, in this case—and you'll be out of here. If you fire Davenport, at least it'll be a sign that you disapprove."

Rose Marie was shaking her head, and said, "Won't do it."

The lawyer nodded at Wolfe and said, "Well, that's it, then."

Wolfe gathered up her purse. "We're definitely going ahead."

Lester said, out of nowhere, "You can go to court, but I don't think we'll lose. We had some good reasons to interview Dr. Wolfe."

Lucas glanced at Lester, uncertainly, then looked at Roux, who raised her eyebrows. She didn't know what Lester was talking about, either.

The lawyer, who had dropped his hands to his lap when he was talking about the five million, resteepled his fingers, then peeked at Lester from behind them. "I know what you're thinking. And if the jury was deciding right this minute, you might get away with it. Ms. Manette and her daughters are in the hospital, the TV people are going crazy, there'd be a lot of sympathy for what Chief Davenport did. But when we get to court, six months from now, or a year from now? You'll lose. And Ms. Wolfe has expressed a determination to follow up on this."

Lester tried to break in during the speech, and finally got in with, "That's not what I'm thinking. I'm not talking about the Manette case at all."

The lawyer stopped and asked, "Then what are you talking about?"

"I'm talking about William Charles Aakers and Carlos Neroda Sonches," Lester said. "Two of Dr. Wolfe's patients . . . and Andi Manette's. We were planning to ask Dr. Wolfe about these cases when Chief Davenport found out where the suspect Mail was hiding, and he had to leave. But we *will* come back to Dr. Wolfe on these . . ."

He had two manila folders in his hands. They were empty, but a cursive feminine handwriting on the tabs said, *Aakers* and *Sonches*. He passed the folders to the lawyer.

"What are these?" the redhead asked, looking at Wolfe.

"Two patients," she hissed. "This man is trying to blackmail me."

"I'm not trying to do anything of the sort," Lester said. "The contents of these two files have been temporarily misplaced, due to some bureaucratic confusion with the other files in the case, but we'll find them and continue our evaluation. We feel that there might well be cause for prosecution."

"What?" the attorney asked. He was looking at Lucas.

Lucas shrugged, and Lester said, "Your client has been treating child molesters without informing the required law enforcement officials. It's all in the records. And we'll find these records. I'm gonna tear the department to pieces if I have to."

Roux leaned back in her chair; Lester looked intent, and Lucas looked away.

After a moment, Wolfe said, "You fuckers."

"BLACKMAIL," WEATHER SAID that night. She was eating the back end of a lobster.

"I suppose," Lucas said. "She reserved the right to do whatever she wanted, but she won't do anything. She'll let it go."

"I don't think I approve," Weather said.

"I could burn the papers, I suppose—if I could find them," Lucas said. "Then we could call her up, tell her we're sorry, and let her sue."

"You were pretty rough with her."

"Shit happens." Lucas yawned, stretched, and smiled. "Just like the bumper sticker says."

"ARE YOU OKAY?" she asked. They'd gone into the living room and parked on the couch, Weather leaning back with her head on his shoulder.

"I'm tired," he said. "I'm so tired."

"I heard a cop was shot, that there had been a shooting, a surgical tech told me . . ." The words were tumbling out in an uncontrolled spate, and her body tensed against him. "I couldn't believe it, I called Phil Orris over at Ramsey. you remember him, the orthopod . . ."

"Yeah."

"He said, 'No, no, it's not Lucas, it's a woman.' I was like, thank you, Jesus, thank you. I was so glad this poor woman was shot, that it wasn't you."

"She's kind of messed up, Sherrill is," Lucas said. "The bone's broken."

"Better than you getting shot," she said. "You've been shot enough."

They sat quietly for a second, then Lucas said, "I think we ought to get married."

She went absolutely still against him, and a second later, said, "So do I."

"I've got a ring for you," he said.

"I know, it's been driving everybody crazy," she said.

He grinned, but she couldn't see it. She was still facing away, the top of her head just under his nose.

"Why don't you go sit in the tub?" she suggested. "Then get in bed. You could use about fifteen hours of sleep."

"All right. Here, move away." He pushed her off a bit, and dug in his pocket, found the ring. "I could never think of what to tell you when I gave it to you," he said. "Except, I love you."

She put it on her finger, and it fit. "You could go on for a while," she said. "But that's certainly an excellent start."

LUCAS SAT IN the tub for fifteen minutes, but he was never any good at re-laxing in hot water. He got out, toweled off, put on a robe, and wandered through the house, looking for Weather, to say good night. He found her on the telephone, and heard her say, "Guess what?"

She was telling friends about the proposal, about the ring. He watched her for a moment, and her face was luminous, like Dunn's had been at the hospital, glowing with a light of its own.

He felt a sudden pang of fear: the moment was too perfect to last. He shook it off, walked into the kitchen, touched her hair, her cheek, kissed her chin.

"Taking a nap," he said.

She dropped the phone to her lap. "Del is pissed," she said. "He had until noon today, in the proposal pool. Some guy named Wood won six hundred and twenty dollars."

Lucas grinned. "Pretty romantic, huh?"

"Go to bed," she said. He walked back toward the bedroom, stopped, and listened.

He heard her punch new numbers into the phone, and heard her say again, "Guess what?"

SUDDEN PREY

1

THROUGH THE SPEAKERS above his head, little children sang in sweet voices, *O holy night, the stars are brightly shining, it is the night of the dear Savior's birth . . .*

The man who might kill Candy LaChaise stood in the cold and watched her through the glass doors. Sometimes he could see only the top of her head, and sometimes not even that, but he never lost track of her.

Candy, unaware, browsed through the lingerie, moving slowly from rack to rack. She wasn't really interested in underwear: her attention was fixed on the back of the store, the appliance department. She stopped, pulled out a black bustier, held it up, cocked her head like women do. Put it back, turned toward the doors.

The man who might kill her stepped back, out of sight.

A minivan pulled to the curb and a chunky woman in an orange parka hopped out and pushed back the van's side door. An avalanche of dumplinglike children spilled onto the sidewalk. They were of both sexes, all blond, and of annual sizes: maybe four, five, six, seven, eight and nine years old. The van headed for a parking space, while the woman herded the kids toward the doors.

The man took a bottle from his pocket, stuck his tongue into the neck, tipped it up and faked a swallow or two. The woman hustled the kids past him, shielding them with her body, into the store and out of sight. That was what he wanted; he put the bottle away, and looked back through the doors.

THERE SHE WAS, still in lingerie. He looked around, and cursed the season: the Christmas decorations, the dirty piles of hard, frozen snow along the streets, the wind that cut through his woolen gloves. His face was thin, unshaven, the skin stretched like parchment on a tambourine. Nicotine had stained his teeth as yellow as old ivory. He lit a Camel, and when he put the cigarette to his lips, his hands trembled with the cold. When he exhaled, the wind snatched away the smoke and the steam of his breath, and made him feel even colder than he was.

AN OILY BARITONE, a man who'd never be Bing Crosby: *. . . Let nothing you dismaaay, Remember Christ our Sa-ay-vior was born on Christmas Day . . .*

He thought, "Christ, if I could only stop the music . . ."

From where he stood, he could see the golden spire atop the state capitol; under the December overcast it looked like a bad piece of brass. Fucking Minnesota. He put the bottle to his lips, and this time let a little of the wine trickle down his throat. The harsh grape-juice taste cut into his tongue, but there was no warmth in the alcohol.

What in the hell was she doing?

She'd cruised Sears Brand Central, taking her time, looking at refrigerators, buying nothing. Then she strolled through the ladies' wear department, where she'd looked at blouses. Then she walked back through Brand Central, checking the cellular telephones.

Again she walked away: he'd been inside at the time, and she'd almost trapped him in the television display. He hit the doors, went through, outside into the wind . . . but she'd swerved toward the lingerie. Had she spotted him? A TV salesman had. Picking up his ragged coat and rotten shoes, the salesman had posted himself near the Toshiba wide-screens, and was watching him like a hawk. Maybe she . . .

There. She was on her way out.

When Candy walked out of Sears, he didn't look at her. He saw her, but he didn't move his head. He simply stood against the outside wall, rocked on his heels, mumbled into his parka and took another nip of the MD 20-20.

CANDY NEVER REALLY saw him, not then. She half-turned in his direction as she left the store, but her eyes skipped over him, like they might skip over a trash barrel or a fire hydrant. She *bopped* down the parking lot, not quite in a hurry, but not dawdling, either. Her step was light, athletic, confident, the step of a cheerful woman. She was pretty, in a thirty-something high-school cheerleader way, with natural blond hair, a round Wisconsin face and a clear Wisconsin complexion.

She walked halfway down the lot before she spotted the Chevy van and started toward it.

The man who might kill her, who still stood by the doors, said, "She just walked past her car."

A Republican state legislator in a wool Brooks Brothers overcoat heard the words and hurried into the store. No time for dialogue with a street schizo: you see them everywhere, mumbling into their wine-stained parkas.

"I think she's going for that van, dude."

CANDY LIKED COUNTRY music and shirt pockets that had arrows at the corners. She liked line-dancing and drinking Grain Belt. She liked roadhouses on country blacktop, pickup trucks and cowboy boots and small blue-eyed children and guns. When she got to the Chevy van, she took out a two-inch key ring filled with keys and began running them through the lock. She hit it on the twelfth one, and popped the door.

The van belonged to a slightly ragged Sears washing machine salesman named Larry. The last time she'd seen Larry, he was standing next to a seven-hundred-dollar Kenmore washer with Quiet Pak and Automatic Temperature Control, repinning his name tag. He was about ten minutes late—late enough that she'd started to worry, as she browsed the blouses and underwear. Had the van broken down? That would be a major problem . . .

But then, there he was, breathing hard, face pink from the cold, leaning against the Kenmore. Larry was a wise guy, she knew, and she didn't care for wise guys. She knew he was a wise guy because a bumper sticker on the back of his van said, in large letters, *AGAINST ABORTION*? And below that, in smaller letters, *Then Don't Have One*. Abortion was not a topic for bumper-sticker humor.

THE MAN WHO might kill her mumbled into his parka: "She's in the van, she's moving."

The voice that spoke back to him was not God: "I got her."

Great thing about parkas: nobody could see the commo gear, the microphones and earplugs. "She's gonna do it," Del said. He put the bottle of Mogen David on the ground, carefully, so it wouldn't spill. He wouldn't need it again, but somebody might.

"Franklin says LaChaise and Cale just went into that pizza joint behind the parking ramp," said the voice in his ear. "They went out the back of the ramp, through a hole in a hedge."

"Scoping it out, one last time. That's where they'll dump the van," Del said. "Get Davenport on the road."

"Franklin called him. He's on the way. He's got Sloan and Sherrill with him."

"All right," Del said, noncommittally. *Not all right*, he thought. Sherrill had been shot a little more than four months earlier. The slug had nicked an artery and she'd almost bled out before they got her to the hospital. Del had pinched the artery so hard that Sherrill had later joked that she felt fine, except for the massive bruise where Del had pinched her leg.

Putting Sherrill's face into this, so soon, might be too heavy, Del thought. Sometimes Davenport showed all the common sense of a . . . Del couldn't think of anything. A trout, maybe.

"There she goes," said the voice in his ear.

THE SALESMAN'S VAN stank of cigar smoke. Candy's nose wrinkled at the smell, but she wouldn't have to tolerate it for long. She eased the van out of the parking space, and checked the gas: half a tank, more than enough. She drove slowly up the block, to Dale, down Dale and onto I-94 toward Minneapolis. Georgie and Duane would be waiting at Ham's Pizza.

She looked at the speedometer: fifty-four. Perfect. Crooks mostly drove too fast. Dick said they didn't give a shit about the traffic laws or the other small stuff, and half the time they'd hit a bank, get away clean, then get caught because they were doing sixty-five in a fifty-five. She wouldn't make *that* mistake.

She tried to relax, checked all the mirrors. Nothing unusual. She took the P7 out of her coat pocket, slipped the magazine, pushed on the top shell with her thumb. She could tell by the pressure that she had a full clip.

Dick always made fun of the little bitty nine-millimeter shells, but she'd stick with them. The small gun felt right in her hand and the muzzle blast was easy to manage. The P7 held thirteen rounds. She could put nine or ten of the thirteen shots into the top of a Campbell's soup can at twenty-five feet, in less than seven seconds. A couple of times, she'd put all thirteen in.

Good shooting. Of course, soup-can lids didn't move. But on the two occasions when she'd been shooting for real, she felt no more pressure than when she'd been outside Dick's double-wide, banging away at soup-can lids. You didn't really line anything up, you kept both eyes open and looked across the front sights, tracking, and just at that little corner of time when the sight crossed a shirt pocket or a button or another good aim point, you'd take up the last sixteenth of an inch and . . .

Pop. Pop, pop.

Candy got a little hot just thinking about it.

DANNY KUPICEK HAD long black hair that his wife cut at home, and it fell over his eyes and his oversized glasses so that he looked like a confused shoe clerk. That helped when he was working the dopers: dopers were afraid of anyone too hip. They trusted shoe clerks and insurance salesmen and guys wearing McDonald's hats. Danny looked like all of those. He pulled the city Dodge to the curb and Del climbed in and Kupicek took off, three hundred yards behind the Chevy van. Del put his hands over the heat vent.

"I gotta come up with a new persona for the wintertime," Del said. "Somebody who's got a warm coat."

"State legislator," Kupicek said. He'd been sitting in the car off the capitol grounds, keeping an eye on Candy's car. He'd watched the politicians coming and going, and noticed how prosperous they seemed.

"Nah," Del said, shaking his head. "I wanna try somebody legit."

"Whatever, you gotta keep your head covered," said Kupicek. He wore heavy corduroy pants, a sweater over a button-down shirt, a wool watch cap and an open parka. "Fifty percent of all heat loss comes from the head."

"What do you think the hood is for?" Del asked, pointing over his shoulder.

"Too loose," Kupicek said, like he knew what he was talking about. He was nine cars behind Candy when they entered I-94, in the slow lane and two lanes to the right. "You need a stocking cap under there."

"Fuck a bunch of stocking caps. I need a desk job is what I need. Maybe I'll apply for a grant."

Kupicek looked at him, the yellow teeth and two-day stubble. "You ain't grant material," he said, frankly. "I'm grant material. Sherrill's grant material. Even Franklin is grant material. You, you ain't grant material."

"Fuck you and your wife and all your little children," Del said. He picked up Kupicek's handset. "Lucas, you there?"

Davenport came back instantly: "We're setting up in the Swann parking lot. Where is she?"

"Just passing Lexington," Del said.

"Stay with her. When she gets off at 280, let me know as soon as she's at the top of the ramp."

"Do that," Del said.

Kupicek was watching the van: "She's got some discipline. I don't think we touched fifty-six since we got on the road."

"She's a pro," Dell said.

"If it was me, I'd be so freaked, I'd be doing ninety. Course, maybe they're not gonna do it."

"They're gonna do it," Del said. He could feel it: they were gonna do it.

GEORGIE LACHAISE WAS a dark woman with blue eyes that looked out from under too-long, too-thick eyebrows. She had a fleshy French nose, full lips with the corners downturned. She locked Duane Cale's eyes across the table and said, "Duane, you motherfucker, if you drive off, I'll find you and I'll shoot you in the fuckin' back. I promise you."

Duane leaned forward over the yellow Formica table, both hands wrapped around an oversized cup of Coke Classic. He had an unformed face, and hair that had never picked a color: one eyewitness might say he was blond, another would swear that he had brown hair. One would say apple-cheeked, another would say fox-faced. He seemed to change, even as you looked at him. He wore a camouflage army jacket over jeans and boots, with the collar turned up, and a Saints baseball hat.

"Oh, I'll do it," he said, "but it don't feel right. It just don't feel right. I mean, we did that one in Rice Lake, I was good there."

"You were perfect in Rice Lake," Georgie said. She thought, *You were so scared I thought we'd have to carry you out.* "This time, all you gotta do is drive."

"Okay, you see right there?" asked Duane, tapping the tabletop with the cup. "You said it your own self: I was perfect. This don't feel perfect, today. No sir. I mean, I'll do it if you say so, but I . . ."

Georgie cut him off. "I say so," she said bluntly. She glanced at her watch. "Candy'll be here in a minute. You get your asshole puckered up and get behind the wheel and everything'll go smooth. You know what to do. You only gotta drive two blocks. You'll be perfect."

"Well, okay . . ." His Adam's apple bobbed. Duane Cale was too scared to spit and the Coca-Cola didn't seem to make a difference.

LUCAS DAVENPORT PEELED off his topcoat and the gray Icelandic sweater. Sloan handed him the vest and Lucas shrugged into it, slapping the Velcro tabs into place, everything nice and snug, except if you took a shot in the armpit it'd go right through your heart and both lungs on the way out the opposite 'pit . . . Never turn sideways.

"Fuckin' cold," Sloan said. He was a narrow, sideways-looking man who today wore a rabbit-fur hat. "We live in fuckin' Russia. The Soviet fuckin' Union."

"Is no Soviet Union," Lucas said. They were in a drugstore parking lot, Lucas and Sloan and Sherrill, and had gotten out of the slightly warm car to put on the vests. A loitering civilian watched them as his dog, wearing a blue jacket, sniffed up an ice-bound curb.

"I know," Sloan said. "It moved here."

Lucas pulled the sweater back over his head, then slipped back into his topcoat. He was a tall man, dark-haired, dark-complected with ice-blue eyes. A scar trailed through one brow ridge and expired on his cheek, a white line like a scratch across his face. As his head popped through the sweater's neck hole, he was grinning at Sloan, an old friend: "Who was trying to start a departmental ski team?"

"Hey, you gotta do something in the middle of the . . ."

The radio broke in: "Lucas?"

Lucas picked up the handset: "Yeah."

"On the 280 ramp," Del said.

"Got it . . . you get that, Franklin?"

Franklin came back, his voice chilled. "I got it. I can see LaChaise and Cale, they're still sitting there. They look like they're arguing."

"Keep moving," Lucas said.

"I'm moving. I'm so fuckin' cold I'm afraid to stop."

"On University . . ." Del said.

"We better go," Sherrill said. Her face was pink with the cold, and nicely framed by her kinky black hair. She wore a black leather jacket with tight jeans and gym shoes, and furry white mittens that she'd bought in a sale from a cop catalog. The mittens were something a high school kid might wear, but had a trigger-finger slit, like hunting gloves. "She'll be picking them up."

"Yeah." Lucas nodded, and they climbed into the city car, Sloan in the driver's seat, Sherrill next to him, Lucas sprawled in the back.

"Here she comes," said Franklin, calling on the radio.

"Check your piece," Lucas said over the seat to Sherrill. He wasn't quite sure of her, what she'd do. He wanted to see. He slipped his own .45 out of his coat pocket, punched out the magazine, racked the shell out of the chamber, then went through the ritual of reloading. In the front seat, Sherrill was spinning the wheel on her .357.

As Sloan took the car through an easy U-turn and the three blocks toward the Midland Steel Federal Credit Union, Lucas looked out the window at the street, and felt the world begin to shift.

The shift always happened before a fight, a suddenly needle-sharp appreciation of image and texture, of the smell of other bodies, of cigarette tar and Juicy Fruit, gun oil, wet leather. If your mind could always work like this, he thought, if it could always operate on this level of realization, you would be a genius. Or mad. Or both.

Lucas remembered a stray thought from earlier in the day, picked up the handset and called dispatch.

"We need two squads on University," he said. "We're tracking a stolen Chevy van and we want a uniform stop as soon as possible."

He recited the tag number and license and the dispatcher confirmed it. "We've got a car on Riverside," the dispatcher said. "We'll start them that way."

CANDY PULLED THE van to the curb outside Ham's Pizza. Georgie and Duane were waiting, and she slid over to the passenger seat, and popped the back door for Georgie as Duane got in the driver's seat.

"Everything okay?" Duane asked.

"Great, Duane," Candy said. She gave him her cheerleader smile.

Duane hungered for her, in his Duane-like way. They'd gone to school together, elementary through high school. They'd played on a jungle gym, smart Candy and not-so-smart Duane. She'd let him see her tits a couple of times— once down by Meyer's Creek, skinny-dipping with Dick, when Dick hadn't seen Duane coming, but Candy had. She was Dick's woman, all right, but wasn't above building extracurricular loyalty for a time when it might be needed.

"Drive," Georgie said from the back. And to Candy: "You set?"

"I'm set."

"This should be a good one," Georgie said.

"Should be great," Candy said. Ten o'clock on a payday morning. The paychecks were issued at eleven. The first employees would be sneaking out to cash their checks by eleven-oh-one. That'd be an hour too late.

"There's the nigger again," Duane said, distractedly.

A giant black man had come into Ham's before Candy had gotten there, ordered a slice, asked if he could pay with food stamps. When told that he couldn't, he'd reluctantly taken two crumpled dollar bills out of his pocket and pushed them across the counter.

"Food stamps," Georgia said in disgust. "He's one of those screwballs. Look at him talk to himself."

Franklin, shambling along the street, said, "One block, fifteen seconds."

DUANE SAID, "THERE it is," and his voice may have trembled when he said it. Georgie and Candy turned away from the black man and looked down the street at the yellow brick building with the plastic sign, and the short stoop out front.

"Remember what I said, Duane. We'll be in there for one minute," Georgie said. She leaned forward and spoke softly into his ear, and when Duane tried to turn his head away, she caught his earlobe and tugged it back, pinched it between her nails. Duane flinched, and she said, "If you drive away, one of us will hunt you down and kill you. If you drive, Duane, you're dead. Isn't that right, Candy?"

"That's right," Candy said, looking at him. She let some ice show, then switched to her God-Duane-I'd-Love-to-Fuck-You-But-I-Gotta-Be-True-to-Dickie look. "But he won't drive. Duane's okay." She patted his thigh.

"Oh, I'll do it," Duane said. He looked like a trapped rat. "I mean, I'll do it. I did it in Rice Lake, didn't I?"

He pulled the van to the curb and Georgie gave him a look, then the two women pulled nude nylon stockings over their faces and took the pistols out of their coat pockets.

"Let's go," Georgie said. She climbed out, and Candy followed a step behind; it passed through Georgie's mind that Candy looked radiant.

"I feel like I might pop one," Candy said to Georgie, as they climbed the four steps to the Credit Union door.

FRANKLIN WAS HALFWAY down the block when they went inside and he said, "The two women are inside. Pulled the nylons over their heads. It's going down."

Five seconds later, Del and Kupicek stopped at the corner behind him, then eased forward so they could see the back of the Chevy van and Cale's head. They were forty yards away.

Sloan stopped at the next corner up, and eased forward until he could see the front of the truck. "You set?" Lucas asked. He cracked the back door.

"Yeah." Sloan nodded, looked almost sleepy and yawned. Tension.

"Let's go," Lucas said. And in the handset he said, "Go."

GEORGIE AND CANDY went in hard, very large, very loud, screaming, masks, guns, Georgie first:

"On the wall," she screamed, "on the wall," and Candy behind her, vaulting to the top of the cash counter, screaming, the gun big in her hand, the hole at the muzzle looking for eyes. "On the wall . . ."

Four women employees and a single customer, a man in a black ski jacket and tinted eyeglasses, were inside the credit union. The woman closest to Candy looked like a carp, her mouth opening and closing, opening and closing, hands coming up, then waving, as though she could wave away a bullet. She wore a pink sweater with hand-darned blue flax blossoms in a line across the chest. Another woman curled up and turned away, looking back at them over her shoulder, and stepped against the back wall, next to a filing cabinet. She wouldn't look at Candy. A younger woman, a cashier, jumped back, yelped once, put her hands over her mouth, backed away, knocked a phone off a table, jumped again, froze. The fourth woman simply backed away, her hands at her shoulders.

Georgie said, rapid-fire, a vocal machine gun: "Easy, easy, everybody take it easy. Everybody shut up, shut up, shut up, and stand still. Stand still, everybody shut up . . . This is a holdup, shut up."

They'd been inside for ten seconds. Candy dropped behind the counter and pulled a pillowcase out of her waistband and started dumping cash drawers.

"Not enough," she shouted over Georgie's chant. "Not enough, there's more somewhere."

Georgie picked out the woman with the best clothes, the woman with the flax blossoms, pointed her finger at her and shouted, "Where is it, where's the rest of it?"

The woman said, "No-no-no . . ."

Georgie pointed her pistol at the man in the ski jacket and said, "If you don't say, in one second I'm gonna blow his fuckin' head off, his fuckin' head."

Georgie was posed in a two-handed TV-cop position, the pistol pointing at jacket-man's head, never wavering. The flax-blossom woman looked around for somebody to help her, somebody to direct her, but there wasn't anybody. She sagged and said, "There's a box in the office."

Candy grabbed her, roughed her, shoved her toward the tiny cubicle in the back. The woman, scuttling ahead, pointed at a box on the floor in the footwell of the desk. Candy shoved her back toward the door, picked up the box, put it on the desk, and popped the top: stacks of currency, tens, twenties, fifties, hundreds.

"Got it," she shouted. She dumped it in the pillowcase.

"Let's go," Georgie shouted. "Let's go . . ."

Candy twisted the top of the pillowcase and threw it over her shoulder, like Santa Claus, and hustled around the cash counter toward the door. The man in the ski jacket had backed against the wall at a check-writing desk, his hands over his head, a twisted, trying-to-please smile on his face, his eyes frightened white spots behind the amber-tinted specs.

"What are you laughing at?" Candy screamed at him. "Are you laughing at us?"

The smile got broader, but he waved his fingers and said, "No, no, I'm not laughing . . ."

"Fuck you," she said, and she shot him in the face.

The blast in the small office was a bomb: the four women shrieked and went down. The man simply dropped, a spray of blood on the tan wall behind his head, and Georgie spun and said, "Go."

They were out the door in seconds . . .

"Do it," Del said, and Kupicek floored it.

Sloan was coming in from the front. Duane saw him coming, had no time to wonder. The car swerved and screeched to a stop three inches from the van's front bumper, wedging him to the curb. From behind, in a flash in his rearview mirror, he saw another car wedge in behind him. In the next half-second, the passenger door flew open and the big black pizza guy was there, and a gun pointed at the bridge of Duane's nose.

"Don't even fuckin' scratch," Franklin said, in his pleasant voice, which wasn't very pleasant. "Just sit tight." He reached across, flipped the shift lever into park, killed the engine, pulled the keys from the ignition and let them fall on the floor. "Just sit."

And then there were more guys, all on the passenger side of the car. But Duane, as interested as he was in the muzzle of Franklin's gun, turned to look at the door of the credit union.

He'd heard the shot: the sound was muffled, but there wasn't any doubt.

"Shit," said the black man. He said, loudly, "Watch it, watch it, we got a shot."

"GO," SCREAMED GEORGIE. She was smiling, like a South American revolutionary poster-girl, her dark hair whipping back, and she covered the inner door while Candy exploded through the outer door onto the stoop and then Georgie was through behind her and the van was right there.

And the cops.

They heard the shouting, though Candy never could isolate a word. She was aware of Georgie's gun coming up behind her and she felt her hand loosen on the bag and the bag falling off to the left, and her own gun coming up. She started squeezing the trigger before the gun was all the way up and she saw the thin slat-faced man, and his nose might have been about the size of a Campbell's soup-can lid and her pistol came up, came up . . .

LUCAS HEARD THE shot inside and he went sideways and saw Franklin reflexively crouch. Off to the left, Sherrill was propped over the top of Kupicek's car, her pistol leveled at the door and Lucas thought, *Hope they don't look out the window* . . .

Then the door flew open and the two LaChaise women were on the stoop and their guns were coming up and he shouted, "No, don't, no, don't," and he heard Del yelling, and Candy LaChaise started firing and he saw Sherrill's gun bucking in her hand . . .

CANDY SAW THE man with the yellow teeth and the black hole at the end of his pistol and the woman with the dark hair and maybe—if she had time—she thought, *Too late* . . .

She felt the bullets go through, several of them, was aware of the noise, of the flash, of the faces like wanted posters, all straining toward her, but no pain, just a jostling feel, like rays of light pushing through her chest . . . then her vision went, and she felt Georgie falling beside her. She was upside down, her feet on the stoop, her head on the sidewalk, and she waited for the light. The light would come, and behind it . . .

She was gone.

LUCAS WAS SHOUTING, "Hold it, hold it," and five seconds after the two women burst from the credit union, there was no reason to fire his own weapon.

In the sudden silence, through the stink of the smokeless powder, somebody said, "Jesus H. Christ."

2

THE MINNEAPOLIS CITY hall is a rude pile of liverish stone, damp in the summer, cold in the winter, ass-deep in cops, crooks, politicians, bureaucrats, favor-seekers, reporters, TV personalities and outraged taxpayers, none of whom were allowed to smoke inside the building.

The trail of illegal cigarette smoke followed Rose Marie Roux down the darkened marble halls from the chief's office to Homicide. The chief was a large woman, getting larger, her face going hound-dog with the pressure of the job and the passing of the years. She stopped outside homicide, took a drag on the cigarette, and blew smoke.

She could see Davenport inside, standing, hands in his pockets. He was wearing a blue wool suit, a white shirt with a long soft collar and what looked like an Hermès necktie—one of the anal numbers with eight million little horses prancing around. A political appointee, a deputy chief, his sideline software business made him worth, according to the latest rumors, maybe ten million dollars. He was talking to Sloan and Sherrill.

Sloan was thin, pasty-faced, serious, dressed all in brown and tan—he could lean against a wall and disappear. He could also make friends with anyone: he was the best interrogator on the force. Sloan hadn't taken his gun out that afternoon and was still on the job.

Sherrill, on the other hand, had fired all six shots from her revolver. She was still up, floating high on the release from the fear and ecstasy that sometimes came after a gunfight. Roux, in her few years on the street, before law school, had never drawn her pistol. She didn't like guns.

Roux watched the three of them, Lucas Davenport and his pals. Shook her head: maybe things were getting out of control. She dropped the cigarette on the floor, stepped on it and pushed through the door.

The three turned to look at her, and she looked at Lucas and tipped her head toward the hall. Lucas followed her back through the door, and shut the door against the inquiring ears of Sloan and Sherrill.

"The request for a uniform stop—when did you think of that?" Roux asked. Her words ricocheted down the marble halls, but there was nobody else to hear them.

Lucas leaned against the cool marble wall. He smiled quickly, the smile here and then gone. The smile made him look hard, even too hard: mean. He'd been working out, Roux thought. He went at it hard, from time to time, and when he'd really stripped himself down, he looked like a piece of belt leather. She could see the shape of his skull under his forehead skin.

"It seemed like a no-lose proposition," he said, his voice pitched low. They both knew what they were talking about.

She nodded. "Well, it worked. We released the voice tape from Dispatch and it's taking the heat off. You're gonna hear some firing-squad stuff from the *Star Tribune*, the editorial page. Questions about why they ever got inside— why you waited that long to move. But I don't think . . . no real trouble."

"If we'd just taken them, it would have come to a couple of witnesses with bad records," Lucas said. "They'd be back on the street right now."

"I know, but the way it looks . . ." She sighed. "If the LaChaises hadn't shot this guy Farris, there'd be a lot more trouble."

"Big break for us, Farris was," Lucas said, flashing his grim smile again.

"I didn't mean it that way," Roux said, and she looked away. "Anyway, Farris is gonna make it."

"Yeah, a little synthetic cheekbone, splice up his jaw, give him a bunch of new teeth, graft on a piece of ear . . ."

"I'm trying to cover you," Roux said sharply.

"Sounds like you're giving us shit," Lucas snapped back. "The Rice Lake bank people looked at the movies from the credit union security cameras. There's no doubt—it was the LaChaises that did it over there. They looked the same with the panty hose, said the same things, acted the same way. And it was Candy LaChaise who killed the teller. We're waiting to hear back from Ladysmith and Cloquet, but it'll be the same."

Roux shook her head and said, "You picked a hard way to do it, though: a hard way to settle it."

"They came out, they opened up, we were all right there," Lucas said. "They fired first. That's not cop bullshit."

"I'm not criticizing," Roux said. "I'm just saying the papers are asking questions."

"Maybe you oughta tell the papers to go fuck themselves," Lucas said. The chief was a politician who had at one time thought she might be headed for the Senate. "That'd be a good political move right now, the way things are."

Roux took an old-fashioned silver cigarette case out of her pocket, popped it open. "I'm not talking politics here, Lucas. I'm a little worried about what happened." She fumbled a cigarette out of the case, snapped the case shut. "There's a feel of . . . setup. Of taking the law in our own hands. We're okay, because Farris *was* shot and you made that call for a stop. But there were six or seven holes in Candy LaChaise. It's not like you weren't ready to do it."

"We were ready," Lucas agreed.

". . . So there could be another stink when the medical examiner's report comes out."

"Tell them to take their time writing the report," Lucas said. "You know the way things are: In a week or so, nobody'll care. And we're still a couple of months from the midwinter sweeps."

"Yeah, yeah. And the ME's cooperating. Still."

"The LaChaises started it," Lucas persisted. "And they were sport killers. Candy LaChaise shot people to see them die. Fuck 'em."

"Yeah, yeah," Roux said. She waved at him and started back toward the chief's office, shoulders slumped. "Send everybody home. We'll get the shooting board going tomorrow."

"You really pissed?" Lucas called after her.

"No. I'm just sorta . . . depressed. There've been too many bodies this year," she said. She stopped, flicked a lighter, touched off the fresh cigarette. The tip glowed like a firefly in the semidark. "Too many people are getting killed. You oughta think about that."

WEATHER KARKINNEN WAS doing paperwork in the study when Lucas got home. She heard him in the kitchen, and called down the hall, "In the study."

A moment later, he leaned in the door, a bottle of beer in his hand. "Hey."

"I tried to call you," she said.

Weather was a small, athletic woman with wide shoulders and close-cut blond hair. She had high cheekbones and eyes that were dark blue and slightly slanted in the Lapp-Finnish way. Her nose was a bit too large and a little crooked, as if she'd once lost a close fight. Not a pretty woman, exactly, but men tended to drift toward her at parties. "I saw a TV story on the shooting."

"What'd they say?" He unscrewed the beer cap and took a sip.

"Two women were shot and killed after a robbery. They say it's a controversial shooting." She was anxious, brushing hair out of her eyes.

Lucas shook his head. "You can't pay any attention to TV."

He was angry.

"Lucas . . ."

"What?" He was defensive, and didn't like it.

"You're really steamed," she said. "What happened?"

"Ah, I'm taking heat from the media. Everybody seems to worry about whether it was a fair fight. Why should the fight be fair? This isn't a game, it's law enforcement."

"Could you have taken them? Arrested them? Gone to trial, with the people at the other banks in Wisconsin?"

"No." He shook his head. "They were always masked, and always used stolen cars. There was a case down in River Falls, two years ago, where Candy LaChaise was busted for armed robbery. The guy she robbed, the car dealer, was mugged and killed two weeks later, before the trial. There weren't any witnesses and she had an alibi. The River Falls cops think her old nutcake pals helped her out."

"But it's not your job to kill them," Weather said.

"Hey," Lucas said. "I just showed up with a gun. What happened after that, that was their choice. Not mine."

She shook her head, still distressed. "I don't know," she said. "What you do frightens me, but not the way I thought it would." She crossed her arms and hugged herself, as she would if she were cold. "I'm not so worried about what somebody else might do to you, as what you might be doing to yourself."

"I told you . . ." Getting angrier now.

"Lucas," she interrupted. "I know how your mind works. TV said these people had been under surveillance for nine days. I can *feel* you manipulating them into a robbery. I don't know if *you* know, but I know it."

"Bullshit," he snapped, and he turned out of the doorway.

"Lucas . . ."

Halfway down the hall, the paperwork registered with him. She was doing wedding invitations. He turned around, went back.

"Jesus, I'm sorry, I'm not mad at you," he said. "Sometimes . . . I don't know, my grip is getting slippery."

She stood up and said, "Come here. Sit in the chair."

He sat, and she climbed on his lap. He was always amazed with how small she was, how small all the parts were. Small head, small hands, little fingers.

"You need something to lower your blood pressure," she said.

"That's what the beer's for," he said.

"As your doctor, I'm saying the beer's not enough," she said, snuggling in his lap.

"Yeah? What exactly would you prescribe . . . ?"

3

CRAZY ANSEL BUTTERS waited for the rush and when it came, he said, "Here it comes."

Dexter Lamb was lying on the couch, one arm trailing on the floor: he was looking up at the spiderweb pattern of cracks on the pink plaster ceiling, and he said, "I told you, dude."

Lamb's old lady was in the kitchen, staring at the top of the plastic table, her voice low, slow, clogged, coming down: "Wish I was going . . . Goddamnit, Dexter, where'd you put the bag? I know you got some."

Ansel didn't hear her, didn't hear the complaints, the whining. Ansel was flying over a cocaine landscape, all the potentialities in his head—green hills, pretty women, red Mustangs, Labrador retrievers—were compressed into a ball of pleasure. His head lay on his shoulder, his long hair falling to the side, like lines of rain outside a window. Twenty minutes later, the dream was all gone, except for the crack afterburn that would arrive like a sack of Christmas coal.

But he had a few minutes yet, and he mumbled, "Dex, I got something to talk about." Lamb was working up another pipe, stopped, his eyes hazy from too many hits, too many days without sleep. "What chu want?"

His wife came out of the back into the kitchen, scratched her crotch through her thin cotton underpants and said, "Where'd you put the bag, Dex?"

"I need to find a guy," Ansel said, talking over her. "It's worth real money. A month's worth of smoke. And I need a crib somewhere close. TV, couple beds, like that."

"I can get you the crib," Lamb said. He jerked a thumb at his wife. "My brother-in-law's got some houses, sorta shitty, but you can live in one of them. You'd have to buy your own furniture, though. I know where you could get some, real cheap."

"That'd be okay, I guess."

Dex finished with the pipe and flicked his Bic, and just before hitting on the mouthpiece, asked, "Who's this guy you're lookin' for?"

"A cop. I'm looking for a cop."

Lamb's old lady, eyes big and black, cheeks sunken, a pale white scar, scratched her crotch again and asked, "What's his name?"

Butters looked at her. "That's what I need to know," he said.

BILL MARTIN CAME down from the Upper Peninsula, driving a Ford extended cab with rusted-out fenders and a fat V-8 tuned to perfection. He took the country roads across Wisconsin, stopped at a roadhouse for a beer and a couple of boiled eggs, stopped again for gasoline, talked to a gun dealer in Ashland.

The countryside was still iced in. Old snow showed the sheen of hard crust through the inky-green pines and bare gray broadleafs. Martin stopped often to get out and tramp around, to peer down from bridges, to check tracks in the snow. He didn't like this winter: there'd been good snow, followed by a sleet storm that covered everything with a quarter-inch of ice. The ice could kill off the grouse, just when the population was finally turning back up.

He looked for grouse sign, didn't find any. The season was too new for bear sign, but in another six weeks or eight weeks they'd be out, he thought, sleek and quick and powerful. A young male black bear could run down a horse from a standing start. Nothing quite cleared the sinuses like bumping into a big old hungry bear when you were out on snowshoes, armed with nothing but a plastic canteen and a plug of Copenhagen.

At two o'clock in the afternoon, heading south, he saw a coyote ripping at something in the foot-high yellow grass that broke through the snow beside a creek. Voles, maybe. He pulled the truck over, got out a Bausch and Lomb laser rangefinder and the AR-15. The rangefinder said 305 yards. He figured a nine-inch drop, maybe two inches of right-to-left drift. Using the front fender as a rest, he held a couple of inches over the coyote's shoulder and let go. The .223 caught the mutt a little low, and it jumped straight up into the air and then came down in a heap, unmoving.

"Gotcha," Martin muttered, baring his teeth. The shot felt good.

Martin crossed the St. Croix at Grantsburg, stopped to look at the river— the surface was beaten down with snowmobile trails—then made his way reluctantly out to I-35. The interstate highways were scars across the country, he thought: you couldn't get close enough to see anything. But they were good when you had to move. He paused a final time at an I-35 rest stop just north of the Cities, made a call and then drove the rest of the way in.

BUTTERS WAS WAITING outside an Amoco station off I-94, an olive-drab duffel at his feet. Martin eased to the curb and Butters climbed in and said, "Straight ahead, back down the ramp."

Martin caught the traffic light and said, "How you been?"

"Tired," Butters said. His small eyes looked sleepy.

"You was tired last fall," said Martin. Martin had passed through Tennessee on one of his gun-selling trips, stopped and done some squirrel-hunting with Butters.

"I'm more tired now," Butters said. He looked into the back of the truck. "What'd you bring?"

"Three cold pistols, three Chinese AK semis, two modified AR-15s, a bow, a couple dozen arrows and my knife," Martin said.

"I don't think you'll need the bow," Butters said dryly.

"It's a comfort to me," Martin said. He was a rough-muscled, knob-headed outdoorsman with a dark reddish beard over a red-pocked face. "Where's this guy we gotta see?"

"Over in Minneapolis. Just outa downtown. By the dome."

Martin grinned his thin coyote-killing smile: "You been studying up on him?"

"Yeah, I have been."

They took I-94 to Minneapolis, got off at the Fifth Street exit, got a pizza downtown, then went back to Eleventh Avenue. Butters directed Martin to a stand-alone two-story brick building with a laundromat on the ground level and apartment above. The building was old, but well-kept: probably a neighborhood mom-and-pop grocery in the forties. Lights showed in the apartment windows.

"He owns the laundromat," Butters said. "The upstairs is one big apartment. He lives up there with his girlfriend." Butters looked up at the lights. "She must be there now, 'cause he's downtown. He runs his boys right to closing time. He got back here last night about two, and he brought a pizza with him."

Martin looked at his watch, a black military-style Chronosport with luminescent hands. "Got us about an hour, then." He looked back out the window at the building. There was just one door going up to the apartments. "Where's the garage you were talking about?"

" 'Round the side. There's a fire escape on the back, one of them drop-down ones, too high to get to. What he did last night was, he pulled into the garage—he's got a garage-door opener in his car—and the door come down. Then, a minute later, this light went on in the back of the apartment, so there must be an inside stairs. Then he come down through the back again, out through the garage, around the corner and into the laundromat. He was in the back, probably countin' out the machines."

Martin nodded. "Huh. Didn't use them front stairs?"

"Nope. Could be something goin' on there, so I didn't look."

"All right. We take him at the garage?"

"Yeah. And we might as well eat the pizza. We only need the box, and Harp ain't gonna want any."

They chatted easily, comfortable in the pickup smells of gasoline, straw, rust and oil. Then Martin, dabbing at his beard with a paper napkin, asked, "What do you hear from Dick?"

"Ain't heard dick from Dick," Butters said. He didn't wait for Martin to laugh, because he wouldn't, although Butters had a sense that Martin sometimes enjoyed a little joshing. He said, "Last time I talked to him direct, he sounded like he was . . . getting out there."

Martin chewed, swallowed and said, "Nothing wrong with being out there."

"No, there ain't," Butters agreed. He was as far out there as anyone. "But if we're gonna be killing cops, we want the guy to have his feet on the ground."

"Why? You planning to walk away from this thing?"

Butters thought for a minute, then laughed, almost sadly, and shook his head. "I guess not."

"I thought about goin' up to Alaska, moving out in the woods," Martin said, after a moment of silence. "You know, when I got the call. But they'll get you even in Alaska. They'll track you down anywhere. I'm tired of it. I figure, it's time to do something. So when I heard from Dick, I thought I might as well come on down."

"I don't know about that, the politics," Butters said. "But I owe Dick. And I got to pay him now, 'cause I am gettin' awful tired."

Martin looked at him for a moment, then said, "When you're that kind of tired, there ain't no point of being scared of cops. Or anything else."

They chewed for another minute and then Butters said, "True." And a moment later said, "Did I tell you my dog died?"

"That'll make a man tired," Martin said.

LIKE THE SEVEN dwarves, Daymon Harp whistled while he worked. And while he collected: unlike Snow White and her pals, Harp sold cocaine and speed at the semiwholesale level, supplying a half-dozen reliable retailers who worked the clubs, bars and bowling alleys in Minneapolis and selected suburbs.

Harp had seven thousand dollars in his coat pocket and he was whistling a minuet from the Anna Magdelena Notebook when he turned the Lincoln onto Eleventh. A pale-haired kid with a pizza box was standing on the corner outside his laundromat, looking up at the apartments. The pizza box was the thing that snared him: Harp never thought to look for the delivery car.

Daymon turned the corner, pushed the button on the automatic garage door opener, saw the kid look down toward him as he pulled in, then killed the engine and got out. The kid was walking down the sidewalk with the pizza box flat on one hand and Daymon thought, *If that fucking Jas has gone and ordered out for a pizza when she's up there by herself* . . .

He was waiting for the kid, when Martin stepped up behind him and pressed a pistol to his ear: "Back in the garage."

Daymon jumped, but controlled it. He held his hands away from his sides and turned back to the garage. "Take it easy," he said. He didn't want the guy excited. He'd had a pistol in his ear before, and when caught in that condition, you definitely want to avoid excitement. He tried an implied threat: "You know who I am?"

"Daymon Harp, a jigaboo drug dealer," Martin said, and Harp thought, *Uh-oh*.

The kid with the pizza followed them inside, spotted the lighted button for the garage door opener, and pushed it. The door came down and Martin prodded Harp toward the stairs at the back.

"Take the position," Martin said.

Harp leaned against the wall, hands and feet spread wide. "Got no gun," he said. He looked sideways at Martin: "You're not cops."

"We'd be embarrassed if you was lying about the gun," Martin said. The younger guy patted him down, found the wad of cash and pulled it out. "Ooo," he said. "Thanks."

Harp kept his mouth shut.

"This is the deal," Martin said, as Butters tucked the money away. "We need some information from you. We don't want to hurt you. We will, if you get stupid, so it's best for you to go along."

"What do you want?" Daymon asked.

"To go upstairs," Butters said, in his soft Tennessee accent. Harp looked at him out of the corner of his eye: Butters had three dark-blue tears tattooed at the inner corner of his left eye, and Daymon Harp thought again, *Uh-oh.*

THEY CLIMBED THE stairs as a trio, and now the southern boy had a pistol barrel prodding Daymon's spine, while the other focused on his temple. They all tensed while Daymon unlocked the door. A woman called down an interior hall, "Day? That you?"

Butters left them, padding silently down the hall, while Martin stayed with Harp. The woman came around a corner just as Butters got to it and she jumped, shocked, as Butters grabbed her by a wrist and showed her the gun. "Shut up," Butters said.

She shut up.

Five minutes later, Harp and the woman were duct-taped to kitchen chairs. The woman's hands were flat on her thighs, with loops of tape around her upper arms and body. She had a sock stuffed in her mouth, held in place with two or three more wraps of tape. Her terrified dark eyes flicked between Harp and whichever of the white men was in sight.

Martin and Butters checked the apartment. The landing outside the front door, Martin found when he opened it, was blocked by a pile of brown cardboard appliance boxes. The boxes made a practical burglar alarm and buffer, should the cops come, but still provided an escape route if one were needed.

Butters checked the two bedrooms and found nothing of interest but a collection of vinyl 33-rpm jazz records.

"Clear," Butters said, coming back to the front room.

Martin sat down in a third chair and, knee-to-knee with Harp, said, "You probably know people like us. Met us in the joint. We don't much care for black folks and we'd be happy to cut your throats and be done with it. But we can't, this time, 'cause we need you to introduce us to a friend of yours."

"Who?" Daymon Harp asked.

"The cop you're working with."

Harp tried to look surprised. "There's no cop."

"We know you gotta go through your routine, but we don't have a lot of time," Martin said. "So to show you our . . . mmm . . . sincerity . . ." He chose his words carefully, softly: "We're gonna cut on your girlfriend here."

"Motherfucker," Harp said, but it wasn't directed at Martin. It was simply an exclamation and Martin took it that way. The woman's eyes bulged and she rattled around in the chair, and Martin let her. Over his shoulder, he said, "Ansel? See if you can find a knife in the kitchen . . ."

There was no one standing in the street outside the laundromat, which was a good thing for Butters and Martin, because Harp wouldn't talk right away, and for one short moment, even with the gag, with the windows shut, in the middle of winter, even with that, you could hear Jasmine screaming.

THE MICHIGAN STATE Prison sent a single escort with Dick LaChaise. La-Chaise was four years into a nine-year sentence, and not considered an escape risk—with good behavior, he'd be out in a couple of years. They put him in leg irons and cuffs and LaChaise and Wayne O. Sand, the escort, flew into Eau Claire as the sun was going down, eight days after the shootings in Minneapolis.

During the flight, Wayne O. Sand read *The Last Mammoth* by Margaret Allan, because he liked that prehistoric shit and magic and all. If he'd lived back then, he thought, he'd probably be a clan chief, or something. He'd be in shape, anyway.

LaChaise read a tattoo magazine called *Skin Art*. LaChaise had full sleeves: tattoos running up and down both arms, a comic-book fantasy of superwomen with football-sized tits and lionish hair tangled around his bunched-up weight-room muscles, interspersed with eagles, tigers, knives, a dragon. His arms carried four names: Candy and Georgie on the right, and Harley and Davidson on the left.

The sleeves had been done on the outside, by commercial tattoo artists. The work on his back and legs was being done on the inside. Prison work, with a sewing needle and ballpoint ink. Though the figures lacked the finish of the commercial jobs, there was a nasty raw power to them that LaChaise liked. An aesthetic judgment.

When the plane's wheels came down, LaChaise put the magazine away and looked at Sand: "How about a McDonald's? A couple of Big Macs?"

"Maybe, you don't fuck me around," Sand said, still in the book. Sand was a flabby man, an authoritarian little prison bureaucrat who'd be nice enough one day, and write you up the next, for doing nothing. He enjoyed his power, but wasn't nearly the worst of them. When they landed, Sand marched LaChaise off the plane, and chained him to the seat post in the back of a rental Ford.

"How about them McDonald's?" LaChaise asked.

Sand considered for a second, then said, "Nah. I wanna get a motel 'fore it's too late. There's a game tonight."

"Hey, c'mon . . ."

"Shut up," Sand said, with the casual curtness of a prison guard.

Sand dropped LaChaise at the Eau Claire County Jail for the night. The next morning, he put LaChaise back in the car and drove him through the frozen landscape to the Logan Funeral Home in Colfax. LaChaise's mother was waiting on the porch of the funeral home, along with Sandy Darling, Candy's sister. A sheriff's car was parked in the street, engine running. A deputy sat inside the car, reading a newspaper.

AMY LACHAISE WAS a round, oily-faced country woman with suspicious black eyes, close-cropped black hair and a pencil-thin mustache. She wore a black dress with a white collar under a blue nylon parka. A small hat from the 1930s sat nervously atop her head, with a crow's wing of black lace pulled down over her forehead.

Sandy Darling was her opposite: a small woman, slender, with a square chin and a thin, windburned face. Crow's-feet showed at the corners of her eyes, though she was only twenty-nine, four years younger than her sister, Candy. Like Candy, she was blond, but her hair was cut short, and she wore simple seed-pearl earrings. And while Candy had that pure Wisconsin milkmaid complexion, Sandy showed a scattering of freckles over her windburned nose and forehead. She wore a black wool coat over a long black dress, tight black leather gloves and fancy black cowboy boots with sterling silver toe guards. She carried a white cowboy hat.

When the rental car pulled up, Amy LaChaise started down the walk. Sandy Darling stayed on the porch, turning the cowboy hat in her hands. Wayne O. Sand popped the padlock on the seat-chain, got out, stood between Amy LaChaise and the car door and opened the door for LaChaise.

"That's my ma," LaChaise said to Sand, as he got out. LaChaise was a tall man, with heavy shoulders and deep-set black eyes, long hair and a beard over hollowed cheeks. He had fingers that were as thick and tough as hickory sticks. With a robe, he might have played the Prophet Jeremiah.

"Okay," Sand said. To Amy LaChaise: "I'll have to hold your purse."

The deputy sheriff had gotten out of his car, nodded to Sand, as Amy La-Chaise handed over her purse. "Everything okay?" he asked.

"Yeah, sure." Sand drifted over to chat with him; LaChaise wasn't going anywhere.

AMY LACHAISE PLANTED a dry lizard's kiss on her son's cheek and said, "They was shot down like dogs."

"I know, Mama," LaChaise said. He looked past her to Sandy Darling on the porch, and nodded curtly. To his mother he said, "They told me about it."

"They was set up," Amy said. She made a pecking motion with her nose, as if to emphasize her words. "That goddamn Duane Cale had something to do with it, 'cause he's just fine, talking like crazy. He'll tell them anything they want. All kinds of lies."

"Yeah, I know," LaChaise said. His mother was worried because Candy had given her money from some of the robberies.

"Well, what'cha gonna do?" Amy LaChaise demanded. "It was your sister and your wife . . ." She clutched at his arm, her fingers sharp and grasping, like buckthorn.

"I know, Mama," LaChaise said. "But there ain't much I can do right now." He lifted his hands so she could see the heavy cuffs.

"That's a fine thing," Amy LaChaise moaned, still clutching at him. "You just let it go and lay around your fat happy cell."

"You go on into the chapel," LaChaise said, with a harsh snap in his voice. "I want to take a look at 'em."

Amy LaChaise backed away a step. "Caskets are closed," she ventured.

"They can open them," LaChaise said, grimly.

Sandy Darling, still on the porch, watched the unhappy reunion, then turned and went inside.

LOGAN, THE FUNERAL director, was a small, balding man, with a mustache that would have been tidy if it hadn't appeared moth-eaten. Although he was gray-faced, he had curiously lively, pink hands, which he dry-washed as he talked. "In a case like this, Mr. LaChaise," he said, looking nervously at La-Chaise's handcuffs, "we can't be responsible for the results."

"Open the boxes," LaChaise said.

Logan, worried, cracked the lids and stepped back. Way back. LaChaise stepped up, raised them.

Candy, his wife.

She'd been shot several times through the body, out of sight under her burial dress, but one shot had gone almost straight through her nose. The nose had been rebuilt with some kind of putty. Other than that, she looked as sweet as she had the day he first saw her at the Wal-Mart. He looked at her for a full minute, and thought he might have shed a tear; but he didn't.

Georgie was worse. Georgie had been hit at least three times in the face. While the funeral home had sewed and patched and made up, there was no doubt that something was massively wrong with Georgie's skull. The body in the box looked no more like the living Georgie than did a plastic baby doll.

His sister.

He could remember that one good Christmas when they'd had the tree, he was nine or ten, she was three or four, and somebody had given her pajamas with feet in them. "Feetsies," she called them. "I'm gonna put on my feetsies." Must have been twenty-five years gone by, and here she was, with a head like a football. Again he felt the impulse toward tears; again, nothing happened.

Logan, the funeral director, his face drained of blood, cleared his throat and said, "Mr. LaChaise?"

LaChaise nodded. "You did okay," he said, gruffly. "Where's the preacher?"

"He should be here. Any minute." Logan's hands flittered gratefully with the compliment, like sparrows at a bird feeder.

"I want to wait back here until the funeral starts," LaChaise said. "I don't wanna talk to my mama no more'n I have to."

"I understand," the funeral director said. He did: he'd been dealing with old lady LaChaise since the bodies had been released by the Hennepin County Medical Examiner. "We'll move Candy and Georgie into the chapel. When Reverend Pyle arrives, I'll step back and notify you."

"That's good," LaChaise said. "You got a Coke machine here somewhere?"

"Well, there is a Coke box in the staff area," Logan said.

"I could use a Coke. I'd buy it."

"No, no, that's fine . . ."

LaChaise looked at the escort. "How about it, Wayne? I'll buy you one."

Sand drank fifteen caffeinated Diet Cokes a day and got headaches if he went without. LaChaise knew that. "Yeah," Sand said. "A Coke would be good."

"Then I'll make the arrangements," the funeral director said. "The Coke box is back through that door."

He pointed back through the Peace Room, as the staging area was called, to a door that said, simply, "Staff."

ON THE OTHER side of the staff door was a storage room full of broken-down shipping cartons for coffins, eight or ten large green awnings, folded, for funerals on rainy days, a forklift and a tool bench. The Coke box was just inside the door, an old-fashioned red top-opening cooler, with a dozen Coke Classic cans and a couple of white Diet Coke cans bathed in five inches of icy water.

"Get one of them Diets," Sand said, looking down into the water. He was watching his weight. LaChaise dipped into the cooler and got a regular Coke and a Diet, and when he turned back to the escort, Crazy Ansel Butters had stepped quietly out from behind the pile of awnings. He had a .22 pistol and he put it against Sand's head and said, "Don't fuckin' move."

Sand froze, then looked at LaChaise and said, "Don't hurt me, Dick."

"Gimme the keys," LaChaise said.

"You're making a mistake," Sand said. His eyes were rolling, and LaChaise thought he might faint.

"Give him the keys or *you'll* be making a mistake," Butters said. Butters had a voice like a bastard file skittering down a copper pipe.

Sand fumbled the keys out of his pocket and LaChaise stuck his hands out. When the cuffs came off, he rubbed his wrists, took the keys from Sand and opened the leg irons. "That deputy still out by his car?" he asked Butters.

"He was when I come in," Butters said. He slipped a Bulldog .44 out of his coat pocket and handed it to LaChaise. "Here's your 'dog."

"Thanks." LaChaise took the gun and stuck it in his belt. "What're you driving?"

"Bill's truck. Around the side."

"Did Mama see you?"

"Shit no. Nobody seen me."

LaChaise stepped close to the escort, and turned him a bit, and said, "All right, Wayne, I'm gonna cuff your hands. Now you keep your mouth shut, 'cause if you start hollering before we get out of here, we'll have to come back and do something."

"I won't say a thing," Sand said, trembling.

"You scared?" LaChaise asked.

"Yeah, I am."

"That's good; keep you from doing anything foolish," LaChaise said. He snapped the cuffs over Sand's hands, then said, "Lay down."

Sand got down awkwardly, and Butters stepped up behind him and threw a half-dozen turns of packaging tape around his ankles. When he was finished, LaChaise took the roll of tape, knelt with one knee in the middle of Sand's back, and took three more turns around his mouth. When he was finished, LaChaise looked up at Butters and said, "Borrow me your knife."

Sand squirmed under LaChaise's knee as Butters passed a black lock-back knife to LaChaise.

LaChaise grabbed a handful of Sand's hair and pried his head back and said, "Shoulda bought me them Big Macs."

He bounced Sand's head off the concrete floor once, twice, then said, "You asshole." He pulled his head straight back, leaned to the side so he could see Sand's bulging eyes. "You know how they cut a pig's throat?"

"We gotta move along," Butters said. "We can't fuck around." Sand began thrashing and squealing through the tape.

LaChaise let him go for a minute, enjoying himself, then he cut Sand's throat from one ear to the other. As the purple blood poured out on the concrete, Sand thrashed, and LaChaise rode him with the knee. The thrashing stopped and Sand's one visible eye began to go opaque.

"Gotta go," Butters said.

"Fuckhead," LaChaise said. He dropped Sand's head, wiped the blade on the back of Sand's coat, folded the knife as he stood up and handed it to Butters.

"Gonna be hell cleaning up the mess," Butters said, looking down at the body. "I hate to get blood on concrete."

"We'll send them some Lysol," LaChaise said. "Let's roll."

"Lysol don't work," Butters said, as they headed for the doors. "Nothing works. You always got the stain, and it stinks."

THEY WENT OUT the service drive on the back of the funeral home, Butters with his thin peckerwood face and long sandy hair sitting in the driver's seat, while LaChaise sat on the floor in front of the passenger seat.

When they turned onto the street, LaChaise unfolded a bit and looked over the backseat, through the cab window, through the topper, and out the topper's rear window, down toward the funeral home. The deputy's car was still sitting in the street, unmoving. Nobody knew yet, but they probably didn't have more than a couple of minutes.

"Are we going up to the trailer?" LaChaise asked.

"Yeah."

"You been there?"

"Yeah. There's electricity for heat and the pump, and a shitter out back. You'll be okay for a day or two, until we get set in the Cities. Martin's down there today, waiting for some furniture to get there."

"You find a cop?"

"Yep. Talked to a guy last night, me and Martin did. We got us a cop the name of Andy Stadic. He's hooked up with a dope dealer named Harp. Harp took some pictures, and now we got the pictures."

"Good one." They crossed a river with a frozen waterfall, and were out of town. "How's Martin?"

"Like always. But that Elmore is a hinky sonofabitch. We told him we needed a place to stay, me 'n Bill, and I had to back him up against the wall before he said okay on the trailer."

"Fuck him," LaChaise said. "If he knew I was gonna be out there, he'd be peein' his pants."

"Gonna have to keep an eye on Sandy," Butters said.

LaChaise nodded. "Yeah. She's the dangerous one. We'll want to get out of the trailer soon as we can."

Butters looked sideways at him. "You and Sandy ever . . ."

"No." LaChaise grinned. "Woulda liked to."

"She's a goddamned wrangler," Butters agreed.

Butters drove them through a web of back roads, never hesitating. He'd driven the route a half-dozen times. Forty minutes after killing Sand, they made the trailer, without seeing another car.

LaChaise said: "Free."

"Loose, anyway," Butters said.

"That's close enough," LaChaise said. He unconsciously rubbed his wrists where the manacles had been.

LOGAN, THE FUNERAL director, ran into the chapel like a small, drunk tailback, knocked down a half-dozen metal folding chairs, staggered, nearly bowled over Amy LaChaise, struggled briefly with the door handle and was gone out the front door.

Sandy looked at Amy LaChaise across the closed caskets.

"What the hell was that?" Amy asked.

"I don't know," she said, but she felt suddenly cold.

Ten seconds later, the cop who'd been parked out front ran in the door with his pistol in a two-handed grip. He pointed the gun at Sandy, then at Amy, then swiveled around the room: "Hold it. Everybody hold it."

"What?" Amy asked. She clutched her purse to her chest.

Logan peeked out from behind the deputy. "Mr. LaChaise is gone."

Amy screeched, like a crow killing an owl, a sound both pleased and intolerable. "Praise the Lord."

"Shut up," the deputy screamed, pointing the pistol at her. "Where's the prison guy? Where's the prison guy?"

Logan poked a finger toward the back. "In there . . ."

"What's wrong with him?" Sandy asked.

The deputy ran through the door into the back, and Logan said, "Well, he's dead. LaChaise cut his throat."

Sandy closed her eyes: "Oh, no."

A HIGHWAY PATROLMAN arrived five minutes later. Then two more sheriff's deputies. The deputies split Amy LaChaise and Sandy, made them sit apart.

"And keep your mouths shut," one of the deputies said, a porky man with a name tag that said Graf.

LaChaise, Sandy thought, was at Elmore's daddy's trailer, out at the hill place. Had to be. That whole story about Martin and Butters needing a place to stay—it sounded like bullshit as soon as Elmore had told her about it.

But the problem was, she was Candy's sister, LaChaise's sister-in-law. She'd been present when LaChaise had escaped and murdered a man. And now LaChaise was up at a trailer owned by her senile father-in-law.

She'd seen LaChaise railroaded by the cops for conspiracy to commit murder: they'd do the same to her, and with a lot more evidence.

Sandy Darling sat and shivered, but not with the cold; sat and tried to figure a way out.

THE TRAILER WAS a broken-down Airstream, sitting on the cold frozen snow like a shot silver bullet. Butters and LaChaise crunched through the sparse snow on four-wheel drive, then they got out of the truck into the cold and Butters unlocked the trailer. "I come by this morning and dropped off some groceries and turned on the heat . . . Can't nobody see you in here, but you might want to keep the light down at night," he said. "You don't have to worry about smoke. Everything's electric and it works. I turned the pump on and filled up the water heater, so you oughta be okay that way."

"You done really good, Ansel," LaChaise said.

"I owe you," Butters said. And he turned away from the compliment: "And there's a TV and a radio, but you can only get one channel—sort of—on the TV, and only two stations on the radio, but they're both country."

"That's fine," LaChaise said, looking around. Then he came back to Butters, his deep black eye fixing the other man like a bug: "Ansel, you ain't owed me for years, if you ever did. But I gotta know something for sure."

Butters glanced at him, then looked out the window over the sink: "Yeah?"

"Are you up for this?"

Ansel glanced at him again, and away: it was hard to get Crazy Ansel Butters to look directly at you, under any conditions. "Oh yeah. I'm very tired. You know what I mean? I'm very tired."

"You can't do nothin' crazy," LaChaise said.

"I won't, 'til the time comes. But I am getting close to my dying day."

The words came out with a formal stillness.

"Well, that's probably bullshit, Ansel," LaChaise said, but he said it gravely, without insult intended or taken.

Butters said, "I come off the interstate, down home, up an exit ramp at night, with pole lights overhead. And I seen an owl's shadow going up the ramp ahead of me—wings all spread, six or eight feet across, the shadow was. I could see every feather. Tell me that ain't a sign."

"Maybe it's a sign, but I got a mission here," LaChaise said. "We all got a mission now."

"That's true," Butters said, nodding. "And I won't fuck you up."

"That's what I needed to know," LaChaise said.

4

A CLERK NAMED ANNA marie knocked on Lucas's office door, stuck her head inside, struggled for a moment with her bubble gum and said, "Chief Lester said to tell you, you know Dick LaChaise?"

"Dick?"

She paused for a quick snap of her gum: "Dick, who was married to that one woman who got shot, and was brother to the other one? Last week?"

Lucas had one hand over the phone mouthpiece and said, "Yeah?"

"Well, he escaped in Wisconsin and killed a guy. A prison guard. Chief Lester said you should come down to Homicide."

"I'll be down in two minutes," Lucas said.

A HEAVYSET PATROL cop, with a gray crew cut, was walking down the hall when Lucas came out of the office. He took Lucas's elbow and said, "Guy comes home from work and he finds his girlfriend with her bags packed, waiting in the doorway."

"Yeah?" The cop was famous for his rotten jokes.

"The guy's amazed. He says, 'What's going on? What happened?' 'I'm leaving you,' says the girlfriend. 'What'd I do? Everything was okay this morning,' says the guy. 'Well,' says the girlfriend, 'I heard you were a pedophile.' And the guy looks at his girlfriend and says, 'Pedophile? Say, that's an awwwwfully big word for a ten-year-old . . .' "

"Get away from me, Hampsted," Lucas said, pushing him off; but he was laughing despite himself.

"Yeah, you'll be tellin' all your friends . . ."

LESTER WAS TALKING to the Homicide lieutenant, turned when Lucas came in, dropped his feet off the lieutenant's desk and said, "Dick LaChaise cut the throat of a prison guard during the funeral of Candace and Georgia LaChaise, and vanished. About an hour ago."

"Vanished?" Lucas said.

"That's what the Dunn County sheriff said: vanished."

"How'd he cut the guy's throat? Was there a fight?"

"I don't know the details," Lester said. "There's a cluster-fuck going on at the funeral home. It's over in Colfax, ten, fifteen miles off I-94 between Eau Claire and Menomonie. Probably an hour and a half drive."

"Hour, in a Porsche," the lieutenant said lazily.

"I think you ought to send one of your group over there," Lester said.

"Hell, I'll go," Lucas said. "I'm sitting on my ass anyway. Do we have any paper on LaChaise?"

"Anderson's getting it now," Lester said. "Anyway, the sheriff over there says LaChaise might be heading this way. LaChaise's mama says he's gonna get back at us for Candace and Georgia. 'Eye for an eye,' she says."

Lucas looked at the lieutenant. "Can I take Sloan?"

"Sure. If you can find him."

Lucas picked up a half-pound of paper from Anderson, the department's computer jock, beeped Sloan, and when he called back, explained about La-Chaise.

"You want to go?" Lucas asked.

"Let me get a parka. I'll meet you at your house."

LUCAS DIDN'T DRIVE the Porsche much during the winter, but the day, though bitterly cold and sullenly gray, showed no sign of snow. The highway had the hard bone-dry feel that it sometimes got in midwinter.

"Are we in a hurry, I hope?" Sloan asked as they rolled north along the Mississippi.

"Yeah," Lucas said. As soon as they got on I-94 at Cretin, he called Dispatch and asked them to contact the Wisconsin highway patrol, to tell that he was coming through on an emergency run. They dropped on the interstate at noon, and at 12:20 crossed the St. Croix bridge into Wisconsin. Lucas put the snap-on red flasher in the window and dropped the hammer, cranking the Porsche out to one-twenty before dropping back to an even hundred.

The countryside looked as though it had been carved out of ice, hard sky, round hills, the creek lines marked by bare gray trees, snapped-off golden-yellow cornstalks sticking out of the snow, suburban homes and then isolated farmsteads showing plumes of straight-up gray wood smoke.

Sloan watched it roll by for a few minutes, then said, "I get to drive back."

DUNN COUNTY SHERIFF Bill Lock was a fussy, officious, bespectacled man, a little overweight, who, if he'd put on a fake white beard, would make an adequate department-store Santa. He met Lucas and Sloan among the coffins in the Eternal Comfort Room at Logan's Funeral Home, where Logan had set up coffee and doughnuts for the cops.

"Come on and take a look," Lock said. "We'd appreciate it if one of our guys could talk to Duane Cale—you still got him over there in Hennepin County jail. He might have some ideas where they went."

"No problem," Lucas said. He dug out a card, scribbled a number on the back and handed it to Lock. "Ask for Ted, tell him I said to call, and what you want to do."

"Good enough." Lock walked them through the staging room, where the bodies of Georgie and Candy LaChaise were still waiting for a funeral. "You want to look?" he asked.

"No, thanks," Lucas said hastily. "So what happened?"

"Logan says LaChaise insisted that he open the coffins. They came back here and he opened them. Then LaChaise asked if there was a Coke machine around, and Logan told them where the machine was. That was one of the cooler things he did: he was so routine, taking his time with the bodies, saying good-bye, then asking for a Coke . . ."

Lock walked them through it, a couple other deputies standing around, watching. They wound up in the back room, next to the Coke box. Sand's body was still on the floor, in the middle of a drying puddle of blood. Sand looked small, white and not particularly tough, his head cocked up at an odd angle, his chin squarely on the floor, his nose off the ground.

"Logan figures he was gone for five minutes. When he came back to the staging room, there was nobody here. He looked into the back, and found this."

"Never saw LaChaise again?" Lucas asked.

"Never saw him again," Lock said, shaking his head. "Never heard any noise, nothing. Now we got the sonofabitch running around the countryside some-where."

"He's long gone," Lucas said.

"Yeah, but we're doing a house-to-house check anyway," Lock said.

"He had to have help." Lucas walked around the body, squatted, and looked at Sand's hands as they stuck out of the cuffs. "There aren't any defensive cuts, so it wasn't like LaChaise pulled a shank on him." Lucas stood up and made a hand-washing motion. "If LaChaise was cuffed and wearing leg irons, there's no way he could have taken this guy without some kind of fight. There must've been somebody else here."

"Unless he'd cut a deal with Sand to turn him loose, and make it look like an escape—then double-crossed him."

"Huh. What'd he have to offer Sand? Candy and Georgie were dead, so the source of money had dried up . . ."

"We're checking with Michigan, see if Sand had any problems back there. Something to blackmail him with . . ."

"Nobody saw him walking away." Lucas made it a statement.

"Nope. Nobody saw nothing."

Sloan jumped in: "I heard his mother says he's coming after us."

"That's what she says," Lock said, nodding. "And she could be right. Dick is nuts."

"You know him?" Lucas asked.

"From when I was a kid," Lock said. "I used to run a trap line up the Red Cedar in the winter. The LaChaises lived down south of here on this broken-ass farm—Amy LaChaise is still out there. I used to see the LaChaise kids every now and then. Georgie and Dick. Their old man was a mean sonofabitch, drunk, beat the shit out of the kids . . ."

"That's how it is with most psychos," said Sloan.

"Yeah, well, I wouldn't be surprised if somebody told me he'd been screwing Georgie, either. She always knew too much, there in school." Lock scratched his head, caught himself and slicked back his thinning hair. "The old man came after me once, said I was trespassing on his part of the river, and they didn't even live on the river."

"What happened?" Sloan asked.

"Hell, I was seventeen, I'd baled hay all summer, built fence in the fall and then ran the trap line. I was in shape, he was a fifty-year-old drunk: I kicked his ass," Lock said, grinning at them over Sand's body.

"Good for you," Sloan said.

"Not good for his kids, though—living with him," Lock said. "The whole goddamn bunch of them turned out crazier'n bedbugs."

"There's more? Besides Georgie and Dick?" Lucas asked.

"One more brother, Bill. He's dead," Lock said. "Ran himself into a bridge abutment up on County M, eight or ten years back. Dead drunk, middle of the night. There was a hog in the backseat. Also dead."

"A hog," said Sloan. He looked at Lucas, wondering if Lock was pulling their legs.

Lock, reading Sloan's mind, cracked a grin. "Yeah, he used to rustle hogs. Put them in the car, leave them off at friends' places. When he got five or six, he'd run them into St. Paul."

"Hogs," Sloan said, shaking his head sadly.

Lock said the only two people who'd showed up for the funeral were Amy LaChaise and Sandy Darling, Candy's sister. "They're both still sitting out there. They say they don't know what the heck happened."

"You believe them?" Sloan asked.

"Yeah, I sorta do," Lock said. "You might want to talk to them, though. See what you think."

AMY LACHAISE WAS a mean-eyed, foulmouthed waste of time, defiant and quailing at the same time, snapping at them, then flinching away as though she'd been beaten after other attempts at defiance.

"You're gonna get it now," she crowed, peering at them from beneath the ludicrous hat-net. "You're the big shots going around killing people, thinking your shit don't stink; but you're gonna see. Dickie's coming for you."

SANDY DARLING WAS different.

She was a small woman, but came bigger than her size: her black dress was unconsciously dramatic, the silver-tipped black boots an oddly elegant country touch, both sensitive and tough.

She faced them squarely, her eyes looking into theirs, unflinching, her voice calm, but depressed.

Sandy had seen Lucas arrive with Sloan, had seen them talking with the sheriff. The big tough-looking guy wore what she recognized as an expensive suit, probably tailored. FBI? He looked like an FBI man from the movies. The other man, the thin one, was shifty-looking, and dressed all in shades of brown. They went in the back, where the dead guard was, and a few minutes later came back out, and talked to Amy LaChaise. She could hear Amy's crowing voice, but not the individual words.

After five minutes, the two men left Amy LaChaise and walked over to where she was sitting. She thought, *Hold on. Just hold on.*

"Mrs. Darling?" The big guy had blue eyes that looked right into her. When he smiled, just a small polite smile, she almost shivered, the smile was so hard. He reminded her of a Montana rancher she'd met once, when she'd gone out to pick up a couple of quarter horses; they'd had a hasty affair, one that she remembered with some pleasure.

The other guy, the shifty one, smiled, and he looked like Dagwood, like a nice guy.

"I'm Lucas Davenport from Minneapolis," the big guy said, "And this is Detective Sloan . . ."

She caught Lucas's name: Davenport. Wasn't he . . . ? "Did you shoot my sister?" she blurted.

"No." The big man shook his head. "Detective Sloan and I were at the credit union, but neither one of us fired a gun."

"But you set it up," she said.

"That's not the way we see it," Lucas said.

Sandy's head jerked, a nod: she understood. "Am I going to be arrested?"

"For what?" the thin man asked. He seemed really curious, almost surprised, and she found herself warming to him.

"Well, that's what I want to know. I came to the funeral, and now they won't let me go anywhere. I've got to ask before I go to the bathroom. Nobody'll talk to me."

"That's routine," the thin man said. "I know it's tiresome, but this is a serious thing. A man's been murdered."

The thin man—Sloan?—made it sound so reasonable. He went on. "We'll talk to the sheriff, see if we can get you some information on how much longer it'll be. I imagine you'll have to make a formal statement, but I'd think you'd be home for dinner."

"If you're not involved," Davenport said. She was sitting in a big chair, and he dropped into another one at a right angle to her. "If you've got anything to do with this, if you know where LaChaise is at, you better say so now," he said. "Get a lawyer, get a deal."

She shook her head, and a tear started down her cheek. "I don't know anything, I just came to say good-bye to Candy . . ."

Three things were going on in her head. When Lucas said, "Say so now," she thought, deep in her mind, *Oh, right.* At another level, she was so frightened she could hardly bear it. And in yet another place, she really was thinking about Candy, dead in a coffin not ten yards away; and that started the tear down her cheek.

LUCAS SAW THE tear start, and he glanced at Sloan. A wrinkle appeared between Sloan's eyes. "Take it easy," Sloan said gently. He leaned forward and touched her hand. "Listen. I really don't think you had anything to do with this, but sometimes, people know more than they think. Like, if you were Dick LaChaise, where would you go? You know him, and you both know this territory . . ."

They talked with her for another fifteen minutes, but nothing came of it. Sandy showed tears several times, but held her ground: she simply didn't know. She was a horse rancher, for God's sakes, a landowner, a taxpayer, a struggling businesswoman. She didn't know about outlaws: "Candy and I . . . she moved out of the house when I was in ninth grade and we didn't see her much after that. She was always running around with Dick, doing crazy stuff. I was afraid she'd wind up dead."

"What'd your folks do?" Sloan asked.

"My dad worked for the post office—he had a rural route out of Turtle Lake. They're both gone now."

"Sorry," Sloan said. "But you don't know anybody they might have run to?"

She shook her head: "No. I didn't have anything to do with that bunch. I didn't have time—I was always working."

"So how crazy is LaChaise?" Lucas asked. "His mother says he's gonna come after us."

Sandy flipped her cowboy hat in her hands, as though she was making an estimate. "Dick is . . . strange," she said, finally. "He's rough, he was good-looking at one time, although . . . not so much now. He was wild. He attracted all the wild guys in the Seed, you'd hear about crazy stunts on his bike, or sleeping on the yellow line. He really did sleep on the yellow line once—on Highway 64, outside a tavern. Dead drunk, of course."

"Do you think he'll come after us?" Lucas asked.

"Are you worried?" asked Sandy, curiously. The big guy didn't look like he'd worry.

"Some," Lucas said. " 'Cause I don't know enough about him. And his wife and his sister—excuse me for saying this, I know Candy was your sister—the things they did were nuts."

Sandy nodded. "That's from Dick," she said. "Dick is . . . he's like an angry, mean little boy. He'll do the craziest stuff, but then, later, he'll be sorry for it. He once got drunk and beat up a friend, and when he sobered up, he beat himself up. He got a two-by-two and hit himself in the face with it until people stopped him and took him to the hospital."

"Jesus," Sloan said, looking at Lucas, impressed.

"But he can be charming," Sandy said. "And you can shame him out of stuff. Like a little boy. Unless he's drunk, then he's unstoppable."

"You keep talking about drinking. Is he drunk a lot?"

"Oh, yeah," Sandy nodded. "He's an alcoholic, no question. So are most of his friends. But Dick's not one of those guys who's drunk all the time—he'll go dry for a while, but then he'll go off on a toot and be crazy for two weeks."

"Somebody cut this prison officer's throat while he was cuffed up and laying on the floor. You think LaChaise could do that?" Lucas asked.

"He could if he was in one of his bad-boy moods," Sandy said. "No question. I don't know if I'm getting this across—but when I say like a mean little boy, I mean just like that. He has tantrums, like fits. He scares everybody when he has one, because he's nuts, and because he's so strong. That's what's going on now: he's having one of his tantrums."

"But a kid's tantrum only lasts a few minutes . . ."

"Well, Dick's can go on for a while. A week, or a couple of weeks."

"Is that how he came to get involved in this murder over in Michigan? A tantrum?"

"Oh, no, he wasn't involved in that," she said. "The cops framed him."

Lucas and Sloan both glanced away from her at the same moment, and she smiled, just a bit. "So you don't believe me—but they did," she said. "I testified at the trial. There was this guy named Frank Wyatt, who killed another guy named Larry Waters. The prosecution said that Waters stole some dope from Wyatt, and that Dick owned part of the dope—which he may have, I don't know. Anyway, the night that the dope was stolen, the prosecution said Dick and Wyatt got together at a tavern in Green Bay and talked about killing Waters."

"That was the conspiracy," Lucas said.

"Yes." Sandy nodded. "They had this informant. They let him off some dope charges for his testimony. He testified that he was at the tavern when Wyatt and Dick talked. Wyatt shot Waters the next day."

"And you say LaChaise wasn't at the tavern?" Sloan asked.

"I know he wasn't," Sandy said. " 'Cause he was at my place. I had a filly who broke a leg, shattered it. There was nothing we could do about it, the break couldn't be fixed, we had to put her down. I hate to do that; just hate it. Dick and Candy were in town, and I mentioned it to them. Dick said he'd take care of it, and he did. That was the night he was supposed to be in Green Bay. I had it written in ink on my income-tax calendar. In fact, Dick and Candy were there that whole week . . . But the jury didn't believe me. The prosecution said, 'She's his sister-in-law, she's just lying for him.' "

"Well." Lucas looked at Sloan again, who shrugged, and Lucas said, "We know it happens. You get some asshole—excuse me—who goes around wrecking people's lives, and you get a shot at him, and some cops'll take it."

"Sort of like you took with Candy and Georgie?" Sandy asked.

"We didn't cheat with Candy and Georgie," Lucas said, shaking his head. "They went to the credit union to rob it—nobody made them do it, or suggested that they do it. They did it on their own hook: we were just watching them."

She looked steadily at him, then nodded. "All right," she said. "If I was a cop, I'd have done the same thing."

THEY TALKED FOR a few more minutes, but nothing developed that would help. Lucas and Sloan said good-bye to the sheriff and headed for the car.

"What do you think about Sandy Darling?" Lucas asked as they skated down the sidewalk.

Sloan shook his head. "I don't know. She's a tough one, and she's no dummy. But she was scared."

"The cops scared her," Lucas said. "They were pushing her pretty hard."

"Not scared that way," Sloan said. Lucas tossed him the car keys and Sloan popped the driver's-side door. "She was scared like . . ."

They got in, and Sloan fired the car up, and after another moment, continued: ". . . she was scared like she was afraid she'd make a mistake. Like she was making up a story, and was afraid we'd break it down. If she isn't involved, she doesn't need a story. But I felt like she was working on one."

Lucas, staring out the window as they rolled through the small town, said, "Huh." And then, "You know, I kind of like her."

"I noticed," Sloan said. "That always makes them harder to arrest."

Lucas grinned, and Sloan let the car unwind down the snaky road toward the I-94.

"We better take a little care," Lucas said finally. "We'll get the word out, that we're looking for anybody asking about cops. And get some paper going on the guy, and his connections. Roust any assholes who might know him."

"I've never had any comebacks," Sloan said. "A few threats, nothing real."

"I've had a couple minor ones," Lucas said, nodding.

"That's what you get for sneaking around in the weeds all those years," Sloan said. Then: "Bet I beat your time going back."

"Let me get my seat belt on," Lucas said.

LACHAISE STRETCHED OUT on a bed, a soft mattress for the first time in four years, and breathed the freedom. Or looseness. Later, he made some coffee, some peanut-butter-and-Ritz-cracker sandwiches, listened to the radio. He heard five or six reports on his escape and the killing of Sand, excited country reporters with a real story. One said that police believed he might be on foot, and they were doing a house-by-house check in the town of Colfax.

That made him smile: they still didn't know how he'd gotten out.

He could hear the wind blowing outside the trailer, and after a while, he put on a coat and went outside and walked around. Took a leak in the freezing outhouse, then walked down to the edge of the woods and looked down a gully. Deer tracks, but nothing in sight. He could feel the cold, and he walked back to the trailer. The sun was nearly gone, a dim aspirin-sized pill trying to break through a screen of bare aspen.

He listened to the radio some more: the search in Colfax was done. The Dunn County sheriff said blah-blah-blah nothing.

Still, nightfall was a relief. With night came the sense that the search would slow down, that cops would be going home. He found a stack of army blankets and draped them across the windows to black them out. After turning on the lights, he walked once around the outside of the trailer, to make sure he didn't have any light leaks, came back inside, adjusted one of the blankets, and climbed back to the bed. The silence of the woods had been forgotten, submerged in his years in a cell, and for a while he couldn't sleep.

He did sleep, but when he heard the tires crunching on the snow, he was awake in an instant. He sat up and took the Bulldog off the floor. A moment later, he heard footsteps, and then the door rattled.

"Who is that?" he asked.

A woman's voice came back: "Sandy."

HER FACE WAS tight, angry. "You jerk," she said. He was looking down at her, the gun pointed at her chest. Coldly furious, she ignored it. "I want you out of here. Now."

"Come in and shut the door, you're letting the cold in," he said. He backed away from her, but continued to look out over her head. "You didn't bring the cops?"

"No. I didn't bring the cops. But I want you out of here, Dick . . ."

"Tomorrow," he said. "We're heading for Mexico."

"At the funeral home, they said you were gunning for these cops that killed Candy and Georgie."

"Yeah, well . . ." He shrugged.

"Why'd you kill the prison guard?" she asked.

His eyes shifted, and she felt him gathering a reason, an excuse: "He was the meanest sonofabitch on the floor. If you knew what he'd done . . ."

"But now they're looking for you for *murder*."

He shrugged: "That's what I was in for."

"But you didn't have anything to do with that," she said.

"Didn't make no difference to them," he said.

"My God, Dick, there *is* a difference . . ."

"You didn't know this guy," LaChaise said. "If you'd known what Sand put my friends through back in the joint . . ." He shook his head. "You couldn't blame us. No man oughta go through that."

He was talking about rape, she knew. She didn't buy it, but she wouldn't press him, either. She wanted to believe and if she pressed him, she was afraid she'd find out he was lying.

"Whatever," she said. "But now you've got to move. Martin was bragging about how good his truck is: If you leave tomorrow, you can be in Arizona the day after, driving straight through. You can be in Mexico the day after that, down on the Pacific Ocean."

"Yeah, we're figuring that out," LaChaise said, but again, his eyes shifted fractionally. "What happened at the funeral home?"

"The police kept us there for a couple of hours—and two detectives from Minneapolis talked to us—and then they took us down to Menomonie, to the courthouse. We had to sign statements, and then they let us go. A couple of deputies came around again, about dinnertime, and checked the house."

"They have a warrant?"

"No, but I let them in, I thought it was best," she said. "They looked around and left."

"What about Elmore?"

"Elmore was at work," Sandy said. "They already talked to him."

"Would Elmore turn us in?" LaChaise said.

"No. He's as scared as I am," Sandy said, and the anger suddenly leaped to the surface: "Why'd you do it, Dick? We've never done anything to you, and now you're dragging us down with you."

"We needed a place to ditch," LaChaise said defensively. "We didn't know what the situation would be. If the cops were right on our ass, we needed some place we could get out of sight in a hurry. I thought of this place."

"Well, I want you out," Sandy said. She poked a finger at him. "If you're not out, I'll have to take the chance and go to the police myself. When you get out, I'll come out here and wipe everything you've touched . . . and I hope to hell if you get caught, you'll have the decency to keep your mouth shut about this place."

"I won't get caught," LaChaise said. "I'm not going back inside. If I get killed, that's the way it is: but I'm not going back."

"But if you do get caught . . . you know, shot and you wake up in a hospital . . ."

"No way I'd tell them about this," LaChaise said, shaking his head. "No way."

"All right." She glanced at her watch. "I better get going, in case those deputies check back. I'll tell you something, though: one of the Minneapolis cops was this Davenport guy. The guy who's in charge of the group that killed Candy and Georgie."

"I know who he is," LaChaise said. "So?"

"He's awful hard," she said.

"I'm awful hard, too," LaChaise said.

She nodded: "I'm just telling you," she said.

When Sandy left, she walked head-down to her car, and sat inside for a moment before she started it. Now she *was* guilty of something, she thought. As a hardworking, taxpaying Republican rancher, she should be in favor of sending herself to prison for what she'd just done. But she wasn't. She'd do anything to stay out—the idea of a prison cell made her knees weak. If Dick had landed anywhere else, she'd have turned him in. But the trailer hideout would be impossible to explain, and she'd had the experience, in LaChaise's earlier trial, of seeing what vindictive cops could do.

Damn. She thought about the weapons in the hall closet back home, a .22, a deer rifle, a shotgun. She'd never considered anything like this before, but she could go home, get Elmore's deer rifle, come back out here . . .

Get Dick outside.

Boom.

She could dump his body in a cornfield somewhere, and nobody would know anything until spring. And if the coyotes got to him, probably not even then. She sighed. She couldn't do anything like that. She'd never wanted to hurt anyone in her life. But she wasn't going under. She'd swim for it.

WEATHER AND LUCAS ate handmade ravioli from an Italian market while Lucas told her about the trip to Colfax. Weather said, "Tell me that last part again. About the eye-for-an-eye."

Lucas shrugged. "We have to take a little care. The guy won't be running around for long, there're too many people looking for him. But everybody involved in the shooting . . . I've told them to keep an eye out."

"You think he'd come here, looking for you?" she asked.

"I don't think so," Lucas said. Then he said, "I don't know. Maybe. He's nuts. We've got to take a little care, that's all."

"That's why you've got the gun under your chair. A little care."

Lucas stopped with a forkful of pasta halfway to his mouth. "I'm sorry," he said. "But it's no big deal—and it's just for a little while."

5

Eᴀʀʟʏ ᴍᴏʀɴɪɴɢ ᴀᴛ the Black Watch.

Andy Stadic pushed through the front door, took his gloves off and unbuttoned his overcoat as he walked around the bar and through the double swinging doors into the kitchen. Opening the coat freed up his weapon: not that he'd need it, but he did it by habit.

Stadic was short, bullet-headed, with close-cropped hair and suspicious, slightly bulging eyes. In the kitchen, he nodded to the cook, who was chopping onions into twenty pounds of raw burger, ignored the Chicano dishwasher, turned the corner past the pan rack and pushed through another set of doors.

The back room was cool, lit with overhead fluorescent, furnished with cartons of empty beer bottles, boxes of paper towels and toilet paper, cans of ketchup, sacks of potatoes—the whole room smelled of wet paper and potatoes and onions and a bit of cigar smoke.

Daymon Harp sat in one of two red plastic chairs at a rickety round table, chewing gum, his feet stretched out in front of him, crossed at the ankles. He wore a bomber jacket, faded Levi's and purple cowboy boots with sterling-silver toes.

"What'd you want?" Stadic asked, standing, hands in his pockets.

"We got a problem." Harp uncrossed his legs, put a foot on the second chair, and pushed it across the concrete floor at Stadic.

"I don't want to hear about problems," Stadic said.

"Can't be helped," Harp said.

"Man, I hate even seeing you," Stadic said. "If the shoo-flies walked in right now, I'd be all done. I'd be on the one-stop train to Stillwater."

"I couldn't help it. Sit down, goddamnit."

Stadic turned the chair and straddled it, his arms crossed on the back. "What?"

"Two guys showed up at my crib last night," Harp said. "Put some guns on me. They were looking for your name."

"My name?"

"Yeah. They knew I was working with a cop, but they didn't know your name."

"Jesus Christ, Harp . . ."

"They said they'd cut one finger off Jas every ten seconds until I came out with it, and had something to prove it by. They were gonna cut off two fingers just to show that they was tellin' the truth. And after they got all ten fingers, they said, they were gonna cut out her eyes and then cut her throat and then they were gonna start on me."

"You told them?" Stadic's voice rose in disbelief.

"Goddamn right I told them," Harp said. "They cut her pointer finger off right there, on a bread board. She was all tied up and gagged and flopping around, and they were like they was killed chickens or something . . . couple of goddamn mean crackers. I been in the joint with these motherfuckers before. They got little tears tattooed under their eyes, one for each man they killed, and when you start tattooing them on, you better be able to prove it to the rest of the crazies. This crackhead kid's got three of them and the fucker with the knife got two."

"You coulda said anything," Stadic said.

Harp shook his head. "They wanted proof. I had a little proof."

Now Stadic was very quiet. "What proof?"

"I had some pictures taken."

"You motherfucker . . ." Stadic stood up, kicked the chair aside, his hand moving toward his pistol. Harp held his hands up.

"It was from way back when, when I didn't know you. And I had Jas's motherfuckin' finger laying there like a dead shrimp, all curled up. What the hell was I supposed to do?"

"You coulda *tried* lying," Stadic shouted. His fingers twitched at the gun butt.

"You wasn't *there*," Harp said. "You don't *know*."

Stadic took a breath, as though he'd just topped a hill, turned in place, then said, "So what'd they want with my name?"

"They need some information from you."

"Tell me." He was nibbling nervously at a thumbnail, ripped off a piece of nail, spit it out, tasted blood. The nail was bleeding, and he sucked at it, the blood salty in his mouth.

"They want personnel files," Harp said. "From the police department."

LA CHAISE HAD SPENT whole days thinking about it, daydreaming it, when he was locked up: the requirements of the coming wars. Us against Them. They would need a base. In the countryside, somewhere. There'd be a series of log cabins linked with storm sewer pipe, six feet underground and more sewer pipe set into the hills as bunkers. Honda generators for each cabin, with internal wells and septic fields.

Weapons: sniper rifles to keep the attackers off, heavy-duty assault rifles for up close. Hidden land mines with remote triggers. Armor-piercing rockets. He'd close his eyes and see the assaults happening, the attackers falling back as they met the sweeping fire from the web . . .

The attackers were a little less certain; some combination of ATF agents and blacks from the Chicago ghettos, Indians, Mexicans. Though that didn't seem to make a lot of sense, sometimes; so sometimes, they were all ATF agents, dressed in black uniforms and masks . . .

Daydreams.

THE REALITY WAS a couple of trucks and a run-down house in a near-slum.

LaChaise and Butters drove down to the Cities in Elmore's truck, with Martin trailing behind. They needed two vehicles, they decided, at least for a while. Butters and Martin caught Elmore in the barn, while Sandy was out riding, and squeezed him for the truck keys.

"Just overnight," Butters said, standing too close. "Martin's got some warrants out on his car, if the cops check—nothing serious, but we gotta have some kind of backup. We won't do nothin' with it."

"Guys, I tell you, we're moving stuff today . . ." Elmore stuttered. Martin and Butters scared Elmore. Martin, Elmore thought, was a freak, a pent-up homosexual hillbilly crazy in love with LaChaise. Butters had the flat eyes of a snapping turtle, and was simply nuts.

Elmore tried to get out of it, but Martin put his hands in Elmore's coat pocket, and when Elmore tried to wrench away, Butters pushed him from the other side. Martin had the keys and said, "We'll get them back to you, bud."

THE HOUSE WAS a shabby two-story clapboard wreck on a side street in the area called Frogtown. The outside needed paint, the inside needed an exterminator. Half the basement was wet and the circuit box hanging over the damp concrete floor was a fire marshal's nightmare. Martin had brought in three Army-surplus beds, a dilapidated monkey-shit-yellow couch and two matching chairs, and a dinette set, all from Goodwill, and a brand-new twenty-seven-inch Sony color TV.

"Good place, if we don't burn to death," Martin said. The house smelled like wet plaster and fried eggs. "That wiring down the basement is a marvel."

"Hey, it's fine," LaChaise said, looking around.

No web of sewer pipe, no Honda generators. No land mines.

That evening, Butters sat in one of the broken-down easy chairs, his head back and his eyes closed. Martin sat cross-legged on the floor with his arrows, unscrewing the field points, replacing them with hundred-grain Thunderheads, a can of beer by one foot. He would occasionally look at LaChaise with a stare that was purely sexual.

"We're gonna do it," LaChaise said. He had a half-glass of bourbon in his hand. "We've been talking for years. Talk talk talk. Now with Candy and Georgie shot to pieces, we're gonna do it."

"Gonna be the end of us," Martin said. His beard was coppery red in the lamplight.

"Could be," LaChaise agreed. He scratched his own beard, nipped at the bourbon. "Do you care?"

Martin worked for another minute, then said, "Nah. I'm getting crowded. I'm ready."

"You could go up north, up in the Yukon."

"Been there," Martin said. "The goddamn Canadians is a bunch of Communists. Even Alaska's better."

"Mexico . . ."

"I'm a goddamn American."

LaChaise nodded and said, "How about you, Ansel?"

Butters said, "I just want to get it over with."

"Well, we got to take our time, figure this out . . ."

"I mean, everything over with," Butters said. "I can take my time with *this*."

LaChaise nodded again. "It's the end for me, for sure. But I swear to God, I'm taking a bunch of these sonsofbitches with me."

Martin looked at him uncertainly, then nodded, and looked away. They worked together, comfortable but intent, like they did in hunting camps, thinking about it all, drinking a little, letting the feeling of the hunt flow through them, the camaraderie as they got the gear ready.

They checked the actions on their weapons for the twentieth time, loading and unloading the pistols, dry-firing at the TV; the good smell of Hoppe's solvent and gun oil, the talk of old times and old rides and the people they remembered, lots of them dead, now.

"If I lived," LaChaise continued, "I'd do nothing but sit in cells for the rest of my life anyhow. Besides . . ."

"Besides what?" Martin asked, looking up.

"Ah, nothin'," LaChaise said, but he thought, *Mexico*. He'd always planned to go, and hadn't ever been.

"It cranks me up, thinking about it," Butters said. His face was flushed with alcohol.

SANDY HAD BLOWN up when she'd come back from her ride, and Elmore had told her about the truck. She jumped in her van and went after them, but they were gone. She got to the St. Croix, realized the futility of the chase, slowed, turned around and went back.

"What were you thinking about?" she shouted at Elmore. "You shoulda swallowed the keys."

That night, Elmore was in the kitchen making a pot of Rice-a-Roni with venison chunks, and she could smell the chemical odor of the stuff as she sat in front of the TV. She heard the rattling of the dishes, and finally, Elmore stood in the hallway behind her. She pretended to watch the sports.

He said, "We oughta talk to the cops."

"What?" She pushed herself out of her chair. She hadn't expected this.

Elmore's voice rose to a nervous warble: "If we stick with this, only two things can happen. We get killed, or we go to jail for murder. That's it: them two things."

"Too late," she said. "We gotta sit tight."

Tears came to his eyes, and one dribbled down a cheek, and Sandy suddenly didn't know what to do. She'd seen Elmore frightened, she'd seen him cower, she'd seen him avoid any serious responsibility, but she'd never seen him weep. "Are you okay?"

He turned his head toward her, the tears still running down his cheeks: "How'd this happen?" he said.

She'd thought about that: "My sister," she said. "The whole of this is because of Candy. And because of your dad's trailer. It's because of nothing that means anything . . ."

"We've got to go to the police."

"But what do we tell them? And why would they believe us?"

"Maybe they won't," he rasped. "But you saw all those guns and all that other shit that Martin had. How're they going to Mexico with all that shit? How are they gonna get across the border with it? And if they do get across, what are they going to use for money? They ain't going to Mexico. They're gonna pull some crazy stunt."

"No—no," she said, shaking her head. "They're out of here. Dick LaChaise is nobody's fool."

"Dick LaChaise is fuckin' nuts," Elmore said. "You want to know what's gonna happen? We got two or three more days, and then we'll be dead or in jail. Two or three more days, Sandy. No more horses, no more trail rides, no more going up to the store or running down to the Cities. We're going to jail. Forever."

They stared at each other for a moment, then she said, almost whispering, "But we can't get out. If we talked to the cops, what would we give them? We don't even know where Dick's at. And there're Seed guys all over the place— look what happened when that guy was going to testify against Candy. He got killed."

"Maybe old John Shanks could tell us something," Elmore said. John Shanks was a criminal attorney who'd handled Candy's assault case. "See if he can cut us a deal."

"I don't know, El," Sandy said, shaking her head. "This thing is all out of control. If they hadn't stayed in the trailer . . ."

"We can clean up the trailer."

"Sure, but if we turn against them, they'll drag us in. How'd you like to be in the same prison with Butters and Martin?"

Elmore swallowed. He was not a brave man. "We gotta do something."

"I'm gonna walk down the driveway," Sandy said. "I'll figure something out."

————

SANDY PUT ON her parka and pacs, and her gloves, and stepped outside. The night was brutally cold and slapped at her skin like nettles; the wind was enough to snatch her breath away. She crunched down the frozen snow in the thin blue illumination of the yard light, thinking about it, worrying it. If she could only keep things under control. If only Dick would disappear. If only Elmore would hold on . . .

Elmore.

Sandy had never really loved Elmore, though she'd once been very fond of him; and still felt the fondness at times. But more often, she suffered with the fact that Elmore clearly loved her, and she could hardly bear to be around him.

Sandy had grown up with horses, though she'd never owned one until she was on her own. Her father, a country mailman, had always wanted to ride the range—and so they rode out of the county stables on weekends, almost every weekend from the time she was three until she was eighteen, three seasons of the year. Candy hadn't cared for it, and quit when she was in junior high; Sandy had never quit. Never would. She loved horses more than her father loved riding them. Walking down the drive, she could smell the sweet odor of the barn, manure and straw, though it was more than a quarter-mile away . . . She could never leave that; never risk it.

She'd gone to high school with Elmore, but never dated him. After graduation, she'd left for Eau Claire to study nursing, and two years later, came back to Turtle Lake, took a job with a local nursing home and started saving for the horse farm. When her parents died in a car accident—killed by a drunk—her half of the money had bought four hundred acres east of town.

Elmore had been working as a security guard in the Cities, and started hanging around. Sandy, lonely, had let him hang around. Made the mistake of letting him work around the ranch: he wasn't the brightest man, or the hardest worker, but she needed all the help she could get, working nights at the nursing home, days at the ranch. Made the mistake of sleeping with him, the second man she'd slept with.

Then Elmore had fallen off a stairwell and wrenched his back: the payoff, twenty-two thousand dollars, would buy some stock and a used Ford tractor. And there wasn't anybody else around. And she *was* fond of the man.

Sandy often walked down the drive when life got a little too unhappy, when Elmore got to be too much of a burden. The ranch, she'd thought, was the only thing she wanted in life, and she'd do anything to get it. When she'd gotten it—and when the breeding business actually started to pay off—she found that she needed something else. Somebody else. Even if it was just somebody to talk to as an equal, who'd understand the business, feel the way she did about horses.

Elmore was an emotional trap she couldn't find a way out of. There was the man in Montana; he was married now, but she thought about him all the time. With somebody like that . . .

She brushed the thought away. That's not who she had.

She turned, circling, crunching through the snow: prison for life. And she got around to the north, and saw the first slinky unfolding of the northern lights, watched as they pumped up to a shimmering curtain above the everlasting evergreens, and decided that she might have to talk to someone about Dick LaChaise.

"But not quite yet," she told Elmore when she was back inside. "Just a couple of more days—we let it ride. Maybe they'll take off. Anyway, we gotta build a story. Then maybe we talk to old John."

ANDY STADIC WENT into the laundromat and sat down. The place smelled of spilt Tide and ERA and dirty wash water, and the hot lint smell of the dryers.

A woman glanced at him once, and again. He was just sitting there, a well-dressed white man, and had nothing to wash. She started to get nervous. He sat in one of the hard folding chairs and read a two-week-old copy of *People*. The woman finished folding her dry clothes, packed them in a pink plastic basket, and left. He was alone. He walked over to the door, turned the Open/Closed sign to Closed, and locked the door.

Stadic watched the windows. A blond-haired hippie strolled by, a kid who might have been the southern boy who'd jumped Daymon Harp. A minute later, a hawk-faced white man walked up to the door, stuck his head inside.

"You Stadic?"

"Yeah."

"Sit tight."

Damn right. He'd told them he wouldn't go anyplace private. He'd told them Harp would be watching.

Another minute passed, and then a bearded man came around the corner, Pioneer seed-corn hat pulled low over his eyes. He walked like a farmer, heavy and loose, and had a farmer's haircut, ears sticking out, red with the cold, and a razor trim on the back of his neck. The farmer took his time getting inside. Stadic recognized the eyes beneath the bill.

LaChaise.

"What the fuck do you think you're doing?" Stadic said. He wanted to get on top of the guy immediately.

"Shut up," LaChaise said. His voice was a tough baritone, and his eyes fixed on Stadic's.

"You don't tell me to shut up." Stadic was on his feet, squared off.

LaChaise put his hand in his pocket, and the pocket moved. He had a gun.

"Go for your gun," LaChaise said.

"What?" As soon as he said it, a temporizing word, uncertain, Stadic felt that he'd lost the edge.

"Gonna give me trouble, go for your gun, give me some real trouble. I already killed one cop, killing you won't be nothing."

"Jesus Christ . . ."

LaChaise was on top, knew it, and his hand came off the gun. "Where're the records?"

"You gotta be nuts, thinking I'd give you those things."

"I *am* nuts," LaChaise said. His hand was back on the gun. "You should know that. Now, where're the records?"

"I want to know what you're gonna do with them."

"We're gonna scare the shit out of a lot of people," LaChaise said. "We're gonna have them jumpin' through hoops like they was in a Russian circus. Now quit doggin' me around: either give them to me, or tell me you don't have them. You don't have them, I'm gone."

When they'd set up the meeting, by phone, LaChaise had said that if he didn't bring the papers, the next call would be to Internal Affairs.

Stadic let out a breath, shook his head. "Scare the shit out of them? That's all?"

"That's all," LaChaise said. He was lying and Stadic knew it. And LaChaise knew that he knew, and didn't care. "Gimme the goddamned papers."

"Jesus, LaChaise, *anything* else . . ."

"I'm outa here," LaChaise said, turning toward the doors.

"Wait a minute, wait a minute . . ." Stadic said, "I'm gonna stick my hand in my coat."

LaChaise's hand went back to his pistol and he nodded. Stadic took the papers out of his breast pocket and held them out at arm's length. LaChaise took them, didn't look, and backed away. "Better be the real thing," he said, and he turned to go.

"Wait," Stadic said. "I gotta know how to get in touch with you."

"We'll get in touch with you," LaChaise said.

"Think about it," Stadic said, his voice tight, urgent. "I want you outa here— or dead. I don't want you caught. Anything but that. If they figure out where you're at, and they're coming to get you . . . I oughta be able to call."

"Got no phone," LaChaise said. "We're trying to get one of them cellulars."

"Call me, soon as you get one," Stadic said. He took an index card from his pocket, groped for a pen, found one, scribbled the number. "I carry the phone all the time."

"I'll think about it," LaChaise said, taking the card.

"Do it," Stadic said. "Please."

Then LaChaise was gone, out the door, pulling the hat down over his eyes, around the corner. Harp came through the back door two minutes later.

"I think three is all of them," Harp said. "I saw the cracker on the street, then a pickup pulls up and this peckerwood gets out—he's new—and the pickup goes off; the driver was probably that other dude."

"Get the plates?"

"Yeah. I did."

"See anybody else? Anybody who looked like a cop?" Harp shook his head. "Just a couple of kids and some old whore."

LA CHAISE FLIPPED THROUGH a computer printout of the police department's insurance program. Some of it was gobbledygook, but buried in the tiny squares and rectangles were the names of all the insured, their addresses and phone numbers.

"Modern science," LaChaise said.

"What?" Martin turned to look at him.

"I'm reading a computer printout; I'm gonna get a cell phone," LaChaise said. "You go along and things get easier."

He started circling names on the printout.

6

WEATHER KARKINNEN WORE a white terry-cloth robe, with a matching terry-cloth towel wrapping her hair. Through the back window she was a Vermeer figure in a stone house, quiet, pensive, slow-moving, soft with her bath, humming along with a Glenn Gould album.

She got a beer from the refrigerator, popped the top, found a glass and started pouring. The phone rang, and she stepped back and picked it up, propped it between her ear and her shoulder, and continued pouring.

"Yes, he is," she said.

Lucas was sitting in his old leather chair, eyes closed. He was working on a puzzle—a tactical exercise involving both a car chase and a robbery.

Lucas had once written strategy board games, had moved them to computers, then, pushed temporarily off the police force, had started a company doing computer simulations of police problems.

He'd made the change at just the right time: His training software did well. Now the company was run by a professional manager, and though Lucas still held the biggest chunk of the stock, he now worked mostly on conceptual problems. He was imagining a piece of software that spliced voice and data transmissions, that would layer a serious but confused problem beneath an exciting but superficial one, to teach new dispatchers to triage emergency calls.

Triage. The word had been used by the programmers putting together the simulation, and it had been rattling around his brain for a few days, a loose BB. The word had a nasty edge to it, like *cadaver*.

"Lucas?"

He jumped. Weather was in the doorway, a glass of dark beer in her hand. She'd brewed it herself in a carboy in the hall closet, from a kit that Lucas had bought her for her birthday.

"You've got a phone call . . ."

Lucas shook himself awake, heaved himself out of the chair. "Who is it?" he asked, yawning. He saw the beer. "Is that for me?"

"I don't know who it is. And get your own," she said.

"We sound like a TV commercial."

"You're the one who was snoring in the chair after dinner," she said.

"I was thinking," he said. He picked up the phone, ignoring her dainty snort. "Yeah?"

The man's voice was oily, a man who gave and took confidences like one-dollar poker chips. "This is Earl. Stupella. Down at the Blue Bull?"

"Yeah, Earl. What's happening?"

"You was in that shoot-out a week or so ago, in the papers. The credit union." He wasn't asking a question.

"Yeah?"

"So this chick came in here tonight and said she'd seen the husband of one of these girls, who like supposedly busted out of prison and killed somebody. It was like La Chase?"

Lucas was listening now. "LaChaise," he said. "That's right. Where'd she see him?"

"A laundromat down on Eleventh. She said she saw him going in and he talked to a guy in the window for a minute and then he left."

"Huh. Who's the chick?" Lucas asked.

"Don't tell her I talked to you," Stupella said.

"No problem."

"Sally O'Donald. She lives somewhere up the line, by the cemetery, I think, but I don't know."

"I know Sally," Lucas said. "Anything else?"

"Nope. Sally said she didn't want to have nothing to do with LaChaise, so when she saw him, she turned right around and walked away."

"When was all this?"

"Sally was in about an hour ago," Stupella said. "She saw the guy this morning."

"Good stuff, Earl. You'll get a note in the mail."

"Thanks, dude."

LUCAS DROPPED THE phone on the hook: LaChaise. So he *was* here. And out in the open. Lucas stood staring at the phone for a second, then picked it up again.

"Going out?" Weather asked from the hallway.

"Mmm, yeah. I think." He pushed a speed-dial button, listened to the beep-beep-boop of the phone.

Del answered on the second ring. "What?"

"I hope that's not a bedside phone you're talking on."

"What happened?" Del asked.

"Nothing much. I thought we might go for a ride, if you're not doing anything."

"You mean, go for a ride and get an ice cream? Or go for a ride and bring your gun?"

"The latter," Lucas said, glancing at Weather. She had a little rim of beer foam on her upper lip.

"Latter, my ass," Del said. "Give me ten minutes."

THE BACK STREETS were ruts of gnarled ice. The Explorer's heater barely kept up, and Del, who didn't like gloves, sat with his hands in his armpits. The good part was, the assholes and freaks got as cold as anyone else. On nights like this, there was no crime, except the odd domestic murder that probably would have happened anyway.

When the radio burped, Del picked it up: "Yeah."

"O'Donald is the third house on the left, right after you make the turn off Lake," the dispatcher said.

"All right. We'll get back."

Lucas cruised the house once, rattling the white Explorer down the ruts. The house showed lights in the back, where the kitchen usually was, and the dim blue glow of a television from a side window. "The thing is," Lucas said, "she has a terrible temper."

"And she's about the size of a fuckin' two-car garage," said Del. "Maybe we should shoot her before we talk to her."

"Just a flesh wound, to slow her down," Lucas agreed. "Or shoot her in the kneecap."

"We shot the last one in the kneecap."

"Oh yeah; well, that's out, then." Lucas parked and said, "Don't piss her off, huh? I don't want to be rolling around in the yard with her."

SALLY O'DONALD WAS in a mood.

She stood on the other side of a locked glass storm door, her hair in pink curlers, her ample lips turned down in a scowl, her fists on her hips. She was wearing a threadbare plaid bathrobe and fuzzy beige slippers that looked like squashed rabbits.

"What do *you* assholes want, in the middle of the night?"

"Just talk, no problem," Lucas said. He was standing on the second step of the stoop, looking up at her.

"Last time I talked to that fuckin' Capslock, I thought I was gonna have to pull his nuts off," she said, not moving toward the door lock. She stared over Lucas's shoulder at Del.

Del shivered and said, "Sally, open the goddamn door, will you? We're freezing out here. Honest to God, all we want to do is talk."

She let them in after a while, and led them back to a television room so choked with smoke that it might have been a bowling alley. She moved a TV dinner tray out of the way, pointed at a corduroy-covered chair for Lucas and sat down in another. Del stood.

"We know you saw Dick LaChaise—you only told about a hundred people," Lucas said.

"I didn't tell no hundred people, I told about three," she said, squinting at him from her piggy eyes. "I'll figure out who it was, sooner or later. Pull his nuts off."

"Jesus, Sally," Del said. "Take it easy on the nuts stuff."

"We just want to know where you saw him, who he was with and what you know about him," Lucas said. "Our source says you used to hang out with him."

"Who is it? The source? I talk to you, you oughta give me something."

"You know I can't tell you that. I could ask Sex to give your place a pass for a couple of months," Lucas said, adding, "if the information is decent."

She nodded, calculating. A two-month pass from Sex added up. She said, "All right. I hung with the Seed, off and on, for maybe ten years? Up until—let's see—four or five years ago. They got me in the business to begin with, turned me out in Milwaukee. Dick was one of the bigger shots in the Seeds when I first met him. He was maybe twenty-five back then, so he'd be what, forty?"

"Thirty-eight," Lucas said. "That's a long time ago."

"Yeah. I remember him especially because he thought he was Marlon Brando. He liked to wear those squashed fisherman hats, and gold chains and shit. I caught him practicing his smile once, in the can at this bar in Milwaukee."

"Practicing . . . ?"

"Yeah."

"I'm not getting a picture of a big leader, here," Lucas said.

"Oh, he was. Maybe a little too nuts, though. You know, most of the Seeds were sort of . . . criminal businessmen. A little dope, a little porn, a few whores. Bad, but not necessarily crazy. Dick . . . you heard about the sleeping on the yellow line?"

"Yeah, heard the story," Lucas said.

"I was there. He did. And he was asleep. And I once saw him try to ride a Harley up an oak tree . . ."

Lucas looked at Del and they both shrugged. "He killed this guard, cut his throat, pretty cold," Lucas said to O'Donald. "Does that sound like LaChaise?"

She thought for a moment, cocking her head, then said, "Well, ten years ago, he would've had to be pissed. But just cold like that . . ." She snapped her fingers. "I don't know."

"His old lady and Georgie LaChaise—they had a rep for stealing money and giving it to nut groups," Lucas said. "He had to have help in the escape. We thought maybe some of the nuts helped out."

"I didn't know his wife or his sister. The Seed had some serious goofballs around, though. Just before I left it was the blacks this and the Jews that and the politicians and media and cops and feminists and television and banks and insurance companies and welfare and food stamps . . . the whole pizza pie."

"Sounds like talk radio," Lucas said.

She laughed, an unpleasant gurgling sound, and her stomach bounced up and down. She pointed her finger at him. "That's good."

"What was he doing at the laundromat?" Del asked.

"Talking to some guy," O'Donald said. "They was standing up, arguing with each other—that's when I came down the street and saw him. He has a beard and he had a beard when I knew him, but he didn't have a beard in the newspaper picture."

"That was the last picture they had of him," Lucas said. "He started growing the beard two or three months ago."

"How'd it look?" Del asked. He'd propped himself against a chest of drawers. "Short and smooth? Special cut?"

"Bible prophet," she said. "Long and scraggly."

Lucas said, "Then what? After he was arguing with the guy?"

"I didn't hang around. I don't need Dick LaChaise seeing me and asking for a favor, if you know what I mean."

"You worried about freebies?" Del asked.

"I don't care about freebies," she said. She looked away, her lips still moving, then she shook her head and said, "If Dick is here, some of his old Seed buddies are probably around, too. You really don't want to fuck with them."

"We did," Del said.

O'Donald nodded: "I read about it—that thing where you guys killed his old lady and his sister."

"Yeah?" Del nodded.

"He's here to even the score on that," O'Donald said. "If I were you guys, I'd move to another state."

Lucas looked at her. "You think he'd come after cops?"

"Davenport, have you been listening?" she asked impatiently. "Dick is a fuckin' fruitcake. You killed his woman and his sister. He's coming after you, all right. Eye for an eye."

She frowned suddenly, then said, "That guy he was talking to—at the laundromat. I think he was a cop."

Lucas said, "What?"

"I don't know who, but I recognized the attitude. You know how you can always tell a cop? I mean, except for Capslock here, he looks like a wino . . . Well, this guy was like that. A cop-cop."

"Would you recognize a mug shot?"

She shrugged: "Probably not. I didn't really look at him, I was sort of looking past him, at Dick. It was the way he stood that made me think cop."

Del looked down at Lucas and said, "That's not good."

"No. That's not good." Lucas looked back through the dark house, the smoke-browned wallpaper, the crumpled Chee-tos bags on the floor, the stink of a cat, and he said, half to himself, "Eye for an eye."

7

MARTIN HAD BROUGHT a foam target with him, a two-foot-square chunk of dense white plastic with concentric black circles around the bull's-eye. He'd nailed it to a wall beside the refrigerator, and was shooting arrows diagonally across the living room, into the kitchen. The shooting made a steady THUMM-whack from the bowstring vibration and the arrows punching into the target.

Form practice, he called it; he didn't care where the arrow went, if the form was correct. As it happened, the arrow always went into the bull's-eye.

LaChaise had been watching a game show. When it ended, he yawned, got to his feet and went to a window. The light had died. He looked out into the gloom, then let the curtains fall back and turned to the room. He cracked a smile and said, "Let's saddle up."

Martin was at full draw, and might not have heard. He held, released: THUMM-whack.

Butters had been playing with their new cell phone. They'd bought it from a dealer friend of Butters's, who'd bought it from one of his customers, a kid with a nose for cocaine.

"Good for two weeks," the dealer had promised. Butters had given him a thousand dollars for the phone, and the dealer had put the money in his jeans without counting it. "The kid's ma is a realtor. She's in Barbados on vacation, left him just enough money to buy food. The kid said his ma made fifty calls a day, so you can use it as much as you want; I wouldn't go calling Russia or nothing."

They'd used it twice, once to call Stadic, once to call a used-car salesman.

When LaChaise said "Saddle up," Butters put the phone down, opened the duffel by his foot, and took out two pistols. One was a tiny .380, the other a larger nine-millimeter. He popped the magazines on both of them, thumbed the shells out and restacked them. Then he took a long, thin hand-machined silencer out of the duffel and screwed it into the nine-millimeter: excellent. He unscrewed the silencer, picked up his camo jacket and dropped the silencer in the side pocket.

"Ready," he said simply. Butters had a thick blue vein that ran down his temple to his cheekbone: the vein was standing out in the thin light, like a scar.

"How about you?" LaChaise asked Martin.

Martin was at full draw again, focused on form: THUMM-whack. "Been ready," he said.

LaChaise parted the drapes with two fingers, looked out again. The street-lights were on and it was snowing. The snow had started at noon, just a few flakes at first, the weather forecasters saying it wasn't much. Now it was getting heavier. The closest streetlight looked like a candle.

LaChaise turned back into the room, stepped to a chair, and picked up three sheets of paper. The papers were Xerox copies of a newspaper article from the *Star Tribune*. He'd outlined the relevant copy with a pen:

Officers Sherrill, Capslock, Franklin and Kupicek were removed from active duty pending a hearing before a weapons review board, a routine action always taken after a line-of-duty shooting incident. Deputy Chief Davenport and Officer Sloan did not discharge their weapons and will continue on active duty.

So Sherrill, Capslock, Franklin and Kupicek were the shooters.

"What?" asked Martin. He opened his eyes and looked up at LaChaise.

"Eye for an eye," LaChaise said.

"Absolutely," Martin said. He was pulling on his coat. "So let's go."

MARTIN DROVE HIS truck to West End Buick-Oldsmobile. He'd called earlier, and asked for the salesman by name: "I talked to you a couple of days ago about a '91 Pontiac, that black one . . ."

"The Firebird?" The salesman had sounded uncertain, since he hadn't talked to anyone about the Firebird.

"Yeah, that's the one. You still got it?"

"Still looking for an owner," the salesman had said. "There's a guy coming around tonight, but nobody's signed anything yet."

Martin had grinned at the car-sales bullshit. "I'll come by in an hour or so."

"I'll be looking for you," the salesman had promised.

Martin carried a Marine Corps combat knife with a five-inch serrated blade. He'd bought it as a Christmas gift for himself, through a U.S. Cavalry catalog, and carried it in a sheath, on his belt. The knife was the only gift he'd gotten in the past few years, except that LaChaise had given him a bottle of Jim Beam the year before he went to prison.

Martin was thinking about the Jim Beam when he got to the Buick store. He parked across the street: he could see light from the windows, but the snow had continued to thicken, and the people on the other side of the glass were no more than occasional shadows.

He had ten minutes. He closed his eyes, settled in and thought about the other men he'd killed. Martin didn't worry about killing: he simply did it. When he was a kid, there was always something around the farm to be killed. Chickens, hogs, usually a heifer in the fall. And there was the hunting: squirrels, rabbits, raccoons, doves, grouse, deer, bear.

By the time he killed his first man, he didn't much think about it. The man, Harold Carter, was owed money by LaChaise, that LaChaise had borrowed to set up his motorcycle parts store. Carter was talking about going to court. LaChaise wanted him to go away.

Martin killed Carter with a knife on the back steps of his own home, carried the body out to his truck and buried the man in the woods. Nothing to it; certainly not as hard as taking down a pig. A pig always knew what was coming, and fought it. Went squealing and twisting. Carter simply dropped.

His second killing had been no more trouble than the first. His third, if he did it right, should be the easiest yet, because he wouldn't have to deal with the body. Martin closed his eyes; if he were the type to sleep, he might have.

LaChaise, driving Elmore's truck, dropped Butters at the Rosedale Mall. Butters carried both pistols, the short .380 in his left jacket pocket, and the nine-millimeter, with the silencer already attached, in a Velcroed flap under his arm.

He cruised past TV Toys. A tall woman talked to a lone customer, and a thin balding man in a white shirt stood behind the counter. Butters stepped to a phone kiosk, found the paper in his pocket, and dialed the number of the store. He watched as the man in the white shirt picked up the phone.

"TV Toys, this is Walt."

"Yes, is Elaine there?"

"Just a moment."

The man in the white shirt called over to the tall woman, who smiled and said something to her customer and started toward the counter. Butters hung up and glanced at his watch.

Five-twenty. LaChaise should be getting to Capslock's place.

Capslock's wife was a nurse at Ramsey General Hospital, according to her insurance file. She finished her shift at three o'clock.

LaChaise stopped at a Tom Thumb store, bent his head against the storm, punched in her phone number—the insurance forms had everything: address, employer, home and office phones—and waited for an answer.

Like Butters, LaChaise carried two pistols with him, but revolvers rather than automatics. He didn't care about the noise he made, so he didn't have to worry about a silencer; and he liked the simplicity of a revolver. No safeties or feed problems to think about, no cocking anything, just point and shoot.

Cheryl Capslock answered on the fourth ring. "Hello?"

"Uh, Mrs. Capslock?" LaChaise tried to pitch his voice up, to sound boyish, cheerful. "Is Del in?"

"Not yet. Who is this?"

"Terry—I'm at the Amoco station on Snelling. Del wanted, uh, he wanted to talk to me and left a number. Could you tell him I'm around?"

"Okay, your name is Terry?"

"Yeah, T-E-R-R-Y, he's got the number."

"I'll tell him," Cheryl Capslock said.

MARTIN WALKED ACROSS the street to the car lot. The Firebird was in a display stand, forty feet from the main side window on the dealership. He walked once around the car, then again, then bent to look in the side window.

As he rounded the car the second time, he saw a salesman, in the lighted room, pulling on a coat. Martin took the knife out of the sheath and put it in the right side pocket of his coat. Ten seconds later, the salesman, shoulders humped against the snow, trotted out to the car. His coat hung open, showing a rayon necktie.

"She's a beaut," he said, tipping his head at the car.

"You're Mr. Sherrill?" asked Martin.

"Yeah, Mike Sherrill. Didn't we meet last week sometime?"

"Uh, no, not really . . . Listen, I can't see the mileage on this thing."

Sherrill was in his mid-thirties, a onetime athlete now running to fat and whiskey. A web of broken veins hung at the edges of his twice-broken nose, and his once-thick Viking hair had thinned to a blond frizz. "About fifty-five thousand actual. Let me pop the door for you."

Sherrill skated around the car, used a gloved hand to quickly brush the snow off the windshield, then fumbled at the locked keybox on the door. Martin looked past him at the dealership. Another salesman stood briefly at the window, looking out at the snow, then turned away.

"Okay, here we go," Sherrill said. He got the key out of the keybox and unlocked the car door.

Martin didn't mess around, didn't wait for the better moment. He stood to one side as Sherrill opened the door. When Sherrill stepped back, he moved close against the other man, put one hand on his back, and with the other, delivered the killing thrust, a brutal upward sweep, like a solar plexus jab.

The knife took Sherrill just below the breastbone, angling up, through the heart.

Sherrill gasped once, wiggled, started to go down, his eyes open, surprised, looking at Martin. Martin guided his falling body onto the car seat. He pushed Sherrill's head down, caught Sherrill's thrashing legs and pushed them up and inside. Sherrill was upside down in the car, his feet over the front seat, his head hanging beneath the steering wheel. His eyes were open, glazing. He tried to say something, and a blood bubble came out of his mouth.

"Thanks," Martin said.

Martin pushed down the door lock, slammed the door and walked away. There was nobody in the dealership window to see him go.

BUTTERS WAITED UNTIL the man in the white shirt had a customer and the woman was free. He walked into the store, his hand on the silenced pistol. At the back of the store, near the door to the storeroom, was a display for DirecTV. He headed that way, and Elaine Kupicek followed. She was a nice-looking woman, Butters thought, for a cop's wife.

"Can I help you?" She had a wide, mobile mouth and long skinny hands with short nails.

"I own a bar, down in St. Paul."

"Sure . . ."

"If I put in DirecTV, would I be able to get, like, the Green Bay games, even when there's no broadcast over here?"

"Oh, sure. You can get all the games . . ."

The man in the white shirt had moved with his customer to a computer display, where they were talking intently about TV cards for a Windows 95 machine.

"We have a brochure that shows the options . . ."

Butters looked at her, then put the fingers of his left hand to his lips. She stopped suddenly in midsentence, puzzled, and then he took the .380 out of his left pocket and pointed it at her.

"If you scream, I'll shoot. I promise."

"What . . ."

"Step in the back; this is a robbery."

He prodded her toward the door. She stepped backward toward it, caught the knob with her hand and her mouth opened and Butters said, conversationally, "Be quiet, please."

She went through, her eyes looking past Butters, searching for the man in the white shirt, but Butters prodded her further into the room, and then closed the door behind them.

"Don't hurt me," she said.

"I won't. I want you to sit down over there . . . just turn over there."

She turned to look at the chair next to a technician's desk: a brown paper lunch sack sat on the table, with a grease stain on one side. Her lunch sack, with a baloney sandwich and an orange. She stepped toward the desk and said, "Please don't."

"I won't," he promised, in his gentle southern accent. She turned back to the chair and when her head came around, he took the nine-millimeter out of the Velcroed flap in one swift, practiced motion, put it against the back of her head and pulled the trigger once.

Kupicek lurched forward and went down. Butters half-turned, and waited, listening. The shot had been as loud as a hand-clap, accompanied by the working of the bolt. Enough noise to attract attention in an ordinary room, but the door was closed.

He waited another two seconds, then stepped toward the door. Elaine Kupicek sprawled facedown, unmoving. Butters put the pistol back in the Velcroed flap, and the .380 decoy gun in his pocket.

When he opened the door, the man in the white shirt was still talking to the customer. Butters strolled out easily, hands in his pockets, got to the tiled corridor outside the store, looked both ways and then ambled off to the left.

LACHAISE CROSSED THE street in the snow, up the walk to the left-hand door of the town house. He carried the .44 in his right hand, and pushed the doorbell with his left. He stepped back, and a gust of snow hit him in the eyes. The gust came just as the door opened, and he wondered later if it was the snow in his eyes that was to blame . . .

A woman opened the inner door, then half-opened the storm door, a plain woman, half smiling: "Yes?"

"Mrs. Capslock?"

"Yes?"

He was coming around with the gun when Del loomed behind her: a shock, the sudden movement, the face, then Del's mouth opening . . .

Capslock swatted his wife and she went sideways and down, and Capslock screamed something. LaChaise's gun, halfway up, went off when Capslock screamed, and Capslock's arm was coming up. LaChaise's gun went off again and then Capslock had a gun, short and black with the small hole coming around at LaChaise's eyes, and LaChaise slammed the storm door shut as Capslock fired. Splinters of aluminum sliced at LaChaise's face and he backed away, firing the Bulldog again, aware that the door was falling apart, more slugs coming through at him.

The muzzle flashes were blinding, the distance only feet, then yards, but he was still standing and Capslock was standing: and then he was running, running toward the truck, and a slug plucked at his coat and a finger of fire tore through his side . . .

DEL FIRED FIVE times, cutting up the door, smashing the glass, then stopped, turned to Cheryl, saw the blood on her neck, dropped next to her, saw the wound, and her eyes opened and she struggled and he rolled her onto her side and she took a long, harsh, rattling breath.

"Hold on, hold on," he screamed, and he ran back to the phone and dialed 911 and shouted into it—was told later that he shouted. He remembered himself talking coldly, quietly, and so he listened to the tape and heard himself screaming . . .

LACHAISE WAS BLEEDING.

He drove the truck, looking at himself in the rearview mirror. Shrapnel cuts on the face, agony in his side. He was holding his side with his hand, and when he looked at his hand, it was wet with blood. "Motherfucker . . ." he groaned.

A spasm of fear seized his heart. Was he dying? Was this how it would end, with this pain, in the snow?

A cop car went screaming past, lights blazing, then another, then an ambulance. Hit somebody, he thought, with a thread of satisfaction. God, it hurt . . .

The man must have been Capslock himself; and he was fast with a gun, blindingly fast. And what had he screamed? He'd screamed *LaChaise* . . .

So they knew.

LaChaise looked into the rearview mirror.

He was bleeding . . .

8

LUCAS WAS ON the west side of minneapolis, pushing the Explorer up an I-394 entrance ramp, when a dispatcher shouted, "Somebody shot Capslock's wife," and a second later, Del patched through: "LaChaise shot Cheryl."

"What?" Lucas was on the ramp, moving faster. To his right, an American flag as big as a bedsheet fluttered in the gloom. "Say that again."

"LaChaise shot Cheryl . . ." From behind Del's voice, Lucas could hear a jumble of noise: voices, highway sounds, a siren. Del seemed to be out of breath, gasping at his radio.

"Where are you?" Lucas asked.

"Ambulance. We're going into Hennepin." Now the words were tumbling out, like a coke-fired rap. "I saw him, man. LaChaise. I shot at him. I don't know if I hit him or not. He's gone."

"What about Cheryl?"

"She's hit, she's hit . . ." Del was shouting; several words came through garbled, then he said, "It's our wives, man; he's going after the families. Eye for an eye . . ."

Weather.

She'd be in the clinic, doing minor patch-up work on post-op patients. The fear caught Lucas by the throat; Del said something else, but he missed it, and then Del was gone.

The dispatcher blurted, "We lost him, he closed down."

"I'm going to the U Hospitals. I want Sherrill, Franklin, Sloan and Kupicek on the line *now*," Lucas said. He fumbled a cellular phone out of an armrest box and punched the speed-dial button for Weather. A secretary answered, then transferred him to the clinic, where another secretary, bored, said Weather was busy with a patient.

"This is Deputy Chief Lucas Davenport of the Minneapolis Police Department and this is an emergency and I want her on the line *immediately*," Lucas shouted. *"GET HER."*

Then Franklin came back through Dispatch: he was in the office.

"Get your wife and kid and go someplace until we know what's happening," Lucas said.

"The kid's in school . . ."

"Just get them," Lucas said. "Have you seen Sloan?"

"I think I just saw him goin' in the can . . ."

"Tell him. Get his wife, get out someplace. Anywhere. Get lost, but stay in touch . . ."

"You think . . ."

"Move it, goddamnit." Lucas was stomping the gas pedal, trying to get more speed out of the Explorer.

Weather came up: "I'm on my way there," Lucas said. He took fifteen seconds to tell her what had happened: "Get out of the clinic and stay away from your office," he said. "Tell the secretary where you'll be. I'll stop and see her when I get there."

"Lucas, I've got things to do, I've got a guy with a skin cancer . . ."

"Fuck the clinic," he snapped, his voice a rasp. "Go someplace where you're not supposed to be, and wait there. If the guy comes after you, he might start killing your patients, too. Everybody can wait an hour or two."

"Lucas . . ."

"I don't have time to chat, goddamnit, just do it." He cut off a white-haired guy in a red Chevy Tahoe and could see the guy pounding the steering wheel as he went by.

Sherrill was working an ag assault in a bar off Hennepin, drunk college kids beating a black guy with bar stools until he stopped moving. He still wasn't moving, but he wasn't quite dead, either. Sherrill called, and Lucas gave her the word on Del.

"Oh, my God, I'm going over there," she said.

"No. Call Mike, tell him to take a walk. Tell him to go sit in a restaurant until you get to him. We want everybody where they shouldn't be until we figure out what's going on."

Dispatch came back: "Del hit LaChaise—there's blood on the sidewalk, going out to where a truck was parked. All the hospitals know, we're covering the emergency rooms . . ."

Kupicek came up. He and his kid were at a peewee hockey match. "Call your wife, you all go out to eat somewhere on the department, catch a movie," Lucas said. "Check with me before you go home. Look in your rearview mirror, stay on the radio."

"How's Del's wife?" Kupicek asked.

"I don't know: we've got people on the way to Hennepin."

"Keep me tuned, dude," Kupicek said.

Thirty seconds later, the dispatcher came back, and asked Lucas to switch over to a scrambled command frequency. "What?" he asked.

"Oh, God." The dispatcher sounded as though she were weeping, a sound Lucas hadn't heard from Dispatch. "Roseville called: Danny's wife's been shot. She's dead. In the store at Rosedale."

Lucas felt the anger rising, building toward a black frenzy: "Don't put this on the air, don't tell anyone outside the center . . . when did this happen?"

"The call came in at five-seventeen, but they think she might have been shot about five-twelve."

"When was Del?"

"About five-fifteen."

So there had to be more than one shooter. How many?

"Who'll tell Danny?" the dispatcher asked.

"I will," Lucas said. "Does Rose Marie know?"

"Lucy's on the way to her office."

Lucas called Kupicek back. "Danny, where are you?"

"Hennepin and Lake. Looking for a phone."

"Change of plans: We got Roseville with your wife, we need you at the emergency entrance to Hennepin General. Right now. You gotta light with you?"

"Yeah."

"Light it up and get it in there . . ."

"I got the kid."

"Bring him: he'll be okay."

When Kupicek was gone, Lucas got back to Dispatch: "Check Danny's file: he's got a sister named Louise Amdahl and they're tight. Get her down to Hennepin General. Send a car and tell them to move it, lights and sirens all the way."

And he thought about Sherrill and Weather. He punched up the phone again, caught Weather, told her about Kupicek's wife: "I'm not coming. But you gotta hide out and I'm not bullshitting you, Weather, I swear to God, you gotta get out of sight, someplace where I can get you. The guy could be in the hospital right now."

"I'm going," she said.

"Take care, please, please, take care," he said.

And he got Sherrill: "Did you reach Mike?"

"No, Lucas, they can't find him." Her voice was high, scared. "He's supposed to be there, but they can't find him. I'm going there."

"I'm sending a squad."

"Lucas, you don't think . . . ?" Her marriage had been on the rocks for a while.

"We don't know what to think," Lucas said. Sherrill didn't know about Danny's wife. He didn't tell her. "Get on up there."

Back to Dispatch: "Two cars, get them up there. You gotta beat Sherrill up there . . ."

LUCAS WENT STRAIGHT though the city traffic, not slowing for any light, green, yellow or red, his foot on the floor: driving the Explorer was like driving a hay wagon, but he beat Kupicek by two minutes, pulling in a car length behind Rose Marie Roux. The chief was pale, nearly speechless: She said, "This . . ." and then shook her head and they ran inside, Lucas banging the doors out of the way.

Del, covered with blood, stood in the hallway, talking to a doctor in scrubs: "Sometimes she gets stress headaches in the afternoon and she takes aspirin. That's all. Wait, she drinks Diet Coke, that's got caffeine. I don't know if she took any aspirin this afternoon . . ."

He saw them coming, Lucas and Rose Marie, and stepped toward them.

"He hit her hard," he said. He seemed unaware that tears were running down his seamed face: his voice was absolutely under control. "But if there aren't any complications, she'll make it."

"Aw, Jesus, Del," Lucas said. He tried to smile, but his face was desperately twisted.

"What happened?" Del said. He looked from one of them to the other. "What else happened?"

"Danny's wife's been shot; she's dead. And we can't find Mike Sherrill."

"The motherfuckers," Del rasped.

Then Danny Kupicek banged through the entryway, a kid tagging along behind, still in his hockey uniform, wearing white Nikes that looked about the size of battleships, a shock of blond hair down over his eyes. He seemed impressed by the inside of the hospital.

"Del," Kupicek said, "Jesus, how's Cheryl? Is she okay?"

"Danny . . ." said Lucas.

Ten minutes later, they found Mike Sherrill. Marcy Sherrill arrived just in time to see the cops gathering around the Firebird, and thrust through them just in time to see the door pop open, and look straight into her husband's open eyes, upside down, dead.

She turned, and one of the uniforms, a woman, wrapped her up, and a moment later she made a sound a bit like a howl, a bit like a croak, and then she fell down.

LACHAISE WAS THE first to get back to the house. Martin had called from a pay phone and LaChaise sent him to get Butters.

"You bad?" Martin had asked, his voice low, controlled.

"I don't know, but I'm bleeding," LaChaise told him. "Hurts like hell."

"Can you breathe?"

"Yeah. I just don't want to," LaChaise said.

"Can you get in the house?"

"Think so. Yeah."

"Get inside. We'll be there in fifteen minutes."

LaChaise hurt, but not so bad that he couldn't make it to the house. That encouraged him. Except for the burning pain, which was localized, he didn't *feel* bad. There was no sense of anything loose inside, anything wrecked.

But when he got in the house, he found he couldn't get the jacket off by himself. When he lifted his arm, fire ran down his rib cage. He slumped on the living-room rug, and waited, staring at the ceiling.

Martin came in first, Butters, stamping snow off his sleeves, just behind him.

"Let's take a look," Martin said.

"You get yours?" LaChaise asked.

Martin nodded and Butters said, "Yep. How about you?"

"I got somebody, there were ambulances all over the place . . ."

They helped him sit up as they talked, and LaChaise told them about making the call, and then Del popping up behind his wife. "And the fucker recognized me . . . careful, there . . ."

They peeled the parka off, then the vest, then the flannel shirt, each progressively heavier with blood. His undershirt showed two small holes and a bloodstain the size of a dinner plate.

"Better cut that," Butters muttered.

"Yeah." Martin took out his knife, and the Jockey T-shirt split like tissue paper. "Roll up here, Dick . . ."

LaChaise tried to roll onto his left side and lift his arm; he was sweating heavily, and groaned again, "Goddamn, that hurts."

Martin and Butters were looking at the wound. "Don't look like too much," Butters said. "Don't see no bone."

"Yeah, but there's an in-and-out . . ."

"What?" LaChaise asked.

"You just got nicked, but there's a hole, in-and-out, besides the groove. Maybe cut you down to the ribs, that's the pain. The holes gotta be cleaned out. They'd be full of threads and shit from the coat."

"Get Sandy down here," LaChaise said. "Call her—no, go get her. I don't know if she'd come on her own . . . She can do it, she used to be a nurse."

Martin looked at Butters and nodded. "That'd be best, she might have some equipment."

"Some pills," Butters said.

"Get her," LaChaise moaned.

9

T HE SANDHURST WAS a yellow-brick semiresidential hotel on the west edge of the business district. The building was three stories higher than anything else for two blocks around, and easily covered. The clients were mostly itinerant actors, directors, artists and museum bureaucrats, in town visiting the Guthrie Theater or the Walker Art Center.

Lucas and Sloan brought Weather in through the back, down an alley blocked by unmarked cars. Two members of the Emergency Response Team were on the roof with radios and rifles.

". . . everything I've been trying to do," Weather was saying. Lucas's head was going up and down as he half-listened. He scanned each face down the alley. His hand was in his pocket and a .45 was in his hand. Sloan's wife was already inside.

"It won't be long," Lucas said. "They can't last more than a couple of days."

"Who? Who can't last?" Weather demanded, looking up at him. "You don't even know who they are, except this LaChaise."

"We'll find out," Lucas said. "They're gonna pay, every fuckin' one of them." His voice left little doubt about it, and Weather recoiled, but Lucas had her arm and marched her toward the hotel.

"Let go of my arm," she said. "You're hurting me."

"Sorry." He let go, put his hand in the small of her back, and pushed her along.

The two hotel entries, front and back, met at the lobby: Franklin and Tom Black, Sherrill's former partner, sat behind a wide rosewood reception desk, shotguns across their thighs, out of sight. The largest cop on the force, a guy named Loring, read a paperback in one of the lobby's overstuffed chairs. He was wearing a pearl-gray suit and an ascot, and looked like a pro wrestler who'd made it small.

In the entry, a uniformed doorman turned and looked at them when he saw movement down the back hall. Andy Stadic raised a hand, and Lucas nodded at him and then they were around a corner and headed down toward the elevators.

"You know, anybody could find out where we are," Weather said.

"They can't get in," Lucas said. "And they can't see you."

"You said they were Seed people, and Seed people are supposed to be in these militias," Weather said. Weather was from northern Wisconsin, and knew about the Seed. "What if they brought one of those big fertilizer bombs outside?"

"No trucks are coming down this block," Lucas said. "We got the city digging up the streets right now, both sides."

"You can't hold it, Lucas," Weather said. "The press'll be here, television . . ."

Lucas shook his head: "They'll know you're here, but they won't get inside. If they try, we'll warn them once, then we'll put their asses in jail. We're not fucking around."

He took her up to the top floor, and down the hall to a small two-room suite with walls the color of cigar smoke; the rooms smelled like disinfectant and spray deodorant. Weather looked around and said, "This is awful."

"Two days. Three days, max," Lucas said. "I'd send you up to the cabin but they know about us, somehow, and I can't take the chance."

"I don't want to go to the cabin," she said. "I want to work."

"Yeah," Lucas said distractedly. "I gotta run . . ."

FOR TWO HOURS after the killings, Rose Marie Roux's office was like an airport waiting room, fifty people rolling through, all of them weighed down with their own importance, most looking for a shot on national television. The governor stopped, wanted a briefing; a dozen state legislators demanded time with her, along with all the city councilmen.

Lucas spent a half hour watching Sloan and another cop interrogate Duane Cale, who didn't know much about anything.

"But if Dick is here, I'd get my ass out of town," Cale said.

The interrogation wouldn't produce much, Lucas thought. He locked himself in his office with Franklin, away from the media and cops who wanted to talk about it. Sloan came in after a while, and started making calls. Then Del wandered in, his clothes still dappled with his wife's blood.

"How's Cheryl?" Lucas asked.

Del shook his head: "She's out of the operating room, asleep. They put her in intensive care, and won't let me in. She'll be there until tomorrow morning, at least."

"You oughta get some rest," Lucas said.

"Fuck that. What're you guys doing?"

"Talking to assholes . . ."

Between them, they called everyone they knew on the street who had a phone. Lucas tried Sally O'Donald a half-dozen times, and left word for her at bars along Lake Street.

A little more than two hours after the killings, Roux called:

"We're meeting with the mayor at his office. Ten minutes."

"Is this real?" Lucas asked.

"Yeah. This is the real one," Roux said.

A minute later, O'Donald called back.

"Can you come down and look at some pictures?" Lucas asked. "The guy you thought might be a cop?"

"I can't even remember in my head what he looked like," O'Donald said. "But I'll come down if you want."

"Talk to Ed O'Meara in Identification."

"Okay—but listen. I talked to my agent . . ."

"Your what?"

"My agent," O'Donald said, mildly embarrassed. "She said she might get five thousand dollars if I talked to *Hard Copy*."

"Goddamnit, Sally," Lucas said. "If you screw me and Del . . ."

"Shut up, shut up, shut up," O'Donald said. "I'm not going to screw anybody. What I want to know is, are you gonna take LaChaise off the street?"

"Yeah. Sooner or later."

"So if I talk, he won't be able to get at me?"

Lucas hesitated, then said, "Look, I'll be honest. If you talk, and then you bag outa here for a few days, he'll be gone. He won't last a week."

"That's what I wanted to know," O'Donald said.

"But you gotta tell me when you're going on," Lucas said. "We'll put a guy on your house—in your house, maybe—just in case LaChaise comes looking."

"Jeez," she said. There was a minute's silence. "You put it that way . . . maybe I won't. I don't want to fuck with Dick."

"Either way, let me know," Lucas said. He glanced at his watch. The meeting was about to start. "Come in, talk to Ed . . ."

"Wait a minute, wait a minute. I thought of something else you might want to know."

"Yeah?"

"You ought to look at the ownership of that laundromat."

"Why don't you just tell me?" Lucas asked.

"I understand that it belongs to Daymon Harp." The name hung there, but Lucas didn't recognize it.

"Who's he?"

"Jeez, Davenport, you gotta get back on the streets a little more. He's a dealer. Pretty big time . . ."

"A Seed guy?"

"No, no, never. He's a black guy; good-looking guy. Ask Del. Del'll know who he is."

"Thanks, Sally."

"You talk to Sex?"

"I'll talk to them tonight."

When he got off the phone, he said to Del, "Daymon Harp?"

"Dealer—semi-small-time. Careful. Reasonably smart. Came over from Milwaukee a few years back. Why?"

"Sally O'Donald says he owns the laundromat where she saw LaChaise."

Del frowned, shook his head. "I don't know what that means. I can't see Harp running with the Seed guys. That's the last combination I could imagine."

"Might be worth checking . . ."

Del looked at Sloan. "Want to run it down?"

Lucas interrupted. "Why don't you get cleaned up first? Sloan and Franklin can stay with the phones. When I get back, we'll all go down."

LUCAS WAS THE last one in the door. The meeting included Roux, the mayor and a deputy mayor; Frank Lester, head of investigations; Barney Kittleson, head of patrol; Anita Segundo, the press liaison; and Lucas.

Rose Marie was talking to Segundo when Lucas eased through the door. She asked, "How bad?"

"CBS, NBC, ABC, CNN and one or two of the Fox cop shows all have people on the way. *Nightline* is doing a segment tonight. They're talking about LaChaise and his group being *militia*. Ever since the federal building was blown up in Oklahoma City, that's a hot topic."

"*Are* they militia?" the mayor asked. "Do these media guys know something?"

"The FBI says LaChaise was on the edge of things, but they don't show him really involved," Lester said. "He knew some of the Order people back in the eighties . . ."

"Didn't the Order kill that radio guy in Denver?" the mayor asked.

Lester nodded: "Yes. But the feds took them out a little while later. LaChaise was a big guy in the Seed, and some of the militia people from Michigan were involved in the Seed back when it was a biker gang. And later on, some of the Seed people got involved with Christian Identity—that's sort of an umbrella group. And we know LaChaise used to sell neo-Nazi stuff in his bike shop: *The Turner Diaries*, and all that. Some people think the Seed got its name from a right-winger who went on the radio and said it was too late to stop the movement, because there were Seeds everywhere. But that could be bullshit."

"We gotta nail that down," the mayor said, jabbing a finger at Roux. "If these are militia, we gotta start thinking in terms of bombs and heavy weapons."

Roux glanced at Lucas, scratched her head and said, "I don't think . . ."

She stopped, and the mayor's eyebrows went up. "Yeah?"

"I don't think that's much of a possibility, Stan. I think we're basically dealing with some goofs, with guns. Three guys, psychos, who maybe rode together in a biker gang. And maybe messed around on the edge of the Nazi stuff."

"Well, you're probably right," the mayor said. "But if they blow up the fuckin' First Bank, I don't want to be standing there with my dick in my hand, trying to explain why we didn't know what was coming."

Roux nodded. "That's one thing: we're gonna need a very tight public relations operation, or we're gonna get run over," she said. "We'll have cops gettin' paid off, we'll have reporters chasing witnesses . . ."

"The guy at Rosedale—the other clerk with Kupicek's wife, in the TV store—he's already signed up for *Nightline*," Segundo said.

The mayor was an olive-complected, bull-shouldered man, with fine curly black hair just starting to recede. He looked at his deputy, then at Roux: "Rose Marie, it's gonna be you and me."

"Sounds like a hit song from the fifties," the deputy said, "Rose Marie, it's you and me."

Everyone ignored him.

"We lay down the law about cops talking to the press: if you do it, you better get a lot of money, 'cause you won't be working here anymore," the mayor said. "We have four major press briefings every day: one early, to catch the morning shows; one just before noon; one just before five; and one at eight forty-five, to catch the late news. You'll have to coordinate with your investigators—we should have a bone to throw them at every press conference. Doesn't have to be real, but it has to be *satisfying* . . ."

The mayor went on for five minutes, laying out the handling of the press.

Then he turned to Lester and Lucas: "Lucas, I want you and your people totally off stage. We don't want any arguments about whether the response was provoked by the shootings at the bank."

"I didn't know that was still a question," Lester said.

"There isn't a question," the mayor said irritably. "But the media'll chew on any goddamned bone they can find. You gotta remember we're dealing with the entertainment industry. *Die Hard*, Oklahoma City, it's all the same. Now it's our turn to make the movie." He rapped on the table with his knuckles, still looking at Lester and Lucas: "We can only bullshit them for so long. We gotta catch these guys."

"We've got a procedure in emergencies," Roux said, and the mayor swiveled back to her. "We run two parallel investigations. Lucas and his bunch play the angles, and Frank runs the main sweep. Everybody coordinates through Anderson. He puts out a book every day on every little piece we get. Nobody hides anything from anybody."

"It works?" asked the mayor.

"So far," Lucas said.

"Then let's do that," the mayor said. "Do we have one single thing we can move on now? Anything?"

"Maybe one," said Lucas. He was thinking about the laundromat: a place to start.

SANDY DROVE WHILE Butters leaned against the window on the passenger side. Elmore followed in Sandy's truck. Elmore hadn't wanted to go at first, and Butters agreed: Butters wanted Sandy, not her husband.

"I'm not going," Sandy had said.

Butters said, "I ain't got time to argue, Sandy. You're going." There was no doubt that she was going: he didn't bother to show her a gun, but it was there. Butters had an affable, southern-boy line of bullshit, but beneath it, he was as cold as Martin. When she went to get her coat, Butters went with her.

"Are you guarding me?" she asked.

"I'm making sure that you come along," Butters said. "I know you don't want to."

"You gonna tell me what happened? Who shot him?"

"No," Butters said. He'd told them that LaChaise had been shot in a fight. Sandy and Elmore had been feeding the stock, and hadn't seen any television.

When it was clear that Sandy was going, Elmore insisted that he go along too. Butters finally agreed, because he didn't want to waste time arguing: "But you come down in the van—Sandy goes with me," Butters said. "We're still gonna need both trucks for a while."

They stopped at the old folks' home, where Sandy still filled in when somebody was sick. A big first-aid kit in the nurse's office gave up bandages, needles and thread, razor blades and antiseptic. A large illegal bottle of Tylenol-3 was kept stashed in the bottom desk drawer, for the miscellaneous aches and pains of old age, and she emptied it. What else? Surgical scissors, a couple of Bic disposable razors, tape. Saline. There was a stock of sterile saline in the storeroom. She took five liters.

The nurses each had a personal drawer in a row of filing cabinets. Nobody bothered to lock them, and Sandy dug around in Marie Admont's drawer and found the bottle of penicillin pills. Marie had gotten them after a crazy old lady had raked her with her fingernails. Marie had only used a few of the pills, and a half-dozen remained in the bottle. Sandy took them.

THE DRIVE TO St. Paul seemed to last forever, the dark strip through Wisconsin, then the winding road out to the interstate on the Minnesota side. Butters said a half-dozen words during the trip, Sandy four or five. Both were caught in their own thoughts.

Once in the Cities, Butters guided them down the interstate, then back into the narrow ice-clogged streets of Frogtown. They parked behind Martin's truck, and got out. Elmore parked behind them, and hurried through the snow, white-faced, and said, "I want to talk to Sandy. One minute. Before we go in there."

Butters said, "Get your asses in there, goddamnit."

"I'm going to talk to Elmore," Sandy said, her voice like the ice in the streets. "I'll get to Dick when I get to him."

"Listen . . ."

"Are you going to shoot me, Ansel? That'd help Dick a lot."

Butters backed off, and Sandy took Elmore twenty yards down the street. "What?"

Elmore was visibly trembling.

"I been listening to the radio," he rasped. "They been down here killing cops' families. That's all they're talking about on the radio, every station I could get. They killed two people and there's a third one might die. Everybody in the goddamned world is looking for them, Sandy."

Sandy looked at him, then turned and looked at Butters, who stood silently waiting. "Oh my God," she said.

"We got to get out," Elmore said.

"Let's go see Dick," Sandy said. "I'll work us out of here. But you're right. We've got to see John."

They walked down the driveway together, Butters lingering just out of earshot. Martin waited at the door.

"Come on in," he said to Sandy. He looked at Elmore and nodded, and Elmore looked away.

The house had one couch, a broken-down wreck in the living room. Martin had pulled the cushions off and thrown them on the floor, and LaChaise was lying on them, his head propped up with a pillow. Martin had covered him with a blanket, and LaChaise grinned at Sandy when she came in.

"How bad?" she asked.

"Not too bad," LaChaise said. "It's more like . . . it's gotta be cleaned up."

"Let me see," Sandy said. "I need a light."

They peeled the blanket off and LaChaise rolled onto his side. The pain had subsided somewhat, and he lifted his arm so she could see more clearly. At the same time, Butters took the shade off a table lamp, and held it like a torch over LaChaise.

Sandy looked at the wound for a moment. An open gash, at the back, became a bluish streak where the bullet had gone beneath the skin. A small round exit wound showed four inches below his nipple and over to the side. A trailing gash showed some rib meat. Sandy looked up at LaChaise. "You gotta go to a hospital," she said.

"Can't do that. You gotta fix it."

She looked at it again. In fact, she could fix it. "It'll hurt," she said.

"Atta girl," LaChaise said, and to Butters: "Told you so."

"I believed you," Butters said.

"What happened?" she asked. "How'd you get shot?"

"Argument over traveling money," LaChaise said. "The guy owed me . . ."

"Did you kill him?"

"No, I didn't kill him," LaChaise said, smiling faintly. "Now, you want to fix me? This hurts like hell." .

"You lying sonofabitch," Sandy said evenly. "You killed some cops' families. I oughta . . ."

Before she could finish, Martin backhanded her. His hand was like a leg of beef, and knocked her flat. For a second, she didn't know what had happened, and then dazed, ears ringing, heard LaChaise say, "Whoa, whoa . . ." Behind him, Elmore: "Goddamnit . . ."

She rolled, tried to sit up, and Martin was there, his face inches from hers: "Stop the bullshit. You fix him or I'll cut you into fuckin' fish bait." Across the room, Butters was smiling at Elmore, half expecting him to make a move, but Elmore swallowed and shut up.

Sandy got back to her feet, turned away from Martin without a word and said to LaChaise, "I brought you some pills. You should take a few before we start."

LaChaise looked at her, then at Martin, and grinned at Martin: "I wouldn't turn your back on her," he said.

LACHAISE TOOK THE pills with a swallow of water, and looked past Sandy at Elmore. "El, I hate to say this, but you better get back. I was recognized, and the cops'll probably be coming by again."

"I thought it'd be best if Sandy come back tonight," Elmore said.

"She's staying," Martin said bluntly. "Overnight, anyway. Until Dick's okay."

"What the hell am I supposed to tell the cops if they come?" Elmore demanded. "They'll want to know where she is."

"Tell 'em she went out to the store, then call us on my cell phone. She can be back in an hour," LaChaise said.

"Sandy . . ." Elmore couldn't say it, but she knew what he was thinking.

"Come on, El, let's get my stuff out of the truck," Sandy said. She nodded at LaChaise. "I'll get my stuff and kiss El good-bye."

"I'll help," Butters said.

"You can stand on the porch," said Sandy.

Outside, at the truck, Elmore whispered, "I'm sorry about that in there. I was gonna say something . . ." He scuffled at the snow with the toe of his boot. "We gotta get out."

"I know." She looked back at the house, at Butters standing there on the dark porch. "But I've got to get clear. If they killed cops' families, then they're dead men. I'll be back home tomorrow, and we'll figure something out."

"Sandy . . ." He stepped up to her, maybe to kiss her. She moved just an inch sideways and pecked him on the cheek.

"You go on; I'll be okay. Just wait 'til I get there, before you call John."

He didn't want to go, but he couldn't stay. He shifted his feet, looked up at the sky, shook his head, then started the low moaning that she'd seen earlier: he was weeping again.

"El, El, hold on," she said. "Come on, El . . ."

"Ah, Jesus," he said.

"I'll see you in the morning," she said.

As Elmore was starting the truck, Sandy walked back toward the house; Butters suddenly dropped off the porch and hurried past her, waving at Elmore. Elmore rolled down the driver's-side window and Butters came up, leaned close to Elmore, grinned and said, "You call the cops, we'll cut off her head."

THE BULLET HAD simply slipped beneath the skin and back out again, but the wound had to be opened and cleaned. Sandy cut through the skin, carefully, with a razor blade. Fresh blood trickled into the gash, but as soon as she had the entire pathway open, she flushed it with saline, then soaked a sterile gauze pad with more saline and dabbed it clean. At the bottom of the wound, there was a flash of white. Rib bone.

"Just touched a rib," she said to Martin.

"I see," he said, peering into the hole. He was interested in bullet wounds.

After a final wash, she repaired the razor cut with a long series of rolling stitches with black nylon thread, then painted the area around the wound with antiseptic. LaChaise wiggled a few times, but kept his mouth shut.

When she'd finished the stitching, Sandy's hands were red with blood. She went to the kitchen, washed, then returned to LaChaise and put a heavy bandage over the wound. She fixed the bandage in place with round-the-chest wraps of gauze, and then tape.

At the end of it, LaChaise sat up.

"Maybe you shouldn't move," she said.

He was feeling the pills, and smiled weakly and said, "Shit, I been hurt worse than this by sissies."

"That's the codeine. You're gonna hurt later on," Sandy said.

"I can live with it," he said. He got shakily to his feet and looked down at the bandaging job. "Jesus, good job. Really good job. You're a little honey," he said.

DEL AND LUCAS were on the way out of the building when Sloan caught up: "I'm coming," he said. "Keep you out of trouble."

All the way out to the laundromat, they argued about the shootings, and the response. Del said the season was open.

"Wouldn't be murder," Del said stubbornly. "I wouldn't just shoot them cold."

". . . and the thing is," Lucas continued, "you'd take all of us down with you. We'd all go out to Stillwater together. Nobody'd believe it was just you."

An unwanted grin popped up on Del's face: "Hell, we know half the guys out there. Be like old home week."

Sloan said, "Lucas is right. I don't even think you should be riding with us. If you pop somebody now, after Cheryl, the media'd crucify us, and the grand jury'd be on us like a hot sweat: the politics would kill us."

"Well, who in the hell's side is everybody on?" Del asked. "What about Cheryl?"

"Don't ask that question," Lucas said. "The answer'll piss you off."

They were in Lucas's Explorer, Lucas driving, beating through the desolate streets to the near south side. Lights showed on the laundromat's second floor. Below them, behind the storefront windows of the laundromat, five women, all of them black, folded clothes, read magazines or sat and stared at the dirty pink plaster walls.

Lucas stopped in a bus zone on the corner, twenty yards up the street from the windows. "When I talked to Lonnie, he said if you go up the main stairway, you get to the top and there's a bunch of junk, cardboard boxes and stuff, all piled up. You can't get through to the door, not in a hurry, anyway," Del said, peering up at the second-story windows. "There's a back stairs that comes down inside the garage. But the garage door's locked, and you can't get through that."

"So you go up the stairs and make a lot of noise—kick the boxes out of the way, bang away on the door," Sloan said to Del. "We'll wait out back. If he opens up the front door, you call us; and if he runs, we'll be the net."

"All right," Del said, "but I think we might be barking up the wrong tree. I can't see Harp having anything to do with a bunch of . . ." He stopped in midsentence, pointed through the windshield. "Hey—look there."

A woman was walking toward them, half skating on the slippery sidewalk, holding what appeared to be a small white bakery sack. She passed under a streetlight and then into the brighter lights from the laundromat window.

"That's Jas Smith, Daymon's old lady," Del said.

Lucas said, "Let's take her. Maybe she'll invite us up."

"Yeah." Del and Sloan hopped out of the right side, while Lucas walked around the nose of the truck, converging on Jasmine. She was wearing a brimmed hat, and her head was down against the snow: she didn't see them coming until they were on top of her.

Then she jumped, and put her hand across her heart: "Goddamn, Capslock, give me some warning."

"Sorry . . ."

"If I was carrying a little piece or something, I might of shot you outa self-defense, popping out like that."

She looked at Lucas and Sloan, worried, and Del said, "This is Chief Davenport and Detective Sloan. We got something we need to talk to Daymon about. Not bust him; just talk."

"Whyn't you call him up?"

"Because we didn't want him hanging up on us," Sloan said pleasantly. "You hear about all those cops' husbands and wives getting shot today?"

"Everybody heard," she said.

"My wife was one of them," Del said. "She's in the hospital now, and she's hurting. We want you to know how serious this is—so why don't you just open up the garage and we'll go on up and talk to Daymon."

She looked from Del to Sloan to Lucas, and said, "He'd kick my ass if I done that. I mean, he'd kick me so bad."

Del looked at Lucas and nodded: he would.

"What happened to your hand?" Lucas asked. Jasmine wasn't carrying a bakery sack; her hand was professionally wrapped in a huge white bandage.

She looked down at it, and her lip trembled: "Paper cutter," she said. "Cut my finger right off." She started to blubber. "It was just layin' there, and I knew it was off, and then the blood squirted out . . ."

Lucas said, "Jeez, that's too bad. Look, Daymon must have an unlisted number, right? Of course he does."

He nodded, and she nodded. He took a cellular phone out of his pocket.

"So why don't you dial him up, and tell him we're down here by the garage, and then he can go brush his teeth or whatever, and we can go on up."

"I'll try," she said, after a moment.

HARP LET THEM up, unhappy about it. The apartment smelled of marijuana, but nothing fresh, just old curtain-and-rug contacts, enough to get you started if you'd gone to college in the sixties. Harp was waiting for them in the kitchen, his butt against the edge of the table, his arms crossed over his chest. He looked at Jasmine as if she were at fault, and she said, "Honey, they snatched me right off the street, they knew you was up here . . ."

Del said, "That's right, Day; we were coming up, one way or another."

"What you want?" Harp grunted.

"You heard about the killings?"

"Didn't do it," Harp said.

Lucas felt a tingle: Harp was a little too tough. "We know you didn't do it personally, but we think you might have a connection," Lucas said. "Two of the people involved met down in your laundromat. We have a witness. We want to know why these two white assholes would come halfway across the country to meet in Daymon Harp's laundromat."

"You think I'd help them peckerwoods?" Harp asked indignantly. "I been inside with those motherfuckers. Daymon Harp ain't helping them no way, no place, no time."

"How'd you know they were peckerwoods?" Sloan asked. "We didn't say they were peckerwoods."

"They all over the TV," Harp said. "They're Seeds, right? I know all about it—you can't get nothin' but TV news. They canceled *Star Trek*."

"Who's your cop friend?" Lucas asked.

Harp's eyelid flickered, a quick twitch. "What kind of bullshit you talkin'?"

They pushed him for twenty minutes, but he wouldn't move. He knew nothing, saw nothing, had heard nothing. On the way out the door, Lucas said to Jasmine, "Take care of the hand."

OUTSIDE, THEY HURRIED along to the truck, blown by the breeze. Sloan said, "I don't know what he knows, but I think he's got a corner on something."

"I'll talk to Narcotics. We'll shut him down," Lucas said. He looked back up at the apartment lights. "Twenty-four hours, maybe he'll be ready."

Del shook his head: "He can't talk. Too many dead people, now. If he's got a connection, he'll do everything he can to bury it." He looked back at the apartment: "I'll bet you anything he books it."

LACHAISE HAD CALLED Stadic with the number of his new cell phone: Stadic had been in the office, and he scribbled it down, stuck the paper in his wallet.

Two hours later, the shit hit the fan. He tried calling the number, but there was no answer. Then he was swept up in the chaos of the response, and eventually found himself wearing a doorman's uniform, working the door at the hotel where the families were hidden. No time to call . . .

At ten o'clock the night of the attacks, the bank time and temperature sign down the block said −2°. Stadic traded his doorman's uniform for street clothes and hurried down the street to his car. The ferocity of the attacks had stunned him. Near panic, he'd spent the evening pacing in and out of the Sandhurst, wondering whether he should run for it. He had almost enough money . . .

But he realized, with a little thought, that it was too late. Cops' families had been attacked. That was worse than killing the cops themselves. If anyone found out that he'd been involved, there'd be no place to hide. If he were to be saved now, salvation would come in one form: the death of LaChaise and all of his friends. Which wasn't impossible . . .

He sat in his car, took out his cellular phone, punched in his home number. Two calls on the answering machine. The first was Daymon Harp, who said two words: "Call me." The second call was nothing.

Stadic erased the tape, hung up, found LaChaise's number in his wallet and punched it in. The phone was answered on the first ring.

"Hello?" A man's voice, a southerner.

"Let me speak to Dick," Stadic said.

LaChaise came on a second later: "What?"

"You're fucked now. You can't walk a block without bumping into a cop."

"We can handle it. What we need is their location. We heard on the radio they were all being moved."

"They're at the Sandhurst Hotel in Minneapolis," Stadic said. "They're sequestered in interior rooms. There are cops all through the place. Snipers on the roof. The streets are being dug up outside, so you can't get a car close."

After a moment of silence, LaChaise said, "We'll think of something."

"No, you won't. There's no way in. And who got shot? One of you is hit, they found blood down Capslock's sidewalk."

"I got scratched," LaChaise said. "It's nothing. We need to know more about this hotel."

"There's no way in," Stadic said. "But there are some people outside you might be interested in—and I don't think there's a watch on them."

"Who's that?" LaChaise asked.

"You know Davenport?" Stadic asked. He looked down the street at the hotel. Another cop paraded the lobby, behind the glass doors, in the doorman's uniform. Stadic was due back in the uniform in the morning. "He runs the group that shot your women."

"We know Davenport. He's on the list," LaChaise said.

"He's got a daughter that almost nobody knows about, because he never married the mother," said Stadic. "She's not on any insurance forms."

"Where is she?"

"Down on Minnehaha Creek—that's in south Minneapolis. I got the address and phone number."

"Let me get a pencil . . ." LaChaise was back in a minute, and scribbled down the address. "Why're you doing this?" LaChaise asked.

" 'Cause I want you to finish and get out of here. You got three of them. You get Davenport's daughter, we set something up on Franklin, and you're outa here."

LaChaise said nothing, but Stadic could hear the hum of the open line. Then LaChaise said, "Sounds like bullshit."

"Listen, I just want you to get the fuck out of here," Stadic said. Then, "I gotta go. I'll call you about Franklin."

Stadic hung up, and dialed Harp's unlisted number. Harp picked it up on the first ring.

"What?" Stadic asked.

"Cops were here. Capslock and Davenport and another guy. Somebody saw you and LaChaise in the laundromat. They think I know something about LaChaise."

"Just hang on," Stadic said.

"I don't know, man. I'm thinking about taking a vacation."

Stadic thought a minute, then said, "Listen, how much trouble would it cause the business, if you were gone for a week?"

"Not much," Harp said. "I make a couple of big deliveries, we'd be all right. You think I should walk?"

"Yeah," Stadic said. "Go somewhere they wouldn't expect. Not Las Vegas. Not Miami."

"Puerto Rico?"

"That'd be the place," Stadic said. "They'd never think of it."

"Great pussy. No pussy like Puerto Rico pussy," Harp said.

"Forget the pussy. Just get your ass down there so Davenport can't get right on top of you. Take Jas."

"What for? She ain't doing me no good," Harp said. "She been weepin' around about this finger."

"You need a witness. There's some heavy shit coming down. You might want to prove that you weren't here. Take a credit card, and buy some stuff down there. Keep the receipts, so you can prove it."

"Yeah, okay. Good idea," Harp said.

"Stay in touch. Call my place, leave a hotel name on the tape. Nothing else, just the hotel name."

"We're outa here," Harp said, and he hung up.

Harp's disappearance would simplify things, Stadic thought: one less problem to worry about. LaChaise would be gone in a week, and in two weeks, nobody would be coming back to Harp.

LUCAS CALLED A meeting for ten o'clock: At nine-fifteen he shut himself in his office and closed his eyes, feet up on the desk, and worked parts of it out. At nine-thirty, he started going through LaChaise's file, everything that Harmon Anderson had managed to put together from Michigan, Wisconsin, Illinois and the FBI.

LaChaise's criminal career had begun when he was a teenager, with game-law violations in Wisconsin, followed by timber rustling off state forestlands—cutting and selling walnut trees out of the hardwood forests in the southern part of the state. He'd been convicted twice of taking deer out of season, and twice on the tree rustling.

Somewhere along the line he'd joined the Seed—called the Bad Seed at the time—a motorcycle club with ties to drug smuggling, pornography and prostitution. Then he'd apparently gone into business: he'd been convicted of failing to remit sales taxes to the state of Wisconsin, and the contents of a motorcycle shop had been seized.

A year later, operating another shop, he'd been closed again, and again, his motorcycle stock was seized, apparently to cover the remaining principal and outstanding interest on the late sales taxes from the first shop.

Two months after that, he was charged with underreporting his income for three years, but was acquitted. The next charges, illegal dumping of industrial waste, were filed in Michigan. Then there were charges of threatening a game warden, trespassing, two assaults that were apparently bar fights and two drunken driving convictions.

The murder count was weak, as Sandy Darling had said it was.

When Sandy Darling's name popped into his head, Lucas dropped the file folder against his chest, thinking: if nothing turned up, he should make a quick run up to Darling's place. She wasn't all that far, and she knew LaChaise about as well as anyone alive. He had to be hiding somewhere . . .

He went back to the file: there was a sheaf of newspaper accounts of La-Chaise's arrest and trial, and the reporters noted the difficulty of conviction—and the jubilation of the prosecutors and local lawmen when the guilty verdict came in.

A county sheriff was quoted as saying, "Sooner or later he was going to kill an honest citizen or a law enforcement officer. Putting Dick LaChaise in prison is a public service."

But the conviction smelled—and he thought of Sandy Darling again.

At nine-fifty, Del showed up, and in the next few minutes, Sloan, Franklin and Sherrill. Kupicek was out of it, for the time being: lost his shit, as Franklin put it, but he said the words with sympathy.

Sherrill was holding tighter than Lucas expected.

"I didn't think there was any feeling left, until I saw him dead," Sherrill said, slumped in her chair. Her face was dead-pale against her dark hair and eyes. "I served the papers on him two months ago, but Jesus, I didn't want him dead."

"You can handle it?" Lucas asked.

"Oh, yeah," she said. She was ten years older in five hours, Lucas thought. She had a little harsh wrinkle running from the left side of her nose to the corner of her mouth, and it was not a smile line. "Yeah, I'll tell you what: I'm in on this."

Lucas looked at her for a moment, then nodded and looked at the others. "I don't know what Del and Sloan have told you, but we think LaChaise and friends of LaChaise might be involved somehow with Daymon Harp, a dealer around town. We're gonna start pushing him. But what we need is to start working through Harmon's paper on LaChaise, and all the paper we can find on Daymon Harp, and see if we get any crossover. LaChaise had to have a good contact here, because they got a list of our relatives. And it's possible that the contact is a cop."

"A cop," Sherrill said. She looked at Franklin, who shook his head once, as though he couldn't believe it.

"Could be," said Sloan.

"We need to chain LaChaise's known associates into the Cities, looking for *their* associates. There must be some. And we start busting ass. And I mean, like, tonight. One more thing: I want everybody to call each and every street contact you've got, and you tell them that there's big money for anyone who calls me with a location. Big money—ten grand. Ten grand, no questions asked, any way they want it."

"Where's that coming from?" Franklin asked.

"Outa my pocket," Lucas said, looking across the desk at him. Lucas had the money, all right: they never talked about it, but they all knew it.

"Way to go," Del said. He looked at the others: "That's what'll get them. We'll buy the motherfuckers out."

The phone rang on Lucas's desk.

———

ALTHOUGH COPS WERE everywhere around the hotel, there were still a few working the neighborhoods, doing the routine.

Barney's Old Time Malt Shoppe pulled in a lot of cops because Barney used to be one, before he retired, and because he rolled free coffee to any cops who stopped in, and always had a booth open. A single patrol car sat in Barney's lot. Stadic noted the number, 603, then cruised the place, peering through the windows. A tall, slender, pink-cheeked sergeant with pale hair and a much darker mustache: Arne Palin, two years behind Stadic at Central High.

Stadic pulled to the curb, kept an eye on the cops through the window. Harp had written down the plates on the truck LaChaise had taken to the laundromat for the meeting. Stadic took the piece of notepaper out of his pocket and called Dispatch on his handset: "Yeah, six-oh-three, run a Chevy S-10, Wisconsin Q-dash-H-O-R-S-E."

"Hang on . . ."

A moment later it came back: the truck was registered to an Elmore Darling, on a rural route in Turtle Lake, Wisconsin.

"Thanks for that . . ."

He looked through the window into Barney's. The cops inside hadn't heard their car number going out. He moved down the street, to a stop signal.

Now. One more call.

He brooded about the idea through the green light: the streets were empty, and he sat staring at nothing, the red-yellow-green bouncing unseen across his face. He knew the phone number, all right. If he had the guts . . . but then, it was hardly a matter of guts anymore. It was a matter of urgent necessity. And he'd already set it up.

If Davenport thought LaChaise was going after his daughter, LaChaise was a dead man: and that's what he needed. Dead men. Stadic pulled himself together and punched in the number. Christ, if they recognized his voice . . .

The phone rang once, then Davenport's voice said, "Yeah?"

"I don't want to say who this is—I don't want to get involved—but you gave me your card, once." He pitched his voice up, made it smooth, syrupy.

"OKAY," LUCAS SAID, an edge of impatience in his tone. He was staring at Sherrill, who was chewing on a cuticle. Lucas didn't need tips about loan sharks, cigarette smuggling, credit card dealing, dope factories.

"I live down by Richard Small and Jennifer Carey." The voice was curiously soft. "That's your little girl with Jennifer, right?"

There was a hard moment of silence, then Davenport said, "Jesus."

"There's been a truck driving around. I saw him twice when I was out walking my dog. Wisconsin plates. I thought I should call."

And the caller was gone.

Lucas exploded out of the chair and ran from the office and through the building to Dispatch. The other four, not understanding, went after him.

———

A PATROL CAR squatted in front of the house, exhaust curling up into the falling snow. Another was parked across the street, and the two cops from the car waited in the back of the house. Lucas arrived fifteen minutes after his dash to Dispatch, carrying his black wool overcoat and a briefcase. Del trailed a few steps behind, like a destitute bodyguard, watching the windows up and down the street. A cop met them at the door.

"We kept everybody away from the windows," the cop said. "There's been nothin' on the street. Nothin' moving."

"Good. And thanks. Keep an eye out," Lucas said.

Jennifer Carey and Richard Small waited for him in the dining room, the blinds pulled.

"Where's Sarah?" Lucas asked, without preamble.

"Upstairs, in bed," Jennifer said. She was still the willowy blonde, but with a few more wrinkles than when Sarah had been conceived. Lucas had wanted— had offered, in any case—to marry her, but though she'd wanted the baby, she hadn't cared for the prospects of marriage to Lucas. Now she and Small, a vice-president at TV3's parent corporation, had put together a family: Jennifer's daughter, his son. Jennifer looked past Lucas at Del, and a tiny smile caught her lips. "How're you doing, Del?"

Del shrugged. "Cheryl's gonna make it."

"What's the threat level?" Small asked. He was short, muscular, blunt, a onetime Navy pilot in Vietnam, and Lucas liked him.

"We don't know," Lucas said. "The call was weird, but we can't take any chances. You're gonna have to move."

"I can't quit working," Jennifer said. "This is too large."

Lucas said, "That pushes the threat quite a bit higher."

"We'll keep her behind security, inside the building," Small said. "We'll make sure she doesn't leave at any expected time. We can use different cars."

"That'll all help," Lucas said. "But we still haven't figured out their capability. We know there are several of them, and we've only got the ID on LaChaise. The other two—we just don't know."

Jennifer looked at Small. "Do you think you could get off?"

Small shook his head: "I'm not going anywhere; I gotta be here." He turned to Lucas. "How safe is this hotel you're putting people into?"

"Safe," Lucas said. "That'd be the best place. We don't really know how much these guys know about us. I don't know how they found out about Jen and Sarah . . ."

"Sloan's wife," Jennifer said.

Small and Lucas looked at her, and she said, "Sloan's wife. She'd take care of the kids—she loves kids. And she's in the hotel, right?"

Lucas nodded. "Give her a call."

Jen headed for the phone, and Lucas turned to Small: "If we can get you guys in the hotel tonight, we'd like to put a few guys in here . . . I'd be with them . . ."

"Use the house as a trap," Small said.

"Yeah."

Small nodded: "All right. So let's get the kids out."

Jennifer came back: "She says she'll be glad to take them."

Small said, "Pack a suitcase. You go with the kids for tonight. Lucas is gonna set up an ambush here . . . and I'm going to stick around. Make sure the cops don't steal anything."

Del looked him over. "You got a gun someplace?"

Small nodded: "Yeah. I do. I don't like people fucking with my kids."

My kids . . .

Lucas never flinched, but as he stepped over to a telephone, he caught Jennifer's reflection in a windowpane. Behind his back, she'd brought a finger to her lips, and Small nodded. Lucas picked up the phone and called downtown: "Sherrill and Franklin are around somewhere," he said. "Get them on the line."

A high-pitched voice said something from back in the house, and Jennifer hurried that way. Lucas stepped into the hall, and saw Sarah standing halfway down the stairs in her fuzzy pink pajamas, rubbing her sleepy eyes. Lucas cleared his voice and said into the phone, "We're making some changes down here."

SARAH WOULD GROW up to be tall and willowy and blond like her mother— like Lucas's mother—but with her father's tough smile and deep eyes. Jennifer let her go and she wandered over to Lucas and took his index finger in her hand, and when he dropped the phone back on the hook, said, "What's going on?"

Lucas squatted, so he could look straight into her eyes. "We have some problems. You have to stay at a hotel tonight. With Mom. And Mrs. Sloan will be there."

"What kind of problems?"

"There are some really bad men . . ." he was explaining when the phone rang. Small picked it up, then handed it to Lucas: "It's Chief Roux. I'll take Sarah," he said.

Lucas nodded. "Yeah," he said into the phone.

"*Nightline*'s coming on: watch it," Roux said. Her words came in a spate. "We picked up a thumbprint off that door in Roseville and damned if the FBI didn't come up with a name that fits. A man named Ansel Butters, from Tennessee, an old friend of LaChaise's. We've got a photo from Washington and we've released it, and it oughta be on *Nightline* in about a minute."

"Anything on Butters? Local contacts?"

"Not as far as I know, but Anderson's working the computers," Roux said. "Nothing happening down there?"

"Not yet," he said. "I'll go turn on the TV."

"The word's out about the money you put on the street, the ten thousand," Roux said. "Channel Three has it, and if they've got it, everybody else will in an hour. I'm not sure it's a good precedent."

"There aren't any precedents for this," Lucas said.

"All right. I hope it dredges something up," Roux said. "By the way, this Butters—his nickname is 'Crazy.' Crazy Ansel Butters."

"That's what I want to hear," Lucas said.

LUCAS, DEL AND Small stood around the television while Jennifer packed the kids: The regular *Nightline* host was on vacation, and an anonymous ABC newsman fronted the show. He started with "a significant bit of breaking news," and a black-and-white photograph of Ansel Butters filled the screen.

"If you have seen this man . . ."

A moment later, he launched into his prepared introduction, and said, "Minneapolis, a city crouched in shock and terror this wintry night," and all three of them—Lucas, Del and Small—said "Jesus" at the same time.

JENNIFER LEFT WITH the kids in a three-car convoy. Neighbors were wakened, and cops installed in corner houses. The snow stopped at midnight, and Lucas, Small and Del, trying to keep the house looking awake, watched on the weather radar as the snow squalls drifted off to the northeast and into Wisconsin.

At 12:30, which Small said was their usual time, they began turning off lights and killed the television. Moving cars were scarce. They sat behind the darkened windows and grew sleepy.

"Maybe it was just a bullshit call," Small said.

"Maybe, but we've got nothing else working," Lucas said. "Whoever it was had my card and my direct line. That says something."

"Maybe somebody's jerking you around," Del said.

Lucas yawned. "I don't think so. The guy knew something."

"I hope they come in," Del said fervently, in the dark. "I hope they come."

10

WHILE LUCAS DASHED to Small's home, stadic crossed the St. Croix at Taylors Falls and headed into the Wisconsin night on Highway 8. The going was slow: there were no lights, and at times, as he passed through the intermittent snow squalls, the highway virtually disappeared. A green sign—Turtle Lake 17—flicked past; and much later a John Deere sign, and then lights.

He was running on adrenaline now: only five hours since the attacks, and it seemed like a lifetime.

At Turtle Lake, he passed a hotel with a No Vacancy sign, and then the casino loomed out of the snow like an alcoholic hallucination. He turned into the lot and had to drive halfway to the back to find a parking space. The casinos were always full, even at midnight, even in a blizzard.

A uniformed security officer stood just inside the doors, eyes watchful. Stadic asked, "Where's the phone?" and the security man pointed down the length of the casino. "Outside any of the rest rooms," he said.

The first phone, mounted on the wall between the men's and women's rest rooms, was occupied by a woman who appeared to be in crisis: she had a handkerchief in her hand and she twisted it and untwisted it as she cried into the phone. Stadic moved on, found another one. The noise from the slots might be a problem, he thought, but he needed the phone. He cupped his hand around the receiver and dialed the fire station.

A sleepy man answered. Stadic, watching the casino traffic, said, "This is Sergeant Manfred Hamm with the Minnesota Highway Patrol out of Taylors Falls, Minnesota. To whom am I speaking?"

The sleepy man said, "Uh, this is Jack, uh, Lane."

"Mr. Lane, you're with the Turtle Lake Fire Department?"

"Uh, yeah?"

"Would you by any chance cover a rural fire route, Mr. and Mrs. Elmore Darling?"

"Uh, yeah." Lane was waking up.

"Mr. Lane, we've got a problem here. Mrs. Darling has been involved in an automobile accident outside of Taylors Falls, and we need to send a man to speak to Mr. Darling. We don't know exactly where his house is, as all we have is a rural route address. Would you have a location on the Darling house?"

"Well, uh . . . Just a minute there."

Stadic heard the fireman talking to somebody, and a moment later he came back: "Sergeant Baker?"

"Sergeant Hamm," Stadic said.

"Oh, yeah, Hamm, sorry. The Darlings live at fire number twelve-eighty-nine. You stay on Highway 8, and you go a little more than a mile past the Highway 63 turnoff, and you'll see Kk going to the south. They're about a mile down that road . . . You'll see a red sign by the driveway, says, Township Almena and the number. Twelve-eighty-nine. Got that?"

"Yes, thank you," Stadic said, scribbling it down. "We'll send a man."

"Was, uh, the accident . . . ?"

"We're not allowed to say more until the next of kin are located," Stadic said formally. Then: "Thank you again."

———

THE SNOWFALL HAD eased as he crept out Kk, trying to stay in the middle of
the road. Although the air was clear, the fresh snow flattened everything: he
couldn't see the edge of the road, or where the ditches started. He crawled
along, past the big rural mailboxes, hunting for the fire signs in the beam of a
six-cell flashlight.

And he found it, just like the fireman had said he would.

The Darling house sat back from the road, and showed a sodium vapor yard
light at the side of a three-car pole barn. The inverted mushroom shape of a
satellite TV antenna sprouted at the side of the pole barn, pointing south. The
house was two stories tall, white and neat. A white board fence led off into
the dark and snow.

A fresh set of tire tracks led to the garage: with the snow coming down as
it had been, there must have been a recent arrival. Stadic continued a half-mile
down Kk to the next driveway, turned around and headed back.

LaChaise had given him a local phone number in the Cities, and another man
had answered when he called. So at least two of them were down there—and
after the fight, they were probably all three hanging together.

He wasn't sure what he'd find at this place: but if they were friends of
LaChaise, they might know where he was . . . and they might know Stadic's
name.

Just short of the Darlings' driveway, he turned off his headlights and eased
along the road with the parking lights. He turned into the end of the driveway
and, keeping his foot off the brake, killed the engine and rolled to a stop.

He had a shotgun in the back, on the floor. He picked it up, jacked a shell
into the chamber, zipped his parka, put on his gloves and cracked the door.
He'd forgotten the dome light: it flickered, and he quickly pulled the door shut.
Watched. Nothing. He reached up, pushed the dome light switch all the way
to the left, and tried the door again. No light. He got out, and headed down
the drive, the shotgun in his hand.

A shaft of light fell on the snow outside the kitchen. Stadic did a quick-peek,
one eye, just a half-second, past the edge of a yellowed pull-down shade. A
gray-faced man in a plaid shirt and blue jeans, with a bare-neck farmer haircut,
sat alone at a kitchen table. He was eating macaroni out of a Tupperware bowl,
washing it down with a can of beer. He was watching CNN.

Stadic ducked under the window and, walking light-footed, testing the snow
for crunch, continued past the house to a detached garage, and down the side
of the garage to a window. He flicked his pocket flash just long enough to see
the truck inside. He checked the plates: Q-HORSE2. So they had two vehicles.
There were probably no more than two people inside the house, because that
was the nominal capacity of the truck. And there was probably only one person
inside, the one he could see, because the other truck was gone.

He stepped back to the house, checked the window again. The man—Elmore
Darling?—was still there, eating. Stadic moved to the back door. The door

opened onto a small three-season porch. He pulled open the aluminum storm
door a half-inch at a time. Tried the inner door: the knob turned under his
hand. Nobody locked anything in the country. Assholes. He opened the inner
door as carefully as he had the storm door, a half-inch at a time, taking care
not to let the shotgun rattle against the door frame.

Inside, on the porch, he was breathing hard from the tension, his breath
curling like smoke in the dimly lit air. He could hear the TV, not the words,
but the mutter. The porch smelled of grain and maybe, a bit, of horse shit: not
unpleasant. Farm smells. The porch was almost as cold as the outside. He eased
the storm door shut.

The door between the porch and the house had a window, covered with a
pink curtain. He peeked, quickly: still eating. He'd have to move before Darling
sensed him here, Stadic thought. He took a breath, reached out and tried the
doorknob. Stiff.

All right. He backed away a step, lifted the shotgun to the present-arms
position, cocked his leg.

Took a breath and kicked the doorknob.

The door flew open, the screws of the lock housing ripping out of the wood
on the inside. Darling, a soup-spoon of macaroni halfway to his face, fell out
of his chair and onto the linoleum floor, and tried to scramble to his feet.

Stadic, moving: "Freeze . . . Freeze." Stadic was on top of Darling, leaning
toward him, the barrel of the shotgun following his face. Stadic shouted, "Police," and "Down on the floor, down on the floor . . ."

With his dark coat blowing around his ankles, the cold wind behind him,
and the black gun, he looked like the figure of death. Darling flattened himself
on the floor, his hands arched behind his head, shouting, "Don't, don't, don't."

SANDY SPENT AN hour watching the TV news, the crisis building in the news-
rooms. Murder and terrorism experts arriving at the networks like boatloads of
war refugees, looking for life on television. You could tell they liked it: liked
the murder, liked the guns, liked having the expertise.

"Bunch of vultures," Butters said.

LaChaise and Butters and Martin were drunk. Martin simply got quieter and
meaner: he'd stare at Sandy, drinking, stare some more. Butters tended to laugh
and lurch around the house, and want to dance. LaChaise talked incessantly
about the old days when they rode together with the Seed, and all the things
the cops had done to him and his daddy.

"Nothing like what they did to my daddy," Butters said once. "He used to
write some bad checks when me and momma got hungry, and they'd be all
over him. Used to beat him up and make him cry. The goddamn sheriff there
liked to see a man cry. I was gonna kill him when I got big enough, but
somebody else did it first."

"So what finally happened?" Sandy asked. "To your old man?"

"Hung himself down the basement one day, right next to this big old rack of empty Ball jars. I come home from school and found him there, just twisting around. Did it with one of them pieces of plastic electric cable, had a hell of a time getting it unwrapped off his neck . . ."

The story angered LaChaise—topped him—and he walked around the house kicking doors down. Then he came back and said, "I don't want to hear no more about your daddy," and dropped into the one big chair and into himself, glowering at them, his disapproval rank in the air.

"Well, fuck you," Butters said, and Sandy felt like something could happen between them. But LaChaise grinned and said, "You, too," and that defused it.

Then *Nightline* came on, with the story about Butters, and they listened to the *Nightline* reporter list his life record.

"How'd they get that?" LaChaise roared, and he glared around the room, as though one of them had given Butters up. "Who'n the fuck is the traitor?"

And then it occurred to him. He swung, the bottle of Jim Beam still in his hand, to Sandy: "That fuckin' Elmore."

Sandy backed away, shook her head. "No. Not Elmore. I warned him to keep his mouth shut, and he said he would." But she thought, *Maybe he did.* Maybe he got on a phone and gave them up to Old John.

"I might have touched something," Butters said calmly, and LaChaise swung around toward him.

"You had gloves," he said.

"Couldn't get the pistol out of my pocket with gloves, so I took them off. Tried to stay away from things, but . . . maybe I touched something. My fingerprints would ring bells with the cops."

LaChaise considered, then said, "Nah, it's that fuckin' Elmore, that's who it is."

"If it was Elmore, he would've given them Martin, too," Butters said. He was holding a bourbon bottle, and took a swig.

"He's right, Dick . . ." Sandy started, but LaChaise pointed at her, a thick forefinger in her face: "Shut up."

And he dropped back into his chair. After a moment he said, "I just fell apart. I saw the guy and I came apart."

Three people had gone out to kill, and only LaChaise had failed. He'd been brooding about it.

"There was no way you could know," Martin said finally. He was as drunk as Butters. "It would have happened to me or Ansel, too. You call, you make the check, who's to know that he's gonna walk in one second later?"

"No, it's my fault," LaChaise said. "I wasn't steady. I coulda took her. I coulda took them both. I coulda shot her, then shot him, let 'em watch each other die. She was right there, but I was gettin' fancy, then this cop pops up behind her. He was fast . . ."

"Lucky that shot caught you in the side, instead of square in the back," Butters said. They knew what he meant, but the word "back" seemed to hang in the air. LaChaise had been running when he was hit.

"I gotta get out of here," Sandy said. She stood up, but LaChaise pushed himself out of the chair and said, "I told you to fuckin' shut up." And quick—quick as a whip—he caught her with an openhanded roundhouse, and knocked her to the floor, as Martin had earlier in the evening. Butters and Martin sat impassively, watching, as she struggled to her hands and knees.

She could taste blood in her mouth. She looked up at him and thought about getting a gun. She should have killed him the night she found out that he'd murdered the cop. She couldn't do it then. She could do it now.

"You gonna shut up?" LaChaise asked.

"Let me go home, Dick," she said. She wiped at her mouth with the back of her hand.

"Fuck that. You're staying here," he said.

But he didn't mention Elmore again that night.

ELMORE TOLD STADIC everything he knew, and only lied in a few spots. "Sandy's not in it at all," he said. "They showed up, and there wasn't anything we could do. They got all the guns in the world."

"Who are the other guys?" Stadic asked.

"Martin, who's like this crazy queer from Michigan who walks around with a bow and arrow, and Ansel Butters. He's from Tennessee and he comes up and goes hunting with Martin."

"Is Butters a fag?" Stadic and Darling sat in wooden chairs, across the kitchen table from each other. The shotgun's barrel rested on the table, pointing at Darling's chest. Stadic had closed the outer door, and the house was getting warm again. The kitchen was a pleasant place, with just enough chintz and country pottery to make it homey. Darling had a nice wife, Stadic thought.

"No, Butters is straight, but he takes a lot of drugs," Darling said. "Martin, now, everybody says he's a fag and he's in love with Dick, but he never does anything homosexual or nothing . . . it's just a thing."

"And that's all," Stadic said. "There's just the four."

"Just the three—you can't count Sandy," Elmore said. "I'd tell you where they were at, but I don't know. I mean, I kinda know . . ."

Darling was holding this one piece back, lying. He was an excellent liar, but Stadic was a professional interrogator. He wasn't sure that Darling was lying, but he also knew that he had no way to control the man. He couldn't take him with him, couldn't hold him. And if Darling got in touch with LaChaise, LaChaise would recognize Stadic's description. A problem.

He sat in the kitchen chair with the barrel of the gun pointing at Darling's chest.

"Tell me again," Stadic said. "You get off at Lexington . . ."

"And it must be about six blocks up the road. North. Then right. Just a little house."

"You didn't see the number or the street name."

"Nope. I was just following behind." He brightened. "But I'll tell you—my truck is on the street. So is Martin's. You could look for my truck, it's got a license plate says, Q-HORSE."

Stadic nodded. "So six or seven blocks."

"No more than that," Darling said. "We could find it. I'd go down there with you."

Stadic thought for another moment, then shook his head.

"Nah," he said.

"What, then?" Darling asked, his eyebrows going up as if mystified, a stupid smile on his face. Stadic shrugged, and pulled the trigger.

The 00s in the three-inch Magnum shell blew Elmore Darling completely off his kitchen chair.

SANDY HUDDLED IN the bedroom, just to be away from them.

LaChaise went to sleep in his chair, and Martin and Butters sat in the living room, the television turned down, talking quietly about the kills.

Martin said, "I had my hands on him and when the knife went in, he kind of rose up, and shook. Like when you cut the throat on a deer, they make that last little try to get goin' . . . you know?"

"Sure, they push up, try to get their feet under them . . ."

"Damn good time to get hurt," Martin said. "There's one old boy, Rob Harris over to Luce County, got down on a spike buck like that, stuck him in the throat with his knife, and that buck rose up and stuck one of them spikes right in Rob's eye. Blinded the eye."

"What happened to the buck?" Butters asked.

"Run off. Rob says it must've been a brisket hit 'cause there was blood all over hell," Martin said. "Probably out there to this day . . ."

"Yeah, well, this Sherrill dude sure ain't."

"Not when I get that close," Martin said. "When I get that close, the boy's a goner . . ."

They both turned and looked at LaChaise, thinking they might have given offense, but LaChaise was unconscious.

"This Kupicek, she never even twitched," Butters said. "Never even knew what hit her. One minute she's talking to me, the next minute, it's St. Peter."

"Silencer work good?"

Butters nodded. "Worked real good. All you hear is that ratchet sound, you know, maybe a little pop, but it's no more'n opening a can of soda."

"Wish I had me a silencer like that."

"If I were gonna do it again, I think I might do it as a single-shot. You know, load one round, carry it cocked-and-locked over an empty clip. Then you wouldn't get the ratchet noise . . ."

They went on, working over the details, the TV turned down. Butters's face would come up every half hour or so. On the first newsbreak of the day, at five o'clock, TV3 produced a series of computer-morphed photos of both LaChaise and Butters, with a variety of hairstyles and facial hair.

"Oughta shave your head," Martin said. "That's the only thing they ain't got."

"Nah. Too late for me," Butters said. He looked at his watch. "Be daylight in a couple-three hours. I'm going out. Check this kid's house, the Davenport kid."

"Better wait for Dick," Martin said.

Butters shook his head as he stood up. "It's about fifty-fifty that it's an ambush," Butters said. "Better that only one of us goes; and Dick's hurt, and they don't know you yet."

"You sober?"

"As a judge."

Martin dropped his hands on his thighs, a light conclusive slap, and nodded. Butters said: "Help me load up."

"What're you takin'?" Martin asked.

Butters grinned: "One of everything."

LaChaise stirred in the chair, half-opened his eyes, shook his head and slept again.

"I better get going," Butters said. "Don't want to disturb Dick's beauty rest."

11

D EL WAS IN the hallway, stretched out on three couch pillows. Small was in bed, still dressed but in stocking feet, alert. Every once in a while, he'd get out of bed and creep through the hallway, and whisper a question down to Lucas.

"Anything?"

"Nothing yet."

Lucas yawned, pushed a button on his watch to illuminate the face. Five forty-five. More than two hours to first light. He walked carefully back toward the bathroom, navigating by feel through the darker lumps of the furniture. The bathroom was for guests, for convenience: small, with a toilet and a sink, a tube of Crest and a rack of kids' toothbrushes for after-meal brushing. There was no exterior window. Lucas shut the door and turned on the light, winced at its brightness, splashed water in his face. His mouth tasted worse than his face looked; he rubbed a wormy inch of Crest over his teeth with his index finger, spat the green slime into the sink, and stood there, leaning over the sink, weight on his arms, watching the water.

There were all kinds of hints and pointers, but none of them solid. Not yet. But the case would go quickly, he thought. If he were alive, if Weather and Sarah and Jennifer and Small were all alive in a week, then it'd be done with.

It'd be done with even if they didn't stay around.

They could walk out now, catch a plane, fly to Tahiti—he had the money to do it a hundred times over—lie on the beach, and when they came back, it'd be done. The difference of a week.

And maybe they should.

But he liked the tightening feel of the hunt.

He didn't like what it had done to Cheryl Capslock or the others, the dead, but he did like the feel of chase, God help him.

He turned out the light, opened the door and went back to the living room.

DEL WAS AWAKE. He said, "Cheryl couldn't feel much of anything after they got her out of surgery."

"She'll feel it today," Lucas said. He unconsciously touched a white tracheotomy scar on his throat.

"Yeah, that's what the docs said."

"They say anything about scars?" Lucas asked.

"She's gonna have some, but they shouldn't be too bad. What there is, she can wear her hair over."

"I know a plastic surgeon over at the U, friend of Weather's. If you need one."

They sat a while in the dark. Then Del said, "If she died, I don't know what I'd do."

"She'll be okay."

"Yeah." Then: "But that's not exactly what I meant. I mean, I never really thought of it until this afternoon. If she was gone, I'd be lost. I been on the streets so long, the whole world looks like it's fucked. Cheryl keeps me from going nuts. I *was* going nuts before I met her. I was a crazy motherfucker . . . I was such a good wino that I could've *become* one."

"Made for each other," Lucas said, with a wry undertone cops affected when they were getting too close to sincerity.

"Yeah. Jesus, I want to kill that motherfucker . . ."

Then the handset:

"Lucas. Got one coming." A surveillance voice. Lucas grabbed the radio and stepped to the front door. He could see out the inset glass windows without being seen himself.

"White male in a pickup, moving slow. He's not delivering papers."

"Can you see the plates?"

"I can't, but Tommy can, he's got the night scope . . . Tommy? He'll be there in a minute."

"Right, I got him coming . . ."

"Lucas, he's coming up to the house now."

Lucas could see the headlights on the snow, then the slowly moving pickup. "Get the plate, get the plate."

"He's going by, but he was looking. Jeff, what'd you think?"

"He was looking, all right."

"We don't want to shoot a goddamn reporter, take it easy . . ."

Lucas said, "Tommy, you got that plate?"

"Front plate's dirty, I can get CV. It's Minnesota . . ."

"Tommy, c'mon . . ."

"I got it, I got it . . ." He read the license out, and Dispatch acknowledged. "He's going around the corner . . ."

"Which way?"

"South. Wait a minute, he's stopping. He's stopping."

"Dick, you guys get down here in the car," Lucas said into the handset. "Come around the block from the back."

"Didn't think it'd happen," Del said. He was wide awake, breathing hard.

"Take it easy," Lucas said.

Small called down the stairs: "What's happening?"

"Nothing," Lucas called back, and then Del led out through the front and down the sidewalk, moving with the wintertime short-step duckwalk of a man on ice.

Lucas still had the handset. Tommy: "He's getting something out of the back. He's got the dome light on and he's doing something in the back."

Lucas brought the radio up: "Everybody take it easy, he could have anything in there."

Dick came back: "We're coming in, we're coming around the corner."

Lucas said, "Let's go," and they started running, moving off the sidewalk into the snow, high-stepping. At the corner, they rounded an arbor vitae, and saw the truck fifty feet away, across the street, the door open now. The driver was turning toward them, he had something in his arms . . .

"Hold it," Lucas shouted. Del was sprinting ahead, and Tommy came in from the side, his long coat whipping around his legs, and Dick came in with the car . . .

BUTTERS HAD SPIRALED in toward the house from a half-mile out, quartering the neighborhood, watching faces in the few cars he'd encountered, looking for lights, looking for motion. In the woods, he'd learned to look not for the animal, but the disturbance in the animal's wake. Deer sometimes sounded like they were wearing jackboots, pounding through the woods; squirrels made tree limbs jiggle and jerk in a way that wasn't the wind; even a snake, if it was big enough, parted the grass like a ship's prow cutting through water.

He watched for the odd motion; and saw none.

Still, there was something not right about this. He understood that the cop might think that the kid was safe, but why would he take the chance? Putting the kid in the hotel would have been the natural thing to do.

Butters saw nothing, but he smelled something: the kid felt like bear bait, a bucket of honey and oatmeal, meant to pull them in. They had to check, because the kid might be one of their last chances to really get even. And that, he thought, made the kid even better bait.

But he turned toward the house, spiraling, moving closer . . .

THE UNMARKED CAR caught the truck in its high beams, and the man turned, hearing Lucas's scream, saw the running men . . . put his back to the truck and said, "What? What?"

Del was twenty feet away and coming in, and the man raised his hands and Del almost popped him: almost . . .

"Freeze. Right where you are." Lucas behind Del, Tommy on the edge, the doors popping on the blocking car.

"What?" The guy was white-faced, shocked, his mouth dropping open. He stepped back away from the van.

There was movement in the van, and Tommy swiveled toward it, his shotgun raised. A blond head. Then a child's voice, tired and frightened: "Daddy?"

SPIRALING: AND CATCHING, down a street that led almost straight into the target house, a dark-night tableau. A car parked diagonally across the street, its headlights on a van. A man outside the van, his hands up. More men in the street.

"There you are," Butters said, with satisfaction. "I knew you were out there."

Lucas saw Butters's truck: noticed it mostly because it was identical to the truck they were standing next to.

Del was apologizing to the owner, who had just gotten home from his parents' farm, and trying to reassure the little girl, who was old enough to be frightened by the men who'd suddenly surrounded them.

The truck in the intersection paused for just a heartbeat, two heartbeats, then casually rolled on. The driver must have seen the commotion in the street, Lucas thought. "I've got a daughter just like you, who lives up the block," Lucas said to the little girl. "Do you know Sarah Davenport?"

The girl nodded without saying anything, but now the world was okay.

"Sure, she knows Sarah . . ." the father was saying, and Lucas made nice and forgot about the other truck.

And walking away, a shaky, white-faced Del said, "Jesus, I gotta ease off. I almost shot the guy. He didn't do a fuckin' thing, I just wanted to do it . . ."

STADIC THOUGHT ABOUT it all the way into the Cities. He was exhausted from the day on duty, from the drive, from the killing. Through the thinning snow, he had flashes, almost visionlike in their clarity and intensity, of Elmore Darling sitting at the table in the instant before the gunshot. Darling was smiling, hopeful . . . afraid. He was alive. Then he wasn't. There was no transition, just a noise, and the smell of gunpowder and raw meat, and Elmore Darling wasn't there anymore.

The visions frightened Stadic: What was happening? Was he losing it? At the same time, his cop brain was working out the inevitable progression. He now knew where LaChaise and his friends were hiding. If he worked it right, if he came up with the right story, he could ambush them. He needed to draw them out of their house, unsuspecting.

He could set up outside the house, in the dark, next to their vehicles. Darling said the trucks would be on the street. Then he could prod them out. He could call and say that the cops had been tipped, that they were on the way. They'd have to run for it.

LaChaise was injured, so only Martin and Butters would be at full strength. He'd catch them as soon as they stepped out on the porch, before they could get the door shut, then he'd go in after the woman.

But how about the shotgun? Darling had been killed with 00s, maybe he ought to change to 000s? Or maybe just go with the pistol. If he was right there, real close, take them with the pistol and forget the shotgun. Of course, if LaChaise was really hurt, if he didn't come out, then he'd have to go in after him . . .

There'd be risk. He couldn't avoid it.

And how would he explain the sequence to the St. Paul cops? He could say he'd been tipped to the location by one of the local dopers, but he hadn't given it much credence. He'd gone to take a look, when he'd stumbled right into them . . .

But why would he go into the house? Why not fall back and call for an entry team?

Stadic chewed it over, worried it, all the way down to the Cities. If he was going to do it, he should stop down at his office and pick up a vest. But when he stopped at the office, the first thing he heard was people running in the hallways . . .

LUCAS STARED OUT through the slats in the venetian blinds. Still dark. "Not coming."

"So it was bullshit," Del said. He yawned.

"Maybe. Strange call, though," Lucas said, thinking about it. "Came straight into me. He had the number."

"We oughta leave a couple of guys here, just in case," Del said. "I gotta get down to Hennepin and see Cheryl."

"Yeah, take off," Lucas said.

Dispatch called: "Lucas?"

He picked up the handset. "Yes?"

"A woman called for you. Says she has some information and she wants the ten thousand."

"Patch her through."

"She hung up. She says her old man might hear her. But she gave her address. She says she wants you to take her out of her house, if her old man gets . . . she said, 'pissed.' " A dispatcher couldn't *say* "pissed," but she could quote "pissed."

"What's the address?" Lucas asked.

"It's over on the southeast side . . . you got a pencil?"

As Lucas took it down, Del asked, "You want me to come along?"

Lucas shook his head. "It's probably bullshit. Half the dopers in town will be calling, trying to fake us out. Go see Cheryl."

"They'll let me in pretty soon," Del said. The light on his watch face flickered in the dark. "I gotta be there when she wakes up."

"Keep an eye out," Lucas said. "The crazy fucks could be around the hospital."

LUCAS, BEGINNING TO feel the weight of all the sleepless hours, looked at the house and wondered: called to a semi-slum duplex, in the early-morning darkness. An ambush?

"What do you think?" he asked.

"You wait here," the patrol cop said. "We'll go knock."

The two patrol cops, one tall and one even taller, were wearing heavy-duty armor, capable of defeating rifle bullets. Two more cops sat in the alley behind the house, covering the back door.

Lucas stood by the car, waiting, while the cops approached the door. One of them peeked at a window, then suddenly broke back toward the door, and Lucas saw that it was opening. A woman, gaunt, black-haired, poked her head out and said something to the cops. The tall cop nodded, waved Lucas in, and then he and the taller cop went inside.

Lucas caught them just inside the door. The taller cop whispered, "Her husband's in the back bedroom, and he keeps a gun on the floor next to the bed. We're invited in, so we can take him."

Lucas nodded, and the two cops, walking softly as they could over the tattered carpet, eased down the hallway, with the woman a step behind them. At the last door, the lead cop gestured and the woman nodded, and the cop reached inside the dark room and flipped on the light. Lucas heard him say, "Police," and then, "Get the gun," and then, "Hey, wake up. Wake up. Hey you, wake up."

Then a man's voice, high and squeaky, "What the fuck? What the fuck is going on?"

The woman walked back down the hall toward Lucas. She was five-six, and weighed, he thought, maybe ninety pounds, with cheekbones like Frisbees. She said, "I heard you're putting up the money."

"If your information is any good," he said.

The two patrol cops prodded her husband out into the hallway. Still mostly asleep, he was wearing stained Jockey shorts and a befuddled expression. His hands were cuffed behind his back.

"Oh, the information is good," the woman said to Lucas. Then, "You remember me?"

Lucas looked at her for a moment, saw something familiar in the furry thickness of her dark brows, mentally put twenty-five pounds on her and said, "Yeah. You used to work up at the Taco Bell, the one off Riverside. You were . . . let's see, you were hanging out with Sammy Cerdan and his band. You were what—you played with them. Bass?"

"Yeah, bass," she said, pleased that he remembered.

He was going to ask, "What happened?" but he knew.

Still smiling, a rickety smile that looked as though it might slide off her face onto the floor, she said, "Yeah, yeah, good times."

Her husband said, "What the hell is going on? Who's this asshole?"

The tall cop said, "He had a bag of shit under his mattress."

He tossed a Baggie to Lucas: the stuff inside, enough to fill a teaspoon, looked like brown sugar.

"This is fuckin' illegal. I want to see a search warrant," the husband said.

"You shouldn't of hid the bag, Dex," the woman said to him. To Lucas, "He never gave me nothin'. I'm boostin' shit out of Target all day and he never give me nothin'."

"Kick you in the ass," Dexter shouted at her, and he struggled against the taller cop, and tried to kick at her. She dodged the kick and gave him the finger.

"Shut up," Lucas said to him. To the woman: "Where are they?"

"My brother rented them a house, but he doesn't know who they are. The one guy, Butters? He was here asking about crooked cops and houses he could rent. As soon as I saw on TV, I knew that was him."

"You cunt," her husband shouted.

Lucas turned to him and smiled: "The next time you interrupt, I'm gonna pull your fuckin' face off."

The husband shut up and the woman said, "I want the money."

"If this pans out, you'll get it. What's the address?"

"I want something else."

"What?"

"When my mom took the kids, they kicked me off welfare."

"So?"

"So I want back on."

Lucas shrugged. "I'll ask. If you can show them the kids, then . . ."

"I don't want the kids back. I just want back on the roll," the woman said. "You gotta fix it."

"I'll ask, but I can't promise," Lucas said. "Now, where are they?"

"Over in Frogtown," she said. "I got the address written down."

"What about the cop?" Lucas asked. "Who'd you send him to?"

The woman shook her head. "We didn't know any cop. Dex just gave him names of some dopers who might know."

Lucas turned to her husband. "What dopers?"

"Fuck you," Dex said.

"Gonna give you some time to think about it," Lucas said, poking a finger in Dexter's face. "Down in the jail. For the shit." He held up the bag. "If you think about it fast enough, maybe you can buy out of the murder charge."

"Fuck that, I want a lawyer," Dex said.

"Take him," Lucas said to the patrolmen. To the woman: "Gimme the address."

LACHAISE WOKE UP sober but hung over. He stood up, carefully, walked down to the bathroom, closed the door, found the light switch and flicked it on, took a leak, flushed the toilet.

He'd been sleeping in his jeans, T-shirt and socks. He pulled up the shirt to check the bandage on his ribs, looking in the cracked mirror over the sink, but saw no signs of blood, just the dried iodine compound. Best of all, he didn't feel seriously injured: he'd been hurt in bike accidents and fights, and he knew the coming-apart feeling of a bad injury. This just plain hurt.

The house was silent. He stepped back out of the bathroom, walked down the hall to the next room and pushed the door open. Sandy was curled on the bed, wrapped in a blanket.

"You asleep?" he asked quietly.

There was no response, but he thought she might be awake. He was about to ask again, when there was a noise in the hall. He stepped back, and saw Martin padding down the hallway, a .45 in his hand. When Martin saw LaChaise, his forehead wrinkled.

"You all right?" Martin asked.

"I'm sore, but I been a lot worse," LaChaise said. "Where's Ansel?"

"He went to see about that Davenport kid."

"Jesus Christ, that's my job," LaChaise said.

Martin's mouth jerked; he might have been trying to smile. "He figured you'd think that. But he thought it might be a trap and he figured, you know, you're the valuable one. You're the brains of the operation."

"Shoulda told me," LaChaise growled.

"You was drunk."

Sandy pushed herself up. Beneath the blanket, LaChaise noticed, she'd been wrapped in a parka. "What's going on?"

"Ansel went after the cop's kid," LaChaise said. He looked at her in the long coat, and said, "What's wrong with you? What's the parka for?"

"It's like a meat locker in here," she said, crossing her arms and shivering.

"Bullshit: she wants to be ready to run," Martin growled.

LaChaise turned to her: "You run, we'll cut your fuckin' throat. And if you *did* get away . . ." He dug in his shirt pocket, and came up with a stack of photographs. Two men sitting at a table, one black, one white. LaChaise riffled them at her like a deck of cards. "We got a cop on the string. The only way he gets out is if we get away, or we're all dead. If you get away from us, and go to the cops, he'll have to come after you, in case you know his name. Think about that: we've got a cop who'll kill you, and you don't know who it is." He put the photos back in his pocket.

Sandy shivered. "I'm not thinking about running," she said. "I'm just cold."

"Bullshit," Martin snorted.

"Whyn't you put some shoes on?" LaChaise said. "Let's go out."

"Go out?" she asked doubtfully. She looked toward a window: it was pitch black outside. Then she looked back at LaChaise. "Dick, you're hurt . . ."

"Hell, it ain't that bad. There's no bleeding. And I can't be cooped up in here," LaChaise said. Despite the headache, he was almost cheerful.

"I'd rather stay here."

"Don't be an asshole," he snapped. "Let's go out and see what's cookin'. One of you can drive, I'll sit in the back."

WHILE SANDY AND Martin got ready, LaChaise turned on the television, clicked around the channels and found nothing of interest but a weather forecast. The snow would diminish during the morning, and the sun might peek through in the afternoon. Big trouble was cranking up in the Southwest, but it was several days away.

"Cold," Martin grunted, coming back from his bedroom. He was wearing his camo parka.

"Better for us, since they plastered pictures of me and Butters all over hell," LaChaise said. "Less people on the street."

"Nothing must've happened with Ansel. They'd be going on all channels if he'd done something."

"Maybe backed off," LaChaise said. "Maybe nothin' there."

Martin looked at Sandy: "You ready?"

"I'm not sure about this," she said. "If somebody sees us . . ."

"We're just gonna ride around," LaChaise said. "Maybe go to a drive-through and get some Egg McMuffins or something."

"Gonna be light soon," Martin said.

BUTTERS GOT BACK to the house and saw the snow-free spot where Martin's truck had been parked, and the tracks leading away. Hadn't been gone for more than a couple of minutes, he thought: wonder what's going on? He parked Sandy's truck over the same spot and went inside. A note in the middle of the entry floor said, "Cabin fever. Gone an hour. We'll check back."

Butters shook his head: Cabin fever wasn't a good enough reason to go out. Of course, he'd been out. Still. LaChaise had once saved his life, LaChaise was as solid a friend as Butters had ever known . . . but nobody had ever claimed that he was a genius.

WHEN LUCAS ARRIVED at the parking lot off University and Lexington, the St. Paul cops were putting together the entry team under a lieutenant named Allport. Four plainclothes Minneapolis cops, all from homicide or vice, were standing around the lot, watching the St. Paul guys getting set.

Allport spotted Lucas and walked over to shake hands: "How're you doing?"

"Anything we can do to help?"

Allport shook his head. "We got it under control." He paused. "A couple of your guys were pretty itchy to go in with us."

"I'll keep them clear," Lucas said. "Maybe we could sit out on the perimeter."

Allport nodded: "Sure. We're a little thin on the ground 'cause we're moving fast. We want to get going before we have too many people on the street." He looked up into the sky, which seemed as dark as ever with snow clouds. But dawn was coming: you couldn't see it on the horizon, but there was more light around. "Why don't you take your guys up on the east side, up on Grotto. You'll be a block off the house, you can get down quick if something happens."

"You got it," Lucas said. "Thanks for letting us in."

"So let's go," Allport said.

Lucas rounded up the Minneapolis cops: "There'll be two squads on Grotto, which is a little thin. We'll want to spread out along the street. St. Paul will bring us in as soon as the entry team pops the place."

A Sex cop named Lewiston said, "St. Paul don't have a lot of guys out here."

"There's a time problem," Lucas said. "They want to get going before they have too many civilians on the street."

Lewiston nodded, accepting the logic, but Stadic said, "I wish we were doing the entry. These fuckin' shitkickers . . ."

Lucas grinned and said, "Hey." Then: "We don't even know if it's anything. Could be bullshit."

The entry team left, followed by the other cops in squads and their personal cars, a morose procession down through the narrow streets of Frogtown, staying two blocks from the target, walking in the last block.

STADIC HUNG BACK as they walked, his shotgun under his arm. He'd been caught up in the rush around the office, when word got back that Davenport's source might have something. Now he was worried: if they got tight on the house, they just might pull some people out of it alive . . .

Davenport pushed on ahead, walking fast with two other Minneapolis cops. This was his first chance, and probably his last: Stadic stepped behind a dying elm, took his cellular from his pocket and pushed the speed-dial button.

"Yeah?" LaChaise answered in two seconds, as though he'd been holding the phone.

"Get out of there," Stadic rasped. "There's a St. Paul entry team coming in right now. Go out the back, go east, they're thin up there. Get out."

After a second of silence, LaChaise said, "We ain't there."

"What?"

"We're in the truck. Where're you at?"

"Old house in St. Paul, north of the freeway a few blocks . . . If that's your place, you stay away. I can't talk, I gotta go."

He heard LaChaise say "Shit" and then Stadic turned the phone off and hurried to catch the others.

BUTTERS HAD WALKED up the stairs toward the bathroom when he glanced out a back window and saw the man dart through the streetlight a block over. The motion was quick, but heavy. Not a jogger, a soldier. He knew instantly that the cops were at the door.

He was still wearing his camo parka. He ran light-footedly down the stairs to the hall, where Martin had stacked the weapons in an open hall closet, out of sight but easy to get to. Butters grabbed the AR-15, already loaded, and four loaded magazines. He jammed the mags in his pocket and jacked a shell into the chamber and kept going, right to the back door.

The rear of the house was still dark, and he listened for a moment. He couldn't hear anything, but the door was the place they'd come. He turned back, crossed the house to the darker side away from the back door, went into Martin's bedroom, and tried a window. Jammed. He went to the next, turning the twist lock, lifting it. There was a vague tearing sound as old paint ripped away; the smell of it tickled his nose, but he had been quiet enough, he thought. The old-fashioned storm windows opened behind some kind of withered, leafless bush. He looked out, saw nobody, pushed open the storm window and peeked. Still nothing, too dark. He took a breath and snaked over the windowsill into the snow behind the hedge.

The snow crunched beneath his weight where dripping water from the eaves had stippled the surface with ice. He lay still for a moment, listening. Listening was critical in the dark: he'd spent weeks in tree stands, turning his head to the tweaks and rustles of the early morning, the deer moving back to bedding areas, the foxes and coyotes hunting voles, the wood ducks crunching through dried-out oak leaves, the trees defrosting themselves in the early sun, the grass springing up in the morning. Ansel Butters had heard corn grow; and now he heard footsteps in the snow, coming from the back, and then more, from the front.

Butters went down the side of the house, listening to the crunch of feet coming in: they wouldn't hear him, he decided. They were making too much noise on their own, city people in the snow, carrying heavy weapons. He went left, to the house next door, pressed himself against its weathered siding. Trying to see, trying to hear . . .

And here they came, through the backyard, three or four of them, he thought. Staying low, he moved to the corner of the house, then around it, to the east. He really had no choice about which way to go . . .

The loudspeaker came like a thunderbolt:

"Halt. By the house, freeze . . ."

And he thought, *Night scope.* Before the last words were out, he fixed on the position of the men coming up from the back.

He could sense the motion.

Butters ran sideways and fired a long, ripping burst across the group, thirty rounds pounding downrange, his face flashing in the muzzle flash like a wagon spoke in a strobe light.

The return fire was short of him, of where he had been. Moving all the time, he punched out the magazine and slammed in another, looking for muzzle flashes, squirting quick three- and four-shot bursts at them, more to suppress than to hit.

And still the return fire was short . . .

Then he was behind a garage; he sensed something in front of him and slowed just in time. He touched and then vaulted a four-foot chain-link fence, crossed a yard, went over the next fence, pushed through a hedge, scratching his face, took another fence, then another, heard garbage cans crashing behind him, screams, another burst of gunfire which went somewhere else, more screams.

He could hear himself breathing, gasping for air, trying to remember about how many shells would be left; he thought maybe six or eight, plus the third magazine in his pocket.

He felt good, he was moving, operating, he was on top of it.

Heading east.

THE LOUDSPEAKER AND the gunfire took them by surprise, Lucas and the other cops standing behind cars, talking quietly among themselves. They stiffened, turned, guns coming out, men crouching behind cars. Then radios began talking up and down the block, and Lucas, running to a St. Paul squad, said, "What? What?"

"Shit, one of them's out, he's maybe coming this way," a patrol sergeant said.

Lucas ran back toward his own people, touched them, "Watch it, watch it, he could be coming . . ."

Butters ran hard as he could, made it to the end of the block, passed between two houses, and in the dark space between them, ran almost headlong into a small tree. The blow knocked him down, but he held on to the rifle. Blood trickled into his mouth, and the sting told him that he'd cut his lip, probably badly. He crawled toward the street, gathered himself.

Across the way, he could hear people talking; more gathered behind him. He had no choice. He slapped the magazine once to make sure it was seated, and ran out into the street.

There: a cop—someone—dead ahead, behind a squad car, not much to see, turning toward him, crouching, hand coming up . . .

Butters, still running, fired a burst at the cop behind the car, saw him go down.

Another cop opened up from his right, then a third, and then he was hit: a stinging blow, as if somebody had struck his bare butt with a hickory switch. He knew what it was, and even as he returned the fire he passed through the line of cars, and cops were firing into each other as they tried to get him, men spilling themselves into the snow to get away from the bullets, others scream-ing . . .

And Butters ran.

A house, straight ahead, with lights on. And there was some pain now, more than an ache, more like a fire, in his thigh. He ran up four steps of the porch of the lighted house, to a stone-faced entry and an almost full-length glass pane in the front door. He fired a short burst at the glass, blew it out, and went through the door.

A man in pajamas stood at the bottom of a stairway; a woman stood at the top, looking down.

Butters pointed the gun at the woman and screamed at her: "Get down here."

And a kid yelled, "What? What's going on? Mom?"

LUCAS SAW HIM coming, down to the right. He fired twice, thought he might have hit him once, but the man was very fast, and ran in an odd, broken, jerky two-step that made him hard to track, especially with the bad light. The man fired a burst and Lucas felt a hard, scratching rip at his hairline, not hard, like a slug, but ripping, like a frag. Then Butters went through the line of cops and Lucas could see muzzle flashes coming at him and he dropped, screaming, "Hold it, Jesus . . ."

And when the firing stopped, he lurched up on his elbows in time to see Butters sprint up the porch steps, and the muzzle flash from the gun as he went through the glass door . . .

"Around back, somebody around back," Lucas shouted.

Two St. Paul cops, frozen by the fire, broke toward the side of a nearby house, heading toward the back, and Lucas and another Minneapolis cop—Lewiston—moved in toward the porch.

"Take him?" Lewiston asked.

"Get in tight," Lucas said. "Let's . . ."

"You're hit," Lewiston said. "There's blood running out of your head."

"Just cut myself, I think," Lucas said. "You go right . . ."

BUTTERS POINTED THE AR-15 at the woman on the stairs and screamed, "Get down here."

And then the kid called, "Mom?"

The woman shouted, "Jim, go back in your room. Jimmy . . ."

Butters couldn't think. His leg was on fire, and the man in the pajamas was frozen, the woman was yelling at the kid: a car rolled by outside and he turned, looked that way, couldn't see anything. The woman was shouting at the kid and Butters yelled at her, "Get your ass down here, goddamnit, or I'll fuck your old man up . . ."

He pointed the gun at the pajama man and the woman came down the stairs, red-faced, terrified, watching his eyes. She wore a flannel nightgown, and something about it, the nightgown, the man's pajamas . . .

Then the kid came to the head of the stairs. He was wearing a T-shirt and Jockey shorts, skinny bare legs, and he looked frightened and his hair stood up where his head had been on a pillow.

And Butters remembered: the winter the cops came, and they got his mother and his old man out of bed, and Butters had come to the stairs in his shorts, just like this . . . He remembered the fear, and the guns the cops wore on their hips, and the way his old man seemed to crawl to them, because of the guns, and his mother's fear . . . They stank of it. He stank of it.

And all of this was exactly the same, but he had the gun.

"Don't hurt us," the woman said.

"Fuck this," Butters said.

He popped the magazine from the rifle, slapped in the third full one, checked to make sure that the half-empty one was ready, easy to reach in his pocket.

"You go back to bed, kid," he said.

He ran straight out the door, across the porch, at the two cop cars that were parked up the street to the right. There were two men close by, one left, one right, and the one to the right looked familiar and he decided to take that one.

He turned toward Lucas and raised the rifle, and saw Lucas's gun hand coming up but knew that he was a quarter-inch ahead . . .

STADIC WAS COMING up the middle, but was still thirty yards out, when Butters came through the door. Davenport and Lewiston were too close to the porch, and below it, to see Butters as he came through, but Stadic, back in the dark, had just enough time to set his feet and lift the shotgun.

Butters turned toward Davenport, the gun coming up. Davenport reacted in a fraction of a second, and maybe an entire lifetime, behind Butters. The shotgun reached out, a cylinder of flame, reached almost to Butters's face, it seemed.

And blew it off.

Butters went down like an empty sack.

THE COPS ALL around froze, like a stuck videotape. After one second, they started moving again. Radios scratching the background. Everything, Stadic thought, moving in slow motion. Moving toward Butters, Davenport looking at him . . .

"Man," Davenport said. "He had me. You saved my ass."

And Davenport clapped him on the shoulder. Back in the furthest recess of his numbed mind, Stadic thought: *That's two.*

LUCAS CLAPPED THE wide-eyed Stadic on the shoulder and then ran down the block toward the car where a cop had been hit. Lucas had seen him go down in the flash of fire from Butters, a fact stored in the back of his head until he could do something about it.

At that moment, a helicopter swept overhead, pivoted around in a tight circle, and they were bathed in light. A cameraman was sitting in the open door, filming the scene in the street.

Two St. Paul cops reached the downed man just as Lucas did. Lucas knelt: the man had been hit in the head, and the top of his skull was misshapen. There was blood out of his nose and ears, and his eyes were dilated, but still moving.

"Gotta take him, can't wait for an ambulance," Lucas shouted at one of the St. Paul cops. "Get him in the car . . ."

Together they picked up the wounded man and put him in the backseat of a squad; one of the St. Paul cops got in the back with the wounded man, and the driver took off, the back doors flapping like big ears as he turned the corner, followed by the lights from the chopper.

"Jesus Christ, get the fuckin' chopper out of here," Lucas yelled at another of the St. Paul cops, a sergeant. "Get them out of here."

The sergeant was leaning against the hood of a squad, and he suddenly turned, head down, and vomited into the street. Lucas started away, thinking now: the house. More people coming in? What happened down there?

Then the sergeant said, "We just never had a chance to say anything . . ."

"Yeah, yeah . . ." And he ran back down the street to the body of the shooter. Butters's face had been obliterated by the shotgun. He was gone.

All right—the house.

He stood, and stepped that way, and saw more running figures, cops, coming in. Another St. Paul lieutenant, a patrol officer, one he didn't recognize.

"What happened . . . ?"

"Got him, and we got one of your men shot. He's bad, he's on his way in."

"Jesus Christ."

"What happened at the house?"

"Jesus Christ, who got hit?" The lieutenant looked around crazily. "Who's hurt?"

"The house, the house," Lucas said. "What happened?"

"Empty. Nobody there. Guns," the lieutenant said.

"Shit."

The lieutenant ran down to the patrol sergeant, who'd stopped vomiting, and was standing shakily against the hood of the squad. "Who was it, Bill, who was it?"

LUCAS LOOKED DOWN at Butters. Gone.

He squatted, felt under Butters's butt. The dead man kept his wallet on the left. Lucas lifted it out, opened it, started riffling through the paper: a Tennessee driver's license, current. The picture was right.

Stadic came around the car, his eyes wide, staring at the dead man. "I hope I just, I hope I just . . ."

"You did perfect," Lucas said. Lewiston came up, and Lucas said, "You okay?"

"Fine. Freaked out."

"Why don't you run Andy into Ramsey?" Lucas suggested.

"I'm okay," Stadic said.

"You're tuning out," Lucas said. "You need to go sit somewhere, get your blood pressure down."

Stadic looked at him, a flat, confused stare, and then suddenly he nodded: "Yeah. Okay. Let's do it."

He used a sharp command voice, out of place, out of time. Lucas looked at the other cop: "Take him." And, as they walked away, "Hey: Thanks again."

LUCAS WENT BACK to the wallet, looking for anything: a scrap of paper with an address, a note, a name, but Butters carried almost nothing: a Mobil credit card, a Sears card, a Tennessee hunting license, the driver's license, an old black-and-white picture of a woman, wearing a dress from the '40s, and a more recent, color photograph of a Labrador retriever. Not much to work with.

The lieutenant ran up, said, "Dispatch is calling the FAA, they'll try to get these assholes out of here." They both looked up at the chopper, and then the lieutenant said, looking at Butters's body, "You know how lucky we are?"

"What?" Lucas looked up. His scalp had begun to hurt, as though somebody had pressed a hot wire against it.

"He was in that house," the lieutenant said, and Lucas turned to look.

A man, a woman and a kid were looking out through the shattered door, past a patrol cop who'd run up to see that everybody was okay. The woman kept pushing the kid back, but the kid wanted to see. "If he'd holed up in there, there wouldn't have been a goddamn thing we could do. We could've had some kind of nightmare out here."

"Yeah . . ." And Lucas suddenly laughed, all the tension of the last ten minutes slipping away. "But look what he did to your cars."

The lieutenant looked at the car, which showed a ragged line of holes starting in the front fender and running all the way to the back bumper. A couple of slugs had grooved the roof, the windows were gone. The lieutenant did a little

Stan Laurel walk down the length of the car and said, "They hurt m' auto-mobile, Ollie."

"I guess. He didn't miss a single piece of sheet metal," Lucas said.

"Sure, it's a little rough," the lieutenant said, switching to a car salesman's voice. "But look at the tires: the tires are in A-1 condition."

They both laughed, shaking their heads. They laughed from relief, the lifting of the fear, the safety of the other cops and the people in the house.

Another chopper, TV3 this time, arriving late, swept over the house with its lights and beating blades and caught them standing over the body of Ansel Butters, looking at the car, laughing, unable to stop.

12

THE DAWN CAME like a sheet of dull steel pushed over the eastern horizon, cold, sullen and stupid. Fifteen cop cars blocked off the neigh-borhood, and yellow crime-scene tape wrapped the trail along which Butters had fled. A half-dozen cops were walking the route, looking for anything he might have thrown from his pockets—a piece of paper, a receipt, anything.

Tennessee cops had been to Butters's broken-down acreage since the night before, when his prints had been nailed down. They'd discovered what looked like a fresh grave in a decrepit apple orchard, opened it and found a Labrador retriever, shot once in the head.

"Old dog, had bones sticking out of his back, all gray on his muzzle," a Tennessee state cop told Lucas. "Probably shot him a couple of weeks ago. It's been cold enough that the body's still intact."

Lucas, standing in the street next to the shot-up cop car, was impatient with the dog information: "We need anything in the house that might point to as-sociates," Lucas said. "Any piece of paper, phone records, anything."

"We're tearing the place apart," the Tennessee cop said. "But when we saw the grave, we thought we had to do something about it."

"Screw the grave, we gotta find out where he's been and who he was hanging out with . . ."

"We're watching you on TV, we know you got a problem," the Tennessee cop said dryly. "We're turning over everything."

LUCAS RECOGNIZED THE truck the moment he saw it: the truck that had slowed through the intersection. He couldn't be absolutely sure, but he was sure enough. Butters had been on his way in to Small's house. Whoever had called him had known, had saved Sarah's life, and probably Jennifer's and Small's and the boy's . . .

"Belongs to Elmore Darling," the St. Paul cops told him when he walked up. "Wisconsin cops are on the way out to his house."

"Goddamnit," Lucas said. The woman had suckered them. They'd had her, they'd let her go, and here was her truck.

The truck produced gas charge slips, maps, empty soda cans, and dozens of prints. The guns at the house had produced nothing but fragments of prints: they'd all been carefully polished with cleaning rags. There were a few good prints on a hunting bow, and more on some hunting arrows. The prints were on the way to the FBI.

St. Paul crime-scene guys had shrouded the truck's license plate from cameras, and asked the local media not to mention it, but the word was going to leak, and probably soon. If the Dunn County cops got to the Darlings' place soon enough, they might surprise them, and anyone staying with them. Lucas had to smother an impulse to run over to Wisconsin, to be in on the raid. The Wisconsin cops would do well enough without him.

As Lucas ran through the bits and pieces of paper coming out of the van, all carefully cased in Ziploc bags, Del wandered up.

"How's Cheryl?" Lucas asked.

"Hurtin'. They were giving her another sedative when I left. Christ, I heard about this, I couldn't believe it."

"It was interesting," Lucas said.

"What happened to your head?"

"Cut, somehow. Nothing much."

"You're bleeding like a stuck pig."

"Nah . . ." He wiped at his hair, and got fresh blood on the palm of his hand.

"Did you hear about the St. Paul cop that got shot? Waxman?" Del asked.

Lucas was trying to find a place to wipe the blood, stopped, and asked, "I didn't know his name . . . What?"

"Just came on the radio: he died."

"Ah, shit." Lucas looked down the street. Everywhere, the St. Paul cops were clustering. The word was getting out.

"Radio says they never got him to the table," Del said. "He was barely alive when he went in the door. They say he was gone thirty seconds later."

ROUX CAME THROUGH with the St. Paul chief and found Lucas and Del eating cinnamon mini-doughnuts at the house. The guns from the closet had been carefully laid out on the living-room floor, waiting for a ride downtown.

"Jesus," Roux said to Lucas, shocked. "You were hit . . ."

"Naw, just cut." He pawed gently at his scalp. The cut was beginning to itch, and when he touched it, a burning sensation shot through his scalp, and he winced. "The bleeding's stopped . . ." He took his hand away and looked at it; blood dappled his fingertips.

"Lucas," she said, "I'm telling you, not asking you. Go get it fixed."

"Yeah . . ."

"Now," she said. Then, looking at the guns: "They brought an arsenal with them. We lucked out."

"Look, you gotta talk to the patrol people," Lucas said. "LaChaise is on the street, now. He'll be looking for a friend—old bikers, dopers, somebody like Dexter Lamb. In fact, we ought to stake out the Lamb place, they could turn up there." .

"Yeah, yeah . . ."

"And you gotta get the patrol guys pushing the street people. Put some more money out there. The money worked. If we start running the assholes around, and there's some money in it, we'll find them."

Roux said, "*We'll* do that. *You* get your head fixed."

DEL DROVE LUCAS a few blocks to Ramsey Medical Center, where a doctor anesthetized, cleaned and stitched the scalp wound.

"Souvenir," the doctor said.

She handed Lucas a scrap of silver metal, like a fragment of Christmas-tree tinsel, but stiff—maybe a scrap of car aerial.

"How many stitches?" Lucas asked.

"Twelve or thirteen, I imagine," she said, sewing carefully.

Del was reading a two-year-old copy of *Golf Digest*, looking up every once in a while to see how it was going. When she finished, the doctor said "Okay," and tidied gauze and disinfectant-soaked cotton away into a steel basket, and then paused and asked, "Why were you laughing after you killed that man?"

"What?" Lucas didn't understand the question. Del dropped the top of the magazine and stared at the doctor.

"I saw it on television," she said. "You were standing there laughing, right over his body."

"I don't think so," Lucas said, trying to remember.

"I *saw* it," she snapped. "I thought it was pretty . . . distasteful, considering what just happened. So'd the anchorpeople: they said it was shocking."

"I don't know." Lucas shook his head, reached toward his scalp, which now felt dead, then dropped his hand. "I mean, I believe you—but I can't remember laughing about anything. Christ, we just finished carrying a shot cop down to a car."

"The cop died," Del said, putting the magazine down.

"And I didn't kill anyone," Lucas said. He hopped off the exam table where he'd been sitting, and loomed over the doctor.

"That's not what they're saying on television," the doctor said, giving no ground. She glanced at Del, pulled off her latex gloves with a *snap!*.

"Don't believe everything you see in the movies," Lucas said.

"This wasn't the movies—it was videotape, and I saw it," she insisted.

"The only difference between TV news and the movies," Del said, "is that movies don't lie about what they are."

"Oh, bullshit," the doctor said.

"If you operated on a cancer patient, and the patient died, and when you came out of the operating room, you saw a friend and smiled at him . . . if somebody took a picture of you, would that represent the way you felt about the patient dying?"

She studied him for a minute, then said, "No."

"I hope not," Lucas said. "I don't remember laughing. Maybe I did. But that doesn't have anything to do with what happened."

ON THE WAY out, Del said, wonderingly, "Are we in trouble or something?"

"I don't know," Lucas said. They tracked through the endless hallways to the back, where they'd ditched the car away from the reporters in the lobby. "More and more, with TV, it's like we fell down the fuckin' rabbit hole."

ANDERSON CALLED: HE'D been tracking the various investigations. "The Dunn County cops hit the Darling place. They found the husband . . . uh, Elmore Darling . . . was shot to death in the kitchen. His wife is missing. His truck is up there, so she's down here, somewhere, if she's still alive."

Lucas shook his head: "Huh. Family feud?"

"Hard to tell what's going on," Sloan said. "They got a charge slip from yesterday—from last night—at an Amoco station off I-94 over in St. Paul, so he was over there, probably at that house. And then he gets shot up there. There's no doubt he was shot in place, there's splatter all over the kitchen. Short range with a shotgun."

Lucas repeated the story to Del, who scratched his chin: "That don't compute."

Lucas said into the phone, "They're printing everything, right?"

"I guess. They've got their crime-scene guy up there."

"Be nice to know who all was in that house," Lucas said. "If Sandy Darling was there with the rest of them."

"I'll push them on it," Anderson said.

LACHAISE, MARTIN AND Sandy had been heading back to the house with a bag of supermarket doughnuts and two quarts of milk, when Stadic had called and told them to get out.

"Shit." LaChaise was stunned. "They got us, they got the house."

"Maybe something happened with Ansel," Martin said slowly. "Maybe they spotted him scoutin' out the Davenport house, and followed him back."

He pulled the truck to the curb, reached out and poked the "power" button on the radio, got old-time rock 'n' roll, and started working down the buttons.

Sandy looked from one of them to the other: "Now what?"

"I'm trying to think," LaChaise said.

"Let me go back home," Sandy said.

"Fuck that," Martin said. To LaChaise: "We gotta get out of sight."

"How about the trailer? We could probably lay low in the trailer for a while."

"If they've got Elmore's truck, they'll bag Elmore for sure, and he'll tell them about the trailer," Martin said. "If they put any pressure on him, he'll talk his ass off."

He was still playing with the car buttons, and finally switched over to AM. They found a news station almost instantly, but no news—nothing but blather.

"Let's get turned around, and get out of here," LaChaise said finally. "If Stadic's right, we're too close."

"If he's right, we ought to hear something on the radio," Martin said.

But he swung the truck around, and they headed west toward Minneapolis. At that moment, a helicopter roared overhead, cutting diagonally across the city blocks, headed for Frogtown.

"Goddamnit," Martin said. "They're doing it."

LaChaise punched the radio buttons again, still found nothing. "Let's get over to Minneapolis. We can figure it out there."

"Maybe it wasn't Butters led them in—maybe it was Elmore," Martin said. "Maybe Butters is still out there."

LaChaise seized on the idea: "That's gotta be it." To Sandy: "You were talking about it last night, weren't you? Bailing out on us."

"No, we weren't," she lied.

"Don't give me that shit," he muttered; he poked spasmodically at the radio, and tripped over the news station again. This time, they were on the air locally:

". . . police are flooding the east side neighborhood around Dale on the possibility that one or more members of the gang escaped the house at the same time as Butters. Residents are asked to report unusual foot traffic through their streets, but not to approach anyone they may see. These men are armed and obviously dangerous . . ."

"C'mon," LaChaise said impatiently, "what happened?"

"They got Butters," Sandy said. "If they know he was one guy coming out of the house, they got him."

"Yeah, but is he dead or alive?"

". . . we've just gotten word from our reporter Tim Mead at Ramsey Medical Center that the St. Paul police officer wounded in the shoot-out has died. We still have no identification, and authorities say the officer won't be identified until next of kin can be found and notified, but our reporter at Ramsey says the officer definitely *has died. With Butters's death, that brings to two the number of people killed in this latest clash between Twin Cities police officers and the LaChaise gang . . ."*

LaChaise groaned: "Oh, goddamn, they killed Ansel. The sonsofbitches killed Ansel."

Martin: "We gotta get under cover. If they got the house, they'll get my prints. If they get my prints, sooner or later they'll get this truck. We don't have much time."

The highway was slippery with the snow, and LaChaise finally told Martin to get off and find someplace to park. "We gotta talk this out. We're in big fuckin' trouble. We lost our gear."

"You got your 'dog, I got my forty-five and the knife."

"We lost the heavy stuff," LaChaise said. He patted his pocket and said, "But I still got Harp's money."

"Dick, you gotta give this up and run for it," Sandy said. "Drop me off, I'll call the cops. I'll tell them I was kidnapped and you let me go. I'll tell them you're headed for Alaska or the Yukon, you can head for Mexico."

"Aw, that ain't gonna work," LaChaise said.

"The whole thing lasted one day, Dick," Sandy said, pressing him. "Now you're on the road, no guns, no transportation, no place to run to."

"But we do have some money," Martin said. "That can get us some guns. And I just thought where we might get a car and a place to hide."

MARTIN TOOK THEM into South Minneapolis, to Harp's laundromat. The laundromat was empty: it was too early and too cold to think about washing laundry. They parked the truck in front of the garage doors, Martin got a claw hammer out of his toolbox, and all three of them walked around to the front. The door that led up the stairs was locked. Martin, with LaChaise blocking, popped the door with the hammer. The lock was old, and not meant to stop much. When Martin pushed the door shut, it caught again.

"Locks are different at the top," Martin said quietly. "Best you can buy. And it's a steel door. But if we can get him to open it, just a crack, there's nothing but a shitty little safety chain after that."

Martin led the way up the stairs. He'd told LaChaise about the pile of cardboard boxes at the top of the stairs. They moved and restacked them until they had a narrow passage to the door.

"Ready?" Martin had his .45 in his hand, and LaChaise drew his Bulldog.

"Try it," LaChaise said.

Martin banged on the door, then tried the doorbell next to it. And then banged some more.

"Open up, Harp," he shouted. "Minneapolis police, open up."

Silence.

Martin tried again. "Goddamnit, open the fuckin' door, Minneapolis police."

They could hear themselves breathing, but felt no vibration, no footfall, no bump or knock that might suggest somebody was home.

"He should be here, this time of day," Martin said.

"Maybe he can't hear us."

"He could hear us . . ." Martin put his ear to the door and stood that way, one hand up to silence LaChaise, for a full minute. Then he looked at LaChaise: "Shit, he's not here."

"We gotta get off the street," LaChaise said.

"I know, I know." Martin looked at the door, shook his head. "No way we're going through that. And the garage door will be locked. We could try pulling the fire escape down."

"The whole city would see us climbing up there," LaChaise said. Then: "Run downstairs and see if there's anybody in the laundromat."

Martin nodded, trotted down the stairs, fought the jammed door for a moment, then disappeared outside. A second later he was back. He shoved the door shut and called up, "Nobody."

LaChaise crushed one of the boxes, pushed others in front of the door, until he had a clear patch of wall.

"What're you doing?" Martin asked, hustling up the stairs.

"This," LaChaise said. He hit the wall with the claw side of the hammer. A square foot of old plaster cracked and sprayed out, showing the laths beneath.

"Jesus, sounds like dynamite," Martin said, looking back down the stairs.

"Nobody to hear us," LaChaise said. "And Harp don't come up this way, so he won't see it." He hit the wall again, a third time and a fourth. "Why don't you go down to the bottom and keep an eye out. This could take a few minutes."

LACHAISE BROKE A six-inch hole through the wall, alternately beating it with the head of the hammer, smashing it, then digging the hole out with the claw. When the hole was big enough, he reached through and popped the locks on the door. They pushed inside, and found an empty apartment.

"Nobody around," Martin said, after a quick reconnaissance. "But his car's downstairs. The Continental. Maybe he ran out to the store."

"Give us some breathing space," LaChaise said. "We gotta be ready, though. Shouldn't cook nothin' until we got him."

Sandy had followed Martin through the apartment. The place had once been four tiny apartments, she thought, remodeled into one big one. A hallway divided the new unified apartment exactly in half—that would have been the old main entry hall.

The place *felt* empty. More than that. Vacated. She looked in the refrigerator: it was nearly bare. She stepped back down the hallway and looked into the master bedroom—she'd peeked in when they first entered, but this time, she pushed in and looked around. A small leather suitcase was lying empty at the end of the bed. The apartment was cold, she noticed. She went back to the living room and checked the thermostat. It was set at fifty-five.

She said, "I think they went on a trip."

"Huh?" LaChaise looked at her. "Why?"

"Well, there're holes in the closet where they took a whole bunch of clothes out at the same time. And there's a suitcase sitting on the floor like they decided to take a different one, but didn't put the first one back. And the thermostat's set at fifty-five, like you'd turn it down before you went somewhere."

"Huh," said Martin, nodding. "It *feels* like they left."

Martin noticed the two telephone answering machines, sitting side by side. "He's got two answering machines," he said. "I wonder if he left a message."

He picked up one phone, and dialed the number posted on the other: the phone rang twice, then a man's voice said, "Leave a message." Nothing there. He hung up, picked up the second phone and dialed the first. And Harp's voice said, "We're outa here. Back on the twenty-sixth or so. I'll check the messages every day."

"He's gone," Martin said to LaChaise. "He says they're gone until the twenty-sixth."

LaChaise made him redial, listened to the message, then looked at Martin with a broad grin. "Goddamn. We landed on our feet," he said, when he'd hung up. He looked around the apartment: "This place is six times better than the other one. This is great. And we got a Continental. A fuckin' luxury car . . ." He started to laugh, and whacked Martin on the back. Even Martin managed to crack a smile.

ROUX AND THE mayor met Lucas in Roux's office, and heard about the laughing incident.

"I didn't believe it was me, until I saw the tape," Lucas said. "I don't know why we were laughing. We just about had a goddamned disaster on our hands, and instead, it was all done with. I guess that's why." The explanation sounded lame.

"The St. Paul cop getting killed—that's not a disaster?" the mayor asked.

"We didn't know the cop was dead. And we thought we were going to get a whole goddamned family shot up. When Butters ran in there, when he blew through that door, I thought we were out of luck."

"The TV people are wondering why there weren't enough people out there in the first place. Enough to take him as soon as he showed," the mayor said.

"Normally, it would have been plenty. Except that he saw us coming and he had a machine gun. And he didn't care if he died. All that—that changes everything. We're lucky only one guy got killed; it could have been three or four. If he'd had some combat experience, he might've waited until the entry team was halfway into the house, and then took them on at close range."

"Anyway, that's all St. Paul's problem," Roux said. "And as far as Lucas is concerned, the laughing thing, I think I can clear it out."

The mayor's eyebrows went up. "How?"

Roux said, "You know Richard Small—TV3? He was on the stakeout last night. He wouldn't leave, and Lucas let him keep his shotgun. I talked to him this morning and he figures Lucas and Del are his war buddies now. I'll call him about the laughing incident, and why they were doing it—out of relief, or hysteria, and how unfair this is, some horseshit like that. He just about runs TV3. If he goes on the air with another perspective, we can turn it around. And he'll do it. When I talked to him this morning, he was still jacking shells in and out of the shotgun."

The mayor looked from Lucas to Roux. "Do it," he said, nodding. "Emphasize the fairness thing, and how he'd be setting the record straight on his combat buddy."

And to Lucas: "You gotta keep your ass down and out of sight."

"I'm trying," Lucas said.

HOMICIDE HAD BEEN turned into a war plans room: file cabinets and desks pushed into corners, two tables shoved together with a six-foot plastic map of the Twin Cities spread across it. Sherrill was there, wearing her .357 in a belt clip.

"You okay?" Lucas asked.

"Yeah. We got the arrangements going on Mike. I'm all cried out."

"We got one of them," Lucas said.

"Not the one I want, not yet," Sherrill said, shaking her head. "We got Kupicek's guy. I want the third man, the one we don't know yet."

Anderson wandered in, spotted Lucas, and stepped over: "I got a lot of new paper, if you want it."

They talked about the paper for fifteen minutes, what the Tennessee cops were doing, the Wisconsin cops, about the death of Elmore Darling. "We've got more pictures of Sandra Darling, we'll put those out. But I don't know. I don't know if she's with this LaChaise, or we're gonna find her dead in a ditch somewhere."

"She's with him," Sherrill said.

"Why do you think that?" Lucas asked.

"I don't know. I just think she's with them. If they were going to kill them, why not kill both of them? I bet she's screwing LaChaise. Or maybe the second guy. I bet she helped set up the funeral home thing with the second guy . . ."

"Bonnie and Clyde," Lucas said.

"More like Dumber and Dumbest," said Sherrill.

LACHAISE, MARTIN AND Sandy Darling were riveted by the images on the television. The pictures came up from a winter street, with a woman in a long wool coat and fur hat talking into a microphone.

". . . rushed the wounded officer to the hospital, but he died seconds after arrival. As that was going on, Chief Davenport and Lieutenant Selle were seen laughing as they stood over the body of the attacker . . ."

Her voice rolled on over a videotape, taken from a high angle, a uniformed cop and a guy in street clothes, standing over what looked like a pile of clothes in the street. Had to be Butters. And the cops were laughing, no doubt about it.

". . . police were refusing to disclose the identity of the officer or officers who actually shot Butters, saying that information would be available after LaChaise and his gang members are caught, but nobody has denied that Deputy Chief Lucas Davenport took part in the gunfight and was himself wounded. At the moment, a police spokeswoman said, the threat to the officers' families will not allow full disclosure . . ."

"Look at the fuckers," LaChaise said.

Martin frowned as the tape of Davenport and Selle was run again. The picture seemed wrong. "They don't look too happy," he said.

"They're laughing," LaChaise shouted at him. "They're laughing."

LaChaise paced in front of the TV, snarling at it, beating his hands together, palms open, the angry claps snapping into the room. He went to the window shades, looked down at the street, listening, then stalked back to the television.

"That cop who was laughing. They said it was Davenport, right? The guy on our list?"

As if to answer his question, the television reporter said, "The chain of events started last night, when Chief Davenport put a surveillance team on the home of his daughter by TV3 correspondent Jennifer Carey, who now lives with TV3 executive vice-president Richard Small . . ."

She went through the story, ending with the tape loop of Davenport and Selle laughing over Butters's body.

"We're gonna mow those fuckers down," LaChaise brayed at Martin.

Martin said, "Dick, we gotta take care. We can't go off half-cocked, if we want to get anything done."

LaChaise stalked around the apartment, kicking walls, then looked at Sandy: "Why'n the fuck don't you do something useful? Go cook something."

She got up, wordlessly, and went to the kitchen and started looking through the cupboards. She found canned food, but not much else. She dumped a couple of cans of Dinty Moore beef stew in a pot, put it on the stove and started a pot of coffee.

"If we're gonna stay here for more than a couple of hours, we'll need food," Sandy said, as she brought the stew out to the living room. The men were on the couch, still watching the television. As they ate, a TV3 television reporter was delivering a eulogy on the dead cop. He was cut off in midsentence. An anchorman came up, quivering with the urgency of his message.

"In Wisconsin, Dunn County sheriff's deputies raided the home of Dick LaChaise's sister-in-law and her husband, Sandy and Elmore Darling. According to first reports, Elmore Darling was found shot to death in the kitchen of the couple's rural home, and his wife, Sandy, is missing."

A five-year-old snapshot of Sandy Darling filled the screen. Sandy screamed, "Elmore."

LaChaise grinned. "You put on a few pounds," he said, pointing at the picture.

She had her hands to her face: "They killed Elmore." She looked from Martin to LaChaise. "My God. They said Elmore's dead. They killed Elmore. Elmore's dead."

"Could be bullshit," Martin said, his voice even, almost uninterested. "They maybe got him in jail. Don't want anybody to know."

"I don't think so," LaChaise said. The TV anchor was going on, then Martin said, "Guess not."

"No, no . . ." Sandy said, riveted to the screen.

"You didn't much like him anyway," LaChaise said.

Tears started down her cheeks: "I didn't want him dead. He wasn't supposed to die."

LaChaise shrugged. "Shit happens."

Martin: "I wonder if the cops killed him?" His voice was flat, with no real emotion; he was only curious.

LaChaise thought for a minute, then said, "Must've. Who else would do it?"

He looked at Sandy, who backed away from the TV and collapsed in a chair. "Nobody was gonna kill Elmore," she said. And after a minute, "Who'd kill Elmore?"

STADIC WAS WALKING down the hall to his apartment, shell-shocked, his mind running at two hundred miles an hour. He was digging for his keys when the cell phone chirped at him. He pulled it out of his pocket. "Yeah."

LaChaise, without preamble, asked, "What happened to Butters? And Elmore?"

"Jesus Christ, where are you?" Stadic said, his voice hushed. "You know what's going on?"

"We're at a friend's," LaChaise said. "We seen it all on TV. Who killed Butters?"

"Davenport, of course. I told you . . ."

"We thought it might be him. What happened to Elmore?"

"I don't know about that. I thought you did it, when I heard."

"We didn't do it," LaChaise said. He pulled his lip. "Maybe the Wisconsin cops."

"Or the guys from Michigan," Stadic suggested. "There're a couple of Michigan guys running around over there. They are *very* pissed about this Sand guy, you cuttin' his throat."

"Yeah, well, that's what you get for working in the fuckin' joint," LaChaise said. "Try to find out who did it."

"Okay," Stadic said. "But listen—the wives up in the hotel . . . I hear they're getting antsy. They want out. Davenport's girlfriend is going back to the University of Minnesota hospital."

"What's her name? We never got any insurance on her."

" 'Cause they're not married and you didn't say what you wanted the information for. Her name is Weather Karkinnen and she's a doctor over there. In surgery."

"Who else? Who's leaving the hotel?"

"Jennifer Carey, the TV news reporter. She's the mother of Davenport's daughter . . . She's going back to work, but there'll be guards all over her and they've got locked security doors and stuff. She'd be hard to get at."

"All right. Find out about Elmore, if you can."

LaChaise hung up, pulled at his lip again, thinking. After a minute, Sandy said, "What?"

"Davenport killed Butters . . . and the women are gettin' unhappy about being locked up. They may be going back to work."

"Probably got guards all over the place," Martin said. "Tell you what: let's get Harp's car, and go on out to a supermarket and buy some food. Maybe dump the truck: hate to see it go, but I think we better."

Sandy was sitting in the chair, folding into herself, not hearing any of it.

Elmore was dead.

The guilt was almost too much to bear.

13

WEATHER KARKINNEN LAY on the hotel bed and fumed: the television had gone into a news loop. The anchorpeople leaned into the cameras with the usual end-of-the-world intensity, but had nothing new to say. Weather looked at her watch: two o'clock.

Lucas had said he'd drop by at noon, then called to cancel. He told her about the laughing incident, which she hadn't yet seen when he called, but saw later. The television stations were showing it every twenty minutes or so, and it had been picked up by the national news channels.

Lucas said the laughter had been hysterical, or on that order. She only half-believed it. She'd lived with him long enough to feel the satisfaction he got from confrontation, and the deadlier the confrontation, the better. A death wish, maybe; sometimes when he talked about his world, she could barely recognize it as the same place she lived. They would drive across town, and she'd see good houses and nice gardens and kids on bikes. He'd see whores and dopers and pedophiles and retired cat burglars.

At first, it had been interesting. Later, she wondered how he could put up with it, the constant stench of the perverse, the lunatic, the out-of-control. Even later, she understood that he sought it out . . .

She looked at her watch again: two-oh-three. Screw it. She wasn't going to sit around anymore. This LaChaise might be extraordinarily bad, but he could hardly have an intelligence system that would tell him where she was—if he even knew to look for her, which she doubted.

And even if he *did* know where to look for her, once she was in a crowd, she'd be just one of a million and a half women wrapped in heavy winter coats, faces obscured by scarves. Then nobody could find her—not the FBI, not the Minneapolis cops, nobody—much less some backwoods gunman.

"All right," she said. She looked at her watch a third time. She'd had to delay a surgery scheduled that morning, but there was a staff meeting at four, and she could make that. And she could set up for tomorrow. The operation in the morning wasn't much—remove some cancerous skin, and patch the wound with a graft—but it would get her going again.

She found her sweater, pulled it over her head, and was checking her purse for money when the knock came at the door. She opened it, and instantly recognized the blonde in the hall, and the small girl with her.

The blonde smiled: "Hi. I'm Jennifer Carey . . ."

"I know who you are," Weather said, smiling back. "Lucas has talked about you. Come in. And hi, Sarah." She and Sarah were old friends.

Jennifer was tall, lanky, a surfer girl with degrees in economics and journalism. She noticed Weather's sweater: "Breaking out?"

"Definitely. I can't stand it here anymore," Weather said. "I'm going crazy."

"I'll give you a ride, if you want one," Jennifer said. "Unless you've got a car."

"Lucas brought me in, I'd like a ride. I understand you're working outside."

"Yeah. Sloan's wife is here, she's taking care of Sarah for me. But there's no point in letting Lucas have all the fun, chasing around with his gun."

"Daddy shot a man," Sarah said solemnly, looking up at Weather.

Weather sat on the bed so her eyes were level with Sarah's. "I don't think so, honey. I talked to him a couple of hours ago, and he said another policeman did the shooting."

"On TV, they said he did," Sarah said. Her wide eyes were the same mild blue as Lucas's eyes.

Weather said, "Well, I think they might be wrong on this one thing."

Jennifer, moving moodily across the room, dropped into a desk chair: "I understand you and Lucas are getting married. Pretty soon."

"That's the plan," Weather said.

"Good luck," Jennifer said. She was looking out the window at the street. "I . . . well, we talked about it, years ago. It wouldn't have worked, though.

I hope it works with you guys. He's a good guy under the macho bullshit, and I would like to see him happy."

"That's interesting," Weather said. "Do you think that might be a problem? Happiness?"

Jennifer shook her head and turned back to Weather: "He has a very dark streak, a Catholic dark streak. And his job . . . I don't know how he stands it. I know what he does, because I've covered it, but I've got some distance. I mean, I see burned-out newspeople all the time, and they are several steps back from what Lucas does."

Weather nodded, and drifted toward the window herself. The sky and the day had the cold midwinter pre-storm look, a brooding somberness. "I know what you're saying—I was just lying here thinking about it," she said. "I can feel it in him. I can feel it in Del, too, almost as bad. I can feel it in Sloan, but with Sloan, it's mostly a job. With Lucas it's like . . . his existence."

"That's the Catholic thing," Jennifer said. "It can be frightening. It's like, when he confronts a monster, he solves the problem by becoming a bigger monster . . . and after he wins, he changes back to Lucas the good guy." Then she blushed: "God, I shouldn't be talking this way to a guy's fiancée. I'm sorry."

"No, no, no," Weather said. "I need it. I'm still trying to figure out what I'm getting into here." She looked at Sarah: "I would like a child before it's too late . . . just like this one."

Sarah said, "I'm gonna be a TV reporter."

Jennifer said, "Over my dead body. You should be a surgeon, like Dr. Karkinnen."

"Did you cover the robbery at the credit union, where the women were killed?" Weather asked Jennifer.

"I didn't cover it, but I talked to all the people who did. I do mostly longer-term stories. We're working on a story now about police intelligence units."

"What do you think? Some people have said it was an execution."

"No, it wasn't. I'll buy the argument that nobody made them do it. But you know Lucas. He has a tendency to arrange things so they come out his way." She stopped again: "Jeez, I really sound like . . . I don't know, like I'm trying to scrag the guy."

"That's okay—I know what you mean," Weather said. She picked up her coat, hat and mittens and smiled at Jennifer. "Ready to make the break?"

LUCAS WAS INFURIATED when he heard that Weather had left the hotel, and Jennifer had taken her out.

He tried to call the university, but was told Weather was in a meeting and couldn't be disturbed. He got Jennifer at TV3, shouted at her and she hung up. He called back, got her again, asked about Sarah.

"She's with Sloan's wife," Jennifer said. "She's fine. She's watching HBO and eating pizza."

"Listen, I want Weather back in that fuckin' hotel . . ."

"Hey, Lucas? You don't own her. If you call her with this attitude, you're gonna get the same answer from her as you're getting from me. Fuck you. Go away."

And she hung up.

LACHAISE SAID, "LISTEN: they're gonna get your prints out of the house. Then they'll have all three of our faces. We've got to move before that happens."

Martin said, "They won't have any new pictures of me . . . but maybe we should change what we look like."

"Like what?"

Martin shrugged. "I don't know—you got that beard, and they show it on the tube as long. Maybe if you trimmed it, and cut it, and dyed your hair gray. Hell, with gray hair, we'd both look older than the hills."

LaChaise looked back toward the master bedroom: Sandy was in there, making up the beds, singing to herself while she did it. Not a happy song. A song like she was losing it, a song to herself, a singsong.

"Sandy could do it," LaChaise said.

"I think it'd be a good move," Martin said. "We could get out and scout around."

"Then let's do it." LaChaise nodded. "I want to get going again. Find this Weather. And Davenport himself. And the cops. Let's go after the cops."

SANDY AGREED THAT she could change their hair color. She had a flatness about her that provoked LaChaise: "What's wrong with you?"

"When we got into this, Elmore said that in two or three days we'd all be dead. He wanted to go to the cops, and I talked him out of it."

Martin and LaChaise looked at each other, and then LaChaise said, "Why? Why'd you talk him out of it?"

"Because I thought I could still fix things. Get you out of here; pretend I didn't have anything to do with anything. Now they've got me on TV, and they'll have Martin pretty soon. Elmore was right: he's dead now and Butters is dead. Not even twenty-four hours yet. If Elmore was right, we've got another two days at the most. Then we'll all be dead."

She looked at LaChaise: "You want to be dead?"

Martin answered: "No big deal."

LaChaise said nothing at all for a moment, then poked a finger at her: "I don't want to hear this shit no more. You go on with Martin, and get the hair stuff."

"My picture . . ."

"You don't look like that picture—nobody'll know you," LaChaise said. "And we need the right stuff."

"I might want to make a couple of extra stops," Martin said. "They'll have my picture out there as soon as the prints come in. But if I get movin', I could tap a couple of friends for some decent weapons . . . guys I know from the shows. And we gotta dump the truck, sooner or later."

"We can do that tonight," LaChaise said. "Take the Continental, put the truck in the garage for now." He smacked his hands together. "Get a couple of ARs if you can . . ." LaChaise dug in his pocket for the money Butters had taken from Harp. "Couple thousand?"

"Better make it four," Martin said.

"Call me before you talk to anybody—I'll watch television for your face," LaChaise said. "And I might try Stadic again. See if he's heard anything."

THEY WENT TO a Snyder's drugstore, Martin sticking close to her. Sandy already knew she was going to run for it, given the smallest opening. But Martin knew it too, she thought. They went through the store, and got bleach and coloring. Martin poked through a large industrial first-aid kit, and finally took it off the shelf. "Gonna have to change Dick's bandage sooner or later," he said in a low voice.

Just short of the cash register line, he bumped into a rack of commercial trail food and twirled it: he'd always kept some of the stuff around. As he was looking at the varieties, Sandy noticed a telephone by the pharmacy desk.

"Got a quarter? I'll call Dick."

"Yeah," Martin said absently. He dug in his pocket, handed her a quarter. She went to the pay phone, dropped the quarter, punched the number in: LaChaise answered.

"Anything?" she asked.

"Not a thing; same old bullshit," he said. "I'm gonna take a nap."

She hung up and saw the note on the bottom of the machine: 911—No charge. She looked at Martin. He'd just stepped into the cash register line, and his back was to her. She picked up the phone again, bit her lip and punched in the number.

A woman answered immediately.

"Is this an emergency?"

"Yes, I need to talk to Detective Davenport."

"I'm sorry, but this . . ."

"Please, please, please, I've got to talk to him, or they'll kill me."

"Are you in immediate danger?"

"No. Yes . . . I don't know."

"Just a minute, please."

Lucas was taking a nap in his office, stretched out on a plastic air mattress. The mattress was uncomfortable and cold, but the office was dark and quiet and he dropped off, slept for an hour and a half. The phone woke him up.

"Lucas, we've got a call coming in on 911. The woman wants to speak to you, but she's not sure whether she's in danger. She's calling from a Snyder's down on the south side. We're not sending anyone yet."

"Okay," Lucas said sleepily. "Put her on."

"You want us to stay on the line?"

"Sure . . . unless I say something."

The phone clicked once, and the dispatcher said, "Go ahead, ma'am. Chief Davenport is on the line."

"Hello?" Lucas said.

"Is this Detective Davenport?" A woman's voice, tentative, vaguely familiar. He sat up. Could this be . . . ? "Yes, who's this?"

"This is Sandy Darling, I'm with Bill Martin and they're gonna kill me."

Jesus, Lucas thought. He prayed that the dispatcher was sending a squad. "If you stay where you are, you'll be safe . . ."

"No, no, Martin's right on top of me. I've got to talk to somebody, I've got to try to get away."

Her voice was a whispered croak: nothing fake about it.

"They're going after more guns," she continued. "They'll kill anybody who gets close to them. They've got a policeman working with them. One of you."

"What policeman?"

"Gotta go . . ."

"Just stay . . ."

"Can you get me a lawyer, let me talk to a lawyer? I haven't done anything, they just took me . . ."

"Absolutely. Absolutely," Lucas said. "We can bring you in, give you all the legal help you need, all the protection you need. Just stay right where you're at . . ."

Sandy was afraid to turn around, afraid that Martin would be coming up behind with his knife. "I can't," she said. "I gotta go. Get me out."

"Call back," Lucas said. "Call us back. You don't even have to talk. Just dial the number, leave the phone off the hook, or just say, 'Sandy,' and we'll come and get you . . ."

"I gotta go . . ."

And she was gone.

"Hello? Hello?"

The dispatcher: "She's gone, Lucas. I've got three cars coming in, we started them as soon as she said her name, but they're at least three or four minutes away."

"Ah, Christ, ah, Christ. Listen: warn the squads that we took automatic weapons off Butters this morning, if they haven't already heard."

"They know."

"Get everything else you can, scramble it down there in case we get a chase going . . . How many people down in your office there know about this?"

"Just two."

"Keep it that way. If we don't pick her up, and word gets around, she's dead."

"Gotcha . . . Are you gonna talk to Chief Roux . . . about the cop thing?"

"Yeah. I'll talk to her."

Lucas hung up, rounded his desk and headed for the door, which almost hit him, opening inward: Anderson said, "Wup."

"I'm running," Lucas said.

"Only need a tenth of a second," Anderson said. "You know a guy named Buster Brown? Like in the shoes?"

Lucas tried to focus on the name. "Buster? Yeah, I do."

"He's trying to get you. Says it's urgent. Life-and-death about LaChaise." He handed Lucas a Post-it with a number on it. "He says he'll be there."

"Ah . . . All right." Lucas turned back to his desk, snatched up the phone, and began punching in numbers. "We've got some heavy stuff coming down," he said to Anderson. "Go get Lester, tell him to meet me at the chief's office. Right now . . . and hey, you got any gum? My mouth tastes like it's had a bird in it."

"No, but Lester's got some toothpaste in his desk drawer."

"I'll be up," Lucas said. The phone was answered on the first ring: "Hey, Buster? Lucas . . ."

REGINALD BROWN WAS a scanner freak, a terminal diabetic, blind, a double amputee. He could be a pain in the ass, but sometimes he came up with nuggets of information: he knew most of the drug dealers in town by voice, from their cellular phone calls.

"Boy, do I have something for you. I think," Buster said.

"What happened?" Lucas asked.

"I heard some guys talking about you: just now, just a minute ago. I think it was this LaChaise guy. I got half the call on tape."

Lucas said, "Play it for me."

"Sure: Listen to this."

". . . need to know where this Weather is, and be good to know where Capslock's old lady is, her room number. And we need to know where Davenport is working, and Capslock, Sherrill, Sloan, Franklin and Kupicek. You know the list."

Long pause.

"That don't sound right; you better be tellin' the truth, or your name'll be on the list, motherfucker . . . Hey, listen to what I'm telling you . . . No, not you. Did you find out anything about Elmore?"

Another pause.

"That's what we thought. We'll look those boys up when we're done here . . . Now listen, we need that shit and we need it right now. We'll call back in . . . two hours. Two hours, got it?"

Pause.

"I don't know. And you let us worry about getting back to you. You might be pulling some bullshit. And if you are, you better think twice . . ."

Pause.

"Yeah, yeah. Two hours."

Lucas told him to play it again.

"I knew the names," Buster said, when it was done.

"A cellular call."

"Yeah, my end of it, anyway. Couldn't tell about the other end."

"Okay. Did you hear anything before what was on the tape?"

"Well, yeah. Something about how your girlfriend wasn't on the insurance."

"What?"

"That's what they said . . ."

"I'm sending a squad over," Lucas said. "They'll bring you down here. I need to talk to you, face-to-face. Bring the tape with you. There'll be a payday in it."

"You bet, chief," Buster said.

He hung up, thought a moment.

Had to be a cop. Or a civilian employee. If they'd gotten their information from insurance forms, they had to have access to inside computers. And the insurance did make sense: it would explain how they had located the spouses, which had been hard to figure.

He picked up the phone and called Roux.

"I understand you're on the way down here. Something good?" she asked.

"Not exactly. You might want to bring in the mayor."

He called Dispatch: "What happened?"

"We've got two squads at Snyder's. Nobody there. They remember her, though. They just missed them."

"Anybody get their vehicle?"

"No. We just got there, the guys are checking around . . ."

MARTIN AND SANDY got back in the Continental and Martin said, "What'd Dick have to say?"

"He hasn't seen anything on the TV. He said he's going to take a nap."

"Getting shot can take it out of you," Martin said, as he eased the car into the street.

THE MAYOR LEANED on the windowsill, hands in the pockets of his sport jacket, fists clenched, head down. Lester lounged in a side chair, looking almost as though he were sleeping. Roux turned back and forth in her swivel chair, her eyes on Lucas.

"Does anybody else know?" the mayor asked.

"Just Anderson. I told him the whole story, and asked him to check the computers, see if he could tell if anybody was messing with the insurance records. And he's running this Bill Martin name, to see if it pans out."

"We gotta keep this one thing quiet, this insurance thing," the mayor said, shaking his finger at Roux and Lucas. "We gotta find this guy, if he exists, and nail him, before anybody else knows."

"Man, I can hardly believe it," Roux said. "Maybe it's bullshit."

"It's got a bad feel," Lucas said. "We've got one source who thought she saw a cop. Then Darling calls, and she says cop."

Roux held up a finger and punched a number into her phone. She said, "This is Roux. Anything?" She listened for a moment, then said, "Damnit. If anything happens, get back."

She hung up and said, "Still nothing at the Snyders. We're sending some guys down to print the phone, make sure it was Darling. I can't imagine that . . ."

She was cut off by a knock at the door, and a half-second later, Anderson stuck his head in: "Lucas said if I got anything . . ."

"Yeah, come on in," Lucas said. "What'd you get?"

"Two things. You want the good news, or the bad news?"

"Good news," the mayor said. "We haven't had much."

"We ran Bill Martin, conventional spelling, against Dick LaChaise, the Seed, Wisconsin and Michigan. We got a bunch of hits—he's pretty well known with the gang. He's a gun dealer, by the way. We're sending all the prints we took out of the house to the FBI, and they'll run them. We should know in ten minutes if we've got a match."

"Excellent," Lucas said. To the mayor: "That'd be the third guy."

"And it'd prove that you were talking to Sandy Darling," Anderson pointed out. "Not just some bullshit artist."

"The bad news," Lucas said.

Anderson had a half-dozen sheets of paper in his hands, and he shuffled them nervously. "When did your source see the cop with LaChaise? In the laundro-mat?"

"Must've been . . . yesterday? In the early morning."

"Oh, God." He shuffled the paper some more, his mouth working. "Yester-day, somebody accessed the insurance files on everybody in your task force."

"Who was it?" asked Roux.

"We don't know," Anderson said. "They were accessed and printed out through Personnel, at six o'clock in the morning. There's nobody in Personnel at six o'clock."

"From what O'Donald said, the guy she saw was a street cop—not somebody from Personnel," said Lucas.

"So we got a cop with a source in Personnel," Roux said.

Lucas shook his head: "Something like this, you might get one bad guy, but not two. Unless . . . any of the women in Personnel married to a street cop?"

Anderson shrugged. "I can find out."

"Do that," Roux said grimly.

"But, uh . . ." Anderson seemed reluctant.

"What?" asked Lucas.

"Personnel has been raided a few times. You know that. Guys want to look at their files, want to look at test scores or salaries. There'd be more than a few guys around here who could get inside, and who probably know enough about computers to pull up the insurance records."

"But when you think about how many, I bet it wouldn't be *that* many," Lucas said. "So make a list. We'll show mugs to O'Donald."

"If there's a cop in on this, we're gonna get hurt," Roux groaned.

"But why would a cop line up with LaChaise? LaChaise is a goner," the mayor said.

"Blackmail," said Lucas. He looked at Anderson. "When you figure out the computer stuff, let's talk about who's got the shaky rep. Somebody LaChaise might get to."

"If it's a cop, he's dead," Roux said to the mayor.

The mayor pushed away from the windowsill. "I don't want to hear that," he said.

"I don't even want to think about it—but somebody would put him down, given the chance. I guarantee it."

THE CHIEF OF surgery took Weather aside and asked, "Are you going to be okay?"

"Sure. I mean, heck, my own secretary can't track me down. I don't think some hillbilly gunman's gonna get me." She flashed a grin at him. "Don't worry about it, Loren. If I thought it'd be a problem, I wouldn't be here."

14

LUCAS FOUND WEATHER and another woman in a thirteenth-floor laboratory, looking at skin grafts on a white rat. Weather was surprised when he poked his head in the door: "We need to talk," he said gruffly.

The other woman looked at Weather as though Weather should be insulted.

But Weather nodded: "Sure . . ." And when they got out in the hall, she asked, "How mad are you? You look kind of white around the eyes."

"Don't joke about it," he said, his voice suddenly rasping. "We have a tape of a phone call and they were talking about you."

"About me?"

"Yeah. They want to get you, because you're with me. I'm out there busting my balls running these assholes down, and now I've got to spend a half hour looking for you because you've run off someplace . . ."

"Hey," she said sharply. "I did *not* run off. I went to a hospital, where I *work*."

"And told everybody you really didn't want to talk to me, so when we get this phone call, I wind up having to ditch the investigation to find you."

"I didn't ask you to do that," she said.

He stopped talking for a second, then said, "Listen, just what the fuck do you think is gonna happen if one of these people shows up here with a machine gun? You think they're gonna ask for you, and take a number? Or you think maybe they'll shoot a couple of your friends to make the point, then ask where you're at. You're not just risking your life. You're risking theirs. There are already six people dead from this thing."

"Eight," she said. "Don't forget the two women at the credit union."

MARTIN DROVE DOWN I-35W to Burnsville, then, by memory, took them through a rat's-nest of suburban streets, and finally to a blue rambler, where a snow-packed driveway led to a double garage. Martin parked in the street. "Hope he's home," Martin said, leaning across Sandy to look out the side window. "He is, most days."

"Want me to wait?" she asked. She'd run, once Martin was out of sight.

"Better come along," Martin said.

"I was so scared in the store, that somebody would recognize me," Sandy said.

"I don't think Dave'll recognize you," Martin said. "He doesn't watch much TV. And he's a little shy."

Martin rang the doorbell, waited, rang it again and the door opened. Dave— Martin hadn't mentioned his last name—was an older man with thick glasses, wearing a Patagonia pullover. He pushed open the storm door, saw Sandy behind Martin and blushed.

"How y' doing, Dave?"

"Bill, come on in." Dave pushed the door wider. "You on a trip?"

"Yeah, I am—heading out to the Dakotas."

"You heard about the trouble we're having?" Dave glanced sideways at Sandy and blushed again.

"On the radio," Martin said.

Dave said, "And they want to take the guns away from the good people. I can't believe these guys in government." He shook his head.

Dave took them to the lower level, where a row of Remington gun safes lined one wall. He didn't have any ARs, AKs, ranch rifles or anything else that Martin was interested in, but he did have a rack of beautiful bolt-action hunting rifles—"Hunting's coming back in with the yuppies, I've been selling used Weatherbys like hotcakes. You see any Weatherby Mark V's in three hundred Mag or less, in good shape, think about me."

"I'll do that," Martin said. He was looking at another rack, short little rifles, and said, "What're all the Rugers for?"

Dave shrugged. "Just regular demand . . . jump-hunting deer. Can't hardly find them anymore."

"How much you get?"

"Upwards of four-fifty, for a good one," Dave said.

"Jeez, they only cost half of that, new."

"Well, they haven't made them for ten years. If Ruger doesn't come out with them again, I'll make a mint . . ."

They talked more guns for a while, Sandy standing silently behind them, and Martin finally bought two used .45s for seven hundred dollars.

"Wish I could help you more," Dave said, as they left.

To Sandy, Martin said, "Two more stops."

At the first stop, a sporting goods store, he bought four green-and-yellow boxes of .45 ammo, a Browning Mantis bow, two dozen Easton aluminum arrows, two dozen Thunderhead broadheads, an arrow rest, a fiber-optic sight, a release and a foam target like the one they'd left in the Frogtown house. They waited while the guy at the store cut the arrows to thirty and one-quarter inches, and seated inserts in the tips, so Martin could screw in the Thunderheads.

Martin looked at a Beretta over-and-under twenty-gauge while they waited, then sighed, put it back, and said, "Not today."

At the second stop, he bought six more boxes of .45 ammunition.

"Do you know where all the gun stores are?" Sandy asked.

"Most of them," he said. "Most of them from . . . well, from the Appalachians to the Rockies . . . and Salt Lake and Vegas and Reno. I don't know the coasts. Well, some in Florida, if that's a coast."

And a moment later, she asked, "Have you thought about getting out of this?"

Martin looked at her. "Have you?"

She shook her head: "No. I'm stuck with Dick, I guess. I just think we oughta move on. Mexico. I really don't want to die."

"Huh." Martin didn't relate well, but for the first time since she'd known him, he started to talk. "I'm like Butters," he said. "Running out of time. All the people like us are: they're coming to get us, there's no way we can win. We just make a stand, and go."

"Who's they?"

He shrugged. "The government—all of the government, the cops, the game wardens, the FBI, the ATF, all of them. And the media, the banks, liberals, whatever you want to call them. The Jews . . . They're all in it together. City people. They don't all *want* to do us harm—they just do."

"The blacks?"

"Ah, the blacks are more like . . . poker chips," Martin said. "The government's just playing a game with the blacks. I mean, they might use the blacks to get us, but the blacks themselves won't get anything out of it. Never have, never will."

"That's pretty bleak," Sandy said.

"Yeah. Well, you know, the people who run things, they want power. And they get power by writing laws and making you depend on them. They can do anything they want to old people, because old people gotta have Social Security and Medicare and all that. And if you try to be independent, they get you with laws. Like Dick. No way he was ever gonna be able to run that bike shop. He screwed up one time with his taxes, and they came after him forever. Never let him go. Makes a man crazy."

"You think Dick is crazy?"

He grinned and said, "We're all crazy. You can't help it. I was thinking about it the other day—you know how you used to burn leaves in the fall? In all the small towns? And how good it smelled, the burning leaves in the air. Can't burn leaves anymore, because they won't let you. No reason for it, in the small towns anyway. You ain't polluting nothing . . . They just make the law to train you. I mean, it starts with the small stuff, and it goes all the way up to the big stuff, like lettin' the Mexicans in, so people like us can't get good jobs no more . . ."

Sandy nodded. "Okay."

"I used to love the smell of burning leaves in the autumn," Martin said, looking out the window at the snow.

SANDY GOT INTERESTED in the disguises.

She got LaChaise to sit on a stool in the bathroom, ran her fingers through his thick, stiff hair. "Can't just layer over your natural color, 'cause it's too dark," she said, half to herself. She got the bleach and LaChaise said, "You sure about this?"

"I see it done all the time, up at Pearl's," she said, and she started working the bleach in. When she was done with his hair she said, "The bleach might be too harsh for your face . . . maybe you oughta shave."

"Try it," he said. She worked it in; the fumes were bad, but LaChaise, eyes closed, sat it out.

When she was finished, bleach had turned LaChaise's normally dark hair and beard to a thin, watery yellow, the color of corn silk. The delicate color contrasted oddly with the harsh contours of his face. "Holy shit, I look like some kind of fag," he said, staring at himself in the bathroom mirror. "Maybe I oughta leave it like this."

"Too weird," Martin said. "You want people to look away from you, not stare at you."

They did the color next, and when he looked again, LaChaise was impressed. With the gray beard, he looked as though he might be seventy. "Get your back humped, nobody'll give you a second look," Martin said.

LaChaise looked at Sandy: "You done really good," he said.

Sandy had been enjoying herself: now it went away, and under her breath, as she turned way, she said, "Fuck you."

LaChaise said to Martin, "Your turn."

ANDERSON HAD PHOTOS of Bill Martin. "We'll put them out at the afternoon press conference," he said. "We've got a line on his truck and license tag, and we're putting that on the street right now."

"All right—have you seen Stadic?"

"Yeah, he was through here. We sent him home. I think he's kind of messed up."

"He's never shot anyone before," Lucas said. He yawned and said, "He saved my bacon this morning . . . Jesus, I got to get some sleep."

"Go get it," Anderson said. "There's nothing going on . . . what happened with Weather and Jennifer?"

"Jen should be okay—they've got armed security at the station, and the kids are gone. But I want to find a couple of cops who'll stick by Weather on an off-duty basis. I'll pay them. She's getting bitchy, she won't stay put."

"You should have got her some knitting stuff," Anderson said. "You know, so she'd have something to do over there at the hotel."

"I don't think . . ." Lucas started. Then he looked at Anderson, whose face was resolutely stuck in neutral.

"I just don't want them hurt, that's all," Lucas said.

"Yeah, I know, you don't want them to take the risks you're taking . . . as much fun as they are."

Lucas looked sideways at him: "Whose side are you on?"

Anderson shrugged. "Theirs."

"A traitor to his sex," Lucas said, and he yawned again. "Listen, I'm gonna grab a few hours. If you need me, I'm at home."

"We'll call," Anderson said.

Lucas said, "Goddamn women."

LACHAISE STARTED LAUGHING when he saw Martin, and made Martin link arms with him and shuffle around the apartment. Martin joined in, almost as though he'd stepped outside his dour personality.

"Don't quite look old," Sandy said. "You look old, but you move young."

"We need some practice," LaChaise said. And then, a spark in his eyes, "Let's go on out to this big fuckin' mall. What do they call it—the Mall of America?"

Sandy was appalled by the idea: "Dick, you're nuts."

His smile vanished. "You never fuckin' say that," he said.

She shut up: Dick, she thought, was losing it. Play to him, look for a chance. Try not to be in the way when the shooting started.

MARTIN TOOK THE truck, and Sandy and LaChaise followed behind in the Continental. Martin left the truck in a neighborhood north of the airport. He patted it once, like he might a horse, looked it over, then got in the Continental.

"Makes you want to cry," LaChaise said.

"Damn good truck," Martin said, looking back at it as they drove away. "You know, it was perfect, mechanically. New engine, new tranny—new about everything. I could go anyplace, and nobody'd give it a second look. Good thing, too, when you're dealing guns."

"Where're we going?" Sandy asked, still behind the wheel.

"The mall," LaChaise said.

"We oughta take care of some business first," Martin said.

"Yeah? What's that?"

Martin had a map of the downtown area. "I want to go look up the hospital where they're taking these people . . . Hennepin General. Then I want to go over to this other one, where Davenport's old lady works. Just a recon, to see where it is."

"All right," LaChaise said. "I'm just glad to be out."

The first hospital, as it turned out, was only six or eight blocks from Harp's apartment. There were cop cars parked by the entrances.

"That'd be tough," Martin said.

"But we could get to it on foot, if we had to," LaChaise said. "If that big storm comes in . . ."

The other hospital was farther away, but easy to get to—straight down Eleventh to Washington, right, a couple of natural turns, across the river and up the hill past a building that looked like it had been built from beer cans—and there it was.

No cop cars.

"This one would be simpler," Martin said.

"But it's big," said LaChaise. "Finding her could be a problem—even knowing for sure that she's in there could be a problem."

"We could work it out," Martin said.

Sandy drove, listening; she was shocked by the coolness of the discussion. They'd done robberies, she was sure: Candy and Georgie hadn't started on their own. Still, she was reluctantly impressed by the cool appraisal of the targets.

"Now: out to this mall," LaChaise said. He stretched out in back, favoring his side. The wound was tightening up. "Feel like I'm being held together by banjo strings," he grumbled. But he sat up as they approached the mall.

"Looks like Uncle Scrooge's money bin," he said.

"You ain't far wrong," Martin said.

Sandy found a parking spot in the ramp, and they went inside. The mall was packed, but nobody gave them a second look. And LaChaise was fascinated.

"Goddamnedest thing I ever seen," LaChaise said, as they stopped outside the Camp Snoopy amusement park. A gang-banger dragged by, looked them over— two old guys with beards and long black coats. They looked like cartoons. The gang-banger smirked, kept going.

LaChaise took them on a circuit of the mall, browsing through the stores, checking out the women, dragging Sandy along.

"We gotta get out of here," Sandy said, after the first circuit.

"We just got here," LaChaise said, enjoying himself.

"Dick, please . . ."

"Tell you what, let's catch a movie."

"We can see a movie back at the apartment, he's got HBO. Please."

"Then let's get a pizza, or something. God, is that cinnamon rolls I smell?"

The gang-banger went by again, this time from the other direction—they'd both made a circuit of the second level—but this time, after he passed, he turned and followed them.

There was something not quite right here, the banger thought. There was something wrong with the old guys, and the blond was nervous. Her nervousness gave the whole trio a sense of vulnerability. The feel of vulnerability brought him in, like a mosquito to bare flesh. Victims . . .

There may have been ten thousand people in the mall, but there were also dead spots. One of them was next to an automatic teller machine. The banger watched as the trio bought cinnamon rolls and Cokes, then sat on a bench next to the ATM.

Nobody real close. The banger put on a grin and wandered up, put his hand in his pocket and dropped the blade on a butterfly knife.

"How's it going, folks," he said to LaChaise. LaChaise bobbed his head, didn't look up, but the banger could see the smile. The victims usually smiled, at first, trying to pretend that the contact was friendly. "Whyn't you just give it up? A few bucks," the banger said.

Now LaChaise looked up at him, his voice soft. "If you don't go away, I'm gonna take that fuckin' blade and cut your nuts off."

The banger took a step back. "I oughta . . ."

"Fuck oughta. You want to do something, do it, pussy," LaChaise said. The banger looked at Martin, and the pale eyes fixed him like a bug.

The banger said, "Fuck you," and walked away.

"We gotta get out of here, Dick," Sandy pleaded.

"Felt kinda good," LaChaise said to Martin, and Martin's head bobbed. "Hey, c'mon; let's go see a movie."

"Dick, please . . ."

LaChaise pulled her close. "You shut up, huh? Quit whinin'. I haven't been outside in years, and goddamnit, I'm gonna enjoy myself one afternoon. Just one fuckin' afternoon, and you're coming along. So shut up."

LACHAISE COULDN'T FOLLOW the movie: buildings blew up, cars got wrecked, and the cops seemed to have antitank missiles. All bullshit. Martin fell asleep halfway through, although he was awake when it ended.

"Let's get out of here," LaChaise muttered.

On the way out, they passed an electronics store with a bank of TVs lit up along one wall. As they were passing, the chief of police came up: they knew her face from the hours of news. "Hold it," Martin said. They watched through the glass, and suddenly Martin's face came up.

"Shit," he said. "They got me."

"That means they got the truck," LaChaise said.

"We knew they would," Martin said.

LaChaise looked him over, then looked back at the TV, and said, "You know, nobody'd recognize you in a million years. Nobody."

Martin looked at Sandy, who looked at the TV picture, back to Martin, and nodded in reluctant agreement.

Martin watched until his picture disappeared, and then said, briskly, "Let's get a beer."

LaChaise nodded. "We can do better'n that. Let's find a bar." And he turned to Sandy and said, "Not a fuckin' word."

THEY FOUND A place across from the airport, a long, low, yellow log cabin with a Lite Beer sign in the window, showing a neon palm tree. The sign looked out over a pile of dirty snow, freshly scraped from the parking lot. Above the door, a beat-up electric sign said either Leonard's or Leopard's, but the light bulbs in the fourth letter had burned out, along with the neon tubes on one side. Seven or eight cars and a few pickups, all large, old and American, were nosed toward the front door. Inside, they found a country jukebox, tall booths, a couple of coin-op pool tables and an antisocial bartender.

The bartender was drying glasses when they walked in, and twenty people were scattered around the bars, mostly in clumps, with a few lonely singles. Two men circled the pool table, cigarettes hanging from their lips. They checked LaChaise and Martin for a long pulse, and then started circling again.

LaChaise said, "Hey, let's get some money in the jukebox, goddamnit. Sounds like a tomb in here." He held up his arms and wiggled his hips: "Something hot."

Martin muttered, "You're an old man."

LaChaise said, "Yeah, well . . . let's get a beer."

LaChaise got Waylon Jennings going on the jukebox, while Sandy found a booth. LaChaise slipped in beside her, and Martin across from them. A waitress stopped, and LaChaise ordered three bottles of Bud and two packages of Marlboros and gave the waitress a twenty.

When the beer came back, LaChaise shoved one at Sandy and said, "Drink it."

She didn't care for beer, but she took it, and looked out of the booth, thinking: Most ladies' rooms had telephones nearby. After a couple of beers, she'd have to pee. She could call . . .

She was trying to work it through when the waitress came by again, and LaChaise ordered another round. She tried to tune in on the conversation: LaChaise and Martin started talking about some black dude in prison who spent all his time lifting weights.

". . . they thought something must've popped in his brain 'cause they found him layin' on this mat, nothing wrong with him except he was dead," LaChaise said. "Somebody said there was a hit on him and somebody stuck an ice pick in his ear."

"Sounds like bullshit," Martin said.

"That's what I say. How're you gonna stick an ice pick in the ear of a guy who can press four hundred pounds or whatever it was? I mean, and not make a mess out of it?"

Martin thought it over: "Well, you could spot for him, maybe. You're right there by his head if he's doin' presses, and when he finishes he sits up, and you're right there . . ."

LaChaise nodded. "Okay, that gets it in his ear, but how come there's no blood? That's the thing . . ."

Sandy closed her eyes. She was in a booth with two men trying to work out a way to kill a guy who'd wring your head off if the attempt failed—and how you'd do it with a weapon you'd have to sneak into the weight room.

Martin was tapping the table with the Bud bottle: "The suspicious thing is, he was found alone. How many times do you see the weight room empty?"

"Well . . ."

WHEN SHE OPENED her eyes, she found herself looking into the face of a cowboy-looking guy sitting with three friends in a booth across the room. He was about her age; she glanced away, but a moment later, looked back. They made eye contact a couple of times, and she saw him say something to one of his friends, who glanced at Sandy and then said something back, and they both laughed. Nice laughs, more or less; nothing too dirty. Sandy looked away, and thought about Elmore. Dead somewhere: she should be making funeral arrangements.

Sandy didn't cry, as a matter of principle. Now a tear trickled down her cheek, and she turned away from the men to wipe it away.

"If I absolutely had to do one of those guys, I might think about getting a piece of steel cable, like a piece of that cable off the come-alongs in the welding shop . . ."

She made eye contact with the cowboy-looking guy again, and he winked, and she blushed and turned back to Martin, who was saying, ". . . two-hundred-grain Federal soft-points. Busted right through its shoulder and took out a piece of the lung . . ."

Talking about hunting, now.

More beer came, and LaChaise was getting louder as Martin slipped into a permanent, silent grin.

"Let's dance," LaChaise said suddenly, pushing at her with an elbow. She'd had three beers, the two men maybe six each.

She flinched away. "Dick, I don't think . . ."

LaChaise turned back to Martin and said, "You know, goddamnit, this is what I missed, sitting around in that fuckin' place. I miss going out to the cowboy joints."

LaChaise trailed off and looked up. The cowboy-looking guy, a Pabst in his hand, was leaning against the back of Martin's seat, looking at LaChaise. "Mind if I take the lady out for a dance?"

LaChaise looked at him for a minute, then at the beer bottle in front of him. "Better not," he said.

Sandy smiled at the cowboy and said, "We're sort of having a talk here . . ."

"Ain't that, I just don't want him dancing with you," LaChaise said.

"Hey, no problem," the cowboy said, straightening up. Sandy realized he was as drunk as LaChaise, his long straw-colored hair falling over his forehead, his eyes vague and blue. "Wasn't looking for trouble, just looking for a dance."

"Look someplace else," LaChaise grunted.

"Well, I will," the cowboy said. "But it'd be a goddamn pleasanter thing if you were one fuckin' inch polite about it."

LaChaise looked up now, and smiled. "I don't feel like I gotta be polite with trash."

Talk in the bar suddenly turned off. Martin moved, just an inch or two, and Sandy froze, realizing that he was clearing his gun hand. The cowboy stepped back, to give LaChaise room to get out of the booth. "Come out here and say that, you ugly old dipshit," the cowboy said.

The bartender yelled, "Hey, none of that. None of that in here."

LaChaise spoke quietly to Martin, barely turning his head: "Barkeep."

"Yeah."

Then LaChaise slipped out of the booth, uncoiling, keeping his distance from the cowboy. Sandy said, "Dick, goddamnit . . ." and LaChaise turned and pointed a finger at her and she shut up.

The cowboy said, "Here you are, old man, what've you got?"

The bartender yelled, "Not in here, goddamnit, I'll have the cops on you."

LaChaise said to the cowboy, "Fuck you, faggot motherfucker, your faggot cowboy boots . . ."

The cowboy took a poke at him. He coiled his arm, pulled his shoulder back, uncoiled his arm: to LaChaise, the punch seemed to take a hundred years to get going. LaChaise brushed it with the back of his left hand, stepped inside, and with the heel of his right palm, smashed the cowboy under his nose. The cowboy went down and rolled, struggled to his hands and knees.

Sandy called, "Dick, stop now."

The bartender yelled, "That's all; I'm callin' the cops . . ."

Martin was out of the booth and he stepped toward the bartender as LaChaise circled to the right and kicked the cowboy in the ribs, nearly lifting him from the floor. The cowboy collapsed, groaning, and blood poured from his face. The other patrons were on their feet, and an older man yelled, "Hey, that's enough."

Sandy was out of the booth. "Dick . . ." she wailed.

LaChaise looked at the old man and said, "Fuck you." The cowboy was crawling on his stomach, a kind of military low-crawl, leaving a snail's track of purple blood, and LaChaise walked around and kicked him in the side of the head and the cowboy stopped crawling.

"Jesus Christ, you're gonna kill him," the old man yelled, and a few other men yelled, "Yeah . . ."

The bartender picked up the phone and Martin was suddenly there with his pistol: "Don't touch that dial."

LaChaise was walking around the cowboy, and the old man yelled, "Give him a break, for Christ's sake," and LaChaise pointed at him and said, "If you don't shut up, I'm gonna kick your ass."

And moving behind the cowboy, he kicked him in the crotch. Sandy caught his shirtsleeve: "Dick, c'mon, no more, Dick, please, please, let's go, he's hurt . . ."

"Get the fuck away from me," LaChaise growled.

Martin, his gun now hanging by his side, said, "She's right, man. We better get going."

The cowboy was not moving. He lay with one hand under his chest, the other thrown to the side. LaChaise said, "All right," and picked up one booted foot and stomped on the outstretched hand, the bones audibly crunching in the silent room. "Let's go."

On the way past the bar, he took a ten out of his pocket: "Four Buds to go: just crack the top."

And Martin said, "Don't nobody come running out to look at our tags, y' hear? I'd have to go and shoot you. So you just stay here inside and talk on the telephone, and don't get shot."

As they were going out the door, LaChaise with the four bottles of Bud, the old man shouted, "Crazy fuckers!"

SANDY HUDDLED IN the back as they took I-494 west, then north up I-35W into town, LaChaise laughing aloud, Martin serious but pleased: "The hair was what done it," he said over and over. "He thought you was an old fuck, and he just sort of lobbed at you . . ."

They felt good, Sandy realized. This was what they liked.

"You know what we shoulda done with the truck? We shoulda driven it over to this Davenport's place, his house, and drove it right through the front of the place. Up the porch and right through the front, and left it there."

"Might be a lot of cops hanging around," Martin said, now a bit more sober. "And they could pick us up on the way . . ."

"Well, shit . . . we oughta do something."

Sandy said, "You oughta take the car and start driving. If you're careful, you could be in Mexico the day after tomorrow."

LaChaise said, "You know what? I bet if we tore up that apartment, I bet we'd find some more cash. I bet he's got a stash around somewhere. I can't believe a dealer wouldn't."

"Maybe in the car . . ." Martin said, and they started talking about money. Sandy sank back into her seat: at least they weren't talking about Davenport anymore.

A minute later, LaChaise said, "I think I got a leak in my side." Sandy sat up. "What?"

"It was itching, so I just reached in there to move the bandage, and got a little blood."

"Probably pulled a stitch in the fight," Martin said.

"So let's get back and take a look," LaChaise said. The ebullience left him, and, deflated, he stared morosely out the window. "Fuckin' place," he said.

15

THEY'D SWEPT UP everybody they could find, running the dopers, dealers, bikers and gun freaks until you could hardly find one on the streets.

"If they're holed up, I'd bet they've got a television," Lucas told his group. He was sitting behind his desk, his feet on the top drawer, the others scattered around the small office. "That's the first thing this kind of idiot gets: a TV. We could use it to talk to Sandra Darling."

"What do we say?" Del asked. "We can't just come out and tell her to run. They'd kill her."

"We make it a plea for information, stress how anyone cooperating with

LaChaise is going away for a long time. We say, 'Just call 911, nobody'll know.' She'll know we're talking to her."

"Maybe get the shrinks into it," Sloan said. He was sitting on a backwards chair, his chin on his folded arms. "You gotta believe she's with them, at least semivoluntarily. Or started out that way. She was at the funeral home when LaChaise escaped . . ."

"And I don't think they would've taken her along if they thought they'd have to watch her every minute," Sherrill said, nodding at Sloan. She was slumped in a swivel chair. Her dead husband's parents were handling the funeral details, and she was torn between the hunt and the relatives.

Lucas sighed: "Listen, goddamnit. We need to push off in a different direction."

"What direction?" Franklin asked. "You show me the direction, I'll push."

Lucas dropped his feet out of the drawer. "We gotta find the cop. If we can shake him out, we'll have them."

"So . . ." Sherrill said.

"So we start pushing people out again—but this time, we want to know who on the force is dealing."

The others looked at each other, then Del said, "Dangerous."

Lucas nodded. "Yeah, but it's gonna get done, sooner or later. And right now, it's an angle nobody's working."

"So let's go," Franklin said.

"Everybody keep your goddamn heads up—and wear your vests. This is bad shit."

LUCAS TOLD LESTER, who said, "Internal Affairs are looking through a few things, but they're not on the street. You guys be careful."

Lucas nodded. "Del and I are gonna talk to Daymon Harp again, shake him pretty hard. He's been around for a while."

"You want somebody from Drugs?"

Lucas shrugged. "We can handle it; and you're a little short right now."

"You could have Stadic," Lester said. "He's not carrying a gun until the board says okay."

"All right. He oughta know about Harp, anyway."

Lester said, "Take him. He's just been playing doorman up at the hotel . . ."

WHEN STADIC SAW Lucas and Del walking toward the front of the hotel, he caught the way their eyes picked him up and held him: and he thought, *They got me.* He took a step backwards, but realized he didn't have anyplace to run.

Lucas came up and asked, "How's it going?"

"Quiet," Stadic said. "The way I like it." To Lucas he said, "Your old lady came through again."

"Yeah, yeah . . ."

"Do you know a dealer named Daymon Harp?" Del asked.

Stadic thought, *Here it comes.* He said, "Yeah, I see him around. We took him down three or four years ago, he did two. Then we took him again last year, but we missed—he wasn't carrying, no money, no dope. Bad information."

Lucas nodded: "Good. We need somebody who knows him and his people. We're gonna go over and push him."

Stadic's eyebrows went up: "You want me to come?"

"That'd be good," Lucas said.

"Give me fifteen seconds to get out of this fuckin' doorman's suit," Stadic said. "You guys are answering my prayers."

They rode down in a plain gray city car, the heater running as hard as it could, and not quite keeping up. They passed a fender bender on Nicollet, slid through a stop sign at the next street. "Fuckin' Minnesota," Del said. "I'm moving to fuckin' Florida."

"I was reading a book by a guy down in Miami," Stadic said. "He says Florida's fuckin' fucked."

"The fuckhead's probably just trying to keep me out," Del grumbled.

"Both of you shut the fuck up," Lucas said. "You're giving me a fuckin' headache."

Del changed the conversation's direction: "You hear what's been happening over in St. Paul with the unmarked cars?"

"No."

"All their cars got these yellow bumper stickers, they said, 'Buckle Up, It's the Law.' "

"Yeah, I seen those," Stadic said.

"So the wiseasses over there have been peeling off the top of the stickers. Cut them in half with a razor, peel them right off. Now it says . . ."

"It's the Law," Lucas said, laughing.

"Not that anybody would drive a piece of shit like this except a cop," Del said. "What color you think this car is?"

After a minute, Lucas said, "Fuck gray," and they all laughed.

ALL OF SANDY'S stitches were intact, but LaChaise's wound showed some pink at the edges, and was leaking at one corner. "I'll rebandage it, but the best thing would be, if you just sat still for a while," Sandy told him.

As she worked, Martin nailed a piece of plywood over the hole in the hallway wall, next to the door. "Gonna get some goddamn junkies coming in, if we don't nail it up," he said.

When he was done, he stepped back inside, pulled the cardboard boxes up to the doorjamb, and closed the door.

A moment later, he was at the window; he saw the car pull up across from the laundromat.

"Cops," he said.

Sandy stood up, hand to her mouth. LaChaise rolled to his feet, started toward the window, but Martin waved him back: "Don't touch the curtain. They might look up."

LaChaise slowed, stepped carefully up to a narrow slot in the curtains, and saw the three men getting out of the car. All he could see was hats and coats, but the plain gray car was the key. They were cops, all right. They started across the street, talking, and the thin one laughed.

"They're laughing. They may be coming, but they don't know we're here," LaChaise said. He stepped quickly across the floor and killed the TV. "Down the back stairs. We can go out through the garage."

"No," Martin said, shaking his head. "We can't see out the back until we open the garage. If there're cops out there, they'd have us cold." He glanced at the window: "Man, I don't think they know we're here, but I don't think we can risk running, either."

"So let's set up and take them," LaChaise said. "Back to the stairs. Then we got a chance to run, anyway."

They padded quietly down the long central hallway, pushing Sandy in front of them. Sandy went to the bottom of the stairs, in the garage, while LaChaise and Martin stopped just below the level of the top steps. Martin crouched, and LaChaise stood on the step below him, LaChaise with his 'dog and Martin with a .45 in each hand.

"If they know we're here, an entry team'll try the garage door," LaChaise whispered. The garage door opener was plugged into an overhead outlet. LaChaise pointed at it with the gun barrel and said to Sandy, "Pull the plug."

Sandy pulled the plug.

"Let 'em get in a few feet. We want all of them in," Martin said. "If they don't know we're here, we have to take them all . . ."

DEL WENT AROUND back, to watch the garage door. Lucas led Stadic up the stairs.

"Bunch of boxes at the top," Lucas said. "Supposed to be some sort of a barrier to keep the door from being rushed."

Stadic said, "I've seen that in a couple places. Whatever works."

At the top, they moved the cardboard boxes out of the way. On the right side of the door, a piece of plywood was crudely nailed onto the wall.

"Wonder what that is?" Lucas asked, looking at the board.

"Probably an extra barrier to keep people from busting through the wall," Stadic said. "The guy ain't taking any chances."

Lucas banged on the door. "Harp, open up."

Nothing.

"Awful quiet," Stadic said.

Lucas banged again. "Huh. Wonder if he booked."

"The way things are going . . ."

Lucas banged a third time. They waited for a few more seconds, Lucas looked at the lock, said, "No way," and they started back down the stairs.

INSIDE, SANDY WAS crouched next to Harp's car, her hands over her ears. After the third set of knocks, they heard what sounded like feet on the stairs. "I think they're going," Martin whispered.

"I can't fuckin' believe this," LaChaise whispered back. "I gotta go look."

Martin caught his arm. "Best not to. Sometimes, people feel it, when something moves."

LaChaise nodded, and they sat on the steps and listened.

ON THE STREET, Lucas and Stadic walked around the corner and yelled down at Del. Del had been leaning against the brick wall by the garage door, and he pushed away from the wall and slouched back toward them. "Nothing?"

Lucas shook his head and they crossed the street to the car.

Stadic got in the back, and saw Sell-More Green walking down the street toward them. Sell-More worked for Harp, but he didn't know Stadic. Stadic made a quick calculation, and as Lucas cranked the car, patted Lucas on the shoulder and said, "Whoa," and pointed.

Lucas and Del looked where Stadic was pointing. A thin black man in an old parka and black sneaks was scuffling along, oblivious of them. "That's Sell-More Green," Stadic said. "He's one of Harp's dealers. Or he used to be."

Lucas said, "So let's ask him where Harp is."

They waited until Sell-More was passing the car, and then popped out, three doors opening at once, and Sell-More turned sideways and thought about running, but then just stopped, hands in his pockets. "What for?" he asked.

"How you doing?" Stadic asked.

"Hungry," Sell-More said. "Haven't ate in two days."

Lucas dug in a pocket, took out a small clip of bills, and pulled out a ten: "Where's the boss?"

Sell-More licked his bottom lip: "Who?"

"Daymon, for Christ's sakes," Lucas said.

"Oh, Daymon." Sell-More looked up at the apartment. "He said the cops was hassling him because of these white boys killing cops. So he went on a trip. With Jas-Min."

"You know where?"

"He said maybe Mexico. Someplace warm," Sell-More said. "Is that good for the ten?"

"You lyin'?" Lucas asked.

"No way," Sell-More said. He shivered. "If the boss was here, I'd be eating."

Lucas handed him the ten and said to Del, "Mexico."

Del looked around at the snow: "Wish I was with him."

Stadic nodded, happy with the story. If Davenport thought Harp was involved, he'd just keep coming back. He didn't want Davenport poking around Harp's operation: not now.

They'd taken a couple of steps away from Sell-More when Lucas stopped and said, "You wanna go for a hundred?"

Sell-More said, "What?"

"We're looking for cops who might be . . . dealing. If you want to ask around, get a name or two, it'd be worth some cash."

Stadic tensed: he hadn't planned on this. "Do I get the bread now?" Sell-More asked hopefully.

"Hell no," Lucas said. "When I get the names—and the names better be good."

Sell-More said, "That's pretty dangerous, what you want."

"Yeah, well, that ten won't last long," Lucas said. He took a card out of his pocket and handed it to Sell-More. "You get hungry again, get a name and call me. Nobody has to know about it."

Sell-More's eyes seemed to roll inward, and after a moment of silence, he looked from Lucas to Del to Stadic, and then he said, "I think I might know somebody."

LACHAISE LOOKED AT Martin: "They're gone."

Martin nodded. "Yup."

"I can't believe it," LaChaise said. He looked down at Sandy and said, "We're good as gold."

Sandy nodded. She could still feel her heart thumping. The cops had hit the Frogtown house the day after the first shootings. She didn't know how they'd done it, but they'd killed Butters and they would have killed all of them, probably. Now they were knocking on the door of the new place. The whole thing was coming apart, just like Elmore had said it would. Elmore had never been bright: now he was looking like a prophet.

She didn't say any of that: instead, she thought, *Telephone*.

16

LUCAS CHECKED ON his crew: Sloan and Sherrill were probing sources in the local biker groups. Del and Franklin were working independently, running more dopers. Anderson, who worked for Lester, was running lists of names though personnel, asking who might know enough to crack the personnel computers. Lucas stopped by his office: "Anything?"

Anderson said, "Your name keeps coming up."

"I think we can eliminate that one," Lucas said.

Anderson yawned and said, "Well, that leaves about sixty more, including everybody in your group, and I'm not finished running the roster."

"Give me a list when you get it," Lucas said.

He also got a copy of Buster Brown's tape and carried it back to his office and listened to it again.

". . . *need to know where this Weather is, and be good to know where Capslock's old lady is, her room number. And we need to know where Davenport is working, and Capslock, Sherrill, Sloan, Franklin and Kupicek. You know the list.*"

Long pause.

"*That don't sound right; you better be tellin' the truth, or your name'll be on the list, motherfucker . . . Hey, listen to what I'm telling you . . . No, not you. Did you find out anything about Elmore?*"

Another pause.

"*That's what we thought. We'll look those boys up when we're done here . . . Now listen, we need that shit and we need it right now. We'll call back in . . . two hours. Two hours, got it?*"

Pause.

"*I don't know. And you let us worry about getting back to you. You might be pulling some bullshit. And if you are, you better think twice . . .*"

Pause.

"*Yeah, yeah. Two hours.*"

He rolled it back and listened for background sounds: he'd seen a movie where they figured out where something was by the sound of a train . . . but there was nothing. Buster thought he could hear a television, but Lucas couldn't pick it out of the tape noise. Then he thought, *What was that about Elmore?*

LaChaise:

Did you find out anything about Elmore? . . . That's what we thought. We'll look those boys up when we're done here . . .

Huh. That sounded like they hadn't killed Elmore Darling. That sounded like they thought they knew who had—and so did the cop talking to them. Lucas puzzled through it: the cop was telling them that Elmore had been killed by other cops, probably the Michigan prison people, in revenge for the killing of Sand. That was absurd—but something a con might believe. But if the Michigan people hadn't killed Elmore, and LaChaise hadn't . . .

Lucas launched himself out of his chair and took a quick turn around his desk. Had to be the cop. But how had he known to kill Elmore? How had he known that Elmore was even involved? Was the cop that deep with LaChaise, that he'd know all of it? Had he been involved in the escape itself?

That didn't seem likely: the voices on the phone had been antagonistic.

So how did he know? They had enough pieces of the picture that he should be able to put it together. And when he found it, maybe the cop . . .

STADIC WAS FRANTICALLY trying to locate Sell-More. The junkie had said he might know somebody. And as one of Harp's dealers, *he might.* Harp and Stadic were careful in their rare meetings, always taking them well out of town. But money had to be moved, information had to be worked through, pictures had to be looked at. And with dopers, you could never tell: they were as likely to wake up in Chicago or Miami as at home, and somehow, somebody might have seen him, and Harp, and put two and two together.

Stadic hit all the spots, braced a few dealers with questions about cops, as cover. Davenport would probably shit if he found out that Stadic was covering the same ground as his own people, but that couldn't be helped.

Just after dark, he talked to a convenience store clerk who had sold Sell-More a doughnut not ten minutes earlier. Sell-More was walking, the clerk said. Stadic crisscrossed the side streets, and five minutes later found Sell-More wandering along a sidewalk, hands in his pockets, eyes glazed. Stadic pulled over, ran the window down: "Get in," he said.

Sell-More looked at him, then spoke slowly, a thin glimmer of intelligence: "I ain't got much."

"We want to talk to you anyway," Stadic said, the car grinding through the lumpy ice at the edge of the road. "Get in."

Sell-More shuffled around the car, got in the passenger side, slumped, then leaned forward and rubbed his hands in the air from the car's heater. "Fuckin' hungry," he said.

"You spent the money on dope?"

"I am a dope," Sell-More said. "What you want, anyway?"

"Where're your gloves?"

"Ain't got no gloves. Where're we going?"

"Just gonna drive around a minute, keep the heat going," Stadic said. "What'd you find out?"

Sell-More shrugged. "My man said that Daymon Harp's got a cop, 'cause every time somebody tries to edge in on Daymon, they get busted the next day. He says everybody knows that."

"That's it?"

"Dude gotta be in narcotics," Sell-More said.

Though he was driving, Stadic closed his eyes for a moment. He felt the world slipping out of control, like one of those nightmares where something goes wrong, and you can't ever get it quite right again. If a dumbass like Sell-More could figure this out, then other people could figure it out, too. He hadn't been given away by the name, but by the pattern. And if anyone looked at the pattern of arrests closely enough, they'd find Stadic's name.

"Hey, man . . ."

The tone in Sell-More's voice snapped his eyes open, and he found that he was drifting toward a parked Pontiac. He wrenched the car back to the middle of the street, missing the Pontiac by a foot.

"You okay?" Sell-More asked.

"Tired," Stadic said. He steadied himself. One thing at a time. When Harp got back, Stadic would have to move him out of town. Kill him? Probably not. The thing was, Harp maybe had stashed Stadic's name somewhere as an insurance policy, the same way he'd taken those pictures . . . Goddamn him.

Stadic slipped his hand inside his coat, found the cell phone. The cold lump of his pistol was next to it. "I need you to make a phone call," he said.

SHERRILL AND SLOAN had come back, still in their parkas.

"Cold?"

"Yeah. Getting bad," Sherrill said. "Supposed to get warmer tomorrow, but they're talking about some big storm is getting wound up somewhere. Somebody's gonna get it in two or three days."

"Doesn't make it easier."

"Nobody on the streets," Sloan said. "You hear anything from Sell-More?"

"Not a thing." The phone rang, and Lucas picked it up.

Sell-More said, "This is the guy you give the ten dollars to."

Lucas grinned at Sloan and pointed at the phone: "Yeah? Sell-More?"

"I got a name for you."

Lucas leaned forward in the chair. "Who?"

"You said a hundred dollars."

"If you got a name."

After a five-second silence, Sell-More said one word: "Palin."

"Say that again?"

"Palin. Like, my Pal . . . in . . . trouble. Pal-in."

"Where'd you get this?" Lucas asked.

"Some homeboy down on Franklin."

"You come up here, ask for Davenport. If the name's anything, you got a hundred. And I want the name of the homeboy. That's another hundred."

"Don't leave," Sell-More said. "I'm on my way."

LUCAS DROPPED THE phone on the hook and looked at Sloan. "Arne Palin?"

Sloan dropped his jaw in mock surprise. "Arne Palin? No way."

"Sell-More says Arne Palin," Lucas said.

"Arne's so goddamn straight he still doesn't say 'fuck' in front of women," Sherrill said.

Lucas scratched his head: "But he used to be a roaring drunk. You remember that, Sloan? He did some pretty wild shit, fifteen years ago."

"Yeah, cowboy shit. But jeez . . ." Sloan shook his head. "If you were gonna pick a name who didn't do it—I'd pick Palin. I don't think he's smart enough to think of doing it."

"Gotta be bullshit," Lucas agreed. "But I wonder where Sell-More got it?" He picked up the phone and called Anderson. "Is Arne Palin on your list?"

Anderson said, "Yeah. He's trying to transfer into personnel. They had him up there a few days. You got something?"

"Maybe. Check and see where he's been the last few days—when he's been on duty and so on. See if he was working that day O'Donald saw the guy at the laundromat."

"How close a check?" Anderson asked. He sounded tired.

"Close. We got the name off the street."

"Arne?"

"Yeah, I know. But check, huh?"

STADIC EASED THE car to the curb. "Out," he said. "And you keep your mouth shut. You keep your mouth shut until Harp gets back, and you won't have to worry about gettin' high, not for a while. You be the man."

"The man," Sell-More said, picking up on Stadic's fake jive. "I be the man."

"That's right," Stadic said. He checked the rearview mirror: nothing in sight. He'd picked the darkest piece of ice-clogged street he could find. "You go on, now."

Sell-More cracked the door and swiveled to clamber out. "And get you some gloves. Your hands are gonna freeze," Stadic said. He groped under his sweater for the stock of the old .38. "Do that," Sell-More said.

He was out, ready to slam the door, when Stadic called, "Hey. Wait a minute."

Sell-More leaned forward to say, "Huh?" but never got the syllable out: As he leaned under the roof, Stadic shot him in the face, one quick shot, a bang and a flash, and Sell-More dropped straight down, banging his head on the doorsill as he fell, a wet snapping sound.

"Shit." Stadic stretched across the seat, and put the muzzle almost against the back of Sell-More's head, and pulled the trigger again. Sell-More's head popped up and down. "If you ain't dead, fuck ya," Stadic said, and he stretched out and caught the door handle and pulled the door shut.

He was in his own car with the murder weapon. He could feel his heart thumping: had to dump the gun. If he got a block away, no jury would convict him, unless he had the gun. But he couldn't ditch it too quick. They'd check close around the body, anyplace a gun might be thrown.

And he listened to the radio; the radio was routine, nothing more. Give it another block. Give it one more. Another one. No calls? He found another dark street, caught the black cut of a storm sewer, pulled up close, cracked the door, dumped the gun. Just before he closed the door, he heard an odd sound, and he hesitated.

What was it? His ears were still ringing from the shots, maybe he was hearing that. He rolled down the window, just an inch, and heard the sound again, over the noise of the wheels. And then he passed the end of the block, and looked down to the right. A group of kids on the sidewalk, with candles.

Carolers.

"Christ," he said. "Little fuckers oughta be in bed." And he went on.

SELL-MORE HADN'T SHOWN, and Del had come and gone—he'd be at the hospital, he said. Sherrill had left for the funeral home. Visitation night. Lucas and Sloan said they'd be along.

"You don't have to come," Sherrill said.

"Of course we have to," Lucas said. He patted her on the shoulder. "We'll be there."

When she was gone, Sloan said, "Why don't we pick up a burger and a beer before we go over?"

Lucas nodded: "All right." He was locking the door when they heard running footsteps. Anderson, white-faced, came around the corner: "It's Palin," he blurted.

"What?" Lucas looked at Sloan, then back to Anderson.

"I had Gina down at Dispatch running tapes, to nail down where Palin was when he was on duty. And night before last, he called in a Wisconsin plate. You won't believe . . ."

"Elmore Darling," Lucas said, snapping his fingers. "That's how he found Darling. Took the numbers off the plate when he talked to LaChaise, ran them, went over there and killed Darling."

"I think so," Anderson said, his oversized Adam's apple bobbing in his thin neck. "We never would have caught him if we hadn't run those old tapes."

"Arne Palin," Sloan said, shaking his head.

"Let's take him," Lucas said.

17

LUCAS MET QUICKLY with Roux and Lester, and Lester got the Emergency Response Unit moving. Palin was at home: his precinct boss called him about emergency overtime. Palin said he'd be happy to work, and was told to stay close to the phone while they figured out a new schedule.

"LaChaise isn't with him. He couldn't be that far gone," Lucas said to Roux and Lester, as they walked out toward the doorway.

"We can't take the chance, we don't want anyone else killed. Let the ERU do the entry," Lester said. "If LaChaise isn't there, you get in there and see if you can crack Palin in a hurry. Maybe we can get LaChaise's location before he figures out that we've got Palin."

"Sloan's here, he can help with the interrogation," Lucas said. They turned a corner and saw Sloan waiting by the door, talking with Franklin. As they walked up, Stadic came in, stamped snow off his feet.

"You want to come?" Lucas asked Franklin.

"If you need the weight," Franklin said. He nodded at Stadic, who nodded back. "I'm trying to sneak out to my house and pick up some clothes for my old lady."

"Do this one thing first," Lucas said. He turned to Stadic. "How about you? You look kind of fucked up."

"Yeah, I am," Stadic said, shaking his head.

"All right," Lucas said. He stuck a finger in Stadic's gut. "Get some sleep."

"But what's happening?" Stadic asked.

"We think one of our guys is talking to LaChaise," Lester said grimly.

Stadic's eyelids fluttered, and he said, "No way." And then, "Who?"

Lucas, Sloan and Franklin were already pushing through the door into the snow.

"Arne Palin," Roux said to Stadic, behind them.

"No way," Stadic said again.

"I gotta think he's right," Franklin said as they stepped out into the snow and the door closed. He looked up at the miserable sky, which was so close that he almost felt he could touch it. "I can't believe it's Arne Palin."

STADIC WENT DOWN to his office; nobody home, just a bunch of empty desks. He kept a half-dozen white crosses stashed in a hole at the back of a desk drawer, where they couldn't be seen even if you emptied out the drawer. He popped one, as an eye-opener, took his phone out of his pocket and started to punch the speed dial, but stopped, frowned, thought about it and turned it off again. Cell phones are radios. He should stay off the air.

Then it occurred to him that LaChaise's calls on the cell phone could be traced. Shit. If they found the phone, and checked the billing, he'd be screwed. Stadic started to sweat. Christ, he had to get that cell phone. Had to.

He thought for a moment, then picked up a desk phone and dialed LaChaise's number: as he dialed, the first of the amphetamine hit his bloodstream, and his mind seemed to clear out a bit.

LaChaise answered: "Yeah."

"I got a guy for you," Stadic said, without preamble.

"Which one?"

"Franklin. He and Davenport and a couple of other guys just left here, they're gonna raid a guy . . . nothing to do with you. But I heard Franklin say he had to sneak over to his house after this raid, to pick up some clothes for his wife. She's over at the hotel."

"When's he gonna get there?" LaChaise asked.

"This raid won't take long," Stadic said. "They'll probably hit this house in twenty minutes or so, and Franklin doesn't live too far away. I'd say, half hour to an hour, depending on what happens with the raid."

"Anybody watching his house?"

"No."

"Gimme the address," LaChaise said.

After he hung up, Stadic worked it through his quickening brain: wait in the snow across the street. If he saw LaChaise and Martin arrive, that was fine. If he didn't, he'd wait until Franklin showed. Franklin would pull out the other two. And when they moved in on him, to kill him, Stadic could come up from behind, and take them out.

Just as he'd planned it at the other house, but with one less guy to worry about. Had to get that cell phone, though.

Leaving the office, locking the door, he heard voices in the hall, and then Lester came around the corner with Lew Harrin, a homicide guy. He heard Lester say, "There's Stadic, let's get him," and then Lester called, "Hey, Andy."

Stadic turned as they came up. "Yeah?"

"We got a homicide down on Thirty-third, somebody ran over a guy laying in the street. The uniforms checked it out, say it looks like he was already dead, couple of bullets in the head. Run down there with Lew, see what's going on."

"Listen, I'm totally fucked . . ." Stadic began.

"Yeah, I know," Lester said. "We're all fried. We can't put you out front because you don't have a gun, but you can do this, this is just bullshit interviewing. Anyway, we hear the guy's a doper. Maybe you'll know him."

"Man, my head . . ."

"I don't want to hear it," Lester said. "Get your ass down there."

LACHAISE AND MARTIN scrambled to get ready for the attack on Franklin. Martin had field-stripped one of the .45s. He walked around finding his boots as he put it back together and reloaded. LaChaise pulled on his parka and said to Sandy, "I'm worried about you. You'd sell us out, just like your old man."

"C'mon, Dick," she said. "Don't scare me."

"You oughta be scared."

"I am scared," she said. "The police are going to kill us."

"Yeah, probably," he said, and he grinned at her.

Martin handed LaChaise a blued Colt .45 and a half-dozen magazines. "A little more firepower," he said. "I wish we had some goddamn heavier stuff. That AR'd be worth its weight in gold."

LaChaise broke his eyes away from Sandy. "These'll work," he said, stuffing them in his parka pocket. He turned back to Sandy. "I thought about taking you, but that won't work. We're gonna have to . . ."

"What?" she asked, suddenly sure that this was it: they were going to kill her.

LaChaise grinned at her. "Gonna have to tie you up a little."

"Dick, c'mon. I'm not going anywhere. I can't . . ."

"Bill and I have been talking: we think you will."

She looked at Martin, who nodded. "You will," he said.

"Down the garage," LaChaise said.

THEY'D FOUND A dozen padlocks in a kitchen drawer, of the kind Harp used as backup locks on his washing-machine coin boxes. And from the garage, they got a chain. Martin brought an easy chair along, and a stack of magazines.

The lockup was quick, simple and almost foolproof: LaChaise, Sandy thought, probably learned it in prison. One end of the chain went snugly around her waist, and was padlocked in place. The other end went around a support beam in the basement, and was padlocked there. She had just enough slack to sit down.

"You can try to get out," LaChaise said. "But don't hurt yourself trying, 'cause it won't do you no good."

"Dick, you don't have to do this," Sandy said, pleading. "I'd be here."

LaChaise looked at her hard: "Maybe . . . maybe we can have some fun when I get back."

"What?"

He said, "C'mon, Bill. We gotta move."

LUCAS KNEW FIVE minutes after they took Arne Palin that they'd made a mistake.

They'd set up a few blocks away, pulled on the vests, ready for anything. The entry team went to the front door, knocked, and when Palin opened, pushed him back. Another team went through the back door at the same moment, breaking the lock. Palin, sputtering, stuttering, his wife screaming, watched as the team flowed through the house, from bedrooms to basement. Lucas, Sloan and Franklin moved in right behind the entry team. Palin had been patted down and pushed back on the couch with his wife. Palin was sputtering, angry, then dumbfounded.

"Nothing here," Franklin said. "Can I split?"

"Yeah, take off," Lucas said. "You coming back to the office?"

"Soon as I get the stuff to my old lady," Franklin said. He nodded at Palin. "Arne," he said, and he was gone.

"What the hell?" Palin asked Lucas. "What the hell?"

"Last night you called in a routine make on a Wisconsin pickup that belonged to an Elmore and Sandy Darling. Why'd you do that?"

Palin's wife looked at him, and Palin's mouth opened and shut, and then he turned his head, thought for a moment, then looked up at Lucas and said, "I never did that."

"We got you on tape, Arne."

"I never," Palin protested.

"Elmore Darling was shot to death last night and Sandy Darling is running, maybe, with LaChaise and these other nuts. We know you ran their tags . . ."

"You wanna fuckin' listen to me?" Palin screamed. He started to stand up but Lucas held a hand out toward his chest. He sat down again and shouted, "I didn't run no Wisconsin plates, and you ain't got it on tape because I never did it."

Sloan said, his soft act, "Arne, you might want to get a lawyer . . ."

"I don't need no fuckin' lawyer," Palin shouted, bouncing on the couch. "Bring the fuckin' tapes in here. Bring the fuckin' tapes in here."

Lucas looked at him for a long beat, then at his wife, who was weeping. "All right," he said. "Why don't you get your coat on? Let's go downtown and listen to the tapes, and see if we can figure out what's going on."

"I want to come, too," Palin's wife said.

Lucas nodded. "Sure, that'd be fine." He'd been about to tell her to get her coat, as well. He didn't want anyone left behind, if they were talking to La-Chaise.

STADIC LOOKED AT the body of Sell-More. Sell-More's head was bent against the curb, twisted hard to the right, and his legs had apparently been crushed by the car that hit him. There was no visible blood.

"Shit," he said to Harrin, the homicide cop. "I just talked to him, a few hours ago. Davenport's gonna freak out. This is LaChaise's work. Wonder what the hell's going on."

Lucas took the call from Stadic on the way back to the office: Sell-More? Why in the hell would somebody hit Sell-More? Because he was asking questions?

FRANKLIN LIVED IN north Minneapolis, in a single-story rambler in a neighborhood of mixed housing styles and ages. Across the street, a brick four-square looked across at him, while to his left, a white clapboard split-level crowded his driveway. Franklin drove slowly down toward his house, tired, feeling the day. There was a little drifting snow around, from the squalls that had come through during the night.

Maybe he ought to get the snowblower out and blast his driveway clean, before it got too deep, or run over too much by the paper delivery guy. He had an insulated jumpsuit in the front closet, along with some pacs; he could clean it out in ten minutes. But had he gassed up the snowblower?

LACHAISE AND MARTIN had cruised Franklin's house, then the side streets.

"If there's anybody around, they sure gotta be inside," Martin said. "Can't see shit out here."

"I been thinking about it," LaChaise said. "No point in both of us taking him on. So, you drop me up the block, where I can walk back. Then you find a place to park—you see that streetlight?"

LaChaise pointed at a streetlight on the corner two houses up from Franklin's. "Yeah?"

"You park where you can see the light. If you can see it, then you can see his car lights when he shows up. As soon as you see him turn in, you come on down. I'll take him as soon as he gets out of his car."

"What if he goes in the garage, stays in the car, drops the door without getting out?"

"Then I'll go right up next to his car window and fill him up from there," LaChaise said. "That might even be easier."

"Wish we had a goddamn AR," Martin said again.

"The 'dog'll do, and the forty-five."

"You'll freeze out there . . ."

"Not that cold," LaChaise said. "We'll wait for an hour. I can stand an hour."

THEY'D BEEN WAITING twenty minutes when Franklin showed, Martin a block and a half down the street, LaChaise ditched behind a fir tree across the street from the mouth of Franklin's driveway.

Four cars had passed in that time, and a woman in a parka and snowpants, walking, carrying a plastic grocery bag. She passed within six feet of LaChaise, and never suspected him. As she passed, LaChaise pointed the 'dog at the back of her head and said to himself, "Pop."

He had six shots in the 'dog. He thought about that for a minute. Martin had given him one of the .45s he'd bought from Dave. Now he took it out of his pocket, racked the slide to load and cock it and flipped the safety up.

WHEN FRANKLIN TURNED onto the street, LaChaise leaned forward, tense. The car was moving slow, and he had a feeling . . . yes. He clicked the safety down on the .45.

The garage door started up, a light on inside, and Franklin took a hard left into the driveway. The door was moving up quickly enough that Franklin could keep rolling into the garage. LaChaise unfolded from behind the fir, stumbled— his legs were cramped, he'd been kneeling too long—recovered, started to run after the car, stumbled again, caught himself and saw the car door swing open. But the stumbles had slowed him down . . .

FRANKLIN WAS A big man, but agile. He swung his feet out of the car and stood up, still thinking about the snowblower, and at that moment saw LaChaise running up the drive, knew who it was and said, "Shit."

LaChaise saw the big man turn toward him and saw his hand drop, and he flashed on Capslock making the same quick move. He was ready this time, and he pulled up and fired the first shot with the 'dog, into Franklin's chest from twenty feet, saw Franklin stagger back. He closed, walking, fired again at fifteen feet, then a third, a quick bang-bang-bang and then Franklin's hand came up and LaChaise jerked off a fourth shot and knew that it had gone wide to his right . . .

And then Franklin's gun was up and LaChaise saw the muzzle flash and he fired once with the .45 with his off hand; missed, he thought. Franklin fired again and LaChaise thought he felt the bullet zip through his beard and he was firing and Franklin fell down but he was still firing and LaChaise turned and ran . . .

Martin was there, skidding to a stop, the door opening. LaChaise piled through the passenger-side door and Martin took off, the back end slewing wildly once, twice, then straightening. LaChaise caught the door and slammed it, and looking back, saw Franklin on the floor of the garage . . .

"Got him," Martin said.

"I don't know," LaChaise said uncertainly. "He was this *big* motherfucker, and I kept shooting him and he kept bouncing around and he wouldn't go down . . ."

"You can shoot a guy in the heart, he can be good as dead, but he can go on pulling the trigger thirty seconds or a minute," Martin said. "That's what happened to them FBIs down in Miami. Those old boys were good as dead, but they kept on shooting, and they took the FBIs down with them."

"I don't know . . ." LaChaise said. He twisted to look back, but Franklin's place was gone in the night.

WHEN THE FIRST slug hit, Franklin felt like somebody had smacked him in the breastbone with a T-ball bat. Same with the second one, and the third. Then he had his own weapon out, but the fourth shot caught his arm, and stung, as though somebody had hit him with a whip, or a limber stick, and turned him. He thought, *Don't be bad*, and he opened fire, knowing that he wasn't doing any good, his left arm on fire. Then another shot hit him in the chest and he fell down, slipping on the snow that had come off his car. He had no idea how many times he'd fired, or how many times he'd been shot at, but a slug ripped through his leg and he rolled, and now was hurting bad, but he kept his pistol pointing out toward the door, and kept it going . . .

And then it all stopped, and he was in silence. Out in the street, he saw LaChaise hurtle into a waiting car.

He said out loud, "What?" And he remembered, Christ, he probably was out of ammo. He automatically went for the second magazine with his left arm, and a tearing pain ran through his arm and shoulder.

"Ahhh . . ." He pushed himself up, and pain coursed through his left leg. He looked down, and saw blood pooling on the floor. Pushing with his right leg, he managed to flop across the driver's seat and grab the radio with his good hand.

"Help me," he groaned.

LESTER CAUGHT LUCAS just as he walked into the office.

"Franklin's down. Two minutes ago. They hit him at his house," he shouted down the long marble hallway. "They're taking him to Hennepin."

"On the way," Lucas shouted back. "They're bringing in Palin, talk to him . . ."

Lucas ran through the snow to the medical center, down the street to the emergency entrance. No cops. A doctor was standing just inside the entrance, a couple of nurses were wrestling with a gurney.

"I'm a cop," Lucas said. "You got a . . ."

"Yeah, you're Davenport, I've seen you on TV. He's on the way," the doctor interrupted. "The paramedics got him, they're working on him."

"How bad?"

"He's shot in the arm and the leg. Sounds bad enough, but not critical. They say he took four rounds right in the middle of his vest."

Lucas flashed back to the street where they'd stopped to pull on the vests, so they could charge in on simple old Arne Palin. How did LaChaise—it had to be LaChaise—know to wait for Franklin?

Then he heard the sirens, and he and the doctor went out to meet the paramedics, and he stopped thinking about it.

18

Lucas hurried through the crowd of media in the lobby, shaking his head, saying, "No, I'm sorry . . . the chief should be out in a minute, I'm really sorry I can't say anything."

Outside, he hurried, slipping and sliding, back toward City Hall. His office was dark, and he went up to Homicide, where he found Sloan, Del and Sherrill.

"How's Franklin?" Sloan asked, standing up. They all were beginning to fade.

"He's in surgery, but it's not critical," Lucas said. "Somebody said he might have some peripheral nerve damage in his arm. I'm not sure, but I think that means he might have some patches of skin where he can't feel anything."

"Could be worse," Del said.

"Where's his wife?" Sloan asked.

"She's at the hospital," Lucas said. "What happened with Palin?"

"We're keeping him around, in case you or the chief wants to talk to him. But it's not him," Sloan said.

"Tell me," Lucas said.

"Have you heard the tapes?"

"No."

"Well, if it's him," Sloan said, "he's disguising his voice. But why is he disguising his voice, when he gives his squad number? And even if you figure it's disguised, it sounds too much not-like him."

"Huh." Lucas nodded. "What was he doing earlier on the tape?"

"That's the other thing," Sherrill said. "I went down and listened to them, and he and Dobie Martinez cleared out a burglary report and then said they were going to stop for a cup of coffee, and they went off the air. Then ten minutes later, there's the request on the Darling car . . . then ten minutes after that, they come back on the air again, ready to go back to work."

"Shit," Lucas said. "Did you talk to Martinez?"

"Yeah. He remembers clearing the burglary, then stopping at Barney's. He says they were in there for fifteen or twenty minutes, that Arne never left him, and then they came back and started working again. He says they never called in any Wisconsin plates. So unless they're working together, the identification was bullshit."

"It's bullshit," Lucas said. "But I'd like to hear the tapes."

"I've got a copy on cassette, I'll get it," Sherrill said.

She stepped away, and Lucas said to Del, "Have you heard about Sell-More?"

"No, I just got here."

"Stadic called just about the time Franklin got shot. He was on a call down south. Sell-More was lying in the street with a couple of bullet holes in his head."

"Sonofabitch," Del said. "They used Sell-More to set up Palin."

"But I don't understand why," Lucas said. "It's gotta be a cop, and he's gotta know that it wouldn't hold up."

They all looked at each other, and then Sloan said, "Maybe he ain't the brightest."

"Bullshit. He's been leading us around by the nose," Lucas said. "Who's working the scene down at Franklin's?"

"Some of Lester's guys, I don't know who—Christ, people are all over the place."

"I want to talk to whoever it is . . ."

Lester came in, and they turned toward him, and a second later, Rose Marie Roux followed Lester through the door. She looked at Lucas and said, "Give me an idea."

Lucas said, "I got nothin' that we aren't already doing. He's gotta be holed up with a friend."

"We've shaken down every biker in the fuckin' city," Lester said. "The question is, who was a good enough friend that they'd put up with this shit? Maybe he's staying with . . . you know."

He didn't say it, but he meant, "the cop."

Lucas shook his head and said, "My brain isn't working right. I need to lie down for a while." Then he said to Roux, "There is one thing. We should talk to Sandy Darling. She's freaked out about lawyers, she thinks we're gunning for her with the rest of them . . ."

"So what do we say? Without giving her away?"

Lucas rubbed his chin. "Suppose we say that we had a source who has been useful, but now is apparently afraid and has gone into hiding. We're asking her to come back out, that we'll protect her and offer her immunity."

"I don't know about immunity," Roux said doubtfully. "What if she's deep into it, and she's just playing an angle?"

"All right, so we just say, 'Protect her.' I mean, there's three ways we can get them: we can take them on the street, we can find the cop who's pulling our dick or we can get Darling to give them up. We're doing everything we can on the street, but we're getting nowhere with the cop . . ."

Roux nodded. "All right. I'll put this out. They're using everything we give them, so it'll be on the air in ten minutes."

Sherrill walked up, carrying a tape recorder, and said, "Something else. What they're doing—they're not gonna back off. I think we've got to set up a combat team anywhere they might show. Everybody's house. The hotel's already covered. But maybe we should set up at the hospital to cover Franklin and Cheryl and whoever."

Sloan said, "And I don't think anybody ought to be running around loose." He looked at Lucas and said, "Weather and Jennifer. Somebody is feeding these guys everything . . ."

Roux said, "Lucas, get those goddamn women under control, will you? Can you do that?"

Lucas said, "I'll talk to them."

SHERRILL PLAYED THE tape, and Lucas listened, eyes closed. The voice wasn't right: too smooth, too high-pitched: faked. Whoever it was would have fooled the Dispatch people, because the unit number was right and the request was routine.

"I think—I can't swear to it—but I think that's the guy who called me and warned me that Butters was cruising Jennifer and Sarah," Lucas said.

"Why?"

"I'll tell you why," Lucas said. "Because that fuckin' LaChaise is blackmailing him, and he figures that if we take them alive, they'll deal him. And they probably will. So he's got to have them dead."

LUCAS HEADED OUT to TV3 in a city car, monitoring the radio, his cell phone in his pocket. This was like nothing he'd ever heard of: this was like a war. He didn't have the usual intervals of quiet, when he could sit and think about patterns, and the way the opponents were working. Puzzle pieces were slipping past him; he could feel it. Maybe if he got some sleep . . .

The TV3 lobby was locked. When he approached the glass doors, four men ranged behind two reception desks waved him off. He stood next to the glass, held up his ID. One of the men, large, in a heavy, dark suit, crossed the lobby to the door. Lucas realized that he was wearing a vest and carried a pistol on his hip. The man looked at the ID, looked at him, then turned the knob on the lock.

"I thought that was you," the man said, looking over Lucas's shoulder as Lucas came through.

"Who're you?"

"Thomason Security," the man said. "We're on all the doors."

Lucas nodded. "Good." Thomason was a heavy-duty security firm, used mostly for moving money at sports events and rock concerts, but also as a source of armed guards and bodyguards for celebrities. He asked for Jennifer.

"We'll call up," the man said. Lucas waited, leaning on a countertop. As the man called, he noticed that the other guard on his side of the lobby had a Winchester Defender twelve-gauge at his feet. Even better.

The first guard turned to Lucas and said, "Go on up. You know the way?"
"Yeah."

Jennifer met him at the elevators: "What's going on?"

"We've decided that we've got to pull everybody in tight—back at the hotel," Lucas said. "These guys are suicidal."

Jennifer shook her head: "I know, but you saw our security. There's no way they can get at me. I'm as safe here as I'd be at the hotel. I've got to work; I'm on camera four hours a day. This is the biggest story of my life."

"Look, goddamnit, we know they were coming after you guys . . ."

"That's all taken care of. They can't find out where the kids are, because nobody knows but you and me and Richard. And I'm safe in here," she said. "I'm sorry, but we've figured the risks. I'm staying here."

He gave up. "All right. But I want to talk to Small. I want to make goddamn sure that you've got a tight communications link between here and City Hall, and the second something happens . . ."

WEATHER WAS WORSE.

When Lucas walked into the suite, Weather was talking with Sarah. When Lucas began the pitch, she picked Sarah up and held her on her lap.

"Listen, Weather . . ." Sarah blocked Weather off, like some kind of psychic barricade. He couldn't operate with Sarah looking at him with his own blue eyes; couldn't sell. He couldn't touch Weather, and he needed to touch her to convince her, he thought.

"Lucas," she said, exasperated, when he finished. "Nobody can find me at the hospital. Nobody. People who work there can't find me, unless they have my schedule—and half the time they can't find me then. I've got jobs lined up all week. I just can't skip them because there are some lunatics running around out there."

"The problem is, you're a lure," Lucas said. "You could bring a hell of a lot of trouble down on the heads of everybody around you. And now we know they've got a cop feeding them information . . ."

"Look," she said. "Let's do this. Let's tell everybody—everybody, including the police—that I'm in the hotel. We can sneak me in at night, and I'll go around and complain about being stuck there, so everybody knows I'm around. Then we'll sneak me out in the morning, and nobody'll know but the two of us."

"Somebody'll know," Lucas said.

"Two or three people. You can use guys you're sure of."

Lucas said, "How about if you were interviewed on TV tonight—ten minutes from now, a half hour—in the hotel? About what it's like to be shut up here, and wait? So it'll be on TV?"

She nodded. "If that will keep me on the job," she said.

"I'll call Jen and see if she can set it up," Lucas said. He made a quick circle of the room, coming back to the pair of them, picked up Sarah and bounced her. "Want to see your mom?"

"She's breaking a major story," Sarah said solemnly.

"I think she could take a minute away to see her kid," Lucas said. "Let's go talk to her."

19

LaCHAISE WAS MANIC: they'd shot the cop, he said, his face alight, as though he expected Sandy to have a celebration prepared.

"What d'ya think about that, huh? What d'ya think?"

Sandy, coldly furious, turned her face away until the chain came off, and then stalked up the stairs, into the back bedroom, the one they said was hers, and slammed the door in LaChaise's face. She said not a word. She'd felt like a dog with the chain around her waist, and a mistreated dog at that.

She lay on the stripped-off bed for half an hour, thinking about Elmore, thinking about horses, smelling the odd lingering body odors of strangers.

Horses. She got up, went out to the living room. LaChaise and Martin were drinking, watching television. "I've got to call a guy, to make sure he's feeding the stock," she said.

LaChaise shrugged. "Use the cell phone. It's in my coat pocket. Don't talk more'n a minute or so, in case there's some way they can trace it. And call from out here, where we can hear you."

She nodded, went to his coat, dug around. She found the stack of photos, the photos of the cop, deep in one pocket. Ten of them, two men at a table, one black, one white. Which one was the cop?

She listened for a minute, then took two of the photos, the two that showed each of the faces best, and slipped them into her jeans pocket. She put the rest back, found the telephone, and went out to the hallway where the men could hear her.

Jack White. She knew the number, dialed in. Jack's wife answered:

"Sandy, where are you, we can't believe . . ."

"It's not what anybody thinks," she said. "I can't talk—but you've got to tell Jack to take care of the stock."

"He's already doing that, as soon as he heard about Elmore."

"Tell him he'll get paid; I swear, as soon as I can get out of this," Sandy said.

"He'd do it anyway."

"Gotta go . . . and thanks. I won't forget it."

She hung up and LaChaise said, "Still think you might get out of it, huh?"

"I'll put the phone back in your coat," she said coldly. She did, and went back to the bedroom, flopped on the bed.

Tried to think. Got up after a while and poked around the room: this was a guest bedroom, and had been used as storage. LaChaise had torn the place apart, looking for money, and found nothing of interest. She went to the window, lifted the blind and looked out. The snow had quit, and distant streetlights seemed to sparkle in the suddenly clear air. Must be an inch of snow, she thought. She leaned forward to peer at the ledge . . .

And thought: *Out the window.*

Bedsheets—but she didn't have any bedsheets. The bed had been folded and pushed against the wall when they got there. She could get sheets, there were sheets in a closet down the hall, that'd be natural enough: but that goddamn Martin would think about the sheets and the window.

She looked back out, then to her right. And the fire escape was there, one window down, at the end of the long hall. Ten feet, no more. The ledge was a foot wide . . . and snow-covered. The fall was twenty feet or more. Enough to kill her.

Still. The snow could be brushed away . . .

The window had a swivel lock, and she twisted it: after some resistance, it went. She tried the window. Didn't budge. She looked closely at it, but it didn't seem to be painted shut. She tried again, squatting to push up with stiff arms . . . and it gave, just an inch, but it'd go.

She looked back at the door. This would be a bad time, with both of the men drinking, both of them awake. As she thought it, LaChaise screamed from the front room.

"Motherfucker . . ."

The police?

Sandy pulled the window back down, locked it, pulled the shade and then quickly tiptoed to the door. Then she opened it and peered down the hall.

". . . can't get it right," LaChaise roared. "Why'd he wear a vest to go home . . ."

The television brought the news that Franklin wasn't dead—that he wasn't even in particularly dangerous condition, that he'd been saved by a bulletproof vest.

"What do I gotta do?" LaChaise shouted at Martin. "What the fuck do I gotta do?"

"You did right," Martin said. "You hit him four times in the chest, is what the news says."

But Martin's efforts to calm him down only made LaChaise angrier. Already full of beer, he got Harp's Johnnie Walker and started drinking it off, carrying a water tumbler full of ice cubes, pouring the whiskey over them, gulping it down like Coca-Cola. He paced as he drank, watching the television.

A blond newscaster from TV3—"She's the one we want to get," Martin said, "Davenport's woman"—reported that "Police are searching for an informant who provided critical information earlier this week, but who has disappeared. They ask that you call the department on the 911 line, as you did the last time, or any police line and ask for Chief Lucas Davenport. Police said they would offer the informant absolute protection from retaliation from Richard LaChaise or any of his accomplices."

"Yeah? How are you gonna do that?" LaChaise brayed at the screen. Then: "I'd like to fuck her," and then: "Who could be talking to them? We don't know anybody."

Sandy shrank back: she knew.

"Probably whoever told them about the house we was in," Martin said. "Ansel had to ask around, talking to a bunch of dopers. Somebody probably gave him up."

"Yeah . . . Goddamn, ol' Ansel. I miss that sonofabitch."

LaChaise's face crinkled, and Sandy thought he'd begun to weep. He turned abruptly, marched down the hall into Harp's stereo room and began tearing the vinyl record albums out of their covers and smashing them, three and four at a time.

Martin looked at Sandy, but showed no sign of disapproval—or approval, either. He showed nothing, she thought.

To the sound of the breaking records, Sandy went back to the bedroom and shut the door. Martin was nuts, but he was controlled. But the booze had pushed LaChaise over the edge, and the very air of the apartment carried the smell and taste of insanity, of the expectation that something crazy was about to happen.

She had to get out.

A moment later, she heard Martin's arrows start to whack into the target outside her door. Martin had put the target next to the window at the end of the main hall. If he pulled an arrow to the right, she thought, it'd go right through the window shade and glass, out over the fire escape and into the roof of the next building . . .

She was sitting on the bed when LaChaise stopped breaking records. A moment later, LaChaise and Martin were shouting at each other, and she heard the thumping of heavy bodies colliding in the front room. She ran to the door and down the hall again, and found Martin on the floor, on top of LaChaise, with a heavy arm around LaChaise's neck. LaChaise was facedown, and trying to get to his hands and knees.

"Let me up, you motherfucker," LaChaise roared.

"Can't do that; can't do that," Martin was saying urgently. "We need the goddamn TV . . ."

He saw Sandy and said, "Tried to kick in the TV."

"Fuckers don't do nothing but lie," LaChaise said, but he sounded calmer.

"But we need to see what they're saying, and what happens with the cops," Martin said.

After a moment of silence, LaChaise said, "Let me up. I won't kick it."

Martin nodded. "All right."

Martin stood up, between LaChaise and the television, and LaChaise grunted as he stood up, a tight grin: "You kicked my ass."

"You're drunk as a skunk."

"Well, that's true," LaChaise said. "But you're pretty fuckin' drunk yourself." Sandy moved away, stepping back toward the bedroom, but LaChaise turned and saw her and said, "What're you lookin' at?" and then, "Hey, wait a minute."

Sandy padded back toward the room, looking for a place to hide, and heard LaChaise say to Martin, "If I can't kick the TV, might as well jump me a little puss."

Sandy turned around inside the bedroom: looking for a way out. There wasn't any. LaChaise came to the doorway and leaned in, and she said, "Dick, don't."

"Bullshit," he said.

"I won't fuckin' move. I'll lie there like a brick. And if I get a chance to kill you, I will."

He stepped toward her and she thought he'd hit her. Instead, his eyes wavered, and he said, "Fuck you," and staggered away.

She shut the door. Had to get out. Had to.

LUCAS AND SLOAN brought Weather into the back of the hotel, while Sherrill and Del brought in Jennifer and a TV3 crew. Weather went to fix her hair and check makeup, and Jennifer, standing aside with Lucas, muttered, "I wouldn't let Weather look at this Sherrill chick too long."

"What?"

"Give me a break, Davenport. Never in your life would you fail to appreciate the young woman's qualities."

"Well, I do appreciate them," Lucas said stiffly. He suddenly felt like an asshole, broke down and grinned. "But I'd never do anything about it."

Jennifer looked at him in an appraising way, and said, "Maybe you really have changed."

"Yeah, well . . ."

Weather came back out and they went down to the lobby for the interview, a two-minute no-brainer on the cops' families suffering from cabin fever, how it felt to be barricaded inside. Jennifer did another quick interview with Sloan's flustered wife, and then went out the back door with her protection.

"That should do it," Weather said, when they got back to her room.

"I hope so. I hope they're watching television," Lucas said. "Jen says they'll run the tape every time they do the updates."

"Are you still angry with me?" Weather asked. She sounded slow, depressed.

"No. I never was as much angry as I was . . . cranked up," Lucas said.

She patted the bed: "You need to get some sleep, I can see caffeine leaking out of your eyes."

"Maybe a few hours," he agreed.

SANDY COULD HEAR LaChaise talking to Martin, both of them still drinking. She got up twenty times to go to the window, to look at the ledge. Long way down. Higher than the hayloft in the barn. She'd lie on the bed, close her eyes, try to rest. Nothing worked.

Eventually, the talk in the living room stopped, and the television was turned off. She went to the window, looked out again. Then a sudden THUMM-whack outside her door. Martin was at it again, shooting the bow down the hall. He fired it twenty times, then quit.

The apartment was quiet for a half hour, an hour, the hands creeping around her watch. She went back to the door, listened, cracked it, looked out. If she could get sheets—or if she could just get out the door, for that matter. The men had been very drunk . . .

The hall light was on, and one more in the living room. A half-dozen arrows stuck out of the target at the end of the hall, five feet away. But nobody was moving. She went down the hall on her tiptoes: the door to the master bedroom was open, and in the half-light, she could see LaChaise sprawled across the king-sized bed.

Martin was wrapped in a blanket, lying on the floor by the front door. She tiptoed down toward him and whispered, "Bill?"

He stirred, but his breathing remained even. She looked back down the hall toward the basement door. Martin's voice, thick with sleep, said, "The door's locked. I got the key in my pants."

She jumped: it was as though he'd snatched her thought from midair. "I wasn't going to the door. I was just making sure that Dick's sleeping it off," she said.

"Are you . . . ?" she was going to ask, *all right*? Before the words could get out of her mouth, he'd rolled and was pointing a pistol at her head. She stepped back and said, *"Please . . ."*

Drunk as he must be—he'd finished LaChaise's bottle of Johnnie Walker and a half-dozen more beers—his hand seemed absolutely steady. "You're gonna call the cops on us, aren't you?"

"No, honest to God . . ." She looked back at the bedroom; the black-and-white target loomed on the wall outside the door, next to the fire escape window.

"Are you gonna fuck him?"

Now, she thought, they were getting to the important issues. She crossed her arms: "Not if I can help it," she said, looking at the hole in the end of the pistol. "If Dick does it to me, I'd have to be unconscious or dead."

The hole at the end of the pistol seemed as large as a basketball hoop, and held between her eyes. He kept it there, kept it, and she closed her eyes . . .

"All right," he said. She opened her eyes and the pistol was pointing at the ceiling. He grinned at her, a wet, sleepy, evil grin, she thought. "Hope nobody down in the laundry heard me and Dick wrestling around."

My God, she thought, he's lying here thinking about it: Martin's turned on. Out loud she said, "They'd have been here, if anybody called the cops." Her eyes drifted toward the telephone: pick it up, 911, leave it off the hook, wait one minute . . .

Impossible. She could handle LaChaise, she thought, but Martin . . . Martin seemed to see everything.

The gun flashed back up and leveled at her forehead again, and Martin said, "Bang." Then, "Go on back to bed."

LUCAS TRIED TO sleep, snuggled against Weather. Though he felt as if he'd been awake for days, his internal clock still said it was too early. And the bed was wrong, not his, and the pillow was no good: it crooked his neck at a bad angle. But most of all, he couldn't stop his mind. He wasn't putting the puzzle together, he was simply reliving the whole long episode, without profit.

A few minutes after midnight, Weather finally spoke in the dark: "You're vibrating," she said.

"Sorry."

"You need the sleep."

"I know," Lucas said. "My brain's all clogged up."

She half-rolled. Her voice was clear, and he realized she'd been lying awake: "How much longer, before you get them?"

"Probably tomorrow, unless they just hide out. If they move, we'll get them. Tomorrow or the next day, I'd say."

"What if they're running?"

"Their pictures have been on every TV in the country; they couldn't stop to get gas. They really can't go out in the open."

After another moment of silence, Weather said, "You think they'll be taken alive?"

"No."

"You guys'll just shoot them?"

"It's not that—if they called up and said they wanted to come in, and they told us where they were, and they came out with their hands over their heads . . . We'd take them. But it's not shaping up that way. The first guy, Butters, might as well have committed suicide. They figure they're dead. They've already written themselves off. And that's scarier'n hell."

"Gotta be their parents . . . you know, who made them like that."

"Always is," Lucas said. "I've watched some kids grow up from little psychos into big psychos: it was always the parents that made them that way."

"If you could intervene early enough . . ."

Lucas shook his head: "Never work. Nobody spends as much time with the kids as their parents, even if their parents don't want them. And usually, nobody knows anything is wrong until the kid's already bent. Maybe you could set up an army of fascist social workers who'd go around to every house once a month and cross-examine every kid, but that'd probably be worse than what we've got. Look·what happened with all these mass child-abuse things. They're all bullshit, and it's the social workers who've done it."

Another silence.

Then Weather said, "I don't believe that more violence is the way to solve the problem. I don't think shooting these people will do it."

Lucas said, "That's 'cause you're a doctor."

"Hmm?"

"Doctors think in terms of illness and cures. The problem is, when one of these guys gets sick, somebody else gets hurt. So we've got two problems, not one. First we've got to protect innocent people. Then we've got to do whatever we can with these guys—cure them or whatever. But first we've got to stop them."

"That doesn't seem to be what you're doing . . ." Then she added, hastily, "Sometimes it doesn't, anyway."

"Yeah, I know. Sometimes we play it a little too much like a game. That's just a way to deal with it . . . but that's not the way it really is. It ain't football, even if TV thinks so."

They talked a bit longer, then Weather said, "I've got to get some sleep. I'm working in the morning."

Lucas kissed her good-night again, and lay on his back, watching the outside light trace feather patterns across the ceiling, and some time later, finally fell asleep.

SANDY MOVED THE window an inch at a time, and the cold air flooded in. That was a problem. Once she committed herself, she could hardly go back. The room would be cold, and if Martin or LaChaise came in, they'd know . . .

But she pushed the window up anyway. Then leaned out, brushed snow off the ledge with her hand. The ledge didn't seem too slippery, but she wouldn't be able to walk it with boots. She dropped to the bed, took off her boots and socks, put the socks in the boots and the boots in her parka pockets, the heels sticking out. Couldn't drop those . . .

She looked down. *I'm going to kill myself.*

She took a breath and stepped out on the ledge: and the shock of the cold on her feet almost pitched her off. She held to the inside of the window frame, then edged to her right. The ledge was plenty wide, almost as though it had been designed to get her to the fire escape. Probably had been, she thought.

She slid another step, and then another, refusing to look down again. She let go of the edge of the window frame, and now was balanced on nothing but her painfully chilled feet, the outside wall pushing against her back. She looked straight out, feeling more balanced that way. Two more steps. Two more.

Reaching out with her right hand, she groped for the steel of the fire escape. Another step. Christ, she was afraid to look to her right, another step, groping . . . and she felt it. Now she turned her head, saw it, grabbed the railing and stepped over to it.

She stopped to check the window above the fire escape. The shade was down, but there was a crack at the bottom between the shade and window frame, and she could see down the hall. In the semidark, Martin looked like an enormous cocoon, rolled up on the floor at the end of the hall.

She stepped over the railing onto the fire escape, breathing hard: she was excited and frightened to death. She took two steps down, onto the drop platform, and bounced gently, to see if that was enough to make it drop. It didn't move. She tried again, harder. Nothing. Hard, this time. There was a metallic clank to the left, but the platform stayed up.

This wasn't the way it was supposed to work, but in the dark, she couldn't see why the platform wasn't dropping. Something was stuck somewhere . . .

She thought about hanging from the bottom, and dropping. But even with a two-step platform drop, and the six feet she'd get by hanging, it'd be a twelve- or thirteen-foot drop onto an uncertain alley surface . . .

She'd break a leg.

But she thought about it, the cold in her feet growing to pain.

THEN SHE FELT the vibration.

She didn't know what it was, but she went to her knees under the window, and put her eye to the crack under the shade. Martin was on his feet, walking down the hall toward her room. He stopped at LaChaise's room, looked in, then went into the bathroom. Sandy took a breath—but Martin was back in three or four seconds, and now he was moving softly down the hall toward Sandy's door.

He stopped at her door, and she ducked, unable to watch, afraid he'd sense her eyes. She waited, then forced herself to look. Martin was at her door, one hand on her knob. Unmoving, listening.

Sandy's feet were burning: she had to move them, but she couldn't. She was afraid that he'd sense anything, any movement.

Then Martin left her door, came down the hall to the fire escape window, pulled arrows out of his target. Then he turned and went back down the hall, looked around once, put the arrows on a shelf and dropped back on the sleeping bag.

Sandy, still holding her breath, ducked below the window again, sat, lifted her feet off the fire escape and cradled them. They hurt, and for a while there was nothing in her world but her heartbeat and her feet. Had to move. She looked through the crack again. Martin was on the sleeping bag again, but awake, twitching. Twitching? She watched: Jesus, he was masturbating.

Now Sandy was breathing like a locomotive, great gouts of steam puffing out into the cold night air: her feet were freezing, the pain excruciating. She looked at the drop, looked at the ledge, and painfully stepped back over the rail onto the ledge.

Back to the bedroom. She moved faster going back, the pain pushing her. She caught the window ledge and crawled back through. Her feet felt as though she were walking on broken bottles, but she ignored them for the moment and focused on closing the window, carefully, not making a sound.

All right. The room was cold, but there was nothing she could do about that, not right away. She couldn't open the door: Martin might catch a draft. She pulled off her coat, took the boots out, sat on the bare bed, and used the inside of her coat sleeves to wipe her feet.

When they were dry, she touched them, ran her fingers along the soles. No feeling, but no blood, either. She put on her socks and lay back. If she were quiet . . .

Wait. She got on her hands and knees, crawled around the perimeter of the room, and found a hot air register. Open, closed? There was no heat coming out. She looked at the light, decided to risk it. She turned it on, just for a second, looked at the register—closed—and turned it off. Went back to the register, in the dark, and opened it as wide as the adjustment level allowed. Still no heat. The furnace wasn't running at the moment.

What else? The lock. She stepped to the window, twisted the lock, pulled the shade. The window ledge and fire escape would have footprints: nothing she could do about it. Hope for some wind.

She dropped back on the bed, wrapped herself in her parka, and tried to feel her feet. And tried to stave off the disappointment. Twenty feet . . . maybe she should have gone for it. Twenty feet.

NUDE EXCEPT FOR the white tape wrap on his wound, LaChaise walked out to the living room, looked at the TV, yawned, scratched himself and said, "What's on?"

Martin wouldn't look at him. He said, "That Weather woman was interviewed in the hotel. Didn't say where she was inside, but they got cops all over the place, with shotguns. Vests. Gas. Inside and outside, on the roof."

"Trying to scare us," LaChaise said.

Martin half-laughed and said, "Well, it's working." Still he wouldn't look, and LaChaise stepped over to the window and pulled the blind back an inch or two. Six o'clock in the morning and still dark.

"Sandy sleeping?"

"Yeah," Martin said. "You scared the shit out of her last night."

"Yeah?" He didn't care.

"We're gonna need some heavier gear if we're gonna keep going," Martin said, staring at the TV.

"What've you got in mind?"

"We can't get the hotel, and they're crazy if any of them are staying at home. We can't just hang out on the street, looking for them, 'cause they know what we look like . . ."

"Not with the hair." LaChaise touched his gray hair and beard.

"Well, we couldn't hang long—they're checking everybody."

"So where?"

"The hospital where Capslock's old lady is, and that other cop, Franklin."

"How do you know they're at the same place?"

"Saw it on TV."

"Goddamn. Glad I didn't kick it in," LaChaise said.

"Yeah. So we need some heavier gear."

"You know where to get it?"

"I know a guy. He's a problem, but we can work something out. We'd need Sandy. And we'd have to get moving."

"All right." LaChaise started toward the bathroom; halfway down the hall, he stopped and looked at Harp's record collection and said, "Jesus Christ, what happened to the records?"

"You got pissed off and broke them up."

"Christ, I must've been fucked." LaChaise bent and picked up half a record. *Sketches of Spain*, by Miles Davis. "Some kind of spic music," he said. He yawned again and flipped the broken record into the room, on top of all the other fragments, and went on down to the bathroom.

SANDY WAS DRESSED, wrapped in the parka, when LaChaise came to the door.

"Let's go," he said, rapping once.

"Where?"

"You gotta do something for us."

LACHAISE DROVE, WHILE Martin gave directions from memory, out this street and down that highway, turn at the lumber store with the red sign. They were somewhere west of the city, around a lake. Dozens of ice-fishing shacks were scattered over the frozen surface of the lake, and pickups and snowmobiles were parked beside some of the shacks.

"The thing is," Martin said, "is that half his business is illegal, 'cause he don't believe in gun controls . . . but I do believe he'd shoot us down like dogs if he had a chance. If he seen us coming." He looked at Sandy. "So you walk up to his front door and ring the bell. I'll be right there, next to the stoop."

"That's . . . I couldn't pull it off," Sandy said.

"Sure you can," Martin said. She remembered the night before, his eyes over the sights of the pistol.

THE HOUSE WAS a brown-shingled rambler on a quiet, curving street. Lights showed from a front window and the back of the house; the car clock said 7:30. Still dark enough.

"Door latches on the right," Martin said. They continued past the house, did a U-turn, dropped Martin and waited as he walked away in the dark. After a minute or so, they started back toward the house. "Quick beep, all the lights, then just run up to the house with the bag in your hand," LaChaise said.

They'd picked up a newspaper at a coin-op box, and wrapped it in a plastic grocery bag they found in the backseat. "Don't fuck it up."

Sandy held on: just this thing, they said.

"Now," said LaChaise.

They pulled up to the house, stopped in the middle of the driveway. Sandy gave the horn a light beep, then hopped out of the car, carrying in the paper. At the same moment, Martin duck-walked down the front of the house, until he was directly beneath the stoop, on the right side of the door under the latch, but pressed to the side of the house.

Sandy saw a white-haired man come to what must be a kitchen window as she hurried up the driveway, shivering from the cold. The man was holding a mug of coffee, his forehead wrinkling at the sight of her. She hurried up the stoop and rang the doorbell. Martin's face was just beside her right pant leg, a .45 in his hand. The door opened, and the white-haired man pushed the storm door open a crack and said, "Yes?"

Sandy pulled the door open another foot, and Martin stood up and pushed his pistol at the man inside. "Don't move, Frank. Don't even think about moving."

"Oh, boy," the man said. He had a surprisingly soft, cultured voice, Sandy thought, for a gun dealer. He backed up, his hands in front of him. LaChaise was out of the car, and Martin pushed Frank into the house, Sandy following, and LaChaise coming up behind.

Inside, Martin said, "He'll have a three-fifty-seven under his sweater, back on his hip, Dick, if you want to get that . . ."

LaChaise patted the man, found the gun.

Martin went on, "And he might have an ankle piece . . ." LaChaise dropped to his knees, and the man said, "Left ankle," and LaChaise found a hammerless revolver.

"You dress like this to have coffee, I'd hate to see you getting ready for trouble," LaChaise said, grinning at the man.

The man looked at him for a moment, then turned back to Martin. "What do you want?"

"Couple of special AKs, out of that safe in the basement. A couple of vests."

"You boys are dead, you know that?"

Martin nodded. "Yeah. Which is why maybe you shouldn't fight us. There's no percentage in it, 'cause we just don't give a fuck anymore."

The man nodded and said, "Down this way."

FRANK HAD THREE gun safes in the basement, aligned along a wall with a workbench and a separate reloading bench. He reached for the combination dial on the middle safe, but Martin stopped him, made him recite the combination, and ordered Sandy to open it. He pressed his pistol to the back of the man's neck: "If anything happens—if there's a bang or a siren, or a phone line, you'll be dead."

"There's nothing," Frank said.

Martin said to LaChaise, "He's probably got a hand piece stashed behind something down here, where he can get it quick. Keep your gun pointed at him." And to Frank, he said, "I'm sorry about this, but you know what our problem is."

Sandy finished the combination, grasped the handle on the safe, turned her head away and tugged. The safe door opened easily; Martin said, "All right." Sandy almost didn't hear him: she'd seen the obsolete black dial telephone on the gun bench.

"You got him?" Martin asked LaChaise.

LaChaise moved a little sideways to Frank, and kept the gun pointed at his ear. Martin brushed past Sandy, reached into the safe and took out an AR-15. *"All right,"* he said, finding the custom selector switch. He quickly field-stripped it, found nothing wrong, put it together. There were three guns in the safe, and two dozen boxes of ammo. Martin took it all, stuffing the ammo boxes in his coat pockets until they were full, handing the rest to Sandy.

"And the vests," Martin said.

"Over in the corner closet," Frank said.

Martin walked across the basement to a closet with a sliding door, pushed it back, found a row of Kevlar vests in plastic sacks. He selected two of them, then glanced at Sandy, and took a third.

"I'm really sorry about this," Martin said. He handed the vests to Sandy, put his gun on Frank and prodded him toward the stairs. LaChaise went up ahead of them, so they could keep the white-haired man covered around corners.

Sandy fumbled one of the boxes of ammo, then another one. They hit the floor, and shells spewed out. "Oh, shit," she said.

"Goddamnit," Martin growled. "Get those . . ."

Sandy stooped, and began picking up the cartridges, stuffing them into her pockets, as the men climbed the stairs.

When they reached the top, and had started down the hall, Sandy darted to the telephone and dialed 911. The operator answered a second later, and she said, "This is Sandy Darling calling for Chief Davenport. We're here buying guns. They're gonna attack someplace. I'll leave the phone off the hook and try to keep them here . . ."

She placed the phone sideways across the top of the receiver and hurried up the stairs after LaChaise and Martin.

20

LUCAS AND DEL were waking up with day-old danish and plastic foam cups of fake cappuccino when Dispatch called.

"Woman called for you and identified herself as Sandy Darling," the dispatcher said without preamble, excitement under her steady voice. "Said they were buying guns and they're gonna attack something, but she didn't say what or when. She left the phone off the hook. We've got Minnetonka started that way, but they've got almost nobody around: it'll be a few minutes."

"Well, Jesus . . ." Lucas jumped up and grabbed his coat as he spoke into the phone: "How long ago did she call?"

"Thirty-five seconds."

"Warn Minnetonka about the guns. Don't let some guy be a hero, just seal off the streets around the address and bring in a team, or whatever they do out there . . . If they need aid, get Lester and see if we can ship some of our ERU guys out, or maybe Hennepin County guys."

"Marie is doing that now, most of it. Are you going?"

"Yeah. Gimme the address . . ."

He scribbled it down and said, "Direct us in there: we'll be on the air in one minute."

He slammed the phone down and Del said, "What?" and Lucas said, "Darling called. She said they're buying guns and she left the phone off the hook." They were already running down the hallway.

LACHAISE AND MARTIN had rolled the rifles under their coats, and when Sandy came up from the basement, Martin asked, "Get it all?"

"I got most of it," she said, rattling the shells in her pockets. She felt herself flushing, and thought, Oh my God; Martin would figure it out. She said, "There's a lot more ammo down there. I think we missed most of it . . ."

"Forget it," Martin said. He turned away and said to Frank, "Here." He handed the white-haired man a wad of cash.

"This is not exactly a purchase," Frank said, tightly.

"Take the fuckin' money," Martin said impatiently. "I feel bad enough anyway. The cash comes off a drug dealer downtown, there's no tracing it, it's all clean. It'll more than cover the cost of the stuff."

"Still not right," Frank said. He took the money.

"I know," Martin said, almost gently. "But there's no help for it. Now walk us out to the car so you can wave good-bye."

They were in the car, rolling, and Frank went back to the house with his hands in his pockets. They turned the corner, headed down another side street, then out to the highway. As they sat at the intersection, waiting for the light, a dark sedan crossed the highway against the light, and flashed past, heading into the welter of streets they'd just left.

"Asshole," LaChaise muttered.

Sandy closed her eyes.

LUCAS PUSHED THE Explorer out I-394, his foot to the floor, the car banging and creaking with the speed, Del braced in the passenger seat, cursing with every slip and bump. Dispatch said the owner of the phone was a guy named Frank Winter, no priors anywhere, but he was a registered federal firearms dealer.

"So she knew what she was talking about," Del said.

Ten minutes after they left City Hall, they found a phalanx of City of Minnetonka and Hennepin County cars blocking access to the subdivision. Lucas hung his badge out the window and a cop pointed at a group of men, some in uniform and some in plainclothes. Lucas parked and he and Del walked over.

The command cops looked up and one of them, in plainclothes, said, "Lucas," and Lucas nodded and said, "Gene, what's happening?"

"We got a couple of guys in the house across the street," the cop said. "There're lights on, but there's no cars out front. There's a set of tracks going up into the driveway, and then backing out. Pretty fresh. We've had this off-and-on snow and the guys say the tracks are crisp."

"Might have come and gone," a uniformed cop said.

"The question is, do we call ahead? Or do we just take the place?"

Lucas shrugged and grinned at him. "You da man."

"Yeah, right," the plainclothes cop said sourly. Then, "Fuck it. He's a firearms dealer, so he could have all kinds of shit in there . . . If we go bustin' in, we could have a fight. If we call ahead, what can they do? Can't get out."

He was thinking out loud. One of the Hennepin cops said, "He can't flush the evidence down the toilet."

"Huh. All right. Let's call."

FRANK WINTER CAME out of the house with his hands over his head, and stood that way in the driveway, until an armored cop directed him down the middle of the street to a blocking car. Winter said on the phone that LaChaise, Martin and Darling had been there—had left only fifteen minutes earlier—but the house was now empty. When he got to the blocking car, where Lucas and Del were waiting with a group of uniformed cops, one of the uniforms turned Winter around and patted him down.

"He's wearing a vest," one of the cops said.

"Why the vest?" Del asked.

"In case one of you officers decided to shoot me," Winter said simply. "The woman called you in, didn't she?"

"What woman?"

"The one with Martin and his friend," Winter said. Then, "Do I need a lawyer?"

"Better give him his rights," Lucas said, and one of the cops recited the code. "You want one?"

"Yeah, I better," Winter said. "I was sitting there, thinking about calling you, when you called me."

"Why didn't you?" Lucas asked.

"Because I figured Martin would kill me, or LaChaise."

"What'd they get from you?" Del asked.

"A couple of pistols, an accurized seven-mil-Magnum Model 70 and a box of handloads and a whole bunch of AR-15 ammo. Martin's an Armalite freak: he's always reworking them. I'd be careful. I'd bet they've got modified with them."

"This Model 70," Lucas said. "Got a scope?"

"Yeah. A Leupold Vari-X III in 3.5 × 10."

"A sniper rifle."

"A varminter," said Winter.

"Yeah, if elk are varmints," Lucas said.

AN ENTRY TEAM swept the house. The basement was an arsenal, but, as one of the cops said cheerfully, "Nothin' illegal about that."

Lucas was looking at a Model 70, a gray synthetic-stocked Winchester .300 Magnum with a Pentax scope. He turned the eyepiece down to two-power and sighted across the basement at a crosshairs target. Winter had opened the gun safes so the weapons could be inventoried, and they'd found fifty handguns, two dozen rifles and as many shotguns. Del was playing with a derringer, snapping it at a wall target, and Lucas was looking at the butt of the Model 70, when a plainclothes cop came halfway down the stairs and said, "We're sending Winter downtown. You got anything else you want to ask him?"

"Naw. I kind of think he's telling the truth," Lucas said.

"So do I, but he should have called us," the cop said. He grinned and said, "Now he claims he tried to call out, but his phone was screwed up and he was afraid to go out. Says he didn't know the phone was off the hook down here, just that it didn't work."

"Not bad, if he sticks to it," Lucas said.

The cop said, "We got guys walking the neighborhood, checking about the car." Winter had said LaChaise, Martin and Darling were in a big brown car, but he didn't notice what kind because he wasn't thinking about it. Maybe a Lincoln or a Buick. The cop went on, "The media are swarming in."

"Jesus, that was quick," Del said.

"They're monitoring everything . . ."

"Can't let them know that there was a tip," Lucas said. "LaChaise'll know where it came from and he'll kill the woman."

"What'll I tell them? They'll want to know."

Lucas scratched his head, formulating the lie: "Tell them that Winter called us. Tell them that we used an entry team because we were concerned it might be some kind of ambush, and Winter was known to be a gun dealer with heavy weapons . . . Get that word out quick, so we don't get anybody speculating about tips . . . I'll get my chief to back us up, and we'll talk to Winter's lawyer about keeping Winter's mouth shut."

"All right." The cop nodded, and hurried back up the stairs.

Lucas turned to Del and said, "Look at this."

Del came over and Lucas knelt by the gun safe and said, "See the dust?"

There was a faint patina of dust on the floor of the middle safe, where Winter said he'd kept the stolen guns.

Del nodded. "Yeah?"

"Three guns were taken out of here. See? You can just barely see the outlines . . ." Lucas traced the dust outlines in the air, his finger a half-inch above them.

"Yeah?"

"Watch this . . ." He put the Model 70 in a rack-slot on the opposite end of the gun safe, and wiggled it in place. When he picked it up, he'd left in the dust an almost imperceptible outline of the gun butt.

"Doesn't look the same," Del said. "Too fat."

"But he said a Model 70 and this is a Model 70." He turned to the Minnetonka cop doing the inventory. "Give me one of those ARs, would you?"

The cop handed him an AR, a legal, unmodified rifle, and Lucas printed the butt in the dust next to the Model 70 imprint. The two prints were distinctly different—but the AR's print matched the dust shadows of the three stolen guns.

"They took the ARs out of here," Del said.

"And they're modified," Lucas said. "That's why he laid that rap on us about Martin modifying guns. He wanted us to know that they're running around with machine guns, but he didn't want to say they came from him."

"I'm getting pretty fuckin' tired of this machine gun shit," Del said.

"Let's get a photographer down here and see if we can get some shots of this," Lucas said, tapping the edge of the safe. "I don't know if we can get Winter or not. He's a smart guy. But maybe we can fuck with him a little."

"Why'd they come out for more guns? They've got guns."

"Because of Franklin," Lucas said. "If they'd shot Franklin with an AR, it would've gone through that vest like it was cheese." He took a slow turn around the basement, looking up at the ceiling: the ceiling was neat, just the way the rest of the basement was. Lucas's basement joists were full of cobwebs, which he had every intention of leaving alone.

"Say they took three ARs off Winter. And he says they took three vests. I'd say they're gonna make a suicide run."

"On what? The hotel?"

"Maybe," Lucas said, but then shook his head. "I really think it's gonna come somewhere else. They gotta figure that none of us are hanging around home, not after Franklin. They can't get at the hotel, we've made that pretty clear."

"They're gonna hit the hospital," Del said, suddenly white-faced. "They're going back in after Cheryl and Franklin, and Franklin's old lady's been over there . . . Shit, where's the telephone?"

STADIC HEARD ABOUT the scramble out to Minnetonka, and called LaChaise, while LaChaise, Martin and Sandy were still driving back downtown.

"They're out there now," he said, with thin satisfaction. "They were about five minutes off your ass."

"What happened to Winter?" LaChaise asked, prompted by Martin.

"They're talking to him. The way I heard it, he's cooperating."

"Fucker must've called them the minute we were gone," LaChaise said. "They got the car?"

"I don't know," Stadic said.

"We better get out of sight."

"Yeah: and one more thing. Me and a half-dozen other guys are supposed to be on the way to Hennepin General. They think you might be on the way there."

"What? Why?"

"I don't know, but we're on the way over there. They talked to Winter, and he must've said something."

"I gotta think," LaChaise said. "Something's screwy."

STADIC SAT BEHIND a desk in the emergency room, a shotgun by his feet, while Lester and another cop named Davis talked about ways of blocking off the drive without being too conspicuous about it. Lucas and Del showed up, cold, damp, hurried.

"You get the new composites on the street?" Lucas asked Lester.

"Yeah, and we got the car out," Lester said. As they talked, they drifted toward a group of chairs a few feet from Stadic. "Big brown car. What the fuck does that mean? What we got to do is break out where they're hiding."

"Until we do that . . ."

Davenport went on talking but Stadic blanked. All he could think of was, Big Brown Car. And he thought, *Oh, shit, they're at Harp's.*

At noon, he was relieved of duty. He stopped at the office just long enough to pick up a pair of 8 × 50 naval binoculars, then drove down toward Harp's place. He stopped a block and a half away and put the glasses on the windows above the laundromat. He hadn't been watching for more than five minutes when he saw the blinds move—somebody looking out at the street.

All right, he had them again. Same deal? He could wait in the street until they came out—they'd be in the car, that'd be a problem. He could maybe park across the street, and wait: and when he saw the garage door going up, he could run over to the driver's side, blow it up from one foot away—press the muzzle of the shotgun against the glass and pull the trigger. That would take out the driver, then the other guy . . . He'd need his vest.

He chewed his thumbnail nervously. A lot could go wrong. There'd be questions, later, too. But he could talk those away. He kept thinking about the death of Sell-More, he'd say, and how Harp seemed to tie into it. He ran Harp's name on the computer and came up with a Lincoln . . . but why wouldn't he tell everybody at that point? Why would he go in by himself?

He tried to work it through, but his mind wasn't right: too tired. He drove past the apartment to a liquor store with a pay phone, and dialed LaChaise again.

"We're looking for a big brown car, a Lincoln or a Buick."

"That's it? No tags?"

"No tags. But they've got a new composite out on you—it won't be on TV until the late news, they want to see if you hit the hospital. But they say you've got gray hair, and gray beards, and you look like old men."

"That fuckin' Winter," LaChaise said. Then, "What's it like at the hospital. Security?"

"Tighter than a drum."

"Goddamnit . . ."

"If I was you, I'd think about packing up and getting out," Stadic said. "Your time's running out."

After a moment, LaChaise said, "Maybe."

Stadic could hear him breathing; five seconds, ten. Then Stadic said, "Really?"

"We're talking about it," LaChaise said. "Mexico."

21

THE WHOLE DAY dragged, the hours squeezing by: every cop in the department was on the street: there were rumors that the local gangs were filling up the Chicago-bound buses, just to get out of the pressure.

Lucas had run out of ideas, and spent half the day at the hospital, with dwindling expectations.

Night came, but no LaChaise . . .

THE HOSPITAL WAS quiet, dark. Nurses padded around in running shoes, answering calls from individual rooms, pushing pills. Lucas, Del and a narcotics cop named McKinney hung out in an office just off the main lobby. There was no telling where LaChaise and Martin would try to crack the place—if they tried at all—but from the lobby, they could move quickly to either end of the building.

"Unless they come in by parachute," McKinney said.

"That'd be good," Del said. "You see that movie?"

"Yeah . . . actually, there've been a couple of them. There was that one where the guy jumps out of the plane without a 'chute, you see that one? Grabs the guy in midair?"

"What's-his-name was in it, the kid, you know, the *Excellent Adventure* guy," Lucas said.

"Yeah, I saw that," said McKinney. "That's what got me jumpin'."

"Hey, you jump? Far out . . ."

They talked about skydiving until they wore it out, then Lucas went back down the hall and crawled into an empty bed. Del sat up with McKinney; when first light came, he put his gun away and went to sit with Cheryl until she woke.

"YOU WANT ME to drive?" Martin asked Sandy.

"No, I'm okay," she said.

"Watch your speed. We don't want to attract no cops," Martin said.

"Maybe we should of stopped in Des Moines," LaChaise said. "This is a long fuckin' way."

LaChaise had spent the trip in the backseat. Whenever they passed a highway patrolman—they'd seen three—he sprawled out of sight.

"Yeah, well, we're almost there," Martin said. "See that glow out there? Way off, straight ahead? That's Kansas City."

They'd made the decision late in the afternoon, LaChaise and Martin, and just after dark, LaChaise had walked back to the bedroom and said, "Get your stuff ready."

Sandy sat up. "Where're we going?"

"Mexico."

"Mexico? Dick, are you serious?" She felt a quick beat of hope. If they made it out of town, they'd have some room. And someplace along the road, they'd forget about her for a while, and she'd walk away. A dusty little restaurant someplace, a small town out on the desert . . . she'd wait until they started eating, then she'd tell them she had to go to the ladies' room and then she'd walk out, leave a note on the car seat, hide until they were gone.

It was all there, in her mind's eye: and when they were gone—long gone— she'd turn herself in. Work it out.

A possibility.

But now Dick was complaining that they'd come too far? What was all that about?

She thought about it, a sinking feeling, and finally asked, "Why is Kansas City too far, Dick?" He didn't answer immediately. "Dick?"

"Because we don't want to drive in the daytime," Martin said. He looked at his watch. "It'll be light in another hour. We've got to find a motel."

Martin spotted an all-night supermarket on the outskirts of the city, and told Sandy to take the off ramp. LaChaise waited in the car with Sandy until Martin returned: he'd bought two loaves of bread, a couple of pounds of sandwich meat, and two big bars of dark green auto mechanic's soap.

"What's the soap for?" Sandy asked, peering into the bag.

"Whittlin'," Martin said, grinning at her.

LaChaise rented a room in a chain motel called the Red Roof Inn. LaChaise went in because he'd shaved just before they left the Cities, and Sandy had given him a neat trim. Wearing one of Harp's suits with a silk tie, he looked like a Republican. He paid cash for the room, two days, said he was alone, and asked that the maid be told not to wake him up.

"Been traveling all night," he said.

"No problem," said the woman behind the desk.

The room was on the back side of the motel, with two double beds and a TV. They slept, restlessly, until two o'clock, when Martin got up and ordered a pizza, Coke and coffee from a local pizza place. The stuff was delivered, no questions, and they ate silently. At four, with the sun slipping down in the west, they went back out to the car.

Martin said, "I'll drive."

"That's all right, I . . ."

"Get in the back and shut up," LaChaise said.

"What's going on?" Sandy asked. LaChaise grabbed her by the jacket and jerked her forward, until his face was only an inch from hers: she could smell the cheese and onions from the pizza.

"Change of plans. Now get in the fuckin' car."

She got in the car. "Dick, what're you going to do? Dick . . . ?"

"We're gonna rob another goddamned credit union, is what we're gonna do," LaChaise said.

LUCAS WAS AT the hospital because he couldn't think of any better place to be: they now hadn't heard from LaChaise for thirty-six hours. Del, Sloan, Sherrill came and went and returned. They were running out of conversational gambits, sitting in dark rooms, out of sight, waiting . . .

Lester called. "Lucas: LaChaise, Martin and Darling just hit a credit union in Kansas City. Not more than an hour ago—four twenty-five."

"Kansas City?" The news came like a punch, left him unsteady. "Are they sure?"

"Yeah, they say there's no doubt. We're getting a videotape relayed through TV3. The Kansas City cops gave it to everybody in sight."

"How soon will you have the tape?"

"Ten or fifteen minutes, I guess. TV3's putting it on the air soon as they get it. We're gonna tape it off them."

Lucas hung up and looked at Sherrill and Sloan: "You ain't gonna believe it," he said.

THE ROBBERY WAS smooth, professional. Martin was in first with an AR-15. He was shouting the moment he came through the door, leveling the rifle, pointing at people.

LaChaise pushed Sandy Darling through the door behind Martin, then vaulted up on the counter. There were only two customers in the place, and three people behind the counter. LaChaise looted the cash drawers, said something to one of the younger women, smacked her on the ass with the palm of his hand and crossed through the counter gate. The camera, taking in the whole office, showed Sandy Darling pressed against the wall, her hands over her ears.

"They ain't no cherries," Del said. They were in Homicide, fifteen guys and four women standing around a small TV.

"You've seen it before," Lucas said. "It's the same goddamn robbery that we broke up, all over again."

"Except for the grenade," Sherrill said.

As they were backing out the door, Martin gave a little speech. "We want everybody into the manager's office, on the floor, behind the desk. We're gonna roll a hand grenade in here . . . now I don't want to scare anyone, 'cause they're nothing like you see in movies. There'll just be a little pop. You'll be fine if you're behind the desk . . ."

Martin held up what looked like a grenade, and the office staff and customers jammed into the manager's office, out of sight. Martin called, "Here we go," and rolled the grenade into the room, and disappeared. The grenade turned out to be a hand-carved lump of green soap that didn't look too much like a grenade, when you looked at it close.

"No plates," Lucas grunted, watching. "They didn't want anybody to run out and see the car and get the plates."

"Darling didn't look too happy to be there. No gun, she looked scared, they had to push her in and out," Sloan said.

"They got eight grand," said somebody else.

"So he says to this chick," Lester began, and then corrected himself, ". . . this woman, the teller, he says, 'You oughta make it to Acapulco sometime, honey.' "

"Sounds like bullshit," said Del.

"I don't know," Lester said. "He's the kind of guy who'd say something like that." He looked around the room: "I wish we'd taken him here, goddamnit."

LATE THAT NIGHT, Sandy sat in the backseat, unmoving, wide awake, not quite believing it. The lights of Des Moines were fading in the rear window. They were headed back to Minneapolis, ahead of what the all-night stations were saying was a major storm coming up from the Southwest. Already blizzard conditions in Nebraska.

They'd be in the Cities by dawn, back in the apartment. The whole thing had been a game, to loosen up the targets.

"A stroke of fuckin' genius," LaChaise said, pounding Martin on the back. "I just wish we had someplace to spend the cash."

22

LUCAS SAT AWAKE, trying to make sense of it. if LaChaise and Martin were on a suicide run—and it had appeared that way from the beginning—what had changed their minds? They couldn't believe that escape was as simple as running to Mexico. The Mexicans would ship them back to the States as quickly as they were found; or kill them.

Maybe it was simpler than he was making it: maybe their nerve failed.

He got up, hands in his pockets, and stared out the window across his snow-covered lawn. In the distance, on the other side of the Mississippi, he could see Christmas lights red, green and white along somebody's roofline. A silent night.

And he was restless. He hadn't wanted Weather to come back to the house—one more night in the hotel, he'd said, just until we find their trail again—but she'd insisted. She wanted to sleep in her own bed. She was in it now, and sleeping soundly.

Lucas was sitting up with a pistol and a twelve-gauge Wingmaster pump. He looked at a clock: four in the morning.

He picked up a TV remote, pointed at a small TV in the corner of the room, and called up the aviation weather service. All day, the weather forecasters had been talking about a huge low-pressure system that was pinwheeling up from the southern Rockies. Snow had overrun all of the southwestern and south-central parts of the state, and now the weather radar showed it edging into the metro area.

If they were coming back, he thought—if this thing was no more than a shuck—and if they'd fallen behind the snow line, they might be stalled for a day. If they'd stayed ahead of it, they'd be coming into town about now.

Nobody thought they'd be coming back. The network TV people were getting out of town as fast as they could pack up and find space on an outgoing plane. Nobody wanted to be stuck out in flyover country the week before Christmas, not with a big storm coming.

The cops were the same way: going home, filing for overtime. Lucas called Kansas City cops, and the Missouri and Kansas highway patrols every hour, looking for even the faintest sniff of LaChaise. Nobody had gotten one: they'd vanished.

Just as if they'd taken country roads east and north, instead of west and south, where the search was focused, Lucas thought. He looked out the window again, then self-consciously went and closed the wooden blinds.

After killing the TV, he wandered through the dark house, moving by touch, listening, trailing the shotgun. He checked the security system, got a drink of water and went back to the living room where he dropped on a couch. In a few minutes, he eased into a fitful sleep, the .45 in a belly holster, the shotgun on the coffee table.

THEY STAYED AHEAD of the snow.

They drove through southern Iowa in the crackling cold, millions of stars but no moon, following the red and yellow lights of the freighter trucks heading into Des Moines, and after Des Moines, up toward Minneapolis-St. Paul. They stopped once at a gas station, the bare-faced LaChaise pumping the gas and paying a sleepy attendant, the hood of his parka covering his head, a scarf shrouding his neck.

"Colder'n a witch's left tit," the attendant said. He looked at a thermometer in the window. "Six below. You want some Heat to put in the gas?"

"Yeah, that'd be good," LaChaise said. A compact television sat in a corner, turned to CNN. As the attendant was ringing up the sale, a security-camera videotape came up, replaying the Kansas City robbery.

"What's that shit?" LaChaise asked.

The attendant glanced at the TV. "Ah, it's them assholes that were up in the Cities. They're making a run for Mexico."

"Good," LaChaise said.

"Wisht I was going with them," the attendant said, and he counted out the change.

As they continued up I-35, the nighttime radio stations came and went, playing Christmas music. Clouds began to move in, like dark arrows overhead; the stars winked out.

"Christmas, four days," Sandy said, sadness in her voice.

"Don't mean a fuckin' thing to me," LaChaise said. "My old man drank up our Christmases."

"You must of had a few," Sandy said.

LaChaise sat silent for a moment, then said, "Maybe a couple." He thought about his sister and her feetsie pajamas.

Martin said, "We had a couple of good ones, when my old man was alive. He got me a fire engine, once."

"What happened to him?" Sandy asked.

"He died," Martin said. "Throat cancer."

"Jeez, that's awful," Sandy said. "I'm sorry."

"Hard way to go," Martin said. "Then it was me and my ma, and we didn't have no Christmases after that."

LaChaise didn't like the subject matter and fiddled with the radio: the scanner locked on "O Holy Night."

"I know this song; my old man used to sing it," Martin said.

And he sang along in a creditable baritone,

O holy night, the stars are brightly shining, this is the night of the birth of Our Lord.

Sandy and LaChaise, astonished, glanced at each other: then Sandy looked out the windows, at the thin snowflakes now streaking past, and felt like she was a long way from anywhere.

They drove in silence for a long time, and Sandy slept off and on. She woke with the sense that it was much later, sat up, and looked out. They'd slowed: the snow was now coming at the front of the car like a tornado funnel, but they were passing through a bridge of light.

"Where are we?" she asked.

"Just south of the Cities," Martin said. "We'll be in town in twenty minutes."

"Lots of snow."

"Started hard about ten minutes ago," Martin said. He looked at LaChaise. "What do you think?"

"Let's do it. Get back, drop Sandy and do it." He looked out the window. "This storm is perfect. We won't get a better shot than this."

"What?" Sandy asked.

LaChaise looked back over the seat. "We're gonna take the hospital."

LACHAISE CAME TO him in a dream. Lucas was on the couch, struggling to wake up, but he couldn't. He was too tired, and whenever he tried to open his eyes, he'd immediately fall back into a deep sleep—and then struggle out again. He *had* to wake up, because LaChaise and Martin and Darling were sneaking through the garage, coming up to the kitchen door, guns in their hands, laughing, while Lucas struggled to wake . . .

"Lucas. Lucas . . ."

He bolted up, and Weather jumped back. "Whoa," he said. "Sorry."

"That's okay. You wanted me to wake you . . ."

"Time to go?"

She was dressed in slacks and a long-sleeved blouse, operating clothes, and was carrying a plastic bag with one of her simple black Donna Karan suits from Saks. Faculty meetings. "Pretty soon. I'll put some coffee on. It's snowing like crazy out there."

MARTIN SKETCHED OUT the layout of the Eighth Street entry of the Hennepin County Medical Center, from the earlier recon.

"Two doors: the main emergency room is locked. We could fake that we're hurt, and they'd let us in, but there'll be a bunch of people there . . ." He tapped the second door. "This one leads back to the main lobby, right past the emergency room—the emergency room is off to the left, down this hall. There's a guard desk just inside. If we was hurt, he'd let us in, I seen hurt people come in that door. But we'd have to take him out . . ."

"No problem."

". . . Then we go on down the hall and the elevators are over to the left. We want the second-floor surgical care . . ."

They worked through it: get the room numbers at the front desk, get up, hit the place, get out.

Martin said, "It's six blocks or so: if we really got in trouble, we could run back here in five minutes, on foot. That snow'd help: can't see shit in the snow, not until dawn. We got almost two hours yet."

"Let's do it."

Sandy didn't want to hear about it. She paced in the bedroom, stared at the walls: but not dumbly. Her mind was a torrent, a jumble of suppositions and possibilities. She looked at the window and thought, *I should have jumped.*

In the front room, Martin and LaChaise geared up—each with two pistols and an AR-15, each wearing a bulletproof vest. "Wish I could take the bow," Martin said.

"Makes no sense," LaChaise grunted.

"What about Sandy?" Martin asked, dropping his voice. "Chain her up again?"

"If we don't, she'll split," LaChaise said.

"Which wouldn't be that terrible, if she didn't tip off the cops."

"She would," LaChaise said. "She's been thinking about how to get out— how to save her ass."

Martin nodded. "Yeah. Well. We could do her."

LaChaise said, "Yeah, we could."

"Can't take her with us," Martin said.

LaChaise pulled on his long winter coat, slipped his arm out of one sleeve, and held the AR-15 beneath it. "How do I look?" he asked Martin.

"Okay, as long as you're a little ways off."

"Huh." LaChaise turned the weapon in his hands, looked back toward the bedroom and said, "If you want to do her, you could. Or we could just chain her up again."

Martin thought for a minute, and said, "If we do this right—if we faked them out—we could be coming back. We might need her."

"So we chain her up," LaChaise said.

"Well—unless you really want to do her."

LACHAISE CAME INTO the bedroom and said, "We're gonna have to chain you up again."

"Dick, for God's sakes . . ."

"Hey, shut up. Listen. We can't let you go to the cops. And you would. So we're gonna chain you up. It's either that, or . . ." He shrugged.

"You shoot me."

"Probably wouldn't shoot you," he said.

The way he said it chilled her. Probably wouldn't shoot her. Probably kill her with a knife, she thought. Martin liked the knife.

"So put your coat on . . ."

She put her coat on, afraid to say anything at all. She was standing on a knife edge. She went ahead of LaChaise, down the stairs, where Martin was waiting like Old Man Death. He was holding the chain.

"Sorry about this," he said, but he didn't sound sorry.

They'd put the chair back next to the post, and they chained her into it again, snapping the padlocks. "You'll be okay," LaChaise said.

"What if you don't come back?" she blurted.

He said, "You better hope we do—you'd have to get pretty damn skinny to get out of that chain." He grinned at his own wit, then said, "We'll leave the keys over on the steps."

He dropped the keys on the steps, far out of reach, and then they got in the car, ran the garage door up, backed out, and dropped the door, Sandy disappearing behind it.

"Glad we didn't do her," LaChaise said.

"Yeah?"

"When we do her, I want to fuck her first. She always sorta treated me like I wasn't . . . good enough."

LUCAS FOLLOWED WEATHER to a parking ramp a block from the University Hospitals, a slippery slog through the heavy, wet snow. On the way, he checked with Del, who was staying at the hospital, to see if he was awake yet.

"Just barely," Del said. "I'm thinking about brushing my teeth."

"Cheryl's still asleep?"

"Like a baby."

"I'm heading into the office," Lucas said. "I'll walk over later."

"Is it snowing yet?"

"Look out the window," Lucas said. "It's gonna be a nightmare."

Lucas followed Weather into the parking ramp, waited until she'd parked her car, then drove her back out of the ramp to the hospital entrance, and saw her as far as the front desk.

"This is a little ridiculous," she said.

"I'll feel funny about it when I hear LaChaise is dead," he said.

Inside, he said, "Call me before you head home." She waved a hand as she headed toward the elevators, turned the corner out of sight.

Lucas headed back to the car. He'd had the shotgun between the seats, and now he put it on the floor in front of the backseats, out of sight. He had to use the wipers to clear the window, and he horsed the Explorer out of the parking circle and headed toward the office.

23

LACHAISE LOOKED AT Martin: "This is it, dude."

Martin nodded. "Could be."

"We could drive north up to Canada, run out of the snow, head west . . ."

Martin said, "The Canadians got computers at the border. We'd set them off like a skyrocket."

LaChaise was silent for a minute: "Probably couldn't get out of the snow anyway." They slowed at a cross street, and a single orange plow truck, its blade raised off the roadway, went banging by: "Look at that asshole. Doing nothing, probably getting overtime." LaChaise's mouth was running: "You scared?"

Martin seemed to think for a minute. "No," he said.

"Tense?"

"I'm . . . thinking."

"Somebody ought to," LaChaise joked.

"We gotta be ready to ditch the car," he said. "I don't think we'll get in and out without running into somebody—we can take them if we're fast enough, that won't be a problem, but in maybe two or three minutes, we'll have cops coming in from the outside, ready for us. If we've got them hot on our trail, you go left and I'll go right. But remember, they can track us: try to stay in the street where you can. That'll slow them down . . ."

"That's just if we have trouble."

"Yeah."

LUCAS CROSSED THE Mississippi on the Washington Avenue bridge, rolled through a couple of turns in Cedar-Riverside and eased the Explorer into the loop. He could make thirty miles an hour, but even in four-wheel drive, the truck's wheels kept breaking loose. The driver's-side windshield wiper, which had never worked right, left a frozen streak just at his eye level. He had the radio going, and the morning show guy on 'CCO said there'd be a foot of snow on the ground when the storm ended.

"We've got school closings all over southwest and east-central Minnesota, and the Minneapolis and St. Paul systems will be making a call in the next ten minutes. The governor'll probably shut down state government, since he does it every time somebody sees a snowflake . . . don't get me started on that, though . . ."

A cop car was pulling out of the driveway at the medical center when LaChaise and Martin arrived. They coasted to the curb and sat for two minutes, letting the cop get well clear, then Martin said, "You're the hurt one. Pull your hat down."

"I'm good," LaChaise said. He was breathing through his mouth again, gulping air. "My fuckin' heart feels like it's gonna explode."

Martin took the car into the emergency entrance drive: "You won't notice when we get inside."

"This is a fuckin' war, man," LaChaise said. "This is like fuckin' 'Nam."

"Especially the snow," Martin said.

MARTIN STOPPED OUTSIDE the first of the two doors and left the car running. If they made it back, it'd be quicker. If they didn't, who cared what happened to the car?

LaChaise got out of the driver's side, and limped toward the door to the lobby. Martin ran around the front of the car and caught him, slipped an arm around him, and they hobbled to the entrance. The door was open, all right, and just like Martin said, a security guard was looking at them from a phone-booth-sized security room just inside the entrance.

"Little help," Martin grunted at the guard. "He's hurt."

The guard didn't even hesitate, but went out a small door on the side of the room into a hall and walked up to them and said, "What's the . . ."

And saw the guns.

"Turn around," Martin said quietly, pointing the AR-15 at the guard's chest. "We don't want to hurt you."

"Aw, shit."

"Yeah, shit," LaChaise said. "Turn around."

The guard wavered and then said, "Naw. Fuck you."

"Fuck me?" Too quickly to see, Martin struck the guard in the face with the butt of the eight-pound rifle, a horizontal stroke that caught the man in the forehead with the force of a small sledge. The guard jerked back into the wall and slid to the floor.

"Go," Martin said, but LaChaise was already moving, heading down the hall to the lobby.

Visiting hours didn't start until midmorning, so only seven people turned to look at them when they walked into the lobby: a woman and two children; two young men who sat together; a teenaged girl who curled on a chair, reading a romance novel; and the woman behind the reception desk, who said, "Great God Almighty."

They did it like a bank job: LaChaise faced the people waiting in the lobby chairs, and made his little speech: "Don't anybody move . . ."

Martin focused on the woman behind the counter: "We want the room numbers for Capslock and Franklin in surgical care. If you don't give them to us quick, we'll kill you."

"Yes, sir." She called up the names on the computers and read off the room numbers. LaChaise could see them over her shoulder.

"Where are those numbers? When we get off the elevators."

"You turn to your right going down the hall . . ." She drew a line on the desk with her index finger. Martin nodded.

"All right, come out of there, and sit with these other people," Martin said. "Keep your hands where I can see them."

They'd been inside for a little more than a minute.

LaChaise pushed the elevator call button as the woman walked from behind the desk. Martin motioned her toward a chair, and as she went past him, struck her with the gun butt as he had the security guard. The butt hit the woman in the nose, which shattered, and she went down with a chopped-off shriek. The teenaged girl yelped at the same instant, but choked it off, a hand over her mouth. The two young men watched them with flat eyes that said they'd seen guns before.

"Anybody calls the cops, we come down here and waste them," LaChaise snarled. "And you know we will."

The elevator car arrived and LaChaise and Martin backed inside. As the door closed, they heard people running.

THE TWO MEN ran for the door while the woman tried to gather up her kids and start moving. She was screaming, "Help us, help us . . ."

The teenaged girl stepped to a wall-mounted fire alarm and pulled the handle down.

Inside the elevator, the alarm went off like a bomb. LaChaise freaked: "Holy shit . . ." and kicked the doors.

"Hang on, we'll be there in one second," Martin said. But it took longer than that, eight or ten seconds, with the alarm screaming the whole time.

DEL WAS BRUSHING his teeth in a rest room when the alarm went off. He spat once, caught his pistol in his right hand and his radio in the left, ran toward the door with white foam dripping down his chin and said into the radio, "Lucas? Lucas?"

Lucas came right back. "Yeah?"

Del was in the hall, running toward his wife's room. "Something's happening here, there's some kind of alarm."

"Be there in one minute," Lucas said. "I'm right straight down on Washington."

"Get some more guys coming . . ."

FRANKLIN WAS ASLEEP when the alarm went off, but it shook him awake and he pushed himself up, reached for the bedside table and pulled his pistol out. He could hear people in the hallways, the night nurses, he thought. But the alarm made too much sense to him. They were coming, he thought, just like Davenport said they might, and there weren't any cops between himself and the door. He'd have to do it alone . . .

And then Del yelled, "Franklin, I'm in Cheryl's room, you awake?"

And he yelled back, "Yeah, I'm up now."

"Can you get to the door?"

"Yeah."

Franklin pulled the IV from his arm and more or less fell off the bed onto his good side, winced at the impact, and low-crawled to the doorway. Two nurses were standing in the hall, looking up and down it, and he shouted at them: "Get out of sight. Get out of sight."

They saw the gun in his hand, froze for a second, then scurried into a doorway. Del peeked from the doorway across the hall two doors down. "Maybe it's not . . ." he shouted.

But as he said it, LaChaise peeked from his end of the hall. His face was clean-shaven but unmistakable, as was the hard black form of his rifle. Del snapped a shot, missing, and Franklin jerked one off and thought it'd probably gone into the ceiling. Then LaChaise was out of sight for a second, and the next second, the muzzle of the rifle came around the corner and began chattering down the hall, a ferocious up-close pounding followed by a hail of plaster from the walls, the bits and pieces of .223 slugs zipping past like bees, the sound of shattering glass, and then the quick hollow boom of Del's automatic.

With plaster pouring on him like rain, Franklin peeked down the hall, saw movement and fired three quick shots. Somebody screamed, "No," a yelp, the sound of a man hit. Then the machine gun opened up again, and more plaster rained down, and the door above his head exploded in plastic and chipboard splinters.

Del, across the hallway, heard the man scream "No," and thought that Franklin had hit one of them. Franklin fired three more times and Del popped back out and fired three evenly spaced shots: Franklin was working a revolver, and he'd need time to reload. There was now so much dust in the hallway that Del could barely see the end of it. Then there was movement again and he jerked his head back and the walls came apart again and something slashed at his throat. He touched it, he could feel something sticking out. A bone? A piece of his jawbone? Shocked, he turned and looked at Cheryl, whom he'd rolled off the bed onto the floor. She was looking at him and began screaming and crawling forward, toward him.

He was hurt, but he didn't feel hurt: he popped out the door and fired another half-dozen shots down the hall, then snapped on an empty chamber.

Franklin came in with two shots: Del groped for another magazine, dropped the empty out of the gun butt, and slapped the next one in and jacked a shell into the chamber. Cheryl was on top of him, trying to hold him, and he was trying to push her away, get back to the door.

Franklin was yelling, and dimly, he heard, "Hold it, hold it. I think they're gone."

Del looked down the hall, but saw nothing. Then Cheryl was screaming something he couldn't make out, fear in her eyes, and she grabbed at his throat.

MARTIN WAS HIT. The slug, a lucky shot, went through the inside part of his thigh, just below his testicles, catching mostly skin. There was a big artery there, he knew, and he pulled back and ripped open his pants leg. His leg showed a raw open wound but no heavy pulse of blood. He was bleeding, all right, but wouldn't bleed to death—not in the next minute or so. LaChaise was screaming at him, "You hit? You hit?" as he slammed another magazine into the AR.

"Yeah, I'm hit. This is no good, man."

LaChaise jumped into the hallway, fully exposed, like in the cop and cowboy shows, and blew the entire thirty-shot magazine down the halls, playing it like a hose. Martin had gone to the elevators. He pushed the "down" button and the doors slid back: "Let's go!"

"One more," LaChaise screamed. He poured another magazine down the hall, then skipped across the hallway and piled into the elevator and the doors closed and they started down.

"Maybe somebody waiting," LaChaise said. He shoved his last magazine into his rifle. The wells around his eyes were white, his nostrils wide as he gasped for breath: "How bad is it?"

"Bad enough, but I ain't gonna die from it," Martin grunted. "Watch the doors," LaChaise said, and they leveled their rifles at the opening elevator doors. Nobody.

The lobby was deserted and they ran out toward the hall that would lead to the car.

They'd been inside for little more than a minute.

LUCAS SKIDDED TO a stop in the parking lot, on the opposite side of the building from the emergency room entrance. Del's wife was screaming on the radio: "Del's hurt, Del's hurt . . . they're going away, but Del's hurt . . ."

Lucas had everything on the street headed for the hospital, and Dispatch said more guys were running down from City Hall. They'd be there in a minute, in thirty seconds . . . He jammed the truck into park and got the shotgun off the seat and ran toward the lobby doors. As he ran up, he saw the elevators open, and LaChaise and Martin lurched out, Martin hobbling.

They turned the other way, not seeing him, heading down a hall that would lead to the emergency room exit. He was behind them, sixty or eighty feet away, on the wrong side of the hospital. He pulled at the door and nearly fell down: locked.

Without thinking, he backed up a step, pointed the shotgun at LaChaise's back through the glass and fired. The glass exploded, and he pumped and fired through the hole, and pumped again, was aware that somebody was screaming, and then the glass panes ten feet to his left blew out and he could see the flash of a machine gun rolling toward him. He went down and automatically ducked his head, and the shattering glass ripped at his coat and pants.

When the long play of the machine gun passed, he got to his knees and fired two more shots as quickly as he could, got no response and stood up.

The hall opposite him was empty. There was a sudden, keen local silence, as though he had suddenly gone deaf. Then the sound of sirens faded in, and he stepped through the holes in the glass doors and ran across the lobby.

He ducked behind the wall at the reception desk, and saw a woman with a bleeding face looking at him from the floor where she'd crawled for cover. He waited, listening, then hurried down the hall, ready to take someone at the corner . . .

Another body, the security guard, breathing but blowing bubbles of blood. There was a double blood-trail, going out the door, one stopping five feet from the curb, the other going all the way to the curb. They had a car, but they were gone.

A cop car skidded into the lot, and Lucas stepped out with his hands up, waved, groped for his radio and said, "They're on the streets . . . look for the brown car, the big brown car. They're not more than fifteen seconds out of the lot. They got machine guns, they're hit . . ."

A doctor was running down the hall toward him. He glanced at Lucas, then bent over the security guard and shouted back toward the emergency room: "We need a cart, get a goddamn cart."

Lucas said, "There's another one by the reception desk."

The doctor screamed, "We need two carts . . ."

As the cops broke out of the incoming car, Lucas turned and ran back to the lobby. The elevator doors were open, the floor a pool of crimson blood. There was only one puddle, he noticed, with two footprints in it. The other man hadn't been hit yet, so he'd got him with the shotgun.

He pushed two, rode up, and when the doors started to open, he yelled, "Davenport coming in."

He could hear a woman shouting, and he hurried around the corner toward Del's room. Del was on the floor, with Franklin and Cheryl, both in hospital gowns, bent over him. A nurse was hurrying down the hall with a cart.

"How bad?" Lucas yelled as he came up.

"He's not gonna be as pretty as he used to be," Franklin said grimly.

Lucas knelt beside Cheryl and Del looked up at him: a splinter of Formica, thin as a knife, and about the width of a pencil, was sticking through Del's neck, inside the lines of his jaw. He looked at Lucas and shook his head, his eyes wobbling.

Cheryl turned to the nurses and shouted, "Hurry," and to Lucas, in a calmer voice, "It goes all the way through, up in the roof of his mouth."

"Jesus, let's get him . . ."

The nurses came up and Lucas picked Del up and laid him on the cart. "Down to the ER," one of the nurses said. The other one pointed at Cheryl: "And you've got to lie back down, you can't be up . . ." And at Franklin: "You too . . ." She pushed Cheryl toward the bed behind them.

Franklin said, "You get them?"

"They made it out, but we got guys coming in all over the place."

"Shit."

"I hit one of them and you guys hit one. We've got one blood trail going in and out of the elevator, and another one starting in the lobby." Lucas started to tremble with the adrenaline.

"Good," Franklin said, and he began to shake as well. He looked down at the wreckage of the hallway, and said to Lucas, "You know what it was like in here?"

"What?"

"It was like one of those scenes in *Star Wars* where the Storm Troopers are shooting about a million shots at the good guys and never hit anything. I mean, more shit went up and down the hall . . ."

Lucas looked at him, covered with plaster dust, and said, "You know, you might want to sit down."

Franklin rubbed his chest, looked at Cheryl, now flat on her back and deathly pale, and said, "Yeah, I might."

24

MARTIN WAS RUNNING, staggering, turning the corner into the hall that would take him out past the emergency room, past the body on the floor, LaChaise a step behind, when the world blew up again, and a hail of glass and lead blew past them.

LaChaise screamed, but Martin could sense him still moving, then another shot pounded past them and LaChaise turned and opened up with the machine gun and Martin went through the door out onto the sidewalk, half expecting to die there.

But the car was waiting, idling peacefully. A woman was a half-block away, walking toward them carrying a bag. She stopped, suddenly, when she saw them, but Martin was already around the car; he threw the gun in the backseat and climbed inside. LaChaise piled in the passenger side and they rolled out of the lot, the passenger side door flopping open, then slamming as they slewed in a circle and headed south.

"Hurt bad . . ." LaChaise moaned. "My fuckin' legs . . ."

"Fire alarm," Martin said. He had one hand clamped over the wound in his leg, and he could feel the blood seeping between his fingers. "Sonsofbitches set off the fire alarm."

"How bad are you hit?" LaChaise asked, then moaned again as they bounced over a curb and around a corner. The streets were empty.

"I'm bleeding heavy," Martin said. "Christ . . . Hang on."

Martin was trying to turn into the side street that led to the garage. But he was moving too fast, and driving with one hand, and they hit a curb again, ran through a small bare tree, bounced off the parking strip and back into the street. LaChaise, groaning, reached over Martin's head to the sun flap and pushed the button on the garage-door opener. Across the street, the door started up, and Martin horsed the car inside.

Sandy Darling was there with the chain, her eyes wide as she moved behind the steel post, and Martin reached up and jabbed the garage-door opener again and the door started down.

They had not been gone more than ten minutes, and were now no more than a minute and a half out of the hospital. Martin pushed his door open and climbed out, leaving the rifle behind, clutching his thigh, trying to stop the flow of blood.

LaChaise was out, got the padlock keys. "Hurt," he said. "Get your first-aid shit . . . we're hurt."

"What happened?" Sandy asked, as LaChaise popped open the padlock at her waist.

"Fucked up," LaChaise said. "They were waiting."

"Are they coming?"

"Don't know," LaChaise said. "Let's get upstairs . . ."

THE TWO MEN pulled off their outer clothes in the living room. Martin's leg looked like somebody had carved out a golf ball–sized chunk of meat with a dull hunting knife: the wound was circular, ragged, choked with blood and chopped flesh, with pieces of thread from his pants mixed in the gore. Sandy handed him a heavy gauze wound pad and said, "Clamp that over the hole . . . let me look at Dick."

All of LaChaise's wounds were in the back of his legs, the back of his arms and the back of his head, and most were superficial cuts from glass. When he first took off his pants and shirt, he appeared to be shredded. But blood was actively flowing from only one wound, and when Sandy dabbed at the rest of him, she said, "I don't think you're too bad. Get to a hospital, and you won't die."

"Kiss my ass," LaChaise groaned. "Wipe it up or something."

"On the other hand," she said, looking at the one wound that was bleeding, "you've got a bullet hole in the back of your arm." She rolled his arm, and found a lump under the skin near the front. "And that's the bullet, I think."

"Cut it out," LaChaise said.

"It's pretty deep."

"I don't give a fuck, cut it out."

"Dick, I'd just hurt you worse."

"All right, all right . . ."

Martin stretched out on the floor and lay silent and motionless as she poured a glass of water over the wound, probed at it, shook her head and said, "All I can do is put some more pads over it and bind it up. You need a doctor. You're going to get infected."

Martin's stomach heaved and she realized he was laughing: hysterical, she thought. Then again, maybe he thought it was funny. "Infection'll take a couple days. We ain't got a couple days." He looked at LaChaise. "We gotta keep moving, boy."

"I'm really fuckin' hurtin', man."

"They'll wonder where we went, and sooner or later, they'll kick their way in here. If we're gonna do any more damage, we gotta move." He looked at the windows. "Before light."

LaChaise groaned, but got to his hands and knees, looked sideways at Sandy and said, "Tape me up where you can."

"I don't have that much tape."

"Well, get the worst ones," he said. To Martin: "That fuckin' shotgun. Somebody had a fuckin' shotgun and he had me dead, but that first shot missed. That fuckin' glass was like a hurricane . . . Second shot hit me in the vest."

Sandy said, "I'll get a towel."

As she ran back to the bathroom LaChaise crawled across the floor to the bulletproof vest he'd taken off. A ragged pattern of pellet holes punctured the nylon back panel. "Probably shooting triple-ought," he said. "Christ, if he'd been a little worse shot and a little high, I wouldn't have a head."

Martin was on the phone, dialing.

"Surgery, please . . . Thanks." Then, after a moment, "This is Chief Davenport, is my wife Weather there?" He listened as LaChaise watched, then said, "No, that's okay. Tell her to call when she gets done, okay?"

"She's not his fuckin' wife," LaChaise said, when Martin hung up. "Was she there?"

"She's scrubbing for surgery."

"That's where we're going, then," LaChaise said. "That motherfucker Davenport set the whole thing up. I wouldn't be surprised if that was him up in the hallway. Jesus, that was something . . ."

SANDY CAME BACK from the bathroom, and overheard the last part of the conversation. "Where're you going?"

"Hospital where Davenport's old lady works," LaChaise said.

"You gonna let me go?"

"Something like that," LaChaise said, and he grinned at her. Her heart lurched: they were going to kill her.

"Turn over," she said. She dabbed his back with the wet towel, cleaning him up as best she could, isolating the biggest cuts, pulling a few pieces of glass out of his back and legs. "I can't patch the ones under your hair," she said.

"Just get the rest."

Martin had slid over to his travel bag, got a pair of camo jeans out, and pulled them on as he sat on the floor. "We wait an hour, and then we head out: if we go right straight across to Washington Avenue . . ."

"Around that curve and down that ramp and across the bridge and the hospital's right there," LaChaise finished, remembering the recon.

"Five minutes from here," Martin said. He pulled on his boots and looked at Sandy. "You about done with him?"

"About as much as I can do," Sandy said.

"We could use some coffee and eggs," Martin said. He found the TV remote and clicked it on. An announcer was barking something into the screen, and he fumbled a minute to get the sound up. ". . . just a few minutes ago. They have been positively identified as . . ."

"I better get the rifles, in case they show up," LaChaise said. He stood carefully, groaned and started down the hall. "Coffee and eggs," he said to Sandy. "Toast."

Sandy followed him down the hall and stepped into the kitchen. LaChaise went on, and she glanced back at Martin. He'd picked up his bow, but he was watching the television. Sandy stepped into the kitchen. She hadn't done this because she suspected that the cops would kill anyone with LaChaise: but now she had no choice. She took the phone off the hook, punched in 911. When it was answered, she said, quietly, "Sandy Darling. They're here."

She put the receiver down beside the phone, leaving the line open, and started banging around in the cupboard, looking for a frying pan. LaChaise came by a minute later, carrying an AR under his arm. He was pushing shells into a magazine as he walked, and he continued by into the living room. "Where'd you put your rifle?" he asked Martin.

"Aw, shit, it's probably on the floor in the backseat," Martin said. "I just threw it . . ."

He stopped, suddenly, at the sound: breaking glass down the stairs, then pounding feet. "They're here," Martin said. He pointed a pistol at the door, and LaChaise ran to the window and looked out. "Nothing on the street."

A man screamed through the door: "LaChaise, they know you're here, they're coming . . ." The screaming continued for a moment but they couldn't make it out, and the feet pounded back down the stairs.

"Aw, shit, aw, shit," Martin yelled. "Down the back . . ."

25

S TADIC WAS UP, dressed but still groggy—he was a hundred hours behind on his sleep, he thought—and thinking about breakfast cereal when he heard the screaming on the radio.

He threw on a parka and gloves, grabbed his gun, and ran for his car. He was five minutes from downtown: he made it in four. The parking lot outside the medical center looked like a used car lot, cops coming in from everywhere in their own cars. Light racks lit up the snowstorm.

He paused, looking at the chaos, then went on by, and took a turn down Eleventh. Yes: Lights shone down from Harp's apartment. Damnit: He went around the block, got a shotgun out of the trunk and loaded it. If he could flush them, unsuspecting, he could finish it. Dispatch said both men were hurt.

He decided to wait a few minutes: if they'd been shot, maybe the woman would be going out for medical supplies. He could take her at the door, and then go right on in. Otherwise, the place was a fort.

A DOCTOR CAME down the hall to the phones and said, "Are you Davenport?"

"Yeah." Lucas was on the phone with Roux. He said, "Hang on," and looked at the doctor.

"We got a picture, you might want to look at it."

"OKAY." OUT THE window, he could see the media vehicles piling up down the street. Cameramen orbited the building, their lights like little suns illuminating the night. "Gotta go, they got an X ray on Del," he said to Roux.

"I'll be there in fifteen minutes," she said.

Lucas followed the doctor back into the emergency room, where two other doctors were looking at an X ray clipped to a lighted glass. Lucas could see the outline of the Formica where it pierced Del's face.

"He got lucky," the doctor said, tapping the film. "It just penetrated into the base of the tongue. Didn't quite make it through: we were afraid that it had penetrated the pal . . . the roof of the mouth, but it didn't. It's just sort of jammed in there. We'll get it cleaned out."

"No damage?"

"He's gonna hurt like hell, but in a couple weeks, he'll be fine. He's gonna need a plastic guy on his neck, though. The thing looks nasty."

"How about his wife?"

Cheryl had ripped some IV tubes loose when she'd crawled across to her husband, and had been bleeding. "That's nothing," the doctor said. "She's fine."

"God bless," Lucas said. "And Franklin?"

"He's okay."

TWENTY-FIVE MINUTES AFTER the firefight, Lucas was talking to a patrol captain, trying to figure out why they hadn't found the car: "Christ, they were no more than thirty seconds ahead of you guys."

The captain was getting a little hot: "Look, a fuckin' mouse couldn't have gotten out of here on its hands and knees. We're looking at every car parked in the loop, they must be in a parking garage, somewhere. We'll get them . . ."

Lucas was staring over his shoulder, his eyes defocused. He said, "Stay put," and put his handset to his mouth and said, "I need a run on Daymon Harp. That's first name D-A-Y-M-O-N, last name H-A-R-P. I need to know what he drives."

The captain looked at him curiously; five seconds later, Dispatch came back, a different voice. "Lucas, Sandy Darling just called. She's left the phone off the hook, she says they're there . . ."

"On Eleventh Avenue?" Lucas asked.

"Yeah . . . how'd you know?"

Then the other dispatcher: "Lucas, he's got a 1994 Lincoln . . ."

"A brown one," Lucas said.

"Yes."

"All right," Lucas said, and he felt the rush, the lift that came at the end of a hunt. "I want to do this right. They're at Harp's apartment on Eleventh, it's a two-story, they're up above a laundromat. There's a front stairs and a garage on the side. I want somebody down there now, and we'll need an ERU team . . ."

Behind him, the patrol captain broke for his car. He shouted back, "I'll get some guys moving."

AGAIN, STADIC HEARD the sudden rush on the radio. And the phrase, "Down on Eleventh."

He knew immediately what it was. He grabbed his phone, punched in Harp's number. Busy. Christ. He couldn't allow a siege: there'd be survivors.

The apartment would be surrounded, there'd be helicopters overhead . . . when it came to outright suicide, LaChaise and the other crazy fucker might change their minds. And once they were out, and behind bars, they'd deal him.

The fear clawed at him, propelled him out of the car door. He ran up the side street past the garage, around the corner, kicked in the glass on the bottom floor door and ran up the stairs. At the top, facing the pile of cardboard boxes, he screamed: "LaChaise, they know you're here. They're coming now. Right now. You've got less than a minute. They've got Harp's car, they've got Harp's car. You hear me? Harp's car, they got it."

And he ran back down, seeing in his mind's eye a cop car pulling up from across the street, leveling a shotgun at him, the questions . . .

The street was empty. Hell, the radio traffic hadn't started more than a minute ago. He ran back around the corner, jumped in his car, started it and rolled away.

And as he went, he noticed the utter silence of the night, the quiet in the snow. Every siren in town had been killed. But every cop car in town was rolling toward him.

He punched the car down the street, one block, two, and stopped: when the first cars came in, he wanted to be with them.

The first car came in as he thought, gliding in silence toward the laundromat on the corner.

26

LaCHAISE RAN TOWARD the back door, saw Sandy in the kitchen, grabbed her, and she screamed, "Let me get my coat, my coat . . ."

LaChaise ran back to the front room, grabbed his own coat and Sandy's. Martin had his bow in his hand, six arrows in the bow-quiver, a fistful more in the other hand, his coat gaping open. He hobbled after them as LaChaise hit the stairs and Sandy followed, pulling on the coat.

When Martin reached the bottom of the stairs, the garage door was halfway up. He heard LaChaise scream, "Aw, shit . . ." and LaChaise's rifle came up and began the stroboscopic flash and stutter, and then LaChaise, with Sandy a foot behind, was out in the snow.

Martin was ten feet behind. He looked left: a cop car, windows shattered, sideways in the street. LaChaise was already running to the right.

"This way, this way . . ." LaChaise was screaming at him. Martin caught up and they turned the corner and Martin said, "Give me the rifle."

"What?" LaChaise's face was white, antic, the skin stretched around his eyes. Sandy was running away from them, down the street. *Let her go.*

"I won't make it. I can't move, my leg's fucked, I pulled something loose again," Martin said. He fumbled at his waistband. "Take my pistol," he said, handing it to LaChaise. "You got yours. That'll be enough. Grab a car, get moving . . ."

"Christ," LaChaise said. He tossed Martin the rifle, fumbled two spare magazines out of his pocket, passed them over, then caught Martin around the neck in a bear hug, held him for a half-second, said, "I'm going for Davenport's woman. I'll probably be seeing you in a while," then turned and ran after Sandy.

Martin went back to the corner and peeked. Fifty yards down the street, a cop was behind a car door, looking at him. He fired a burst, then pulled back and hobbled away, across the street, a thin trickle of pink in the snow where he passed.

He could hear the sirens now, coming in from everywhere.

LUCAS AND AN out-of-uniform patrol cop named Bunne rode toward Eleventh in Lucas's Explorer. Bunne wore a baseball jacket, the first thing he'd seen when he'd run out of a locker room before heading down to the hospital on foot. They were six blocks from Harp's: one minute. A half-minute after they left the hospital, they got the choked call on the radios, almost unintelligible over the panicked, harsh, into-the-mike breathing, "We got fire, we're shot, we're taking fire, Dick's shot, for Christ's sake, get help."

"Goddamn," Bunne said. Lucas had been following the patrol captain. Now he put the Explorer on the wrong side of the slippery street and they roared along, side by side, sirens everywhere. At the same time, he was shouting, "Where'd they go, you dumb shit?"

The cop came back, as though he'd heard, "They're on Eleventh, they're on Eleventh heading toward the Metrodome, they're on foot."

"Ten seconds," Lucas said.

Bunne drew his pistol and braced himself, white-faced, but at the same time showing Lucas a shaky grin: "This stuff scares the shit out of me," he said.

Lucas, focused on the driving, said, "The snow isn't that bad, it's the fuckin' night that's killing us."

"Nah, it's the fuckin' snow," Bunne said.

A red car, a small Ford, pulled out of a side street and Lucas nearly hit it. The Ford jumped a curve and piled up on a street sign, and they went by, the ultra-pale face of a redheaded kid peering at them through the glass. "Lawsuit," Bunne said, and they went around the corner, on the outside, and then they were on Eleventh on top of Harp's place, the patrol captain fifteen yards behind them. A squad was parked sideways in the intersection. A cop ran toward them, as Lucas and the patrol captain, in the other car, slid to a stop. The cop was pointing back past them: "They're on foot," he hollered. "We gotta get a perimeter up. They're not more'n a minute ahead. You must've come right past them . . ."

Lucas got out of the car and another plainclothes guy, Stadic, joined them, carrying a shotgun. Lucas got his own shotgun out of the car and tossed it to Bunne and said, "Let's go."

The three of them started off, and then another cop ran up behind, carrying another shotgun, and the four of them went off into the snow. The last cop, in uniform, said, "Charlie said they crossed the street . . ."

Lucas led the way, said, "Don't bunch," and the others self-consciously spread out. Lucas said, "Everybody got a vest?" Stadic and the uniform cop said yes; Bunne shook his head, he was bareheaded, barehanded, and wearing penny loafers. "Go back and get a vest," Lucas said.

"Fuck that, I'm coming," Bunne said. Lucas opened his mouth to object, but Bunne pointed at the ground ahead of them: "Look at that. Blood trail."

They all stopped and Stadic said, "He's right," and they all looked down the street toward a row of old brown brick apartment houses. "This is them," Bunne said, pointing at the fresh tracks in the snow. "See the different sizes of holes . . . that's the woman, this one guy is dragging his leg, that's the blood trail."

"Can't see shit; it'll be light in an hour," the uniform cop said, looking around. He was nervous, nibbling at his brushy black mustache. "Got snow on my glasses . . ."

They pushed into the snow, past the apartment houses and small businesses, a Dairy Queen, a jumble of parking lots and fences, the occasional hedge, Dumpsters behind buildings, all good cover: following the blood which appeared as ragged, occasional sprinkles in the snow, black in the dim light. As they moved up under a streetlight, Lucas said into his handset, "We're tracking them . . ." and gave the position.

No way they could get out of the neighborhood, he thought, but there was an excellent possibility that they'd take a house somewhere, and they'd have a siege. "Better get a hostage team down here," he said. "They could hole up . . ."

At that minute there was a sharp slap and Bunne said, "Oh, Christ," and fell down. Lucas screamed "Shooter," and they scattered. But they could see nothing, and hear nothing but sirens, the traffic on the highway and the peculiar hushed purring of the snow.

The uniform was screaming, "Where is he? Which way, which way?"

Lucas put the radio back up and shouted, "Man down, get a goddamn ambulance up here." He scrabbled crabwise to Bunne and asked, "How bad?" while Stadic was shouting, "Over to your left . . ."

Bunne said, "Man, hurts . . . Can't breathe . . ."

Lucas unzipped the baseball jacket coat and found a torrent of blood pouring from a chest wound, and more, sticky and red, in the back. The hole in the coat looked more like a cut than a bullet puncture. Lucas pressed his palm against the chest wound and looked back in the street, and saw it lying against a car. A fuckin' arrow? No sound, no muzzle flash . . .

"He's shooting a bow," Lucas shouted at the others. "He's shooting a bow, you won't hear it, watch it, he's shooting a bow, stay out of the streetlights."

One of the cops yelled, "What the fuck is this? What the fuck is this?"

An ambulance turned the corner, the lights blood-red, and Lucas waved at it. When it came in, he said to the EMT, "Hit by an arrow, he's bleedin' bad," and left her to it, running after the other two men.

He found them zigzagging up the street, still following the blood. "Ten feet at a time," the uniform said. The uniform was sweating with fear and was wet with melting snow. His eyes were too big behind his moisture-dappled spectacles, his breathing labored, but he was functioning. He ran left, and dropped, pointing his shotgun down the blood trail. Stadic went right, dropped. Lucas followed up the middle, dodged and dropped. Stadic went past, and then the uniform cop.

On a patch of loose snow, Lucas saw that they were only following one track.

"What happened to the other two tracks?" he shouted.

"I don't know. They must've turned off back in the street," Stadic shouted back, as the uniform cop leapfrogged past him. Stadic scrambled to his feet, and as he did, he grunted and dropped, and Lucas saw an aluminum arrow sticking out of his chest and just a flicker of movement up the trail. He fired three shots, saw another flicker, and fired two more, the last two low, and then the uniform cop fired a quick shot with his twelve-gauge.

"How bad?" Lucas shouted at Stadic.

"Nothing. Hit the backing plate in the vest," Stadic said, getting to his feet. "He's a good fuckin' shot." He broke the arrow off and they moved forward again, found a puddle of blood, and some blood spatter. "You hit him," the uniform cop said.

"Maybe you," Lucas said.

"Naw, I couldn't see bullshit, was just shooting 'cause I was scared." He looked around and said, "Maybe we ought to wait until daylight. He can't be far. He ain't going anywhere, he was already bleeding before you hit him."

"I want him," Lucas said. He put the handset to his face and told the dispatcher that the three had broken up, two apparently together, the third hurt bad. He gave the location and said, "We're following up."

"There are people coming straight into that block," the dispatcher said. "You're heading right into them. We've got guys with armor coming up, so take it easy . . ."

WHEN THEY SPLIT up, Sandy had run on ahead, LaChaise trailing her by fifty feet, with Martin hobbling behind. They ran a block, LaChaise catching Sandy, then a red Ford stopped at an intersection ahead of them. Sirens were coming from all directions: the Ford wasn't moving. Without breaking stride, LaChaise swerved behind it, jerked open the passenger-side door, and pointed his pistol at the driver: "Freeze, motherfucker."

The driver instinctively stepped on the brake, and LaChaise was inside, his gun in the redheaded kid's face. Sandy, when she saw LaChaise turn toward the car, dropped back a few steps. When he jerked open the car door, she turned and ran the other way. When LaChaise turned back, she was gone in the snow.

"Fuck it, fuck it . . ." LaChaise pointed his pistol at the redheaded driver: "Take off. Slow. Go, go . . ."

He slid to his knees in the passenger-side foot well, his head below the level of the dash, the pistol pointed at the kid's chest. They went a block, then the driver said, "No," and swerved, and they hit something, and LaChaise yelled, "Motherfucker," and the driver put his hands up to ward off the bullet.

But LaChaise levered himself up, and the kid babbled, "They almost hit us . . ." and LaChaise saw the two cars—a cop car and a four-by-four—disappearing down the street.

"Go," he said to the kid. "That way. Down toward the dome."

SANDY FOUND AN alley and stuck with it, loping along behind the apartment buildings. LaChaise had told her, teasing, that if she turned herself into the wrong cop, she was dead. True enough: she had his picture, but not his name.

And he'd be looking for her. Her best option, she thought, was to find a phone and call Davenport.

Now, if she could find someplace open. But what would be open at seven o'clock on a day like this? The city was a wilderness, the snow pelting down in buckets. She stepped out in the open, then back into the dark as a car roared by, then into the open again to look down the street. There was light on the side of the Metrodome. If she could get in there, there'd be lots of phones. She started that way.

LUCAS, STADIC AND the uniformed cop moved slowly up the blood trail, peering into the dark, starting at every shadow; the uniform fired once into a snowblower as it sat beside a house; Lucas nearly nailed a gate, as it trembled in the blowing snow. They shouted back and forth to reassure each other, and to pressure the bleeding man. Keep him moving; don't let him think about it.

MARTIN FIGURED HE was dying, but he wasn't feeling much pain. Nor was he feeling much cold. He was reasonably comfortable, for a man who'd torn open a thigh wound and had taken a gunshot hit in the butt. The butt shot had come in from the side, and nearly knocked him down. But he kept moving, feeling the blood running down his legs. He'd have to stop soon, he thought dreamily. He was running out of blood; that's probably why he felt so good. The shock was ganging up on him, and pretty soon, things would start shutting down.

One more shot with the bow, then he'd dump it. And when they came in again, for the last time, he'd go to work with the AR-15. His final little surprise, he thought, and grinned to himself.

LUCAS HIT THE ground next to a bridal-wreath hedge. A handful of snow splashed up in his face, and he snorted and tried to see past the corner of the apartment building, thrusting his .45 that way. He could feel Bunne's blood on the pistol stock, a tacky patina that'd be hard to get off. "Go," he yelled, and the uniform went past and immediately screamed and went down, and Lucas flopped beside him, thought he saw movement, and fired, and the cop was screaming, "Got me, he got me . . ."

Lucas pulled him back. The arrow was sticking out of the cop's leg, just above the knee: it had apparently hit the bone square on, and was stuck in it. "Gonna be okay," Lucas said, and yelled at Stadic, "Stay back, forget it, just hold your ground." He called for another ambulance on the handset and asked Dispatch, "Where's the help?"

"They oughta be right ahead of you, they're all over that block."

"You can't see the guy," Lucas sputtered. "You can't see him in the snow . . ."

Stadic hunched up beside him. "What do you want to do?"

"Hold it here for a minute. Get the ambulance . . .?"

The uniformed cop picked up on it. "Where's the fuckin' ambulance . . . "

An ambulance swung in behind them, and Stadic turned and ran back to wave it down.

"One more push," Lucas said. He spoke at the downed cop, but he was talking to himself. He got halfway to his knees, then launched into a short dash and dropped behind another hedge. Up ahead, powerful lights were breaking out around the block, and, behind the lights, he sensed moving figures.

"Davenport," he yelled.

"Where are you?"

"Straight ahead; I think he's between us . . ."

And somebody else shouted, "We don't know that's Davenport, watch it, watch it . . ."

Then Lucas saw Martin. He'd been hunkered into the side of a shabby old apartment, next to a line of garbage cans. He broke across toward the next apartment, and Lucas shouted, "There he is," and fired two quick shots, missing.

"He's coming around the apartment, look that way, he's coming around, watch it . . ."

And one second later, the lightning-stutter of the AR-15 lit up the back side of the apartment. Lucas half-ran that way, aware of the slipperiness underfoot, the shotgun already at his shoulder, leading the way. The automatic fire stopped before he was halfway there, then started again with a fresh clip. Glass was breaking, more cops were firing. Lucas reached the corner and peeked.

MARTIN WAS FIFTEEN feet away, in an alleyway stairwell. On his right, he was protected by the building. Ahead of him, and to his left, all along the length of a vacant lot, cop cars blocked the route. The cops were returning fire, but they didn't know he was below the level of the stairwell wall. With the snow, they probably couldn't see anything but the muzzle flash.

He crouched for a second, then popped up and fired another burst at one of the cars, aiming low, figuring the cops would be behind it.

LUCAS SAID TO the handset, "Tell everybody to cease fire. Cease fire, for Christ's sakes, you're gonna kill me. I got him if you can make them cease fire."

Three seconds later, he heard yelling on the other side of the street, and the fire diminished. He peeked at the corner again. Martin had reloaded, and was about to pop up again, to hose down the line of cars.

Lucas shouted, "Freeze!"

Martin turned, and his mouth dropped open. He posed like that for an instant, looking at the shotgun, then said, "Fuck you," and the AR came around. Lucas waited for a microsecond longer than he should have, then shot Martin in the head.

27

LUCAS YELLED, "GOT him," stepped out and waved, and a line of cops broke toward him. He stepped through the snow and down the steps to the body. Most of the top of Martin's head was gone, but his face looked almost placid, his eyes closed, his lips turned up in a not-quite smile.

There was little point to it—he was dead—but out of reflex Lucas patted the body, felt the solidity of the body armor under the coat. And something else. A pistol, Lucas thought, but when he touched it, it was rectangular and he slipped it out of Martin's pocket just as Stadic arrived at the top of the stairs.

"He's dead?"

Lucas said, "Yeah," and stood up, a cell phone in his hand. Where'd they get it? Probably a street buy. He frowned at the phone, then stepped up the stairs toward Stadic: "Watch the muzzle," he said. Stadic's shotgun muzzle had drifted toward him as Stadic peered down the stairwell to Martin. "One down, one to go."

"One?" Stadic asked. "What about the woman?"

"She's been talking to us. We're not sure about her status," Lucas said.

"Okay." Stadic nodded, and he thought: *Shit. They're gonna talk with her.*

Lucas brushed past him on the way up the stairs and said, "So let's find them."

The line of cops arrived and Lucas shouted, "There're two more. They're headed up the street toward the dome . . ."

A PATROL LIEUTENANT trotted over and they began talking search techniques, and whether they should put it off until light: Lucas wanted to keep the pressure on. Stadic watched them as they talked. Lucas still had the phone in his hand, then unconsciously stuck it in his coat pocket. Had to get it. Stadic stared at the pocket. Had to get it, had to get it, had to get it . . . the chant rang through his mind like a mantra.

"Come on," Lucas called to him. Stadic, jolted back to the present, said, "I'm here," and Lucas clapped him on the back and led the way back behind the building. He was six feet ahead, unsuspecting. Stadic had the shotgun: and there were more cops everywhere. But the temptation . . . an accident.

Nobody would believe it.

Had to get him alone. He had a piece-of-shit Davis .380 in his pocket. A piece of shit but it'd do the job, but he had to have him alone. Alone with either LaChaise or the woman would be best . . . But Christ, who knew what would happen in that chase?

Davenport was electric, animated, and if you didn't know what was going on, you might think *Happy*. Stadic thought about the arrows coming out of the snow, silent razors in the dark, the whack in the chest. If it'd been eight inches higher, it'd have carved a hole right through his throat and he'd be lying in the street with a plastic bag over his face. He shuddered, and followed Davenport.

THE SEARCH GOT under way. Groups of cops swept the streets, parking lots and yards inside a perimeter thrown up in the first few minutes after finding LaChaise's location. Any house that showed fresh tracks was approached, the door banged on, the occupants asked and warned. But there were few of them this early in the day.

Lucas stayed along Eleventh, the billowing top of the dome a few blocks straight ahead, like the Pillsbury Doughboy's butt. Then a uniformed cop who'd lost his hat and gloves, his blond hair soaked with snow, his hands white as ice, ran up and said, "We've f-f-f-found a line of t-t-t-tracks. Small tracks, a woman or a kid, and whoever it was kept stopping behind b-bushes and around c-corners . . ."

"That's her," Lucas said. "Show me the way."

They ran off together, Stadic a few steps behind. Four uniformed guys with flashlights and shotguns were leapfrogging up the track, which wandered through the maze of old houses, apartments, small brick businesses and parking lots. They were moving quickly, but nervously: everybody'd heard about the arrows.

They were staying out of the trail, and Lucas stopped, just a moment, to look at it. "Looks the same," he said to Stadic.

"Yeah, gotta be her," Stadic said.

They ran harder, caught up with the uniforms. Lucas said, "Listen up, guys, this woman has been talking to us. She actually called in and left the phone off the hook so we could follow it in to the apartment. We gotta be a little careful, but I don't think she's dangerous."

"G-g-g-good," chattered the bareheaded cop. "I'm f-f-fuckin' freezing."

"Well, Jesus, go get some clothes on," Lucas said. And to the others, "Come on . . ."

They ran along the track, and as they approached a cross street, saw cops ahead. A spotlight beam broke down toward them, and the uniforms waved their flashlights.

"She broke the perimeter before we set up," Lucas said. "That means LaChaise probably did, too."

He fumbled in his pocket, pulled out first the cell phone, then his handset, and said into the handset, "The woman's outside the perimeter . . . we've got to spread it. The woman's outside for sure, LaChaise probably."

He thrust the phone and handset back in his pocket and they ran along again, the cop cars behind them squealing in circles and then heading out to new positions. The larger the square got, the thinner the cops would be: but cops were pouring in from everywhere, from Hennepin County, from St. Paul. No ordinary dog hunt.

As they followed on the trail, Lucas said, "You know what? She's going to the dome."

"You think?" Stadic asked.

"She's trying to find a phone," Lucas said. He took the handset out again, and relayed the idea to Dispatch. "Get her through to me if she calls."

The streets were getting wider as they got closer to downtown, and then they lost the track: she'd turned into a cleared-off street.

"Still bet it's the dome," Lucas said. "Tell you what," he said to Stadic and two of the uniforms, "you guys go that way, we'll go this way, push both sides of that apartment. But I bet she headed for the dome. I'll see you on the other side and we'll go on over."

"All right."

They split up, and Lucas and the other uniform headed off to the left. As they approached the apartment, Lucas thought of the cellular phone, took it out, then the handset and called Dispatch. "Get somebody at the phone company. I need a number I can call where they can trace a cell phone. I'll call them on the cell phone, and I want them to figure out the number, and then give me a list of calls billed from the phone . . . who's at the numbers. Got that?"

"Got it."

They pushed around the apartment, found nothing but pristine snow. Stadic was waiting on the other side, and they all looked over at the dome.

"Let's go," Lucas said, but as he was about to step off the curb, Dispatch called. "That was fast," he said.

"Lucas, Lucas . . ."

"Yeah?"

"LaChaise . . ." The dispatcher was sputtering. "LaChaise is at the University Hospitals."

"Oh, shit."

Lucas look around wildly, spotted a cop car, waved at it, started running toward it, barely heard the dispatcher, "Got your wife . . ."

"What?" he yelled into the handset. And to Stadic: "Stay with her, stay with Darling."

He ran toward the squad car, and as the car stopped and the window came down, Lucas shouted, "Pop the back door, pop the back."

The driver popped the back door and Lucas dove inside and shouted, "University Hospitals, go, go . . ." And to the handset, "What about Weather? What about Weather?"

"They think he might . . . have her."

28

THE KID BEGAN to cry as they passed the metrodome, and when LaChaise yelled at him, told him to shut up, he simply cried harder, holding on to the top of the steering wheel with both hands, tears pouring down his face.

LaChaise finally pushed himself up into the seat beside him and pointed the way: down to Washington, right, around a curve to a lighted sign that said several things, but concluded with "Jesus Saves," down a ramp and onto a covered bridge.

"Shut up, for Christ's sakes, you do this right, I won't hurt you."

"I know you," the kid said, "you're gonna kill me."

"I ain't gonna fuckin' kill you if you do right; I got no quarrel with you."

But the kid started up again and LaChaise said, "Jesus Christ," in disgust, and they rolled off the bridge past the beer-can building, up the hill to Harvard Street.

"Turn," LaChaise said. The kid stopped weeping long enough to get around the corner, and before he could start again, LaChaise said, "Go straight ahead to that turnaround and then stop."

"You gonna kill me there?"

"I'm not gonna fuckin' kill you, unless you get smart," LaChaise said. "Just stop there and let me out, and go on your way."

There were a half-dozen people on the street, coming and going from the hospital, slip-sliding down the sidewalks. Operations took place early in the morning. LaChaise had had two operations himself, for an appendix and to get a skin patch put over a bad case of road rash, and both times, they'd woken him up at dawn for the trip down to the operating room.

"Right there," he said, "behind that red Chevy."

The kid pulled in behind the Chevy, and LaChaise eased himself out, the backs of his legs on fire. The kid was looking at the gun and LaChaise grinned at him and dug into his jeans, found the remnant of the cash they'd taken from Harp, pulled out the wad of bills and threw it on the passenger seat. A couple of thousand dollars, anyway. "Thanks for the ride," he said, and he stepped away from the car and slammed the door, and walked up to the hospital entrance.

He felt like a cowboy.

He carried his own pistol, the 'dog .44, in his right hand, and pulled Martin's pistol out of his left pocket, and pushed through the doors using his elbows.

An information counter was just inside the doors to the right. A security guard sat behind the desk, watching a portable television. Three more people, two women and a man in a white medical jacket, were scattered around the lobby chairs, the women reading, the man staring sightlessly at the wall, as though he'd made an unforgivable error somewhere.

LaChaise walked over to the guard, who looked up only at the last minute, a smile dying a sudden death. LaChaise pointed the two guns at the guard's chest and said, "Walk me up to the operating rooms or I'll kill you."

The guard looked at the guns, then at LaChaise, and then, slowly, stupidly, at the television: "They're looking for you," he said.

"No shit. Now get out of there and walk me up to the operating rooms. You got five seconds, then I kill you."

"This way," the guard said. He came out from behind the desk, his hands held at shoulder height. He was unarmed. The three people in the lobby were looking at them, but nobody moved from their seats. "There's another guy coming in, in one second," LaChaise said to the room in general. "If anybody's moving, anybody's standing up, he'll kill you. Sit tight and you'll be okay. I'm Dick LaChaise, that you seen on TV, and I'm here on business."

The sound of the line pleased him; it *sounded* cowboy-like. They walked a few feet down a corridor, around a corner to the right, to a bank of elevators. The guard pushed the elevator button and the doors slid open. "Three," he said, as they got inside. "You gonna kill me?"

"Not if you do what I tell you," LaChaise said. "When we get to three, you stay in the car and ride until you get to the top." LaChaise pushed all the buttons higher than three, and a bell rang and the door opened, and LaChaise waved the gun at the guard and said, "I'll stand here until the doors are closed. If you get off before the top, somebody'll shoot your ass. Got that?"

"Yes, sir," the guard said, as the doors closed.

AT THE END of the hall, double doors led to the operating suite. To his right, an elderly man sat in a chair reading *Modern Maturity*. He looked up, sucked on his teeth, and looked back at the magazine. LaChaise had the odd impression that he hadn't noticed the guns.

Nobody else in sight. LaChaise went to the double doors, pushed through, found himself in a nursing station. Two nurses were looking at a clipboard, and one of them was saying, ". . . must be stealing scrubs again. They're all his size, and it's only the new ones . . ."

They both looked up at the same time. LaChaise was there in his heavy dark coat, dripping water from the melting snow, his eyes dark and two guns in his hand. He said, "Ladies, I need to see Dr. Weather Karkinnen."

The taller and younger of the two nurses said, "Oh, shit," and the older, shorter one shook her head and said, "You can't. She's operating."

"Then let's go down to the operating room and see her."

"You're not authorized," the older woman said.

"If you don't show me, I'm going to kill one of you, and then the other one will show me, I bet. Who do I kill?" He pulled back the hammer on the 'dog, and the catches ratcheted in the silence. The two nurses looked at each other, then the older one began to sniffle, the way the boy in the car had; and the younger one said, finally, "I'll show you."

She led the way through another set of doors, stopped outside of a single wide door, stood on tiptoe to look through a window and then stepped back and said sadly, "In there."

"If she's not, I'll be back," LaChaise said, holding her eyes. The woman looked away, and LaChaise bumped through the door.

WEATHER HAD HER eyes to the operating microscope while her hands made the delicate loops that produced square knots in the nearly invisible suture material. She'd just said, "If you actually listen to The Doors you start to laugh; listen to the words of 'L.A. Woman' sometime and tell me they're not . . ."

The door banged open and she almost jumped, and everybody turned and, without looking up, she said, "Who in the fuck did that?"

"I did," LaChaise said.

Weather finished the knot and then looked up from the scope, blinked and saw him there, with the two pistols.

"Who's Weather Karkinnen?"

"I am," Weather said. He pointed a pistol at her and she closed her eyes. "Come out of there."

She opened her eyes again and said, "I can't stop now. If I stop now, this little girl will lose her thumb and she'll go through life like that."

LaChaise took a mental step back, confused: "What?"

"I said, if I quit now . . ."

"I heard that," he snapped. "What're you doing?"

"I'm hooking up an artery. She had a benign tumor and we removed it and now we're hooking up the two ends of the artery to get the blood supply going again."

"Well, how long will it take?"

Weather looked back through the operating microscope. "Twenty minutes."

"You've got five," he said. And he said, "You're really short for a doctor."

Weather looked away again, and asked, "Are you going to kill everybody in here?"

"Depends," LaChaise said.

"If I get another doctor in here, he could finish for me."

"Get him."

"Not if you're going to hurt him, or the others."

"I won't hurt him if he doesn't fuck with me."

Weather looked at the circulating nurse and said, "Betty, go down and ask Dr. Feldman to step in here, if he would."

LaChaise looked at the nurse and said, "Go. And if you fuck with me . . ."

Weather went back to the microscope and they all waited, silently, her hands barely moving, for two or three minutes, when a man in an operating gown bumped hip-first into the room, his hands at chest level. "What's going on?"

LaChaise pointed one of the guns at him, and Weather said, "We've got a gentleman with a gun. Two guns, in fact. He wants to talk with me."

"The police are coming," the new doctor said to LaChaise. In the sterile operating theater, LaChaise looked like a rat on a cheesecake.

"They're always coming," LaChaise said.

"However this works out, we've got to finish this," Weather said to Feldman, her voice steady. "Could you take a look?"

The operating scope had two eyepieces, and Feldman, his hands still pressed to his chest, stepped to the operating table opposite Weather and looked into the second eyepiece. "You're almost done."

"I need to put in two more knots, and then it's a matter of closing . . ."

She gave him a quick brief on the operation, and finished one of the two knots. "One more," she said.

"I've got to go down and back off mine," Feldman said.

"How far are you in?" Weather asked.

"Not in," Feldman said. "We were just getting the anesthesia started . . . I'll be back."

He went with such authority that LaChaise let him go without objection. Weather was working in the incision again, and one of the nurses said, "If I stay here, I'll pee my pants."

"Then go," Weather said. "Everybody else okay?"

They were okay. The nurse who thought she might pee her pants decided to stay with them.

Feldman returned: "Where are we?"

"Just finishing," Weather said calmly. "See?"

Feldman looked through the scope and said, "Nice. But I think you might need one more, at . . ."

He was stalling. Weather said, "I think that should be all right." Feldman looked at her and she gave a small shake of the head. "You sure?"

"Better to get him out of here," Weather said.

"What's going on?" LaChaise demanded.

"Trying to figure out what we can do here," Feldman snapped. "We're right in the middle of things."

Weather stepped back from the table. "But I'm done," she said. She looked at LaChaise. "Now what?"

"Outa here. We need a phone. Someplace where they can't get at me."

"There's an office at the end of the hall."

"Let's go," he said, waving the pistol at her.

THE OUTER AREA was deserted. The nurses had gone, and the cops hadn't arrived yet. Weather pulled off her mask and peeled off the first of her gloves and said, "What're you going to do?"

"Talk to your old man," LaChaise said.

And kill her, while they were on the phone, she thought. She came to the office and said, "In there. There's a phone."

She gestured and she went through ahead of him, turned. "You have a lot of choices to make," she said.

"Shut up. What's your old man's number?"

"You could probably dial 911 and they could patch you through. He's out there in his car."

"Do it, and hand me the phone . . ."

Weather punched 911 and handed it to him. He listened a minute, the gun muzzle steady on her chest, and said, "This is Dick LaChaise. I want to talk to Lucas Davenport. I'm at the hospital and I'm pointing a gun at his old lady, Dr. Karkinnen."

Weather said, "You don't have much time left: you better start thinking this through."

"I said, shut up."

"Why? Because if I don't you're gonna kill me? You're already planning to kill me."

"You don't want it to come no sooner than it has to . . ." Then he said to the phone, "Well, get him on. Well, when is he gonna be . . . Yeah? You tell him to call . . ." He looked at the phone, but there was no number, and he looked at Weather.

"The surgery suite," Weather said. Lucas wouldn't get on the phone. He knew what LaChaise would do.

"The surgery suite," LaChaise repeated, and he hung up. "He's on foot somewhere. They're getting him."

Weather said, "I've got to sit down," and she dropped in the chair on the other side of the desk. "Look, you're either going to have to shoot me or listen to me, and I think you better listen: My friend Davenport will get here in a few minutes, and if you kill me, he'll kill you. You can forget all about rules and regulations and laws; he'll kill you."

"Like he killed my old lady and my sister."

She bobbed her head. "Yes. He set that up. I talked to him about it, because I couldn't believe he did it. It's caused us some trouble. But when he thinks he's right, he won't turn. And if you kill me . . ." She shrugged. "That's the end for both of us. You won't walk out of here."

"I ain't walking out anyway."

Now he looked at her, and she saw that she was still wearing one glove, and she pulled it off slowly, watching his eyes.

"There's no death penalty either in Wisconsin or Minnesota. You escaped once. You might have to wait for a while, but there's always the chance that you could be free again. One way or another."

"Bullshit, they're gonna kill me."

"No, they won't. Not if you wait a while. They have all kinds of rules. And once you're on television, they won't be able to take you off and shoot you somewhere. Once you're in the system, you'll be safe. My husband, my friend . . ."

"Is he your husband or your friend?"

"We're planning to get married in a couple of months. We live together . . . If you make a deal with him, he won't kill you. But if you shoot me, you can make any kind of deal you want—you can make a deal with the President— and he'll kill you anyway."

He grinned, and said, "Yeah, tough guy," but he was thinking. He thought about Martin, probably dead already, going cold in the snow somewhere, and he said, "They'd stick me in the Black Hole of Calcutta."

"Probably, for a while," she agreed. "Then something bigger and dirtier would come along, and they'll start to forget about you, and they'll give you a little air. Then you'll have a chance. If you die now . . . that's it. No court, no TV time, no interviews, no nothing."

"Well, fuck that," LaChaise said. "Let's see what your old man says."

Weather took a breath: it was a start. "You're bleeding," she said. "We could get a first-aid kit."

29

THE DRIVER OF the squad had his foot to the floor, his partner, braced for impact, screaming, "Slow it down, slow it down," and they skidded through the first corner and nearly off the street, then they were on Washington headed toward University Hospitals.

Dispatch came back: "We don't know what the situation is, but she's still alive. He's got her on the third floor, in surgery. Wait a minute, wait a minute, he's calling in on 911, he wants to talk to you . . ."

Lucas shouted, "No. I don't want to talk. He wants me to hear him shoot her. Tell him you're trying to get in touch."

"Got that."

He sat clutching the handset, the street reeling by. Then Dispatch again: "You asked for a number at U.S. West."

"Yeah, yeah." He'd almost forgotten, but he took the cellular phone from his pocket and punched the number in as the dispatcher read it.

The phone was answered instantly: "Johnson."

"This is Lucas Davenport. I was supposed to call here to find out what numbers this phone has been calling."

"Yeah. We've got the number now, we're reading it now, we'll check the billings and get back to you. You can hang up."

"Get it quick," Lucas said. "Soon as you can."

"It'll take a few minutes."

"Whatever. Call me back at the number," Lucas said, and he hung up, got on the handset, and said, "What's happening?" and the cop in the passenger seat lifted his hands to ward off an oncoming car, but the driver slipped it to the left and then hooked down a ramp and they were on the bridge.

Dispatch: "He's still in the operating room. Another doctor's going in and out. We've got two cars there, we've got an ERU team a minute away. Listen, the chief wants to talk . . ."

Lucas said, "You're breaking up . . . I'll get back."

He turned the handset off and said, "Stay off the radio, guys."

"Why?" asked the white-faced cop in the passenger seat.

"Because Roux wants to take me off this, and I can't do that."

THEY FLASHED UP the hill on the far side of the river, made the turn and slewed down Harvard toward the hospital's front entrance. As they braked to a stop, Lucas said, "Pop the door," and they popped it, and he climbed out with the cops and said to the driver, "I owe you big time," and they all ran into the building.

A half-dozen security guards were in the lobby, and Lucas held up his ID and said, "What's the deal?"

"They're out of the operating room. They're in an office."

"Any cops up there?"

"Yeah, but they can't see down through the doors."

"Let's go up," Lucas said. He'd observed at several of Weather's operations, trying to learn a little about her life. He knew the operating suite, and most of the adjoining offices and locker rooms. They rode up in the elevator, and when they got off, were met by two uniforms, who saw Lucas and looked relieved.

"He's down there, Chief. He's got her in a back office, and he's asking for you," one of the cops said.

"You got a phone line into him?"

"Yeah, but he says don't call unless it's you."

"All right." He turned to the security guard. "I need an exact floor plan, and all the nurses and doctors who work inside."

"You gonna call?" one of the cops asked.

"Not yet," Lucas said. "And I don't want anyone to tip him off that I'm here. We gotta figure something out."

WEATHER WAS FIGHTING LaChaise. She'd come out from behind the desk, rolling out of the office chair, and she said, "I hope everything goes okay for Betty. I wish you'd come a half hour later."

LaChaise was standing, holding the door open just a crack, peering down the long hall to the double doors. Davenport, when he arrived, should be coming around the corner just in front of the doors, a thirty- or forty-foot shot. But he was half listening to Weather, and he said, "Yeah?"

"She's a farm kid," Weather said. "If she loses that thumb, she'll have a tough time of it. I don't know how you work around a farm without a right thumb. I know I couldn't."

"What do you know about farms?" LaChaise snapped, looking at her now.

"I grew up in northern Wisconsin—I'm a country kid," Weather said. She didn't say, *like your wife and sister.* "Other doctors start out dissecting frogs or something; I started out taking Johnson twenty-fives apart, and putting them back together again."

"I had a Johnson twenty-five once," LaChaise said. "Hell, I guess everybody did, who had a boat up north."

"Just about," she agreed. "My old man . . ."

She went on for a bit, talking about her family. She got LaChaise to talk about Colfax and the UP, and she told him about ski trips to the UP, and it turned out that they both knew some of the same bars in Hurley. "From Hayward to Hurley to Hell," she said.

He laughed abruptly, winced and said, "Ain't that the truth."

"Are you hurt bad?" she asked.

"I got some shit in my legs . . . cop at the other hospital got me with a shotgun."

"Want me to look?"

"No."

She was about to push him on it, when the phone rang. "That's him," LaChaise said. His eyes flicked over to her.

Not yet, she thought. *Please, not yet.* She had him going . . .

LUCAS MUTTERED TO the cop, "Remember about Martin . . ."

"Yeah, yeah."

He dialed and LaChaise picked it up.

"Chief Davenport is on the way. He was in the ambulance with your friend, the Martin guy."

"Martin's alive?"

"Yeah, but he's hurt," the cop said. "He got hit in the legs and he surrendered. He'll be okay."

"Martin?" There was wonderment in LaChaise's voice. "You gotta be shittin' me."

"You got a radio or TV? They'll be carrying him into the hospital."

"Ain't got no TV," LaChaise said, looking around the office. "What about Sandy?"

"Who?"

"Sandy Darling, she was with us."

"Oh. Yeah. I guess they can't find her," the cop said. Then, "Anyway, Chief Davenport wants you to know that he's coming. He'll be here in five minutes."

"Don't call back until he gets here," LaChaise said.

LACHAISE TURNED TO Weather and said, "They say Martin made it."

"Good."

"I don't believe them."

"You can't tell what a person'll do when he's hurt bad enough. I've had all kinds of weird confessions when I was working in an emergency room. A person thinks he's going to die in the next couple of minutes . . . something changes," Weather said. She looked at his gun. "I wish you wouldn't keep that pointed at me. I'm not going to beat you up."

He shifted the muzzle of the gun, just slightly, and she said, "Thanks," and thought, *Maybe.*

THE ERU TEAM included a young blond Iowan who was carrying a Sako Classic .243 with a fat black Leupold scope. Lucas stepped away from the medical people, who were working out a floor plan, and said, "How good are you?"

"Very," he said.

"You ever shoot anyone?"

"Nope, but I got no problem with it," the Iowan said, and his flat blue eyes suggested that he was telling the truth.

"You'll be shooting just about sixty feet, close as we can tell."

"At sixty feet I won't be more than a quarter-inch off my aim-point."

"You're sure?"

The kid nodded. "Absolutely."

"We need him turned off. He may be pointing a gun at Weather or me."

"I got a low-power, wide-view scope. I'll be able to see his move—if he's got the gun right at her head, if the hammer's down, I can take him, and your wife's okay. If the hammer's cocked . . . then it's not so good, maybe fifty-fifty. If he's got the gun at her head, if you can get him to take it away, I'll be able to see it and I'll take him. You need to get him to take it away just a second, just an inch."

"He can't have any time to recover—not even a millionth of a second."

The kid shook his head. "I'm shooting Nosler ballistic tips—I didn't want anything that'd go through and ricochet around the halls. So all the energy'll get dumped inside his skull. If I hit him anywhere on the face—and I will—he'll be gone like somebody turned off a switch. That fast."

Lucas looked at him for another long moment, and said, "I hope you can do it right."

"No problem," the kid said, and he stroked the rifle like he might stroke his girlfriend's cheek.

Lucas nodded and went back to the medics and to look at the floor plan. Basically, the suite was one long hall with double doors in the middle, dividing the operating rooms from the support offices. He'd put the sniper at the far end of the hall, open the doors himself and talk to LaChaise, who was in one of the offices at the other end of the hall.

"We'll put the gun on a gurney," Lucas said. "We're gonna need an office chair . . . and then I'll call, and go through the doors. . . . Will the doors stay open?"

"You've got to push them back hard," one of the doctors said.

A cop said, "Lucas, the chief . . ."

"Tell her to call back," Lucas said. He looked back at the sniper and said, "Let's do it."

" . . . PEOPLE DON'T UNDERSTAND that," LaChaise said. "People don't understand how country folks get ripped around by the government. Christ, you start out just trying to get ahead . . ."

Weather was quietly amused at her own reaction: in some way, she liked the guy. He was like two dozen high school classmates back in Wisconsin, kids who didn't have much to do if they stayed around home. You'd see them trying to put together lives with part-time jobs in the resorts, out in the woods, trying to guide . . . willing to work, but without much hope, afraid of the cities.

LaChaise was like that, but gone down some darker, more twisting trail. He hated his father; didn't much like his mother. Idolized his younger sister, and even his wife.

"Candy sounds like trouble, though," Weather said. "Sometimes people push too hard."

"Yeah, I guess. But she was so damn lively . . ."

LUCAS GOT THREE big stacks of surgeon's scrub suits, all green, from the laundry. The sniper took off his jacket and pulled one of the scrubs on, and tied a pair of pants around his head. They put one stack of scrubs in the middle of a low stainless-steel instrument gurney. The sniper sat in an office chair behind the gurney, and dropped the rifle across the top of the stack, and put a couple more scrubs on top of it. The other two stacks went on either side of the center pile.

Lucas walked down the hall toward the double doors and looked back. He could see the glass of the scope and the rifle barrel, but they made no visual sense. He couldn't tell exactly what they were, and LaChaise would be twice as far away. The sniper himself was invisible with the green scrub pants tied around his head.

"Good," Lucas said, hustling back. "If we can drop one more suit right here . . ." He spread one across the barrel.

Lucas and another member of the ERU walked down the length of the hall again, and looked back a second time. The other cop said, "This scares the shit outa me."

"Me, too," Lucas said. He nodded at the sniper. "But can you see him?"

"I can only see him because I know he's there. LaChaise . . . no chance."

Lucas walked back. "All right," he said to the Iowan. "I hope to God you haven't been bullshitting me."

The kid said, "You wanta quit fuckin' around and get the show on the road? And stay to the right side of the corridor. The slug'll be coming right past your ear."

THE PHONE RANG again, and LaChaise bent over to pick it up: pain shot down his leg and he grunted, almost stumbled, caught himself, and lifted the phone.

Lucas said, "I'm right down the hall from you. If you look out, I'll open the double doors, and you'll see me."

He was that close? LaChaise put his eye to the door crack and looked at the double doors. "Let's see you."

The first of the two doors opened, slowly at first, and then quickly, pushed against the wall; it stayed open. The man who'd pushed it open was standing behind the other door. He peeked out at LaChaise.

"All right, here I am," Lucas said. "We got a lot to talk about."

"You killed my goddamn wife and sister," LaChaise said. "And I say, 'Eye for an eye.' "

"When your sister was killed, she was firing a gun at us," Lucas said. "She went down shooting. We didn't just shoot her out of hand: we gave her a choice to give up."

"Bullshit, everybody says it was over in one second, I saw the TV . . ."

"Doesn't take long to have a gunfight," Lucas said. "Anyway, what're we going to do here?"

"Well, we've been talking about that, your old lady and me," LaChaise said.

THE SNIPER COULD feel just the lightest sweat start on his forehead, just a patina. Through the scope, he could see the crack in the door, and even, from time to time, LaChaise's eye. He thought about taking the shot, but he didn't know what Weather's situation was. He'd seen training films where the crook's gun was taped to the hostage's head, the hammer held back on the gun with thumb tension. Shoot the crook, the hammer falls, and the hostage is gone.

He wouldn't take it, yet. Not yet. He moved his eye a bit farther from the scope: he didn't want the glass to steam up.

I DON'T WANT to talk on the phone anymore," Lucas said. "I want to talk face-to-face. I want to see if Weather's okay, what you've done to her . . ."

"I haven't done nothin' yet," LaChaise growled.

"I'm gonna push open this other door. I won't have any cover. I'm gonna keep my gun in my hand. You shoot her, you're a dead man. But come on out here—talk to me."

Lucas pushed the second door open, and stood in the center of the hall, his gun by his side, the phone still by his face.

"Trick of some kind," LaChaise called down the hall.

"No. We're just trying to get everybody out of here alive," Lucas said. "Your friend Martin would probably tell you to give it up. He went down shooting, but he seemed happy enough to be alive on the way to the hospital."

"You swear that's true—man to man," LaChaise said.

"Yeah, I do," Lucas said. "Now let me see your face."

After a moment of silence, LaChaise said, "We'll come out to talk. Your old lady'll be in front of me and the gun'll be pointing right at her head. Anybody tries any shit . . ."

"Nobody's gonna try any shit," Lucas said.

LaChaise looked at Weather. "He *is* a tough guy," LaChaise said. "Let's go out there. You just stay right ahead of me."

"Don't hurt me," Weather said.

"Let's see what happens. Maybe this'll work out."

She touched him with her fingertips. "You should give yourself a chance. You're a smart man. Give it a chance."

Then she stepped in front of him, and felt the cold steel of LaChaise's gun muzzle touch her scalp just behind her ear. They edged into the hall together, and LaChaise nervously looked behind him—nothing but a blank wall—and then down at Davenport, who loomed large and dark standing in the double doors. He held the gun at his side and LaChaise again thought, "Cowboys."

If he got out of this—he was thinking that way, now—if he got out of this, it'd be a long time before he played any cowboy games again.

"I'm here by myself," Davenport said from the doors. "And I'm pleading with you. Weather takes care of little kids . . . that's what she's doing. For Christ's sake, if you gotta shoot somebody, go for me; let her go."

"You killed my Georgie . . ." But now Georgie was a bargaining chip.

"We didn't want to. Look, for Christ's sake, don't shoot her by accident, huh? Look, here is my gun."

Weather could feel the muzzle on the bone just behind her ear. But she wasn't thinking about it. She was listening to Lucas's tone of voice, and she thought, *Oh, no, something's going on.* She opened her mouth to say something, but LaChaise, behind her, said, "This one time, I'm going to take your word for it . . ."

Now there was a pleading tone in LaChaise's voice, and Weather felt the pressure from the gun muzzle move away from her ear.

THE SNIPER COULD see Weather from the shoulder up, and all of LaChaise's head, and the muzzle of the pistol. He could hear what LaChaise was saying, but was mentally processing it in the background. Everything else was focused on the muzzle. He saw it start to move, mentally processed the words, *going to take your word for it,* realized that the muzzle was about to come away from Weather's head, and then the muzzle lifted out of Weather's hair and the sniper let out just a tiny puff of breath and squeezed . . .

THE DISTANCE WAS sixty-two feet. In two one-hundredths of a second, the slug exploded from the barrel and through LaChaise's head, his skull blowing up like a blood-filled pumpkin.

LaChaise never sensed, never knew death was on the way. He was there one instant, moving the muzzle, ready to quit, even thinking about jail life; in the next instant, he was gone, turned off, falling.

WEATHER FELT THE muzzle move, and the next instant, she was on the floor, blind. She couldn't see, she couldn't hear, she was covered with something—she was covered with blood, flesh, brains. She tried to get to her feet but slipped and fell heavily, tried to get up, then Lucas was there, picking her up, and she began to scream . . .

And to push him away.

30

THREE DOCTORS, PHYSICIANS and friends, bent over Weather, trying to talk with her. She was disoriented, physically and psychologically. The explosion of blood, bone and brain had done something to her. The doctors were talking about sedatives.

"Shock," one of the cops said to Lucas. The doctors had pushed Lucas away— his presence seemed to make her worse. "We'll get her cleaned up, get her calmed down, then you can see her," they said.

He went reluctantly, watching from the back of the room. Roux showed up, looked at the body, talked to the kid from Iowa, then came over to see Lucas.

"So it's done," she said. "Is Weather all right?"

"She's shook up," Lucas said. "She freaked when we shot LaChaise."

"Well, look at her," Roux said quietly. "She looks like she was literally in a blood bath. A bath of blood."

"Yeah, I just . . . I don't know. I did right, I think."

Roux nodded: "You did right." She asked, "Did you talk to Dewey?"

Dewey was the shooter. Lucas looked across the room at the Iowa kid, who had the rifle cradled in his left arm, like a pheasant hunter with a shotgun. He was chatting pleasantly with the team leader. "Never had a chance," Lucas said. "I need to thank him."

Roux said, "He scares the shit out of me. He seems to think the whole thing is very interesting. Can't wait to tell his folks. But he doesn't seem to feel a thing about actually killing somebody."

Lucas nodded, shrugged, turned back toward Weather. "Jesus, I hope . . ." He shook his head. "She acts like she hates me."

THE PHONE IN his pocket rang and Lucas fumbled for it. Roux said, "What about Darling?"

"We've got some guys trying to find her over at the dome." Lucas got the phone out—his own phone. The ringing continued in his pocket. "Uh-oh," he said, as he dug out the second phone. "This could be bad news."

He turned the phone on and said, "Yes?"

"This is Johnson, over at U.S. West."

"What'd you get?"

"The phone was registered to a Sybil Guhl, she's a real-estate broker in Arden Hills. There were forty-two calls in the last few days, both businesses and private phones . . ."

"Private phones," Lucas said.

"There were calls to a Daymon Harp residence in Minneapolis," Johnson said in his fussy corporate voice. "To an Andrew Stadic residence . . ."

"Oh, shit," Lucas said.

"Beg pardon?"

"How many calls to Stadic?"

"Uh . . . nine. That was the most frequently called personal phone—actually, it's another cellular."

"Who else?"

There were other calls, but they could be discounted. Lucas said "Thanks," hung up and looked at Roux. "Andy Stadic," he said. "He's the guy."

"Damnit." She brushed her hand across her eyes, as though that would make it go away. "Let's get a team out to his house."

"He's not at his house," Lucas said, backing away, heading toward the elevators. He looked one last time at Weather, sitting head down on the cart, the doctors crouched around her. He should stay; but he'd go. "He's leading the hunt for Sandy Darling."

SANDY HEARD THE knot of cops coming up behind her. She needed to talk to somebody on a phone before she turned herself in. One of the cops—maybe one of those behind her, maybe not—would have a face that matched the photos in her pocket.

If he was behind her, she might not get a chance to talk. When she heard the cops calling back and forth, she thought about running over to the dome, but the street was too wide, too open, and they were too close. She'd been leaving tracks, but there'd been no way to avoid that. Now she ran a few feet into the street, through fresh snow, heading toward the dome. As she got into the street, onto snow compacted by traffic, she swerved left.

An old house, with four or five mailboxes mounted next to the door, was only a few dozen feet away, and behind it, a ramshackle garage. All the windows in the house were dark, but somebody had left it not long ago. A set of tire tracks came out of the garage, into the street.

Sandy hurried to the drive, tiptoed up the car track, crouched, looked around, then lifted the garage door. The door rolled up easily. The garage was empty, except for three garbage cans and a pile of worn-out tires stacked on one side. She dropped the door, and in the pitch-blackness, felt her way across to the stack of tires and sat down.

She felt as though she'd been physically beaten, but there was hope now. If she could get to a phone . . .

Through the walls of the garage, as if from a distance, she could hear the cops calling back and forth, and then more sirens. She sat and waited.

STADIC AND TWO uniformed cops crossed the street to the Metrodome. A ramp led up from the street to the concourse level, and they climbed it, spread out in a skirmish line. Four cars were parked in the tiny parking area above the ramp. Footprints led from the ramp area to the doors at the base of the dome. They couldn't tell if anyone else had walked up the ramp.

"Protect yourself, boys," Stadic said to the others. "Davenport might be right that she's helping out, but he don't know everything. If you come up on her, be ready."

The uniforms nodded, and as they approached the line of doors, they saw that one was propped open with a plastic wastebasket. "Five'll get you ten that she came in here," one of the cops muttered. They eased through the first set of doors, then went through a revolving door onto the circular concourse.

Nobody in sight. The concourse was only dimly lit, but somewhere, somebody was running a machine that sounded like an oversized vacuum. Stadic said, "You guys go that way. Holler if you see anything. She could be anywhere."

At that instant, one of the cops saw movement over Stadic's shoulder. He yelled, "Hold it . . . You! Hold it."

Stadic spun, and saw a figure in the dim light. The figure had stopped in the center of the concourse, and then the other uniform yelled, "Minneapolis police, hold it." All three of them trotted toward the figure. A man; a janitor.

"What happened?" the man asked. He was holding a hot TV dinner in one hand, a plastic fork in the other.

"Sorry," the first cop said. He put his pistol away. "You work here?"

"Uh, yeah . . ."

"Did you see a woman come through here? Hiding out?"

"Haven't seen anybody but the guys down working on the rug," the man said.

"The rug?"

"Yeah, you know, the Astroturf."

"All right: we're looking for a woman. If you see anybody, you let us know. We'll be walking around the concourse."

"What'd she do?" the janitor asked.

"She's that woman with the guys killing the cops," Stadic said.

"Yeah?" This was something different. "Is she, like . . . armed?"

"We don't know," Stadic said. "Don't take any chances. If you see her or any of your guys see her, get to a phone." He waved over his shoulder. There were phones all along the concourse. He scribbled a number on a business card. "Call this number. It'll ring me, right here, and we'll come running."

The janitor took the card. "I'll tell the other guys. We don't try to take her?"

"No. Don't go near her," Stadic said. "We know her sister used to shoot people for sport."

"I'll tell you what I can do—I can go up on top and look down," the janitor said. "We can get up there, see almost everything inside."

"Good. Give me a call," Stadic said. To the uniforms he said, "You guys go that way. Check all the stairwells, go up and down, look in the women's cans. I'll meet you on the other side."

"Got it."

"And I'll go up on top," the janitor said.

CARS WENT BY every few minutes, some fast, some slow. Sandy could hear nothing else, except the whisper of the falling snow. Finally she stood up and edged back to the door, lifted it two feet, squatted and looked out. Nobody. She pushed it up another foot, duckwalked out into the snow. She looked at the house, the windows still dark, then across the street at the dome. She could knock on the door of the house, maybe get somebody up, get a phone.

But there had to be a phone right there, across the street. No cars coming.

She ran across the street and up the approach ramp. A number of car and foot tracks went up the ramp. As she followed them, she brushed past a green pole set into the concrete. The pole was a modernistic phone kiosk, with a phone hanging on the other side—dial 911, no charge—but she never saw it.

Instead, she went on to the door, opened it, stepped through into the dead space between the inner and outer doors, then pushed through the revolving door onto the concourse. Nobody in sight, just a bunch of wet foot tracks. But she could hear rock music coming from somewhere. Tom Petty, she thought.

Down the hall she saw a sign: rest rooms and phones. She went that way and found a bank of phones. She picked up a phone, listened, got a dial tone, punched in 911. The call was answered instantly.

"This is Sandy Darling . . ."

"Ms. Darling, where are you?"

"I'm at the Metrodome, I'm inside."

"Okay. We'll put you through to Chief Davenport. He's on his way there."

A moment later they clicked through. "Ms. Darling? This is Lucas Davenport. The policeman working with LaChaise—his name was Andy Stadic?"

"I don't know," Sandy said. "They wouldn't tell me. They said if I turned them in, the cop was paid to come kill me. I've got some pictures of him. I took them out of Dick's pocket."

"Okay. I'm two minutes away and we've . . ."

"Listen, I think Dick is going to the hospital where your wife works. You've got to get over there first."

"Dick LaChaise was killed at the hospital," Lucas said.

"He's dead?"

"Yes."

"Thank God . . ." She said it half to herself, but Lucas picked it up.

"I'm just about there and we've got more people on the way," Lucas said. "Stadic is in the dome with you, so you've got to stay out of sight."

"He's in the dome?" She could hear voices and footsteps.

"Yes."

"Oh, God," she whispered. "Somebody's coming."

"Run," Lucas said. "Run and hide."

Sandy dropped the phone and ran across the hall. Two doors and a stairway led down to the first tier of seats: she pulled on a door, not expecting it to open. It did. She went through, down the stairs to the field of blue plastic seats, and turned left. Below her, on the football field, a half-dozen people were doing something to the dark green carpet. Stretching it? She couldn't tell.

She went down six rows, apparently unseen by the people on the field, slid halfway down the row of seats, and lay on her back. They'd have to look down every single row to see her, and she only had two minutes to go. Two minutes, Davenport had said. She thought she saw movement at the peak of the roof, but when she focused on the spot, there was nothing.

Less than two minutes, she thought.

STADIC'S PHONE RANG.

"This is the building engineer, I talked to you . . ."

"Yeah, yeah."

"She's hiding third row down, lower tier, right behind the goalposts."

He had her. "Which end?"

"South."

"What the fuck end is that?" Stadic snarled. North, south, he couldn't tell anything in this place.

"The, uh, hmm, I know: she's on the opposite end from where they're working on the rug."

Stadic said, "Go on back up there and watch in case she moves," then turned the phone off and started running. If he could get her. If he could get the phone away from Davenport. Christ, if LaChaise had Davenport's old lady, they could be there all day. He was still alive, if he could get the girl.

Stadic rounded the end of the concourse and saw people milling around. One of them yelled, "Sandra Darling. Sandra Darling, where are you?"

Who was that? That couldn't be Davenport . . .

He dodged left, went down the stairs to the first tier. He was halfway around.

He went down three rows and started running sideways. He was on the thirty-yard line, the twenty, the ten, but still a way to go.

A uniformed cop came out of one of the staircases, saw him and yelled, "Andy Stadic. Stadic. Stop there, Andy."

They had him.

No doubt. But he kept going, he was almost to the woman: he could do that, anyway. He could say that he didn't hear, that he was about to arrest her. He had the .380 in his pocket, if he could drop it, if they found her with the gun . . .

Sandy heard the cops shouting, heard somebody banging toward the seats. She peeked: the man in the photos was a hundred feet away, running right toward her. He *knew* where she was. She began to crawl down the space between the seats, got to the stairs, scrambled up them, hands and feet churning.

"Sandy Darling, stop," Stadic screamed. He brought the shotgun up, centered it on the back of her head and jerked the trigger. The shot boomed inside the stadium and he saw her go down. Had she gone down before the shot? Had he hit her?

Somebody shouted and he turned, dizzy, and a cop fired a pistol and a chair splintered behind him.

Then he saw the woman, scrambling, disappearing into a stairwell. He ran that way, and somebody fired another shot at him, but Stadic had lost it.

The woman, he thought. If he could just get the woman. He forgot about the phone: he thought about the small figure disappearing into the stairwell.

There was his problem. *The woman.*

DAVENPORT APPEARED, LARGE, hair standing out from his head as though somebody had deliberately mussed it, his long black coat dangling down his legs. He was a quarter of the way around the stadium, a pistol in his hand. "Stadic, goddamnit . . ."

But Andy Stadic, too many days with no sleep, one inch from having pulled it off—Stadic was locked into a loop. Find the woman. He jerked the shotgun toward Davenport and pulled the trigger, once, twice, three times, four, and then the gun was empty. Lucas dropped and the shotgun blasts rattled harmlessly off the seats twenty yards away. Not even close. The cops farther up the dome fired three more shots, missing.

Stadic ignored them, dropped the shotgun, drew his pistol, a Glock nine-millimeter, and ran up the stairs, into the stairwell, going after the woman.

And he found blood.

A SMEAR ON the concrete, then a dribble. He'd hit her with his quick shot. He followed the blood around the corner and up. She'd moved to the next tier. Somebody was screaming at him: "Stadic. Stadic . . ."

Not Davenport, one of the other cops.

He was so close.

SANDY WAS HURT. She didn't know whether she'd been hit with shotgun pellets, or pieces of the plastic chairs, but she was bleeding from the right hip, thigh and calf, and maybe from her back. Her back hurt, anyway, a scratching pain, like a cut.

She emerged on the second level, saw a TV booth to her left. *Try to hide.* She ran to the booth. The door was locked. She went back down the stairs, thinking she might hide in the seats again—and noticed that the booth window was open. She stood on the back of a seat, and pulled herself in.

Not a broadcast booth, but a camera position. Empty, except for a heavy camera stand. No playoff games this year. She crouched below the window and listened to the cops yelling out in the stadium.

THE THOUGHTS WERE making a little tune in Stadic's head: get the woman, fuckin' Davenport; get the woman soon as you can . . .

He ran up the stairs, paused, looked for blood. Heard the cops calling behind him: "Where'd he go? Get out in the goddamn concourse . . . I think he went up."

More blood. Yes. Going up.

He followed, poked his head out of the stairwell, and a cop at the far end shouted, "There he is. He's up on top."

LUCAS RAN UP a stairwell, paused at the top, and peeked. Stadic was in the next well, with a pistol. Lucas poked his head around the corner and yelled, "Andy. Give it up, man."

"Fuck you, Davenport." Stadic swiveled and fired. "You caused this shit."

Somebody shouted, "He's gone, he went back down."

STADIC JUMPED BACK into the stairwell, paused a second, then came back out: and caught him. Lucas, hearing the other cops yelling, had come out of his stairwell and was headed down the aisle toward him. Stadic had his gun up: Lucas's gun was out to his side, as he balanced himself trying to run down the too-narrow row of seats. Stadic fired and Davenport flipped over, went down between the chairs.

WHEN SANDY HEARD Lucas shout, she stuck her head up and peeked. Stadic was twenty feet away, Davenport beyond him: she recognized him from TV, the funny shock when you realized that the TV image actually represented a person. Then Stadic fired and Davenport flipped over the chairs, going down.

Sandy looked wildly around the booth, saw the TV stand. The camera mounting-head was fixed to the end of a steel cylinder, which disappeared into a heavy steel base, fixed with two collars held by wing nuts. She loosened the wing nuts and pulled the cylinder out of the base. The cylinder was a chromed-steel pipe four feet long, an inch and a half in diameter. She grabbed it like a baseball bat, hefted it.

STADIC FROZE AFTER firing at Davenport: stunned. He'd just killed a cop, for Christ's sake. He stood for a second, looking at his pistol. Maybe he could tell them Davenport was the one, that Davenport had set him up.

Glassy-eyed, he turned back to the trail the woman had left. Blood trail . . .

LUCAS'S HEAD CRACKED one of the blue plastic chairs as he went over the side. The bullet had missed—he didn't have time to think about it, but he was whole, dizzy, disoriented, struggling to get up . . .

THE BLOOD TRAIL ran toward a door on a TV booth, then away from the door and up toward the window.

"ANDY, ANDY . . ." THE uniformed cops, still half a stadium away, were firing at him. Stadic looked up at the window, climbed on the chair back, pulled himself up. A bullet clipped his coat, another the back of his neck, and he fell.

"Andy . . ."

That was Davenport? He popped up, gun in hand, and saw Lucas again, fired quickly, saw Lucas duck, go down.

He looked up. Christ, the window was right there. Blood on his hand, on his neck, blood on everything, slippery . . .

He went straight up, leaping, caught the window and hauled himself up, heard the cops yelling, "Andy, Andy, Andy," a regular football cheer, doing the wave for Andy Stadic.

He hauled himself up, hands slippery with blood . . .

Sandy was there, looking down at him.

SANDY HEARD HIM scrabbling at the booth, saw his hand catch the edge, saw him fall. There were more shots, and then he was up again, bullet-headed, like a gorilla, like King Kong, climbing up the outside of the booth.

Back home, Sandy had always been the one who split wood for the wood stove. She liked doing it, feeling the muscles work.

Now here was this blood-covered man coming to kill her. A man she didn't know, with a gun, crawling up the wall . . .

She swung the steel cylinder with everything she had: for Elmore, for the times Martin and LaChaise had knocked her down, for the fear during the ledge walk, for all the blood. She swung the pipe like a wood-splitting maul.

STADIC LOOKED UP. Saw it coming. Had just enough time left in the world to let go of the window.

LUCAS WAS ON his knees, his gun coming up, thinking, *Vest; he's wearing a vest* . . .

The gunsight tracked up Stadic's back to his neck, just as Stadic's head went over the lip of the window, and Sandy loomed in front of him. Lucas snapped the barrel upright, afraid to touch off the shot . . .

He saw the steel cylinder come down.

Heard the crack.

Saw Stadic drop like a rag.

THERE WAS NO sound in the stadium. Everything had stopped: the workmen, the running cops. Lucas. Sandy. Stadic's body upside-down in the blue chairs.

After a long, long beat, the world started again. "You can come down," Lucas said to Sandy as the other cops ran toward them. "You'll be all right now."

31

SANDY DARLING LAY in the hospital bed, tired, dinged up, but not seriously injured. Her most pressing problem was her left foot, which was cuffed to the bed frame. She could sit up, she could move, but she couldn't roll over. The simple presence of the cuff gave her the almost uncontrollable urge to roll, and a powerful sense of claustrophobia when she couldn't.

She'd spoken to a lawyer. He said the Hennepin County District Attorney might come up with a charge, but there wasn't a case if what she said was true. She was a victim, not a perpetrator.

Sandy had told the truth, generally, with a few critical lies. She hadn't seen them, she said, until Butters came to get her, to patch up LaChaise. After Butters showed up, she hadn't been free to leave. She'd tried to get free every way she could.

There remained the problem of LaChaise's fingerprints and other traces in the Airstream trailer: but nobody but Sandy knew he'd been there—nobody alive—and probably not more than five other people in the world were aware of the Airstream. If they *did* find the trailer, and bothered to fingerprint it, she could attribute any cooperation to Elmore. Otherwise, when she got out, she'd wait a few days, and then go out to the trailer with cleaning rags and a bucket of detergent.

And she should get out—in a couple of days, with any luck, the lawyer said.

She turned on her side, felt the tug of the cuff and looked out the window. She had a view of a snow-covered rooftop and a hundred yards of anonymous street.

Elmore. Elmore would be the problem, she thought. The guilt she felt about Elmore was deeper, more intractable than she would have believed. He haunted her thoughts, in death, the way he never had in life.

She'd babbled something about it to a doctor. The doctor told her that grief was natural, would stay, but could be borne and would eventually fade.

Maybe, maybe not.

God, if I can only get out . . .

She needed to be outside, working with the horses. This was a pretty time of year, if you liked the north woods, the white fences of the training rings, the dark trees against the snow.

The horses would be out in it now, running over the hillside, the blankets flowing over their backs, gouts of steam snorting from their nostrils.

Sandy Darling shut her eyes and counted horses.

THE PLAINCLOTHES GUYS gathered in Homicide, where there really wasn't enough space, like mourners at a wake, muttering among themselves. Much of the talk was about the Iowa boy and his rifle.

And Stadic, of course.

Stadic dead was better than Stadic alive, everybody agreed on that. But already, the amateur lawyers were talking: he'd never been found guilty in a court of law. What would happen to his benefits? He had an ex-wife and kid, would they get them?

"Andy was a greedy sonofabitch, he was always bitchin' about not havin' enough, not makin' enough," Loring said. "All the guy ever thought about was money. That's why his old lady split. But I never thought he'd . . ."

Lester came in and cleared his throat and said, "Listen up, everybody. We're all done. Unless you're on the schedule or you're making a statement, go home. Finish your Christmas shopping. And get the goddamn overtime forms in, and anybody who wants comp time instead of money, come see me, and I will personally kiss you on the ass and shake your hand . . ."

"At the same time?"

A little laughter.

A detective from Sex said, "What about Stadic?"

"What about him?" Lester asked.

"I mean . . . we were talking . . . what's gonna happen?"

Lester said, "Aw, shit, let's not get into that. We got a long way to go with the county attorney."

"What about Harp?" asked a drug guy.

"We're looking for Mr. Harp," Lester said. "And pay attention here: if anybody except the chief or the mayor talks to the press about Andy Stadic, without checking with us first, well, that's your First Amendment right, but we *will* cut your nuts off with a sharpened screwdriver."

"Hey, are we gonna be on *Cops?* . . ."

SLOAN AND SHERRILL found Lucas sitting in a waiting room at the University Hospitals, looking at a sheaf of papers in a manila file.

Sherrill stuck her head in and said, "What's happening, dude?"

Lucas closed the file and said, "Just . . . hanging out."

Taking that as permission to come in, they dropped into chairs facing him, and Sloan asked, "Have you seen Weather?"

"She should be waking up," Lucas said. "I'm waiting to go in."

"Has she said anything to anybody?" Sloan asked.

"Yeah, but she's disoriented," Lucas said. "She really seems . . . hurt. I think I really hurt her."

Sloan shook his head: "You didn't hurt her. You did what you had to."

Sherrill, exasperated, said, "C'mon, Sloan, that's not gonna help."

"What?"

"Clichés," Sherrill said. She turned to Lucas. "Maybe you *did* hurt her. You ought to think about that."

"Aw, Jesus," Sloan groaned.

"The problem that's got me is, it's my fault," Lucas said. "I didn't see Stadic—I should have seen him. If I'd seen Stadic, we would've had them all."

Sloan was irritated: "C'mon, Lucas, how could you have seen Stadic? He saved your life with Butters."

Lucas waved him off: "You remember when we were getting ready to raid poor old Arne Palin? We were talking at the door, you and me and Franklin? And Lester was there, and Roux? Stadic came in, and Franklin said something like, he wanted to sneak back to his place to pick up some clothes for his wife. An hour later, he was ambushed."

"Lucas . . ."

"Listen, after he was ambushed, I ran over to the hospital, and I kept thinking, how could they know he was coming? How could they know? They couldn't just hide outside his house twenty-four hours a day, waiting for him to come along. Why would they? We'd had it on TV that everybody was safe in the hotel . . ."

Lucas pointed a finger at Sloan: "The answer was right there in front of me: Stadic told them. He was the only one who could have."

Sherrill shook her head. "Seeing that might seem possible when you're working it out backwards. At the time, nobody would have figured it out."

"I should have," Lucas said.

"You're feeling sorry for yourself," Sloan said. "Get your head out of your ass."

"Since I didn't see it . . . well, I don't know what else I could've done at the hospital," Lucas said. He spread his hands, looked around the waiting room as though an answer might be written on the walls, then back at Sherrill and Sloan. "I sit here thinking about what I could've done, and I can't think of anything better. Not that that'd given her the best chance of staying alive, with what we knew at the time. Everything we knew said that LaChaise was insane."

"That's exactly right," Sloan said.

"The way I hear it, from what Weather told the docs, she spent the whole time with LaChaise working on him, convincing him he ought to stay alive . . . that *she* oughta stay alive. And it worked. They were both getting out of it and then boom! He blows up, and she freaks out," Lucas said.

"That's got to have some kind of effect on you," Sherrill said.

"What kind of effect? He was a giant asshole," Sloan said. "Getting shot was too good for him."

"That might not be the way she sees it," Sherrill said.

"Well." Sloan looked away. "I mean, what're you supposed to do?"

"I don't know," Lucas said. He pushed the conversation away. "Have you seen Del?"

"Yeah, he's gonna hurt for a while," Sloan said. "He's not, you know, *injured* that bad, but he *hurts* like hell."

"His wife is pissed," Sherrill said. "She says we should have had more people up there, besides Del."

"She's right," Lucas said.

"What about Sandy Darling?" Sloan asked Lucas. "I hear she's talking."

"Yeah." Lucas nodded. He'd spent the best part of an hour listening to the interrogation, before leaving Hennepin General for the University Hospitals. "Basically, she was kidnapped."

"Who killed her old man?"

"She doesn't know. She said it wasn't LaChaise or Butters or Martin."

"Stadic?" asked Sherrill, in a hushed voice.

"I think so," Lucas said. "He was trying to get rid of everyone. He got the truck tags, somehow, and figured out where they lived. He probably thought they were hiding up there, and went up to take them out. He had to see everybody dead to get free—and they all *would've* been dead if Sandy Darling hadn't tripped over her goddamn cowboy boots and fallen on her face in the stadium."

"It's a hell of a story," Sloan said. "The question is, how much of it is bullshit?"

"Maybe some," Lucas said. "Maybe not, though. There were a couple of things: she said while they attacked the hospital, they chained her to a post in Harp's garage. There's a chain around the post, and there're two padlocks, just like she said, and there's paint missing from the post and it's on the chain, as if somebody was trying to pull it free. The chain's got latents all over it, so we'll know if she was handling the chain. I think she was. Then she says she tried to climb out a window on Harp's building, walk down a ledge and go down the fire escape, but that the fire escape was jammed. There are fingerprints on the window, and the fire escape *is* jammed—it's actually an illegal latch, but you can't see it. So that's right. And walking that ledge in her bare feet, on snow, you'd have to be pretty desperate. And when she called from the dome, she didn't know it was all over, and she tried to warn me that LaChaise was going after Weather . . ."

"All right, so she walks," Sloan said. He stood up, yawned, and said, "The big thing is, *you* gotta take care of *yourself*."

"I gotta take care of Weather, is what I gotta do," Lucas said.

Sloan shook his head: "Nope. Nobody can take care of Weather except Weather. You gotta take care of yourself."

"Jesus, Sloan," Sherrill said. She was getting angry. "You know what he means . . ."

Sloan opened his mouth and shut it again: A few years earlier, Lucas had gone through an episode of clinical depression, and since then, Sloan had thought of his friend as somewhat . . . *delicate* was not quite the right word; dangerously poised, perhaps. He said, "Well . . ." and let it go.

A nurse poked her head in, spotted Lucas and said, "Weather's up."

Lucas pushed himself out of the chair and said, "See you guys later," and hurried down the hall after the nurse.

Weather had a private room, and when Lucas walked in, she was on her feet, in a hospital gown, digging into a lockerlike closet for her clothes. Her face was intent, hurried.

"Weather . . ."

She jumped, turned, saw him and her face softened: "Oh, God, Lucas." She reached toward him.

"How are you?" He wrapped her up in his arms and her feet came off the floor.

"If you don't smother me, I'll probably be okay," she gasped.

He put her down. "Probably?"

"Well, when they had me sedated, they talked me into this ridiculous hospital gown." She pulled it out to the side, as if she were about to curtsy. "Every doc I know has been down to check on me, and every one has taken a good look at my ass."

"Just like you: bringing light into people's lives."

"I gotta get out of this gown," she said, digging into the locker again. "Shut the door."

Lucas shut the door, and as she tossed the balled-up gown on the bed, he said, "Really now—don't bullshit me. How are you?"

She was pulling on a blouse, and stopped, suddenly, as her hands came through the cuffs. "I'm sorta . . . messed up, I think. It's the weirdest thing." She rubbed her temple, looking up at him. Then her eyes drifted away, focused in the middle distance past his shoulder. "I'll be going along, thinking about something else, and then all of a sudden, there I am again, back in the hall with this man and you're standing there and then . . ."

She shuddered.

"Don't think about it," Lucas said.

"I'm not thinking about it. I refuse to think about it. But it's like . . . like somebody else holds up a picture of it, right in front of my eyes. It just comes, boom!" she said.

"Post-traumatic stress," he said.

"That's what I think," she said. "But in some way, I never really believed in it until now. It's like people who had it were . . . weaklings, or something."

"It'll go away," he repeated. "There in the hall—I didn't know what was happening with you and LaChaise, I couldn't take any chances, there wasn't any way to really know."

"I worked that out," she said. "And God, the whole thing was my fault. What was I doing here? When he came in the OR, I thought I was dead. I thought he'd kill me right there, and all my friends, the people with me. I felt so *stupid* . . ."

"You can't anticipate lunatics," Lucas said. "None of this made any sense."

Weather was rambling on: "Then he made the fatal error. I didn't see it, because we were talking so . . . normally. But I see it now: he'd maneuvered himself, by what he'd done, the way he was acting, into a spot where all the solutions were drastic and narrow. Thinking about it, I'm not sure he would have surrendered. At the time I thought he would: No, I was *sure* of it. But now, I'm not sure. When we were talking, he'd keep changing his mind, like . . . like . . ."

"A child," Lucas said.

"Yes . . . Well, not quite. Like a crazy child," she said.

She was staring out the window when she said that, looking down at the trees along the Mississippi, when suddenly she focused again, and turned to look up at him. "What about you?" she asked. "We heard about the policeman, that he was killed and you were there . . . are you all right?"

"Oh, yeah, I'm fine." He stood back from her, holding on to her shoulders but at arm's length, looking her over. She seemed so bright, so focused, so normal, so *all right*, that he suddenly laughed.

"What?" she asked, trying on a smile.

"Nothing," he said. He wrapped her up again, and her feet came off the floor again. "Everything. Especially the way that gown showed your ass off."

"*Lucas . . .*"

SECRET PREY

1

THE CHAIRMAN OF the board pulled the door shut behind him, stacked his rifle against the log-sided cabin, and walked down to the end of the porch. The light from the kitchen window punched out into the early-morning darkness and the utter silence of the woods. Two weeks of nightly frost had killed the insects and had driven the amphibians into hibernation: for a few seconds, he was alone.

Then the chairman yawned and unzipped his bib overalls, unbuttoned his pants, shuffled his feet, the porch boards creaking under his insulated hunting boots. Nothing like a good leak to start the day, he thought. As he leaned over the low porch rail, he heard the door opening behind him. He paid no attention.

Three men and a woman filed out of the house, pretended not to notice him.

"Need some snow," the woman said, peering into the dark. Susan O'Dell was a slender forty, with a tanned, dry face, steady brown eyes, and smile lines around her mouth. A headlamp was strapped around her blaze-orange stocking cap, but she hadn't yet switched it on. She wore a blaze-orange Browning parka, snowmobile pants, and carried a backpack and a Remington .308 mountain rifle with a Leupold Vari-X III scope. Not visible was the rifle's custom trigger job. The trigger would break at exactly two and a half pounds.

"Cold sonofabitch, though," said Wilson McDonald, as he slipped one heavy arm through his gun sling. McDonald was a large man, and much too heavy: in his hunting suit he looked like a blaze-orange Pillsbury Doughboy. He carried an aging .30–06 with open sights, bought in the thirties at Abercrombie & Fitch in New York. At forty-two, he believed in a certain kind of tradition——his summer car, a racing-green XK-E, was handed down from his father; his rifle came from his grandfather; and his spot in the country club from his great-grandfather. He would defend the Jaguar against far better cars; the .30–06 against more modern rifles, and the club against parvenus, hirelings, and of course, blacks and Jews.

"You all ready?" asked the chairman of the board, as he came back toward them, buttoning his pants. He was a fleshy, red-faced man, the oldest of the group, with a thick shock of white hair and caterpillar-sized eyebrows. As he got closer to the others, he could smell the odor of pancakes and coffee still steaming off them. "I don't want anybody stumbling around in the goddamn woods just when it's getting good."

They all nodded: they'd all been here before.

"Getting late," said O'Dell. She wore the parka hood down, and the parka itself was still unzipped; but she'd wrapped a red and white kaffiyeh around her neck and chin. Purchased on a whim in the Old City of Jerusalem, and meant to protect an Arab from the desert sun, it was now protecting a third-generation Irishwoman from the Minnesota cold. "We better get out there and get settled."

Five forty-five in the morning, opening day of deer season. O'Dell led the way off the porch, the chairman of the board at her shoulder, the other three men trailing behind.

Terrance Robles was the youngest of them, still in his mid-thirties. He was a blocky man with thick, black-rimmed glasses and a thin, curly beard. His watery blue eyes showed a nervous flash, and he laughed too often, a shallow, uncertain chuckle. He carried a stainless Sako .270, mounted with a satin-finished Nikon scope. Robles had little regard for tradition: everything he hunted with was new technology.

James T. Bone might have been Susan O'Dell's brother: forty, as she was, Bone was slim, tanned, and dark-eyed, his face showing a hint of humor in a surface that was hard as a nut. He brought up the rear with a .243 Mauser Model 66 cradled in his bent left arm.

Four of the five—the chairman of the board, Robles, O'Dell, and Bone— were serious hunters.

The chairman's father had been a country banker. They'd had a nice rambling stone-and-redwood home on Blueberry Lake south of Itasca, and his father had been big in Rotary and the Legion. The deer hunt was an annual ritual: the chairman of the board had hung twenty-plus bucks in his forty-six years: real men didn't kill does.

Robles had come to hunting as an adult, joining an elk hunt as a thirtieth-birthday goof, only to be overwhelmed by its emotional power. For the past five years he'd hunted a half-dozen times annually, from Alaska to New Zealand.

O'Dell was a rancher's daughter. Her father owned twenty miles of South Dakota just east of the Wyoming line, and she'd joined the annual antelope hunt when she was eight. During her college years at Smith, when the other girls had gone to Ivy League football games with their beaux, she'd flown home for the shooting.

Bone was from Mississippi. He'd learned to hunt as a child, because he wanted to eat. Once, when he was nine, he'd made soup for himself and his mother out of three carefully shot blackbirds.

Only McDonald disdained the hunt. He'd shot deer in the past—he was a Minnesota male, and males of a certain class were expected to do that—but he considered the hunt a pain in the ass. If he killed a deer, he'd have to gut it. Then he'd smell bad and get blood on his clothing. Then he'd have to do something with the meat. A wasted day. At the club, they'd be playing some serious gin—drinking some serious gin, he thought—and here he was, about to climb a goddamned tree.

"Goddamnit," he said aloud.

"What?" The chairman grunted, turned to look at him.

"Nothing. Stray thought," McDonald said.

One benefit: If you killed a deer, people at the club attributed to you a certain common touch—not commonness, which would be a problem, but contact with the earth, which some of them perceived as a virtue. That was worth something; not enough to actually be out here, but something.

THE SCENT OF woodsmoke hung around the cabin, but gave way to the pungent odor of burr oaks as they pushed out into the trees. Fifty yards from the cabin, as they moved out of range of the house lights, O'Dell switched on her headlamp, and the chairman turned on a hand flash. Dawn was forty-five minutes away, but the moonless sky was clear, and they could see a long thread of stars above the trail: the Dipper pointing down to the North Star.

"Great night," Bone said, his face turned to the sky.

A small lake lay just downslope from the cabin like a smoked mirror. They followed a shoreline trail for a hundred and fifty yards, moved single file up a ridge, and continued on, still parallel to the lake.

"Don't step in the shit," the woman said, her voice a snapping break in the silence. She caught a pile of fresh deer droppings with her headlamp, like a handful of purple chicken hearts.

"We did that last week with the Cove Links deal," the chairman said dryly.

The ridge separated the lake and a tamarack swamp. Fifty yards further on, Robles said, "I guess this is me," and turned off to the left toward the swamp. As he broke away from the group, he switched on his flash, said, "Good luck, guys," and disappeared down a narrow trail toward his tree stand.

The chairman of the board was next. Another path broke to the left, toward the swamp, and he took it, saying, "See you."

"Get the buck," said O'Dell, and McDonald, O'Dell, and Bone continued on.

THE CHAIRMAN FOLLOWED the narrow flashlight beam forty-five yards down a gentle slope to the edge of the swamp. The lake was still open, but the swamp was freezing out, the shallow pockets of water showing windowpane ice.

One stumpy burr oak stood at the boundary of the swamp; the kind of oak an elf might live in. The chairman dug into his coat pocket, took out a long length of nylon parachute cord, looped it around his rifle sling, leaned the rifle against the tree, and began climbing the foot spikes that he'd driven into the tree eight years earlier.

He'd taken three bucks from this stand. The county road foreman, who'd been cleaning ditches in preparation for the snow months, told him that a twelve-pointer had moved into the neighborhood during the summer. The foreman had seen him cutting down this way, across the middle of the swamp toward this very tree. Not more than two weeks ago.

The chairman clambered into the stand fifteen feet up the tree, and settled into the bench with his back to the oak. The stand looked like a suburban deck, built of preservative-treated two-by-sixes, with a two-by-four railing that served as a gun rest. The chairman slipped off his pack, hung it from a spike to his right, and pulled the rifle up with the parachute cord.

The cartridges were still warm from his pocket as he loaded the rifle. That wouldn't last long. Temperatures were in the teens, with an icy wind cutting at exposed skin. Later in the day, it would warm up, maybe into the upper thirties, but sitting up here, early, exposed, it would get real damn cold. Freeze the ass off that fuckin' O'Dell. O'Dell always made out that she was impervious to cold; but this day would get to her.

The chairman, wrapped in nylon and Thinsulate, was still a little too warm from the hike in, and he half dozed as he sat in the tree, waiting for first light. He woke once more to the sound of a deer walking through the dried oak leaves, apparently following a game trail down to the swamp. The animal settled on the hillside behind him.

Now *that* was interesting.

Forty or fifty yards away, no more. Still up the ridge, but it should be visible after sunrise, if it moved again. If it didn't, he'd kick it out on the way back to the cabin.

He sat waiting, listening to the wind. Most of the oaks still carried their leaves, dead brown, but hanging on. When he closed his eyes, their movement sounded like a crackling of a small, intimate wood fire.

The chairman sighed: so much to do.

THE KILLER WAS dressed in blaze orange and was moving quietly and quickly along the track. Dawn was not far away and the window of opportunity could be measured in minutes:

Here: now twenty-four steps down the track. One, two, three, four, five, six, seven, eight . . . twenty-three, twenty-four. A tree here to the left . . . Wish I could use a light.

The oak tree was there, its bark rough against the fingertips. And just to the right, a little hollow in the ground behind a fallen aspen.

Just get down here . . . quietly, quietly! Did he hear me? These leaves . . . didn't think about the leaves yesterday, now it sounds like I'm walking on cornflakes . . . Where's that log, must be right here, must be . . . ah!

From the nest in the ground, the fallen aspen was at exactly the right height for a rifle rest. A quick glance through the scope: nothing but a dark disc.

What time? My God, my watch has stopped. No. Six-seventeen. Okay. There's time. Settle down. And listen! If anybody comes, may have to shoot . . . Now what time? Six-eighteen. Only two minutes gone? Can't remember . . . two minutes, I think.

There'd be only one run at this. There were other people nearby, and they were armed. If someone else came stumbling along the track, and saw the orange coat crouched in the hole . . .

If they came while it was dark, maybe I could run, hide. But maybe, if they thought

I was a deer, they'd shoot at me. What then? No. If someone comes, I take the shot then, whoever it is. Two shots are okay. I can take two. It wouldn't look like an accident anymore, but at least there wouldn't be a witness.

What's that? Who's there? Somebody?

The killer sat in the hole and strained to hear: but the only sounds were the dry leaves that still hung from the trees, shaking in the wind; the scraping of branches; and the cool wind itself. *Check the watch.*

Getting close, now. Nobody moving, I'm okay. Cold down here, though. Colder than I thought. Have to be ready . . . The old man . . . have to think about the old man. If he's there, at the cabin, I'll have to take him. And if his wife's there, have to take her . . . That's okay: they're old . . . Still nothing in the scope. Where's the sun?

DANIEL S. KRESGE was the chairman of the board, president, and chief executive officer of the Polaris Bank System. He'd gathered the titles to him like an archaic old Soviet dictator. And he ran his regime like a dictator: two hundred and fifty banks spread across six midwestern states, all wrapped in his cost-cutting fist.

If everything went exactly right, he would hold his job for another fifteen months, when Polaris would be folded into Midland Holding, owner of six hundred banks in the south central states. There would be some casualties.

The combined banks' central administration would be in Fort Worth. Not many Polaris executives would make the move. In fact, the whole central administrative section would eventually disappear, along with much of top management. Bone would probably land on his feet: his investments division was one of the main profit centers at Polaris, and he'd attracted some attention. O'Dell ran the retail end of Polaris. Midland would need somebody who knew the territory, at least for a while, so she could wind up as the number two or three person in Midland's retail division. She wouldn't like that. Would she take it? Kresge was not sure.

Robles would hang on for a while: a pure technician, he ran data services for Polaris, and Midland would need him to help integrate the separate Polaris and Midland data systems.

McDonald was dead meat. Mortgage divisions didn't make much anymore, and Midland already had a mortgage division—which they were trying to dump, as it happened.

Kresge turned the thought of the casualties in his head: when they actually started working on the details of the merger, he'd have to sweeten things for the Polaris execs who'd be putting the parts together, and the people Midland would need: Robles, for sure. Probably O'Dell and Bone.

McDonald? Fuck him.

KRESGE WOULD LOSE his job along with the rest. Unlike the others, he'd walk with something in the range of an after-tax forty million dollars. And he'd be free.

In two weeks, Kresge would sit in a courtroom and solemnly swear that his marriage was irretrievably broken. His wife had agreed not to seek alimony. In return for that concession, she'd demanded—and he'd agreed to give her—better than seventy-five percent of their joint assets. Eight million dollars. Letting go of the eight million had been one of the hardest things he'd ever done. But it was worth it: there'd be no strings on him.

When she'd signed the deal, neither his wife nor her wolverine attorney had understood what the then-brewing merger might mean. No idea that there'd be a golden parachute for the chairman. And his ex wouldn't get a nickel of the new money. He smiled as he thought about it. She'd hired the wolverine specifically to fuck him on the settlement, and thought she had. Wait'll the word got into the newspapers about his settlement. And it *would* get in the newspapers.

Fuck her.

Forty million. He knew what he'd do with it.

He'd leave the Twin Cities behind, first thing. He was tired of the cold. Move out to L.A. Buy some suits. Maybe one of those BMW two-seaters, the 850. He'd been a good, gray Minnesota banker all of his life. Now he'd take his money to L.A. and live a little. He closed his eyes and thought about what you could do with forty million dollars in the city of angels. Hell, the women alone . . .

KRESGE OPENED HIS eyes again with a sudden awareness of the increasing cold: shivered and carefully shook the stiffness out. Looking to the east, back toward the cabin, he could see an unmistakable streak of lighter sky. There was a ruffling of leaves to his right, a steady trampling sound. Another deer went by, a shadow in the semidark as the animal picked its way through a border of finger-thick alders at the fringe of the swamp. No antlers that he could see. He watched until the deer disappeared into the tamarack.

He picked up the rifle then, resisted the temptation to work the bolt, to check that the rifle was loaded. He knew it was, and working the bolt would be noisy. He flicked the safety off, then back on.

The last few minutes crawled by. Ten minutes before the season opened, the forest was still gray to the eye; in the next few minutes, it seemed to grow miraculously brighter. Then he heard a single, distant shot: nobody here on the farm.

Another shot followed a minute later, then two or three shots over the next couple of minutes: hunters jumping the gun. He glanced at his watch. Two minutes. Nothing moving out over the swamp.

THROUGH THE SCOPE, the target looked like an oversized pumpkin, fifteen or twenty feet up the tree. His body from the hips down was out of sight, as was his right arm. The killer could see a large part of his back, but not the face.

The crosshairs of the low-power scope caressed the target's spine, and the killer's finger lay lightly on the trigger.

Gotta be him. Damn this light, can't see. Turn your head. Come on, turn your head. Look at me. Have to do something, sun's getting up, have to do something. Look at me. There we go! Keep turning, keep turning . . .

THIRTY SECONDS BEFORE the season opened, the crackle of gunfire became general. Nothing too close, though, Kresge thought. Either the other guys were holding off, or nothing was moving beneath them.

What about the deer that had settled off to his left?

He turned on the bench, moving slowly, carefully, and looked that way. In the last few seconds of his life, Daniel S. Kresge first saw the blaze-orange jacket, then the face. He recognized the killer and thought, *What the hell?*

Then the face moved down and he realized that the dark circle below the hood was the objective end of the scope and the scope was pointed his way, so the barrel . . . ah, Jesus.

JESUS WENT THROUGH Kresge's mind at the same instant the bullet punched through his heart.

The chairman of the board spun off the bench—feeling no pain, feeling nothing at all—his rifle falling to the ground. He knelt for a moment at the railing, like a man taking communion; then his back buckled and he fell under the railing, after the rifle.

He saw the ground coming, in a foggy way, hit it face first, with a thump, and his neck broke. He bounced onto his back, his eyes still open: the brightening sky was gone. He never felt the hand that probed for his carotid artery, looking for a pulse.

He would lie there for a while, head downhill, would Daniel S. Kresge, a hole in his chest, with a mouth full of dirt and oak leaves. Nobody would run to see what the gunshot was about. There would be no calls to 911. No snoops. Just another day on the hunt.

A real bad day for the chairman of the board.

2

LOOKING AS THOUGH he'd been dragged through hell by the ankles, a disheveled Del Capslock stumbled out of the men's room in the basement of City Hall, fumbling with the buttons on the fly of his jeans. Footsteps echoed in the dark hallway behind him, and he turned his head to see Sloan coming through the gloom, a thin smile on his narrow face.

"Playing with yourself," Sloan said, his voice echoing in the weekend emptiness. Sloan was neatly but colorlessly dressed in khaki slacks and a tan mountain parka with a zip-in fleece liner. "I should have expected it; I knew you were a pervert. I just didn't know you had enough to play with."

"The old lady bought me these Calvin Kleins," Dell said, hitching up the jeans. "They got buttons instead of zippers."

"The theory of buttons is very simple," Sloan began. "You take the round, flat thing . . ."

"Yeah, fuck you," Del said. "The thing is, Calvin makes pants for fat guys. These supposedly got a thirty-four waist. They're really about thirty-eight. I can't get them buttoned, and when I do, I can't keep the fuckin' things up."

"Yeah?" Sloan wasn't interested. His eyes drifted down the hall as Del continued to struggle with the buttons. "Seen Lucas?"

"No." Del got one of the buttons. "See, the advantage of buttons is, you don't get your dick caught in a zipper."

"Okay, if you don't get it caught in a buttonhole."

Del started to laugh, which made it harder to button the pants, and he said, "Shut up. I only got one more . . . maybe you could give me a hand here."

"I don't think so; it's too nice a day to get busted for aggravated faggotry."

"You can always tell who your friends are," Del grumbled. "What's going on with Lucas?" He got the fly buttoned finally and they started up the stairs toward Lucas's new first-floor office.

"Fat cat got killed," Sloan said. "Dan Kresge, from over at Polaris Bank."

"Never heard of him."

"You heard of Polaris Bank?"

"Yeah. That's the big black-glass one."

"He runs it. Or did, until somebody shot his ass up in Garfield County. The sheriff called Rose Marie, who called Lucas, and Lucas called me to ride along."

"Just friends, or overtime?"

"I'm putting in for it," Sloan said comfortably. He had a daughter in college; nothing was ever said, but Davenport had been arranging easy overtime for him. "Great day for it—though the colors are mostly gone. From the trees, I mean."

"Fuck trees. Kresge . . . it's a murder?"

"Don't know yet," Sloan said. "This is opening day of deer season. He was shot out of a tree stand."

"If I was gonna kill somebody, I might do it that way," Del said.

"Yeah. Everybody says that." Davenport's office was empty, but unlocked. "Rose Marie's in," Sloan said as they went inside. "Lucas said if he wasn't here, just wait."

As Lucas stood up to leave, he asked Rose Marie Roux, the chief of police, why she didn't do something simple, like use the Patch.

" 'Cause I'd have to put patches all over my body to get enough nicotine. I'd have to put them on the bottom of my feet."

She was on day three, and was chewing her way through a pack of nicotine gum. Lucas picked up his jacket, grinned faintly, and said, "A little speed might help. You get the buzz, but not the nicotine."

"Great idea, get me hooked on speed," Roux said. "Course, I'd probably lose weight. I'm gonna gain nine hundred pounds if I don't do something." She leaned across her desk, a woman already too heavy, getting her taste buds back from Marlboro Country. "Listen, call me back and tell me as soon as you get there. And I want you to tell me it's an accident. I don't want to hear any murder bullshit."

"I'll do what I can," Lucas said. He stepped toward the door.

"Are you all right?" Roux asked.

"No." He stopped and half turned.

"I'm worried about you. You sit around with a cloud over your head."

"I'm getting stuff done . . ."

"I'm not worried about that—I'm worried about *you*," she said. "I've had the problem—you know that. I've been through it three times, now, and doctors help. A lot."

"I'm not sure it's coming back," Lucas said. "I haven't tipped over the edge yet. I can still . . . stop things."

"All right," Roux said, nodding skeptically. "But if you need the name of a doc, mine's a good guy."

"Thanks." Lucas closed her office door as he left and turned down the hall, by himself, suddenly gone morose. He didn't like to think about the depression that hovered at the edge of his consciousness. The thing was like some kind of rodent, like a rat, nibbling on his brain.

He wouldn't go through it again. A doctor, maybe; and maybe not. But he wouldn't go through it again.

DEL SAT IN one of Lucas's visitor's chairs, one foot on Lucas's desk, blew smoke at the ceiling and said, "So what're you suggesting? We send him a fruitcake?"

Lucas's office smelled of new carpet and paint, and looked out on Fourth Street; a great fall day, crisp, blue skies, young blond women with rosy cheeks and long fuzzy coats heading down the street with their boyfriends, toward the Metrodome and a University of Minnesota football game.

Sloan, who was sitting in Davenport's swivel chair, said, "The guy's hurting. We could . . . I don't know. Go out with him. Keep him busy at night."

Del groaned. "Right. We get our wives, we go out to eat. We talk the same bullshit we talk at the office all day, because we can't talk about Weather. Then we finish eating and go home with our old ladies. He goes home and sits in the dark with his dick in his hand."

"So what're you saying?" Sloan demanded.

"What I'm saying is that he's all alone, and that's the fuckin' problem . . ." Then Del lifted a finger to his lips and dropped his voice. "He's coming."

LUCAS STEPPED INTO the office a moment later, with the feeling he'd entered a sudden silence. He'd felt that a lot, lately.

Lucas was a tall man, hard-faced, broad-shouldered, showing the remnants of a summer tan. A thin line of a scar dropped through one eyebrow onto a cheek, like a piece of fishing line. Another scar slashed across his throat, where a friend had done a tracheotomy with a jackknife.

His hair was dark, touched by the first few flecks of gray, and his eyes were an unexpectedly intense blue. He was wearing a black silk sweatshirt showing the collar of a French-blue shirt beneath it, jeans, and a .45 in an inside-the-pants rig. He carried a leather jacket.

He nodded at Del, and to Sloan said, "Get out of my chair or I'll kill you."

Sloan yawned, then eased out of the chair. "You get your jeans dry-cleaned?" he asked.

"What?" Lucas looked down at his jeans.

"They look so crisp," Sloan said. "They almost got a crease. When I wear jeans, I look like I'm gonna paint something."

"When you wear a tuxedo, you look like you're gonna paint something," Del said.

"Mr. Fashion Plate speaking," Sloan said.

Del was already wearing his winter parka, olive drab with an East German army patch on one shoulder, an Eat More Muffin sweatshirt, fire-engine-red sneaks with holes over the joints of his big toes, through which were visible thin black dress socks—Del had bunion problems—and the oversized Calvin Kleins. "Fuck you," he said.

"So what's happening?" Lucas asked, looking at Del. He circled behind the desk and dropped into the chair vacated by Sloan. He turned a yellow legal pad around, glanced at it, ripped off the top sheet and wadded the paper in his fist.

"We're trying to figure how to snap you out of it," Del said bluntly.

Lucas looked up, then shrugged. "Nothing to do."

"Weather's coming back," Sloan said. "She's got too much sense to stay away."

Lucas shook his head. "She's not coming back, and it doesn't have anything to do with good sense."

"You guys are so fucked," Del said.

"You say 'fuck' way too much," Sloan said.

"Hey, fuck you, pal," Del said, joking, but with an edge in his voice.

Lucas cut it off: "Ready to go, Sloan?"

Sloan nodded. "Yeah."

Lucas looked at Del: "What're you doing here?"

"Seeking guidance from my superiors," Del said. "I've got an opium ring with fifty-seven members spread all over Minneapolis and the western suburbs, especially the rich ones like Edina and Wayzata. One or two in St. Paul. Grow the stuff right here. Process it. Use it themselves—maybe sell a little."

Lucas frowned. "How solid?"

"Absolutely solid."

"So tell me." Lucas poked a finger at Del. "Wait a minute . . . you're not telling me that fuckin' Genesse is back? I thought he was gone for fifteen."

Del was shaking his head: "Nah."

"So . . ."

"It's fifty-seven old ladies in the Mountbatten Garden Club," Del said. "I got the club list."

Sloan and Lucas looked at each other; then Sloan said, "What?"

And Lucas asked, "Where'd you get the list?"

"From an old lady," Del said. "There being nothing but old ladies in the club."

"What the hell are you talking about?" Lucas asked.

"When I went over to Hennepin to get my finger sewed up after the pinking shears thing, this doc told me he'd treated this old-lady junkie. She was coming down from the opium, but she thought she had the flu or something. It turns out they've been growing poppies for years. The whole club. They collect the heads at the end of the summer and make tea. Opium tea. A bunch of them are fairly well hooked, brewing up three or four times a day."

Lucas rubbed his forehead. "Del . . ."

"What?" Del looked at Sloan, defensively. "What? Should I ignore it?"

"I don't know," Lucas said. "Where're they getting the seeds?"

"Seed stores," Del said.

"Bullshit," Lucas said. "You can't buy opium seeds from seed stores."

"I did," Del said. He dug in his parka pocket, pulled out a half-dozen seed packets. Lucas, no gardener, recognized the brand names and the envelopes.

"That's not—"

"Yes, it is. They got fancy names, but I talked to a guy at the university, and brother . . ." He tossed them on Lucas's desk. ". . . them's opium poppies."

"Aw, man." Now Lucas was rubbing his face. Tired. Always tired now.

"The hell with the old ladies," Sloan said. "Let's get out of here."

"I'll talk to you later," Lucas said to Del. "In the meantime, find something dangerous to do, for Christ's sake."

LUCAS AND SLOAN took Lucas's new Chevy Tahoe: Kresge's body, they'd been told, was off-road.

"I'm not gonna push you about being fucked up," Sloan said. "Just let me know if there's anything I can do."

"Yeah, I will," Lucas said.

"And you oughta think about medication . . ."

"Yeah, yeah, yeah . . ."

"Is . . . How's Weather?"

"Still in therapy. She's better without me, and gets worse when I'm around. And she's making more friends that I'm cut off from. She's putting together a new life and I'm out of it," Lucas said.

"Christ."

"When she moved out," Lucas said, "she left her dress in the closet. The green one, three thousand bucks. The wedding dress."

"Maybe it means she's coming back."

"I don't think so. I think she abandoned it."

Much of the trip north was made in gloomy silence, through the remnants of the autumn's glorious color change; but the end was coming, the dead season.

JACOB KRAUSE, THE Garfield County sheriff, was squatting next to the body, talking to an assistant medical examiner, when he saw Lucas and Sloan walking down the ridge toward them. They were accompanied by a fat man in a blaze-orange hunting coat and a uniformed deputy leading a German shepherd. The deputy pointed at Krause, and turned and went back toward the house.

"Is this him?" Krause asked.

The AME turned his head and said, "Yeah. Davenport's the big guy. The guy in the tan coat is Sloan, he's one of the heavyweights in Homicide. I don't know the fat guy."

"He's one of ours," the sheriff said. He had the mournful face of a blue-eyed bloodhound, and had a small brown mole, a beauty mark, on the right end of his upper lip. He sighed and added, "Unfortunately."

A few feet away, two crime scene guys were packing up a case of lab samples; up the hill, two funeral home assistants waited with a gurney. The body would be taken to Hennepin County for autopsy. Krause looked a last time at Kresge's paper-white face, then stood up and headed back up the path. He took it slowly, watching as Davenport and Sloan and the fat man dropped down the trail like Holmes and Watson on a Sunday stroll with Oliver Hardy. When they got closer, Krause noticed that Davenport was wearing loafers with tassels, that his socks were a black and white diamond pattern, and that the loafers matched his leather jacket. He sighed again, the quick judgment adding to his general irritation.

"HELLO. I'M LUCAS Davenport . . ." Lucas stuck out his hand and the sheriff took it, a little surprised at the heft and hardness of it; and the sadness in Davenport's eyes. "And Detective Sloan," the sheriff finished, shaking hands with Sloan. "I'm Jake Krause, the sheriff." He looked past them at the fat man. "I see you've met Arne."

"Back by the cars," the fat man said. "What do we got, Jake?"

"Crime scene, Arne. I'd just as soon you don't come up too close. We're trying to minimize the damage to the immediate area."

"Okay," the fat man said. He craned his neck a little, down toward the orange-clad body, the AME hovering over it, the crime scene boys with their case.

"Accident?" Lucas asked.

Krause shrugged. "C'mon and take a look, give me an opinion. Arne, you better wait."

"Sure thing . . ."

ON THE WAY down to the body, Lucas asked, "Arne's a problem?"

"He's the county commission chairman. He got the job because nobody trusted him to actually supervise a department or the budget," Krause said. "He's also a reserve deputy. He's not a bad guy, just a pain in the ass. And he likes hanging around dead people."

"I know guys like that," Lucas said. He looked up at the tree stand as they approached the body and asked, "Kresge was shot out of the stand?"

"Yup. The bullet took him square in the heart," Krause said. "I doubt he lived for ten seconds."

"Any chance of finding the slug?" Sloan asked.

"Nah. It's out in the swamp somewhere. It's gone."

"But you think he was shot out of the tree stand," Sloan said.

"For sure," Krause said. "There's some blood splatter on the guardrail and threads from his coveralls are hanging from the edge of the floorboards up there—no way they should be there unless they snagged when he fell over the edge."

Lucas stepped over next to the body, which lay faceup a foot and a half from a pad of blood-soaked oak leaves. Kresge didn't look surprised or sad or any of the other things he might have looked. He looked dead, like a wadded-up piece of wastepaper. "Who moved him?"

"The first time, other members of the hunting party. They opened up his coat to listen to his heart, wanted to make sure he wasn't still alive. He wasn't. Then me and the doc here"—Krause nodded at the AME—"rolled him up to look at the exit wound."

Lucas nodded to the assistant medical examiner, said, "Hey, Dick, I heard you guys were coming up," and the AME said, "Yup," and Lucas said, "Roll him up on his side, will you?"

"Sure."

The AME grabbed Kresge's coat and rolled him up. Lucas and Sloan looked at the back, where a narrow hole—a moth might have made it—was surrounded by a hand-sized bloodstain just above the shoulder blade. Lucas said, "Huh," and he and Sloan moved left to look at the entry, then back at the exit. They both turned at the same time to look at the slope, then at each other, and Lucas said, "Okay," and the AME let the body drop back into place.

Lucas stood and brushed his hands together and grinned at the sheriff. The grin was so cold that the sheriff revised his earlier, quick, judgment. "Good one," Lucas said.

"What do you think?" Krause asked.

"The shooter got close," Lucas said.

"You wouldn't get that angle through the body, upward like that, unless the shooter was below him," Sloan explained. "And if the shooter's below him"— they all looked back up the slope—"he couldn't have been more than thirty or forty yards away. Of course, we don't know how Kresge was sitting. He could have been looking out sideways. Or he could have been leaning back when the slug hit."

Krause said, "I don't think so."

"I don't either," Lucas said.

"So it's a murder," Krause said. He shook his head and looked from the body to Lucas. "I wish you'd keep this shit down in the Cities."

"MIND IF I check the tree?" Lucas asked the crime scene cops.

One of them said, "We're done, if it's okay with the sheriff."

"Go ahead," Krause said.

Lucas began climbing the spikes, looked down just as he reached the platform, and asked, "What about motive?"

Krause nodded. "I asked those people down at the cabin about that. Instead of a name, I got an estimate. Fifteen hundred, maybe two thousand people."

Sloan said, "Yeah?"

"There's this merger going on . . ."

Lucas listened to Krause's explanation of the merger as he carefully probed the backpack hung on the tree. He remembered seeing bank-merger stories in the *Star-Tribune*. He hadn't paid much attention—more corporate jive, as far as he could tell.

"Anyway, he was up here hunting with a bunch of big shots from the bank," Krause said, unwinding his story. "Some of them, maybe all of them, are set to lose their big shot jobs."

"Those are the people we saw down at the cabin?" Lucas asked. He'd finished with the backpack, left it hanging where he found it, and dropped back down the tree.

"Yeah," Krause said sourly. "They filled me in on the merger business."

"Shooting him seems a little extreme," Sloan said.

"Why?" Krause asked. The question was genuine, and Sloan glanced at Lucas and then looked back at the sheriff, who said, "Close as I can tell, he was about to mess up the lives of hundreds of people. Some of them—hell, maybe most of them—will never get as good a job again, ever in their lives. And he was doing it just so he could make more money than he already had, and he had a pile of it. Shooting him seems pretty rational to me. Long as you didn't get caught."

"I wouldn't express that opinion to the press," Lucas said mildly. He went back to the body, knelt on one knee, and began going through Kresge's pockets.

"I never say anything to the press that I haven't run past my old lady," Krause grunted, as he watched. "She hasn't turned me wrong yet." A second later, he added, "There is one other possibility. For the shooting. His wife. He's right in the middle of a divorce."

"That could be something," Lucas agreed. He squeezed both of Kresge's hands through their gloves, then stood up and rubbed his hands together.

"These folks at the cabin said the divorce is signed, sealed, and delivered, that the wife really took a chunk out of his ass."

"Makes it sound less likely," Sloan said.

"Yeah, unless she hates him," Lucas said. "Which she might."

Sloan opened his mouth to say something, then shut it, thinking suddenly of Weather. Krause asked, "Find anything new in the backpack?"

"Couple of Snickers, couple packs of peanut M and M's, half-dozen hand-heater packs."

"Same thing I found," Krause said.

"Do you deer hunt, Sheriff?" Lucas asked.

"Nope. I'm a fisherman. I was gonna close out the muskie season this afternoon, beat the ice-up. I was loading my truck when they called me. Why?"

"It gets as cold on a tree stand as it does on a November day out muskie fishing," Lucas said.

"Colder'n hell," Krause said.

"That's right. But he hadn't eaten anything and hadn't used any heat packs, even though he brought them along and must've intended to use them," Lucas said. "So he was probably shot pretty soon after he got to the stand."

"Did anyone hear any early shots?" Sloan asked.

"I asked the other people about unusual shots, but nobody said anything was out of order. Bone said he thought either Kresge or one of the other guys, a guy named Robles, had fired a shot just after the opening. But Robles said he didn't, and his rifle is clean, and so's Kresge's."

"How long had they been sitting?"

"About forty-five minutes."

Lucas nodded: "Then that was probably the killing shot. He'd still have been pretty warm up to that point."

They talked for a few more minutes, then left the AME with the body and headed back through the woods toward the cabin. As they passed the mortuary attendants, now sitting on the gurney, Krause said, "He's all yours, boys."

"Been a nice month, up to now," the sheriff said, rambling a bit. "No killings, no rapes, no robberies, only a half-dozen domestics, a few drunk-driving accidents, and a couple of small-time burglaries. This sort of blots the record."

Lucas said, "The killer had to find the place in the dark—so he had to know where it was, exactly."

"Unless he came after daylight," Krause said. "That's possible."

"Yeah, but when we were coming in, your deputy—the one with the dog?—pointed out where this Robles guy was sitting, and generally where the other people were. So the killer would have to take a chance on being seen, unless he really knew the layout."

"And if he knew all that, he'd probably be recognized by the others," Sloan said. "Which means he probably came in when it was dark."

"Unless he's one of these guys," Krause said. "These guys would have all the information, plus an excuse for walking around with guns . . . and they'd know that nobody would come looking at the sound of a shot."

"It could be one of these guys," Lucas said. "But it'd take guts."

"Or a crazy man," Sloan said.

AT THE END of the track they could see a half-dozen people sitting and standing on the cabin porch, a man in a red plaid shirt talking animatedly to the others. A short man in a blue suit sat apart from them.

"What's the situation with these people?" Lucas asked as they started down the slope toward the cabin. "Who questioned them?"

"I did, and one of our investigators, Ralph—that's Ralph in the blue suit."

"Is he good?" Lucas asked.

The sheriff thought for a minute and then said, "Ralph couldn't pour piss out of a boot with the instructions written on the heel."

Sloan asked, "So how come . . . ?"

"I try to keep him out of the way, but he was at the office and answered the phone this morning."

"Did he collect all the guns?" Lucas asked.

"No, but I did," Krause said. "Two of them had been fired—both people had deer to show for it. The others look clean."

"I saw the deer hanging down by the cabin . . ." Lucas said. Then: "Get your crime scene guys to check their hands and faces for powder traces. And count shells—find out what they claim to have fired, and do a count."

"I'm doing all that, except for the shells," Krause said. He looked up at Lucas. "I'm going by the book. The whole book. My problem is more along the lines of interrogation and so on. Expertise."

Lucas tipped his head at Sloan: "Sloan is the best interrogator in the state."

Sloan grinned at the sheriff and said, "That's true."

"Then we'd like to borrow you for a while," Krause said. "If you got the time."

"Fine with me," Sloan said. "Overtime is overtime."

"Is there any possibility that you could do some running around Minneapolis for me?" Krause asked.

Sloan looked at Lucas. "I've got a couple of things going . . . Sherrill is doing research on that Shack thing, but she's not getting much. Maybe she could do some running around."

Lucas nodded. "I'll call her this afternoon, on my way back. Anything you break out of these guys, call it down to her. I'll have her talk to Kresge's wife, check for girlfriends . . ."

"Or boyfriends," Sloan said.

"Or boyfriends. And I'll have her start talking to people in his office— secretaries and so on." Lucas looked at Krause. "I don't want to take over your investigation . . ."

"No-no-no, don't worry about that," Krause said hastily. "The more you can do, the better. My best guys are busier'n two-dick dogs in a breeding kennel . . . And my other guys would have a hard time finding Minneapolis, much less anybody in it."

"Sounds like you have some problems," Sloan said. "First Arne, then Ralph . . ."

"We're going through a transitional period," Krause said grimly. Then: "Look, I'm the new guy up here. I was with the highway patrol for twenty-five years, and then last fall I got myself elected sheriff. The office is about fifty years out of date, full of deadwood, and all the deadwood is related to somebody. I'm cutting it down, but it takes time. I'll take any help I can get."

"Whatever we can do," Lucas said.

Krause nodded. "Thanks." He'd been prepared to dislike the Minneapolis guys, but it hadn't turned out that way. Actually, he sort of liked them, for city people. Sloan especially, but even Davenport, with his shoe tassels and expensive clothes. He glanced at Davenport again, quickly. From a little bit of a distance you might think *pussy*. You didn't think that when you got closer to him. Not after you'd seen his smile.

He added, "I don't think I'm gonna get too far up here. Matter of fact, I don't think I'm going to get anywhere—everything about this shooting was set up in the Cities."

They were coming up to the porch, and Sloan said, quietly, "So let's go jack up these city folks. See if anybody gets nervous."

3

THE FOUR SURVIVING hunters sat on the porch in the afternoon sunlight, in rustic wooden chairs with peeling bark and waterproof plastic seat cushions. They all had cups of microwaved coffee: Wilson McDonald's was fortified with two ounces of brandy. James T. Bone sat politely downwind of the others, smoking a cheroot.

The sheriff's investigator perched on a stool at the other end of the porch, like the class dummy, looking away from them. If one of the bankers suddenly broke for the woods, what was he supposed to do? Shoot him? But the sheriff had told him to keep an eye on them. What'd that mean?

And the bankers were annoyed, and their annoyance was not something his worn nerves could deal with. He could handle trailer-home fights and farm kids hustling toot, but people who'd gone to Harvard, who drove Lincoln and Lexus sport-utes and wore eight-hundred-dollar après-hunt tweed jackets, undoubtedly woven by licensed leprechauns in the Auld Country—well, they made him nervous. Especially when one of them might be a killer.

"DAVENPORT IS THE bad dog," Bone said from downwind, as they watched Krause lead his parade down through the woods toward the cabin. He bit off a sixteenth-inch of the cheroot and spit it out into the fescue at the bottom of the porch. "He oughta be able to tell us something."

"Mean sonofabitch, by reputation," O'Dell said. She said it casually, looking through the steam of the coffee. She wasn't impressed. She was surrounded by mean sonsofbitches. She might even be one herself.

"Just another c-cop," Robles stuttered. Robles was scared: they could smell it on him. They liked it. Robles was the macho killer, and his fear was oddly pleasing.

"I talked to him a couple of times on the transfers with his IPO—you all

SECRET PREY —— 485

know he used to be Davenport Simulations?" Bone said. They all nodded; that was the kind of thing they all knew. "He sold the company to management and walked with better'n ten, AT." He meant ten million dollars, after taxes.

"So why doesn't he quit and move to Palm Springs?" Robles asked.

" 'Cause he likes what he does," Bone said.

"I wish he'd get his bureaucratic ass down here and do what we have to do; I wanna get back to town," McDonald grumbled. Back to a nice smooth single-malt; but he'd stay here as long as the others did. Sooner or later, they'd start talking about who'd be running the bank. "No point in keeping us here. We've told them everything we know."

"Unless one of us killed him," Bone said lazily.

"Gotta be an accident," Robles said, nervously. "Opening day of deer season . . . I bet there're twenty of them. Accidents."

"No, there aren't," Bone said. "There are usually one or two, and most of the time, they know on the spot who did the shooting."

"Besides, it wasn't an accident," O'Dell said positively.

"How do you know?" McDonald asked. He finished the loaded coffee and rubbed his mouth with the back of his hand. He could use another.

"Maybe she did it," Robles said. He tried to laugh, but instead made a small squeaking noise, a titter.

O'Dell ignored him. "Karma's wrong for an accident," she said.

"Great: we're talking karma," McDonald said. "Superstitious hippie non-sense."

Bone slumped a little lower in his chair and a thin grin slipped across his dry face: "But she's right," he said. "Dan was a half-mile onto his own property. Who's going to shoot him through the heart from more'n half a mile away? Nope. I figure it was one of us. We all had guns and good reasons."

"Bullshit," McDonald said.

AS THEY WATCHED the parade approaching, O'Dell said, "We should decide who'll speak for the bank. The board'll have to appoint a CEO, but somebody should take over for the moment. Somebody in top management."

"I thought Wilson might do it—until a decision is made on a CEO," Bone said. He looked over at Wilson McDonald, whose eyes went flat, hiding any reaction; and past him at O'Dell. The top job, Bone thought, would go either to himself or O'Dell, unless the board did something weird. Robles didn't have the background, McDonald wasn't smart or skilled enough. "If you think so," McDonald said carefully. This was the moment he'd been waiting for.

O'Dell had done her calculations as well as Bone, and she nodded. "Then you've got it," she said. She put her battered hunting boots up on the porch railing and looked past McDonald at Bone: "Until the police figure out if one of us did it. And the board has a chance to meet."

After a moment's silence, Robles said, "My gun wasn't fired."

Bone rolled his eyes up to the heavens: "I'll tell you what, Terry. It would take me about three seconds to figure a way to kill Kresge and walk out of the woods with a clean weapon." He took a final drag on the cheroot, dropped the stub end on the porch, ground it out with his boot, and flipped it out into the yard with his toe. "No sir: I figure a fired weapon is purely proof of innocence."

He was breaking Robles's balls. Bone and O'Dell had the two dirty rifles, while McDonald and Robles were clean. Usually, Bone wouldn't have bothered: Robles wasn't much sport. But Bone was in a mood. Davenport and the others were dropping the last few yards down the trail to the clearing around the house, and Bone muttered to the others, "Bad dog."

LUCAS LED THE parade up the porch steps, with Krause and Sloan just behind, and the four bankers all stood up to meet them. Lucas recognized Bone and nodded: "Mr. Bone," he said. "Did Sally get the Spanish credit?"

Bone's forehead wrinkled for a second; then he remembered and nodded, smiling: "Sure did. She graduated in June . . . Are you running things here?"

"No, I was just about to leave, in fact. Sheriff Krause runs things up here. We'll be cooperating down in Minneapolis, if he needs the backup."

"So why did you come up?" O'Dell asked. She put a little wood-rasp in her voice, a little annoyance, so he'd understand her status here.

Lucas grinned at her, mild-voiced and friendly: "Mr. Kresge carried a lot of clout in Minneapolis, so it's possible the motive for the shooting will be found there. Quite possibly with the bank, from what I hear about this merger. Detective Sloan"—Lucas looked at Sloan, who raised a hand in greeting—"has been assigned to help Sheriff Krause with his interviews, so we can get you folks on your way home."

"Are you s-s-sure it wasn't an accident?" Robles stuttered.

Lucas shook his head and Krause said, "He was murdered."

"So that's it," O'Dell said, and the bankers all looked at each other for a moment, and then Bone broke the silence: "Damn it. That'll tangle things up."

McDonald, ignoring Krause, asked Lucas, "Do you think . . . one of us . . . ?"

Lucas looked at Krause. "We have no reason to think so, in particular. Since we know you were here, we've got to talk to you," Krause said. "But we've got no suspects."

SLOAN SUGGESTED THAT he would prefer to talk to the four of them individually, inside, while the others waited on the porch. "Nice day, anyway," he said, pleasantly. "And it shouldn't take long."

"Let me go first," McDonald grunted, pushing up from his chair. "I want to get back and start talking to the PR people. We'll need a press release ASAP. God, what a disaster."

"Fine," Sloan said. He turned to Lucas: "You gonna take off?"

"Yeah. The sheriff'll send you back with a deputy."

"See you later then," Sloan said. "Mr. McDonald?"

McDonald followed Sloan and Krause into the cabin. When they'd gone, Bone said to Lucas, "I'd feel better about this if you were running things."

"Krause is a pretty sharp cookie, I think," Lucas said. "He'll take care of it."

"Still, it's not something where you want a mistake made," Bone said. "A murder, I mean——when you're a suspect, but you're innocent."

"I appreciate that," Lucas said. He glanced at the other two, then took a card case from his jacket pocket, extracted four business cards and passed them around. "If any of you need any information about the course of the investigation, or need any help at all, call me directly, any time, night or day. There's a home phone listed as well as my office phone. Ms. O'Dell, if you could give one to Mr. McDonald."

"Very nice of you," O'Dell said, looking at the cards. "We just want to get this over with."

"You shot one of the deer, didn't you?" Lucas asked her. The two gutted deer were hanging head down from the cabin's deer pole in the side yard.

"The bigger of the two," she said.

"I like mine tender," Bone said dryly. "Always go for a doe."

"Good shot," Lucas said to O'Dell. "Broke his shoulder, wiped out his heart; I bet he didn't go ten feet from where you shot him."

She didn't feel any insinuation; he was just being polite. "Do you hunt?" she asked.

He smiled and nodded: "Quite a bit."

WHEN LUCAS HAD gone, O'Dell said to Bone, "That's not a bad dog. That's a pussycat."

Bone took another cheroot out of his jacket pocket, along with a kitchen match, which he scratch-lit on the porch railing; an affectation he acknowledged and enjoyed. "He's killed four or five guys, I think, in the line of duty. He built a software company from nothing to a ten-million AT buyout in about six years. In his spare time. And I'll tell you something else . . ."

He took a long drag on the cheroot, and blew a thin stream of smoke out into the warming afternoon air, irritating O'Dell. "What?"

Bone said, "When we did the transfers on the IPO, I talked to him for ten minutes. While we were doing it, my daughter called on my private line, from school. All upset. She was having a problem with a language credit, and she was afraid they'd hold up her graduation. I mentioned it to him, in passing—— just explaining the phone call. This was seven months ago. He remembered me, he remembered Sally's name, and he remembered the language she was taking."

Bone looked at O'Dell. "You can take him lightly, if you want. I wouldn't. Especially if you pulled the trigger twice this morning."

"Don't be absurd," she said. But she looked after Lucas, down by the parking area, just getting into his truck. "Nice shoulders," she said, thinking the comment would irritate just about everybody on the porch.

THE TRUCK WAS very quiet without Sloan: Lucas didn't need the quiet—in the quiet, his mind would begin to churn, and that would lead . . .

He wasn't sure where it would lead.

He was tired, but he needed to be more tired. He needed to be so tired that when he got back home, he could lie down and sleep before the churning began. He put a tape in the tape player, ZZ Top, the *Greatest Hits* album, and turned it up. Interference. Can't churn when there's too much interference.

The killing at the hunting camp was not particularly interesting: one possible motive, the bank merger, was already fairly clear. Others of a more personal nature might pop up later—Kresge was in the process of getting a divorce, so there might be other women. Or his wife might have something to do with it.

Routine investigation would dredge it all up, and either the killer would be caught or he wouldn't. Whichever, Lucas felt fairly distant from the process. He'd been through it dozens of times, and the routine greed, love, and stupidity killings no longer held much interest.

Evil was interesting, he would still admit; this a residue from his term in Catholic schools. But so far he detected no evil in the killing. Spite, probably; stupidity, possibly. Greed. Anger. But not real evil . . .

HE RODE MINDLESSLY for a while, the winter fields and woods rolling by, Holsteins out catching a few uncommon November rays, horses dancing through hillside pastures; a few thousand doomed turkeys . . . Then he glanced out the side window, caught the boles on the oaks, recognized them, shivered. Turned up the tape.

He'd been dreaming again, lately; he hated the dreams, because they woke him up, and when he woke, in the night, his mind would begin running. And the dreams always woke him . . .

One dream had an odd quality of science fiction. He was being lowered, on some kind of platform, into a huge steel cylinder. Nearby was a steel cap, two feet thick, with enormous threads, which would be screwed into place after he was inside, sealing him in. The process was industrial: there were other people running around, making preparations for whatever was about to happen. He was cooperating with them, standing on the platform obviously expectant. But for what? Why was he about to be sealed inside the cylinder? He didn't know, but he wasn't frightened by the prospect. He was engaged by it, though. He'd start thinking about it, and then he'd wake up, his mind churning . . .

The other dream was stranger.

A man's face, seen from a passing car. There were small beads of rain on the window glass, so the view was slightly obscured; in his dream, Lucas could not quite get a fix on the face. The man was hard, slender, wore an ankle-length black coat and a snap-brim hat. Most curious were the almond-shaped eyes, but where the surfaces of his eyes should be—the pupils and irises—there were instead two curls of light maple-colored wood shavings. The man seemed to be hunched against a wind, and the drizzle; he seemed to be cold. And he looked at Lucas under the brim of the hat, with those eyes that had curls of wood on their surfaces.

Lucas had begun to see the almond shapes around him on the street. See them on the faces of distant men, or in random markings on buildings, or on trees. Nonsense: but this dream frightened him. He would wake with a start, sweat around the neckline of his T-shirt. And then his mind would start to run . . .

He turned up the ZZ Top yet another notch, and raced toward the Cities, looking for exhaustion.

AN HOUR AFTER Lucas had passed that way, James T. Bone hurtled down I-35 in a large black BMW. As he crossed the I-694 beltline he picked up the cell phone and pushed the speed-dial number. The other phone rang three times before a woman answered it, her voice carrying a slight whiskey burr. "Hello?"

"This is Bone. Where are you?"

"In my car. On my way back from Southdale."

"I'm coming over," he said. "Twenty minutes."

"Okay . . . you can't stay long. George is—"

"Twenty minutes," Bone said, and punched off. He pushed another speed-dial button, and another woman answered, this voice younger and crisper: "Kerin."

"This is Bone. Where are you?"

"At home."

"Dan Kresge's been killed. Shot, probably murdered. Had you heard yet?"

"No. My God . . ."

"I'll be at the office in an hour, or a little more. If you have the time . . ."

"I'll be there in ten minutes. Can I get anything started before you get there?"

"Names and phone numbers of all the board members . . ."

They talked for five minutes; then Bone punched out again.

A THREE-CAR FENDER bender slowed him a bit, but he pulled into the downtown parking garage a little less than a half hour after he made the first call. He'd gotten out of his hunting clothes and was wearing a Patagonia jacket with khakis and a flannel shirt. He pulled the jacket off as he rode up in the elevator.

Marcia Kresge met him at the door in a blue silk kimono. "You like it? I bought it an hour ago."

"I hope you're not celebrating," he said.

He said it with an intensity that stopped her: "What happened?"

"Your soon-to-be-ex-husband was shot to death up at the cabin this morning. I'm undoubtedly one of the suspects."

Kresge looked mildly shocked for a quarter-second, then slipped a tiny smile: "So the fucker's dead?"

"I hope to Christ you didn't have anything to do with it."

"*Moi?*" she asked mockingly, one hand going to her breast.

"Yeah, Marcia, you're really cute; I hope you're not that cute when the cops show up."

"The cops?" Finally serious.

"Marcia, sit down," Bone said. Kresge dropped onto a couch, showing a lot of leg. Bone looked at it for a moment, then said, "Listen, I know you think you fucked over Dan pretty thoroughly. You're wrong. Last week the board granted him another two hundred and fifty thousand options to buy our stock at forty, as a performance award. If the merger goes through, and it's botched, the stock'll be worth sixty in a year. If the merger is done exactly right, it could be at eighty in a year. That's ten million dollars, and if it's held for a year, you'll take out eight after taxes."

"Me? I—"

"Marcia, shut up for a minute. The options have value. They become part of his estate. You'll inherit. You'll also get the rest of his estate, that you didn't get in the divorce. No taxes at all on that. In other words, Dan gets murdered, you get ten million. I'm up there with a gun, and guess who's fucking Marcia Kresge?"

"Jesus," she said.

"I seriously doubt that he's involved."

"But they can't think I . . . ?"

"You didn't, did you? You know all those crazy nightclub characters . . ."

"Bone: I had not a goddamned thing to do with it. I really *did* think I'd taken him to the cleaners . . . and I mean, I didn't like him, but I wouldn't kill him."

He knew her well enough to know she wasn't lying. He exhaled, said, "Good."

"You honest to God thought . . ."

"No. I didn't think you went out and hired some asshole to kill him," Bone said. "What I was afraid of is, you'd mentioned to one of your little broken-nosed pals that if Dan died, you'd get another whole load of cash."

"Well, I didn't," she said. "Because I didn't know that I would."

"Okay . . . I don't think it would be necessary to mention to the police that we've been involved," he said dryly.

"Good thought," she said, matching his tone precisely.

"All right." He stood up and started toward the door. "I've got to get down to the bank."

"The bank? God, when you called, I thought maybe . . ." She'd gotten up and come around the couch.

"What?" He knew what.

"You know." She slipped the belt of the kimono; she was absolutely bare and pink beneath it. "I just got out of the shower."

"I thought George was coming over."

"Well, not for a couple of hours . . . and you gotta at least tell me what happened."

"Take off the kimono."

She took it off, tossed it on the couch. He was staring at her, like he always did, with an attention that both disturbed and excited her.

"What?" She unconsciously touched one arm to her breastbone, covering her right breast as she did it. Bone reached out and pushed her arm down.

"Put your hands behind you," he said. "I want to look at you while I tell you this."

She blushed, the blush reaching almost to her waist. She bit her lower lip, but put her hands behind her back.

"We started out like we always do, walking back into the woods. You know how that trail goes back around the lake . . ."

As he told the story, he began to stroke her, his voice never faltering or showing emotion, but his hands always moving slowly. After a moment she slowly backed away, and he stepped after her, still talking. When her bottom touched the edge of a couch table, she braced herself against it, closed her eyes.

"Are you listening?" he asked; his hands stopped momentarily.

"Of course," she said. "A few minutes before six and the shooting started."

"That's right," he said. He pushed her back more solidly into the couch table and said, "Spread your legs a little."

She spread her legs a little.

"A little more."

She spread them a little more.

"Anyway," he said, gently parting her with his fingertips. "Any one of us could have killed him. It was just a matter of climbing down from the tree, sneaking back up the path . . ."

"Did you do it?" she asked.

"What do you think?"

"You could have," she said. And then she said, "Oh, God."

"Feel good?"

"Feels good."

"Look at me . . ."

She opened her eyes, but they were hazy, a dreamer's eyes, looking right through him. "Don't stop now," she said.

"Look at me . . ."

She looked at him, struggled to focus on his dark, cool face. "Did you kill him?"

"Does the thought turn you on?"

"Oh, God . . ."

SUSAN O'DELL'S APARTMENT was a study in black and white, glass and wood, and when she walked in, was utterly silent. She pulled off her jacket, let it fall to the floor, then her shirt and her turtlenecked underwear, and her bra. The striptease continued back through the apartment through her bedroom to the bathroom, where she went straight into the shower. She stood in the hot water for five minutes, letting it pour around her face. When she'd cleaned off the day, she stepped out, got a bath towel from a towel rack, dried herself, dropped the towel on the floor, and walked back to the bedroom. Underpants and gray sweatsuit.

Dressed again, warm, she walked back to the study, stood on her tiptoes, and took a deck of cards off the top of the single bookshelf.

Sitting at her desk, she spread the cards, studied them.

She'd once had an affair, brief but intense, with an artist who'd taught her what he called Tarot for Scientists. A truly strange tarot method: business management through chaos theory, and he really knew about chaos. An odd thing for an artist to know, she'd thought at the time. She'd even become suspicious of him, and had done some checking. But he was a legitimate painter, all right. A gorgeous watercolor nude, which nobody but she knew was O'Dell herself, hung in her bedroom, a souvenir of their relationship.

After she realized the value of the artist's tarot method, he'd bought her a computer version so she could install it on her computer at work—the cards themselves were a little too strange, and a little too public, for a big bank. They'd done the installation on a cold, rainy night, and afterwards had made love on the floor behind her desk. The artist had been comically inept with the computer. He'd nearly brought down the bank network, and would have, if she hadn't been there to save him. But she could now access electronic cards at any time, protected with her own private code word.

Still. When she could, she preferred the cards themselves: the cool, collected flap of pasteboard against walnut. Hippielike, she thought. McDonald referred to her as a hippie, but she was hardly that. She simply had little time for makeup, for indulgent fashion, or for the flattering of men—all the things that Wilson McDonald expected from a woman. At the same time, she obviously enjoyed the company of men, and her relationship with the artist and a couple of other men-about-town had become known at the bank. And she was smart.

As McDonald had thumbed through his box of mental labels, he'd been forced to discard *housewife* and *helpmeet, lesbo* and *bimbo.* When word inevitably got around about the tarot, McDonald had relaxed and stuck the *hippie* label on her. The label might not explain the hunting, or the manner in which she'd cut her way to the top at the bank . . . but it was good enough for him.

Fuckin' moron.

O'Dell laid out the Celtic Cross; and got a jolt when the result card came up: the Tower of Destruction.

She pursed her lips. *Yes.*

She stood up, cast a backward glance at the spread of cards, the lightning bolt striking the tower, the man falling to his death: rather like Kresge, she thought, coming out of the tree stand. In fact, exactly so . . .

She shivered, pulled a cased set of books out of the bookcase, removed a small plastic box, opened it. Inside were a dozen fatties. She took one out, with the lighter, went out to her balcony, closing the glass doors behind her. Cold. She lit the joint, let the grass wrap wreaths of ideas around her brain. Okay. Kresge was dead. She'd wanted him dead—gone, at any rate, dead if necessary, and lately, as the merger deal crept closer, dead looked like the only way out.

So she'd gotten what she wanted.

Now to capitalize.

TERRANCE ROBLES HOVERED over his computer, sweating. He typed:

"Switch to crypto."

You're so paranoid; and crypto's boring.

"Switching to crypto . . ."

Once in the cryptography program, he typed:

"What have you done?"

Why?

Oh shit. "Somebody shot Kresge today. I'm a suspect . . ."

My, my . . .

Even with the crypto delay, the response was fast. Too fast, and too cynically casual, he thought. More words trailed across the screen.

So, did you do it?

Robles pounded it out: "Of course not."

But you thought I did?

He hesitated, then typed, "No."

Don't lie to me, T. You thought I did it.

"No I didn't but I wanted you to say it."

I haven't exactly said it, have I?

"Come on . . ."

Come on what? The world's a better place with that fucking fascist out of it.

"You didn't do it."

A long pause, so long that he thought she might have left him, then: *Yes I did.*

"No you didn't . . ."

No reply. Nothing but the earlier words, half scrolled up the screen.

"Come on . . ."

A label popped up: *The room is empty.*

"Bitch," he groaned. He bit his thumbnail, chewing at it. What was he going to do? Looking up at the screen, he saw the words.

Yes I did.

MARCIA KRESGE OPENED her apartment door and found two uniformed cops standing in the hallway.

"Yes?"

"Mrs. Kresge?" The cops looked her over. Late thirties, early forties, they thought. Very nice looking in a rich-bitch way. She was wearing a black fluffy dress that showed some skin, and was holding a lipstick in a gold tube. She had a lazy look about her, as though she'd just gotten out of bed, not alone.

"Yes?"

They kept it straightforward: her husband had been killed in a hunting accident.

"Yeah, I heard," she said, leaning against the doorpost. Her eyes hadn't even flickered; and to the older cop they looked so blue he thought he might fall in. "Should I do something?"

The cops looked at each other. "Well, he's at the county medical examiner's office. We thought you'd want to make, er, the funeral arrangements."

She sighed. "Yeah, I suppose that would be the thing to do. Okay. I'll call them. The medical examiner."

The older of the two cops, his experience prodding him, tried to keep the conversation going. "You don't seem too upset."

She thought about that for a moment. "No, I'd have to say that I'm not. Upset. But I'm surprised." She put one hand on her breast, in a parody of a woman taken aback. "I thought the asshole was too mean to get killed. Anyway, I just don't . . . mmm, what that's colorful redneck phrase you policemen always use in the movies? I don't give a large shit."

The cops looked at each other again, and then the younger one said, "Maybe we got this wrong. We understood . . ."

"Yeah, I'm his wife. In two weeks we would've been divorced. We haven't lived together for two years, and I haven't seen him for a year. I don't like him. Didn't like him."

"Uh, could you tell us where you were . . . ?"

She smiled at him sleepily. "When?"

"Early this morning?"

"In bed. I was out late last night, with friends."

"Could anybody vouch for you being here last night?" The older cop was pressing; once you had somebody rolling, you never knew what might come out.

But she nodded: "Sure. A friend brought me home."

"I'm talking about later, like early this morning."

"So am I," she said. "He stayed."

"Oh, okay." Neither one of them was a bit embarrassed, and she was now looking at him with a little interest. "Could we get his name?"

"I don't see why not. Come on in," she said. "I'll write it down."

They followed her into the apartment, noted the polished wood floors, the Oriental carpets, the tastefully colorful paintings on eggshell-white walls.

"You haven't asked me how much I'd get from him, if he died before the divorce," she said over her shoulder.

The older cop smiled, his best Gary Cooper grin. He liked her: "How much?"

"I don't know," she lied. "My attorney and I took him to the cleaners."

"Good for you," he said. She was scribbling on a notepad, and when she finished, she brought it over and handed it to him. "George Wright. Here's his address and phone number. I'm going to call him and tell him about this."

"That's up to you," the older cop said.

"That's my number at the bottom, in case you need to interrogate me. It's unlisted," she said. She looked at him with her blue eyes and nibbled on her lower lip.

"Well, thanks," he said. He tucked the slip of paper in his shirt pocket.

"Do I sound like a heartless bitch?" she asked him cheerfully. And as she asked, she took his arm and they walked slowly toward the door together.

"Maybe a little," he said. He really did like her and he could feel the back of his bicep pressing into her breast. Her breast was very warm. He even imagined he could feel a nipple.

"I really didn't like him," she said. "You can put that in your report."

"I will," he said.

"Good," she said, as she ushered him out the door. "Then maybe I'll get to see you again . . . You could show me your gun."

The cops found themselves in the hallway, the door closing behind them. At the elevator door, the younger one said, "Well?"

"Well, what?"

"You gonna call her?"

The older one thought a minute, then said, "I don't think I could afford it."

"Shit, you don't have to *buy* anything," the young one said. "She's rich."

"I dunno," the older one said.

"Take my advice: If you call her, you don't want to jump her right away. Get to know her a little."

"That's very sensitive of you," the older one said.

"No, no, I just think . . . She wants to see your gun?"

"Yeah?"

"So you wanna put off the time when she finds out you're packing a .22."

"Jealousy's an ugly thing," the older cop said complacently. As they walked out on the street to the car, he looked up at the apartment building and said, "Maybe."

And even if not, he thought, the woman had made his day.

AUDREY MCDONALD, COMING in from the garage, found her husband's orange coveralls on the kitchen floor, and just beyond them, his wool shooting jacket and then boots and trousers in a pile and halfway up the stairs, the long blue polypro underwear.

"Oh, shit," she said to herself. She dropped her purse on a hallway chair and hurried up the stairs, found a pair of jockey shorts in the hallway and heard him splashing in the oversized tub.

When Wilson McDonald got tense, excited, or frightened, he drank; and when he drank, he got hot and started to sweat. He'd pull his clothing off and head for water. He'd been drunk, naked, in the lake down the hill. He'd been drunk, naked, in the pool in the backyard, frightening the neighbor's daughter half to death. He'd been in the tub more times than she could remember, drunk, wallowing like a great white whale. He wasn't screaming yet, but he would be. The killing of Dan Kresge, all the talk at the club, had pushed him over the edge.

At the bathroom door, she stopped, braced herself, and then pushed it open. Wilson was on his hands and knees. As she opened the door, he dropped onto his stomach, and a wave of water washed over the edge, onto the floor, and around a nearly empty bottle of scotch.

"Wilson!" she shouted. "Goddamnit, Wilson."

He floundered, rolled, sat up. He was too fat, with fine curly hair on his chest and stomach, going gray. His tits, she thought, were bigger than hers. "Shut up," he bellowed back.

She took three quick steps into the room and picked up the bottle and started away.

"Wait a minute, goddamnit . . ." He was on his feet and out of the tub faster than she'd anticipated, and he caught her in the hallway. "Give me the fucking bottle."

"You're dripping all over the carpet."

"Give me the fucking bottle . . ." he shouted.

"No. You'll—"

He was swinging the moment the "no" came out of her mouth, and caught her on the side of the head with an open hand. She went down like a popped balloon, her head cracking against the molding on a closet door.

"Fuckin' bottle," he said. She'd hung on to it when she went down, but he wrenched it free, and held it to his chest.

She was stunned, but pushed herself up. "You fuck," she shouted.

"You don't . . ." He kicked at her, sent her sprawling. "Throw you down the fuckin' stairs," he screamed. "Get out of here."

He went back into the bathroom, and she heard the lock click.

"Wilson . . ."

"Go away." And she heard the splash as he hit the water in the tub.

DOWNSTAIRS, SHE GOT an ice compress from the freezer and put it against her head: she'd have a bruise. Goddamn him. They had to talk about Kresge: this was their big move, their main chance. This was what they'd worked for. And he was drunk.

The thought of the bottle sent her to the cupboard under the sink, to a built-in lazy Susan. She turned it halfway around, got the vodka bottle, poured four inches of vodka over two ice cubes, and drank it down.

Poured another two ounces to sip.

Audrey McDonald wasn't a big woman, and alcohol hit quickly. The two martinis she'd had at lunch, plus the pitcher of Bloody Marys at the club, had laid a base for the vodka. Her rage at Wilson began to shift. Not to disappear, but to shift in the maze of calculations that were spinning through her head.

Bone and O'Dell would try to steal this from them.

She sipped vodka, pressed the ice compress against her head, thought about Bone and O'Dell. Bone was Harvard and Chicago; O'Dell was Smith and Wharton. O'Dell had a degree in history and finance; Bone had two degrees in economics.

Wilson had a B.A. from the University of Minnesota in business administration and a law degree from the same place. Okay, but not in the same class with O'Dell or Bone. On the other hand, his grandfather had been one of the founders of Polaris. And Wilson knew everyone in town and was a member of the Woodland Golf and Cricket Club. The vice chairman of Polaris, a jumped-up German sausage-maker who never in a million years could have gotten into the club on his own, was now at Woodland, courtesy of Wilson McDonald. So Wilson wasn't weaponless . . .

SHE HEARD HIM thumping down the stairs a minute later. He stalked into the kitchen, still nude, jiggling, dripping wet. "What ya drinking?" he asked.

"Soda water," she said.

"Soda water my ass," he snarled. Then his eyes, which had been wandering, focused on the cold compress she held to her head. "What the fuck were you taking my scotch for?"

"Because we've got things to think about," she said. "We don't have time for you to get drunk. We have to figure out what to do with Kresge dead."

"I already got his job," he said, with unconcealed satisfaction.

"What?" She was astonished. Was he that drunk?

"O'Dell and Bone agreed I could have it," he said.

"You mean . . . you're the CEO?"

"Well . . . the board has to meet," he said, his voice slurring. "But I've already been dealing with the PR people, putting out press releases . . ."

She rolled her eyes. "You mean they let you fill in until the board meets."

"Well, I think that positions me . . ."

"Oh, for Christ's sake, Wilson, grow up," she said. "And go put some pants on. You look like a pig."

"You shut the fuck—"

He came at her again and she pitched the vodka at his eyes. As he flinched, she turned and ran back into the living room, looked around, spotted a crystal paperweight on the piano, picked it up. Wilson had gotten the paperweight at a Senior Tour pro-am. When he came through the doorway after her, she lifted it and said, "You try to hit me again and I swear to God I'll brain you with this thing."

He stopped. He looked at her, and at the paperweight, then stepped closer; she backed up a step and said, "Wilson."

"All right," he said. "I don't want to fight. And we gotta talk."

He looked in the corner, at the liquor cabinet, started that way.

"You can't have any more . . ."

She started past him and he moved, quickly, grabbed her hand with the paperweight, bent it, and she screamed, "Don't. Wilson, don't."

"Drop it, drop it . . ." He was a grade school bully, twisting the arm of a little kid. She dropped the weight, and it hit the carpet with a thump.

"Gonna fuckin' hit me with my paperweight," he said, jerking her upright. "Gonna fuckin' hit me."

He slapped her again, hard, and she felt something break open inside her mouth. He slapped her again, and she twisted, screaming now. Slapped her a third time and she fell, and he let her go, and when she tried to crawl away, kicked her in the hip and she went down on her face.

"Bitch. Hit me with, hit me, fuckin' bitch . . ."

He went to the liquor cabinet, opened it, found another bottle. She dragged herself under the Steinway, and he stopped as though he was going to go in after her, but he stumbled, bumped his head on the side of the piano, caught himself, said, "I'm the goddamned CEO," and headed back up the stairs to the tub, his fat butt bobbling behind him.

Audrey sat under the piano for a while, weeping by herself, and finally crawled out to a telephone, picked it up, and punched a speed-dialer.

"Hello?" Her sister, Helen, cheerful, inquiring.

"Helen? Could you come get me?"

Helen recognized the tone. "Oh, Jesus, what happened?"

"Wilson's drunk. He beat me up again. I think I better get out of the house."

"Oh, my God, Aud, I'll be right there . . . hang on, hang on . . ."

4

LUCAS ARRIVED AT the office late Monday morning, neatly dressed, neatly shaved, dead tired. The simpler things in life could be done on automatic pilot: take the clothes to the cleaners, shower, shave, and eat. Anything more complicated was difficult. Exercise took energy, and a heavy workout was impossible after a month without sleep.

He'd been the route before. The last time over the edge, he hadn't recognized what was happening, hadn't seen it coming, and it'd almost killed him. This time the process felt slightly different. He could feel it out there—the depression, the breakdown, the unipolar disorder, whatever the new correct name for it was—but it didn't seem to be marching on him with the same implacable darkness as last time.

Maybe he could fight it off, he thought. But he still dreaded the bed. The minute his head touched the pillow, the brainstorm would begin. Sleep would come only with exhaustion, and then not until after daylight . . .

IN THE WINTER just past, Weather Karkinnen, the woman he'd been about to marry, had been taken hostage by a killer looking for revenge against Lucas. Weather had managed her attacker: she'd talked him into surrender. She'd given him guarantees. But nobody on the outside knew.

When Lucas closed his eyes at night, he could see the two of them walking down the narrow hospital corridor toward him, Weather in front, Dick LaChaise using her as a shield, with a pistol to her head. He could also feel the pressure at his back, where a hidden police sniper, a kid from Iowa, was looking at LaChaise through a rifle scope.

Lucas's job was to talk the gun away from Weather's head, if only for half a second. If he could just get LaChaise to move the muzzle . . . And he did. The Iowa kid was cold as ice: Dick LaChaise's head had been pulped by the mushrooming .243 slug.

Weather, whose face was only inches away from LaChaise, had been showered with bone, brain, and blood. She had recovered, in most ways. She could work; she could even forget about it, most of the time. Unless she saw Lucas. They tried to pull the relationship back together, but three months after Dick LaChaise died in a hospital hallway, she was gone.

Gone for good, he believed.

And Lucas was staring into the darkness again.

"Hey, Lucas?"

Lucy Ghent, a secretary, was calling down the hall from the chief's office door. She was one of the older women in the office, who competed with her peers on hairdos. "Chief Roux is down in Identification. She wants to see you right away."

"Trouble?"

Ghent flopped a hand, dismissively. "Just . . . weirdness."

Rose Marie Roux was sitting at a cluttered desk in Identification, chewing Nicorette, paging through a document Lucas recognized as the departmental budget. She looked up when Lucas came in and said, "I swear to God, if you killed the smartest guy on the city council, the average IQ in Minneapolis would go up two points. Don't quote me."

"What happened?"

"The York case."

"Yeah?"

Morris York, two years on the force, found with a half-ounce of Mexican bud in a Marlboro box behind his patrol car visor. His marijuana habit had been detected by a departmental mechanic who claimed he was getting a contact high off the car's upholstery. Internal Affairs made movies of York getting mellow on the job.

"Tommy Gedja says this morning, at the council meeting, if that's all we're doing in our cars, why do we need new cars? I think he was serious. I think they're gonna try to pull twelve cars out from under us."

Lucas shrugged: "Life sucks and then they cut your budget. What're you doing down here?"

"More budget problems." A piece of white paper, wrapped in a plastic folder, lay on the desk's otherwise empty typewriter tray. She picked it up and handed it to him. "Came in the mail, first thing this morning."

> Dear Chief of Police Roux:
>
> One week ago, Mr. Kresge sent a memo to Susan O'Dell which said that her department would not be allowed to continue with a planned expansion because of budget constraints. Mrs. O'Dell has worked on the expansion for a long time and when she got the memo, her quote was, "God Damn him, I'm going to kill him." There were three people in the room at the time: Sharon Allen (assistant to the vice president), Michelle Stephens (executive secretary), and Randall Moss (assistant head cashier). I can't tell you my name, but I thought you should know.

"Not much here," Lucas said. He snapped the paper with his index finger. "We could interview Stephens to see how serious she thinks it is. Or if she's just trying to torpedo O'Dell."

"Stephens?" Roux had the gene that allowed her to lift one eyebrow at a time, and her left brow went up.

Lucas nodded. "She's probably the one who sent it—sounds like somebody who actually heard O'Dell say it, but she misuses the word 'quote,' which means not a lot of education. On the other hand, everything is spelled right, and secretaries spell things right. She's very aware of titles and refers to Kresge as 'mister,' which means she saw him as somebody with a lot more status than she has: not an associate. She wouldn't put herself first on the list, because that would make her nervous. And an assistant head cashier probably has a college education."

"So how's she dressed, Sherlock?"

Lucas smiled, but a droopy, tired smile: "Navy jacket and skirt or tan jacket and skirt with an older but neatly ironed white shirt and some kind of tie. Practical heels. Single mother. Tense. Anxious. Angry with O'Dell for personal reasons. Hurting for money."

Roux said, "Smart-ass." She turned and shouted into a closet-sized office: "Beverly! Bring the other thing out so Sherlock Holmes can take a look."

The department's document specialist, a dark-haired woman with a faint Moravian accent, bustled out of the closet with another slip of paper wrapped in plastic.

"Also in the mail," Roux said. "Beverly's checking for fingerprints."

"There are none," the woman said. "Not on the letter or the envelope. Standard twenty-pound copier paper, no watermark. Printed with a laser printer." Lucas took the paper.

Chief Roux:

Daniel S. Kresge was shot by Wilson McDonald, who was hunting with Kresge when the shooting occurred. I have known Wilson McDonald for many years and I believe that he has killed two other people to further his career. These people were:

A man named George Arris, who was killed about 1984, in a shooting outside a restaurant in St. Paul.

Andrew Ingall, who was killed in a boating accident in 1993 on Lake Superior. (He was from North Oaks and his wife still lives there.)

I hope you catch him on this one. He can't go on like this.

A Concerned Citizen.

Lucas looked at Roux, and she caught the small light in his eye. "Interesting?"

"More than the first one," Lucas admitted. "No waffling about the presentation. He gets right to it: Daniel S. Kresge was shot by Wilson McDonald."

"You think a man wrote it?"

Lucas hesitated for a minute, then said, "Maybe not. Could be a woman."

"When I read it, I assumed it was a woman. I don't know why," Roux said.

"Something about the wording," said Beverly. "I think it's a woman too.".

"Would you look into it?" Roux asked Lucas. "Sort of . . . carefully? Lot of rich people involved."

Lucas said, "Sloan and Sherrill are on it."

"Sloan is working on the Ericson killing. That's getting complicated. Sherrill's doing the routine for the sheriff up there. I'd just like you to look at this letter. It sounds so . . . sure of itself."

"You want me to look into it because you think it's necessary?" Lucas asked. "Or because you're worried that I'm going crazy?"

Roux nodded: "Both. It'd be nice if we could catch whoever killed Kresge."

"Are you getting pressure?"

"No, not really. Kresge was divorced, no family around here, not all that well liked. But I mean, hey, it's what we're supposed to do, right?"

"The paper this morning said that McDonald would be speaking for Polaris, at least until the board of directors meets," Lucas said. "The infighting could get pretty intense; something could fall out. In fact . . ." He tapped the first letter with the second. "Something already has."

"So catch up with Sherrill, tell her you'll take this angle. Get away from your desk."

Lucas nodded: "Okay; I'll look at it. And listen, I'm gonna send Del Capslock around with a problem."

"That goddamn Capslock *is* a problem," Roux grunted.

"Good cop," Lucas said.

"Yeah, but I can't stand to look at him: I keep wanting to give him a buck, or send him out to get his teeth fixed . . . What's the problem?"

"He turned up an opium ring."

"Drugs can't handle it?"

"You might want to think about it first," Lucas said. Again, the droopy grin: "I suspect most of the members are friends of yours."

SLOAN WAS DRINKING a Cherry Coke and reading a *Star-Tribune* story about sex in the workplace when Lucas wandered in, carrying xerox copies of the two letters. Sloan dropped the newspaper in the wastebasket, leaned back, and said, "You know what the thing is about you?"

"What?" Lucas pulled another chair around.

"You can't have an adulterous affair, because you're not married. So if you go down to Intelligence, say, and pick out some single chick and fuck her brains loose, well, that's just what bachelors do. But if I did it, that would be adultery and the *Star-Tribune* thinks I should be fired."

"If you did it, your old lady'd kill you anyway, so you wouldn't need a job."

"I'm talking in theory," Sloan said.

"Did you pick out the guilty guy on Saturday? In theory?"

Sloan shook his head. "They're a pretty tough group. Robles was in a sweat, but I think he might sweat everything. Bone seemed to think that Kresge getting murdered was mildly amusing; he was cooperative, though. And he had to stop to think at all the right places. O'Dell was almost too busy figuring out the consequences to talk to me about whether she did it . . . and that made me think she didn't. If she had, she'd have already figured out the consequences. I had a harder time getting a reading on McDonald. He acted like the whole thing was a plot to personally inconvenience him."

"Cold? Sociopathic?"

"Mmmm." Sloan scratched his chin. "No . . . If he is, he covers it," he said after a minute. "I'd say he's more like . . . unpleasant. Arrogant."

"So what's it all mean?"

"If Robles did it, we might get him, eventually. If it's one of the others, forget it. Unless the guy does something really stupid, like tell somebody else about it. Or if it was a group effort. But that's . . ."

"Unlikely," Lucas said.

"More like ridiculous."

"Perfect crime?"

"Just about," Sloan said. "Lots of people probably heard the shot, but nobody thought anything about it. Nobody was looking for the shooter. Once he was off the scene . . . there's no way we're gonna get him. The only chance to get him was to have somebody see it happen, and recognize the shooter. That was it."

"But we know some stuff," Lucas said. He leaned back in the chair and put his feet on the edge of Sloan's desk. "The shooter knew his way around there, in the dark. And he knew which tree stand Kresge would be in. That means that he was either close to Kresge or he worked for him, maybe out at the cabin. Is Krause checking any employees out there?"

"Yeah. There were only two or three people—a handyman who'd do maintenance work around the place, an old guy who patrols some of the cabins, just checking on them two or three times a day. And some guy who plows out the driveway in the winter. None of them had any apparent problem with Kresge. The sheriff doesn't think they're suspects."

"If this was a movie, the handyman would have done it," Lucas said, staring blankly at the ceiling. "He'd be like a Stephen King character, a secret psycho who everybody thinks is retarded . . ."

". . . but who's really pretty smart, but only behaves the way he does because he couldn't get a date to the prom, which is why he burned down the high school."

"How about Sherrill? Is she around?"

"I don't know. She was working yesterday, but I haven't seen her today. I know she was going to try to nail down people in Kresge's office and talk to the ex-wife."

"All right . . ."

"But suppose it is somebody close to Kresge," Sloan said. "Suppose we find a guy who hated Kresge, but knew the farm, knew where the tree stand was, knew Kresge would be in it, and we can prove that he has a rifle, is a great shot, and has no alibi for opening day. You know what? We got all that, and we still ain't got shit."

"There might be one more way," Lucas said.

"Like what?"

"We build a pattern around him."

"Good luck."

"Rose Marie got some mail this morning," Lucas said. He leaned forward and slid the copies across Sloan's desk. "One letter nominates O'Dell, the other one McDonald."

Sloan read them slowly, then read the McDonald letter a second time, and finally looked up at Lucas: "Two more dead ones, huh? But we'd need more than a pattern. We'd have to push him out in the open."

"That could be done," Lucas said. "If it's McDonald."

"Are you buying into the case?" Sloan asked.

"Rose Marie asked me to take a look . . . if you don't mind. If Sherrill doesn't mind."

"I don't mind," Sloan said. "I've got the Ericson file. I could use some extra time."

"I thought the boyfriend did it—the Ericson thing. I thought he admitted it."

"Not exactly," Sloan said. "He says he might have. He doesn't deny it. But we can't come up with any physical evidence, and he was so fucked up at the time, he can't remember anything. And I'm wondering, if he was so fucked up—and he was, he had enough chemicals in him to start a factory—what'd he do with his clothes? They had to have blood all over them."

"You've got nothing physical? No hair or semen . . ."

"No semen. And he had no blood on him, under his nails or in his hair. And the problem is, she was killed on the bed and he slept there every night and half the day. So he's all over the place . . . but so what? He's gonna be. And I'm really worried about the clothes. He says he's not missing any, and I think he might be telling the truth. He doesn't have all that much to begin with. Couple pairs of jeans, couple T-shirts, a coat, some sneaks."

"Huh. Check the drains in the bathroom? Maybe he was naked . . ."

Sloan nodded: "Yeah. The lab looked at it. No blood."

"Okay. So I'll take the McDonald thing," Lucas said. "I'll talk to Sherrill about it."

"She'll go along," Sloan said. He said it with a *tone.*

"Yeah?"

"She's got the great headlights," Sloan said.

"Not exactly a key criterion for a police investigation."

"Yeah, but . . ."

"You've been married too long; all you can think about is strange tits and adultery complaints," Lucas said.

"Not true. Sometimes I think about strange asses . . . Seriously, I heard them talking about you—some of the women. The idea was, don't rush him, let him get a little distance away from Weather."

"Fuck 'em," Lucas said, pushing away from Sloan's desk. "I'll take McDonald. I'd like to see the interviews you did Saturday . . ."

"Krause tape-recorded them, he's getting a transcript made. Probably today. He said he'd shoot a copy down as soon as it's ready."

"All right," Lucas said. "Ship it over."

"And you'll talk to Headlights? I mean, Sherrill?"

Lucas grinned. "Yeah. If you see her, tell her I'm looking for her; I'll be around later in the day."

5

DAMASCUS ISLEY WAS a very smart fat man with a taste for two-thousand-dollar English bespoke suits that almost disguised his size. Lucas spotted him at a back table at the Bell Jar, hovering over a chicken breast salad that had been served in what looked like a kitchen sink. Lucas told the maître d', "I'm with the fat guy," and was nodded past the velvet rope.

"Lucas," Isley said. He made a helpless gesture with his hands, which meant, *I'm too fat to get up.* "Are you coming to the reunion? Gina asked me to ask."

Lucas shook his head, and took a chair across from Isley, who was sitting on the booth seat. "I don't think so. I've busted too many of them."

"Mary Big Jo's gonna be there," Isley said.

"Fuck Mary Big Jo."

"I certainly did," Isley said cheerfully. "Made all the more glorious by your abject failure to do the same."

Lucas grinned: "No accounting for taste," he said. Isley was six-five, a bit taller than Lucas. He'd once been a rope instead of a mountain, a basketball forward when six-five was a big man; Lucas had been hockey, and they'd chased several of the same women through high school and college.

A waitress stepped up behind Lucas, slipped a menu in front of him, and said, "Cocktail, sir?"

"Ah no, I just want . . ." He thought for a second, then said, "Hell, give me a martini. Beefeater, up, two olives."

"I could give you three olives, if you need more vegetables in your diet," the waitress said.

"All right, three," Lucas said; she was pretty in a dark-Irish way.

The waitress went to get the drink, and Isley, following her with his eyes, said, "The way she looked at you, something would be possible. Maybe you'd have to come back a couple of times, get to know her, but it'd be possible." He looked down at the vast salad, the chunks of chicken breast, avocado, egg, tomato, cheese, and lettuce, covered with a bucket of creamy herb dressing, then back up at Lucas. "You know how long it's been since that was possible with me? With all this fuckin' . . ." He couldn't say "fat" ". . . lard?"

Lucas tried to put him off: "So you work out for a couple months."

"Lucas . . . when I was playing ball, my last year, I weighed two-oh-five. So I go to this fat doctor and say, 'Give me a diet I can stay on, something simple, that'll get me back to two-oh-five.' He says, 'Okay, do this: Go to lunch every day and eat one Big Mac with all the fixings. And as much popcorn as you want, all day. Nothing else.' I say, 'Jesus Christ, I'll starve.' He says, 'No you won't, but you'll lose a lot of weight.' "

Isley looked at Lucas. "You know how long he said it would take to get to two-oh-five?" Lucas shook his head. "A year and a half. A fuckin' year and a half, Lucas . . ."

"I'll tell you what, Dama," Lucas said bluntly. "You're either gonna lose it, or you're gonna die. Simple as that."

"Not that simple," Isley said.

"Oh yeah it is," Lucas said. "After all the bullshit, that's what it comes down to."

"I don't even like food that much . . . and I'd like to live awhile longer," Isley said wistfully. "I'd like to quit the company, go to London and study money . . . find out what it really is."

"Money."

"Yeah, you know. *Money*," he said. "Not many people really know what it is, how it works. I'd like to spend some time finding out."

"So start hitting the McDonald's," Lucas said.

"Fat chance."

The waitress arrived with the martini, and Isley's wistfulness disappeared, replaced by the steel-trap investment banker. "So what's going on? Starting another business?"

"No." Lucas sipped the martini. "When you took my company public, we ran some of the money stuff through Jim Bone over at Polaris. You seemed to know him pretty well. He was hunting with Kresge when Kresge got shot, and I need a reading on him. Bone, I mean. And Susan O'Dell, if you know her. And Wilson McDonald."

Isley's face went cautious: "Is this official?"

"No, of course not. I'm just trying to get a reading. Nobody'll be coming back to you."

Isley nodded. "Okay. I know them all pretty well—socially and business, both. Either Bone or O'Dell has the guts to shoot Kresge, but I don't think either one did. These people are very smart and very serious. If they'd wanted to lose Kresge badly enough, they would have done it another way."

"What about Robles or McDonald?"

"Robles is a software genius. He does the math. But he's more of a technician than a manager. He also doesn't have the motive. With his math, he could go about anywhere. McDonald . . ." Isley looked away from Lucas, pursed his fat lips, then turned back. "There are McDonalds who are good friends of mine— same family. Not Wilson, though. There've been rumors . . ." Again, he paused.

"What?" Lucas asked.

"No comebacks?"

"No comebacks."

"There're rumors that he occasionally beats the shit out of his wife," Isley said. "I mean, she goes to the hospital."

"Huh."

"Alcohol, is what you hear," Isley said. "He's a binge drinker. Sober for two months, then has to take a few days off."

"Smart?"

"Pretty smart. Not world-class, but he got through law school with no problem."

"I didn't know he was a lawyer."

"He never worked at it. He's always been a salesman, and a damn good one. Knows everybody. *Everybody.* Access to all the old money in town—his family built a mill over on the river, hundred and some years ago, and eventually sold to Pillsbury to go into banking and real estate. Like that."

"Okay," Lucas said. "So here's another question. Everything I've heard about him says McDonald's rich, he comes from an old family, and all that. Why would he kill Kresge, just 'cause Kresge's gonna merge the bank? He's got all the money in the world anyway."

"No, not really," Isley said. He dabbed at his lips with a linen napkin, tossed the napkin aside, and made a steeple out of his fingers. After a moment of silence, he said, "He's maybe worth . . . seven or eight million. The older generation was a lot richer, relatively speaking, but there were a lot of kids, and a lot of taxes, and the money got cut up. After taxes, and including his after-tax salary, I'd imagine his real expendable income is something in the range of a half-million. If he doesn't dip into his capital, and assuming he puts aside enough to cover inflation."

"Well, Jesus, Dama, that just about *is* all the money in the world," Lucas said.

"No, it's not. It's a lot by any normal standard, but having ten million dollars is nothing compared to being the CEO of a major corporation. Being an American CEO is like being an old English duke or earl." He paused again, his eyes unfocusing as he looked for the right words. "Say you have a spendable income of a half-million a year, and your wife likes to fly first-class to Hawaii or Paris every so often. You can spend fifteen thousand after-tax bucks flying a couple first-class to the islands. You go out of town a half-dozen times a year—Hawaii, the Caribbean, Europe—you can spend a hundred and fifty grand, no trouble. And it's all out of your own pocket. Plus you've got big real estate taxes, you're probably running a couple of fifty-thousand-dollar cars . . . I mean, you can spend a half-million a year and feel like your collar's a little too tight. But if you run a business the size of Polaris, screw first class—you've got your own Gulf-stream waiting at the airport. You've got several thousand people kissing your ass day and night. You've got people driving your cars, running your errands. From everything I can tell by watching it, this all must feel better than anything in the world . . ."

"So even if he had a lot of money, a guy might have reason to waste old Kresge."

"Especially McDonald. Bone, O'Dell, and Robles are essentially hired guns. They are very good at what they do, but they're *here* mostly by chance. They could go anywhere else. But everything Wilson McDonald is is tied to the Twin Cities. In New York or L.A. or even Chicago, they could give a rat's ass about a Wilson McDonald."

"Do you think Bone would talk to me about McDonald? Off the record?"

Isley shrugged: "Maybe. If the idea appealed to him. He played a little ball at Ole Miss."

"Yeah?"

"Yeah. Good quick guard. Probably not pro quality, but he would've been looked at. Called him T-Bone, of course. If you want, I could give him a ring. Just to say you asked about him, tell him you're okay."

Lucas grinned. "Maybe I'm not."

Isley said, "Ah, you're okay . . . if he's innocent. And I'm pretty sure he is."

"Anybody mourning Kresge?"

Isley had been about to stuff a slice of chicken in his mouth, and stopped halfway to the target. Shook his head. "Not a single person that I know. He spent his life fucking people in the name of efficiency." He stuck the chicken in his mouth, chewed, swallowed. "Why would you do that?" he asked. "I know all kinds of people who do, but I can't figure out why."

"Make money."

"Hell, Lucas, I've made a pile of money, and I don't fuck people. You made a pile, and your ex-employees think you're a hell of a guy. But why would you do things in a way that you'd end up in life with a pile of money, but not a single fuckin' friend?"

"Maybe you figure that if you get enough money, you could buy some."

Isley nodded gloomily. "Yeah, probably; that's the way they think."

Lucas finished the last of the three olives, and the last of the pleasantly cool martini, and said, "Listen, Dama. I got a pickup game once a week, bunch of cops, couple lawyers. You start eating those Big Macs and I'd like to get you out there."

"Goddamnit, Lucas . . ."

"Feel good, wouldn't it? Playing horse in the evening. Down on Twenty-eighth?"

Isley tossed his fork in the salad bowl. "Get out of here, Davenport."

Lucas stood up. "Call Bone for me?"

"Yeah, yeah, soon as I get back." He looked at his Patek Philippe. "Give me twenty-five minutes."

LUCAS GOT BACK to the office, stuck his head into Administration, and said, "Got anything for me?"

The duty guy said, "Computer's down."

"How long?"

"I don't know, it's not just us. Some state road guys cut a major fiber-optic. Half the goddamn city's down."

"Road guys?"

"Shovel operators."

JAMES T. BONE'S secretary suspected Lucas of making sport of her. When she told him, peremptorily, on the phone, that Mr. Bone was making no new appointments, Lucas had answered, "Go tell Mr. Bone right now that a deputy chief of police wants to talk to him, and if he says no, I'll have to come down and shoot him."

"I beg your pardon?"

"I think you heard me," Lucas said. He almost added, "sweetheart," but decided that might push it too far.

She went away for a moment; then another voice came on, feminine, cool: "Mr. Davenport? This is Kerin Baki, Mr. Bone's assistant. Can I help you?"

"I need to talk to Mr. Bone."

"When?"

"As soon as possible."

"Come over, and we'll get you in," she said.

BAKI WAS A chilly northern blonde, with an oval face and pale blue fighter-pilot eyes. She met him without any softening smile. In the spring, Lucas thought, she probably had genetic dreams of turning her tanks toward Moscow . . .

She led him through into Bone's office, said, "Mr. Bone, Mr. Davenport," and left them, shutting the door behind her.

Bone was dressed in a subdued single-breasted wool suit with a crisp white shirt and an Italian necktie; but somehow the ensemble came off as a wry comment on Yankee bankertude. He had a telephone to one ear and a foot propped on the N-Z volume of the *New Shorter Oxford English Dictionary*, which lay flat on his desk. He waved Lucas in, and as Lucas dropped into a bent-oak chair across the desk, said into the phone, "Two? That's as good as you can do? Last week it was one and seven . . . Yeah, yeah, yeah. I'll get back to you, but I think we might have to talk to Bosendorfer or Beckstein . . . Yeah, yeah. By four."

He hung up, made a notation on a legal pad, and said, "I can give you all the time you'd need this evening, but if you gotta talk now, you gotta talk fast. And this is all off the record at this point, right?"

Lucas nodded. "Yes. If we need an official statement, we'll send you a subpoena and get a formal deposition."

Bone leaned forward. "So?"

"So do you think McDonald did it?"

"If one of us did it, it was McDonald. I didn't do it. Robles, no motive. O'Dell, too smart. Unless I'm missing something. And to tell you the truth, I don't think it's McDonald. Way down at the bottom, I don't think he's got the grit to pull it off."

"Then why's he running the place?"

"He's not. He's only speaking for it. And that'll only last until O'Dell and I get the board sorted out. Then it'll be one of us."

Lucas said, "Huh," and then, "Have you ever heard of George Arris? Does the name ring a bell?"

"Yes, of course. He was a famous case around here, around the bank. He was murdered—this must've been a few months or maybe a year or so before I came here. Must've been back in '85."

"How was it famous? The name doesn't ring a bell with me . . ."

"It was over on the St. Paul side of the river. Somebody started shooting white guys who were walking in the black areas—there were like three or four of them in a few weeks, shot in the back of the head."

"Ah, jeez, I remember that," Lucas said. "Never solved. And Arris was one of them?"

"Yup."

"What'd he do here?"

"Worked with the trust department, setting up portfolios for rich folk."

"Would he have worked with McDonald?"

Bone said, "Probably. I'd have to look up the exact dates, but they probably overlapped. They certainly both went through that department. I don't really know the details. I wasn't here yet. I just heard about the killing later."

"Okay. How about Andrew Ingall?"

"Andy? He was a vice president, also in the trust department, but he died a few years ago in a boating accident up on Superior. You think Wilson had something to do with it?"

"Why would he?" Lucas asked.

Bone leaned back, then spun his chair in a circle, stopped it with one foot, reached into a desk drawer where he apparently had a stereo tuner hidden. A Schumann piano piece, simple, easy, elegant, and sweet, sprang into the office, and Bone said, "Schumann," and Lucas said, "I know—*Scenes from Childhood*," and Bone said, "Christ, we're so cultured I can't stand it," and Lucas said, "A friend of mine used to play them. Why would McDonald do Andy Ingall?"

"Because they were both candidates to run the operation. Then Andy sailed out of Superior Harbor one day, just moving his boat up to the islands. He never got there. No storm, no emergency calls, nothing. Just phhht. Gone. The theory was that he had a leaky gas tank—he had some kind of old gas engine, an Atomic, or something like that—and gas leaked into the bilge, and he fired up the engine out on the water somewhere, and boom. He was gone before he could call for help. That was the theory, but nobody ever knew for sure. No wreckage was ever found."

"So McDonald got the job." .

"Well, no. When Andy disappeared, everything was screwed up for a while; then we had a general shuffling around, and McDonald wound up as a senior vice president in the mortgage company."

"Huh," said Lucas, and Bone said, "Yeah," and asked, "Can't you get this stuff from the FBI or somewhere?"

"Probably not. Besides, the computer's down."

"You too? Christ, it's chaos downstairs . . ."

"Did you ever hear that McDonald might whack his wife around from time to time? Pretty seriously?"

Bone nodded. "I heard it. I went out with a lawyer lady for a while, old family, she knows that whole country club bunch; and she said something to me about it. She might have some details . . . You could talk to her if you want."

"That'd be good . . ."

Bone scratched a name and phone number on a piece of notepaper and pushed it across the desk. "Sandra Ollsen, two *l*'s. That's her office phone over at Kelly, Batten."

"What kind of law?"

"Estate planning, wills, trusts." He looked at his watch and said, "Listen, I've got to go to a meeting, but I can talk to a guy who's gonna be there, and find out if there was anything between Wilson and Arris."

Lucas said, "Thanks," stood up, and as they shook hands, said, "I understand you used to play a little ball."

"Yeah, a little," Bone said.

"How well do you know Dama Isley?"

"Reasonably well—I heard he played for the Gophers, back when. Hard to believe."

"Yeah. Listen, next time you see him, take a couple of minutes and talk a little ball, old-time stuff, like college days."

Bone shrugged. "Sure. Why?"

"Private project," Lucas said. "You still play?"

Bone, grinning, said, "I still shoot around a little bit on Saturdays. Always a couple of kids trying to take advantage of me."

Lucas said, "A banker? Playing for money?"

"Good grief, no," Bone said. "Not for money. That'd be illegal."

ON THE WAY out, Lucas paused in the open door of Bone's office, saw Kerin Baki talking to the secretary, and said, loud enough for her to overhear, "I'm probably going to want to talk about McDonald again."

Bone, already settling back into his desk, distracted, missed the double-directed comment, nodded, said, "Okay," and Lucas pulled the door shut. He smiled at Baki on the way out and said, "Thank you."

By the time the elevators reached the bottom floor, he thought, the word on McDonald would be out. If Baki was as efficient as she looked, she could never pass on the chance to screw one of her boss's competitors.

LIKE BONE, SANDRA Ollsen was really too busy to talk to Lucas; but he mentioned Bone's name and was admitted to the mahogany offices of Kelly, Batten, Orstein & Shirinjivi. Ollsen was a tall, coordinated woman who looked as though she might once have played some ball herself.

"How's Jim?" she asked casually as Lucas settled into the chair across her desk.

"Looks fine; something of a power struggle going on over there," Lucas said.

"Yes. With Susan O'Dell. I hope she kicks his butt."

"Really?" Lucas asked.

"Really," she said. Lucas, bemused, watched her for a moment, waiting, and then she said, "He sort of dumped me."

"Ah. I know the feeling," Lucas said.

She looked him over. "I don't think so," she said after a minute.

"You'd be wrong," Lucas said. "Anyway . . . he seems to think of you as a friend."

"Right." She rolled her eyes. "Actually, I don't think he was actually looking for friendship when he started squiring me around. He was looking . . ." She grinned at him, not a bad smile at all. "Why am I telling you this?"

"Because of my open face and genuine curiosity?"

" 'Cause you're a trained interrogator, that's why. When I was in college, we called you pigs."

"When I was in college, I called us pigs," Lucas said. "So what was he looking for when he started taking you around?"

"Sex," she said, ingenuously. "Any place, any time . . . Some of the girls around the bank call him the Boner, if you know what I mean."

"All right," Lucas said. "Listen, the reason I came by . . ."

"Bet nobody would ever call you that," Ollsen said. "The Boner."

"Only 'cause I carry a big leather sap in my pocket," Lucas said. "I'd beat the tar out of them."

"Oh, it's a sap. And I just thought you were happy to see me."

Lucas held up his hands: "All right, you win the war of wits." And they both laughed. "But listen, the real reason I came around: You know about the Kresge killing, of course. We're investigating it, and I'm wondering how well you know Wilson McDonald?"

A sudden wariness appeared in her eyes, and she put a hand to her throat. "You think Wilson did it?"

"No, we don't think anything, just yet. But he was one of the four people up there when Kresge . . ."

"Bit the bullet?"

"Exactly the words I was looking for," Lucas said. "Anyway: How well do you know McDonald?"

"My parents knew the family quite well . . ."

"Does Wilson McDonald beat his wife?"

"Ah, Jesus," she said, softly. "I wondered what Jim told you. What are you going to do, blackmail him with it? Wilson?"

"Domestic violence is not my department," Lucas said. "I'm just trying to get a reading on him, what kind of a guy he is."

Again, she hesitated, and Lucas added, "This is all informal. There won't be any record of what you say."

"But you could subpoena me."

"If it got to that point, you'd be morally obliged to tell us anyway," Lucas said.

She thought about that for a moment, then said, "I was at a pool party last summer—Rush and Louise Freeman, he runs Freeman-Hoag."

"The advertising agency."

"Yes. Wilson got drunk. He was getting loud and he went into the pool with his clothes on—Audrey said he fell, but I saw it, and he looked like he was jumping in. Anyway, we got him out, and Audrey walked him around the house out toward their car, and they started arguing. And Louise went over to Rush— I was talking to Rush—and she said something like, 'Rush, you better go around, they're starting to argue.' Something about the way she said it. So Rush went around the house, and I followed, and we both came around the corner just in time to see Wilson hit her right in the head. He just swatted her and knocked her down. Rush ran over and they started arguing, and I thought Wilson was going to fight him. But Audrey got up and said she was all right, and I got between the two guys. And they went off."

"Nobody called the police?" Lucas asked.

"No."

"I thought that was the correct thing to do," Lucas said. "I mean with the lawer-doctor-advertising set. No violence."

She nodded. "I'll tell you what, buster. If any guy ever hit me like that, his ass would be in jail ten minutes later. But . . . sometimes things are more complicated. Audrey didn't want it. She said he was drunk and didn't mean anything."

"So that was the end of it."

"Yes. Then, anyway. I was talking to Louise afterwards, and she said that he'd beaten her up before. A couple of times a year."

"And she'd know?"

"Yes . . . She's a little younger. Louise is. She's Rush's second wife, used to be his secretary. She knows Audrey's younger sister pretty well, I don't know how. The sister told Louise that Wilson beats up Audrey a couple of times a year. Sometimes pretty badly."

"Do you think Wilson McDonald could have killed Kresge?"

"Yes," she said. "Not just because I saw him hit Audrey. I was always a little afraid of him. I knew him when I was little—he was five or six years ahead of me at Cresthaven, and my brother knew him. He's big and fat and mean; he's got those little mean eyes. He's a goddamned animal."

Lucas nodded: "Okay."

"Even if he did it, you won't get him. He's pretty smart, but most of all, he's a McDonald," she said. "The McDonalds . . . they've got this family thing. They don't care what a family member does, as long as he doesn't get caught at it." She stopped: "No, that's not quite right: they don't care what he does, as long as he's not convicted of it. In their eyes, not being convicted is the same as not doing it. That comes from way back. The first McDonalds were crooks, they stole from the farmers with their mill. The second or third generation were still crooks, and they made millions during the Depression with real estate scams that they ran through Polaris. And they're still crooks. And they've got very good legal advice."

"But don't quote you."

"Subpoena me first," she said. "Then you can quote me."

"Do you think Louise Freeman would talk to me?"

"Probably. She's the kind who'd have all the dirt, if I do say so myself."

6

A GRIM-FACED HELEN BELL steered her Toyota Camry into the driveway at her sister's house and said, "Audrey, you're crazy."

"It's all right," Audrey McDonald said sharply. She had a small black circle under her left eye, now covered heavily with makeup, where one of Wilson McDonald's blows had landed. "He must be sober by now. He had to work today."

"He could have gone to work this morning and be drunk all over again," Bell said. She was four years younger than her sister, but in some ways had always been the protective one. "That's happened."

"I'll be okay," Audrey said.

"You'll never be okay until you leave him," Helen said. "The man is an animal and doesn't deserve you. Even the police know it, now—you said so yourself."

"But I love him," Audrey said. On the drive over, Helen had gotten angrier and angrier with her sister, but now her face softened and she patted Audrey on the thigh.

"Then you're going to have to see a doctor, together," she said. "There's a name for this—codependency. You can't keep going like this, because sooner or later, it won't just be a slap, or a beating. He's going to kill you."

"You know what he's said about that, about a doctor," Audrey said. "They don't go to psychiatrists in the McDonald family."

"But it'd all be confidential," Helen protested. "Times have changed . . ."

"After this bank thing is done with," Audrey said, as she pushed open the car door. "Maybe then."

Bell watched her go. She hated McDonald. She'd never liked him, but over the years distaste had grown into this curdling, bitter-tasting hatred. Audrey would never remove herself from McDonald. Somebody else would have to do it for her, like a surgeon removing a cancer.

She liked the metaphor: Dan Kresge had been a cancer on the bank, and he'd been removed. Good for the bank and everybody employed there. McDonald was a cancer on her sister: the sooner he was cut out, the better.

AUDREY EASED INTO the house, moving quietly, wary of an ambush. Was he in the tub again? In the study? She stepped into the kitchen, and the board that always squeaked, the one she'd sworn two hundred times to fix, squeaked.

"Audrey? Is that you?" He was in the study; he sounded sober.

"It's me," she said tentatively.

"Jesus Christ, where have you been? I've been calling Helen, but nobody ever answers." He'd been lurching down the hall as he spoke, a yellow legal pad in his hand, and when he turned into the kitchen, he spotted the black eye and pulled up. "Holy cow. Did I do that?"

She recognized the mood and moved to take advantage of it: "No, of course not," she said sarcastically. "I've been hitting myself in the face with a broomstick."

"Aw, Jesus . . ." That was all she'd get. He went on, "But Jesus, we gotta talk. I got a cop following me around. And the board's gonna meet on Wednesday, but probably won't make a decision. They're talking about a search, for Christ's sake."

"A search? That's just a way of slowing everything down."

"I know that. It's me or O'Dell or Bone."

"Have you talked to your father?"

"Just for a minute, to ask him to stay out of it for the time being. I thought it might be a little too obvious if he got out there. At this point."

"Good thought . . . What about the cop?"

"It's this fuckin' Davenport," McDonald said impatiently. "He was talking to Bone today, and the word is, he's asking about me."

"What's he asking?" Audrey asked. "He doesn't think you . . ."

"I don't know; I'm finding out. He could be a problem."

"How can he be a problem? You didn't shoot anybody."

His eyes slid away from hers: "I know . . . but he could be a problem." He looked back: "I mean, Jesus, if there's a search, you think they're gonna pick a guy who the cops are investigating?"

"Okay."

"And the thing is, the sheriff up there, Krause, he's just about signed off on the thing, from what I hear. He's dead in the water. If it wasn't for Davenport, it'd be pretty much over with."

"Maybe that's something your father could help with right now."

"Come on in here," Wilson said, and turned back toward the study. The study was a large room with a window looking out on the front lawn, and two walls of shelves loaded with knickknacks, travel souvenirs, and small golf and tennis trophies going back to Wilson's days in prep school and college. Framed photos of Wilson and Audrey with George Bush, Ronald Reagan, and in much younger days a tired-looking Richard Nixon, looked down from the third wall. Wilson dropped into the brown-leather executive's chair behind the cherry desk, while Audrey perched on a love seat below Nixon's worn face.

"So call your father on Davenport. On the board, we can call Jimmy and Elaine," Audrey said. "Elaine is very close to Dafne Bose, and Jimmy's been trying to get into the trust department's legal work *forever* . . ." Dafne Bose was on the board. "If we can get to Dafne, we're halfway there."

"You know who else?" He looked down at the legal pad. "We're carrying two million bucks in land-and-attachments paper on Shankland Chev, which they couldn't get a half-million anywhere else. And Dave Shankland . . ."

". . . is married to Peg Bose." Peg Bose was Dafne's daughter. "We couldn't use that right away, it'd look too much like blackmail. But if we got in a squeak . . ."

"Here's the list I've got so far," Wilson said. He passed the legal pad to Audrey. "Seventeen board members, so we need nine. Four I can count on—Eirich, Goff, Brandt, and Sanderson. If we can get Dafne, we can probably get Rondeau and Bunde, 'cause they pretty much do what she suggests. Then we'd need two . . ."

"How about Young? You know he wants to get into Woodland."

"Oh, man, I don't know if I could swing that," Wilson said doubtfully.

"We need a black member anyway, because of that government thing, and who'd be better than Billy Young? His father was a minister and he's really pretty white. And he must be worth . . ."

They began working down strings of possible supporters, analyzing relationships, working out who knew who, who owed who, who could be bought, and with what.

Later, getting coffee, Audrey without thinking brushed her cheek, and flinched at the sudden lancing pain. The black eye: she'd forgotten about it, and Wilson had never really paid any attention to it anyway. The excitement of conspiracy, she decided: some of their tenderest moments had occurred in the study, working over legal pads . . .

MARCUS KENT WAS an assistant vice president in corporate operations, working for Bone; he sat on one end of Susan O'Dell's couch. Carla Wyte, who technically worked for Robles in the currency room, lounged on the other end. Louise Compton, wearing blue jeans and a Nike sweatshirt, sat cross-legged on the floor.

". . . either Bone or me," O'Dell was saying. She was on her feet, as though she were a junior exec making a presentation to the board of directors. "McDonald can't get more than six. He's the obvious first thought, because of his family, but twelve members would be dead set against him. When that becomes obvious, things will start to move. I can see myself with eight votes; and I can see eight for Bone, but only a couple are solid for each of us. Everything is very fluid . . . So I think we're gonna have to start maneuvering here."

"How about Robles?" Wyte asked.

"No chance," O'Dell said. "It's gonna be Bone or me."

"Bone is good," Wyte said. "His division makes the big bucks."

"Most of it by me," Kent said.

O'Dell looked at Kent: "But it's his division, not yours. He gets the credit."

Kent said, "Before we get any further in this, let me ask . . . What do we get out of it? Carla and Louise and me? We know what you get."

O'Dell said, "You get Bone's job. He won't stay around long if I'm picked for the top spot. And Carla's eventually going to move into Robles's slot. But right away—and I mean right away—she gets money."

"How much?" Wyte's eyebrows went up.

"Fifty more. Fifty is the number I had in mind."

"Fifty is a nice number," Wyte said.

"And it'll be twice that when Robles leaves."

Compton said, "How about me?"

"You're gonna be my executive assistant. You're gonna be my ears. My intelligence department. You'll do real well—in terms of clout, if not in title, you'll be number two in the bank."

"So how do we do this?" Wyte asked. "What do we do . . . assuming we're all in."

O'Dell looked around the room. After a second, Kent said, "I'm in," and Compton said, "Yeah." Wyte nodded.

"So . . ." O'Dell said. "I'm going to start putting together a pitch for the board. It's got to be good, and it'll take time. And I'll start working the board: that's something I have to do personally."

"To some extent, it's gonna be like a political campaign, but with fewer voters," Compton said. She'd come to the bank from the state capitol. "One thing we can do is, we can make the point with the newspapers that you'd be the first woman ever to run a major bank in Minnesota. Or anywhere, as far as I know. Any other major bank CEOs are women?" She looked around, then answered herself. "No. Okay. I'll check that out, but I can also start working the papers."

"That's good," O'Dell said. "But we've got to get it going. How long before we could see it on the news?"

Compton looked at her watch: "I've got time today. I'll have to talk to a couple of people, but we should see some action by tomorrow morning. When they call, you've got to be modest and all that . . . you know, the board has to make a decision."

"I know," O'Dell said. "I can do that."

Kent leaned forward, took a cinnamon candy out of a bowl on the coffee table, peeled off the crinkly cellophane wrapper, and popped the candy into his mouth: "Speaking of negative campaigning . . ."

"Were we speaking of that?" Compton asked, with a quick, cynical smile. They would have come to it sooner or later.

"We are now," he said. "We all know Bone's weakness."

"Women."

O'Dell shook her head. "That won't help. We just don't have the time—even if we could find somebody willing to dig into it, it'd take weeks."

Kent was shaking his head. "Not really. Not if the cops look into it and if somebody tips the papers that the cops are looking into it."

"Why would they?" Wyte asked.

" 'Cause of the woman," Kent said, sitting back, savoring his little nugget.

"Marcus . . ." O'Dell said.

"James T. Bone is fucking Marcia Kresge. And has been for a while."

O'Dell's mouth had literally fallen open. "You're kidding me."

Kent shook his head: "Nope. I saw her one night at Bone's place—I was in the ramp, I'd been over at Casper Allen's, about his idiot trusts . . ."

"Casper lives right downstairs from Bone," O'Dell said to the others.

". . . and she'd been fuckin' *somebody*, believe me. And as she's getting into her car, who should come out after her, carrying something? James T. Bone."

"The cops need to know that," Wyte said, with an effort at sincerity. "I mean, even if we weren't trying to . . . to . . . help Susan, they'd need to know that. Dan's death is worth millions to her, and opens the top job for her lover."

"That's what I thought," Kent said, leaning back on the couch, sucking on the cinnamon.

Two hours later, O'Dell ushered Compton into the elevator, the last of them to go, and stepped pensively back into her apartment. Kent was a rat: she'd have to remember that. Starting now. The other two should be okay . . .

She spotted her rifle case, dumped in the corner Saturday morning. The case was empty: the Garfield sheriff still had the rifle. She picked it up, carried it back to a storage closet, and slipped it inside. Stuck on the wall of the same closet was an instant-open gun safe. Acting on impulse, she jabbed at the number pads, rolling her hand like a piano player, and the door popped open. Inside lay an Officer's Model Colt. She took it out, pulled the magazine, pulled the slide back to make sure the chamber was empty, let it slam forward.

She moved slowly through the apartment, dry-firing the pistol from various hiding spots and corners; corny but fun. After ten minutes, she carried the pistol back to the safe, reseated the magazine, and shut the safe door.

She'd have to get out to the range one of these days; she was losing her edge.

MARCIA KRESGE WAS getting comfortable on James T. Bone's couch: "Are you going to get the job?"

"I don't know. O'Dell's pretty strong."

"How about McDonald?"

"We can handle McDonald."

"Good. He's an asshole. O'Dell, you know, smokes dope."

"So what?" Bone said. "So do you."

"I'm not trying to get to be a bank president," Kresge said.

"I don't think that's enough to disqualify her," Bone said.

"It would if she was arrested for possession," Kresge said. "The board wouldn't touch her with a ten-foot pole."

"You'd really wish that on her?" Bone asked with real curiosity.

"I'd like to see you get the job," Kresge said. "And I could fix the bust."

"How?"

"We've got the same dealer," Kresge said.

Bone laughed despite himself. "How'd that happen?"

She shrugged, not seeing anything funny in the coincidence. "You know, we all hang out at the same places, and word gets around. This guy, Mark, used to be a waiter at The Falls. He's working his way through college."

"Selling grass?"

"Grass, speed, acid, coke, heroin, ecstasy. PCP probably. Anyway, he deals to Susan. If somebody tipped off the police, maybe they could catch him making a delivery. You know, socialite dope ring. The cops would like that."

"What if they got your name?" Bone asked.

She shrugged. "I'd get rid of everything before I tipped them, and I wouldn't buy any more. What're they going to do? If they even got my name, I'd sue their butts off if they let it out."

"Listen," Bone said, now serious, leaning toward her: "Forget it. I swear to God, Marcia, if anybody tips off the cops about Susan, I'll whip your ass."

"Oooh . . . that could be fun," she said lightly.

"No. It wouldn't be fun," he snapped.

Sometimes he frightened her, just a bit, she thought. But a bit more than she found pleasant. "You're not gonna get this job by looking pretty, you know," she snapped back.

"I know that. I'm working on it," he said.

"I could talk to a couple of people."

"Anything you could do I'd appreciate . . . but let me know first."

"Hey: If I go into banker's-wife mode, I could probably deliver two or three votes off that board. That damn Jack O'Grady has been trying to get my pants off for fifteen years: I bet he could pull a couple votes for you."

"I think Jack's already with me," Bone said. "But encouragement would be good."

"Even if I have to take my pants off?"

"How big a change would that be?" he asked.

A pause. Then Kresge, smiling prettily, said, "Really great fuckin' thing to say, Bone."

"Tell you the truth, I'm surprised the police haven't spent more time with you. You're not the most discreet person in the world, and you weren't divorced when Dan was killed."

"I can be discreet when I wanna be," she said. "Look at us."

"Okay."

"Besides, a woman cop *did* come around and talk to me—Sherrill, her name was. Last name. She had that big-tit look you go for. And hell, I told her everything."

"But not about us."

"She didn't ask."

Bone stood up, turned. "Anyway: I think McDonald's in trouble. We know O'Dell's gonna get a certain number of votes, and I'll get mine, but it's McDonald's that are up for grabs."

"How's McDonald in trouble?"

"This cop—Lucas Davenport, assistant chief . . ."

"I know him, actually."

"He thinks McDonald's involved. I've talked to him a couple of times and he's a smart guy. He's talking to McDonald's pals and the word is getting out. If there's even a whiff of involvement, the board'll drop him like a hot rock."

"So anything that would encourage Davenport to look at McDonald . . . that would help."

"As long as it didn't turn back on us."

"I'll see what—" The doorbell rang, and Kresge turned her head.

Bone stepped across the room and opened the heavy paneled door. Kerin Baki was there, struggling with an oversized briefcase. As she brought it in, her glasses slipped down her nose, and she jabbed them back as though they'd mutinied. She saw Kresge on the couch and said, "Mrs. Kresge. Have you spoken to Mr. O'Grady?"

"We were just talking about that," Kresge said pleasantly. "Your boss was giving me a very hard time."

Baki turned, said, "Mr. Bone, you should listen to Mrs. Kresge on this."

"Christ, you're conspiring against me," he said.

"*Working* for you," Baki said. "I printed everything I could find on the mortgage company performance since McDonald took over. There are a few things we can use—not necessarily his fault, but you know how mortgages have been performing . . ."

"Let me get a Coke," Bone said. "What would you like, Kerin? Marcia already has a—"

"Bloody Mary," Kresge said. "And it's all gone. I'll help you . . ."

"Just sparkling water," Baki said. She began spreading her papers on a coffee table as Bone and Kresge went to the kitchen to get drinks. When Baki finished with the papers, she heard Kresge laugh, a low, husky laugh with a little sex in it; she could see them moving around Bone's small kitchen, inside each other's personal space, casually bumping hips.

Their relationship had been clear to Baki for a while now; she wouldn't tolerate it much longer. She got so deep into that calculation—the end of Bone's relationship with Marcia Kresge—that she almost didn't notice them walking toward her.

"Kerin?" Bone said curiously. "Are you home?"

He was standing next to her, holding out a glass and a bottle of lime-flavored Perrier. "Oh. Sure. Preoccupied, I guess." She pushed the Perrier aside and went to the papers. "This stack of papers is the annualized return on . . ."

BONNIE BONET DYED her hair black, the dense, sticky color of shoe polish. She dressed in black from head to toe, wore blue lipstick, and carried thirty-five extra pounds. But she was almost smart and could write poetry in Perl-5. She sat across the table from Robles and said, "Because the motherfucker was going to kill a couple of thousand people, that's why."

"I know you're lying," Robles said. He'd broken a sweat.

"No you don't. I'm not lying."

"So tell me what kind of a gun you used," he said.

"My father's .30–30."

"Bullshit. You never fired a gun in your life."

She sneered at him: "You think I couldn't figure out a gun? Every redneck in Minnesota can shoot a gun, but I can't?"

"I'm gonna tell the cops about this," Robles said.

"Go ahead," she said. "You've got no proof."

"Jesus Christ, Bonnie. I know you're lying, but you're pushing me into a corner. You get this fantasy going, you'll tell somebody else, like one of your fuckin' novels . . ." Bonet laughed but looked away. Robles said, "Oh, Jesus, who'd you tell?"

"He doesn't believe me either."

"You told goddamned Dick . . ."

"Well, you started it . . . the whole fantasy thing."

"I was joking," Robles insisted. "I didn't want him dead . . ."

"You got him."

"But I was joking . . ."

"Too late now. You tell the cops about me, I'll tell them about you."

Robles left the bar, sweating, half drunk. Okay, she was lying. But she'd never admit it. She was crazy. Almost for sure . . .

Terrance Robles had made just shy of a half-million dollars the previous year, and he'd spent only a small part of it. With his access to information, he could grow his stake at twenty to thirty percent per year, on top of earnings. If he could hang on for another five years, he could quit. Get out. Buy an old used Cray computer somewhere, and do some *serious* shit.

But he had to hold on.

He could turn Bonet in. Or, alternatively, he could kill her—nothing else would shut her up. She was having too good a time.

Robles bit on a thumbnail, stumbled along the street.

————

LATE NIGHT: THE mixed smells of vinegar and gasoline, one pungent, one metallic; the combination smelling like blood. The vinegar went into the washtub and down the drain, followed by a steady stream of water that would carry it away.

A glass cutter: this had been in the book, which went on to say that it was probably unnecessary, but why take chances? Deep scored lines up and down the bottle, then more, horizontally, until the bottle was checkered with shaky, intersecting lines. Then the bottle sprayed with Windex, carefully and meticulously wiped with paper towels. No fingerprints here.

Now the gasoline, mixed in the bottle with two four-ounce cans of chain saw oil. A strip of old T-shirt for a wick.

The bottle was heavy; a little better than seven pounds.

But it wouldn't have to be thrown far.

Just far enough.

7

"NOW WE'RE GETTING some heat," said Rose Marie Roux. She was drinking coffee from a bone china cup; a matching saucer sat on her desk, and on the saucer, a wad of green chewing gum. "Harrison White called, and said if you need to interview Wilson McDonald, or if you would like to bring him before a grand jury, McDonald will come over anytime and testify. Without immunity. He will answer any questions, without reservation. Under oath."

"And if we don't need him to do that?" Lucas asked. He was facing Roux's window, the sun streaming in. Another good day. Cold.

"Then knock off the innuendos—the snooping around asking other people about him. White says the snooping could cost McDonald the top job at the bank, and if it does, he'll see that the city picks up the difference in what he makes now, and what he would have made in twenty-some years as bank president. He thinks it might be forty or fifty million."

Lucas grinned. "Would we have to pay it all up front?"

Roux smiled back: "He didn't say. But he also talked to a couple of people on the city council, and McDonald's father has been calling around . . . but fuck them. Do what you need with McDonald. I thought you should know that glaciers are starting to move."

"Thanks," Lucas said.

"And, of course, what White says is true. McDonald could be completely innocent, and we could be screwing him out of his lifetime job. In fact, we could even have been set up to do it, with the letter."

"Tell you what," Lucas said. "Let me talk to White. I wanted McDonald bumped, I wanted him nervous, but I don't need to push much harder. We could back off a bit."

"Whatever you think," Roux said. She finished the coffee, peeled the gum off the saucer, and popped it back in her mouth. "Nicotine," she said. "Too expensive to throw away before I chew it out."

"So I'll . . ." Lucas was getting to his feet.

"Sit down," Roux said. She probed her desk for a moment. "We have a couple of things to talk about. First, the opium ring . . ."

"Oh, shit," Lucas groaned.

"And then Capslock has put in for thirty hours accumulated overtime for investigating it."

"Rose Marie . . ."

"He's your guy, goddamnit. Now, this thirty hours. He took the thirty hours when he was supposedly on disability leave after the pinking shears incident. Now what I'm trying to figure is how . . ."

"Aw, Rose Marie, c'mon . . ."

ROUX WAS AMUSING, and he laughed with her, and convinced her to sign off on the thirty hours. But the laughter was like a water bug on a pond, skating across the surface of his mind. He was amused and he laughed, but nothing was deeply funny; life was simply stupid most of the time. Going downhill, again, he thought. He walked back to his office, tired, a little unnerved by the overnight rattling in his brain, and found Sherrill waiting for him.

Sherrill was lanky and dark-eyed, with short black hair and—Sloan's words— the good headlights. Her estranged husband had been killed by a crazy outlaw, who was himself killed by Lucas in a close-quarters firefight in the middle of a freak blizzard. It all happened just minutes before the cold-eyed Iowa boy had blown up both Dick LaChaise and Lucas's marriage prospects. Last winter had been a bad one.

"There you are," Sherrill said. "Want to come detect?"

"Detect what?"

"An anonymous caller phoned the Garfield sheriff's office and said that a US West lineman saw the killer, or might have seen him. The lineman was working on an exchange box near Kresge's place. Said that he was talking about it in a bar, thought about calling the cops but didn't because he didn't want to get involved. So the sheriff tracked him down, and guess what?"

"He confessed and threw himself on the mercy of the court."

"Nope. He's down here. They sent him to an NSP warehouse to pick up a bunch of splicer things . . . The sheriff talked to him and called me. He's the only eyewitness we have so far. I'm going over."

"How far?"

"Ten minutes?"

"Let's go," Lucas said.

SHERRILL HAD A city car parked at the curb. They took I-394 west, falling into routine cop chitchat that covered a vaguely uncomfortable tension between them. Sherrill was at least somewhat available, and, rumor had it, would not be averse to exploring possibilities with Lucas. At the same time, word was around that Lucas hadn't quite recovered from the loss of Weather, and nobody wanted to be the first woman afterwards.

Lucas, on the other hand, with a small reputation as a womanizer, had been expected to make a run at Sherrill ever since her marriage began going bad. He'd never done that. There lingered about them the sense that somebody ought to make a move, almost as a matter of common politeness.

"Did you get anything good out of Kresge's office?" Lucas asked after a while.

"Naw. But there are some newly humble secretaries and assistants around the place, I'll tell you," Sherrill said cheerfully. "Especially around Bone and O'Dell and McDonald. Everybody thinks one of them will get the job."

"What about the merger?"

"That's apparently on hold."

"Hmph. So if somebody shot Kresge to stop the merger, it worked."

"Yup. For the time being, anyway."

"And this telephone guy . . ."

"Harold Hanks."

". . . saw the killer."

"Maybe. But there's something odd about the whole thing. Whoever called the sheriff's office said she heard him talking in a bar. Harold Hanks is a hard-shell Baptist. He told the sheriff he hadn't been in a bar for fifteen years, since he was born again. But he did see somebody, just like the caller said. But he never connected whoever he saw with the killing."

"The caller was a woman?"

"Yeah."

"They knew where the call came from?"

"A pay phone off I-35. I wrote it down, it's up north somewhere."

"Nothing there, then."

"Nope."

"Both letters to Rose Marie were probably written by women—one of them for sure, and the one pointing at McDonald has a female feeling to it . . ."

"Yeah, it does," Sherrill agreed. "So we've got somebody out there who knows a lot more than we do, and she's leading us in."

"Which makes you wonder . . ." He looked out the window.

"What?"

"McDonald's wife," Lucas suggested.

"Hmm."

"He beats her up," Lucas said.

"Yeah?" Old story.

"Something to look into," he said.

They rode in the slightly tense silence for another few minutes, then Sherrill blurted, "Seeing Weather at all?"

"No. The shrink thinks we ought to spend some time apart." Everybody in the department knew about the shrink.

"But eventually get back?" Sherrill asked.

"Maybe," Lucas said moodily. Three teenagers in reflective vests were peering through a surveying total station just off the interstate. All three wore their caps backward.

"You know," Sherrill said, plowing ahead, "you've really got your head up your ass in a lot of ways. You walk around with this cloud over you, mooning over her. Why don't you do something to get her back?"

"I'm afraid it's more complicated than that," Lucas started, a distinct chill in his voice.

"Oh, bullshit, Lucas. If you love her, get her back. Don't wait for her to work it out—plot something. Suck her in. The thing is, if she gets a little freaky when she sees you, then you've got to hang around more. Screw the shrink: the thing is, life goes on, and if you're around all the time, and life keeps going on . . . the freakiness will go away. It'll get boring. Tiresome. And if she basically loves you, and you love her . . ."

"Can we knock this off? You're bumming me out."

"Jesus, what a crock," Sherrill said, angry now.

Lucas was just as angry: "It's a crock, all right. I should trick her back? How would I do that? Huh? Get somebody to set up a blind date, and it's me? Hide in her closet, and pop out when she goes to iron a blouse?"

Sherrill rolled her eyes and nearly took the car into the oncoming lane; Lucas flinched and she jerked it back to the right. "Lucas, this is Marcy Sherrill you're talking to. I was there when you suckered John Mail, remember? I helped you track the LaChaise women. I heard you order up a traffic stop that you knew would never be made, so when we wasted them, our asses would be covered with the press. I was there, for Christ's sake. I heard you work it out. So don't tell me you couldn't work out some little scheme to get close to her. When it came time to finish off John Mail, you didn't get moody—"

"Shut the fuck up," Lucas said.

"Fuck you."

"There's US West," Lucas said, pointing to the right.

"Maybe you don't want her back," Sherrill said. She missed the turn.

"You missed the goddamned turn," Lucas fumed.

"I'll make the goddamn turn," Sherrill said, and she braked, looked quickly left, then did an illegal U, bouncing across a median strip.

"Jesus Christ," Lucas said, startled, bracing himself, as the muffler dragged over the curb.

"You want the fuckin' turn, I'll make the fuckin' turn," Sherrill snarled and, ignoring a red light, turned left across two lanes of traffic into the US West parking area. They lurched to a stop in a visitor's space.

"Satisfied?" she asked.

"Yeah," Lucas said. "Really."

SHERRILL WAS OUT of the car, steaming toward the warehouse entrance. Lucas trailed behind, deflected the door as it slammed on his face, and finally caught her at the service counter, where she flashed her ID at a guard and said, "We're here to see Harold Hanks."

"Oh, yeah," the guard said. "He's waiting up in the canteen on two."

"Second floor?"

"Take those elevators."

She steamed on back to the elevators. "Like you're Miss Social Life," Lucas said at her back.

Then she was suddenly calm: "Lucas, I have an active social life. You just don't see it." A blatant lie, and they both knew it. The elevator went ding and they got inside.

"Maybe Weather and I don't recover quite as quickly as you do," Lucas said, as the doors slid shut.

"That's a horseshit thing to say," Sherrill shouted, really angry now. "You take that back."

"I take it back," Lucas said meekly.

"I'd already signed off on Mike when he got killed," she shouted.

Now he just wanted to quiet her down. "I know, I know . . ."

"Jesus, what a jerk."

THE ELEVATOR DOORS opened, and a short, rotund man in a brown suit was staring at them owlishly; he'd obviously heard the shouting. "Is there a problem?"

"Yeah, him," Sherrill said, tossing her thumb at Lucas, who hovered, embarrassed, in the doorway.

"There are some police officers coming up," the man ventured.

"We are the police officers," Sherrill said. "We're looking for a man named Harold Hanks."

"The canteen . . . that way, left around the corner."

They went left around the corner and Lucas said, "That was really cute."

"Shut up," she said.

HAROLD HANKS WAS a gangly, rawboned man who wore a billed hat over plaid shirt, jeans, and boots, and though he'd spread out on a couch, he looked as though he'd be even more comfortable standing in a ditch somewhere. He was drinking a Welch's grape soda from the can while he paged through a copy of *Guns & Ammo*.

"Anything good?" Sherrill asked, tipping her head to look at the magazine cover.

"Some. But it's mostly pistol bullshit . . . You're Miz Sherrill."

"Yes. And this is Chief Davenport. Sheriff Krause says you saw somebody up by the Kresge place."

"Yeah, I guess—but I didn't tell anybody about it in no bar."

"Did you tell anybody about it at all?" Lucas asked.

"No, I never did," Hanks said. "No reason to. Just somebody in the woods during deer season. Only saw him for a minute. And see, I was up on the south side of Kresge's place, way around from the driveway. I didn't even think of it being up that far . . . I never put it together."

"So what'd he look like? The guy you saw?"

" 'Bout what you'd expect at that time of day, that day of the year. Blaze-orange hat and coat. Carrying a rifle."

"Couldn't see his face?" Sherrill asked.

"Nope. He was wearing a scarf."

"A scarf?"

"Yeah. Covered the whole bottom part of his face. His hood covered the top part of his face, down to his forehead, and the scarf came right up to his eyes."

"Wasn't that a little weird?" Sherrill asked.

"Nope. It gets damn cold out there, sitting in a tree."

"Big guy?" Lucas asked.

Hanks thought for a minute, then shook his head: "Mmm, hard to tell. I only saw him from about the waist up, walking along back in the trees. Not real big. Maybe average. Maybe even smaller than average."

Lucas looked at Sherrill: "Have you seen McDonald?"

She shook her head. "Not yet."

"Six-three, six-four, maybe two-sixty."

"Wasn't anybody that big," Hanks said, shaking his head. "With them coveralls and the blaze-orange coat, a guy that big would look like a giant."

"Did you hear a shot before you saw him?"

"Heck, it was a shooting gallery out there. I was wearing blaze orange myself, just to stand in a ditch. I was happy to get out of there alive. But there was a shot, sort of close by, and in the right direction. About five, ten minutes before I saw him."

"That'd be right," Lucas said to Sherrill.

Sherrill nodded and went back to Hanks. "But that's all. Just a guy in orange. Nothing distinctive?"

Hanks shrugged. "Sorry. I told the sheriff I couldn't help much."

"Didn't see any cars coming or going?"

"There were a couple of trucks and maybe a car or two. I don't know. I wasn't paying any attention."

"What were you doing out there, anyway?" Lucas asked. "Six-thirty, on a Saturday morning?"

"Aw, there's this place called Pilot Lake, full of city people. They got maybe fifty phones around the lake, and some idiot put their exchange right on top of a spring. About once a month, the whole damn place goes down and then they all raise hell until somebody fixes it. It's a priority for us, until we can redo the exchange."

"When did they go down?"

"About ten o'clock Friday night."

"Including Kresge's place?"

"Nope. He'd be the next exchange up the road. Like I said, I was on the south side . . ."

"Okay." Lucas thought for a moment, then asked, "What'd the scarf look like? Black? Red?"

"Red," Hanks said. He scratched his jaw, thinking about it. "Or pink."

"What else? Was it wrapped on the outside, or inside . . . ?"

"Inside—like he covered his face, then pulled the hood up over."

"Okay . . ."

They dug for another five minutes, running him through it again, but came up with nothing more, until they both stood up. Then Lucas asked, "Where would this guy have been walking to? Assuming he had a car?"

"I don't know," Hanks said. His eyes drifted off to the ceiling. "Probably . . . well, he could have been heading back to the Kresge cabin. He was sort of going that way, in a roundabout way."

"Could he have been going anywhere else?"

"Not that I know of."

"How about this Pilot Lake place?"

"Nope. I was on that corner and he was walking . . ." He made a hand gesture, like a time-out signal. "This way to the access road."

"Perpendicular," Sherrill suggested.

"Yeah. Like that," Hanks said.

"You didn't hear a car start?"

"Nope. But I was quite a way from the house, and I was wearing my hat with earflaps . . . So I probably wouldn't have."

"Pink scarf," said Lucas.

"Pink scarf," Hanks said.

"WHAT'S THE PINK scarf?" Sherrill asked, after they let Hanks go. They were sitting alone in the canteen, eating Twinkies from the coin-op.

"Susan O'Dell wears a kaffiyeh as a scarf. It's pale red and white—she was wearing it when I saw her Saturday."

"What's a kaffiyeh?"

"You know, one of those head wraps like Arabs wear," Lucas said. "Like what's-his-name, the Palestinian guy, always wears."

"Oh, yeah. Him. But his is black and white."

"There's another kind that's red and white. And it would look pink from a distance, or pink and white."

"He said pink."

"O'Dell said she never left her tree before seven-thirty, when she shot her buck," Lucas said. "Then she gutted him and dragged him up to the trail and sat down next to her tree to wait until nine, which was the agreed-on time to take a break. Didn't go anywhere."

"I think it's the car that's interesting. If there wasn't a car, it almost had to be one of those guys. Whoever it was had to know the Kresge place pretty well, and there's no way you could walk in from very far away."

"Yeah, but he's pretty shaky on that car stuff," Lucas said. "O'Dell would have been walking *away* from her tree stand if she was going in the direction Hanks said she was. She was definitely at her tree when Bone came by to pick her up at nine o'clock."

"Maybe we push Miz O'Dell," Sherrill said. "See which way she goes."

"Not yet," Lucas said. "I want to go back up there, to Kresge's, look around. And we need to know more about the bank-merger idea—of the three realistic candidates to run the bank, we have accusations against two of them, McDonald and O'Dell. All the accusations came in anonymously, from women. At least, we think the accusation pointing at McDonald came from a woman . . . So the question is, are they legit? Or are they meant to drag O'Dell and McDonald into an investigation that would eliminate them from contenders to run the bank."

"You mean, by Bone? Or somebody working with Bone?"

"I'd hate to think so," Lucas said. "Because I kinda like the guy. But all of them are smart and tough. And the stakes are pretty big. Bone would be looking for an edge."

"So we push Bone."

"Let's wait before we push anyone. Just a day or two . . . Let me get back up north."

"Want me to come?"

Lucas looked at her as he finished his Twinkie. "If you want to. If you stay out of my goddamned life while I'm trapped in the car."

She flushed and said, "I meant what I started out to say, before we got sidetracked. If you still want her, you've got to get off your ass and go after her. If you don't, you'll just . . . drift away. And you'll never know for sure that it's over. If you go after her, you'll know pretty soon whether there's any hope."

"I'll think about it," he said.

"So when are we going up north?"

"Tomorrow," Lucas said, looking at his watch. "We should have some biographical stuff about the people McDonald supposedly killed: Let's take a look at that."

THEY WERE SIX blocks from police headquarters when Sherrill's telephone chirped. She fumbled it out of her jacket pocket one-handed, said, "Yeah?" and then passed the phone to Lucas. "Sloan," she said.

Lucas took the phone: "What's going on?"

"I solved the Kresge case," Sloan said laconically. "I had a little break from the Ericson thing, and I thought I might as well clean it up."

"That's good," Lucas said. "It's a burden off my mind."

Sloan's tone of voice changed: "Terrance Robles just walked in and said he may know who did it."

Lucas, uncertain, and not wanting to bite too hard, said, "You're kidding."

"I'm not kidding. He's out sitting at my desk. Where are you?"

"About two minutes away."

"See you in two minutes," Sloan said.

8

ROBLES WAS SITTING at Sloan's desk when Lucas and Sherrill arrived at Homicide. He was talking to Sloan, and Lucas watched for a minute. Robles was crossing and recrossing his ankles under his chair, twisting his hands together, rubbing the back of his neck, squirming in the chair. Serious stress, Lucas thought. Lucas walked up behind him, trailed by Sherrill, and when Sloan looked up, Robles turned, then got to his feet.

"D-D-Detective Davenport," he stuttered. "I've b-b-been talking to Detective Sloan, he thinks you should know about this."

Lucas took a chair and Sherrill pulled one out of a nearby desk.

"So . . . you think you know who did it?" Lucas asked.

"No. I know somebody who *says* she did it, but I don't think she really did. But if I didn't tell you, I thought . . . I don't know what I thought."

"So?" Lucas grinned at him and made a *What?* gesture with his hands.

Robles had a friend, he said, a woman, a computer freak he'd met in an Internet chat room, and then in person, when it turned out that she lived in Minneapolis. When the news hit the papers that Polaris was considering a merger, and a large number of administrative and clerical personnel in Minneapolis could lose their jobs, she called him to ask him if the merger could be stopped.

"Her mother works at Polaris, routine clerical stuff, exactly the kind of job that would probably be wiped out," Robles said.

"And you told her that the merger couldn't be stopped."

"Not exactly. I told her that nobody much wanted it except Kresge and a small majority of board members, and the only reason the board was going for it was the stock premium . . ."

"Explain that," Sherrill said. "I don't understand stocks."

"Well, see, Midland has offered to buy all the outstanding Polaris shares by trading with their shares, one to one. When they made the offer, they were trading in the sixties—sixty-plus dollars per share—and we were trading in the upper thirties. Their stock dropped on the offer, down to about fifty-three right now. But ours went to forty-six right now, and the closer we get to the merger, and the more certain it looks, the more ours will go up. If we finally merge, and nothing else happens, it'll probably be around fifty dollars a share. Polaris needs ten board members to okay the deal. If you look at how many board members own how much stock, the tenth biggest holder . . ." Robles looked at Sherrill, who seemed to be having trouble following the explanation. "What I'm saying is, of those ten members needed to approve the merger, the one with the smallest holding is Shelley Oakes. He has ninety thousand shares, plus options for fifty thousand more at an average price in the thirties. If the sale goes through at fifty bucks, he'll make a couple of million bucks over what the stock was worth before the merger talk started."

"Ah," Sherrill said, as though she understood.

"The biggest holder, Dave Brandt, has better than four hundred thousand shares, plus God only knows what he has in stock options, which he could exercise before the deal goes down. He'll make tens of millions. Literally tens of millions."

"So the board and Kresge make millions, and everybody else gets fired," Lucas said.

"No, not exactly. Some people would make it. There're rumors that the investment division will be kept intact, that Midland wants the division. Then there are other executives who could make a stink, but most of them have stock options."

"Do you have options?" Lucas asked.

"Yeah, yeah. I've got options on five thousand shares at a bunch of different prices that average out to about thirty-five, so if it goes to fifty, I'd make seventy-five thousand. But I'll tell you what, that's about six weeks' pay for me. And the government would get most of it anyway. I mean, it's nothing."

"Nothing," Sherrill said.

"Nothing."

"Jesus, I make forty thousand a year," Sherrill said. "And I've been shot for it."

"For your big shots, forty ain't a salary," Sloan said from behind Robles. "It's more like the price tag on something they might buy next week."

"Okay, okay," Lucas said. "So this woman . . ."

"Bonnie Bonet."

". . . told you she killed Kresge, and she has some motive."

"Yes."

"Why'd she tell you?"

"Ah, God. Because I asked her." He twisted his hands nervously, and Lucas noticed that he seemed to sweat all the time, and copiously. "See, the thing is, when she came on the 'net and asked if the merger could be stopped, I told her, not unless we killed Kresge. I didn't mean it, we were just joking on the 'net. But she came right back and said, 'Let's do it.' "

"And you said . . ."

"I said maybe we could figure a way to blow his car up," Robles said.

"Blow his car up," Sloan said, repeating the phrase as though he were astonished.

"I was *joking*. I really was—I'd never hurt anyone, it was just all bullshit. We went back and forth about ways to kill him, all ridiculous, like sci-fi stuff, and then . . . we stopped."

"Stopped?" Sherrill's eyebrows went up.

"Yeah. It never came up again," Robles said. "It was like, a couple of nights, then we wore the subject out, and it never came up."

"Until somebody killed him," Lucas said.

"Why didn't you tell me this Saturday?" asked Sloan.

"Because I didn't think there was any chance she'd done it. And if she hadn't done it, talking about it could only get me in trouble. So I wanted to check with her. I came back, and I couldn't find her online, and I didn't know where she lived. She's unlisted, and I'd only gotten together with her at Uncle Tony's. That's a bar . . ."

"We know," Sherrill said. "The one with the porno on computers."

"Porno? You mean the TV Three story? That was all bullshit . . ."

"Yeah, yeah, yeah," Lucas said. "Go ahead."

"Anyway, when I did find her, yesterday, I asked her if she'd heard about it, and she said yeah, she'd done it," Robles said.

"But you don't believe her."

"No. She's never fired a gun. She doesn't even go outside, for Christ's sake. She's white as a sheet . . . she doesn't know about walking around in the woods. Her old man's got something wrong with his bowel or something and never worked, and they never went anywhere when she was growing up. She said she shot him with her father's .30–30, and I bet she doesn't even know what a .30–30 looks like or that he has one."

"Could be the right kind of rifle," Lucas said. "The medical examiner says Kresge was killed with a large-caliber rifle, which around here probably means thirty-caliber . . ."

"That's why I decided to tell you," Robles said plaintively. "I'm ninety-five percent sure she didn't do it—but I'm five percent not sure."

"And you don't know where she lives," Sloan said.

"No, but she uses her driver's license as an ID, and I figured you could get that."

"Bonnie Bonet?"

"B-O-N-E-T," Robles said, spelling it out. "Is this gonna be in the newspapers?"

Sherrill looked at Lucas: "Want me to pick her up?"

"Yeah. Do that. Get some uniforms to back you up. Call me when you've got her." When Sherrill had gone, Lucas turned back to Robles, looked at him for several seconds, then said, "We'll need a statement. Detective Sloan will take it."

And to Sloan: "Read him his rights on the tape."

"My rights?" Robles threw his head back to peer at Lucas. "To a lawyer? Do I need a lawyer?"

Lucas shrugged: "Purely up to you . . . Anyway, talk to Sloan." And to Sloan: "I'll be down at my office. I've got some paper to look at."

TWO FILES WERE waiting for him: files on the people mentioned in the anonymous letter as victims of Wilson McDonald.

Lucas took off his jacket, hung it on an antique oak coatrack, and dropped in the chair behind his desk. He picked up the first file, put his heels on his desk, and leaned back. And then let the file drop to his lap for a few seconds. He was not particularly introspective, but he was suddenly aware that the constant mental grinding in the back of his head—the grinding that had gone on for weeks, a symptom of the beast prowling around him—was fainter, barely distinguishable.

A book project, he thought: *Serial Murder: A Cure for Clinical Depression?* by Lucas Davenport.

GEORGE ARRIS WAS killed on a rainy night in September 1984 while walking down St. Paul's Grand Avenue toward a restaurant-bar generally regarded as a meat rack. Somebody unknown had fired a single shot from a .380 semiautomatic pistol into the back of Arris's head, and left him to die on the sidewalk.

St. Paul homicide investigators had torn the city apart looking for the killer, because Arris was only the last of four nearly identical killings, spaced about two weeks apart.

All the victims were younger white men, all relatively affluent, all walking alone at night. All of the killings were within twenty blocks of each other. A racial motivation was suspected, and black gang members were targeted as the primary suspects.

Four different pistols had been used in the killings. Two of the guns had been found.

The first, a .22-caliber Smith & Wesson revolver which had been used in the second killing, was found by a city work crew trying to open a clogged storm sewer a half-mile from the killing. That set off a general inspection of storm sewers, and the second pistol, a .25-caliber semiauto, was found three blocks from the .22. Neither of the other two pistols was found.

The lead detective on the case was George Jellman.

JELLMAN WAS RETIRED, and it took two phone calls to locate him. "He's out back," his wife shouted. "I'll go get him." She must have been shouting. Lucas mused, because they lived in Florida, which was a long way from Minnesota.

Jellman came to the phone a second later: "Davenport, you miserable piece of shit. I never thought I'd hear from you again."

"How are you, Jelly?"

"Well, I'm looking out at my backyard," he said. "There are two palm trees and two orange trees and a lime tree—Denise makes key lime pie from it. It's just a bit shy of eighty degrees right now, and I can smell the ocean. About an hour from now, I'll be hitting golf balls on the greenest golf course you ever saw in your life . . . How's it up there?"

"Cool, but nice."

"Right. Nice in Minnesota means the snow's not over your boots yet . . . So what's happening?"

"You remember a bunch of killings you handled back in '84, four guys shot in the back of the head?"

"Oh, hell, yes," Jellman said. "Never got the guys who did it."

"I'm interested in the last one—George Arris."

"Why him?"

"We got an anonymous letter with the name of the supposed killer."

"I bet it ain't no goddamn Vice Lord," Jellman said.

"Why is that?"

"Is it? A Vice Lord?"

"No. It's a bank vice president."

"Hah. I knew it. Trust the letter, Lucas—if it was a bullshitter, he would've said it was a Vice Lord, 'cause that was on all the media. The Vice Lords did the other three, but that fourth one, that was a copycat."

"Are you sure?"

"Pretty sure. That was the word on the street, though nobody had any names for us. But the word was, the fourth one came out of the blue. That the Vice Lords who'd done the shooting had split for Chicago before the fourth one ever happened."

"So it was pretty much street talk about the fourth one."

"There was something else too—the first three were all up there in the colored section. But the last guy was down on Grand Avenue. You look on a map, it looks pretty close, but you don't see many blacks over there. Not walking on the street—especially not then, not as tight as everybody was about the first three shootings. And there's Wylie's Market used to be over there. You remember Wylie's?"

"Sure."

"They had a surveillance camera in the back of the store, looking at the cashier's cage and the front door, get people's faces coming in. Anyway, on the film, you can see the street through the window, and we picked out Arris strolling down the street, just a minute or so before he was shot. But there weren't any blacks, either before or after."

"Huh. Is the tape still around?"

"Yeah, someplace. Since the case is still open . . ."

"Did you ever look at the people around Arris? Friends and coworkers?"

"Oh, sure. Went over to that bank where he worked, came up empty. He'd been dating a few women, but hadn't had anything serious in a couple of years. All he did was work: that's what everybody said. Wasn't interested in pussy, gambling, booze. Just interested in work."

"Huh. And he was dead when they found him."

"Yup. Never knew what hit him. Probably never saw it coming. Entry wound right below the bump on the back of his head, exit wound right between his eyes."

"Exit wound? So how'd you know it was a .380—was there a shell?"

"Yeah, we found it in the grass next to the curb. There was a partial print, but really partial—not enough even to start looking for a match."

"Slug fragments?"

"Yeah, one piece. Hollow point of some kind, nothing that would identify a pistol."

"Not much of anything, then."

"Nope. Listen, if you want, I'll call Doug Skelly over in St. Paul and get him to run down that tape for you."

"Thanks, Jelly. Wish you were still on the job."

"Wish I was too, man. I hate this fuckin' place."

THE FILE ON Andrew Ingall consisted of one sheet: His boat had been reported missing on Superior on a clear, fine day with good sailing winds. The Coast Guard, the Civil Air Patrol, and the local sheriff's departments in adjacent Minnesota and Wisconsin counties had done a search. Nothing was ever found, not even a life jacket.

An address and phone number were listed in the town of North Oaks. Lucas punched the number in, got an answering machine, a woman's voice. He hung up, dialed Dispatch, had them check the cross-reference index for numbers on both sides of that address, dialed the first one.

"Hello?" Another woman.

"Yes, my name is Lucas Davenport and I'm with the Minneapolis Police Department. I'm trying to get in touch with Annette Ingall, but all I get at her home is an answering machine."

"Oh my God, nothing happened to Toby?"

"No, no, I just need to talk to her about her husband. Do you know if she works? Where I could call her?"

"Well, she has a bridal wear boutique downtown . . ."

THE BRIDAL SHOP was a brisk ten-minute walk from City Hall, among a cluster of boutiques on Marquette Avenue. Annette Ingall was a tall woman with auburn hair and pale blue eyes; motherly, Lucas thought later, though she was probably five years younger than he was. She did a smiling double take when he walked into the store, and when a clerk came over and he asked for her, she said, "That would be me. Can I help you?"

He stepped closer and pitched his voice down: "I need to talk to you privately for a moment. I'm with the Minneapolis Police Department—nothing happened with your boy, it's a completely different matter."

Her hand went to her throat as the smile died on her face. "How do you know about my son?"

"Because I called one of your neighbors to find you, and she said, 'Oh my God, nothing happened to Toby?' "

"Oh. Okay." The smile flickered back. "Why don't you come back to my office."

Ingall led the way through a door into the back of the store, to a small office cubicle that stuck out into a stock-storage area. There were two chairs inside, and she sat behind her desk and crossed her legs.

Lucas sat down and said, "I'm investigating the death of Daniel Kresge."

"Yes? I read about it."

Lucas picked up the tone. "You didn't like him?"

"No. Not especially. He once made a pretty heavy pass at me, when he and his wife were still together. This was after my husband died, and I was feeling pretty vulnerable."

Lucas nodded: "I'm actually here because I want to know more about your husband. I have an abstract of a Douglas County file about his disappearance, but there's not much in it."

"There wasn't much to say." Her lower lip trembled as she said it; she was twisting a ring on her finger, and Lucas noticed that it was a wedding ring. "He just got on the boat and vanished."

"But there isn't any doubt that the boat sank?" Lucas asked.

"What? Have you found out something?"

"No-no-no. Just . . . your tone of voice."

"Well . . ." Again, the trembling lip. "It's been almost impossible to put this behind me, because nothing was ever found. No body, no boat debris, nothing. After he disappeared, all kinds of inspectors went to the bank, and they came and questioned me to make sure he hadn't taken off with some money. I mean, every time I get a phone call at home that I'm not expecting, I halfway think it's going to be his voice."

"But you really think the boat sank."

"Yes." She nodded firmly. "In fact, I even think I know what happened. Do you sail, Mr. Davenport?"

"I have. I'm not particularly good at it." Weather was a sailing fanatic, as her father had been, and they'd gone out almost every warm weekend, and for a long two weeks in the Caribbean.

"When a boat goes down, there's almost always lots of debris," Ingall said. "You know the enormous amount of stuff sailors carry around with them—books and logs and guides and all kinds of paper. Andy had even more of it than most people. Business papers and references and so on. Plus the boat had a lot of wood. So if it had blown up, like some people thought, they'd have found *something*. But they didn't find anything. So you know what I think?"

"What?"

"What I think is, it was a cool day, and Andy had the autopilot on and he'd gone below. While he was down there *. . .* the keel fell off," she said.

"The keel?"

"Yes. The keel on our boat was about four thousand pounds of lead, held in place with four huge steel bolts. You normally couldn't even see the bolts, without pulling up parts of the sole—the flooring."

"Yeah." He knew what a sole was.

"Anyway, I think the nuts worked off the bolts, from vibration, and then, with some sudden strain, the keel simply fell off," she said. "If that happened, the boat would have turned turtle just instantly, and water would have started pouring down the companionway and the whole thing would have sunk in a minute or two. There are cases known like this. They're rare, but it sort of explains everything. There wouldn't have been time for life jackets or anything, and the inflow of water would have kept everything inside. It would've been just . . . glug."

"But that's a rare thing."

"Yes—but."

"But."

"We kept the boat in Superior, and there's this old guy up there who pretty much lives on his boat. Not technically, because they don't allow that, but he's around day and night. When I was up there during the search, he told me that Andy'd had somebody working on the boat the night before he disappeared. He didn't pay much attention, but he said he'd noticed the guy had pulled up the sole and stuck it in the cockpit, out of the way of whatever he was doing. He assumed the guy was working on the plumbing, but he could have been working on the bolts. Maybe there was something wrong with them. Or maybe he did something that messed them up."

"Huh. Was your husband there that day? When the work was being done?"

"No, not that day."

"Did he often hire people to do work when he wasn't there?"

"From time to time. I mean, good boat-repair people are like plumbers or electricians. They'll schedule you for some work, but something happens on another job and it gets stretched out, or they get free earlier than they think. So lots of times we'd just give them the key and the go-ahead to do the work whenever they could get there."

"Did you know that work was being done?"

"No. But sometimes he didn't tell me. The boat was more Andy's thing than mine."

"Did anybody ever talk to the guy who did the work?"

"Nope. We looked around, but nobody ever figured out who it was. We had a guy we'd used quite a bit, but he said he didn't know anything about it. And nobody ever really saw the guy doing the work. He did it in the evening, mostly after dark. And he wasn't there very long—so that made me think it wasn't the plumbing, which would take a while. The only thing I could think of that you'd pull up the sole for, and wouldn't take long, would be the bolts."

"Look," Lucas said, "I don't want to upset you, but . . . was there any possibility of suicide?"

"No." She said it positively.

Lucas said, "Okay."

"Andy was a happy guy," she said. "He was doing great in his job, he was up for a promotion, we were talking about putting a big garden in behind the house, we were talking about another child. I was supposed to bring Toby up to the islands the next day, and we were all going sailing, and Toby was all excited . . . No. He didn't commit suicide. And he didn't take off with any money or anything. He was just a heck of a good guy and well adjusted and his folks are nice and my folks liked him and they liked him at the bank . . ."

"This promotion," Lucas said. "Who got it? After he died."

"Well . . . Wilson McDonald."

"Would Andy have gotten the promotion if he hadn't died? For sure?"

"*He* thought so. He said he'd aced Wilson out of the slot. I mean, it's never for sure until it's done, and Wilson has all those family connections . . . Why?"

"We're just trying to run down all possibilities," Lucas said vaguely.

She was too smart for that. One hand went to her throat and she leaned toward him and said, "Oh my God, do you think Wilson McDonald killed Andy to get promoted, and then shot Dan Kresge? He got Dan's job, didn't he?"

"Temporarily. There seems to be some doubt about it in the long run . . ."

She pointed a finger at him, excited: "Do you know about George Arris?"

"Yes . . ."

"Wilson got *his* promotion too."

"I haven't been able to establish that. Not clearly."

"Believe me, George would have gotten the job. My God, this never occurred to me," she said. She pushed the palm of her hand against her forehead. "How could I have missed it? It's so obvious."

"There's probably nothing to it," Lucas said.

"Oh, bull . . . feathers, Mr. Davenport. Three people dead and Wilson gets all the promotions? My God, he murdered Andy!"

"No-no-no. There's no evidence of that at all."

"Then why'd you bring it up?"

"Because I'm checking everything . . ."

"Wilson McDonald," she marveled. "Who would've thought."

"Please, Mrs. Ingall . . ."

He halfheartedly tried to talk her out of the sudden conviction that Wilson McDonald had killed her husband; then said goodbye.

He was out the door and on the sidewalk when she called after him: "Mr. Davenport?"

"Yes?" He turned and she came down the walk to him.

"If this was murder—just say it was, that somebody loosened up the bolts on the keel, okay? They couldn't have taken them all the way off, because then the only thing that would be holding it on would be some adhesive and sealer. Then, with a good bump, the keel might have fallen off in the harbor."

"Yeah?"

"So they had to leave the bolts partway on, expecting them to work off, which they eventually would have. But they couldn't know *when*. Toby and I usually went up with Andy, so whoever it was . . . wasn't just killing Andy," she said. "If Andy'd made the islands, we'd have been on the boat the next day, and it might've fallen off with us aboard. This guy, whoever it is—he was willing to kill all three of us."

LUCAS HAD LAST seen Sherrill when she left to pick up Bonnie Bonet, Robles's friend. When he got back, Sherrill and a uniformed cop were marching a young woman down the hall, her hands cuffed behind her back. Lucas caught up with them, said, "Bonet?"

"Yeah," Sherrill said.

Bonet snarled, "Who the fuck are you?"

"Sit her down in Homicide," Lucas said. "I'll be there in a minute."

"She wants an attorney," Sherrill said.

"Got any money?" Lucas asked.

Bonet shook her head defiantly. "No. You gotta appoint one."

Lucas nodded: "So call the public defender," he told Sherrill. "I'll be right back."

He dumped his coat and the file on Ingall in his office, and made a quick call: "I want everything we can find on Wilson McDonald. Everything."

BACK AT HOMICIDE, Bonet was sitting next to Sherrill's desk, while the uniformed cop lounged at another desk between her and the door. She'd been uncuffed and Sherrill was scratching notes on a legal pad.

When Lucas walked in, Bonet looked up and said, "I want the attorney. I'm not answering any questions without an attorney."

"I called. Somebody's walking over," Sherrill said.

"I'm not going to ask you a question, Ms. Bonet," Lucas said. "I'm gonna make a little speech. Mr. Robles says you told him you shot Daniel Kresge because you thought Kresge was setting up a bank merger and your mother would lose her job. But he says he really doesn't think you shot him, that you're making a grandstand play, because you like the attention. For the experience of it. To fuck us over. Do you know the first thing that will happen when the word of your arrest gets out? The bank's gonna fire your mother."

Bonet, naturally pale, went a shade paler. "They can't do that. That's discrimination . . ."

Lucas was shaking his head: "No. There's no union at the bank. They can fire her for any reason they want, as long as the firing isn't illegal—because of race or religion or like that. If her daughter is accused of murdering the bank president on her behalf . . . you think that's not a reason? I'll tell you what: Your mother's gonna be on the sidewalk in about half an hour, as soon as the *Star-Tribune* guy checks out the day's arrest reports. And they check every couple of hours."

Bonet looked at Sherrill, who nodded, then back at Lucas. "But I didn't shoot him," she blurted.

Sherrill dropped her pencil and said, "Oh, shit."

Lucas said, "Again, I'm not going to ask you any questions, but I'll say this: If there's anything that would prove that you didn't shoot him, this would be a good time to mention it."

"Friday night," Bonet said. "I was at a friend's house until almost four in the morning, we were on-line, gaming."

"How many people?" Lucas asked.

"Four . . . three besides me."

"She'd still have time to drive up there," Lucas said.

"It'd be tight," Sherrill said.

"But she could make it," Lucas said.

"I didn't shoot anybody," Bonet wailed. "I don't even know where the asshole lived."

"You were never up there?"

"Never. Why would I be?"

"After you left your friends, you went right home? Did you see anybody who knew you?"

"No . . . Well, I bought some Pepsi at the gas station, but they don't know me there. Maybe they'd remember me."

"What gas station?"

"It's an Amoco down off 494, like 494 and France."

"Did you pay with cash or a credit card?"

"Credit card!" Her face brightened. "The goddamn credit slip has the time and location on it. And it comes on my statement—I bet you can call Amoco and find out."

Lucas nodded and said, "Why'n the hell did you tell Robles that you shot McDonald?"

"Just to jerk his chain," Bonet said. "He called me up and he pretended to be all freaking out and worried, and the next thing I know, he's turned me in."

"He pretended to be freaking out?"

"Yeah. Pretended. He's a cold fish," Bonet said. "I'll tell you what, I wouldn't be surprised if he did it, and he deliberately set me up with that talk on the 'net about how to kill McDonald. I mean, he started it, I didn't. And then he fed me to you."

"Why do you think he might have done it?" Sherrill asked.

"Because of the way he plays with guns all the time," she said. "I think if you pretend to be killing people long enough, pretty soon you want to try it. Don't you think?"

Lucas's and Sherrill's eyes locked: they'd both killed people in gunfights. "I don't know," Lucas said finally. "Maybe."

Sherrill said, "What do you mean, plays with guns?"

"He's always out shooting. You know, rifles and pistols and sometimes he goes out to Wyoming and shoots prairie dogs. He calls them prairie rats. Or prairie pups. And he does that whole paintball thing. You know, runs around in the woods in camouflage clothes with other guys and they shoot each other."

"Robles," Lucas said.

"Yeah. He doesn't come off that way, does he?"

"Have you ever done the paintball thing with him?"

"No—he doesn't even know that I know about it. But I know a friend of his, and he saw us together, and he told me. I thought it was weird."

"Huh." Lucas rubbed his chin, then looked at Sherrill. "What do you think?"

"I think I should check with Amoco," Sherrill said. "And maybe start talking to people about Robles."

Lucas pointed a finger at Bonet: "If this checks out, we'll forget about it. But you keep your mouth shut about what happened. And what you told us. You don't talk to Robles about it, or anyone else. And remember what's at stake here. I'm talking about mom."

"Okay," she said, solemnly. A tear started in one eye.

"Okay," Lucas said. And to Sherrill: "Call Amoco."

ON THE WAY back to his office, Lucas bumped into an assistant public defender heading toward Homicide. She was carrying two briefcases, apparently full of briefs, which bumped alternately against her thighs as she walked. Her hair stood out from her round face in an electrocution halo. Her face was drawn with lack of sleep.

"On your way to see Marcy Sherrill?" Lucas asked.

She stopped and said, "Yeah. But if you're not done with the rubber hoses, I could wait. Maybe catch a nap."

"We're all done. We beat the truth out of her and she's innocent," Lucas said. "We're turning her loose in a few minutes."

"Really?" The lawyer yawned and said, "God, I've gone to bed with men who've said less pleasant things to me."

"Yeah, well . . . sleep tight."

"Won't let the bedbugs bite," she said with another yawn, and humped the briefcases on down the hall toward Homicide. Had to see for herself.

LUCAS SAT IN his office, his feet on his desk, and added up the accusations. After a while he picked up the phone and called Sherrill. "All done?"

"Yeah. She checked out with Amoco. She's gotta do some paperwork, then she's outa here."

"Who's loose? Besides you."

"Tom Black is sitting in a corner, reading *Playgirl*," she said. From somewhere behind her, her regular partner shouted, "I am not." Black was gay, but still mostly in the closet.

"Why don't you guys come on down? I'll tell you about it," Lucas said.

"Almost time to quit."

"It'll take ten minutes, and we won't do anything until tomorrow."

BLACK, PRETENDING TO be disgruntled, slumped in one of Lucas's two visitor's chairs, while Sherrill looked out the window at the street.

Lucas was saying, ". . . if somebody accused, say, Sloan of deliberately setting out to murder somebody, and actually doing it, I'd say, 'Nope, he couldn't do that.' The idea might occur to him, but someplace along the way, he just wouldn't do it."

"So?" Sherrill asked.

"We've got too many people to worry about, all of them with motives. So what we do is, we go around to people who know them well, and ask for a confidential assessment. Could they do it? Would they do it? What would have to be on the line for them to do it?"

Black cocked his head to one side and thought about it for a moment: "That's weird."

"And it could ship us off in a completely wrong direction," Sherrill said. "You've already decided Bone didn't do it, because you like him."

"No," Lucas said, shaking his head. "I do like him, but I haven't decided anything about him."

"But if you like him, you're sort of predisposed not to believe bad stuff."

Black ticked a finger at her: "Psychobabble," he said.

"Sorry," she said. Then, "What about O'Dell and the kaffiyeh? Who's gonna check that?"

"I'll ask her," Lucas said.

"Tomorrow?"

"Yeah." He yawned. "Tomorrow."

9

MARY WASHINGTON CALLED at nine-thirty, and when Weather Karkinnen picked up the phone, Mary said, "Oh good, you're still up," and Weather rolled her eyes and lied: "Just barely."

"Henri asked about you again today. He's interested," Washington said.

"Oh, my God, Mary, why don't *you* go after him?" Exasperation, but also a little tingle of pleasure?

" 'Cause I'm 'Let's have a couple beers and go bowling,' and Henri's 'Let's have a couple of glasses of champagne and talk about monoclonal antibodies.' "

"Well, thanks for the news," Weather said.

"Would you go out with him if he called?"

Henri was six three and had big eyes and long black eyelashes, was thin as a beanpole, balding, and spoke with a French accent. People who knew him well said he was almost too smart: Weather liked him. "I don't know, Mary," she said. "I'm still pretty messed up."

"I think I'm gonna suggest he give you a ring," Washington said.

"Mary . . ." Like being trapped in a high school locker room.

"Then maybe you can introduce me to one of those cops you know; somebody who bowls."

WEATHER HAD BEEN reading *The Wall Street Journal* when Mary called. When she got off the phone, she yawned, tossed the paper in the recycling pile, and headed for the bedroom.

Weather was sleeping again, finally. Her problem had been no less difficult than Lucas's, but hers had less to do with errant brain chemicals. Her problem was plain old post-traumatic shock. She'd pulled the academic studies up on MedLine, knew all the symptoms and lines of treatment, recognized the symptoms in herself—and was powerless to do anything about them.

The unbreakable barrier was Lucas Davenport.

She'd never really been in love with anyone before Lucas. But she'd been in love with him, all right—she'd recognized all those symptoms too. Then the shooting . . .

There'd always been something in Lucas that was hard, brutal, and remote. She'd been sure she could reach it, smooth it out. He needed that as much as she did: he didn't know it, but his taste for the street, his taste for violence, was killing him, in ways that weren't obvious to him. But she'd been wrong about reaching him: the violence was essential to him, she now believed.

The shooting in the hallway, which Lucas had set up, had all the earmarks of that immutable trait. He'd risked his own life, he'd risked hers, and he'd absolutely condemned Dick LaChaise to death, all on his own hook, without consulting anyone, without even much thinking about it. He'd just *done* it. When the Lucas Davenport machine was in gear, nobody had a way out—and when LaChaise had agreed to walk down the hall with Weather, he was dead no matter what else happened.

Weather could never quite put her finger on exactly how she objected to the killing of Dick LaChaise. Intellectually, she knew that she might easily have been killed by LaChaise if Lucas hadn't done what he'd done. Further, LaChaise was an undoubted killer, who deserved anything he got. She could say to herself—intellectually—*All right. It worked.*

Which had nothing to do with her emotional state.

Something had turned in her, the instant the bullet tore through LaChaise's skull. She couldn't talk to Lucas without experiencing the flash of terror when the gun went off, followed by the horror of the death. There, in the hallway, with LaChaise slumping to the floor, with the pistol spinning down the hallway . . . she was actually *wearing* LaChaise, the dead and dying remnants of the part of LaChaise that actually made him human . . .

SHE'D GOTTEN PAST the pills now. She was still talking to her shrink, Andi Manette, and Manette was pushing her to consider and reconsider Lucas.

But Weather wasn't doing that anymore. She'd realized that however deeply she loved him before the shooting, that feeling was dead. And the psychological flashes that carried her back to the killing were no longer tolerable. Lucas brought them on. The sight of his face, the sound of his voice.

She'd learned that she could live without him. She was going to do that. And she was beginning to suspect that sooner or later, she'd even start enjoying herself again. If she could keep him away . . .

She hadn't yet told this to Manette, much less to Lucas. She dreaded the idea: but the time was coming. Time to get on with her life.

WEATHER WENT TO bed early, as most surgeons did: she was on staff at three separate hospitals now, and the workload was increasing. She was operating five or six times a week, starting at seven in the morning. She'd be in bed by ten-thirty, up by six in the morning, walking into the women's locker room by six forty-five.

Went to bed every night feeling cool and lonely. But sleeping again.

She was in the very pit of the night when her subconscious picked up the sound of a car rolling to a stop outside the house, a subtle change from those few cars that simply tolled on by. In her dreams she thought, *Lucas?* though when awake she'd never remember the thought. But she was there, just rising to the cusp of consciousness, when the front window blew out.

SKEEEEEEEEEEEE.

The explosion shook her out of bed: she was up in an instant, not quite awake, but on her feet and moving; and as she moved, the smoke alarm in the living room went SKEEEEEEE.

She lurched into the hallway toward the living room; she was first aware of the light, then the heat, then the realization that she was staring into a fireball.

"No! No!"

And all the time: SKEEEEEEEEEE.

Weather moaned, registered her own moan as though she were standing out-of-body, then ran back down the hall to the bedroom, snatched up the bedside telephone and punched in 911. She got an immediate answer, and said, "My house just blew up. It's burning, I'm at . . ." And she dictated the address and said, "I've got to get out."

"Get outside immediately," the cool voice said. "Just drop the phone and—"

And the kitchen smoke alarm triggered, a slightly lower, less energetic note than the first, but just as loud: SKAAAAAAAAAAA.

She'd dropped the phone, almost stumbled over a pair of loafers on the dark floor, slipped them on, hit a light switch, was rewarded with lights. She padded back down the hall. The fireball seemed to have receded, or to have pulled back within itself: the flames were confined to the front room, to an area not much longer than her couch. There wasn't yet much smoke, although the fire was roaring ferociously.

Weather moved in three quick steps to the kitchen, pulled a fat semiprofessional fire extinguisher from under the sink, pulled the pin as she walked back to the living room, aimed the nozzle at the flames, and squeezed the trigger. Whatever kinds of chemical were in the extinguisher blew out in a fog, and the fire seemed to cave in, but just for a second, and then it was back: no matter how much of the chemical estinguisher she poured on, the fire would only retreat and spring up on another perimeter.

SKEEEEEEE, SKAAAAAAAA . . .

She stepped closer, working the chemical, felt it slackening in force. To her right, she felt the photo of her parents and grandparents staring down from the walls, black-and-white and hand-tinted photos she'd grown up with, memories she'd imported from her former home in the North Woods. With the extinguisher chemical almost gone, she tossed the container behind her, turned to the wall, and started pulling down the photos. Behind her, the fire burned with new authority, and she could feel the heat on her back and legs. She ran with the photos to the kitchen, fought her way back into the living room, tore open the low buffet, and took out a half-dozen photo albums and a box of photos she'd always meant to put in more albums.

And that was all she could do. The fire was growing quickly now, and she ran through the kitchen, well out onto the back lawn, dropped the albums, ran back inside—the smoke was heavy now, and she coughed, staggered—found the framed photos, and carried them through the smoke out back.

SKEEEEEEEEEEEEEEEE, AAAAAAAAA.

She could hear sirens: the nearest fire station was no more than three quarters of a mile away. She started back inside one last time, unaware that she was panting, that her hair was frizzing and uncurling with the heat, that she'd taken spark burns on her hands and arms, that she'd walked on broken glass and cut her feet. She felt it all as discomfort, but she wanted to save the last things, some dishes her mother gave her . . .

She couldn't reach them. The rug in the living room had ignited, and thick gray smoke was rolling through the house. She staggered back through the door just as the first of the fire engines arrived. She ran around the house as the firemen hopped off the truck, and yelled, "The front room . . ."

THE NOISE NEVER stopped: SKEEEEEEEEEE, SKAAAA-AAAAA.

Weather sat on the curb and watched the fireman knock down the front door.

And after a minute, she began to cry.

10

TEN O'CLOCK IN the morning was an early hour for a man to be recalcitrant, Lucas thought, especially if he wasn't a cop, but Stephen Jones was recalcitrant.

"Of course I'd like to help, but I have the damnedest feeling that if I talk to you, it's going to find its way into a gossip column."

"Not from me it won't," Lucas said.

A piece of art hung from the wall behind Jones's desk. The print was colorful and maybe even beautiful, though it resembled a woman hacked up with a pizza cutter. Lucas, who knew almost nothing about fine art, suspected it was a Picasso.

"And the thing is, if it does, I'd be severely damaged . . ."

"I can assure you it won't happen," Lucas said patiently.

Jones rubbed the back of his neck and said, "All right. If somebody absolutely pushed T-Bone up against the wall, when the only option was kill or be killed, he'd kill. But this situation isn't like that. He's already got a lot of money, and he's good enough that he could go somewhere else in a top job. So I don't see it."

"Assume that somehow, we don't know how, he was pushed to the wall. Emotionally, psychologically, or maybe he gambles and we don't know it."

Jones shook his head. "Even then . . . he's the kind of guy who'd always figure he could recover. Always get back. The thing is, he grew up poor. Did you know that?"

"No."

"Yeah, some cracker family down south somewhere, Louisiana, Mississippi, Alabama. He made it all on his own. He's a guy who figures he can always do it again. I don't think he'd . . ."

His voice died away.

"What?" Lucas asked.

"You know . . . If you come at this from another angle . . . We're talking about whether he'd cold-bloodedly kill someone because he'd lose money or his job; and I don't think he would. But I can see him killing somebody if the other person had something on him," Jones said. "Blackmail, for instance. If Kresge had something really serious on him, and threatened to use it, for some reason, I can see Bone killing him for that reason. Not to keep it from being used, but because the threat, or the extortion, would . . . besmirch his honor." He mused over the thought, then jerked his head in a nod: "Yep. That would do it. That's the only way I see Bone deliberately killing somebody. But it would have to be deadly serious, and it would have to be deadly personal."

"What about Terrance Robles?"

"I don't know him well enough to answer. I really don't."

"Susan O'Dell?"

"Susan couldn't do it. She's crusty and calculating and all that, but she's got a soft interior."

"I've seen a deer that would disagree with you," Lucas said.

"You mean the hunting? That's cultural," Jones said. "People from out there, out on the prairie, farmers, have a whole different attitude toward the life and death of animals than they do the life and death of people. I really don't think she could kill anyone. I'm not even sure she could do it in self-defense, to be honest with you. Nope. You're barking up the wrong tree with Susan."

"Wilson McDonald."

Jones frowned. "I can see him killing somebody, but it'd be in hot blood, not cold blood. If he was drunk and angry, he might strike out. He's got a violent streak, and he can be sneaky about it. But as for pulling off a calculated killing . . . I don't think so. Actually, I think he'd be chicken. He'd start imagining all the things that could go wrong, and, you know, being thrown in prison with a bunch of sodomites. I don't think so."

"What about the moral equation—would it be . . ."

"Oh, it wouldn't be a moral problem for him. He'd just be chicken. Wilson McDonald's a classic bully, with all the classic characteristics of a bully: he's a coward at heart."

LUCAS MET SHERRILL in the skyway off City Center, and she was shaking her head as she came up. "They're all innocent," she said. "What happened with Louise Freeman?"

Louise Freeman was the gossip mentioned by Bone's attorney friend Sandra Ollsen. "She and her old man went to New York," Lucas said. "She's back on Friday. I talked to Jones instead."

"How about Black? Did he get anything?"

"Haven't talked to him yet. He's supposed to call when he's done talking with Markham. So: You'll take Bennett, and I'll take Kerr."

"Why don't we go over to Saks first," she suggested. "You can buy me something expensive."

"I've got about twenty dollars on me," Lucas said.

"So let's go to the bank and you can take out a bunch of money."

"Give me a break, huh? I don't—" The phone in Sherrill's purse buzzed, and Lucas said, "Probably Black."

Sherrill fished the phone out of her purse, said, "Hello," listened, and passed the phone to Lucas. "Dispatch, looking for you."

Lucas took the phone: "Yeah?"

THE DISPATCHER SAID, "Lucas, a woman named Andi Manette is trying to get you. She says it's about a personal friend of yours and it's extremely urgent. You want the number?"

"Oh, Jesus," Lucas said. Andi Manette was Weather's shrink. "Hang on." He patted his pockets, found a pen and a slip of paper, and said, "What is it?"

He copied the number, punched the power button, punched it again, and dialed.

Manette picked it up on the first ring: "Yes?"

"Andi? This is Lucas."

"Lucas, I need to tell you something, but I don't want you running off to help. Nobody needs help."

"What? What?"

"Weather was . . . Somebody firebombed Weather's house last night. She was singed a little, and has some small cuts, but she's not badly hurt. She's going to be staying with us for a while, until this is straightened out."

"Firebombed! What do you mean, firebombed? Where is she?"

"The thing is, it would be best if you didn't go looking for her. She's pretty freaked out, and having you around, with all the associations, won't help."

"Well, Jesus Christ, Andi, what happened? Do I get to know that?"

"Nobody knows what happened. It's being handled by the Edina police."

"You don't mean just an explosion or something, you mean somebody threw a firebomb through her window."

"That's exactly what happened," Manette said. "Somebody threw a firebomb through her picture window."

"Andi, I swear to God I won't come after her, but where is she? Tell me that. Just tell me."

"She's at my house, taking a nap right now. She's had a couple of sedatives, she's feeling better. But we figured that people would let you know, and that I'd better talk to you."

"Let me know? My God, Andi, I'm probably a suspect. And even . . . I gotta call those guys."

"Don't call . . ."

"Not Weather. I've got to call Edina."

"Okay. But please don't come out, okay?"

"Okay."

"Thanks. You know I'm trying to bail this out for the two of you, and I'm bailing as hard as I can."

"Hey listen," Lucas said. "Thanks for calling me."

He punched off and Sherrill said, "Weather? Firebombed?" She looked perplexed.

"Yeah. Last night. Listen, you go after these other guys. I'm running out to Edina."

HE CALLED FIRST: The chief's name was Peter Hafman and Lucas barely knew him.

"Don't have much to show you," Hafman said. "Somebody walked up last night and pitched a gallon jug of gasoline through the front window. We've got bits of the wick, looks like a piece of ordinary cotton cloth, I'm told. There is one odd thing . . ."

"What?"

"The bottle was scored so it'd break easier. Scored with a glass cutter. The guys out here say that sounds like a pro."

"I never heard of that," Lucas said. "Look, could I come out and talk to your guys?"

"Come on ahead."

He rang off and handed the phone back to Sherrill, and it immediately beeped again. She answered and handed it back: Dispatch again.

You've got another call coming in. They say this one is urgent too."

"Put it through."

There was a click, and a woman said, "Chief Davenport?" She had a purring voice, a little smoky.

"Yes, this is Davenport. Who is this?"

"Did you know that Jim Bone was sleeping with Dan Kresge's wife? For a long time? And now she'll get all those options that used to be worthless?"

And the phone went dead. Lucas looked at it, looked at Sherrill.

"Now what?"

"That was our woman, I think."

"Really? What'd she say?"

"She said Jim Bone is sleeping with Kresge's wife. And that she's gonna get a pile of stock options now that he's dead."

Sherrill's eyebrows went up: "Any more goddamn clues and we'll have to get a secretary to keep track of them."

"Jim Bone," Lucas said. "Huh."

When Weather left Lucas, she'd stayed with the Manettes for a couple of weeks, then had taken over the lease on a small house being vacated by a University Hospitals surgical resident. Lucas had cruised it in city cars a half-dozen times, hoping to get a glimpse of her. He never had, but he knew the house.

Now he cruised it again, a ranch-style house of stone and clapboard that reminded him of his own house. It looked much the same as it always had, except that the front picture window, which looked out across the flagstone walk, was covered by a piece of unpainted plywood; and the eaves over the window were stained with soot.

He pulled into the driveway, got out, walked up to the front of the house, and peered through the small windows that flanked the center window. He was looking in at the front room: the place was a jumble of scorched furniture and carpeting, with burned drywall panels hanging down from the ceiling, books scattered across the floor in sodden clumps. He could smell the smoke and the water and the burned fiberglass insulation. No gasoline.

He stepped back, and as he turned to leave, noticed a woman watching from next door: she wasn't hiding, and didn't pretend to be doing anything else. She'd come outside to watch him. He headed toward her, dug out his identification.

"Hello. I'm Deputy Chief of Police Lucas Davenport from Minneapolis; I'm a friend of Weather's."

The frown on her face eased a bit, and she tried on a smile. "Oh, good. I've been trying to keep an eye on the place since last night."

"Thanks. I, uh, I'm on my way to talk to your police chief out here, and I thought I'd take a look . . . Listen, do you know if anybody saw anything last night? Or heard anything?"

"Nobody in my house heard anything until the fire engines, but Jane Yarrow across the street heard the window break. She said she didn't know it was a window breaking until later. She just heard *something*. And then she heard a car door slam, but she didn't get up until she heard the sirens. And that was about it—nothing like this ever happened here before."

THE CHIEF WAS out when Lucas arrived at Edina, but he was routed to a Detective James Brown. Brown was a tall, shambling man with a shock of white hair; he wore a rough tweed sportcoat with suede elbow patches, a blue oxford cloth shirt, and khakis with boat shoes. He looked like a professor of ancient languages.

"Not *the* James Brown?" Lucas asked.

"Why yes, I am," Brown said modestly. "This is my disguise: keeps the groupies off."

"Excellent strategy," Lucas said. He dropped into a chair beside Brown's desk.

Brown looked down at a file open on his desk, sighed, and said, "I understand you have a personal relationship with Weather Karkinnen."

"Had one; she broke it off," Lucas said. "I can't prove to you where I was at three o'clock this morning, 'cause I was home in bed, alone. But . . ." He shrugged. "I didn't do it."

"And even if you did, that's a pretty goddamn unbreakable alibi," Brown said.

Lucas said, "Hey . . . I didn't do it."

Brown sighed again and asked, "The chief told you about the scoring on the bottle?"

"Yeah. He said it looked like a pro job."

"That's what the fire guys say. You get a regular bottle, it might bounce, it might not even break. But with the scoring, it explodes when it hits the floor. Very fast, very efficient. What we think is, the bomber came in from the north, idled to a stop in front of the house, got out, leaving the car door open, walked up to the front of the house with the jug, flashed the wick with a cigarette lighter, and heaved it through the window. The whole thing, I timed it, would be ten to fifteen seconds, walking, from the time he got out of the car to the time he got back in. Then he rolled off down the street, around the corner, four blocks down to the highway, and back to Minneapolis. He was on the highway before Ms. Karkinnen even called 911."

"Who owns the place?"

"A couple named Bartlett—they're down in Florida. They'd rented it to a doctor for the past eight years, and then to your friend. Strictly an income property for them."

"Any reason they might want to torch it?"

"Nothing obvious—it's a good neighborhood, they could probably sell it for a lot more than they'd ever get from insurance. And they're pretty reputable people."

"Shit," Lucas said.

"All that stuff that was in the paper last winter . . . The LaChaises . . ."

"Yeah. That's what I'm afraid of," Lucas said.

Brown tapped his desk: "But one thing doesn't fit with that. Whoever did this wasn't trying real hard to kill her. I mean, if it was a pro job. They didn't even come close. She was in the back bedroom, ran out when she heard the window break, saw the fire, called 911, and if she hadn't tried to save her pictures, she wouldn't have been hurt at all."

"She was hurt?" Lucas sat up, angry now. "I was told she wasn't . . ."

"Not bad, not bad," Brown said. "She got a couple of small cuts on her feet from broken glass, and her hair was singed, and she got some small spark burns on one hand. But she told us she has some operations tomorrow and she expects to do them."

LUCAS TOOK IT slow driving back to Minneapolis, pulling threads together. Black checked in on Lucas's car phone: "I had to do some psychotherapy on this Markham asshole, but the bottom line is, he thinks O'Dell couldn't do it."

"All right. You got another one yet?"

"L. Z. Drake," Black said. "Went to school with McDonald."

"Call when you get done."

"Yeah. Hey, you know about Weather?"

"Yeah. How'd you hear?"

"They had some pictures of the house in a news brief . . . Markham had his TV on the whole time I was talking to him. They said she was okay."

"Yeah, yeah . . ."

"You think there's any chance it's another comeback from LaChaise?"

"I don't know what to think."

"All right," said Black. "I'll call you after I talk to Drake."

SLOAN AND FRANKLIN were waiting outside Lucas's office when Lucas got back. Both of them had been involved in the shoot-out that killed the two LaChaise women the winter before, though Sloan hadn't fired his weapon and hadn't been a direct target of the reprisal attacks. Franklin, on the other hand, had been shot in his own driveway.

"We've been talking, man," Franklin said in his booming voice. Lucas was large; Franklin dwarfed him. "We gotta look into this, unless there's some motive for somebody hittin' Weather."

"How'd you hear about it?"

"It's all over the department, it's been on TV," Sloan said.

"You think I oughta call my folks, get them out of the house?" Franklin asked.

"I don't know," Lucas said. They were milling in the hall, and he saw Sherrill starting down toward them. "I don't know what's going on. Nobody's got a motive that I can figure, and there's a possibility that it was a pro job."

"Why a pro job?" Sloan asked. As Sherrill came up, Franklin said to her, "Could've been a pro job."

"You're sure?" Sherrill asked.

Lucas told them about the scored bottle. "That's it," Franklin said. "I'm putting the old lady in a motel."

Black arrived as they were talking about it, stood on the edge of the discussion: he hadn't been in the shoot-out, hadn't been a target.

"I think what we need to do before we panic, is we need to get everybody we got out on the street," Lucas said. "I'll talk to Intelligence and Narcotics and the gang people, I'll talk to St. Paul, and every one of us has got people . . . Let's get out there and dig for a few hours. If this is a group, somebody'll know."

"Loring's got the good biker contacts," Franklin said. "He's been working nights, he's probably home asleep. You want me to roust him?"

"Get him moving," Lucas said.

"I'll find Del, get him started," Sloan said.

"I'm outa here," said Franklin.

As the group started to break up, Black said, "Lucas, I talked to this guy Drake about McDonald."

"Oh, yeah." Old news; he wasn't thinking about McDonald anymore.

Black continued: "I had to push him, but he says he knew McDonald all the way through school, and he has a real violent streak. Bottom line was, Drake thinks he could kill somebody if he decided it was necessary. He said McDonald was a big guy, played a little high school football, and he and a couple of other guys stalked another kid for a couple of years, a little wimpy guy, beat him up a half-dozen times just because they knew they could make him cry in front of the girls . . ."

"Yeah, yeah," Lucas said impatiently. "We can pick that up later."

And as Black left, Sherrill, who'd been drifting away, said from down the hall, "You were gonna talk to O'Dell today . . ."

"No time now," Lucas said. He remembered the phone call about Bone sleeping with Kresge, but pushed the memory away. "Let's get out on the street."

11

THE POLARIS BANK tower was a rabbit warren of meeting, training, and conference rooms, but only one of them was The Room.

The Room was on the fortieth floor, guarded by two thick oak doors.

No Formica here, no commercial carpeting or stainless steel. The conference table was twenty feet long and made of page-cut walnut; the chairs were walnut and bronze and plush crimson cushions; the lighting was subtle and recessed. The floor was oak parquet, accented with Quashqa'i rugs.

An alcove at one side of the room contained a refrigerator stocked with soft drinks and sparkling water. A small bar was tucked discreetly away under a countertop, and a coffeemaker kept fresh three flavors of hot coffee, as well as hot water for anyone who wanted to brew tea. A Limoges-style sugar bowl and creamer waited next to an array of delicate cups and small serving plates. On the countertop itself was a tray of sandwiches cut into equilateral triangles, cookies, and a freshly opened box of Godiva chocolates.

Constance Rondeau probed the box of chocolates, her sharp nose moving up and down like a bird going after a worm. O'Dell watched her work over the box, and realized that she recognized individual types among the Godiva variety, and was picking out the good ones.

O'Dell pulled herself back: she was drifting. Oakes was talking.

". . . do agree that somebody had to take the reins. We've got too much going on, and it's too dangerous out there right now. And somebody's got to work with Midland . . ." If Rondeau looked like a bird, Shelley Oakes looked like a porkpie—all puffy and round-faced.

"But my point is," said Loren Bunde, "we can't take forever finding someone. We don't have the time, with this merger going on. We probably ought to go over to Midland and get one of their mechanics, and just pull the thing together."

"Where would his loyalty be?" asked Bone. "It'd have to be with Midland, because that'll be the successor bank. He'd find a way to screw us: hell, that'd be his job. I definitely think we should go with the merger: but on our terms. They need us. We don't really need them. We've got the fifty-dollar price in play, but if everything shakes out right, we'll get seventy-five."

"Nobody ever mentioned seventy-five," said Rondeau, looking up from the Godiva chocolates with a light in her eye.

"I think that would be a minimum. I don't know what was going on between

Midland and Dan Kresge, but something was going on," Bone said. "Fifty dollars is ridiculous. One-for-one is ridiculous. We should get cash as well: I don't think a hundred is out of the question."

"I think it is," O'Dell said bluntly. "I think seventy-five is on the outer edge of any sane possibility."

"You don't know what you're talking about," Bone said.

O'Dell ignored him, and looked around at the other board members: "Listen: We *must* reconsider the possibility of continuing as an independent," she said. "An immediate merger on the proposed terms would turn some quick profits for all of us, myself included. But the merger talk alone has pushed the stock price, and we'll keep most of that whether or not we merge. So that much is locked in. And the fact is, if the new management were to take what I think is a proper view of the board and its duties, and the top management and its duties, then additional compensation would be provided anyway. There are also benefits available to board members and top management that we will lose in a merger, no matter how much money we got right away."

After a moment of silence, somebody asked, "Like what?"

O'Dell smiled and said, "There's quite a wide range of possibilities . . . A little research on what other boards get as compensation could point to some interesting alternatives. Tax-free alternatives, I might add."

McDonald sat at the far end of the table, where Kresge had always sat, watching the talk, struggling to keep up with it. Bone and O'Dell were clearly at odds, Bone pushing for the proposed merger, O'Dell resisting.

"All these possibilities should be explored," he ventured ponderously. "But I do think that we should consider Polaris's position as a major community asset. We've been here for a hundred years and more, and a lot of us wouldn't be where we are today if we hadn't had the ear of some friendly people at Polaris . . ."

He droned on, losing most of the board immediately. John Goff had the right to buy almost forty thousand shares of Polaris at prices ranging from twelve dollars a share to forty-one dollars, most of it at the lower end. Using a scratch pad and a pocket calculator, he began running all the option prices against Bone's suggestion that they might get a hundred.

Dafne Bose was drawing an airplane on her scratch pad. The bank had a small twin-prop, mostly used for flying audit and management teams to small banks out in the countryside. But what if the bank were to buy something really nice—a small jet—and what if it were available to the board? It probably should be, anyway. A plane like that would be worth tens of thousands of dollars a year, none of it visible to the IRS. O'Dell said there were other possibilities. Bose underlined the plane and looked up at O'Dell, who smiled back.

"Yeah, yeah, that's all fine," Goff said, when McDonald appeared to be running down. "So we've all got a lot to think about. I would propose that we leave everything as is: Wilson speaks for us, but we ask Susan and Jim each to prepare a report on their respective ideas, deliverable before Friday noon to each of us. That's quick, that's only a couple of days, but we gotta move on this. I further suggest that we meet again next Monday to consider the reports. We'd want a complete discussion of all the, uh, options, and at that time we can consider how to go forward."

He looked around, got nods of assent. For just a fleeting, tiny part of a second, O'Dell and Bone locked eyes. Only two of them were left. McDonald had just been cut out. Whoever's report was adopted would be running the place in a week.

McDonald didn't understand that yet. He harrumphed, allowed that the reports were probably a good idea, and after a few more minutes of talk, the board adjourned.

O'DELL ORDERED CARLA Wyte and Louise Compton to her office as soon as she got out of the meeting. Marcus Kent, her other major ally, was too exposed to meet with her publicly, since he technically worked for Bone.

"Everything I said was true," O'Dell told Wyte and Compton. "The trouble is, it's not money in hand. I need exact, specific examples of the kind of payoff we can deliver to board members and top management if they adopt my approach."

She turned to Wyte: "You're the numbers person. I want you to nail down the numbers on this stuff, so they'll know what they'll get, and how much it'll cost the bank, and what the tax consequences will be. Do you know Pat Zebeka?"

Wyte was scribbling on a yellow pad: "I've heard of him. A lawyer."

"Tax guy, one of the best, and he's done a lot of compensation work. Get with him—on my budget, I'll fix it—and get a laundry list of everything we can offer that will provide tax advantages."

And to Compton, who never took notes on anything, because if you never took notes, nobody could subpoena them: "I want charts from you. Get the details from Carla, and put them together in a package. It's gotta be good, and it's gotta be clear. Not so simple they'll be insulted, but they've got to see what they'll get. It has to be as real as the dollars they'd get from a merger. And another thing—there are some pretty big advantages to being on the Polaris board. We need to put together a list of those advantages. Social status stuff."

"Good. What about polling the board?" Compton asked.

"I'm talking to them, the ones I can get. And I've got to talk to McDonald. Tonight, if I can. I'm not sure if the idiot knows he's out of it, but he's got to find out sometime."

"From you? Do you think that's smart? He might be insulted."

O'Dell shook her head: "Has to be done. I've got to get to him before Bone, and I can make him an offer Bone can't."

"What?" Wyte asked.

"I'm president and CEO, but he's board chairman. Talking is what he does best anyway. In a couple of years, when the bank's mine . . ." She flipped a hand dismissively. ". . . he can go away."

"Why couldn't Bone offer him—" Compton stopped herself, shook her head. "Sorry. Stupid question. If Bone gets it, the bank's gonna go away."

BONE TOLD BAKI to coordinate a graphics package on how much money would be available through the merger: he would provide the details. "If you do this right, Kerin, and by that I mean if you do this perfectly . . ."

"What?" Kerin Baki was like a piece of blond ironwood, he thought, brutally efficient, great to look at, but cold. Distant. A Finn, he'd heard. Sometimes she was so chilly he could feel the frost coming off her. He couldn't see her with a southern boy, but thought she might go well with somebody like, say, Davenport.

"You'll be the most important person in the bank, since I can't do shit without you." She disapproved of extraneous vulgarities, which is why he sometimes used them. And what she did next surprised him—almost shocked him. She sat down across his desk and crossed her legs. Good legs. Maybe even great legs.

"I hope you've talked with the board members. Privately, I mean," she said.

"I've started . . ."

"You've got to do better than start," she said. "This is a campaign, not a party."

"Well, I'll—"

"Have you talked to McDonald?"

"No. He's out of it . . ."

"I know. But he's got friends on the board. He can possibly throw them to O'Dell. So you've got to talk to McDonald and do it soon. Call Spacek at Midland and find out if they can find some kind of figurehead job for him after the merger. Vice chairman of the merged banks, or something . . ."

Bone nodded: "Good idea. I'll do that." He looked at her, gauging the change in their relationship, then took the step: "What else?" he asked.

"I've only got one more thing—well, two more things. First, your old pal Marcus Kent works for O'Dell. Everything you tell him goes to her."

Bone's eyebrows went up. "Since when?"

"Since he decided he wanted your job, which was about two minutes after you hired him."

"Little asshole," Bone grumbled, not particularly surprised. "I'll take care of him later. You said two things. What's the other one?"

"I want you to do me a favor."

"Sure. What?"

"I'll tell you when you're given the job. All you have to do now is promise to do me a favor."

"You mean . . . blind? You won't tell me what favor?"

She nodded. She was so serious, so cool, so remote, that he nodded in return. "All right. I hate to do it blind, but if it's anything like rational, I'll do you a favor."

She nodded once again, quickly, ticking the commitment off some mental list.

"I mean, money? A title?" he asked.

"I'll tell you later," she said. And for a fraction of a second, he thought she almost smiled. "Now: I can get a graphics guy to actually put our presentation together, but we might also want some kind of short video presentation from Midland, from Spacek himself, probably. That means we'll need to check the VCR up in The Room."

Bone slapped his forehead: "That's great. I'll talk to Spacek as soon as we're done here." He looked at his watch: "Plenty of time."

"What else?" she asked.

"I need to talk to a guy named Gerry Nicolas. Today. He runs the state pension fund, I don't know the formal name."

"I'll get it," she said. "May I ask why? Just so I can stay current and see how you're thinking?"

Oddly enough, Bone thought, he trusted her: "Because his constituents don't know anything about the stock market, but they know he hasn't gotten them fifteen percent on their money this year, and they want to know why. He's feeling a little shaky, and he also happens to own almost six million shares of our stock which, until the merger talk started, had been sitting in his portfolio like a brick. He's now up sixty million, and due to go up quite a few more if the merger goes through. If it doesn't, he's sucking wind again."

"So if you tell him the board is thinking about backing out . . ."

"He'll be on the phone to the board. And he's got some serious clout when it comes to electing board members."

"Good. That's exactly how we've got to think." She stood up. "I know this changes our relationship somewhat, Mr. Bone, but I really think you'll have a much better chance at this job if you listen seriously to my proposals. And I'll critique yours."

"Of course," he said.

"Don't dismiss me like that," she snapped. "I'm as smart as you are. I might not know as much about investments, but I know a lot more about the way this place really works. If I'm going to save my job, you've got to listen to me."

He laughed despite himself, and again, was somewhat shocked: "Is that what this is all about? Saving your job?"

"That's half of it," she said.

"What's the other half?"

"The favor you're going to do me—that's the other half."

As she was going out the door, he said, "Maybe you better start calling me Jim."

She stopped, seemed to think for a minute, pushed her glasses up her nose, and said, "Not yet."

"THEY'RE GONNA SCREW you," Audrey McDonald shouted. Wilson was in the den, staring at a yellow pad. Audrey had gone to the kitchen to get a bowl of nacho chips and a glass of water; she snuck the vodka bottle out of the lazy Susan, poured two ounces into the glass, gulped it down, took a pull at the bottle, screwed the top back on, put it back on the lazy Susan, turned it halfway around, and shut the cupboard door. Then she stuffed a half-dozen nachos in her mouth to cover any scent of alcohol, got a full glass of water and the bowl of chips, and carried them back to the den.

"If they were gonna give you the job . . ."

"I heard you, I heard you," Wilson McDonald snarled. "I heard you a dozen fuckin' times. You're so full of shit sometimes, Audrey, that you don't even know you're full of shit. I'm running the board—I chaired the meeting today—I can handle them."

"Yeah? How many board members have you talked to, who were willing to commit?"

He was shoving a fistful of chips into his mouth, chewed once, and said, "Eirich and Goff and Brandt . . ."

"You told me that Brandt—"

"I know what I said," he shouted. "I'll get the fucker. That sonofabitch." Brandt had equivocated.

"You can't count on—"

The phone rang, and they both turned to look at it. "Did you talk to your father?" Audrey asked.

"Yes."

"Huh." She stood up, took two steps, picked up the phone. "Hello? . . . Yes, this is Audrey." She turned to look at Wilson. "Why yes, he's here, somewhere. Let me call him."

She pressed the receiver to her chest and said, "It's Susan O'Dell. She said she needs to talk to you right away."

"Okay. Jesus, I wonder what she wants, right away?"

"It won't be good news," Audrey said. She was seized by a sudden dread, looking at her husband's querulousness. This wasn't going right.

Wilson took the phone. "Hello?" He listened for a moment, then said, "Sure, that'll be okay. Give us an hour . . . Okay, see you then."

"What?"

"She's coming over. She wants to cut a deal."

Audrey brightened: "If we can cut a deal, we knock Bone right out of contention. For that, we could offer her quite a bit."

"That's right. And we basically agree on—" The phone rang again, and he turned and picked it up, expecting to hear O'Dell's voice again. "Hello?"

Again he listened, and finally: "Really can't until about, say, ten o'clock. We've got guests . . . Okay, we stay up late anyway. See you then."

He hung up and Audrey raised her eyebrows.

"Bone," he said. "And *he* wants to cut a deal."

Audrey smiled, almost chortled: "My my. Aren't we popular tonight. Aren't we popular . . ." The half a glass of vodka was brightening the world, right along with the phone calls. "We've got some planning to do."

O'DELL CAME AND went.

Bone came and went.

McDonald went up to the bedroom, found a bottle of scotch he'd hidden in the closet, ripped off the top and took a long pull. "Jesus fuckin' Christ," he bellowed. "What's wrong with me? What the fuck is wrong?"

Audrey cowered in the doorway. "Are they right? Are they right, Wilson?" She'd been back to the lazy Susan, this time for a full glass of the vodka.

"That motherfucking Brandt, that traitor," McDonald screamed. He took another long pull at the bottle, two swallows, three, four. When he took the bottle down, he seemed stunned. "How could the fuckers do that?"

And suddenly he was blubbering, his face red as a stop sign, the bottle hanging by his side.

"Call your father," Audrey offered. "Maybe he—"

"Fuck that old asshole," McDonald screamed. "I'm dying. I'm fucking dying." He began pulling at his shirt and when it came off, threw it in a wad on the floor. Audrey retreated to the hall, saw him trot into the bathroom, heard the water start in the oversized tub. A moment later, his trousers flew out the door, followed by his shorts.

"Wilson, we really don't have time for this. We've got to get ourselves together. Just because they said—"

"They were right, you stupid fuckin' cow," McDonald screamed. And he ran out of the bathroom, nude now, his penis bobbing up and down like a crab apple on a windy day. "I'm gone. I'm out of it. I'm dead in the fuckin' water . . ."

He spun around, looking for booze, found it in his hand. He was already drunk: he'd finished half a fifth downstairs before he ran up to get the new bottle. Audrey, desperate, tried to rein him in. O'Dell and Bone couldn't be right. The job couldn't be gone. He couldn't be out of it.

"Maybe O'Dell's offer, the chairmanship . . ."

"I'd be out of there in a month," he shouted. "I'd be nothing . . ."

"Wilson, I think if we—"

"And you, you bitch." McDonald turned, his small eyes going flat as he moved toward her. "You sure as shit didn't do anything to help. *We've got some planning to do*," he mimicked, quoting her from early in the evening. "*We've got yellow pads to fill up . . .* And then they waltz in and tell me I'm done."

"They're wrong."

"Shut up," he bellowed, and he hit her, open-handed. The blow picked her up, smashed her head against the doorjamb, and she went down, dazed, tried to crawl away. "You fuckin' come back here, you're gonna answer for this." He kicked her in the buttock, and she went down on her stomach. He stopped, nearly fell, caught himself, grabbed one of her feet and dragged her toward the bedroom.

"Wilson," she screamed. She rolled and tried to hold on to the carpet, then the doorjamb. "Don't, please don't." Tried to distract him "Wilson, we've got to work."

"Shut up," he screamed again, and he dropped her foot and grabbed the front of her blouse. Made powerful by the booze, he picked her bodily off the floor and hurled her at a wall. She hit with a flat smack and went down again. "Crazy fuckin' bitch . . ." he mumbled, and he took another pull at the bottle. "When I get fuckin' finished with you, you won't be able to fuckin' *crawl* . . ."

12

V ERY EARLY IN the morning. Cold, damp, with the sense that frost was sparkling off exposed skin.

Loring wore a suit that was almost exactly lime green, with a yellow silk shirt and tan alligator shoes, and a beige ankle-length plains duster, worn open. On someone else, the outfit might have looked strange. On Loring, who was slightly larger than a Buick, it was frightening.

"Now just take it easy in there," Loring rasped. "Everything is cool with everybody."

They were in an alley on the south side, walking toward a clapboard garage with silvered windows. "Whose garage?" Lucas asked.

"A friend of Cotina's. The guy's straight, they rode together before Cotina got wild. He's the only guy in Minneapolis that Cotina knew who'd loan them a spot to meet with the cops."

"Could've fuckin' done it downtown," Lucas grumbled.

Loring shook his head: "He's got those warrants out and he's paranoid. He says he's gonna turn himself in."

"Right," Lucas said.

"But he's got some shit to do first."

"Like peddling a ton of Ice to make bail and pay legal fees."

"Probably; but it ain't like the warrants are any big deal. Assault and shit like that."

"All right," Lucas said. They walked up to the garage and Loring banged on an access door. A man opened it, peered out.

"Just the two of you?"

"Yeah, just the two," Loring said.

The man let them in: he was thin, wore a T-shirt with bare arms, despite the chilly weather. A leather jacket hung on a single chair that sat in the middle of the garage, while a jet-black Harley softtail squatted against the overhead door, ready to run.

Lucas looked around: "So where is he?"

"Be here in a minute," the man said.

"Who're you?"

"Bob," the man said. He'd taken a cell phone out of the jacket pocket, punched in a number, waited a minute, and spoke: "Yeah, they're here. Yeah. Okay." He punched off and said, "They're just gonna cruise the neighborhood for a minute, then they'll be here."

Lucas turned and looked out the windows—the silver film was one-way, so anyone inside could see out, but people outside would see only their own reflection—and after a few seconds of silence, Bob asked Loring, "You still ride?"

"Yeah, when I can. My old lady's kind of gone off it, though."

"You been to Sturgis lately?"

"Went this year," Loring said. "Pretty decent."

"Not like the old days, though."

"No. Everybody gettin' old."

"That's the truth. Everybody's got gray hair. We look like the Grateful Dead."

Loring nodded: "Half the people out there brought their bikes in vans, just rode in the last five miles."

"Were you there the year we burned the shitters?"

"Yeah, that was good," Loring said.

Lucas broke in: "This is them? Two red bikes?"

Bob leaned sideways to look out the window. Two bikers in jackets, sunglasses, and gloves were rolling slowly toward the garage. "That's them," Bob said.

The bikers coasted to the side of the alley, killed the engines, climbed off, a little stiff, maybe a little wary. Lucas dropped his hand in his pocket around the stock of his .45, which he'd cocked before they went in. His thumb found the safety and nestled there. Loring's hand drifted to his hip: Loring carried a Smith .40 in the small of his back. A second later, the door popped open, and Charlie Cotina slouched through the door, pulling off his gloves. He was dressed in a plain black leather jacket and jeans, with black chaps and boots. His escort wore Seed colors with a red bandana. Cotina looked quickly at Loring, nodded, then at Lucas, at Lucas's hand, and then back to his face.

"Is that a gun?"

"Yeah."

"Bet you can get it out of there fast," he said.

"I took the jacket to a tailor, and had him fix the pockets," Lucas said.

Cotina nodded, looked at Loring: "This was supposed to be friendly."

"This is friendly, if you've got anything to say," Lucas said.

"I ain't got much," Cotina said, looking back to Lucas. "Just this: We didn't have nothin' to do with that firebomb. Nobody in the Seed is looking for the cops. Whatever happened to LaChaise and his friends is their business. They was out of the group when they come after you. None of us have nothin' against you, and we're stayin' away."

"Maybe you've got some crazy in the group," Lucas said.

But Cotina was shaking his head, again looking at Loring: "You know this bunch of fuckin' hosers: if anybody threw a bomb through this broad's window, it'd be all over town in fifteen minutes. Nobody's said shit, which means to me that nobody we know did it. And I been askin'."

Lucas looked at him for ten seconds without speaking, and Cotina stared back, eyes small and black, like a fer-de-lance. Finally, Lucas nodded, put his free hand in his opposite coat pocket, pulled out a business card, and handed it to Cotina. "If you hear anything, call us. Might be worth something to you someday . . . if you ever go to court."

"Do that," Cotina grunted. And he turned and left, his escort pulling the door shut behind them.

Lucas relaxed a notch, and Bob said, "It'd be polite to give them a minute to get out of here."

"Fuck 'em," said Lucas. But he handed a card to Bob as the bikes fired up: "Same thing applies to you. If you hear anything, it could be worth something in the future."

Bob took it: "Get out of jail free?"

Lucas said, "Depends on what you're in for. But could be."

"Good deal," Bob said. He tucked the card in his hip pocket.

Lucas nodded and Loring led the way through the door, squinting in the brighter light outside. Cotina and his escort were just disappearing around the corner, leaning into the curve. Lucas bent over and picked up his card where Cotina had dropped it. "Must not want to get out of jail," Lucas said.

"He had to do it; he'd have to face problems if he kept it," Loring said. As they walked back to the city car, Loring asked, "What do you think?"

"You're the expert," Lucas said.

"I think he was telling the truth."

Lucas nodded. "So do I. Which creates some problems. Like, who the fuck bombed Weather?"

THEY MET SLOAN and Del at a Northside diner, and Sloan pushed the business section of the *Star-Tribune* across the table at Lucas.

"The bank deal has people freaking out—turns out three or four public pension funds own a big piece of Polaris, and if this merger caves in, so does the stock price," Sloan said. "I don't know if that could have anything to do with Kresge."

"Don't see how," Lucas said. He took the paper and scanned the article. Bone was quoted as saying the merger was still on track, and the bank was continuing to work toward the merger. Further down in the article, an unidentified executive said that the merger was being "reconsidered."

"Snakepit," Sloan said.

"Yeah, they're setting up for a fight over there," Lucas said. He pushed the paper back to Sloan and picked up a menu. Everything featured grease. "I bet Susan O'Dell is the unidentified executive."

"Whatever. But this sounds like pretty heavy pressure to keep the merger going; which would piss off the killer if he was trying to stop it."

Lucas had been preoccupied by the firebombing, but now looked up from the diner menu and said, "Bone's the main guy behind keeping it moving . . . which is sort of odd, when you think about it."

"Why?"

"Because most of those kinds of guys dream about being at the top. Running something. If this goes the way the papers have it outlined, the Bone gets the job, he'll be putting himself out in the cold in a few months."

"With about a zillion dollars," Del said.

"Yeah, there's that . . . The thing is, should we put a watch on him? If some goofball is roaming around out there, trying to stop the merger, he'd be the next target."

"Maybe talk to him, anyway," Sloan said.

LUCAS TOOK A call on the car phone, transferred in from Dispatch: "Why haven't you arrested Wilson McDonald?" A woman's voice, angry, but under tight control.

He said, "Who are you? Who is this?" and in the passenger seat beside him, Del took a phone out of his coat pocket and started punching in a number.

"A person who is trying to help," the woman said. "He almost beat his wife to death last night. You've got to arrest him before he kills someone."

Click. She was gone. Del was talking to Dispatch, but Lucas said, "She's off," and Del said into the phone, "So do you have a number?"

They did. "Find out where it came from."

Pay phone. Up north, off I-694. Nothing there.

"Who is it?" Lucas asked Del. "She knows everything."

"Who'd know that Wilson McDonald beat up his wife last night? Especially if they both try to keep it quiet?"

Lucas thought about it, then said, "Somebody in the family, maybe—and then there's Mrs. McDonald herself."

"Anonymous calls—she doesn't take the rap if her old man finds out about them."

"Yeah . . . you remember Annette what's-her-name?"

"Honegger: I was thinking the same thing. And what happened to her."

"Yeah." Lucas bit his lip. "They ever find her hands and feet?"

"Not as far as I know."

SHIRLEY KNOX WASN'T a particularly good receptionist, but she did know a cop when she saw one. As Lucas and Del climbed out of Lucas's Porsche, she muttered, "Oh, shit," picked up the telephone, pushed the intercom button, and said, "Mr. Knox—Mr. Johnson is here to see you."

Out in the warehouse, Carl Knox was standing next to a foot-tall pile of illegally imported Iranian rugs. He looked up at the speaker as his daughter's voice died away, said, as she had, "Oh, shit," and then, "Wonder what they want?" To the man standing next to him, he said, "I'll slow them down, you throw the rugs back in the box. If you got time, put a couple nails in the lid. Hurry."

Carl Knox didn't know exactly how it had happened, but over the years he'd become the Twin Cities' answer to the Mafia—or to organized crime, at any rate. He'd gotten his start twenty-five years earlier, stealing Caterpillar earthmoving equipment, a line which he still pursued with enthusiasm. Half of the Caterpillar gear north of the 55th parallel had gone through his hands, as well as most of the repair parts when they broke down.

He'd done well stealing Caterpillar. So well, in fact, that he'd piled up a couple hundred thousand unexplainable dollars, which inflation—this was back in the late seventies—began eating alive. Then he'd met a man named Merchant, who explained to him the street need for quick untraceable cash, which led Knox to becoming the Cities' largest prime-lending loan shark. He didn't actually shark himself, he simply loaned to sharks . . .

And that led to his introduction to gambling, and it occurred to him that you could run a pretty sizable book with the computer equipment he was using to locate the Caterpillar equipment he was planning to steal . . . and pretty soon one of his subsidiary partners was running the Cities' largest sports book. But he'd never put any hits out on anyone, and while the occasional broken bone didn't necessarily make him queasy—especially when the bone wasn't his own—his Twin Cities attitude toward violence was, "Damn it, that sort of thing shouldn't be necessary."

Carl Knox hustled his skinny butt into the showroom. A nice rehabbed Caterpillar 966 wheel loader was on display, with a fresh yellow paint job, just outside through the big front windows where he could admire it. As he walked in, he saw Del Capslock slouching toward the reception desk, where Shirley was concentrating on her gum chewing. Capslock was followed by another man, bigger and darker. Knox knew both the face and the name, though he'd never met him.

"Mr. Capslock," he called, a smile on his face. The smile was almost genuine, because Capslock usually wanted nothing more than information. Del spotted him, and drifted over, in that odd street-boy sidle of his.

"Mr. Knox," he said. He lifted a thumb over his shoulder to the dark man behind him. "This is Mr. Davenport."

"Mr. Davenport—Chief Davenport—I've heard much about you." Knox beamed.

"And I've heard about you," Lucas said.

"What can I do for you gentlemen?" Knox asked. "A D9 for that gold mine, maybe?"

"We need you to call up your assholes and have them ask about a firebomb thrown through the window of Weather Karkinnen over in Edina," Lucas said. His voice was friendly enough, and Knox presumed.

"My assholes? What—"

"Don't pull my weenie, Knox," Lucas said, and the friendliness was gone— snap—without transition. "This is a serious matter, and if I have to pull down this fuckin' warehouse with a crowbar to convince you it's serious, I'll call up and get some crowbars."

The hail-fellow disappeared from Knox's face: "How the fuck am I supposed to know about somebody gets a bomb?"

"You saw it on TV?" Del asked.

"Saw it on Channel Three, they were talking about the Seed coming after your asses again. I got nothin' to do with the Seed . . ."

"We're off the Seed," Lucas said. "We're looking for a new angle. So we want you to call up all your particular jerk-offs and tell them to start asking around. You can call me at my office in say . . . four hours. Four hours ought to be enough time."

"Jesus Christ, I'd need more time than that," Knox said. "I can't do nothing in four hours . . ."

"We don't have any time. We want to know where this is coming from, and why," Lucas said.

"So I can ask—"

"Ask," Lucas said. He held out a business card, and Knox took it. "Four hours."

"WE'RE SPINNING OUR wheels," Lucas said, as he settled behind the wheel of the Porsche.

"You know what you gotta do?" Del asked.

Lucas shook his head and started the car.

"You gotta talk to Weather," Del said. "We gotta know that it's not coming from her direction, instead of ours."

"Can't do it," Lucas said.

"Get Sherrill to do it," Del said. "Another woman, that oughta be okay."

"I'll think about it," Lucas said.

"Gotta do it, unless something comes up," Del said. "I told the old lady to hang out at her mom's tonight. Until we find out."

Del had an improbably good marriage, and Lucas nodded. "Good . . . God-damnit, I can't go see Weather."

Del didn't answer. He simply stared out the passenger-side window, watching the darkening fall landscape go by. "Hate this time of year, waiting for winter," he said finally. "Cold coming. Wish it was August."

COPS WERE WANDERING in and out of Lucas's office—nobody had anything—when Knox called back.

"You owe me," Knox said. "I came down on everybody, hard."

"I said four hours, it's been six," Lucas said.

"Fuck four hours," Knox said. "I had to take six, because in four I wasn't getting anything."

Lucas sat up: "So what'd you get in six?"

"Same thing: nothing," Knox said. "And that makes me think that whoever did it is nuts. This isn't a *guy*, this is some freak. Bet it was a neighborhood kid has the hots for her, or something like that. 'Cause it's coming out of nowhere."

"Thanks for nothing," Lucas said.

"Hey: I didn't give you nothing," Knox objected. "I'm telling you serious: There's nothing on the street. Nothing. Zippo. This was not a pro job, not a gang job, not bikers. This had to be one guy, for his own reasons. Or we woulda heard."

Lucas thought about it for a minute, said, "Okay," and dropped the phone on the hook.

"What?" Sherrill asked. She was parked in a chair across the desk and looked dead tired.

"Knox got nothing, says there's nothing on the street."

"He's right."

"Damn it." He turned in his chair, staring out the window at the early darkness.

"Want me to talk to Weather? Del mentioned something . . ."

"Damn it . . ." He didn't answer for a moment, then sighed and said, "I'm gonna do it."

"Want me to come along?"

"No . . . well, maybe. Let me talk to her shrink."

ANDI MANETTE WAS angry about the interview: "You're not helping any-thing."

Lucas's anger flashed right back: "Not everything can be resolved by counseling, Dr. Manette. We've got somebody throwing firebombs, and I've got cops hiding their wives and kids. They're afraid it's another comeback from the crazies. I gotta talk to her."

After a moment: "I can understand that. Weather's probably at her house right now, salvaging what she can—there's smoke in everything. It'd be better if you talked to her here, at my place."

"All right. When? But it's gotta be soon."

"I'll call her. How about . . . Give us two hours."

"Do you want me to bring another cop? I can bring Marcy Sherrill if that'd help—maybe it'd make it seem more official and less personal. If that'd be good."

"I don't know if it'd make any difference, but bring her along. Maybe it'll help."

HE HADN'T SEEN Weather in almost a month; and when Lucas walked in the door of Andi Manette's house, trailed by Sherrill, the sight of her stopped him cold. She was curled in a living room chair, a physical gesture that he knew too well. She was a small woman, and often curled in chairs like a cat, her feet pulled up, her nose in a book—and when she turned toward him, she smiled reflexively and it was almost like everything was . . . okay.

Then the smile faded, and Sherrill bumped him from the back. He stepped forward and nothing was okay.

"How've you been?" he mumbled.

"Well: the firebomb . . ."

"Sorry; stupid question. But you know."

"I know: I've been okay." The smile was long gone now, and her face was tense, her voice controlled. "But the firebomb—do you think it might be the Seed?"

Lucas shook his head, found a chair, sat down. Sherrill was wearing a leather jacket, and she pulled it off to reveal a very large cherry-stocked .357 Magnum in a black leather shoulder rig. She looked like an S-and-M magazine's cover girl. "Not the Seed," Lucas said. "I talked to their head guy, and we've had feelers out everywhere. It's not the Seed."

"A crazy man?"

"That's the consensus right now."

"Unless you've got something going on that we don't know about," Sherrill interjected. "Have you had any serious problems with unhappy patients, or relatives of unhappy patients, or maybe state cases from the psycho hospitals . . . like that?"

Weather frowned, thought for a moment, then shook her head: "Not that I know of."

Sherrill leaned forward a bit: "I only know you a little bit, and I don't want to step on either your feet or Lucas's feet. But how about new relationships?

Or men who think you might be interested, who you blew off? There's usually some kind of emotional basis for a nut attack."

Weather was shaking her head: "Nothing like that."

"Any kids?" Lucas asked. "Any teenage boys trying to cut your grass for you, water your lawn? Just hanging around?"

"No . . . Lucas, I've been racking my brains trying to think of anybody who might do this. Any hint. People from back home, people from the hospital, from the university, cops, but . . . there's nobody. Not to just come walking up some evening and throw a bomb through the window."

"Goddamnit," Lucas said.

"My best idea was that somebody was trying to get at you through me," Weather said. "Remember that newspaper article after the thing with Andi and John Mail? 'The Pals of Lucas Davenport'? Maybe somebody who goes way back read that article—maybe somebody in prison at the time—and decided to come after me. There'd be no way for an outsider to know that we'd broken off the relationship. So . . . I think you might look at your past, more than mine. That is, if it's not just some random crazy man."

"How about the landlords? Would they—"

"Oh God, Lucas, no. They're the nicest people in the world. I called to tell them about the house, and they were worried about *me*. No. Not them."

"All right." Lucas looked at Sherrill: "Anything else?"

"Not if she's sure she's not the target. But Weather, if you think of *anything* . . ."

"I'll call Lucas the next minute," she said.

"So is that it?" Andi Manette asked.

Lucas looked at Weather for a long five seconds, then to Manette: "Yeah, that's it."

Outside on the sidewalk, with the door closing behind them, Sherrill pulled on her jacket and said, "Whew."

"What?"

"She said that thing about breaking off the relationship, and you never even flinched. And she just said it like . . ."

"It was done."

"Yeah."

"I flinched," Lucas said.

"God," Sherrill said. Then, after a while, "Bad day."

REAL BAD DAY.

That night, a little after ten-thirty, Wilson McDonald was shaking his hand in James T. Bone's face, sputtering, "Vice chairman. That's nothing! Nothing! You're treating me like a piece of shit."

Bone said, "Look, Wilson—you're not gonna get the top spot. You're just not. I can commit to leaving you as top guy in the mortgage company. I can get you the vice chairman's job with the merged bank. But I can't say what'll happen after the merger."

"Not gonna be any fuckin' merger," McDonald said. He'd never taken off his coat. He headed for the door, turned when he got there, and said, "And you're never gonna run the goddamned bank. Maybe I can't get it myself, but I can fuck you up."

And he was gone.

Kerin Baki said, "If they go to O'Dell, we may have a problem."

Bone shook his head. "Not necessarily. O'Dell needs ten. I can't see more than seven or eight. And frankly, I don't think McDonald can swing votes. Why should people swing on his say-so? He's gone."

"It's not all power and money equations," Baki said. "Some of it's family and friendship. And all he has to do is swing maybe two votes . . ."

"I don't think he can do it," Bone said.

"You're underestimating O'Dell," Baki said.

"No. I just know what I'm willing to do, and what I'm not. If she gets it—so be it. But I don't think she will."

REAL BAD DAY.

Susan O'Dell took a small red diabetic candy from a bowl on her coffee table, unrolled the cellophane with her fingertips, popped the candy in her mouth, and said, "I'm sure about Anderson, Bunde, Sanderson, Eirich, Sojen, and Goff. If you can give me Spartz, Rondeau, Young, and Brandt, then we've got it: we've got ten."

"We can. Wilson talked to his father today, and he's got Rondeau's commitment. Spartz, Young, and Brandt have already committed to whatever Wilson wants to do," Audrey McDonald said. Audrey was sitting on a love seat, her feet squarely on the floor, her purse squarely on her lap. Her whole body hurt, but nothing had been broken. When Wilson beat you, he did it carefully. Thoroughly, but carefully.

"We've got to be sure," O'Dell said.

"I'll get written commitments if you wish," Audrey said stiffly. She hated O'Dell, but this was necessary.

"That's absurd," O'Dell said. "Nobody would do that. And it's not necessary. No—I want to talk to them. It'll all be very pleasant, but we have to talk."

"I'll arrange it," Audrey said. "But we do want your commitment in writing. We won't be able to show it to anyone, of course, if you go through with your end . . . but if you don't do what you say, we'll . . . hurt you with it."

O'Dell shook her head. "Can't do it."

"You can if you want the job," Audrey said. She twisted slightly, trying to ease a cramp in her back. He really *had* hurt her.

O'Dell sat silently for a moment. Then: "Can I call you tomorrow? First thing?"

"First thing," Audrey said. "There's not a lot of time left."

Audrey looked old, O'Dell thought, looking after her as she scuttled away toward the elevator. They were of an age, but already Audrey was bent over, stiff.

O'Dell worked out, both for strength and flexibility. She was a long-range planner, and had every intention of living to a nice ripe ninety.

AFTER LETTING AUDREY out, O'Dell went to the refrigerator, got a bottle of Dos Equis, popped the top, and sat down on the couch to think about it. Five minutes later the telephone burped from the end table, a single half-ring. She waited, but whoever it was had rung off. She took a couple of sips of the beer, leaned sideways and picked up the phone, punched in Louise Compton's number.

Compton picked it up on the third ring, and O'Dell said, "Audrey McDonald was just here. She said she can deliver Spartz, Rondeau, Young, and Brandt. But there are some conditions."

"Like what?"

"Like they want a written statement: I'm president and CEO, but Wilson gets the chairman's job. He'd just be a figurehead, but the salaries would be the same."

"That sounds . . ."

"Illegal. It might be."

"Why don't you see if you could commit yourself with a couple of witnesses—maybe a couple of the board members—rather than putting it in writing. Then in a couple of years, when we've got the place under control . . ."

"We bump him off."

"Exactly."

"I like your thinking," O'Dell said. The doorbell rang, and she turned, frowned. "Somebody at the door. Hang on."

O'Dell hopped off the couch and hurried across the living room, looked through the peephole into the hallway, frowned, and opened the door.

"I . . ." Then she saw the muzzle of the gun. "No," she said.

In the narrow space of the reception hall, the shot sounded like the end of the world, and for O'Dell, it was. The slug hit her in the eye, and knocked out the back of her skull.

She went down on her back, and a second later another shot hit her in the forehead: but she was already dead.

The telephone lay on the couch, and a tiny, tinny voice screamed "Susan? Susan, what was that? Susan?"

A real bad day for Susan O'Dell.

13

LUCAS STEPPED OUT of the elevator, brushed past a couple of uniformed cops in the hallway, stopped in O'Dell's door and looked down at the body. She was lying flat on her back, her feet toed in, her nose pointed straight up. Her face had been ruined by the two gunshots; a small bloodstain was visible in the carpet below her skull. He could smell the blood.

"What the fuck is this?" Lucas asked in anger and utter disgust. "What the fuck is it?"

An older plainclothes cop named Swanson was sitting in a ladder-back chair, flipping through an appointment book. "Same old shit," he said. Swanson had seen maybe six hundred murders in his career. "Watch your feet, nothing's been processed."

His partner, who was named Riley, said, "We got that McDonald woman coming over. She was here just before the shooting."

"Audrey McDonald? How do we know that?" Lucas asked. He was walking around O'Dell, peering down at the body as though a clue might be written on it.

"O'Dell was on the phone with a friend from the bank when she was killed. The friend—uh, let me see, Louise Compton—called us, called 911. But anyway, just before O'Dell was killed, she told this Compton that Audrey McDonald had just left. We understand you've been talking to her. Audrey McDonald."

"Never laid eyes on her," Lucas said. "Talked to her husband." He squatted next to O'Dell, picked out the powder burns on her face. Small- to medium-caliber pistol, fired from a few inches away, he thought. "Got a slug?"

Swanson pointed a pistol at an entryway wall. "Right there . . . we'll get it. And it looks like maybe the second shot was fired when she was already down, so it might be right under her head. Wooden floors."

"What about this friend? Compton?"

"She's on her way—ought to be here any minute, actually."

"Let's get something over her then," Lucas said. "Cover her up."

"I'll get it," Riley said.

"What time we got?" Lucas asked.

"Compton called 911 at eleven-oh-four," Swanson said. "She say she was on the phone, heard the shots, and when O'Dell didn't come to the phone after she screamed for a few seconds, she called. So we figure it was a minute or two after eleven o'clock."

"You know, Sloan and Sherrill have already interviewed everybody involved," Lucas said. "Maybe you ought to get them up here."

"All right I'll give 'em a ring."

"Christ, what a mess," Lucas said, turning away from the body. "She opens the door and bang. That's all."

"That's about the way we see it . . . We called you because you're up-to-date on this bank thing—we figured if it's a goofball knocking off the top guys . . ."

"Doesn't make sense," Lucas said. "She's the wrong one to get shot."

"Huh?"

"We thought Kresge was shot because he was pushing a merge with a bigger bank. But O'Dell was going after his job on the basis of *stopping* the merger."

Swanson said, "Maybe the merger doesn't have anything to do with it. Maybe they were killed for some bank reason, but nothing to do with the merger."

Lucas said, "I don't know."

"Whatever happened with the firebomb business?" Swanson asked.

"Nothing. Just fuckin' nothin'," Lucas said. His mind switched tracks to the firebomb. And Knox, the Caterpillar man, was probably right, he thought. A kid in the neighborhood who liked to watch fires. But not a street action.

RILEY PULLED A rubber sheet over O'Dell's body and stood up and turned. People in the hall. Then Wilson McDonald stepped through the door, jerked to a halt when he saw the figure on the floor, and said, "My God, is that her?" Audrey McDonald followed reluctantly, a foot or two behind, and peeked around her husband at the covered body. She reminded Lucas of a small, brown hen.

Swanson was just punching off his cell phone: Sloan was on the way. "Who're you?" Swanson asked.

"Wilson and Audrey McDonald . . ." McDonald spotted Lucas emerging from the kitchen hallway. Lucas had taken a quick tour of the apartment after talking to Swanson, but had found nothing that meant anything to him. "Officer Davenport . . . what happened?"

"Somebody shot O'Dell," Lucas said flatly. He examined McDonald, then his wife, then said, "Where were you tonight at eleven o'clock?"

McDonald flushed: "Are you questioning *me?*"

"Do you have an answer to the question?"

McDonald looked at his wife, then said, "I was driving home. I'd just left Jim Bone's place."

"Your wife was here, and you were at Jim Bone's?"

"Yes. We were trying to put together a deal on the succession to Dan Kresge. We needed to talk to the two of them simultaneously."

Lucas shifted his gaze to Audrey: "And you were driving home as well."

"Yes." She touched her throat. "I was."

Her voice touched a memory cell: "How long were you here?" Lucas asked. "And what did you decide?"

"We were arranging—" Wilson McDonald started, but Lucas waved him down.

"Please let your wife answer," Lucas said.

McDonald looked down at Audrey, who said, falteringly, "Well, we were arranging . . . talking about . . . votes on the board of directors. The board appeared to be split three ways, and if we could arrange an alliance with one or the other of them . . ." She shrugged.

And Lucas recognized the voice as the woman on the telephone earlier that day. He wasn't absolutely positive, but he would have bet on it. The timbre of her voice and the pacing of the words were very close.

"Did you see anyone in the hall when you left? Or downstairs?" Swanson asked, swerving off the topic.

"There were some people downstairs, but nobody I recognized," Audrey said. "There wasn't anybody up here. The hallway is short . . ." She pointed back to the hall through the open apartment door. "There're only two apartments."

Lucas pulled them back to the meeting: "What did you decide? Did you get your alliance?"

"Well . . ." Audrey looked at her husband, whose lips were pressed tight in anger.

"This has nothing to do with who killed Susan O'Dell, does it?" he asked. "You're trying to screw me so your pal Bone gets the CEO's job."

"He's not my pal," Lucas snapped back.

"No? Who handled the money for your IPO and the management buyout? And you were in his office last week talking about me. I haven't done anything and you've been spreading rumors that are killing me."

Lucas shook his head: "Routine . . ."

"Bullshit. My lawyer used to be a cop, and he says it's nothing like routine."

"So get your lawyer down here if you want," Lucas said. "But I want an answer: Did you strike a deal with Susan O'Dell?"

Wilson McDonald looked down at his wife, who stared back, then nodded almost imperceptibly. Wilson turned back to Lucas: "Yes, we did. Between the two of us, we had the votes. She becomes president, I become chairman. I work on strategic issues, she works on day-to-day matters."

"How about Bone?"

He shook his head: "Bone is committed to the merger. We couldn't talk."

"So, if O'Dell hadn't been shot, you'd have had the job."

"And Bone would have been out," McDonald said. "Why don't you go ask your pal about that one?"

Swanson stepped in: "Mr. McDonald, we're gonna ask you to step out into the hallway while we talk to your wife. No big problem, you can take a chair if you wish, but we need a statement from her, a sort of blow-by-blow account of everything that happened."

"I thought she had a right to an attorney," McDonald blustered.

"She does," Swanson said, "And if she wants one, we can wait until you get somebody here. But we're not accusing her of anything at all. We just want to hear what happened."

"Then why can't I stay?"

"Because you have a way of answering her questions for her. We've been through this before, and we've just gotten to the point where we ask the spouse to step outside. An attorney's fine, if she wants one now, or she can ask for one at any time."

McDonald looked at his wife for a moment, as if weighing the possibility that she would say something strange under questioning, then looked back at Swanson and nodded. "I'll take a chair." And to Audrey: "The minute they push the wrong button, you come get me, and we'll have Harrison get up here."

"Okay," she said, swallowing nervously. "Don't go far away."

WHEN WILSON MCDONALD had gone, Lucas said, "Detective Swanson is going to talk to you for a few minutes, then Detective Sloan will want to ask a few questions—Detective Sloan has already spoken to your husband . . ."

"Up at Dan's cabin—he told me about it," Audrey said. She seemed more assertive when her husband wasn't around.

"I have to leave in a minute or two, but I'd like to talk to you privately just for a moment, you and I," Lucas said. He looked at Swanson. "I just need to speak to her for a second."

"Sure."

Lucas escorted her into O'Dell's kitchen, lowered his voice: "I believe I spoke to you earlier today."

"What?" Was she really surprised? he wondered. There was an instant of surprise in her eyes. "I don't believe so."

"Mrs. McDonald, you have a rather nasty bruise on your leg, just above your ankle: Is that new?"

"I just . . ." She looked away, groped for a word. ". . . bumped myself."

"No, you didn't," he said. "Your husband beat you up last night. Would you like a call from the domestic intervention people?"

"No, no, we only had a little argument."

"If we took you downtown and had one of our policewomen take a look at you, she'd find a lot of bruises, wouldn't she?"

"That's illegal. I want to see my husband."

"Okay." Lucas raised his hands. "Like I said, this is just between you and me. If you don't want to make a complaint, I'm not going to insist on it. But you should. It never gets better, it always gets worse."

"Things will get better. Wilson's been under a lot of stress. This job . . ."

"Just a job," Lucas said.

"Oh, no." She was shocked. "This . . . this is everything."

BEFORE HE LEFT, Lucas took Swanson aside: "Treat her very carefully. Get as much as you can on her—personal history, everything—and tell Sloan that I want her wrung out, but not scared. Don't push her into getting an attorney."

"Are we trying for anything in particular?" Swanson asked. He turned half sideways to look at Audrey, who was perched on a chair in O'Dell's home office.

"If we can do it—very gently—it'd be nice to get a wedge between her and her husband. Don't be obvious, but if the opportunity comes up, it'd be good to let her know that her interests and her husband's are not necessarily the same."

BACK IN HIS car, Lucas picked up the car phone and called St. Anne's College, which was located a few blocks from his house in St. Paul. He told the St. Anne's operator that he knew it was late and nuns commonly don't take calls from men in the middle of the night, that this was an emergency and perhaps a matter of life and death, that he was with the police department . . . and he got his nun.

Sister Mary Joseph, a psychology professor and childhood friend he'd always known as Elle Kruger: "Lucas? Is somebody hurt?" A sharp, somewhat astringent voice, becoming more so as they got older.

"Nothing like that, Elle. I'm sorry to disturb you, but I have a couple of questions on a case."

"Oh, good. I was afraid . . . Anyway, have you read the *Iliad* lately?"

"Uh, no, actually." He looked at his watch. Had to get to Bone's place.

"Have you ever read it?"

"That's the one . . . No, that's the *Odyssey*. I guess not. Same guy, though, right?"

"Lucas . . ." She sounded exasperated. "I keep forgetting you were a jock. Listen, go down and get the *Iliad*, the one that's translated by Robert Fagles, that's the one I'm reading now, and I'll tell you what parts to read if you don't want to read the whole thing."

"Elle . . ."

"The thing is, this translation is much coarser, in all the right places, than the old ones—my goodness, the Trojan War resembled one of your gang wars. That was always obscured by the language of the other translations, but this one . . . the language is brilliantly apt."

"Elle, Elle—tell me later. I'm calling from my car and I've got a serious question."

She stopped with the *Iliad*: "Which is?"

"If a woman is routinely beaten by her husband, is it likely that she might betray him behind his back, while defending him when he was around?"

"Of course—wouldn't you if you were in her shoes?"

"No."

"No, you probably wouldn't. You'd probably go after him with a baseball bat . . . But yes, a woman might do that."

"I'm not talking about some kind of *pro forma* defense. I'm talking about really believing in the defense. But at the same time, betraying him to the police anonymously, then denying it even to the police."

"This isn't a theoretical question."

"No."

"Then you're dealing with a badly abused woman who needs treatment—if it's not too late for treatment. Some people, if they're abused badly enough, will identify with and even love their abusers, while another side of their personality is desperately trying to get out of the relationship. Just to use a kind of layman's terminology, you could say you have a condition of . . . mmm . . . stress-induced multiple-personality disorder. The part of her personality that sincerely defends her husband may not even know that the other part of her personality is betraying him."

"Shit . . . Excuse me," Lucas said. "So even if I broke her out from her husband in, say, a murder case, she could be impeached as being nuts."

" 'Nuts' is not accepted terminology, Lucas," she said.

"But she could be impeached . . ."

"Worse than that. If she were required to testify in the presence of her husband, she might flip over and start defending him—lying—because he so dominates her personality."

"All right."

"Will I be meeting this woman?"

"Probably not, Elle. I'll tell you about it next time we talk. Right now, I'm running."

"Take care."

"You too."

BONE LIVED IN a high-security building much like O'Dell's, and not more than a five-minute walk away. Lucas dumped the Porsche in a no-parking zone outside the glass front doors, and when a security guard came to the doors, flashed his ID and was admitted to the lobby.

"I need to talk to James T. Bone," Lucas said.

"Don't know if Mr. Bone is in. He often goes out at night," the guard said, moving behind the security console.

"Ring him and let it ring about fifty times," Lucas said.

The guard did that, and after a few seconds, said into the phone, "Mr. Bone, this is William downstairs. I'm sorry to bother you, but there's a police officer here asking to see you . . . Yes, Deputy Chief Davenport, and he says it's urgent. Yes sir."

He hung up the phone: "Mr. Bone is on fourteen," he said. "Take the elevator on the right."

BONE WAS WAITING in the hallway outside his apartment door: as Lucas got off the elevator, he realized that this hallway also had only two doors, as had O'Dell's. Something ticked at the back of his mind, but the thought was gone as Bone stepped out and said, "What's going on?"

Bone was wearing jeans and a T-shirt, but was barefoot.

"You alone?"

"No, actually, I have a friend here . . . Come on in. What happened?"

Lucas stepped inside. A woman, about Bone's age, was sitting on the couch.

"This is Marcia Kresge, Dan Kresge's wife. We were just talking strategy."

"Was Wilson McDonald here an hour ago?" Lucas asked.

Bone looked at his watch: "Well, more than an hour. He left here probably at ten-thirty or ten forty-five."

"Ten-thirty. Have you been here ever since?"

"Yes . . . Marcia got here about . . ."

"About eleven-twenty," said Kresge.

"So what happened to McDonald?" Bone demanded.

"Did you make a deal with McDonald?" Lucas asked, ignoring the question.

Bone looked at Kresge, then back at Lucas: "No. What's he done?"

"So you're out of the job. Because he made a deal with Susan O'Dell."

"Oh, no, I'm not out of it at all." Bone shook his head. "Wilson thinks he can deliver several votes to Susan. He doesn't know it, but he can't. Well, maybe one. The rest are still up for grabs. Now what the hell happened?"

Lucas looked at Kresge, then back at Bone, interested in their reactions. "A couple of minutes after eleven o'clock, somebody rang the doorbell at Susan O'Dell's apartment, and when she opened the door, shot her twice in the head with a handgun. O'Dell's dead."

And they were, as far as Lucas could tell, stunned. Astonished.

Bone, who didn't seem given to sputtering, sputtered, "That's not possible. I just talked to her tonight."

"What time?"

"Seven o'clock or so." He looked at Kresge. "About the Community College deal."

Kresge was solemn: "You know what? It's a crazy man. We could be next."

"Mr. Bone, I don't want to imply anything, but you're the obvious beneficiary of all this—the top job is opened up by a murder, then the main competition is eliminated. Again, I don't mean to imply anything, but we really have to pin down where you were, and what you were doing all evening." He turned to the woman. "And the same with you, I'm afraid."

"Do you really think I'd do this?" Bone asked. He sounded more curious than afraid.

Lucas thought for a moment and then said, "I don't know you well enough to say. But even if I didn't, I have to make sure. If McDonald left here a little after ten-thirty, and you were here alone, and the woman didn't get here until eleven-thirty . . . who has an alibi?"

"I wasn't alone," Bone said. "I'm sorry, I should have said so . . . My assistant, I think you met her at the bank, the blonde? Kerin Baki? She was here. We were working on a presentation for the board."

"When did she leave?"

"A few minutes after Wilson—she was heading down to the bank. She's probably still there," Bone said. "And between the time she left and the time Marcia got here, I made a half-dozen phone calls. There must be some way to get at phone records."

Lucas nodded. "We'll get those."

And Bone said, "I'll tell you something else: We know exactly how many votes I've got, which is nine. And we know how many Susan had, which is seven. I'm one vote away. At least three votes are uncommitted, and we were just working out ways to get one of those three. Because when we get one, all the others will come." He hopped off the couch, and started to prowl the apartment as he talked. "So what I'm saying is, I think I had the top job. This might knock me out—or slow things down. If the board thinks there's the slightest chance that I'm implicated, I'm dead meat. Better to hire somebody else, and apologize to me later, if I'm innocent, than get stuck with a CEO who turns out to be a killer."

"You know who the real beneficiary is?" Kresge said. "Wilson McDonald."

"He made a deal with her," Lucas said.

Kresge made a rude noise: "She might have made a tactical agreement with him, just to grab the top slot. But after she'd gotten rid of Bone and a few other people, she'd have gotten rid of McDonald. She and Jim were actually friends, in a way—but she hated McDonald."

"But everybody says McDonald's out of it."

"Not if there's nobody else left," Kresge said. She looked at Bone. "Jim darling, I'd be very careful if I were you. Very careful."

BONE AND KRESGE agreed to stay at the apartment until Sloan got there. Lucas talked to Sloan by phone, and Sloan said he was nearly done with the McDonalds.

"What do you think?" Lucas asked.

"When I talk to Mrs. McDonald alone, she's pretty straight," Sloan said. "When I get her around her old man, she's a fucking ventriloquist's dummy."

"I talked to Elle Kruger about that. She said severely abused women can get like that."

"We need to give McDonald a good look," Sloan said. "Something tells me he's involved. I don't know if I think that because he's really involved, or because I just don't like the sonofabitch."

"Listen, when you get to Bone's . . . get him aside and talk to him about his sex life. Who he's screwing. Because I think that tip about him sleeping with Kresge is right. You'll understand what I mean when you see them together. And find out if he's screwing his assistant. She's a little chilly, but that's probably just me. Maybe Bone can warm her up."

"I'll do that," Sloan said.

"And you'll need to talk to the assistant. I'll give you her name and you can call her, and get her over to Bone's."

"Where're you going?"

"Home to make a list," Lucas said. "This fuckin' thing is starting to confuse me."

14

LUCAS LIVED IN a ranch-style house in St. Paul, on a road that ran along the top of a Mississippi River bluff. From his front window he could see the lights of Minneapolis across the river. The neighborhood was quiet, fine for walking, and he and Weather had walked a lot when they were together.

Weather.

Why would somebody hit Weather? The Edina cops had exactly nothing. Zero. Zip. No likely neighborhood kids. One of the Edina guys had checked on Lucas—would he do it, why wouldn't he do it. He'd been told emphatically that Lucas would not, and the cops had gone away.

But Lucas couldn't accept it as a nutcase. Nutcases didn't pick out random houses to bomb; or if they did, the chances of hitting someone with Weather's history were . . .

Impossible. Not just slim. Impossible.

HE'D ONCE CONVERTED the master bedroom to use as a den, but after Weather arrived, he'd converted it back to a bedroom, and moved his drawing table into one of the smaller bedrooms. He hadn't worked on a commercial game for years now: everything had gone to computers, and while he might still develop ideas and scenarios, he was rapidly moving away from game development.

Too much money, he thought sometimes. He'd made too much money, almost inadvertently, as sometimes happened in the computer age. He'd drifted from writing tabletop war games to writing game scenarios, which a University of Minnesota computer freak turned into games, to writing simulations of police emergencies to be played out on police computers. And his company had simply grown, first run out of his hip pocket, then with the computer freak, and finally by a professional businessman who'd taken the company public.

And now that he really didn't need to write games, didn't need to sit up until three in the morning thinking of new sci-fi beasts to challenge computer geekdom . . . he didn't. He missed it, but he didn't do it.

NOW HE SAT at his drawing table, cleared away detritus from earlier skull sessions, pulled out a sheet of heavy paper and started making a chart.

The situation at the bank was too complicated. There were too many suspects, and all of them had motives. He needed to simplify and clarify.

But the firebombing prowled around the edge of his consciousness: that's what he needed to settle. The bank killings were almost technical problems, problems that cops solved. The firebombing was personal. What if it was aimed at him rather than Weather? But why would it be?

What if Weather had a new boyfriend, a freak of some kind? Naw. That wasn't Weather. She had a built-in bullshit detector, and nobody would get past that. Maybe she snubbed somebody . . .

Goddamnit. Work. The suspects:

Wilson and Audrey McDonald. What appeared to be a possibly explosive relationship; who knew what might be brewing in that little perfecta? And the more he thought of it, the more he thought that Audrey McDonald was the woman who'd called him—who was pointing the finger at her own husband.

JIM BONE. AND Marcia Kresge and Kerin Baki.

He chewed on the end of his pencil. Baki was a little thin—what would she get out of the killings? Her job? An assistant's job didn't seem heavy enough, but hell, it might to the assistant. Bone, of course, had that reputation as a ladies' man, and supposedly had been sleeping with Kresge's wife. What if he was also sleeping with the assistant? And if he was, so what? There might be some kind of twisted connection between an illicit relationship between Bone and Marcia Kresge, and the killing of Dan Kresge, but even if they had a relationship, how could that lead to the killing of O'Dell?

Blackmail? He remembered one of Bone's colleagues saying that Bone wouldn't tolerate blackmail. Could O'Dell have tried? But Bone, if he wasn't bullshitting about the phone records, pretty much had an alibi. Of course, the phones could be finessed.

Then there was Mr. X.

A Mr. X who might be killing for the reason everybody suspected—to stop the merger—either to save his job or simply as an expression of the general feeling at the bank. But if the killer was a Mr. X, he'd be almost impossible to find. And nobody knew what jobs would be lost yet. And why would he kill O'Dell, who'd taken a stand against the merger?

The killing of O'Dell, Lucas decided, had been an insane risk. Neither the McDonalds nor Bone's group had enough to gain by killing her, to take the risk. If anybody had come along while the killer was going up and down in the elevator, they'd have been cooked . . .

Lucas frowned, thought about that for a minute, then called Dispatch. "Is Swanson still at the O'Dell apartment?"

"Yes, I believe so. You want his phone number?"

"Give it to me." He wrote the number at the top of his suspect sheet, then punched it into the phone.

"Yeah. Swanson."

"This is Lucas. Is Louise Compton there yet?"

"Yeah, right here, want to talk to her?"

"Put her on."

"HELLO?"

"Ms. Compton, sorry to bother you . . . Could you tell me the exact words that Ms. O'Dell said to you when the doorbell rang? Did you actually *hear* the doorbell ring?"

"No, I didn't hear the bell . . . She just said, 'There's somebody at the door,' and the next thing I heard was the shots." Compton's voice was breaking up under the stress of the killing, and ranged from hoarse squawks to sudden squeaks; every word was like a nail on a blackboard.

"Was she a good friend of yours?"

"No, not socially—she was my boss. Oh, God, I can't believe . . ."

"You wouldn't know who she was seeing socially . . . in a sexual sense, I mean."

"I . . . I don't think she was seeing anyone. Not at the moment. Not for quite a while. She has a friend over at North, but he's gay. They sort of squire each other around, when she needs an escort. Or he does."

"And she said that Audrey McDonald had already left?"

"Yes. She said she put Audrey in the elevator, and ran right back to call me."

"She put Audrey in the elevator."

"That's what she said. And that's what she usually does—you know, the elevator is right by her door, she steps out to see you off. Like stepping out on the porch to say goodbye to someone."

"And she always did that?"

"She always did for me."

"Thank you. Let me talk to Officer Swanson again." Swanson came back and Lucas said, "So why'd she say, 'Somebody's at the door'?"

"I dunno. To get to the other side?"

"I'm serious. Why'd she say that? She's got a guard downstairs, who calls up before he lets anyone in. Or you can get up from the second floor skyway, but you've got to have a key card to run the elevator. At least I think you do. I noticed a key card slot when I was riding up . . ."

"Huh. You're right. And I would have thought of that too in about five minutes."

"So it had to be a friend with a key card who was coming over unexpectedly."

"Or somebody else who lives in the building."

"You heard what she said about Audrey?" Lucas asked.

"Yeah, O'Dell put her in the elevator."

"The elevator dings whenever the door opens, right?"

"So if Audrey had just stood there, and let the doors open again after they closed . . ."

"It would've dinged and if O'Dell was out there she probably would've seen the doors opening."

"Goddamnit. See what happens if you get on there and push the *door close* button, or the *door open* button, or both at the same time. See if you can get back off the elevator . . ."

"Okay."

"And check and see if Audrey went out past the guard or what . . . what time she left the place."

"I already checked. She left at ten fifty-three."

"And the guard says that's right?"

"That's what he says. He checked her out."

"Shit."

"Besides, if Audrey'd just made a deal, why'd she kill O'Dell five minutes later?"

"I don't know," Lucas said. "There could be a million fuckin' reasons."

"I'll tell you what," Swanson said. "I bet it's a fuckin' boyfriend that we don't know about. Either somebody in the building she'd been screwing, or somebody at the bank. I vote for a key card."

"I've got the same problem with that as I've got with this firebombing of Weather. People start saying it could be random, but I'm saying if it's random, it's weird. *Anyone* could get firebombed by a random nut, but *not* Weather: not with her recent history. *Anyone* could get shot by a pissed-off boyfriend, but *not* O'Dell—not with her recent history."

"I see what you mean," Swanson said.

"Still: Check with the guards and see how many key cards O'Dell had, and see if you can find them."

"Do that," Swanson said. "What else?"

"Nothing else."

"I could go over and beat up Audrey McDonald for a while."

"Hell, just phone her old man and tell him to do it. Then you can drop by for the confession."

"You see her leg?" Swanson asked, his voice dropping.

"Yeah, I saw her leg."

"I once saw a stripper in a carnival who had bruises like that. Her old man beat her with a rolling pin."

"That's some business we're going to do after we finish with this," Lucas said. "We're gonna haul McDonald's blubber-butt down to City Hall and put him away."

He rang off Swanson and called Sloan. Sloan answered on the second ring: "Sloan."

"Can you talk?" Lucas asked.

"Not really. I could step outside."

"Did you ask Bone about Kresge?"

"Let me step outside."

After a moment of shuffling around and some conversation that Lucas couldn't make out, Sloan came back and said, "Well, I'm in the can. Bone says the phone reception here is better."

"So what'd they say?"

"Yeah, they have a relationship, and it started before her old man died—but not until after the separation. At least, that's what they say."

"How did you read it?"

"I think they're telling the truth about that. They got together at a particular party, and a number of people know about it and know that the party is when it started. I can check all that, but I think they're probably telling the truth. One thing—I took Bone back in the kitchen to ask him about Kresge, and he said he'd appreciate it if I didn't talk about Kresge around his assistant. He said he didn't want the gossip getting around the bank, but I got the feeling that he was lying about that. I think the reason was a little more personal, and I'm wondering if he's boning the assistant?"

"One more bone joke from anybody and they're fired . . ."

"Fuck you, I'm civil service. Anyway . . ."

"I don't know; she's pretty chilly," Lucas said.

"Really? I think she's pretty comfortable with Bone."

Now Lucas was surprised. Sloan was the personality-reading genius in the department. "Is that so? Huh."

"She also doesn't have a completely solid alibi. Kresge does, sort of. She was talking to some other guy—and I get the feeling she may be boning this other guy too—when Bone called with the news that McDonald had left and there was no deal. But this was like on call waiting. She told Bone she'd come over, and then she switched back to this other guy and told him that something had come up with the bank, and they talked about it for a few minutes. Maybe five, ten minutes, because they talked about some other stuff too. And then she hurried right over to Bone's place and got there about twenty after eleven, and from her place she really doesn't have time for another stop."

"Okay."

"And to tell you the truth, she's a pretty funky chick; I don't think she'd kill anyone. She's not crazy enough."

"What about Baki?" Lucas asked.

"I don't know. I can't read her very well. Very pretty; and she looks at Bone like a wolf looks at a sheep."

"Huh. You about done there?"

"Yeah. Unless you want me to torture somebody."

"Not tonight. I'll see you in the morning."

"Shit's gonna hit the fan tomorrow morning, dude. The *Star-Tribune* has the police guy standing outside of O'Dell's, and a business guy standing downstairs here."

"Freedom of the press," Lucas said.

15

JIM BONE HAD his head in his refrigerator when the phone rang. He picked up the kitchen extension and Kerin Baki said, "Mr. Bone, this is Kerin."

"Jesus, Kerin, it's five-thirty. Have you been to bed?"

"No. Too much to do." She sounded wide awake. "Nancy Lu just called me. McDonald called Brandt out at his farm, and Brandt's asking for an emergency board meeting at ten o'clock. We've got to be ready." Nancy Lu was the board secretary.

Bone had been drinking milk out of the carton. He swallowed and said, "All right. Do they want the pitch today? What'd she say?"

"No pitch. They just want to sort things out. But I think you've got to go for it today. If you wait, things could get out of control."

Bone scratched his head: "I don't think they'd give it to me today, but we might kill McDonald off."

There was a second of silence, and then Baki said, "Try to be more careful with your language. You talk that way all the time, and it could cause trouble."

Bone grinned at the phone and said, "Yes ma'am."

"Bring in your blue suit with the thin chalk line—is that clean?"

"Yes . . ."

"And the red-horsey Hermès necktie and the usual shoes and so on. Also, wear jeans and one of those mock turtlenecks and the black leather motorcycle jacket and your cowboy boots. I'm not sure which you should wear and we have to talk about that. Don't shave—you still have that electric razor in your office bathroom?"

"Yes."

"Good. Mr. Bone, I think you should leave your apartment in ten minutes and meet me at the bank in fifteen. You should be here before anybody else."

"I'll be there. And listen. Call Gene McClure and tell him to get his ass in there. We've got to start looking at what Susan was doing. If there's anything about the murder in her computers, we've got to know about it. I've been thinking about it all night."

"Yes. That's good."

"Fifteen minutes," he said. He hung up the phone, looked at it for a moment, said, "Whoa," and headed for the shower. No shave? Motorcycle jacket and cowboy boots? Wonder what that was about.

BONE CARRIED THE suit and tie with a white shirt and a pair of black dress loafers into the elevator, and was met by Baki on the twelfth floor.

"Good," she said, taking the clothes. She was dressed in a tack-sharp blue suit and her hair was perfect. "Gene McClure is on the way in. He should be pretty quick. I scared him a little."

"Good. Get him to me as soon as he comes in. Now: What's this about the boots and jacket?" He looked down at himself.

"We may want to reflect the image of a man who has been working all night to keep the bank going. Nobody else is in. I checked on McDonald, and he hasn't been in, so as far as anybody knows, we've been working all night. Not even McClure knows you're just coming in. I told him you were out for coffee."

"I see . . . Listen, you gotta start calling me Jim."

"Not yet," she said. "Go get your computers up, and get ready for McClure. I've got to mess up my hair."

"Here . . ." He reached out and pulled a few strands over her eyes, a couple out at the sides: "My God, you look different," he said. And he thought that in the six years she'd worked for him, this was the first time he'd ever touched her, in any way. "But you've got to try to look a little tired."

"I am tired," she said.

MCCLURE ARRIVED TEN minutes later, wearing a rumpled suit over a clean shirt; the skin on his face was a scuffed pink, as though he'd scraped off his beard with an emery board. McClure was technically O'Dell's second-in-command, although his position was bureaucratic rather than executive, and he had not been part of her inner circle. Pushing sixty, he was simply waiting for retirement and enjoying himself. But as O'Dell's technical second-in-command, he was now running her department, if only for a few days.

"Jim. Kerin told me about Susan. My God . . ." Bone peered at him and realized that he was really shocked. He liked that.

"Murdered," Bone said. "I'm as upset as you are, but we've got some things to get straight. We've got to balance everything out, tear through everything Susan was doing. We've got to make sure she wasn't up to something . . . unusual."

"Shouldn't we wait for the board?" McClure asked doubtfully.

"No. There's an emergency board meeting this morning at ten o'clock, and they're gonna need this information to put together some kind of response," Bone said. Baki walked into the room with a piece of paper in her hand. "If there's anything unusual in the record, they're going to want to know ASAP."

"All right," McClure said. "I'll get some of the computer cowboys on the way in."

"They're on the way," Baki said, lifting the sheet of paper so they could see a list of names. "All of them."

McDonald was shaken out of bed at eight forty-five; Audrey was up with a cup of coffee.

"What?"

"Board meeting at ten. Nancy Lu called an hour ago. I let you sleep as long as I could. You've got to be good," she said.

"Coffee?"

"Yes," she said. "You go get cleaned up. I'll get your suit . . . the charcoal one, I think, since O'Dell's dead. Wouldn't that be appropriate?"

"Whatever . . ." And he staggered off to the bathroom.

The Polaris Bank's board of directors met at exactly ten o'clock in emergency session. All the members were present, plus Bone and McDonald. Bone showed up at the last minute wearing jeans, a motorcycle jacket, and cowboy boots. Wilson McDonald raised an eyebrow at the costume, and turned to see if Brandt had gotten it.

Before anyone else could say anything, Oakes blurted, "What in the Sam Hill is going on here? Jim? Wilson? Anybody?"

Wilson McDonald steepled his fingers: "There's no reason to think that the O'Dell incident is related to the bank. I understand drugs were discovered in her apartment last night . . ."

"Drugs?" Brandt buried his hands in his face. "Sweet bleedin' Jesus. Is the press gonna find out about this?"

"I would think that the police would make every effort to keep this private.

However, I think there's a good possibility that Susan, as with any drug user, was involved with very unsavory people . . ."

"Bullshit," Bone snapped. He was chewing on an unlit cheroot, scowling. "It's gonna get in the papers. I'd be surprised if it's not out by tomorrow. And her dealer was a waiter at The Falls."

"How do you know about this drug thing, anyway?" Anderson asked querulously, looking from Bone to McDonald. And to Bone: "How do you know her dealer?"

"The police told us about the drugs," Bone said. "Several of us were questioned last night. Another person told me who her dealer was. Told me in confidence."

"We may have to know who it is," McDonald said.

"If the cops ask, I might tell them," Bone said. "But right now, nobody knows that I know, except the person who told me, and the people in this room. If it gets out of this room, it'll hurt the bank and I'll want to know why it got out." He looked straight at McDonald.

"What kind of drugs?" asked Bose, toying with a string of pearls.

"Just an old piece of hash and a little pot," Bone said. "Nothing serious."

"Nothing serious?" McDonald said. This time his eyebrows rose almost to his hairline. "Nothing serious? How can you say it's nothing serious?"

"Because it's not," Bone said.

"I'd disagree," McDonald said. "I think this must be handled very carefully . . ."

"More bullshit," Bone said. He looked at McDonald over the walnut table, his eyes glittering. "And I'm getting pretty goddamned tired of your bullshit, Wilson."

"Listen, pal," McDonald said, but Bone's voice rode over his.

"First, it's *not* important," he told the board. "If it were heroin or cocaine or crack or methamphetamine, it'd be much more important. With this, it's a misdemeanor, and we simply issue a press release saying that we were unaware of any drug use on O'Dell's part, say it may have been related to her glaucoma."

"Glaucoma," McDonald said. "I didn't know she had glaucoma."

"Neither do I, dummy, but by the time the newspapers find out for sure that she didn't, nobody'll give a shit."

McDonald was half out of his chair: "You're asking to be hit in the mouth, Bone. I'm no damn dummy and I want an apology."

Bone waved him down into his chair, closed his eyes: "I'm sorry, I apologize. But I've been here half the night, ransacking O'Dell's files with Gene McClure. We've established that her department is apparently completely on the up-and-up. Everything is absolutely clean."

Brandt said, "Good going. I worried about that all the way in from the farm."

"And we've got to stay on top of it," Bone said. "My assistant has prepared a press release . . ." He opened his briefcase, took out a sheaf of papers, and started passing them around. "It's all very standard, full cooperation with police, the glaucoma thing, an overnight review of her department with her top subordinates indicates exemplary management with no hints of any banking issues in the murder."

Brandt was reading the paper, put it on the table and said, "Excellent."

"We're going to have to tell Spacek at Midland," said Constance Rondeau.

"I already did," Bone said. "Kicked him out of bed at seven o'clock this morning, briefed him. He's issuing a press release that says that Midland is standing behind the merger proposal and that he has full confidence in the integrity of Polaris."

"All right . . . all right," said Anderson.

"Do you think, uh, any of the rest of us might be in danger?" Bose asked.

Bone grinned at her and said, "That's the first question I asked when the cops came over last night." After a bit of uneasy laughter, he said, "The police have nothing. I can't see any connection, and no threats have been made . . . but then, O'Dell wasn't threatened either."

"You think we could use a vacation?"

Bone shrugged. "That's up to you."

The board members looked at each other; then Brandt said, "I really don't think that's necessary. But I do think it's necessary for this board to talk privately amongst ourselves. We have some issues."

Several of the other board members nodded, and Bone pushed back from the table and said to McDonald, "Wilson, I think they're kicking us out." He looked down at himself. "And I could stand a change of clothes."

"Not kicking you out," Brandt objected. "In fact, I'd appreciate it if you both would hang around for a while. I know you're both tired, so we'll give you a call in a half hour or so. Get you out of here for the rest of the day."

In the hallway outside the room, McDonald said, "You called me a dummy."

"I apologized," Bone said. Baki was standing just behind him, prim with a bundle of papers.

"Fuck apologies," McDonald said. "You're going down, you prick."

"Yeah? What's that supposed to mean?" Bone asked. "You walking around with a little handgun, Wilson?" Bone's voice was quiet, and he looked almost as if he might be joking. But McDonald could see his black eyes, and knew that he wasn't.

"Kiss my ass," McDonald said; and Bone, in his turn, took a mental step back. This was not the hail-fellow he knew. Baki caught the hem of Bone's jacket and pulled. "No," she muttered, an inch from his ear. McDonald nodded at the two of them, then turned on his heel.

"Fat fuckin' . . ."

"Some other time," she said. "Did it work out in there?"

"I don't know."

"WHAT HAPPENED?" AUDREY demanded, as soon as the door shut behind her husband.

"I damned near punched Bone out in the hallway, the prick," McDonald said. "Christ, I could use a drink."

"Punched him?" Audrey was confused, and her voice turned shrill. "Wilson, what are you thinking about? Punched him?"

"Ah, shut up," McDonald rapped. He peeled off his coat and tie. "Board wants us to wait around until they're done."

"Are they going to pick someone? We're not ready. We were going to work on Bose this weekend."

"The O'Dell thing spooked them," McDonald said. "I think half of them are getting ready to leave town. Hide out until it's over with."

"But . . ." Audrey was flabbergasted. "They said next week . . ."

"I don't know." Wilson shrugged. He turned to look out his window, down at the street. "Bone turned up looking like a motorcycle bum. He sure as hell didn't look like a CEO, so that's something."

"Okay," she said. She folded her skirt beneath her as she sat down on a plush chair. "So we wait."

THE WAIT WAS an hour long, and seemed to take most of the day. A few people came and went; McDonald stared at a computer screen while Audrey read *Vogue*. Then Jack O'Grady came down, smiled at Audrey, and said, "Wilson, could you step back into The Room for a minute?"

Audrey patted him on the back and Wilson followed O'Grady out the door.

"Going to the Gophers game?" O'Grady asked.

"Always do," McDonald said brightly. "Good year, bad year, I don't care . . ."

But he trailed off when he walked through the door. Bone was already sitting at the long conference table, but this time he was wearing a dark banker's suit with a thin chalk stripe. And he'd shaved.

"Wilson, sit down," said Brandt, and McDonald's stomach turned. He sat down. "Wilson, we've decided we need to get a new leader in place immediately; somebody who can handle the bank and give us a single voice to speak with. We've elected you and Jim Bone to the board of directors. I'll be taking over as the board chairman, and if you'll accept the job, you'll be vice chairman, as well as maintaining the presidency of the mortgage arm. We've asked Jim to take over as president and chief executive officer. And we've directed him to continue with the merger plans."

Brandt looked at Bone, then back to McDonald. "So that's it. Welcome to the board."

"I, uh . . ." McDonald shook his head as if he'd been struck. Vice chairman: he was dead meat. "I, uh, thank you."

BAKI MET HIM in the hall, eyes wide, almost vibrating with caffeine and anxiety, Bone thought, and demanded, "Well?"

He grinned. "I got it. Brandt is chairman, for now, and McDonald is vice chairman. For now."

She smiled back and six years' worth of frost melted for a moment: "I'm very pleased for you, Mr. Bone."

"Jim."

"Not yet," she said; she refrosted.

"And we have to talk about that favor."

"Tomorrow," she said. "I've got some more thinking to do, and we've got some work. I should call Spacek, and tell him that you're now the man to deal with on the merger."

"That's the first thing," he said. "Second thing is, we've got to start talking about how to screw the merger."

"That's not entirely consistent with your previous position," she said, with absolute equanimity.

"I didn't used to be the CEO," he said. "So let's go. We're gonna need coffee and cookies. We've got some minor receiving to do."

"Down in your office," she said. "I ordered everything we'll need this morning."

16

ST. PAUL POLICE headquarters resembles a Depression-era WPA post office, but with new windows. Lucas dumped his Porsche in a reserved-parking space at the front of the building and went inside to a glass security window, where a woman at the desk didn't recognize him, didn't care about his Minneapolis ID, wasn't sure that Lieutenant Mayberry had time to see him, and told him to take a seat in the reception area next to a kid with green hair.

Lucas sat down, said, "Nice hair," crossed his legs, and stared at the opposite wall. The kid, whose brain was moving in slow motion, struggled with the sentiment for twenty seconds before he said, "Thanks, dude," with sincerity.

Lucas waited another twenty seconds, then asked, "What're you here for?"

Another twenty seconds and the kid said, "Fuckin' smokin' weed."

"Were you doing it?" Lucas asked.

"Fuckin' yeah."

THE CONVERSATION WITHERED after that; then Mayberry pushed through the security door and said, "Hey, Lucas, what're you doing out here?" Mayberry had a head the size and shape of a gallon milk jug, right down to the handle, which was a tiny blond ponytail tied into his hair at the back. He pushed through the security door and said, "Come on back . . . How ya been, I haven't seen you since that goat-fuck over at Ronnie White's place."

"Ah, ups and downs," Lucas said. "You heard about Weather?"

"You mean the bomb? Yeah, in the paper—and somebody said you guys busted up."

"I don't know, we're kind of working on things."

"She's a good one," Mayberry said. He guided Lucas to an elevator, up a couple of floors and into a meeting room with a dozen chairs with red plastic seats, a blackboard, a wide-screen color television, and a VCR. Mayberry shoved the tape into the VCR and punched a few buttons, bringing the television up. "I looked at the tape last night . . . man, it's been a long time. I could hardly remember who was who. Anyway, Arris shows up at about 224 on the dial . . ."

He was running through the tape; at the index number 210 he stopped the tape, then restarted it at real-time speed. They were both standing to look at the picture.

"Okay," Mayberry said, tapping the screen. "Here we have a parade of people going by . . . lots of women, going down to the meat rack. Half a dozen guys."

The tape was black-and-white, focused on a thin man with a mustache selling soda, cigarettes, bread, and gasoline over a small counter in a convenience store. In the background, through a window and past two pair of gas pumps, people occasionally walked by the store, most of them on the far side of the street.

"Okay," Mayberry said. "Here we come up to Arris . . . This woman goes by and there he is." He jabbed at the screen. Arris was wearing a light-colored shirt and what might have been tan slacks.

"Pretty blurry," Lucas said, his eyes less than a yard from the screen. "Can't see his face."

"Not very well," Mayberry agreed. He stopped the tape, rewound it a few turns, and Arris rolled through the picture again, this time in slow motion. "We got the ID by having a bunch of his friends look at it, and they picked him out by, you know, general appearance, the flappy way he walked. And the dress was right. You can see his sleeves were rolled up, and that's right."

"Nobody looks like McDonald," Lucas said, watching the people parade past the store.

"You sure he's your guy?" Mayberry asked.

"He's the guy we got a hard tip on," Lucas said.

"Most of these people were going down to the rack," Mayberry said. "But

Arris was just out for a walk, and he went on beyond it. So he was just about alone when he was shot, a block and a half further on. So if you're looking for the killer . . . he's quite a bit further down."

"Jelly told me he didn't think it was random."

"He's usually right," Mayberry said.

"If it wasn't random, the shooter'd almost have to be following him," Lucas said. "He couldn't expect just to walk down the street and run into Arris at a convenient place to shoot. Especially not if Arris would recognize him. He'd want to come up behind him."

"Well, Arris walked every night. Nobody knows if he took the same route every night, but his neighbors say he usually started out the same way. You want to look at this again?"

"Nah, that's okay. What about the print on the shell?"

"We know McDonald's got a fingerprint file, we've got NCIC confirmation on that—he had a secret clearance with the National Guard," Mayberry said. "They're supposed to be sending us something right away, but it wasn't here five minutes ago. I had Chad Ogram pull up the print file on the shell. You know Ogram?"

"Think I met him," Lucas said.

Mayberry had been rewinding the tape, now popped it out of the VCR and handed it to Lucas. "This is for you. Let's go see Ogram."

Ogram worked in a bathroom-sized office stuffed with filing cabinets. At least one clock sat on each flat surface in the office, and a half-dozen more hung on the walls. Ogram, a thin man with vanishing hair, bent over his green metal desk, his bald spot as pink as a newborn's gums.

"Chad," said Mayberry, and Ogram sat up with a start. "You know Lucas."

"Yeah, hey," Ogram said vaguely, glancing at Lucas and then bending over his desk again. "I got the fax."

"What do you think?" Mayberry asked.

"Well, heck," Ogram said. "You know there's not enough for a match."

"Yeah," Lucas said, "I was just wondering . . ."

"But McDonald's right thumb matches what we've got," Ogram said. "We got a piece of a whorl and he's got a whorl that looks just like our piece."

Mayberry and Lucas looked at each other. "Are you sure?" Lucas asked.

"Pretty sure: I have to rescale the fax to get an overlay, but yeah: it looks just like it."

"What are the chances it's someone else?" Lucas asked.

Ogram scratched his bald spot with his right middle finger. "I don't know. Ten to one against. Hundred to one. Not enough for court, but if you come to me and say we've got a partial and a suspect, and we get this much . . . I'd say we got him."

"Jesus," Lucas said to Mayberry. "This can't be true."

"Why not?" Mayberry asked.

"It's too easy," Lucas said. "It's never this easy." And to Ogram: "I kind of need to pin down the odds."

"I know a guy at the FBI who could give you an idea. He fools around with that sort of math thing. Statistics and odds and chances."

"Call him," Lucas said. "And call me in Minneapolis when you find out. Wilson motherfuckin' McDonald."

Lucas headed for the elevators with Mayberry two steps behind. Lucas pushed the call button, turned and jabbed a finger at Mayberry: "Hey: You've got a slug, right?"

"Piece of one, anyway."

"And the ME took a piece of one out of O'Dell—the banker woman who got shot. Let's get them together and do an analysis and see if they match."

"Okay—you guys want to do it?"

"Sure. Send it over."

"It'll be twenty minutes behind you," Mayberry said. "Hot dog, I love this. This case has been open forever."

LUCAS CALLED SLOAN from his car, said, "We got a break in the Kresge case: get Sherrill and Del if they're around, and meet me at my office in twenty minutes."

"Who done it?"

"Our pal, Wilson McDonald."

"You're shittin' me."

"I shit you not," Lucas said. "The problem is gonna be proving it."

He punched Sloan off, found his notebook, looked up the number for Bone's office, and punched it in as he accelerated out onto I-94. Bone's assistant took the call: "Chief Davenport: Everybody's up in the boardroom right now. I think they may be picking a new CEO. So unless it's a major emergency . . ."

"Is Wilson McDonald in there?"

"Yes, of course. He's one of the candidates."

"Thanks. I'll call back." She'd told him what he wanted to know: that McDonald was there, at the bank.

SHERRILL WAS SKEPTICAL.

More than skeptical: she was absolutely nasty. "We got diddly, Lucas. I don't care what the odds are, if it doesn't work in court, it doesn't work. And the goddamn killing is so old that there's no chance of making a case."

"Helps to know who did it," Del said. Sherrill had come in wearing jeans, high-top Nikes, a suede jacket, and a slightly too tight fuzzy white sweater that showed her figure to exceptional advantage. Lucas, Sloan, and Del were resolutely meeting her eyes, though the pressure eventually got to Del and he slumped back in his chair and looked up at the ceiling.

"C'mon, Del, look at the Cat case," Sherrill said. "Everybody in the office knows George Cat killed his old lady. It doesn't do any good, because we can't prove it. It's gonna be even harder with McDonald, because McDonald has every lawyer in the world."

"Still helps to know," Del muttered.

"Because we think Wilson's done about four of them," Lucas said. "If we can put together a pattern, argue it, and have semiconvincing evidence on one, a jury'll pack him away."

"So what do you want?" Sloan asked.

"I want to tear him apart. I want to look him over with a microscope. I want to get a search warrant and pull his house down."

"Don't think we've got enough for a warrant," Del said.

"So let's fuckin' get it," Lucas said. "Sloan, can you break away from the Ericson case for a couple of days?"

"For a while," he said.

"Ask Frank. And if he says okay, look at O'Dell again. See if there's any way McDonald could have finessed it to get into the apartment. Del, you look at Arris again. See if there's anything else. Marcy, you take Ingall. I'm going up north again, right away. I want to think about the Kresge thing again. See if I can figure out how he did it. Let's meet again tomorrow at nine o'clock. And I've got my car phone if you need me before then."

"Why don't you get a real walk-around phone?" Del asked. "Everybody else has one."

"'Cause then people would call me up," Lucas said. "And I couldn't say I must've been out."

Sloan nodded and he and Del left. Sherrill lingered. "You're going up north?"

"Yeah. I want to talk to—" His phone rang and he grabbed it, lifting a finger to Sherrill so she'd wait: "Davenport."

"Lucas this is Sergeant Ogram over in St. Paul. We talked—"

"Yeah, yeah. What'd you get?"

"I talked to my pal in the FBI and he called down to the fingerprint people and then he called me back: he says it's maybe a hundred to one against having the wrong guy."

"So we got him."

"You got him. And listen, that slug fragment's on the way over in a squad. Oughta be there about now."

"Thanks. See ya."

Lucas hung up: "We got him . . . Anyway, I want to go up north and talk to the caretaker and walk the place a little."

"Okay." She turned to go, but she was going slowly.

"You got a problem?" Lucas asked.

She stopped again, looked at him and said, "No," and turned back toward the door. Lucas thought, *Uh-oh*. He'd never in his life gone through a little sequence like that when the woman *didn't* have something to say, and one way or another, he almost always wound up getting his ass kicked.

"Okay, if you're sure."

"I may give you a call tonight," she said. She was nibbling the inside of her lip, as if distracted by something. "I do have something I sort of want to talk about."

LUCAS CALLED KRAUSE at the Garfield County courthouse before he left and arranged to meet Kresge's part-time caretaker at the cabin. The trip north was a good one: quick up the interstate, dry and fast on the back highways. The small towns were buckling down for winter: a man on a small green and yellow John Deere was mowing what must have been a glorious summer garden, now all brown stalks and dead leaves; a man in a camouflage jacket was shooting arrows across his backyard at two archery butts made of bundled wood shavings; an Arctic Cat dealership was running a special on snowmobile tune-ups and a closeout on Yamaha ATVs.

Krause was waiting at the cabin, stepped into the yard and frowned when he saw the Porsche slipping down the driveway. Lucas punched it into an open space next to a Ford truck, climbed out. Below the cabin, the small lake showed a collar of ice, now out six feet from the shoreline.

"Didn't recognize the vehicle," Krause said. "Boy, that's something; don't see many of those around here."

"Had it for years," Lucas said, looking back at the 911. "I'm thinking about trading it in for something a little larger."

"Wouldn't imagine it'd do you too much good out here in the winter."

"Not too much," Lucas agreed. A weathered, white-haired man in his late sixties or early seventies had come around a corner of the cabin, carrying a gas-powered brush cutter. He put it down by the cabin steps and Krause said, "Marlon, this here's Chief Davenport from Minneapolis, and Chief, this is Marlon Wiener."

They shook hands, and Lucas said, "I just sorta need to walk around the place and chat for a while . . ."

"I'll leave you to it," Krause said. "I got some paperwork with me, I'm gonna sit inside with Mrs. Wiener and drink some coffee. Holler if you need me."

LUCAS WANTED TO look at all the tree stand locations. The transcripts of Sloan's interrogations had given the order in which the hunters had dispersed to the stands, but said nothing about the terrain itself.

"We got a six-wheeler here, we could ride up, unless you rather walk," Wiener said.

"Let's walk," Lucas said. "They all walked the morning of the shoot, right?"

"That's right," Wiener said.

"So tell me about Kresge," Lucas said, as they started through the fallen leaves toward the track around the lake. "Good guy, bad guy, what do you think?"

"Wouldn't have wanted to work for him on a daily basis—you know, right next to him," Wiener said. "He was all right with me. Told me what he wanted done and sometimes I'd suggest stuff, and he usually told me to do that too. My wife'd keep the place clean, come down a couple of times a week to dust and vacuum and so on."

"That seems like quite a lot of work," Lucas said.

"Well, he liked to have cars in his driveway. He was always worried he was gonna be burglarized or something. Not saying that it couldn't happen. He told me once that instead of working all day on a job, he'd be happier if I'd break it up so I'd be around here every day, one time or another."

"Did he have parties, or lots of guests? People coming and going?"

"No, not a lot of them—but he did have one big party every summer for management people at the bank," Wiener said. "They'd come up here and swim off the dock and drink and the kids'd fish for bluegills and everybody'd go down to the range and shoot for a while."

"He's got a gun range here?"

"Just a gully, shooting against the end of it. You know, twenty-five feet to a hundred yards."

"Twenty-five feet? These are handguns?"

"Yeah, and .22 rifles for the kids. You know, just fartin' around."

"Huh. Handguns." A handgun would be interesting, especially a big one, like a .44 Mag or a .45 Colt or a .357 Maximum. McDonald could have carried it in concealed, come back, shot Kresge, thrown the gun away. Although the ME thought the killing shot had come from a rifle, a powerful handgun might be an alternative. "The sheriff took an inventory of guns in the cabin. I didn't see any handguns on the list."

"I don't know, they never asked me about it. They just cleaned out the gun cabinet, and that was it."

"Was Kresge big on handguns?"

"Naw, not really. I mean, some. Most of the handguns were brought down by the guests. City people don't get to shoot that much, and they all seemed to like it, get a few beers in them. Mr. Kresge had a handgun, because I saw it: it was a Smith and Wesson .357 Magnum, silver. But I think he brought it with him, when he came up from the Cities."

"A .357 Magnum? Or maximum?"

"Oh, I think . . . a Magnum. Never heard of maximum."

"And he brought it with him."

"I think. Then, it's not exactly a handgun, or maybe it is . . . but he had a Contender. That should have been on the sheriff's list. That was up here."

"A Contender?" A Contender would be perfect."

"You know, one of the—"

"I know Contenders. Scoped?"

"Yeah."

"I don't think that was on the inventory."

"Should have been. He keeps it in the gun cabinet. At least, he did. Unless he took it back."

"We'll check that," Lucas said. "Do you know Wilson McDonald? Big guy?"

Wiener nodded. "Yeah, I've seen him a time or two."

"What'd he shoot when he came up here?"

Wiener shook his head: "Couldn't tell you. Don't even know if he was a shooter, tell you the truth. Mr. Robles, he was a shooter: he'd help instruct the kids and shoot off his mouth about everything about guns. But I think Mr. McDonald was mostly a drinker. That's what I remember about him."

THEY FOLLOWED THE shoreline around the lake to the first stand, where Robles had been stationed. Lucas went down to the stand, climbed the tree, and eased himself out onto the platform of two-by-fours.

"Did you build the stands?" Lucas called down to Wiener.

"Naw, a couple of boys up from Wyoming built 'em," he said. "They were joking about putting in electricity."

The tree stand was one of the more comfortable that Lucas had been in. He could stretch his legs, lean back against the tree trunk, and still look out over the hillside edging the alder swamp. The swamp itself was dotted with stands of aspen, signs of higher ground, with a big, thick island in the middle. Here and there he could see shiny lenses of ice, where a stretch of open water lay at the surface. All around, he could make out the faint telltale trails threading through the brush, signs that deer were working the place. Robles's stand was uphill from what looked like a major deer interchange.

"There's a finger of land goes out into the swamp from there," Wiener called. "Deer can walk right out into that stand of aspens in the middle. Man'd probably drown if he tried to follow; before freeze-up, anyway."

"Okay . . ."

They checked all the other stands in turn, spread out over three quarters of a mile of trail, but all focused on the swamp, and pathways into it and out of it. McDonald's stand was uphill and not far to the left of one of the big lenses of thin ice.

Suppose, Lucas thought, *McDonald had lifted the Contender from the gun cabinet in the early morning just before the group left the cabin. That would explain why it was missing. And the Contender, long for a pistol, was still short enough that he could have concealed it under a hunting parka. Then, in the dark, he walks back down the track to the hillside above Kresge's stand, waits for the shooting to begin, fires a shot killing Kresge, walks back to his stand, and pitches the Contender into the swamp. Climbs the tree . . . shazam. He's up in his tree stand just like the others, and never fired his gun . . .*

"Let's go," he said to Wiener, as he climbed down.

"You figure anything out?" Wiener asked.

"Maybe," Lucas said. "What time did you get here the day Kresge was shot?"

"About ten o'clock, after I heard . . . I was supposed to come in around noon with my trailer and we'd haul any deer carcasses into the registration station and then over to the meat locker. They figured to be out of there about noon, one way or the other," the old man said. "The sheriff asked me about the guy the telephone man saw—the one walking along the edge of the woods— but I just wasn't around. Sorry."

The hunter in the woods. Lucas had almost forgotten. Of course, it could have been anybody, another hunter just crossing the property to get back to his car. "Damn it," he said aloud. Another hunter didn't feel right; Lucas was a believer in coincidences, except when they explained too much. And if the man in the hunting coat was the killer, and if the telephone man had been right about his size, then McDonald wasn't the killer.

"Beg pardon?"

"If somebody was walking in the woods like the telephone guy said, where'd he be going?"

"Sounds like he was heading back to the cabin."

"That'd be a problem," Lucas said.

KRAUSE WAS WORKING on the kitchen table when he got back, a battered leather briefcase next to his foot. Mrs. Wiener was washing dishes, and the odor that came from the cabin's oven was so wonderful that Lucas almost fainted with the impact.

"What's cooking?"

"Cinnamon rolls—they should be just about ready," she said, turning from the sink. She was a chubby, pink-faced woman with kinky white hair. She took a dish towel from the stove handle, dried her hands, and opened the oven. "Perfect," she said.

Krause had gotten up from the table to look. "I get the first one," he said.

"They've got to cool," she said firmly. "And I've got some frosting. You all go sit down."

Krause retreated to the table and his papers. "Anything good?" he asked Lucas.

Lucas said, "You know what a Contender is? Long pistol, single-shot, breaks open like a shotgun?"

"I've seen 'em," Krause said.

"You didn't show one on the inventory of guns taken out of the house."

"There wasn't one," Krause said. "There were three rifles and two shotguns."

"You got a diver on your staff?" Lucas asked.

"Sure. You think you know where the gun is?"

"Maybe. It'd be nice if it were right downhill from McDonald's stand. There's a big patch of water there . . . I wouldn't be surprised if he pitched it in there."

"I don't know about diving in swamps," Krause said doubtfully. "It might mess up the scuba gear. I can check."

"He'll need a metal detector," Lucas said.

Mrs. Wiener said, "There's a gun just like that in the drawer in the gun cabinet."

Lucas looked at Krause and Krause closed his eyes, leaned back in his chair, and said, "Shit." Then at Mrs. Wiener, "Excuse the language," and then at Lucas: "I told Ralph to take the guns out of the cabinet. I didn't check."

Wiener said, "Well, let's go look," and Mrs. Wiener said, "I saw it while I was cleaning. I dusted the cabinet 'cause they left it open, and that's one place I usually can't dust."

The gun cabinet was built into an internal wall, behind a set of shallow shelves. A key fit into a small lock that was out of sight below one of the shelves, and the entire unit swung out. Inside was an empty gun rack with space for eight long guns, and below the rack, two closely fit drawers.

"Was this a big secret, or did everybody know about it?" Lucas asked Wiener.

"Hell, all his friends knew—all the guests. It was just supposed to hide the guns from burglars. But when he had one of those parties, the cabinet'd just be standing open."

"Okay."

"Top drawer," Mrs. Wiener said.

"Did you move the gun?" Lucas asked.

"No. I never touched it. As soon as I saw a gun in the drawer, I shut it."

"She don't like guns," Wiener said, as Lucas gently pulled the drawer open.

And there was the Contender, with a Nikon scope, sitting neatly on a black plastic pad with two boxes of .308 ammunition off to the side.

"That goddamn Ralph," Krause said. "He never opened the drawers."

Lucas took a pen from his pocket, slipped it through the gun's trigger guard, lifted it out of the drawer, and carried it over to the kitchen table and placed it carefully on the table. Then, using a paper napkin to unlock the barrel, and touching only the tip of the stock and the tip of the barrel, he pushed the barrel down and open. A spent shell ejected onto the table.

"Don't touch it," Lucas said. He knelt and looked through the barrel, said, "Yeah. Fired and never cleaned." He looked at Wiener: "Do you know anything about Kresge's gun habits?"

Wiener shrugged: "He always cleaned them. Big thing, you know, sit around and bullshit about the Army and shooting and chain saws and clean the guns."

Krause again said, "Goddamnit," and then, a moment later, "That's the gun, you betcha. That goddamn Ralph."

"Mrs. Wiener . . ."

"Sophia," she said.

"Sophia, do you have any plastic bags . . . garbage bags or anything?"

"Sure. Right here."

Sophia produced a box of kitchen garbage bags. She stripped one out and held it open, while Lucas stuck a pencil in the barrel of the Contender and gently slipped it inside. The shell went into a sandwich bag.

"I'll have them in the lab tonight," Lucas said. "I'll get somebody in to look at them right away."

Krause was still fuming, pushing papers into his briefcase. "I gotta go. I'm gonna find that sonofabitch and I'm gonna choke him to death. He couldn't—"

Sophia Wiener broke in: "You don't have time for a roll?"

Krause's eyes clicked to the tray of cinnamon rolls, cooling on the stovetop with the pan of warm frosting next to them.

"Well," he said. "Maybe one."

17

THE DAYS WERE getting shorter, two or three minutes of sunlight clipped off each afternoon; and the sky had gone dark by the time Lucas was within cell phone range of the Cities. He called the dispatcher, told her to locate the fingerprint specialist and get her down to the office. A half hour out, the car phone rang and he picked it up: "Yeah, Davenport."

"Lucas, this is Marcy . . . Sherrill." Her voice was tentative, as though he might not know her first name. "Are you on the way back?"

"Yeah. I'll be at the office in a half hour. We maybe found the gun."

"What? Where?" Her voice suggested that she was on solider ground now, talking about the investigation.

"In a drawer in the gun cabinet. In the cabin."

After a moment of silence, Sherrill said, "Oh brother. I'm glad I'm not the one who missed it."

"You oughta see the sheriff: he's talking manslaughter . . . Anyway what've you got going?"

"I'd like to stop by your office and talk about it. If you've got a minute."

"Sure. Where are you?"

"Out in Bloomington," she said. "At the Megamall."

"See you in a while."

HARRIET ASHLER SHOWED up two minutes after Lucas, wearing an ankle-length wool coat and a frown, and trailed by her husband: "Dick and I were going to a movie," she said.

"Jeez . . . Is it too late to go?"

She looked at her watch. "If we go, we gotta be in the car in twenty minutes."

Lucas handed her the cardboard box he'd used to transport the guns: "A pistol and a fired shell. If there's anything on the shell, I gotta have it ASAP. If it's a matter of going over the whole pistol, that could wait until morning."

Ashler took the bag and said, "I'll call you in ten minutes—you'll be in your office?"

"Yeah . . ."

"We could come back after the movie and take a look at the pistol, if you're willing to pay the OT."

"That'd be good—but tomorrow morning, early, would be okay."

"I'll do it tonight. Dick can hang around. Then I can sleep in tomorrow."

"I like fingerprinting," Dick said cheerfully. He was a letter carrier and had a six handicap in golf. "I'd just as soon watch her fingerprint as go to a movie."

"Well, we're going to the movie," Ashler said.

"Art movie," said Dick, as his wife started off down the dimly lit hall. "Made by some Jap."

"You have my sympathy," said Lucas.

"Coulda been worse: coulda been a Swede," Dick said, looking after his wife. "Gotta go: I guess I'm just a goddamn culture dog."

LUCAS HEADED DOWN to his office, flipped on the lights, pulled off his coat and hung it on the antique government-issue coatrack. Then he walked up and down his ten-foot length of carpet a couple of times, rubbing his hands, looking at the phone, waiting. Wanted to call someone, but there was no one to call.

Sherrill. Where in the hell was she? If she'd been in Bloomington, she should be here. Or close. He'd left the door open, and he stepped out and looked up and down the hall. Nobody: he could hear a radio playing somewhere, a Leon Redbone piece. He listened for a moment, groping for the name, pulling it from the few muted notes flowing down the hall. Ah: "She Ain't Rose."

Despite what Sherrill had argued earlier, knowing that McDonald was the killer was a huge advantage. If they could pull together enough bits and pieces on all the killings, they could indict him on several counts of murder, let the jury throw a couple of them out, and nail him on the easiest one. All they needed was one. One first degree murder was thirty years, no parole. McDonald was unlikely to pull the full load. He'd die inside.

So one was enough.

Lucas hummed to himself, caught it: Jesus, he hadn't been humming to himself in months. And with all the shit happening, he should be . . . He listened to the back of his mind. No static. Not much going on back there. He let himself smile and took another turn around the carpet, looked at his watch.

And the phone rang.

He snatched it up, said, "Davenport," and at the same time, heard footsteps in the hall.

"This is Harriet Ashler. There's nothing on the shell. It looks like it was lifted out of the box, maybe with gloves, loaded up, and fired. It's absolutely clean. Polished, almost."

Sherrill appeared in the doorway, saw him talking. He gestured for her to come in as he said, "Damn it: I was hoping . . . Well, check the gun. I thought maybe he didn't think about the shell, just like he didn't think about the other one."

"Not this time," Ashler said. Sherrill stepped into Lucas's office, pulled the door shut, and took off her leather jacket as Ashler continued: "I took a look at the pistol, and I think I can see some smudges. As soon as I get back I'll start processing them. Ogram over in St. Paul sent McDonald's prints over this afternoon, so I can give you a quick read."

"Good, I'll be at home. Call me whenever."

Lucas hung up and said, "No prints on the shell, but there's something on the pistol. She's gonna process it tonight."

"He'd have to be suicidal to leave prints on the pistol but not on the shell," Sherrill said. She tossed her coat in a corner, and the motion of the coat in the air stirred up a slight scent, something light, like Chanel No. 5. "And why'd he carry the pistol back to the cabin? He could've pitched it into the woods, and who'd ever find it?"

"I don't know why," Lucas said. He leaned back against his desk. "But why would *anybody* carry a pistol back to the cabin? *Anybody*, no matter who it is?"

Sherrill shrugged: "Maybe they got it there, and thought if they put it back, nobody would know."

"Leaving a fired shell in the chamber?"

"That's a question," she admitted.

Lucas scratched his head and said, "We'll ask him, if we can't figure something out . . . So what's happening with you?"

She peered at him, almost as if she were nearsighted, which she wasn't. "I've got this thing going around in my head and it won't go away."

"Uh-oh," Lucas said. "I've had that problem . . ."

"No-no-no. Nothing like that. I'm not depressed. But, you know that old thing about, 'Women don't want sex, women want love'?"

"What?" She was talking fast, and he was suddenly aware of how quiet the building was, how dark the hallway had been outside, and how the two of them were alone in a not very big office.

"Yeah, well maybe I've heard something like that."

"The fact is, I always liked sex," she said. "A lot. And I haven't had any for a year and a half before Mike was killed, while we were breaking up, and none since he was killed, and right now I just really don't need love, but I really would sorta . . ."

As she spoke, she was moving to his left, and he was on his feet moving to her left, in a narrow circle, Lucas edging toward the door. "Jesus," he said.

"Look, you don't have to," she said. "Where're you going? You're running for it?"

She almost started to smile, a sad, tentative smile, but Lucas only saw part of it. He flipped the latch on the door and hit the light at the same time, and in the next half-second his hands were all over her. She gasped and went a few inches up in the air, and then they were dancing around, half struggling, mouths locked together, Sherrill's blouse coming off, and five seconds after that they were on the floor.

AND TEN MINUTES later Sherrill whispered, "Was that loud?"

"Pretty loud," Lucas whispered back.

"Jesus, I want to do it again." He could only see her face dimly in the light coming through the door's glass panel. And he thought: *This rug smells weird.* But he *said*, "My place," and he reached out and pressed the warm palm of his right hand over one of her breasts.

"I'll follow you," she said.

"No: Come with me. We can be there in ten minutes."

"Can't find my underpants," she said. "What'd you do with my underpants?"

"Don't know . . ."

She pulled on her jeans and untangled her bra from around her neck, buttoned her blouse as Lucas pulled himself together, half turned away from each other, a small piece of still-necessary privacy. Neither of them wanted the light—when Lucas was dressed, Sherrill opened the door and Lucas found her cotton underpants hooked over the top of his wastebasket. Lucas stuck them in his pocket: "Let's go."

"What a fuckin' terrible idea this was," she said, as they jogged down the hall. "Screwing your boss." She looked at him. "You can't screw your boss."

"I'm not your boss," Lucas said. "Keep moving."

LUCAS CONCENTRATED ON driving, out of Minneapolis past the dome, onto I-94 across the Mississippi and off at Cretin, south to the stoplight at Marshall. The light was a long one and Sherill was suddenly on top of him again, one hand fumbling at his belt while he tore at her blouse and finally freed her breasts, his mouth on her neck and then . . .

"Christ, we're a movie," she said suddenly. He looked up, past her: a couple of St. Thomas students were walking past, and one of them flashed him the V-for-victory sign.

"Gotta go," Lucas said, as the light went green, and Sherrill subsided, but still half turned in the passenger seat, her hand on his chest. He dodged one red light, got down toward the river, then out on the boulevard heading south. Home in ten minutes, into the garage, then through the kitchen, stumbling with each other.

"Where's the bedroom?"

She was turned around, but with an arm over his shoulder, and he picked her up and carried her back, dumped her on the bed and kicked off his shoes.

"Hurry," she said.

AND LATER, SHE said, "Man, that rug in your office sure smelled weird. What'd you do in there, anyway?"

Lucas sighed and rolled away from her and said, "This was really a bad idea."

"That's what I said an hour ago."

"Yeah, well . . ."

"What?"

"So even if it's a bad idea, I wanna do it some more."

"We should maybe wait a few minutes."

Lucas laughed and said, "It might be more than a few minutes."

"I think I could cut down the turnaround time."

"I'm sure you could," he said. "But you know what? I'm starving. I've got some bologna in the fridge, and some beer, and I think there's some hamburger buns."

"Three of the major food groups," she said. "We'll live to be a hundred."

"Let's go."

"Show me the shower first."

He showed her the shower; the turnaround time was eliminated, and the bologna sandwiches temporarily forgotten.

BUT THEY GOT to the sandwiches, eventually, spreading mustard over the discs of mystery meat in the light from the refrigerator, and then sat in the dark to eat them with bottles of Rolling Rock.

"I think we oughta keep this quiet," she said finally.

"Yeah, right. We're in an office full of investigators. You're gonna walk in and you're not gonna look at me and Sloan is gonna come up later and he's gonna say, 'You're fuckin' her, aren't you?' "

"So romantic. Coming over here and getting fucked."

"Hey, you know the talk."

She laughed and said, "Yeah, and it's not that hard to take from Sloan. He can be a pretty funny guy."

"He thinks you've got nice headlights."

"I do."

"What can I say?" he said, talking through the bologna sandwich. "The evidence is on your side."

"I better get going," she said. "My car is downtown . . ."

"Oh, bullshit," he said. "You're staying. I'll give you a T-shirt."

"Lucas . . ."

"Shut up. You're staying."

"Okay. Um, was that the last of the bologna?"

SHE SLEPT ON the left side of the bed, a good sign, since Lucas slept on the right. They'd settled down, talking, her hand on his stomach, when the phone rang.

Lucas glanced at the bedside clock. Ten after eleven. "Bet it's Harriet Ashler."

And it was. "We've got a few bits and pieces, and a couple of good prints, but none that I can identify as from McDonald," Ashler said. "None of the good ones are, for sure. In fact, I'm pretty sure that none of the fragments are either."

"Okay."

"Sorry to wake you."

"No problem," Lucas said. And he imagined a wry questioning tone in her voice. It was impossible, he thought as he headed back to bed, that anybody knew yet.

18

ELEVEN O'CLOCK AT night, and Wilson McDonald was savagely drunk.

Stunned by the board's impetuous decision and a patronizingly courteous afternoon meeting that Bone had called with the bank's top managers, he'd stopped at the liquor store on the way home and purchased three-fifths of the finest single-malt scotch, which he proceeded to gargle down as though it were Pepsi-Cola.

After the board decision he'd been, in sequence, angry, despairing, resigned, and finally faintly upbeat. He imagined that he might have a future in the merged bank, until Audrey dismissed the idea with such withering contempt that he lapsed back to despair.

AUDREY HAD SPENT the afternoon in the backyard, wrapped in a winter parka, staring at the sky. The cold air and the hint of burning leaves—an illegal act in Minnesota, sure to be avenged by a politically correct neighbor—reminded her of the bad old days of her childhood on the farm with Mom and Pop and Helen. Hated the farm. Hated this suburb, rich as it was. She should have had a place in Palm Beach and Malibu to go with it.

The very top job at Polaris had always been their goal and intent, the one goal that she and Wilson could agree upon, without reservation. There were other jobs that would have been as good—running First Bank, or Norwest, or 3M, or Northwest Airlines or General Mills or Pillsbury or even Cargill—but they'd been Polaris people, and Polaris was Wilson's one real shot.

Few people outside of the top-management community realized the difference between, say, president and CEO on one hand, and executive vice president on the other. One was an American aristocrat, who held the lives of thousands of people in his hands, while the other was just another suit, a face, a yellow necktie. A CEO had the company plane and a car and driver; an executive vice president had to fight to go business class. And the spouse took status from the CEO: Audrey'd been a half-step from becoming a duchess. Now she was a rich housewife, but a housewife nevertheless.

And the things she'd done to get here: She'd married a brutal, drunken lout, because he seemed to have a chance to go the distance. And though she'd come to love him, at least a little, somewhere down in her heart, she knew exactly what he was . . . And she'd turned herself into a self-effacing beetle of a woman, staying out of sight, out of mind, producing the perfect office parties when they were needed, at which she was never noticed, advising the lout on each and every career move . . . advising against the move to the mortgage company, where he had the title of president, which he'd been so proud of at that time, but now would be fatal . . .

EARLY IN THE evening, with Wilson upstairs drinking and raving, the phone had rung, and a woman named Cecely Olene said, "There was a police officer just here asking about Wilson. I told him that I didn't want to discuss my friends behind their backs and would call you and tell you they'd been asking."

"Well, *thank you*,"Audrey said. "I can't imagine what they must think . . ."

"They think he killed Dan Kresge, is what they think," Olene said bluntly. "And they were also asking about a lot of other people who've died in the past. George Arris and Andy Ingall. They said they have evidence. Fingerprints."

"That's absurd," Audrey said. "Wilson can get angry, but he'd never in his life *kill* anyone. I suspect James Bone is leading them on."

"Well, I don't know about that," Olene said. "In any case, I called you like I said I would. I hope things work out for you."

And she was gone; and given that last sentence, Audrey thought, probably wouldn't be calling back. Ever. *I hope things work out for you.*

Things never just "work out," Audrey thought. They were worked out. Always. When Audrey lived on the farm with Mom and Pop and Helen, she'd had to take any number of harsh decisions. She took another one now, sad in her heart.

She moved around downstairs, cleaning up; watched television for a while. Wilson came down once, dripping, raving. She avoided him, hiding in the basement, running the washing machine. By eleven o'clock, he was far gone, along with two of the bottles. She went to the kitchen, poured two inches of vodka into a water tumbler, drank it down, and went upstairs to confront the Whale.

MCDONALD WAS IN the oversized tub, his gut sticking up through the water level like the top of an apple pie, while the tip of his penis hung offshore of the pie, like a fishing bobber. He was reading a water-spattered copy of *Golf Digest*; off to his left, an open bottle of scotch sat on the ledge.

"Well?" Audrey demanded. "Are you gonna drink all night?"

"Maybe," he said. "Don't let the door hit you in the ass on the way out."

"You're such a pig," she said, surveying his whale body. "Little pathetic fucking dick floating around like an acorn. You oughta get a pair of fingernail clippers and snip it off, worthless little wart. What a sap you are . . ."

McDonald recoiled from this, astonished. They'd had their fights, but she'd never come on like this. He stared at her in stupefaction; then his face went rapidly from pink to red, and he heaved himself up, a sheet of water rolling out of the tub and onto the floor.

"You bitch," he bellowed. "I'm gonna beat your ass . . ."

He was fast on his feet for a fat man, but she was ready for it. She was several steps out into the bedroom, heading for the stairs, before he was out of the tub. Once he was angry enough, she knew, he'd keep coming, and he was angry enough. She ran down the stairs—the alcohol still a warm glow in her stomach, but not yet reaching toward her head—punched her sister's number on the speed-dial, listened, prayed she'd answer. In any case, Helen had an answering machine, which would do almost as well . . . she could hear Mc-Donald thundering down the stairs, two rings, three—and then Helen: "Hello?"

"Helen," she screamed. "Wilson is coming, Wilson—"

"Get the fuck away from there," McDonald shouted. His face was twisted, purple, all the pent-up rage of the day now flowing out toward her. She'd never seen his face like this, not even at the beginning of the worst of the beatings she'd taken from him. But she gave him the finger and he ran toward her and when he was close enough, she swung the phone at his head like a hammer. He deflected it with his forearm, then grabbed it, but she held on, screaming, "Let me go, Wilson, let me go," while he shouted, "Let go of the fuckin' phone . . ."

He was trying to twist the phone free, and when she held on, he stepped back and slapped her hard, knocking her down. She went facedown, slamming hard into the floor, closing her eyes just an instant before impact, deliberately letting her head snap forward; felt the crunch of her nose, the taste of blood in her nose and mouth.

"Oh, Christ . . ." She tried to get up and McDonald kicked her and she went down again, and he was shouting into the phone, "You keep your nose out of this, Helen, this is between Audrey and me, if you stick your nose into this I'll kick your ass too . . ."

Audrey launched herself toward the living room, blood streaming from her nose; the blood left long trails across the gray tile floor and onto the rug. McDonald had hung up the phone, and was coming: she got to her feet, spotted the crystal golf trophy, picked it up and threw it at his head. He ducked, and it bounced off a bookshelf, and he turned and tried to catch it as it bounced across the floor; it was unbroken until the last bounce, when it hit the tile of the kitchen and an arm shattered.

McDonald groaned and picked up the biggest chunk of it and began blubbering: "You fuckin' broke it, you broke my golf man . . ."

He came after her hard then, with a balled fist. She screamed at him, "Wilson, don't," but he clubbed her with a balled fist, and she crashed into the music stand on the Steinway; more blood spattered across the music books, and she went down again.

"Get up!" he screamed. "Get the fuck up . . ."

Instead, she tried crawling under the piano, where she wrapped her arms around the pedal mechanism: and a very small part of her mind assessed the damage she had taken, and was pleased.

"Get out here," McDonald screamed. He'd fallen to his hands and knees, the golf trophy set to one side, and grabbed her ankle and pulled. She hugged the pedal housing, kicking at his face; he dug his fingernails into the skin of her leg, holding on, pulling, and she jerked her leg up sharply and kicked again, connecting with his hands.

"You fuckin' bitch!" he screamed, and he pivoted and began kicking her legs with his heavy bare feet, the kicks landing on her calves and thighs. She abandoned the pedals, crawled toward the other side, where a row of silk plants lined the edge of a low window. Behind her, she left traces of blood; when she kicked his hands off her legs, he'd peeled two-inch strips of skin away and her legs were bleeding profusely; and she was still bleeding from her nose, blowing bubbles of blood out on the beige carpet.

"Oh no you don't," McDonald said, as she crawled toward the plants. He stood up and lurched to the far side of the piano, kicked one of the fake plants out of the way, and stooped over to meet her.

But she'd already reversed herself and squirted out the other side of the piano; she spotted the broken golf trophy on the floor, picked it up, and turned to face him.

"This what you want to do, Wilson?" she shrieked. She hit herself in the face with the trophy, and the edge of it cut her cheek from the corner of her left eye almost to her jawline. McDonald had been trying to get across the jumble of plants; now he stumbled, stopped.

"What the hell are you doing?"

"I'm beating myself up, so you won't have to do it," she screamed. "Here, I'll do it again," and she hit herself again, slashing back at her skull with the broken edge. This drew real blood, and McDonald gawked at her.

"Now," she said, more quietly, "you take your turn . . ." And she pitched the trophy at him, hitting him square in the chest.

McDonald, reflexes working, trapped the trophy against his chest, still gawking at the bloody hulk of the woman ten feet away. Audrey turned and ran toward the back bedroom, and McDonald, carrying the trophy in one hand, drunk but struggling now for self-control, said, "Jesus Christ, Audrey, I knew you were fuckin' nuts, but what the hell is this?"

Audrey pushed back out of the bedroom, carrying Granddad's favorite twelve-gauge. She looked like a nightmare from a horror film, blood matting her hair, running down her cheek into her blouse, bubbling from her nose over her lips and chin down her neckline, and running from her legs down to her feet; she'd left a row of bloody footprints into and out of the bedroom.

"You loser," she said, through the dripping blood.

A sad look came over McDonald's bully face as he looked into the muzzle of the gun: "I was afraid you'd killed all those people; but I didn't want to know," he said.

"Well, now you do," she said.

"You don't have to kill me."

"Wilson, that goddamned Davenport is snuffling around after you, and he's going to get you. He already knows about some of the other killings, and once he has those figured out—you'd cave in like a house of cards. My problem is, you might still be able to prove you were out of town for a couple of the killings. And I'll tell you what, Wilson, after all the shit I put up with married to a goddamn loser . . ." The booze was beginning to have an effect, and she blinked once, twice, almost lost her line of thought. "After all that shit, I couldn't stand going to jail for it."

"You don't have to," he said, hastily. He took a step back. "You gotta think about this."

"I have thought about it," she said. "I would have had to do it sooner or later anyway."

"You goddamn hillbilly," he said, taking another step back.

"You . . ." She couldn't think of an answer to that, so she fired the shotgun, the load of buckshot blowing straight through the broken golf trophy McDonald had moved up over his chest, through an inch of yellow fat, and into McDonald's heart. He wasn't blown backward, the way people hit with shotguns were in the movies; he simply took another step back, tried to say something else, and then toppled.

Audrey checked to make sure he was dead, and then called 911.

"I killed my husband," she choked; and she really choked, because she had loved him, more or less. "I shot my husband," she moaned. "Send somebody . . ."

And when they said they would, she dropped the phone, tossed the gun at McDonald's sightless body, and staggered into the kitchen for another drink.

19

Lucas woke in full light, with the phone ringing again. He hopped out of bed, nearly stumbled on cramped legs, lurched through the bedroom door to the study, picked up the extension on the sixth or seventh ring and said, "Yeah?"

"Lucas, this is Dan Johnson." Johnson ran the overnight Homicide. "Listen, you know this McDonald guy you've been tracking?"

"Yeah?"

"We caught a call from his old lady last night. Audrey McDonald. She killed him with a shotgun."

"What?" He heard the words, but they didn't make sense.

"Killed him," Johnson said. "Hit him in the chest with a goose load, range of about six feet. He'd beaten the shit out of her. There was blood all over the goddamn place."

"Aw, man." Lucas thought for a moment. "Where is she right now? Audrey?"

"Over at the hospital. We got a preliminary statement from her, on the way downtown. She admitted shooting him, then asked for an attorney. Her sister, Helen, is here, making a statement. She says Audrey called her, looking for help, while her old man was chasing her around the house."

"That sounds a little strange. What'd they do, call a time-out so she could use the phone?"

"Well, you gotta hear the whole story, but it holds together."

"Okay."

"So Helen called 911 and asked us to send out a car, that her sister was being beaten to death. The next thing, we get a 911 from Audrey, saying she shot her old man. They were both pretty drunk, Audrey and Wilson. We got blood alcohols on both of them, the old man was two-point-one, she was one-point-four, and big as he was, he had to drink a shitload of booze to get up to two-point-one. We got an empty fifth of scotch and another bottle with about an inch left. He had been drinking part of the afternoon and all evening."

"You think Audrey and Helen could've set it up?" Lucas asked.

"I don't think so. You gotta see Audrey. I mean, McDonald beat the *shit* out of her. She's gonna need plastic surgery. In fact, she might be getting it right now."

"Ah, Christ. Okay, I'll be in."

"No rush. She won't be able to talk for a couple hours, as close as I can tell."

LUCAS WENT BACK to the bedroom, where Sherrill was still curled under the covers. "What?" she asked.

Lucas told her: "McDonald's dead. Shot to death by his old lady in a drunken fight. Or maybe, while her old man was beating her. Like that."

Sherrill sat up, letting the blankets fall away. Lucas decided she was beautiful. "How can that be right?"

"What do you mean?"

"It solves too many problems," she said.

"Yeah." He nodded and remembered his talk with the St. Paul fingerprint specialist—remembered saying that the discovery of McDonald's prints was just too easy. "But it happens that way."

"The first time it happened to me was with that Bonnie Bonet chick. And that was on this case too. Weird case . . . Are you going in?"

"Got to," he said. He dropped down on the bed next to her. "But not this exact moment."

"Oh, God, morning sex," she said. "I never understood what men see in it. I think they just wake up with hard-ons and don't know where else to put them." She yawned and said, "My mouth tastes really bad. Like that drawer in Sex that Rigotto used to spit into."

"Sweet image. You oughta be a fuckin' writer," Lucas said.

"A fuckin' scribe."

"A fuckin' hack. Anyway, I got a new toothbrush you can use," he said.

"Yeah, you would."

"Hey . . ." He was offended.

"Sorry. I make, like, a total retraction." She rolled her eyes.

"You should. Anyway, you could brush your teeth and then I could show you the shower again."

She brightened. "That's not a bad idea; I only got part of the tour last night."

"Did we get to the soap on a rope?"

"I don't believe we did . . ."

LUCAS HAD NEVER thought of himself as a cheerful person, because he wasn't; he wasn't usually morose either. He simply lived in a kind of police-world mélange built of cynicism, brutality, and absurdity, leavened by not infrequent acts of selflessness, idealism, and sacrifice. If a cop brought a continuing attitude of good cheer to that world, there was something wrong with him, Lucas thought. His own recent problems he recognized as involving brain chemicals: he could take other chemicals to alter his mental state, but he was afraid to do that. Would the brain-altered Davenport actually be himself? Or would it be some shrink's idea of what a good Davenport would look like?

All that aside, he was feeling fairly cheerful when he arrived downtown, alone. Sherrill would not get in the car with him: she would not arrive downtown at the same time.

"If we keep doing this, they're gonna know anyway," Lucas said.

"Yeah. Later. And that's what I want. Later."

"But you want to keep doing it?"

"Oh jeez, yeah. I mean, if you do," she said. "A couple, three times a week, anyway. Don't think I could handle every night."

"Don't have to worry about that," Lucas grunted, as he looked in a dresser mirror to tie his necktie. "Another night like last night'd probably kill me."

"You're in pretty good shape for an old fuck," Sherrill said. She was still lounging on the bed, pink as a baby.

"If you make me think of things to say, I won't remember how to tie a necktie," he said, fumbling the knot.

"Who picked out your suits?" she asked. She hopped off the bed to look in the closet. Not only was she beautiful, he thought, her ass was absolutely glorious; and she knew it.

"I did. Who else?"

"You've got pretty good taste." She pulled out a suit, looked at it, put it back, pulled out another. "I can remember, you always wore good suits, good-looking suits, even before you were rich."

"I like suits," he said. "They feel good. I like Italian suits, actually. I've had a couple of British suits, and they were okay, but they felt . . . constructed. Like I was wearing a building. But the Italians—they know how to make a suit."

"Ever try French suits?"

"Yeah, three or four times. They're okay, but a little . . . *sharp*-looking. They made me feel like a watch salesman."

"How about American suits?" she asked.

"Efficient," he said. "Do the job; don't feel like much. You always wear an American suit if you don't want people to notice you."

"Jeez. A real interest." She was being cop-sarcastic. "Never would have guessed it. Suits."

He wasn't having it: "Yeah, sorta," he said. "I like to watch the fashion shows on TV, sometimes, late at night."

Now she was amazed. "Now you're lying."

"No, I'm not. Fashion is interesting. You can tell just about everything you need to know about somebody, by looking at their fashion."

"What about me?"

"Ask me some other time; like three years from now."

"C'mon, Davenport . . ."

"Nope. I'm not going to tell you," he said. "Women get nervous when men have insights into their personalities, and we're too early in this whole thing for me to reveal any."

"You've had some?" Her eyebrows went up.

"Several, over the years, and more last night," he said. "Some of them unbearably intimate; I'll list them for you. Like, three years from now."

"Jeez," she said. "What an enormous asshole . . ."

LUCAS DUMPED THE car and strode into City Hall, jingling his car keys. Sloan spotted him in the hallway.

"What happened to you?" Sloan asked.

"What? Nothing."

"You look weird," Sloan said. "You look . . . happy."

"Any fuckin' happier I'd be dancing a jig," Lucas said. "You talking to McDonald?"

"I was just on the way."

"I want to watch, if that's okay."

"Sure. It's over on the ward, at Hennepin."

HENNEPIN GENERAL HOSPITAL was just down the block and over one; Sloan and Lucas walked over in the brilliant, clear morning light, just a fresh touch of winter in the wind.

"Her lawyer says she'll make a statement," Sloan said, as they crossed the street. "They're trying to hurry things along, get a bond hearing this afternoon."

"They're talking self-defense?"

"Man, it *was* self-defense," Sloan said. "I was just out at the house, there's blood all over the place. And wait'll you see her. He chopped the shit out of her head with a golf trophy. She got like forty stitches in her scalp."

"She sure sold you on it."

"If it's a setup, it's the best one we're ever going to see. The ME says he's got her skin under his fingernails, and she's got big stripes on her legs where he peeled it off. Her legs are a mess, her back and ribs look like she's been in a gang fight, her face is completely blue with bruises, except where it's cut. Her old man's fingerprints are all over the golf trophy. In blood."

"Okay . . ."

"But just in case," said Sloan, reversing direction, "we should bump her a little. I was gonna get Loring to do it, because's he's such a mean-looking sonofabitch, but I can't find him. If you're gonna be around, after we get the statement, could you do it?"

"Yeah, sure."

"Bump" was Sloan's private code word for frighten. He'd be the nice guy and get all the basic information, but even with a voluntary statement it sometimes helped to shake up the suspect. You could never tell ahead of time just what might fall out . . .

A tall, white-haired attorney named Jason Glass, known for handling spousal abuse cases, a court reporter, and Sloan gathered around Audrey McDonald's bed. She was propped half upright, with a saline solution dripping into one arm through an IV. Lucas stepped into the room and looked at her. He hadn't seen much worse, he thought, where the woman actually survived. He stepped back outside the open door and leaned against the wall to listen.

Sloan led McDonald through the routine, with interjections by her attorney: Yes, she was making the statement voluntarily. No, she hadn't been offered anything in return for making the statement. No, she hadn't been asked to answer police question before her attorney arrived, but yes, she had told police that she'd shot her husband, Wilson McDonald, with a twelve-gauge shotgun.

As Lucas listened to her recount the sequence of violence, Frank Lester, the other deputy chief, straggled down the hall, peeked in the door, and said, "How's it going?"

Lucas shrugged: "She ain't arguing. She says she did it. And McDonald was the guy: nothing she's saying makes it seem any other way."

"We're getting some preliminary stuff back from the lab. Everything is consistent with what she said early on."

"They had a history," Lucas said. "The question now is, can she live without him?"

"She's got a problem?"

"When I saw her, at O'Dell's, she was virtually a hand puppet. She had no personality left that he didn't supply."

"Well . . . you know they're pleading self-defense," Lester said.

"Yeah."

"If the lab comes through, I doubt she'll even be indicted."

"If the lab comes through, she shouldn't be," Lucas said. "Speaking of the lab, did we ever get that spectrographic analysis on the slug fragments?"

"Mmm, I heard somebody say something about it. I think it's back, but I don't know what they said."

"All right . . ."

They listened for a minute: Audrey was telling of the pursuit down the stairs, of the panicky call to Helen. "You gonna bump her a little?" Lester asked.

"Yeah, when she's done. I'm starting to feel kinda bad about it, though," Lucas said.

"I don't know," Lester said, peering up at him. "I thought you were looking pretty cheerful."

"Yeah?"

"Yeah. You getting laid again?"

"Jesus, you married guys don't think about anything but sex."

"That's true," Lester said. "Well, let me know what happens."

Lucas nodded. "I will."

"And say hello to Sherrill for me. You know, when you see her."

SLOAN HAD GOTTEN through the shooting, and now was working backward: Did Audrey McDonald know that her husband was suspected of committing a number of murders?

"No . . ." A little fire now, but in a prissy way. "That ridiculous Davenport person is pushing this. Wilson would never kill anybody. He'd lose control and he'd beat me up, but sometimes I was asking for it. Last night . . . last night I just couldn't help myself, I ran into the bedroom to hide and there was the shotgun and the shells on the floor and he was coming and I knew how to load it . . ." She started rambling down the path to the shooting again, and Sloan cut her off.

"Did your husband own a pistol?"

"No. Well, yes, years ago . . ."

"State firearms records indicate he purchased a .380-caliber Iver Johnson semiautomatic pistol at North Woods Arms in Wayzata in 1982."

"I'm sure you're right. But he never used it. He called it his car gun because he had to work down in the colored area sometimes, way back when."

"Do you know where he kept it?"

"No, I assumed he gave it away. Or disposed of it."

"He doesn't have it in his car now?"

"I don't think so; I think I would have known . . ."

"Do you remember how you heard the news that Andy Ingall was lost up on Lake Superior?"

"Well . . . I think somebody from the bank called and told us."

"Mr. McDonald was with you when you found out?"

"Why, yes. Somebody called him, not me."

"You don't know if he'd been in Duluth about that time."

"I'm sure he wasn't; it would have stuck in my mind."

Sloan was pushing a dead end. Lucas waited a few more minutes, listening, then breezed into the room, as though he was in a hurry. Sloan looked up and said, "Chief Davenport . . . Mrs. McDonald."

She seemed to shrink away from him, what was left of her. Most of her face was black with bruises and subcutaneous bleeding around the cuts; a row of tiny black stitches marched up one cheek like a line of gnats; her hair was cut away on one side of her head, and a scalp bandage was damp from wound seepage.

"Mrs. McDonald, I'll be brief," Lucas said. "We're virtually certain that your husband was involved in the deaths of Kresge, Arris, and Ingall. And we're wondering how, if he killed all those people, you could not have known about it."

"Why . . . why . . . he didn't do that."

And her attorney, Glass, was sputtering, "Hey, hey, hey . . . we're not answering those kinds of questions."

"You should," Lucas said. "If Mrs. McDonald doesn't cooperate, well, Mr. Glass . . . you know how it looks. I mean, if a person has ambitions to resume her life in society."

"What?" Audrey McDonald looked dazed, swinging her face from Glass to Lucas. "Resume my life?"

"That's a lot of horse pucky, Lucas," Glass said. To Audrey McDonald: "Ignore him."

"At your own risk," Lucas said. "You know how people talk."

"People," she said.

Lucas added, "We will be executing a search warrant at the McDonald home this morning, looking for more evidence. But we already have substantial support for the idea that Wilson McDonald killed all three of them. And we will want to understand what your role was in the killings . . . if you had one."

"You can't . . ."

"Mrs. McDonald," Lucas said, suddenly going soft. "I mentioned this the other night. I recognize your voice."

"What?" As though she hadn't heard him correctly. And Glass peered at her, a frown on his face.

"You've called me," he said. "You knew your husband was killing people."

"That's utterly——" She groped for a word other than "ridiculous," but couldn't find one. "——ridiculous."

"What are you doing, Lucas?" Glass asked.

And Audrey seemed so genuinely nonplussed that Lucas, puzzled—why would she deny it now? Having helped stop him could only be to her credit, now, and he wasn't around to strike back—backed away, and tried again. "Mrs. McDonald, how often did you visit the Kresge cabin?"

"Why, why . . ." She struggled to think. "It's so hard to *think* with these things they are putting into me."

"You don't have to answer these questions," Glass said. "And I would recommend that you don't."

"You suggest that she not tell me how often she went to Kresge's? Why wouldn't she tell me that?" Lucas asked.

"Because you might try to make your pig's ear into a silk purse, and there's no reason to help you do that," Glass said.

"Maybe six times," she said.

"Mrs. McDonald, you don't have to answer," Glass said. "In fact, I'm telling you: Keep quiet. Lucas—Chief Davenport—if you have any more questions about Mr. McDonald, ask me first. I may advise Mrs. McDonald to answer them. But she won't answer any more questions about herself." Glass looked at the stenographer. "Could you read that back to me?"

"Sure, just a minute."

"No need to," Lucas said. "We got it, and I'm outa here. We'll be checking the McDonald house. And we may be back with more questions." He looked straight into Audrey McDonald's eyes, held them for a second, then turned and walked out.

GLASS CAUGHT LUCAS in the hallway. "What the hell was that all about?"

Lucas shrugged. "Bumping her along a little."

"Well, Jesus . . ." Glass scratched his head. "You don't think she had anything to do with these things, do you? The killings? That old lady?"

"What do *you* think, counselor?"

"Don't *counselor* me, butthead. This is J. B. fuckin' Glass you're talking to. What I want to know is, do I have to start thinking about a defense? Or were you just blowing smoke?"

"Mostly smoke," Lucas admitted.

"All right," Glass said. "How you been?"

"Not too bad . . . You heard about Weather?"

"Yeah, the bomb. Jesus. What do you think, a crazy?" Glass asked.

"We don't know. We've got no theory."

"Shoot. Well, keep your ass down," Glass said, and slapped Lucas on the arm before he started back to McDonald's room.

"Hey, J. B.——how old do you think your client is, anyway?"

Glass spread his hands. "I never asked. Fifty . . . two?"

"She's thirty-eight," Lucas said.

Glass looked at McDonald's room, then said with a hushed voice, "No way."

"She's got some hard miles on her, J. B. And she might not be quite what she looks like."

20

LUCAS WAS SITTING in McDonald's study, flipping through a batch of American Express statements that went back, apparently, forever. Both Wilson and Audrey McDonald were Platinum Card holders, upgraded six years earlier from the Gold. The most interesting statement involved charges on McDonald's card in the days before Andy Ingall sailed off on Lake Superior and vanished.

"The day before Ingall disappears, McDonald spends four hundred bucks at Marshall Field in Chicago. That night, and the night before, he's at the Palmer House," Lucas said to Franklin. "That means if he rigged the boat, he had to have done it at least a couple of days beforehand, or, if he came home that day, he had to go right up to Superior and rig the boat the night before. That seems tricky."

Franklin, enormous in a plaid shirt and jeans, had been going through the check stubs and investment papers. "I ain't finding anything here. It's all too general. They were pretty well off, though. He's got a trust account at Polaris with about three-point-four million divided between stocks and bonds, heavy on the bonds. Plus an account at Vanguard worth another three million, all in the stock market. And if I'm reading it right, he's got another nine hundred thousand in stock at Merrill Lynch. Cash in bank accounts, about twenty-four thousand, plus a money market account with a hundred and seventy thousand . . . that's apparently a tax account." He put the papers down, and looked at Lucas. "I don't know. With that much—that's gotta be more'n seven million—you think he'd be killing to get even richer?"

"I asked the same thing," Lucas said. "The answer is, he was chasing power, not money. He was a bully in high school, he beat his wife, he killed people to eliminate competition for the promotions. He got off on power trips. He'd be running the lives of a couple thousand people if he took over the bank."

Franklin sighed: "I'd like to get a *nice* killer sometime."

A uniformed cop stuck his head in the door: "You know how you told us to find that Jag?"

Lucas nodded without looking up. According to a file they found in the house, and confirmed by the Department of Motor Vehicles, Wilson McDonald owned a 1969 XK-E, which was not in their three-car garage.

"We talked to McDonald's old man," the uniformed cop said. His name was Lane, and he wanted to be a detective. "The car was in a downtown parking garage, already covered up for the winter. And guess what?"

Lucas looked up now. "What?"

Lane stepped fully into the room, held up a transparent plastic baggie. Inside, a small automatic pistol. "Ta-da."

"I don't believe it," Lucas said. He took the bag, held it up, and peered at the gun. The caliber, .380, was stamped on the slide. "That's the one . . . You touch it?"

"No, of course not. The safety's on, and we just bagged it. Figured, who knows—if he didn't shoot it much, maybe it's got some of the same shells from the Arris or O'Dell deals."

"Get it downtown," Lucas said, handing it back.

"Do I get a medal?" Lane asked.

"Yeah. You'll get a size eleven medal right in the ass if you don't get it downtown."

Lane left, and a few minutes later, Franklin, who'd fallen into an odd reverie sitting in an overstuffed chair with the bank statements in his hands, staring at an English hunting print on the wall above McDonald's desk, suddenly said, "I know what it is."

"I'm glad somebody does," Lucas said.

"You know what's wrong with this place?"

Lucas looked around. "Looks pretty nice."

"There are no fuckin' books," Franklin said. He got up, walked around the study, checking the shelves full of ceramic figurines. "They even got a couple of bookends, with no books between them—they got these fuckin' Keebler elves, or whatever they are."

"Hummels," Lucas said. "But they do have a computer." He nodded at the Hewlett Packard crouched on the desk.

"Ain't a book," Franklin said. "I'm going to look around."

Lucas finished the American Express statements, extracted the statement that showed McDonald in Chicago, and stacked the rest on the desk. Slow going. He'd just gotten up when Franklin came back: "I could find five books in this whole fuckin' house. A dictionary, a cookbook, a bartender's guide, and travel books on California and Florida."

"Maybe they took turns reading the dictionary," Lucas said.

"You don't think it's weird?"

"The pinking shears thing with Del—that was weird," Lucas said. "No books? That's not weird, that's just a little unusual."

"I think it's weird," Franklin insisted. "People with seven million, they oughta have books." He frowned, and said, "Hey, you know what else?"

He left the room, and Lucas trailed after him. "There's no CD player. I don't think they've got any CDs. They got no goddamn record player, Lucas."

"Yeah, well . . ."

Franklin turned and said, "These people are very strange." He looked around the room again, spotted a studio portrait of Wilson and Audrey McDonald smiling down from another knickknack shelf. The photo was so heavily re-touched that the two of them looked like puppets. "Look at her eyes," Franklin said. Lucas looked. "They follow you. Man, they are *very* strange."

AUDREY MCDONALD LAY in her hospital bed and thought about Davenport. He seemed to know something. To know *her*. The others had shaken their heads when they saw her, had essentially apologized for their maleness in view of what another male had done to her. The hospital had provided female attendants to care for her, as if a male doctor or male nurse might somehow further the damage done.

Not Davenport. He was ready to crucify her. She would have to move on this.

She dozed for a while, in a little pain, and woke up, calculating.

The lawyer said she'd be here overnight, and then would be wheeled into court for a preliminary hearing on an open charge of murder. She would be allowed to enter a plea—not guilty—and bail would be set. If she was willing, he'd said, she could use her house as security. The assistant county attorney handling the case had already indicated that the state would have no objection, so the deal was as good as done, and she could go straight home from the courthouse.

"Murder?" She'd croaked. "They're charging . . . ?"

"Don't worry: they're already backing off," Glass had said. "When the police finish investigating, they'll almost certainly find that it was self-defense. Right now, it's ninety-ten for no charges at all."

So Audrey had agreed to use the house as security, and had given him a limited power of attorney so that he could get all the paperwork. She'd be out tomorrow afternoon.

And that would be the time to handle the Davenport problem.

She'd thought she was doing that when she pitched the Molotov cocktail through Weather Karkinnen's window. From what she could tell by questioning Wilson, and careful questions to others at the bank, Davenport had been the only reason that Wilson had been looked at so closely. Audrey had attacked Karkinnen in an effort to turn Lucas around—the same tactic had worked in the past, with the McKinney situation and the Bairds. And from what she could tell of the investigation's pace, and from stories in the newspapers, the attack *had* diverted him for a time. Investigators had vanished from the bank, there'd been two days of silence from the police . . . and then suddenly, they were back, and all over Wilson.

Wilson.

She sighed, and let a little tear start at the corner of her eye. She already missed Wilson. She'd known, in her heart of hearts, that someday she'd have to kill him, the love of her life. He would inevitably get in her way, or even become a danger to her. And he finally had. If the police had put pressure on him, he would've pointed them at her, because he was basically a coward. He had no grit. Wilson . . .

She wrenched her mind back to Davenport.

The problem with the Karkinnen diversion was that the police investigation hadn't led anywhere. The newspapers said the police were simply mystified. They'd run down every single clue and they'd found nothing at all. After a while, there was nothing left to do, so they went back to Wilson and had apparently stumbled over something that pointed at the Arris killing. If they'd been preoccupied with Karkinnen a little bit longer, they might never have found whatever it was.

Now they were looking at her. Or at least, Davenport was. She didn't quite understand why. She'd given him an answer to his question—her own dead husband.

She'd actually given him an earlier answer, the answer to who killed Kresge, but he either hadn't gotten the message or had ignored it.

The Kresge murder weapon had the fingerprints of Kresge's caretaker all over it. He'd been the one who put it away the last time Audrey saw it. A few of the lingering partygoers had been sitting around with Kresge, talking and cleaning the guns. When they were done with each one, they'd pass it to the caretaker, who'd put it away.

Kresge had told her, on the shooting range, that she shot the Contender better than he did. That he'd never shot it at all, after the first few times. So the caretaker's prints should still be on it. But the papers hadn't had a whisper about the gun, and Wilson said nobody had even bothered to interview the caretaker. Something was screwed up, she thought. Typical. Very few people could act with her intellectual rigor . . .

Audrey was crazy and smart and she knew how to do research: she'd taken an undergraduate degree in English from St. Anne's, and then, while she was pushing Wilson through law school, she'd taken a master's degree from the University of Minnesota in library science. She was still working in the library when computers moved in, and she'd more or less kept up with them over the years, and when the bank went on-line. When Davenport became a problem, she'd looked him up in the *Star-Tribune* library node on the Internet.

And there she'd found a treasure trove.

The *Star-Tribune* had done a lengthy feature on Davenport after he'd cleared the kidnapping of a psychologist and her two daughters by a madman named John Mail. "Davenport and His Pals" had pictured Davenport with Weather Karkinnen, with Sister Mary Joseph—whom he'd known since their childhood together—and with a variety of cops, lawyers, TV and newspaper reporters, doctors, jocks, and street people, all friends of his.

The two obvious targets for a diversionary attack were the nun and the surgeon—Davenport's oldest friend and his lover. She decided on Karkinnen because Karkinnen was simpler.

Audrey knew Sister Mary Joseph from her college days: the nun had been her instructor in basic psychology, and Audrey remembered her as an intense young woman with a face terribly scarred by adolescent acne. But the nun, who was still at St. Anne's, lived in a communal dormitory-style setting in which intruders would be instantly noticed. And attack would be risky.

Karkinnen, on the other hand, was out in the open. Audrey had been puzzled that the year-old article implied that Karkinnen was Davenport's live-in lover, while Audrey's search turned up different addresses, but she assumed there was something that she didn't know. She considered the possibility that they'd broken up, but then found an engagement announcement only a few months old . . .

So she'd gone for Karkinnen. She'd thrown the bomb through the window, concerned not a whit for the possibility that she might kill the woman, but very concerned at the possibility of being caught. The final attack—out of the car, across the lawn, throw, back in the car, ten seconds—minimized the possibility, but it had still taken nerve.

She'd need the nerve again: but nerve had never been a problem for her. Audrey McDonald had nerve, all right.

She thought again about the possibility of going after Davenport himself. There were two problems with that: First, he was large and tough-looking, and carried a gun. He would be difficult to get at quickly without exposing herself. She couldn't get close enough for poison, couldn't risk a gun attack; if she missed, she'd be dead. And he was a cop, so might be a little more wary than the average citizen. Further, she didn't have time to research him as she had Arris and Ingall. And the second big problem was that killing him might lead the cops investigating *his* killing to take a harder look at his current investigations, including *her*.

A diversion would lead them away from her . . . So it would have to be the nun.

Her legs twitched down the bed, a kind of running motion, as she began working out a possible plan. She'd have to do it the minute she got out. She'd have to emphasize her injuries, complain of cracked ribs, something that wouldn't show on X rays, but would keep her from doing anything heavy. She'd have to hobble and whimper and limp and make people feel sorry for her, and the instant she was alone, she had to go for the nun.

She'd have no trouble with this. She'd been undercover for more than twenty-five years now. She might not ever come out.

FRANKLIN HAD BEEN in a longtime 401K plan. The stocks had gone through the roof during the summer, so, like any Good American, he'd borrowed against the fund to buy a new black Ford extended-cab pickup truck, which he and Lucas walked around, Lucas shaking his head. Finally Franklin said, "So what next? Just wrap it up? We're done?"

"Wrap it up," Lucas said. They were standing at the curb outside McDonald's house. "McDonald's the man, and he's dead: outa reach. I'll spend a couple days trying to figure out the firebomb thing with Weather, then maybe go up to the cabin."

"Going up alone?" Franklin asked.

"Cut some firewood, put the snow blade on the Gator, haul the snowmobiles out and get them checked," Lucas said.

"Going up alone?"

"Get the batteries out of the boat, put the boat away. Maybe figure out some way to cover it. I had some squirrels get in it last year, in the shed, and the damn thing was full of decapitated acorn shells when I got it out this spring."

"Jesus, I wish I was single again, sometimes," Franklin said. "And had a cabin up north. Nothing like a little strange pussy in November."

"If you'd asked me, I could have advised you against getting a Ford," Lucas said. "Anyway, see you around."

"See you around," Franklin said. Lucas walked back up the long driveway to the house, where he'd parked, while Franklin strolled once more around the truck, rubbing out a couple of imaginary blemishes with the cuff of his coat. "I love you," he said aloud. He was back at the driver's side door, and about to get in, when Lucas arrived at the Porsche, a hundred and fifty feet away.

"*Going up alone?*" Franklin bellowed.

Lucas threw him the finger and got in the car.

21

WHEN AUDREY MCDONALD opened her eyes the next morning, she knew something she hadn't known when she closed them the night before.

"Helen," she said.

Helen had been talking to Davenport. Helen had always hated Wilson, and must have called Davenport anonymously. That's how Helen would have done it, maneuvering to get rid of Wilson without damaging her relationship with her sister—and that would explain why Davenport thought he'd spoken to Audrey. Helen and Audrey spoke with the same soft Red River Valley accent, with the rounded and softened *o*'s of the Swedes; they said "boot" when they meant "boat."

Davenport had picked that up, but hadn't known of Helen.

But this was new: Helen had realized that people were being murdered? Believed that Wilson had done it, and moved against him? Helen didn't keep secrets very well: give her a secret, and she usually blurted it out the first chance she had.

Audrey would have to think about this: How much did Helen know, and how much had she guessed? How early had she caught on? Had she taken any notes, mental or otherwise, that might point away from Wilson and toward herself? And did she know about all the incidents? Did she know about McKinney and the Bairds?

WHEN LUCAS WOKE, he thought about Sherrill.

The woman would sooner or later be a problem; maybe even a disaster. They worked too closely, on problems too complicated, for a romance to work very well. And when the word got out—and the word would get out—there would be serious sniping to deal with. He hoped Sherrill understood that: she was smart enough, she should.

He wished she was in his bed now. He rolled over, awake, feeling fresh, pivoted and put his feet on the floor, realized that he hadn't felt quite this good for months.

And then he thought of Weather, and a touch of sadness came over him. He'd wanted to marry her. If she suddenly changed, and came back to him, he'd accept her in an instant.

But she was falling away now. Her influence was fading: he didn't think of her as much. Like Mom's death, he thought. When Lucas's mother died, of breast cancer, he'd thought of her every few minutes for what seemed like a year. Things she'd said, images of her faces, moments of their life together. That was all still there in his head, and the images came back from time to time, but not like those first few months. His mother had gone gently away, and now came back only when he reached for her.

Like Weather.

He sighed, and headed for the bathroom. He was a late riser, and he looked back at the clock as he went: he wanted to be there when Audrey McDonald made her court appearance.

AUDREY'S ATTORNEY, JASON Glass, showed up with a woman photographer, a load of photo equipment, a pair of gym shorts, and a soft halter top.

"This is Gina," Glass told Audrey. "We need to take some photographs of you, showing your injuries. This is absolutely critical for the case. Gina brought some terry cloth for modesty purposes . . ."

They shot the pictures in an unoccupied hospital room, against the white drape that ran around the bed. At Gina's direction, Audrey limped into the small bathroom and put on the shorts and halter top, carefully brushed her hair, and went out to face the cameras.

"I'm sorry," Gina said before she started shooting. "I should have told you to leave your hair as it was. Nobody will ever see these photos except attorneys, and frankly, we want them to look as . . . severe . . . as possible."

Audrey nodded; she knew what was needed. She trundled back into the bathroom and flipped her hair back and forth, stirred it around, then brushed it away from the scalp wound. In the mirror, she looked like a photo of a nineteenth-century madwoman in Bedlam. And that, she supposed, was what they wanted.

"Excellent," Gina said, as she set up a couple of spindly light stands. "That is just beautiful."

When the photos were done, Glass, who'd waited in the hall, said to Audrey, "You look like you still hurt."

"I do," Audrey said, deliberately vague. She peered around as though she'd lost a pair of glasses, or her shoes, and her lip trembled. "I can't believe Wilson is gone."

"I'm going to put you in a wheelchair before we head over to the courthouse," Glass said. "I think you'll be more comfortable that way."

"Thank you," Audrey muttered.

A MAN NAMED Darius Logan was saying, "I know I shouldn't have done it, Your Honor, but the dude flipped me off, you know?" when a sheriff's deputy wheeled Audrey into the courtroom, the two of them trailed by Glass.

Lucas was sitting in the back row, reading the St. Paul paper. Del sat next to him, thumbing through *Cliffs Notes on Greek Classics*. Two dozen other people were scattered around the courtroom, half of them lawyers, a couple of defendants' wives, reporters for the local television stations and newspapers, waiting for the McDonald hearing, and two or three courthouse groupies following the TV people.

McDonald looked bad, Lucas thought. Her head was patched with white bandages, stark against her gray face. She was wearing a gingham dress with short sleeves, a summer dress really, but one that beautifully showed off the bruises on her arms and lower legs. She looked beaten, both physically and psychologically: then, as the bailiff wheeled her toward the defense table, she saw Lucas. And for a vanishingly small instant—a time so short that it must have been imaginary—Lucas felt her eyes spark. Not sparkle, but actually *spark*, as with electricity.

The judge, a prissy little blonde who was known for occasional bouts of judicial intemperance, had grown impatient with Logan. He said, "That's all very well, Mr. Logan, but you've been here a number of times before and we're getting a little tired of it. I'll put bail at five thousand dollars and expect to see you back here at . . ." As he thumbed through a calendar, there was a meaty smack from the audience, as though somebody had just been punched. The impact came from the forehead of a young woman who'd just slapped herself with one heavy hand. The judge looked up and said, "Do you have something to say, young lady?"

The woman stood up and said, "Your Honor, if we got to pay some bail bondsman seven hundred and fifty dollars to get Darius out of jail"—she pronounced it "Dare-I-us"—"where in the hell am I gonna get the money for the kids' dinners?"

The judge's eyes clicked to the face of a well-known TV reporter, then back to the woman. "Why don't you leave Dare-I-us in jail for a while?"

"Don't dare do that," the woman said.

"Why not?"

"Just don't dare."

"Okay. Sit down. Dare-I-us, are you gonna show up for the trial?"

"I sure will, Your Honor."

"All right. Bail's set at one thousand dollars, and you've got the young lady to thank for it."

"Thank you, Your Honor."

As Logan left, the judge said, "Call the next one," and the bailiff called out, "Audrey McDonald."

"Here, Your Honor," Glass called back.

The woman who'd gotten the bail reduced on Darius Logan wedged herself down a line of spectators, out to the center aisle, and headed for the door. As she passed, she saw Del, and Del said, quietly, "Quick pregnancy."

"Shush," she said, and was gone. Del looked at Lucas and said, "Didn't have any kids last week."

"It's a miracle," Lucas said, turning to sports.

AUDREY MCDONALD SAT hunched in her chair, her back to Lucas, as the hearing routine broke around her, speaking only two words: "Not guilty."

"Your Honor, Mrs. McDonald's attorney has offered Mrs. McDonald's house as security for her appearance, and the state has no objection to that. As you may know, the circumstances around this particular incident could lead to a change in the charges against Mrs. McDonald . . ."

And a while later, it was all done. Audrey waited as Glass talked to the assistant county attorney over a few details, then said, "We've got to sign the papers and then I'm going to talk to the press. If I don't, they'll be parked outside your house, hassling you . . ."

She liked that, the press, though her face was determinedly grim.

". . . I don't really expect you to say anything," Glass was saying.

"I'll talk to them, if that will keep them away," Audrey said.

THE PRESS CAUGHT them outside the courthouse, at the curb, where Helen Bell was waiting in her car. Glass made a short speech about spousal abuse, said he anticipated that all charges would be dropped, then asked Audrey if she wished to answer questions.

She bobbed her head. "Did you kill your husband, Mrs. McDonald," a woman reporter blurted.

She bobbed her head again. "Yes," she said weakly. "I couldn't . . . I couldn't . . . He was hurting me so bad . . ." She touched the bandage on her scalp and peered at the camera lens. "Oh, God . . ." A tear trickled down her cheek. "God, I miss him. I'm so sorry . . ."

"Why do you miss him?"

"He was my husband," she wailed. "I wish he could come back . . . But he can't." She seized Glass's arm. "I can't . . ." She gasped.

"All right, all right," Glass said. "She's really weak. She's got to go. I'm pleading with you all. If you have any sensitivity, leave her alone."

"Mrs. McDonald . . ."

Then she was in the car and Helen was driving them away. "My God," Helen said. "My God, Audrey . . ."

"Just take me home."

"No, no. You're coming to my place."

"No. I want to go home," Audrey said. "Helen, please don't argue with me. Just take me home. Please. I just want to turn off the phones and get some sleep."

AND BACK AT the courthouse, Lucas said to Glass, "Quite a performance."

Glass was staring after Helen Bell's car, turned to Lucas and said, "The last thing I expected."

"You didn't prep her?"

"Hell, no. I figured she was such a sad sack, we couldn't lose. I didn't think we was gonna get Greta Garbo. Did you see that tear?"

"I didn't get that close."

"A real tear," Glass marveled. "Ran right down her cheek, and it was the cheek that was turned toward Channel Three. Tell you what, Lucas—if I lose this case, I'm gonna want to borrow one of your guns, so I can shoot myself."

THE HOUSE WAS silent: Audrey entered, listening for the footfalls of Wilson's ghost. She heard creaks and cracking that she hadn't heard before—but she'd never before listened. Helen came in behind her, tentatively. "You're sure you'll be okay?"

"I'll be okay," Audrey said, peering around. The police had been through the place, and though they hadn't been deliberately messy, the house looked . . . disheveled. "I hope the police didn't steal anything."

"Do you want me to come over tonight?"

"No . . . no. I'm going to take a couple of pills and try to sleep. I just really need to sleep, I haven't slept since before . . . before . . ."

"Okay. If you're sure you'll be all right."

"Do you, uh . . . You used to take Prozac," Audrey said. "Do you still use that?"

"Well, sure. Could hardly get along without it," Helen said.

"Do you think it would help? In the next few days?"

Helen shook her head. "I don't think it's for your kind of problem, honestly. I could give you a few and you could try them, but I think a doctor could give you something better."

"Maybe if I could just try a couple. If I don't sleep tonight . . ."

"Sure. We'll talk tomorrow."

When Helen was gone, Audrey prowled through the house, already planning: she'd bundle up his suits, dump them at Goodwill and get a tax deduction. She got a notepad and wrote: "ACCOUNTANT/Taxes and Deductions," and under that, "Suits." Wilson had all kinds of crap she'd want to get rid of, starting with that XK-E. She wrote "Jag" under "Suits." And he had a whole wall full of bullshit awards and plaques—chairman of this charity in 1994, director of that community effort in 1997. All worthless: straight into the garbage can, she thought.

So much to do.

Audrey really did hurt from Wilson's beating, and from her own enhancements to the damage. The scalp wound, in particular, felt tight, like a banjo head, its edges seeming to pull against the stitches. After half an hour of cruising through the house, she went up to the bedroom, set the alarm clock for nine P.M., and tried to sleep.

But sleep, she found, wouldn't come easily. Too many images in her head, a mix of plans and memories. If Wilson had only landed the chairmanship, none of this would have happened. She'd believed in him from the start, and the belief had only begun to falter after Kresge got the top job six years earlier. Kresge was a technocrat, and brought in other technocrats like Bone and Robles. They had no respect for family name, for fortune, for breeding or society. All they knew was how to make money. Wilson, running the mortgage division, which had always been one of the pillars of the bank, was suddenly out on a limb.

She didn't know that sleep had come, but it must have. The clock went off: she sat up, a bit groggy, realized that the room was dark. She groped around the bedstand, found the clock, and silenced the alarm. Then she touched the light and swung out of bed.

A little tension now. She went straight to the shower and stood under it, breathing deeply, flexing the muscles in her back and shoulders. Stiff. When she got out of the shower, she downed four ibuprofen tablets, then dressed: black slacks, a deep red sweater, and a dark blue jacket over the sweater. She found a pair of brown cotton gardening gloves, and pulled them on. The best she could do for nighttime camouflage. Now for a weapon.

The police had been all through the house, but she remembered that when the closet rod broke in the front closet a year or so earlier, Wilson had tossed the broken dowel rod up in the rafters of the yard shed, where it lay with other scrap wood. She found a flashlight in the kitchen, let herself out the back, and walked in the dark to the shed. Inside, she turned the flash on. She could see the scrap wood overhead, but couldn't reach it. The lawn tractor was there, and she stood on the seat, stretched to push the wood around, and saw the two pieces of the dowel rolling to one side. She got both of them down. One was a little more than six feet long, including the split; the other a little more than two feet long, including the sharp split end.

She carried them both back to the house in the dark, and inside the porch gave the shorter of the two pieces a test swing. A little lighter than a baseball bat, but it swung just as well. Wearing the gloves, she rubbed both of them down with WD-40, eliminating any fingerprints.

In the garage, she put both pieces in Wilson's Buick, then climbed on top of the car hood, pulled the cover off the light on the garage door opener, and unscrewed the lightbulb. She climbed down from the car and put the bulb on the passenger seat.

Ready. She took a deep breath, started the car, pushed the garage door opener. The door came up, but no light came on. She backed out of the garage, lights out, then rolled down the long driveway to the street. The houses were far enough apart, and the street dark enough, that she should be able to get out without being seen . . . a calculated risk. If anyone saw her driving without lights, they'd remember it. A risk she'd take. She rolled into the street, drove a hundred feet, and turned on the lights. She'd gotten away with it, she thought.

On the south side of Minneapolis, she stopped in a beat-up industrial area and threw the longer of the two pieces of dowel rod into a pile of trash; the other waited beside the passenger seat.

ST. ANNE'S COLLEGE—St. Anne's College for Blond Catholic Girls, as Audrey thought of it—was a leafy, red-brick girls' college in St. Paul, a short walk from the Mississippi. Davenport lived somewhere in the neighborhood, Audrey knew. The newspaper article didn't say exactly where: just the Highland Park neighborhood.

Maybe to be close to the nun, she thought.

Audrey had spent four unhappy years at St. Anne's, getting finished. She'd needed the finish, with her Red River farm background. And the unhappiness hadn't counted for much, since she couldn't ever remember being happy. She'd plowed through her courses, a smart, reasonably pretty brunette, and had carefully weeded out the likely husband prospects from St. James's—St. James's College for Blond Catholic Boys.

Wilson McDonald had been the result of her four years of winnowing.

ON THE SOUTHWEST side of the campus, the Residence squatted in sooty obscurity. A near-cube built of red brick like most of the other buildings on campus, it housed the declining numbers of the sisterhood of nuns who ran St. Anne's. The newspaper article, "The Pals of Lucas Davenport," had mentioned that Sister Mary Joseph lived on campus, and continued to wear the traditional black habit on public occasions, including the classroom, though she sometimes went out in civilian clothing when working in area hospitals.

Audrey had never seen her in anything but traditional dress, and wasn't sure she'd recognize her in civilian clothing. Still, she thought, she could pick her out.

AUDREY PARKED ON the street, and after sitting for a moment in the dark, looking up and down, she got out, leaving her purse but carrying her cell phone, the dowel rod held by her side. She walked to the Residence along the sidewalk, and, in the dark space between streetlights, turned into the parking lot and moved quickly to the far corner of the building. She stood there, between two tall junipers, an arm's length from the ivy-twined walls—the bare ivy like a net of ropes and strings climbing the bricks—and listened. She could hear voices, but far away; and a snatch of classical music from somewhere. More the *feel* of the conversation than the actual words and notes. The parking lot itself held only a dozen cars, most of them nunlike—black and simple; along with a few civilian cars.

She remembered this moment from the other times. The moment before commitment, when she could still back away, when, if discovered, she hadn't done anything. The moment where she could wave and say, "Oh, hello, I was a bit confused here, I'm just trying to find my way."

And the thrill came from piercing that moment, going through it, getting into the zone of absolute commitment.

She took the phone from her jacket pocket, and punched the numbers in the eerie green glow of the phone's information screen.

"St. Anne's Residence." A young woman's voice. Audrey had done this very job, answering the phone as a student volunteer, two nights a week for a semester, six o'clock to midnight.

"Yes, this is Janice Brady at Midway Hospital. We have a family-emergency call for a Sister Mary Joseph . . ."

"I think Sister is in chapel . . ."

The chapel was in the Residence basement. "Could you get her please? We have an injured gentleman asking for her."

"Uh, just a moment. Actually, it'll be two or three minutes."

"I'll hold . . ."

Then she heard more voices, close by. A man came around the corner, said something, laughed, walked into the parking lot.

Shit. This could ruin everything . . .

The man waved, walked to a car, fumbled with his keys, got in. Sat for a moment. Then started the engine, turned on the lights, and drove to the street.

And Sister Mary Joseph was there: "Hello?" Curiosity in her voice.

"Is this Sister Mary Joseph, a psychologist at St. Anne's College?"

"Yes, it is . . ."

"There's been a shooting incident, and one of the victims asked that you be notified. An Officer Lucas Davenport."

"Oh no! How bad is he?"

"He's in surgery. I really don't have any more information; a priest on the staff has been notified—we assumed he was Catholic."

"Yes, he is. Is the priest doing extreme unction?"

"No, Officer Davenport is in surgery, but we thought a priest should be notified; it's purely routine in these cases . . ."

"I'll be right there."

"If you will check with the information desk at the front entrance, not the emergency entrance, you will be directed to the surgical waiting area."

And the nun dropped the phone on the hook.

AUDREY BRACED HERSELF against the wall. If the nun came out the main entrance, the entrance closest to the parking lot, and headed straight toward the lot, she'd pass Audrey at little more than an arm's length. Audrey would have only a moment to determine if she was alone. If she wasn't, Audrey would follow her to Midway Hospital and try there—the nun would have to walk some distance to the main entrance, and would probably be dropped off.

She was rehearsing it all in her mind when she heard the main door open. No voices, just the clank of the push bar on the door, and the door opening. Three seconds later, a woman in a black habit swept by, and down the walk. Audrey instinctively knew she was alone: she was moving too quickly, with too much focus, to be with another person. Audrey swung out from behind the junipers, her heart gone to stone in her chest, a step and a half behind the nun.

And she struck, like an axman taking a head.

The heavy rod hit the nun on the side of the head, glanced off, hit the nun's shoulder; the woman sagged, her knees buckling, one hand going to the ground. She started to turn.

And Audrey struck her again, this time full on the head, and the nun pitched forward on her face . . . Audrey lifted the dowel rod, her teeth bared, her breathing heavy, and struck at the nun's head again, but from a bad angle: the rod this time bounced off the side of the nun's head and into her shoulder.

With building fury, with the memory of all these decades of slights and slurs against her, with the thought of all the people who'd held her back and down, with her father, her mother, with all the others, Audrey struck again and again, hitting the nun's neck and back and shoulder . . .

And heard the clank of the door again, froze, looked wildly around—nowhere to run, not at this instant, this was the very worst moment for an interruption—and stepped back in the shadow of the junipers. The girl came around the corner no more than a second later, saw the nun, said, "Sister!" and bent over her.

And Audrey struck at her, hitting the girl on the back of the head. Like the nun, the girl pitched forward, onto her face. Audrey hit her again, and again, breathing hard now. Stopped, hovered over the two motionless women for an instant, jabbed at the nun's leg with the end of the dowel rod, got no response, then scuttled away. Around the corner, onto the sidewalk, down the sidewalk to the car. Nobody on the sidewalk. Inside the car, dowel rod on the floor— a sudden touch of panic: she felt her pocket. Yes! The phone was there—and the car started and she eased away from the curb.

This was always the hardest part, staying cool after an attack. With her heart beating an impossible rhythm, Audrey drove slowly off the campus, to the Mississippi, left to the bridge and across to Minneapolis.

She stopped once, on a dark street, to throw the dowel rod down a sewer. She went on, dropped the cotton gloves one at a time out the window. She hadn't seen any blood from either of the women, but it had been dark: she should burn these clothes, or get rid of them, anyway.

That would have to wait—she could wash them tonight, immediately—and throw them out tomorrow.

But now, there was more to do.

Twenty minutes later, headlights on, she pulled into her driveway, and into the darkened garage. She dropped the garage door, groped to the kitchen entrance, went inside and flipped on the light.

Upstairs, she took off her clothes, inspected them closely. Nothing she could see. Still, they'd go in the washing machine. She picked up the phone: no messages. Good.

She dialed, got Helen: "Hello?"

"Helen . . . I just . . . can't sleep," she said, her voice crumbling. "I hate to bother you, have you come over here, but I'm just so blue, I'm just lying here thinking about Wilson." She began to weep, a bubbling, pathetic wail. "Help me."

"Oh God, hang on, Audrey, I'll be right there."

"And H-Helen . . . b-b-bring a few of those Prozacs. Maybe they would help. I've got to try *some*thing."

"I'll be right there. Hang on."

She hung up, satisfied. Cleared her face, gathered her clothes for the wash. She might not ever need the Prozac, she might not ever need Helen coming up the drive with her lights on, to muddy any witness statements—but who knew what the future might hold? Better to work all the possibilities now, than to regret it later.

She thought about the nun, lying on the sidewalk.

Wonder if she's dead?

She never thought about the other woman at all; the other woman was irrelevant.

22

SHERRILL HAD BROUGHT with her a votive candle scented faintly with vanilla, and a crystal candleholder, and their second night together took on the feel of college days, making love in the yellow flickering candlelight. And Sherrill said, as they lay comfortably warm under a sheet, "Do you think you could go for somebody like Candy LaChaise?" Sherrill had put four .357 slugs through Candy LaChaise's chest during an abortive holdup at a credit union.

"I don't think so," Lucas said. He was lying on his back, hands behind his head. "I think she'd smell pretty bad by now."

Sherrill made a quick move toward his groin and he flinched and said, "Don't do that, I almost killed you with my karate reflexes."

And she said, "Yeah, right. Answer the question."

He didn't have to think about it: "Nope. She was pretty, but she was missing a couple of links. You know those kinds of people—basically, they're a little stupid. Maybe they don't get bad grades in school, or maybe they even get good grades, but somewhere, down at the bottom, they're fuckin' morons. They don't connect with the world."

"You remember Johnny Portland?"

"Yeah. Asshole."

She got up on one elbow, looking down at him. "I went out with him a couple of times."

Lucas turned his head to look at her: "Jesus. Did he know you were a cop?"

"I wasn't. This was like my sophomore year in college, I met him at this Springsteen concert. He liked younger girls, I was like twenty; he picked me up at my mom's house in a Rolls-Royce."

"That will turn a girl's head," Lucas said.

"He never touched me. I wasn't gonna sleep with him anyway, he was too old for me, but he never made a move. I thought maybe, you know, he couldn't."

"There were some stories around that he sorta liked wrestling with guys . . ."

"That occurred to me too—you know, not like I was Miss Queen of the May and everybody's drooling over me, but he was showing me off to the guys, like, 'Look what I got.' But he never seemed much interested in really getting me. Just showing."

"Yeah . . . Listen, don't tell anyone else you went out with John Portland. He *was* an asshole."

"I think he might've been missing a couple links too," she said. "And all these other missing-linkers would come around, acting like they were Robert De Niro or something, like wise guys, but they were really like bartenders and tire salesmen."

"De Niro's old man was a famous artist and De Niro grew up with the intellectual artsy crowd on the East Coast," Lucas said. "Somebody told me that."

"Really? He seems pretty real to me. Like he grew up on the streets, and I thought—"

The phone rang, and Lucas rolled out of bed.

"Every goddamned time," she said, eyes following him. "You *could* skip it."

"Not when they call at this time of night," he said. "Back in a sec." Lucas picked up the phone in the den: "Yeah?"

SHE HEARD HIM pounding down the hall; it might have been funny if she hadn't heard him virtually screaming at the telephone. Lucas thundered into the bedroom, found Sherrill pulling up her underpants, snapping on her bra.

"My pants . . ." He seemed confused.

"On the floor, by the foot of the bed."

"My friend Elle . . ."

"I heard. She's hurt and you've gotta go," she said. She rocked back on the bed to pull her jeans on. "I'll drive."

"Bullshit, you will," Lucas said.

"I don't think you'll be in any shape—" she protested, but Lucas cut her off.

"I'm fuckin' driving," he snapped. "Shoes?"

"I think one of them is under the bed, I think I kicked one under . . ."

She was one garment ahead of him, stepping into her Nikes, collecting her revolver and purse from beside the nightstand, heading for the door. Lucas was ten seconds behind, out through the kitchen, into the garage, into the Porsche, slipping out under the garage door before it was fully up.

"Flasher," she said, as they hit the street.

"Busted," Lucas said.

"Better go over to Cretin then, it's better lit and you'll hit some college kid if you run like this on Mississippi."

Lucas grunted, downshifted and slid through a corner, punched the car two blocks down to Cretin, ignored the stop sign and cut across the street in front of a small Chevy van and gunned it again; Sherrill braced herself and asked, "How bad is she?"

"She's bad," Lucas said.

"Take her to Ramsey?"

"Yeah."

"They notify Minneapolis?"

"That was one of the nuns at the Residence calling, another friend." They clipped the red light at Grand Avenue, barely beat the red at Summit, came up behind a line of cars, and Lucas threw the Porsche into the oncoming lane, whipped by a half-dozen vehicles. "She was just calling because she knew I'd want to know."

"Better call Sloan or Del," she said, digging a cell phone out of her purse. "This is the second run at you. Until we figure out what's going on, the rest of the guys ought to know."

Lucas risked a glance at her: she was sitting comfortably in the passenger seat, one hand forward to brace herself, the other hand working the cell phone. She was calm and composed, maybe a slight pink flush to her face. He looked to the front again, ran the red light at Randolph, burned past the golf course, and dove down the ramp onto I-94.

They made a four-and-a-half-minute run to Ramsey Medical Center; Sherrill hooked up with Sloan one minute down the road, filled him in. "Tell him to find Andi Manette's home phone number and call her," Lucas said. "Weather's staying with the Manettes. Tell Weather about it. She and Elle are pretty tight."

Sherrill passed the word, clicked off the phone, looked at the speedometer. "That all you can get out of this thing?"

"No," he said, and the needle climbed through 120.

She watched his face for a moment—a brick, a stone—then looked out at the cars flicking by. Good thing, she thought, that she hadn't driven. She'd never moved this fast on a vehicle that didn't have a stewardess.

LUCAS DUMPED THE Porsche in an ambulances-only zone and they banged into the emergency room. A startled nurse turned toward them from the reception desk, and Lucas said, "I'm Deputy Police Chief Lucas Davenport from Minneapolis and a nun named Elle Kruger was brought in here . . ."

"Yes, yes, she's in X ray, she just got here, the doctors are working—"

"Where?"

"Sir, I can't let you go—"

"Where?" He shouted it at her, and she stepped back and a couple of male white-coated orderlies started down the hall toward the desk.

"Hold it," Sherrill said. "Miss, can you tell us who the doctor in charge is? Jim Dunaway?"

"No, Larry Simone . . ."

"Okay, he's a friend of mine. Could you tell him Chief Davenport and Detective Sherrill are here asking about . . ."

"Sister Mary Joseph. Elle Kruger," Lucas said.

"I'll be right back."

As the nurse started down the hall, waving off the orderlies, a thin, ill-tempered man stuck his head in the door and called, "Hey, whose car is this out here?"

"I'll get it," Sherrill said to Lucas. "Gimme the keys."

Lucas dug the keys out and handed them to her. The ill-tempered man raised his voice: "I'm asking, who the hell left their car out here—"

"I'll move it," Sherrill said, walking toward him.

"You goddamn well will move it," the man said. "Or I'll push that thing right into the wall."

Sherrill stepped to within four inches of his face, her voice low and controlled. "You shut your fuckin' pie hole or I will break all your teeth out," she said. She pulled one hand back on her hip so the ill-tempered man could see the wooden butt of the .357. His eyes slid away from hers, and she pushed through the door to the car.

A BALDING, HATCHET-FACED doctor walked out of a back room, trailed by the reception nurse. He looked around, spotted Lucas. "Are you with Marcy Sherrill?"

"Yes. Elle Kruger—the nun—is my best friend."

"This is Chief Davenport," said the nurse.

"Come on back," he said. "Where's Marcy?"

"Outside, moving a car off the ramp. How's Elle?"

"Not good, but she's better than the other one. We've got head injury but no direct brain damage, like the girl. We've got to manage the swelling and so on, which is gonna be a problem, but I'm more worried about blunt trauma to her kidneys and liver. Somebody beat the hell out of her with what looks like a baseball bat."

"Baseball bat?"

"Yeah . . ."

Sherrill caught up with them and said, "Larry, how are you?" and the doc said, "I'd like to look at that leg of yours again."

"I think it's okay," she said.

"Oh, I know; I just wanted to look for aesthetic reasons." And Sherrill snorted and said, "Aesthetic, my ass," and he said, "That too . . ." and Sherrill said to Lucas, "Larry was one of the docs that took care of me after that thing with John Mail."

"Ah." Lucas said, and looked wildly at Simone, who said, "Through there."

HE COULD BARELY see her. She was flat on her back, under an operating drape, her head tilted back, her head already shaved and painted with iodine-colored disinfectant. A drip flowed into her arm, and her mouth was propped open. She looked like a saint who was about to be committed to fire.

"Elle," Lucas whispered.

"She can't respond," Simone said. "She might hear you, somewhere in her head, but she's too doped up to show it."

"Gonna be all right," Lucas said, his face a foot from her ear. She didn't look like any Elle Kruger he remembered: separated from the habit and other paraphernalia of the church, she looked stark; and the disinfectant added a strange otherworldly touch, like an image from Heavy Metal. "Gonna be all right, we're here with you; we're waiting."

"Come on," Simone said. "They've got to finish getting her ready for the OR."

LUCAS RELUCTANTLY FOLLOWED Simone out of the prep room, Sherrill a step behind him. "You want to look at the X rays?" Simone asked.

"Can I see anything?"

"C'mon."

The X rays were clipped to wall-mounted view boxes and a man in a tweed sportcoat was peering at them. Simone said, "Jerry, what do you think?"

"I've already called Jack Bornum in; we're gonna have to do them both at the same time. I'll take the kid, she's gonna go if we don't get in quick. Jack can have the nun."

"How bad's the nun?" Lucas asked.

"Who're you?"

"I'm a cop—and her best friend. Oldest friend."

"Whoever hit her missed; looks like two or three blows, hard, but never quite brought it down over the top of her head, like with the kid. Everything sort of skidded off."

"What about the blunt trauma?" Lucas asked.

The tweed man shrugged: "I don't know; I do brains." He glanced at his watch. "And I better go do this one."

"How long before the other guy gets here?"

"Five minutes maybe. He'll be here before she's ready to go," Tweed said gruffly. "He's a good guy too—he'll take care of her."

THE OTHER DOCTOR, Bornum, arrived in the allotted five minutes, and disappeared into the back. Simone caught a knife wound to the liver area, and also disappeared. Twenty minutes later, Weather pushed through the door, with Andi Manette a step behind. She saw Lucas and Sherrill and said, "Lucas, my God, what happened?"

"Somebody beat her up. Almost killed her," he said. His voice got shaky and she touched his arm.

"How bad?"

"Pretty bad. They're getting her ready for the OR. They've got a neurosurgeon working on her."

"Oh, no . . ."

He wanted to wrap her up and hold on, but there was a wall between them: he could feel it, pressing them away from each other. "I don't know what happened . . . In fact, I think I'm gonna . . ."

He walked over to the reception desk. "Could somebody let me know when Elle Kruger goes into the OR, and get an idea of how long it'll take?"

"I'll check," the nurse said.

WEATHER STEPPED CLOSER to Sherrill and asked, "How is he?"

She shrugged: "Freaked out. Really freaked."

Weather smiled, a thin, tentative smile but a real one, Sherrill thought. "Take care of him," Weather said.

Sherrill blushed and nodded, then said, "If I can."

Lucas wandered back, and Weather said, "The bomb through my window, and now Elle."

Lucas shook his head: "I can't figure it. It'd have to be somebody who knows me, to know about you two. But who? And why not come after me? And why with the bomb and now a beating, for Christ's sake? There's too much risk involved. If they really want to get at me . . ." He rubbed his chin, wandered away, deep in thought.

A moment later, the nurse appeared in the hallway, busily stepping down toward the reception area; Lucas went to meet her.

"She's in the operating room now," the nurse said. "They're just putting in the anesthesia. Doctor says he can't tell how long it'll be, anywhere from two to six hours."

"Okay, okay . . ."

"He said she's strong," the nurse said.

Lucas turned back to Weather and Sherrill: "Did you hear that?"

They nodded and Weather said, "Have you been to the scene?"

"No, that's where I'd like to go . . ."

"You guys go ahead," Weather said. "I'll wait here, and if anything comes up, I can handle it."

"Thanks, Weather," Lucas said. To Sherrill: "You wanta come?"

"Yeah, I do." She glanced at Weather and quickly nodded.

They'd just started toward a door when a middle-aged couple hurried in, and the woman, tightly controlled, went to the reception desk and said, "My daughter was just hurt in some kind of accident at St. Anne's and we were told she was here, but I don't see her, do you know . . ."

And Lucas shook his head at Sherrill and they hurried out: "I didn't want to see that," Lucas said. "I don't need it."

A ST. PAUL lieutenant named Allport was running the crime scene at St. Anne's when Lucas and Sherrill arrived. He spotted Lucas getting out of the car, and yelled at a patrolman, "Send that guy over here."

The patrolman whistled at Lucas to get his attention, and pointed at Allport. Lucas waved, took Sherrill by the elbow, and they walked along the side of the Residence building to a cluster of cops duckwalking around the parking lot.

"I heard," Allport said. "The nun's an old pal of yours. She gonna be all right?"

"She's in the OR. So's the girl; the girl's in trouble."

"Ah, jeez. She's some kid from the neighborhood here. One of the neighbors said her parents sent her here because she could live close to home and it's safe."

"You figure out what happened?" Lucas asked.

"Yeah. What there is. You ain't gonna like it."

"I already don't like it . . ."

"No, no. I mean, you *really* ain't gonna like it. There's a girl sitting in by the switchboard, she's talking to one of her friends—they're doing homework together. So a call comes in for Sister Mary Joseph—family emergency."

"She doesn't have a family anymore," Lucas said.

"Yeah." Allport looked up at the night sky. "But that's what they said. So the girl runs down and gets the sister and the sister takes the call and she listens and she freaks out and she hangs up, and she says to this girl, 'Lucas has been shot; they're taking him to Midway. I've got to go.' "

"*What?*"

"So she ran to get her keys and her bag and she ran back out and the girl at the phones says to the other one, 'I don't think she should drive,' and the other one says, 'I'll take her,' and she runs out. Then the girl sits there by the phones, and ten minutes later . . . or sometimes later . . . another kid comes in and says there're two people hurt on the sidewalk and to call an ambulance."

"Jesus," Lucas said.

And Sherrill said, "It *is* aimed at you." To Allport: "You know Lucas's former fiancée was firebombed last week."

Allport nodded: "I read about it. You had guys running all over town, kicking ass."

Lucas looked around at the duckwalking crime scene cops: "You finding anything?"

Allport shook his head. "Nope. Not a thing. We're walking around the neighborhood, looking for the weapon—a ball bat, or a big stick—but we haven't found it yet."

"Goddamnit . . ." A thought flew through Lucas's head, quick as a scalded moth; he grasped at it, missed. He shook his head, turned to Sherrill: "Nothing to do here. I'm going back to the hospital."

"I'm coming."

"You don't have to."

"I'm coming."

Allport, arms akimbo, said, "I hate this shit. If the assholes want to beat each other up, or even us, that's one thing. A nun and a kid?"

In the car, Lucas said, "Something's happening, and we don't know what it is."

"I knew that a long time ago," Sherrill said.

Lucas shook his head: "I don't mean that somebody is trying to get at me, or even get at Weather or Elle. There's some kind of apparatus here. Somebody's set up a machine, and it's not some simpleminded revenge. It's doing something . . ."

23

ELLE KRUGER CAME out of the operating room just after four A.M. and the doctor, yawning, came to see Lucas, Sherrill, and Weather: "I'd say the prognosis is good—she's gonna have a few days in the ICU, but there wasn't any direct mechanical damage that I could see. We've got swelling, but we're controlling it. We're going to keep her sedated, keep her quiet, so she won't be talking for a couple of days."

"She's gonna make it," Lucas said.

"Unless we missed something—or if there's just a further natural complication. But it's about as good as you could have hoped for, given the circumstances."

"How about the other girl?" Weather asked.

The doc shook his head: "She *did* have some mechanical damage. I think she's gonna live, we're just gonna have to wait and see. She might be fine, she might be . . . not so fine."

Lucas turned away, suddenly exhausted. "Man."

"Let's go home," Sherrill said.

Weather said, "I'll be back tomorrow—every day until she wakes up."

"You got a ride?" Lucas asked. Andi Manettte, who'd brought Weather over, had left earlier.

"I'll get a cab. They can have one here in a minute."

"We came in the Porsche," Lucas said. Two seats: Weather smiled; she understood the math.

Out the door, walking to the car, Sherrill asked, "Did Weather and Elle have some kind of relationship?"

"Yeah, they liked each other a lot," Lucas said.

"Think Elle will like me?" Sherrill asked.

Lucas nodded. "She likes almost everybody. You two'll get along fine."

ROSE MARIE ROUX talked to the St. Paul chief, and St. Paul put together a group of four detectives to work with two Violent Crimes detectives from Minneapolis.

"You can do what you want, personally, but I want you to stay clear of these guys," Roux told Lucas. "You've set up this paradigm: you think these attacks on Sister Mary Joseph and Weather are aimed at you. Maybe they are, but I want to keep these guys outside the paradigm. I want them to take a cold look at it."

Lucas agreed. "That's smart. But I'm putting Del on the street, looking into a few things; and I'll be looking around. Sherrill, Sloan, and Black are going back to Homicide now that we're done with McDonald."

DEL AND LUCAS spent the day cruising the street, talking to druggies, thieves, bikers, gamblers—anyone smart enough to take revenge on Lucas by attacking his friends; and checking in every hour with the hospital. No change on Elle Kruger.

At the end of the day, they sat in Lucas's office, Del with his feet on the edge of Lucas's desk, Lucas with his feet on an open desk drawer, looking for new ideas.

"All day, absolutely nothing. I've never seen it this dry. Usually there's rumors, even if the rumors are bullshit."

"Nobody wants to get involved with a run at a cop," Lucas said.

"Tell you the truth, *I've* been thinking of terminating our friendship, at least for the time being. Maybe take out an ad in the *Star-Tribune*."

"I once talked to a guy, a lawyer—defense attorney—whose son was arrested for stealing some stereo gear from a Best Buy," Lucas said. "The kid was one of those ineffectual audiovisual freaks, didn't know which way was up. Anyway, the judge gave him six months in the county jail, and this was a first offense."

"Oops."

"Yeah. And this attorney tells me, he knows it was because the judge didn't like *him*, the attorney. Thought he was sleazy, because he did personal injury and DWI and made a lot of money at it. So anyway, the kid does most of the time, like four months, and gets out, and he's okay. But the attorney spent the whole time worrying that he was gonna hang himself in his cell or something."

"Something to worry about, with kids like that," Del said.

"The attorney'd go down every day to visit the kid, keep him connected. But he still worried. And what he told me was that he decided in the middle of the kid's jail term that if the kid killed himself, he'd kill the judge. He made the decision, he worked it all out. He wasn't irrational about it, it wasn't a big macho thing. He'd just do it, and try not to get caught. The first thing he'd do was, he'd wait two years before he made his move. Wait until his son's death was way in the past. Then he'd find a way to kidnap the judge—he said that in his fantasies, he had to explain to the judge why he was going to kill him, he couldn't sleep if he didn't do that—and then he was gonna tie him up or chain him to a tree, and douse him with gasoline and set him on fire."

"Jesus."

"Yeah. He said he'd decided this, but when his kid got out okay, it wasn't necessary, so he let it go. He hates the judge, but he says he'll get at him politically, he doesn't have to burn him up."

"What you're saying is . . ."

"What I'm saying is, I hope it's not something like that," Lucas said. "I hope it's not somebody I bumped into years ago, took care of business, didn't even think about it. And he's been plotting all this time."

"We checked all recent prison releases."

"That's what I mean. What if it's not recent? What if it's somebody from ten years ago, somebody I busted on a solid felony, say, who did a couple of years but figures I ruined his life and his family? And now he's coming after me, by going after my family? I mean, I might never figure out who it is."

A TENTATIVE KNOCK interrupted the thought. Del looked at the door, then back at Lucas, show-shrugged. "Come in," Lucas called.

A woman stepped inside. He remembered her face instantly, and her last name. He pointed a finger at her and said, "The bridal shop, Mrs. Ingall."

"Annette," she said.

"This is Detective Capslock," Lucas said. "Del, this is Mrs. Ingall; her husband disappeared in that yacht up on Superior. The McDonald case."

"Oh, sure."

Lucas: "Sit down. What can we do for you?"

Ingall looked doubtfully at Del, who tried to smile pleasantly without showing too much of his yellowed teeth, and sat in the chair beside him, clutching her purse on her lap. "I saw on TV Three about your friend the nun who was attacked last night. I hope she's going to be okay."

"She should be," Lucas said.

"I've been bothered by it all day," she said. "It kept nagging at me, and nagging at me, and finally I said, 'Annette, go over and talk to Chief Davenport for goodness' sake, and let him worry about it.' "

"Well . . ." Lucas spread his hands, waiting, an edge of impatience barely suppressed.

"After you told me that Wilson McDonald was probably responsible for killing Andy . . ."

"Mrs. Ingall, I didn't exactly say——"

She waved him down and continued: ". . . I was pretty satisfied, because it made a nice pattern. He killed George Arris, shooting him with a gun. Then he killed Andy, by sabotaging the yacht. And then he killed Dan Kresge, shooting him, and Susan O'Dell, shooting *her*."

"Yes?"

"But then—this is what was nagging me—when I read about what happened with you, with your fiancée firebombed, and then this morning, with your friend the nun being hurt . . ."

"Yes, yes."

"Look: There were two other incidents which helped Wilson McDonald's career, that nobody probably told you about, because they didn't involve any-body being killed at the bank, where it would be obvious."

"Two others?" Lucas leaned forward, now interested.

"Two weird . . . accidents," Ingall said. "One involved a man named McKin-ney, who was in the investments department and was also competitive for promotions with Wilson. They were sort of neck and neck. This is way back, when Wilson was still selling out of the investments division, before he went to mortgages. And all of a sudden, this other man's son was killed in a hit-and-run accident. If I remember, he was riding home in the evening on his bike, in the summer, I think he had a paper route or something, and he was hit and killed and they never found out who did it. Anyway, McKinney just fell apart. He couldn't do anything, and when the job came up, which was right after that, Wilson got it."

"Huh," Lucas said. Del was looking at Ingall with interest.

"Then, and this must've been, oh, about 1990, there was sort of a bank recession going on. Lots of banks were restructuring and jobs were being cut. Wilson was one of a half-dozen people in the mortgage division as a vice pres-ident, and people knew some jobs were going to be cut over there. The man who was in charge of the cuts was named Davis Baird, and he had an assistant named Dick McPhillips. Davis Baird didn't like Wilson, he thought he was a fat pompous oaf. He might have cut him. But Dick McPhillips was always under the influence of Wilson's father. If Davis Baird had wanted to cut Wilson, McPhillips couldn't stop it. But . . ." She paused dramatically.

"But," Lucas said, and Del nodded at her.

"But, while they were working out the cutbacks, all of a sudden Baird's parents were killed in a fire at their cabin up north. I thought about this because of the firebomb at your friend's house. Something exploded in the Bairds' house—they even called it a firebomb in the paper, I think—and they were killed, and Baird had to take time off to deal with all of it. McPhillips was in charge of making the cuts, and he got rid of two of the five vice presidents over there . . ."

"But not Wilson," Lucas said.

"Not Wilson."

"Go ahead," Lucas said.

"So I started thinking, this took a strange mind. Not to attack the principal target directly, but to incapacitate the principal by attacking someone close to them. Distracting them in a really awful way. And I thought, you know, that's what's happening to Chief Davenport. He's investigating these murders, and suddenly his fiancée's house blows up, and then an old friend is almost killed. If Wilson McDonald weren't dead, I would say he was doing it for sure. Especially since Andy's death almost might be an accident, and Arris's death was also easy to blame on somebody else—that gang. Nothing is what it looks like."

"Wilson McDonald *is* dead," Del said.

"Yes. Shot to death," Ingall said. "And that's very curious."

Lucas closed his eyes, rubbed his face: "Jesus."

"Do you think this line of thought might be useful?" Ingall asked.

"I don't know," Lucas said. "But you are a very smart lady."

"Yes, I've always thought so," she said.

24

M OST OF THE file on Audrey McDonald had been developed since she killed Wilson: name, age, weight, distinguishing marks. She had a number of scars; too many, Lucas thought. Her only prior contact with police had been two traffic tickets, one for speeding, one for failure to yield, which had resulted in a minor collision.

He made quick calls to the Department of Natural Resources and the Department of Public Safety: she'd never had a hunting license, never taken gun safety training, never applied for a handgun permit.

She'd graduated from St. Anne's. That was interesting—she'd know her way around out there, she'd know what would happen if she called the Residence. She might even have overlapped with Elle Kruger, if just barely. He made a note to ask. After college, she'd worked as a librarian, then with a couple of charitable organizations.

He mulled over the file for a few minutes, then glanced at his watch. Almost time to see Elle. But first he picked up the phone book and looked up Helen Bell, Audrey's sister. She was listed in South Minneapolis. Not expecting too much, he punched in her phone number. She answered on the second ring.

"I'd like to come talk to you about the whole case," he said, after he introduced himself.

"I . . . thought it was just about done," Bell said. He noticed her voice immediately: she sounded like Audrey, who sounded like the woman who'd called him to press him on McDonald.

"Well, we haven't settled the Kresge thing," Lucas said. "I just want to come over and chat. Get some opinions."

"Okay. I'll be here the rest of the day."

THREE NUNS, ALL in traditional dress, were perched on chairs in Elle's room, watching a young nurse change a saline drip. When Lucas stepped in, easing the door closed, one of them chirped, "Hi, Lucas. She's awake."

Lucas stepped around the beige curtain that masked Elle's bed from the outside, and looked down at his oldest friend. They'd gone to Catholic grade school together, goofing along the sidewalk, her long golden hair shimmering in the autumn sunlight, her blue eyes happy, smiling at him . . . His first clear memory of a female other than his mother. Now, her head was swathed with bandages, her face bruised, showing yellow disinfectant, her eyelids drooping over blue eyes that seemed more hazy than happy. She smiled weakly and he thought she looked wonderful.

"You look terrible," he said. "Like somebody beat the daylights out of you."

"That's funny," she mumbled. "I sort of feel that way too."

He touched her foot. "You're gonna make it."

"Yes, probably. Do you know what happened?"

"Pretty much. You got a phony phone call. Somebody pulled you out of the building, and ambushed you."

"I don't know," she said. "I can't remember much after about six o'clock, but that's what I've been told."

"How bad is the memory thing?" He swallowed as he said it: he didn't need bad news, not about Elle.

Again she smiled weakly: "Just a couple hours of amnesia, nothing unusual. I've taken a few tests: there's no impairment. Permanent impairment."

"All right," he said. "All right."

"The girl . . ."

The girl would live. She smelled vanilla when a nurse wiped her arm with an alcohol swab; smelled fried eggs in a glass of apple juice, celery in oatmeal. When asked to read aloud from a chart, she'd read quite well—except that she'd read some words backward, pronouncing them correctly in their backward form.

"She could recover," Elle said. "I feel so bad that she was running after me . . ."

"Nothing you could do," Lucas said.

"Does anybody have any idea who might've done it?" A shadow of fear in her eyes, something he'd never seen before.

He shook his head. "Not yet."

They talked for ten minutes before Elle's eyelids grew heavy; Lucas kissed her on the cheek, with much approval from the squad of nuns who perched like blackbirds on their row of red leatherette chairs. Before he left the hospital, he talked to her doctor for a minute, picked up a pack of X rays and some preoperative photos at the radiology department.

THE HENNEPIN COUNTY Medical Examiner's Office was just down the street from police headquarters, connected by what the cops half seriously referred to as the secret tunnel. Lucas dumped his car in one of the cop slots on the street and then took the tunnel to the ME's office. He showed the photos and films to one of the forensic pathologists.

"Probably right-handed, and probably not too tall," the ME said, sucking on an illegal Winston. "The blows all hit on the side and back of her head, rather than coming down on top. But if it were a man, swinging flat, like a baseball bat, he would've knocked her head off. This looks more like somebody coming down, but from a relatively low swinging position."

"Possibly a woman?"

The ME pushed his lips out and blew a capital O. "Could be. Whoever it was, wasn't all that strong. Jumping somebody from behind, with a club—a strong guy would have killed her, hitting her like that."

"Huh."

LUCAS HAD SEEN Helen Bell at the arraignment of her sister, and had been struck by how little they resembled each other, in the sense of a total package, for two women who looked so much alike. Audrey at thirty-eight was a beetle, hunched, fussy, dressed all in earth colors, her movements small and nervous. Bell at thirty-four was not exactly a butterfly, but seemed even in the restrictive circumstances of a legal hearing to be much more outgoing, much more like a woman in her thirties. Her hair was touched with color, she wore a bit of makeup, and at the arraignment, she'd worn a pretty red silk scarf with a conservative blue business suit; and she smiled.

Helen Bell lived in a small white house with green shutters, backed onto an alley, a shaky-looking garage standing behind the house. Lucas left his car in the street and walked up the narrow seventy-year-old sidewalk to the front door and knocked. Bell was there in a minute, smiling nervously when she opened her door and said, "Chief Davenport? Come in."

The living room had a just vacuumed look, and magazines, mostly about homemaking, were stacked carefully on a coffee table. "Coffee?" she asked. "It's only microwave instant."

"Yes, that'd be nice." The voice again: this was the tipster, all right. Lucas mentally kicked himself: he'd known that Audrey McDonald had a sister.

"Decaf or regular?" She was bustling around, making sure he was comfortable; he felt as though he were on a first date.

"Whatever you have . . . Regular is fine."

She went to get it, and he looked around the small living room, checked a shelf of paperbacks: self-help, mostly. How to succeed in business. "Where do you work?" he called.

He heard the door slam on the microwave: "Fisher Specialties down in Bloomington. You know—truck accessories. I'm in charge of the orders department." She came out of the kitchen carrying two mugs of coffee. "Sit on the couch—I'll take the easy chair."

"Any children?"

"A daughter. Connie. She should be home from school any minute."

"I wanted to talk to you about some background involving the death of Dan Kresge and then later, of Wilson McDonald . . ."

"Are they going to drop the charges against Audrey?"

"I don't know, I don't work in that area," Lucas said. "Mrs. Bell . . . did you write to us about your brother-in-law? Call me on the phone?"

She looked too surprised by the question; she wasn't surprised, but she acted as though she were, her eyebrows going up, her head cocking to one side. "Why . . ."

"I can get phone records, if I want to," Lucas said. "And there's nothing at all illegal about what you did. You were simply recommending an investigation."

She took a sip of coffee, then ran the index finger of her free hand around the rim of the cup. After a second, she said, "Yes, that was me. You'd already figured it out, I guess. But it couldn't be from the phone—I called from Rainbow."

Rainbow was a supermarket. Lucas shook his head: "It's just your voice. You sound a little, I don't know—Canadian."

"Aboot," she said.

He nodded. "The first time I talked to your sister, I thought she was the one who called. So: How long ago did you decide Wilson McDonald was killing people?"

"I . . . thought there'd been a lot of deaths, to get him where he'd gotten. But it was only when Mr. Kresge was shot that I was really sure. You know that Mr. Kresge was going to merge the bank . . ."

"Yes."

"And Wilson's job was gone. I mean, *gone.* Then Mr. Kresge gets killed, and Wilson's job was saved. And maybe he's even in line for Mr. Kresge's job. That was too much. There'd been too many of these things."

"How long had he been beating your sister?"

"He beat her up before they got married," Helen said. "She told me that later."

"Then why'd she marry him?"

"Because she loved him," Bell said simply. "She still loves him."

"That's a very odd relationship."

"A kind of codependency," Bell said. "You know . . . Never mind."

"No. Say it."

"My father, before he died, used to beat up my mother. And Audrey. And he would've started on me, if I'd been old enough. And somehow, I think that did something to Audrey's brain—she thinks women *deserve* to get beaten. I mean, she'd never say that, but way deep down, I think she might *feel* it. I used to plead with her to leave the man."

"Where do you come from? You and Audrey?" He knew, but if he could get her rolling, anything might come out.

"Oxford. It's up in the Red River Valley," she said. "The closest big town is Grand Forks."

"Sugar beets?"

"No, we never really farmed. We lived just outside Oxford—we could walk to school—and my dad was a mail carrier. Both of my grandfathers were farmers, though. Dad grew up on a farm, and so did Mom, but he just wasn't interested."

"Your folks still live up there?"

"No, they both died. My father died when I was little, when I was ten, that was . . . twenty-four years ago, now. Just about this time of year. Mom died four years later. In the spring. After Mom died, I went to live with my aunt Judy in Lakeville and Audrey went to college. She went to St. Anne's."

"I know . . . Listen, I assume that you didn't talk to us directly because you didn't want to offend your sister. Or alienate her. Is that right?"

Bell nodded. "You know, she kept talking about how she loved him and what a great provider he was, but I really thought he was an animal and that sooner or later, he'd kill her. He *was* a killer. You said on the phone that the Kresge thing wasn't finished yet, but you know, it really is. Wilson killed him. Maybe I should have come forward earlier, but . . . I wasn't sure. And he was my sister's husband."

"The good provider."

"Easy to laugh off if you're a police officer, down here in Minneapolis," Bell said. "But if you were poor in Oxford, Minnesota, and we pretty much were, then 'good provider' isn't something you laugh at."

Lucas glanced around: "Are you married? Or . . ."

"Divorced," she said. "Four years now." She shook her head at the unstated question. "Larry never laid a hand on me. We just found out that we weren't very much interested in each other. We were dating when I got pregnant, and we got married because we were supposed to."

"All right," he said.

They talked for a few more minutes, then Lucas stood up. "Thanks."

"What about Dan Kresge? Are you all done now?"

Lucas shrugged. "I don't know. There doesn't seem much more to look at. We'll keep picking at little corners, but there's not much left."

"I'm glad that man's gone—Wilson, not Mr. Kresge. I know it's a sin, but I'm glad he's gone."

LUCAS HAD JUST taken a step toward the front door when the door opened and a slender teenager stepped in, dressed head to foot in black, carrying a black bookbag. Her hair was blond, no more than an inch long, and a tiny gold ring pierced one eyebrow. She looked quickly at her mother, then to Lucas, gave him an assessing smile and said, "My. This is a studly one."

"Connie!"

"He *is* . . ." Slightly seductive, intended to tease her mother.

"Please! This is Chief Davenport from the Minneapolis Police Department."

"A cop? You can't be asking if Aunt Audrey really killed him—she admits it," the teenager said. She dropped her bookbag in the entry. "I don't think she killed anyone else."

"We're just making routine calls," Lucas said.

"The chief of police makes routine calls?"

"I'm not the chief, I'm a deputy chief," Lucas said. "And sometimes I make routine calls, if the case is important enough."

"We were just finishing here," Bell said.

"Well, good luck with Aunt Audrey," the girl said. "The meanest woman alive."

"Connie!" And Bell looked quickly at Lucas: "Connie and Audrey don't get along as well as they should."

"She is such a tiresome little bourgeois," Connie said, rolling her eyes. "The only interesting thing she ever did was kill Wilson."

"Which was, when you think about it, pretty interesting," Lucas said.

Connie nodded: "Yup. I gotta admit it."

Lucas smiled at her, deciding he liked her. The girl picked it up, and smiled back, a touch of shyness this time. Lucas said to Bell, "If anything else comes up, I'd like to give you a call."

As Lucas passed Connie, he picked up just the slightest whiff of weed; he glanced at her, and she picked *that* up too. Smart kid, he thought, as he walked down the sidewalk.

Thinking: More dead people. Audrey's parents, dead and buried.

From his car phone, he called Sherrill: "I'm gonna run up to the Red River Valley tomorrow, up by Grand Forks. Can you go?"

"Yup: this is my weekend. Can we stay overnight in one of those sleazy little hotels with the thin walls and fuck all night so the people can hear us on the other sides of the walls?"

"I don't know about all night . . . maybe, you know, *once.*"

"I'll start practicing my moaning. Call me tonight."

The phone rang a minute later, and he thought it was Sherrill calling back. It was Lucas's secretary. Rose Marie wanted to see him.

ROSE MARIE ROUX was working on the budget when Lucas stepped in. "Sit down," she said, without looking up. She worked for another moment, humming to herself without apparently realizing it: she was happy doing budgets.

"So," she said eventually, dropping her yellow pencil and linking her fingers. "Are you sleeping with Marcy Sherrill?"

Lucas got frosty: "We're seeing each other. I don't think it's much of any-one's business what happens——"

"Lucas, for Christ's sake——are you living in a goddamn cave?" she asked in exasperation. "A deputy chief of police can get away with sleeping with one of his detectives only if——"

"She's not one of my detectives," Lucas said. "I don't have any regular su-pervisory control . . ."

"Oh, bullshit——she works for you when you need her. And besides, the media won't give a shit about technicalities. You're a deputy chief, she's a sergeant. I don't care——I really don't. What I was about to say is, a deputy chief can get away with sleeping with one of his detectives only if he's very, very careful. Not secretive, but careful. Now: You left a message that you were going off to this place . . ." She looked at a notepad. "Oxford. Tomorrow. Up in the Red River Valley? Were you planning to take Sherrill?"

"I thought——"

"If you take her, she's gonna have to take vacation time. Or she puts in her regular hours, and you go up on her days off and she doesn't get paid at all."

"Look . . ."

"No, you look: I'm not trying to save *her* ass. I'm not trying to save *my* ass. I'm trying to save *your* ass. I can guarantee you that if you go up there with her, and she's paid for it, and the press finds out, you'll wind up being fired. I'd back you up, but it wouldn't do any good——you'd get it in the neck any-way."

"Maybe we just oughta forget the whole thing," he said. "Me 'n' Marcy."

She softened a quarter-inch: "I didn't say you gotta do that. But you've got to be discreet, and you've got to be politically careful. She can't be on the payroll when you're off together."

"All right," he said. "That's it?"

"Elle Kruger seems to be doing okay."

"I was just talking to her, and her doctor. She's gonna have a lot of pain for a long time," Lucas said. "But her brain wasn't affected. At least, not as far as they can tell. Motor is all right, memory, language."

"Nothing on it?"

"Nothing yet. But that's why I'm going up to the Red River. There's a question about whether Audrey McDonald might be involved."

Roux's genetically enabled left eyebrow went up: "Seriously?"

"Seriously. We might have the edge of something pretty interesting," Lucas said.

"Okay. But remember what I said about Sherrill."

"She's off the next couple of days. We should be all right."

"No expense accounts, no meals, no nothin' . . ."

"Nothing," he said. "Not a nickel. For either of us."

"All right," she said. "Good luck."

"With Marcy? Or the case?"

"Whatever," she said.

LUCAS, BACK IN his office, called the county attorney's office and asked for Richard Kirk, the head of the criminal division. He waited for a moment, and Kirk came on: "What's up?"

"How long can you hold off on a decision about Audrey McDonald?"

"Why?" Just like a lawyer.

" 'Cause."

"Just like a fuckin' cop: *'Cause*," Kirk said. "Anyway—we're gonna take McDonald's story to the grand jury and let them decide. That's the democratic way, and also lets our beloved county attorney off the hook if something goes wrong."

"So when do you go to the jury?"

"Next Wednesday, but it'd be no problem to hold off for a while. We could present the basic case Wednesday and hold the decision for the meeting one after that."

"That'd be good," Lucas said. "Some odd stuff has come up."

"So we'll do that—and don't surprise us at the last minute."

"Okay. And tell your boss to hold off any speeches to the Feminist Fife and Drum Club, about it being an obvious case of self-defense."

"Okay. But if something happens, call me, so we know which way to lean," Kirk said.

"I'll call."

"Goddamnit, Davenport, you're old enough to know . . ."

"What?"

"That too much investigation will screw up a perfectly good case."

25

MORGAN BITE HAD such a beatific look on his face as he stood at the edge of the Bite Brothers parking lot, at the end of the line of black Cadillac limousines, still holding the check, that Audrey McDonald actually thought of killing him; actually thought that after she received all the money she was due, after all the legal matters were cleared away, after all the police were gone, she might come back some night and murder the man, for the simple pleasure of doing it.

Bite was speaking in clichés: ". . . able to achieve such a natural appearance that the loved one seems to be undoubtedly present among us . . ."

She wanted to say, "Yes-yes-yes," and run away down the sidewalk; she limped instead, putting on a stunned expression, as though she might at any moment suffer a relapse. Though, now that she thought of it, Bite might find a relapse attractive, given his profession.

". . . not regret this in any way, and do not hesitate for a moment to call me at any time, day or night, with any concerns . . ."

She'd just given him a blank check to handle Wilson's funeral—well, blank to the tune of twenty-five thousand dollars, which he thought would be adequate to protect Wilson's image in the business community. Whenever she'd mentioned anything having to do with Wilson's death, Bite had seemed intimately aware of every detail, while somehow remaining unaware that she'd had anything to do with it. Come to think of it, she sort of liked that. Maybe she wouldn't kill him.

Well: She could decide that some other time.

Audrey McDonald came with a full set of the negative emotions: hate, anguish and anger, pain, fear, dread and loathing were her daily bread, illuminated by an active imagination. Love and pleasure were not quite a mystery. She thought she might have loved Wilson, and her parents, and even Helen. She felt pleasure with the prospect of money—not with what it could buy, but the lucre itself; she loved handling it, reading account statements. She had talked Wilson into buying a hundred gold coins, American Eagles, which she kept in a box in a cubbyhole in the kitchen. Once a week she would take them out and handle them, so smooth, so beautiful and cool to the touch.

And she certainly felt pleasure with the prospect of killing.

Killing was the most interesting thing she'd ever done, and that alone was a powerful attraction. Added to the attraction was the simple reality that a killing was always done to decrease her own fear—fear of poverty, fear of helplessness, fear of low status—and to increase the amount of money she would someday have. So far, she hadn't killed idly: so far, she'd always made a profit on her killings.

But it was dread that hung over her fifteen minutes after she left Bite Brothers, as she pulled the car to the curb in front of her sister's house. Helen had been talking to Davenport again: she'd called to confess it, and to admit that she'd written to Davenport that Wilson had killed people.

But Wilson hadn't. She had.

And if Davenport was still sniffing around, he might trip over something inconvenient. She was beginning to fear the man, not because he seemed to be particularly bright, or especially hard-driving, or even mean, but because he simply wouldn't go away. Now he was visiting Helen. This was all supposed to be done with. What did he want?

Helen was standing in the doorway as she limped up the sidewalk. Putting on the limp.

"I'm sorry," Helen said. "He was hurting you so badly that I don't think I had a choice."

Audrey nodded abruptly and let Helen take her coat at the door. "Still hurt," she mumbled. And she looked terrible. The bruises were going yellow, and her hair, unwashed since the attack, looked like sticky pieces of dirty brown kite string.

"Let me get you a coffee," Helen said, bustling around.

"Why aren't you working?" Audrey asked. Audrey hadn't worked since Wilson's second promotion, the one that carried him into mortgages. She'd always talked about Helen's having a "career" in a way that made both Helen and her ex-husband feel like rag-pickers.

"I had personal time coming, and since the fight with Wilson, I thought . . . I just thought I ought to be around," Helen said from the kitchen. She appeared a moment later with the coffee. "How are you?"

Audrey shook her head: "I still hurt. I still feel like I've been in an auto accident . . . and Wilson . . ." She sniffed.

"When's the funeral?"

"They released him today. His father's secretary called and said his father wanted to handle the funeral, but I said no, I would handle it. It's at Bite Brothers, day after tomorrow, at two o'clock."

"I'll take you," Helen said.

"Thank you. I think we should go in Wilson's Lexus, though."

"No problem; I'll come over to your place with Connie, and we'll all go together in the Lexus."

They talked for a few minutes about the funeral, sipping the coffee as they talked. Then Audrey asked, "What all did Detective Davenport want to talk about?"

"Oh, he just figured out that I was the one who wrote the letter about Wilson," Helen said. "And he wanted to know why I thought Wilson did it."

"You know, I'm not sure Wilson did all those things," Audrey said tentatively.

Helen looked away, flushing just a bit; this embarrassed her. "Oh, Audrey . . . I know you loved him."

"Yes. And sometimes . . . I don't know."

"What?" Helen asked. Audrey almost never opened up. Now she seemed about to.

"I sometimes wondered myself. Something you don't know—and please don't tell Detective Davenport this, I mean, Wilson is gone—but I began to wonder myself. And after Andy Ingall disappeared on his boat, well, Wilson was gone the night before. He came home at three o'clock in the morning, and he'd been drinking, and we had an awful fight. And the next day, Andy sailed away. That's when I began to wonder."

"You should have said something," Helen said.

"I . . . really did love him," Audrey said. "And he loved me. Nobody ever loved me before, no man did. I'm not so good-looking as you are . . ."

"Oh, shut up, Audrey," Helen said. "As soon as this is all over with, we'll take you to a friend of mine for a makeover, and you'll be amazed. You'll have guys coming around. You've got the whole rest of your life to look forward to."

"Unless they send me to jail," Audrey said piteously.

"No way," Helen declared. "I asked Detective Davenport about that, and he said that the county attorney was ready to declare that it was self-defense. Which it obviously was . . ."

Audrey perked up a bit at that. "Maybe I *could* do a makeover," she said, brushing some of her sticky hair away from her face. "That would be good . . ."

"So you'll be okay?"

"I think so. I have to go now, there's more funeral things to be done. I talked to Wilson's father; he seemed to think the whole thing was like a bad business deal. I was afraid he'd hate me. But he didn't seem any different."

"Well, you know the old man," Helen said. She'd met him two or three times at the McDonalds' house; he was, she thought, a spectacular horse's ass. "Though usually, they say, having a child die is the worst thing that can happen to a person."

"Not for that old man; he is a monster," Audrey said.

"I was just talking about our folks with Detective Davenport," Helen said. She'd gone to get Audrey's coat from a chair, and didn't see her sister jerk around toward her.

"What?"

"Oh, you know, we were just talking, nothing serious," Helen said, as she held the coat.

"I mean, about them dying, or just that they were gone?"

"Nothing, really—just something that came up in passing."

He *was* sniffing around. Audrey didn't push it, because it seemed unlikely to produce much, and she didn't want Helen wondering about the conversation. But she would have to think about this. Go after Davenport directly? That was one possibility, as long as it wouldn't push more investigators her way. As for Helen, she had to do something to interrupt this relationship with Davenport, which was altogether too cozy.

All this was going through her head as she went through the forms of departure, ending with, "So you'll be at the house at noon?"

"Noon," Helen said. "And if you need anything before then, call me. Please. This is the reason I took the time off."

When Audrey pulled away from the curb, Helen was still at the door. Audrey touched the horn, emitting a polite Japanese tone, and thought, *"Connie."*

AND NO TIME like the present.

She drove to a Rainbow supermarket, looked up Child Protection in the phone book. "I don't want to give you my name—I'm a teacher at South High and I'm going out of channels here—but there's a student named Connie Bell who has been smoking a great deal of marijuana and I've heard from another student that she gets it from her mother; and I've heard that she and her mother have been fighting, and that Connie has been beaten up several times by the men who hang around with her mother. Thank you."

She hung up.

Connie smoked marijuana—Helen had confessed that; she had told Audrey weeks before that she'd slapped Connie after an argument over marijuana. There was just enough truth in her call to cause Helen some inconvenience. That was all Audrey needed for now: for Helen to look away from Davenport.

26

MARCY SHERRILL WAS banging on Lucas's door at seven o'clock. He stumbled out to open up, his hair still a mess from the night, wearing a T-shirt and jeans, one sock on, one sock off; his alarm had gone off ten minutes earlier.

"You look terrible," she said cheerfully. "I got up early and went for a run."

"God will someday strike you dead for that kind of behavior," he said. He was not a morning person. "If I could only get the glue out of my eyes."

"Quit pissing around; let's get going," Sherrill said. "I'll drive. You can sleep, if you want."

He perked up, but just slightly. "If you drive, I might survive."

"So, I'll drive," she said. "C'mon, c'mon. Go." He turned back to the bedroom and she slapped him on the butt.

"Christ, it's like having a coach," he grumbled, but he tried to hurry.

MINNESOTA IS A tall state; Audrey McDonald's hometown, Oxford, was in the Red River Valley in the northwest corner, on land as flat as the Everglades. They took Lucas's Porsche out I-94, Sherrill driving the first two hours, giving it to Lucas, then taking the car back four hours out. Sherrill was a cheerful companion, not given to long stretches of silence. As she chattered away about the landscape, the various road signs and small towns, the river crossings, animals dead on the road, Lucas began to wonder what, exactly, he was doing with her. He began to check her from the corner of his eye, little peeks at her profile, at her face as she talked. Over the years, he'd had relationships, longer or shorter, with a number of women, and in the transition zone between them, had often felt ties to the last woman even as the ties to the new woman were forming.

In this case, there were more than simple ties back to Weather. Weather had been something different—the love of his life, if Elle Kruger wasn't—while Sherrill was much more like the other women he'd dated: pretty, smart, interesting, and eventually, moving on.

He wasn't sure that he wanted a relationship with a woman who'd be moving on, especially when she really wouldn't be out of sight. Sherrill was a cop, who had a desk right down the hall from his office: even when he wasn't trying to see her, he saw her four or five times a day.

"You sighed," she said.

"What?"

"You just sighed."

"A lot of shit going on," Lucas said.

She patted him on the leg. "You worry too much. It's all gonna work out."

They followed the interstate northwest to Fargo, crossed the Red River into North Dakota, took I-29 north past Grand Forks, then recrossed the Red into Minnesota on a state highway to Oxford.

"Starting to feel it in my back," Sherrill said to Lucas. Lucas was behind the wheel again. "Probably would've been more comfortable in my car."

"Yeah, I'm getting too old for this thing, I need something a little smoother," Lucas said. "Good car, though."

"Too small for you. Though you'll probably start to shrink a little, as the age comes on. You know, your vertebrae start to collapse, your hair thins out and sits lower on your head, your muscle tone goes . . ."

"You go from a 34-C to a 34-long . . ."

"Oooh. That's mean. But I kinda like it," she said.

They passed a sign warning of a reduction of speed limits; Lucas dropped from eighty to sixty as they went past the 45 sign. Past a farm implement dealer with a field of new John Deeres and Bobcats and antique Fords and International Harvesters; past competing Polaris and Yamaha snowmobile dealerships, both in unpainted steel Quonset huts; past a closed Dairy Queen and an open Hardee's, past a Christian Revelation church and a SuperAmerica; and then into town, Lucas letting the car roll down to forty-five by the time they got to the 25 sign. Past a redbrick Catholic church and a fieldstone Lutheran church and then a liquor store that may once have been a bank, built of both fieldstone and brick.

"Just like Lake fuckin' Wobegon," Sherrill said.

"No lake," Lucas said. "Nothing but dirt."

"If I had to live here, I'd shoot myself just for the entertainment value," Sherrill said.

"Ah, there're lots of good things out here," Lucas said.

"Name one."

Lucas thought for a moment. "You can see a long way," he said finally, and they both started to laugh. Then Sherrill pointed out the windshield at the left side of the street, to a white arrow-sign that said, "Proper County–Oxford Government Center."

The Proper County Courthouse and Oxford City Hall had been combined in a building that resembled a very large Standard Oil station—low red brick, lots of glass, an oversized nylon American flag, and a large parking lot where a grassy town square may once have been. Lucas spotted three police cruisers at one corner of the parking lot, and headed that way.

"Watch your mouth with these people, huh?" Lucas said, as they got out of the car.

"Like you're Mr. Diplomat."

"I try harder when I'm out in the countryside," he said. "They sometimes resent it when big-city cops show up in their territory."

THE OXFORD POLICE Department was a starkly utilitarian collection of beige cubicles wedged into a departmental office suite twenty-four feet square. The chief's office, the only private space in the suite, was at the back; the department itself seemed deserted when Lucas and Sherrill pushed through the outer door.

"A fire drill?" Sherrill asked.

"I don't know. What's that?" An odd, almost musical sound came from the back; they walked back between the small cubicles, and spotted a man in the chief's private office, hovering over a computer. As they got closer, they could hear the boop-beep-thwack-arrghh of a computer action game. Sherrill gave Lucas an elbow in the ribs, but Lucas pushed her back down the row, walking quietly away. Then: "Hello? Anybody home?"

The boop-beep-thwack stopped, and a second later a young man with a round face and a short black mustache stepped out of the chief's office.

"Help you folks?"

"We're looking for the chief of police, or the duty officer . . ."

"I'm Chief Mason." The young man hitched up his pants when he saw Sherrill, and walked down toward them. Lucas took out his ID and handed it over. "I'm Deputy Chief Lucas Davenport from Minneapolis, and this is Detective Sherrill . . ."

He explained that they had come up to review documents and interview people who might have any information about the death of George Lamb, Audrey McDonald's father, twenty-four years earlier. The chief, who had been staring almost pensively at Sherrill's breasts, started shaking his head. "I been a cop here for four years; nobody in the department has been here more than twelve. Better you should go up and talk to the county clerk, she might be able to point you at some death records or something."

"Second floor?" Lucas asked.

"Yee-up," the chief said.

THE COUNTY CLERK was even younger than the chief, her hair dyed an unsuccessful orange: "Okay, twenty-four years. About this time of year, you say?"

"About this time."

"Okay . . . We're computerizing, you know, but all this old paper is hard to get on-line," she said, as she dug through a file cabinet. "Here we go. George Lamb? Here it is."

"You got anything in there on an Amelia Lamb? George's wife? Four years after George?"

She went back to the cabinet, dug around, then shook her head. "Nothing on an Amelia."

She straightened up, stepped to the counter, pushed a mimeographed form across the counter at them, said to Marcy, "I really like your hair," and Marcy said, "Thanks. I just got it changed and I was a little worried about doing it . . . used to be longer."

The death form was filled out on a typewriter, and signed by a Dr. Stephen Landis. Lucas scanned the routine report and asked, "Is Dr. Landis still practicing here?"

"Oh, sure. He's over at the clinic, right down the street to Main, take a left two blocks."

Marcy looked over Lucas's arm: "Heart attack?"

"That's what it says."

"You know, Sheriff Mason would've been a deputy back then; I bet he would know about it," the clerk said, reading the file upside down. She tapped a line on the file with her fingertip. "This address isn't right in town—it's out at County A—so they would have been the law enforcement arm involved in a death."

"We just talked to a *Chief* Mason," Sherrill said. "They're not the same guy?"

"Second cousins, though you could never tell," the clerk said. "Sheriff John Mason's grandparents on his father's side, and Chief Bob Mason's great-grandparents on his father's and grandfather's side, are the same people, Chuck and Shirley Mason from Stephen."

"Thank you," Lucas said. "Where can we find the sheriff's office?"

"Down the hall all the way to the end."

As they left, Sherrill asked, "Are Chuck and Shirley still alive?"

"Well, sure," the clerk said. "Hale and hearty. Course, they'd be down in Arizona right now."

———

THE SHERIFF WAS out, the receptionist said, but if it was a matter of importance, he'd be happy to come right back. Lucas identified himself, and the receptionist's eyebrows went up, and she punched a number in her telephone. A minute later, the phone rang, and she picked it up and said, without preamble, "There're some Minneapolis police officers here, looking for you."

The sheriff was a chunky, weathered man, going bald; he wore an open parka and was carrying a blaze-orange watch cap when he stepped into the office five minutes later.

"You want to see me?"

"Yes," Lucas said. He introduced himself, produced his ID, and mentioned the death of George Lamb.

"George Lamb? You mean about a hundred years ago, that George Lamb?" The sheriff's voice picked up a hint of wariness.

"Twenty-four years," said Lucas.

"Come on back," the sheriff said. And to the receptionist: "Ruth, go get Jimmy and tell him to come back too."

To Lucas: "You folks want some coffee?"

"That'd be fine," Lucas said. They were passing a coffeepot in a hallway nook, and Sherrill said, "I'll get it. Sheriff? Sugar?"

As the sheriff settled behind his desk, and Sherrill brought the coffee, Lucas said, "We're sorta digging through the background on Lamb. The county clerk said you were around at the time, I don't know if you'd remember it or not."

"Yeah, I do. He used to be a mail carrier outa here, he had the rural route. Died of a heart attack. Why're you looking into that? If I might ask?"

"We've got a case going on in the Cities, woman just shot her husband," Lucas said. "She's charged second degree, but that could get dismissed as self-defense. We're looking into all the deaths that have been associated with her, and we found out that both her father and mother died young . . ."

"I know the woman," the sheriff said. "Audrey. McDonald. Used to be Lamb. Been reading about the case in the *Star-Tribune*. What the heck is a chief of police doing way up here on a case like that?"

"Actually, uh, Marcy and I are friends," Lucas said, tipping his head toward Sherrill. "We were both working the case, and we sorta wanted to get away for a weekend . . . and we were sorta curious about Lamb."

The sheriff glanced at Marcy and then back at Lucas, nodded as if everything was suddenly clear. "I didn't take the first call on Lamb, but when we got word that somebody out there was dead, I came in," the sheriff said. He spun in his office chair, looking out of the office window toward the back of a line of Main Street stores. "This was early in the morning. I mean real early, like four o'clock. He was dressed in gray long johns, and he was laying on the kitchen floor. One of the girls had called us—Audrey I think, the other one was still pretty young—and the two little girls had their mom out in the living room, and she was sitting on the couch all wailing away. And Lamb was deader'n a mackerel. It was his practice to wake up in the morning by breaking a raw egg in a double-shot glass, then pouring the glass full with rye, and drinking it down. We found him laying on the floor in a puddle of rye, with the egg all over his face. Took him off quick."

"Egg and rye. That'd open your eyes, all right," Sherrill said.

" 'Spose," said the sheriff. Another man, tall, lean as a fence post, ten years older than the sheriff but with a full head of hair, propped himself in the office doorway.

"You wanted me?"

"Yeah, Jimmy, come on in . . ." The sheriff introduced Lucas and Sherrill and said, "They're checking around about the time George Lamb died down there on A. You remember that?"

"Yeah. Long time ago. Don't quite see what you'd be checking on. Dropped dead of a heart attack."

"Was there anything unusual about the circumstances?" Lucas asked. "Something to make you wonder if it was more'n a heart attack?"

The sheriff shook his head, and Jimmy scratched his head and said, "Well, no. Not really. The population up here is older'n average—not much to hold the younger people anymore—so we see a lot of heart attacks. Probably once or twice a week we get a call, and a fair number of times, the victim is dead before the ambulance gets there. I probably seen a few hundred of them in my time, and . . ." He shrugged. "Soon as I saw him, I thought, *Heart.*"

"Shoot," Lucas said. "How about the mother? Amelia?"

The sheriff shook his head. "They left here after George died—sold the place off and moved down to your territory, I think."

"Really?" Lucas shook his head ruefully. "You know, I never asked. I just assumed . . ." Lucas glanced at Marcy, then said to the sheriff, "I didn't see a motel coming in. Is there a place we can stay?"

The sheriff seemed to relax a half-inch. "North out of town a half-mile, there's the Sugar Beet Inn. Real clean place."

"Good enough," Lucas said. They all stood up and Lucas shook with the sheriff and Marcy said, "Thanks for the coffee."

And then they were outside and Lucas looked up at the building and said, "That's the goddamnedest thing, huh?"

"He seemed a little tense," Marcy said.

"They oughta be a little tense," Lucas said. "They're covering something up."

They were at the car, and Marcy looked at him over the roof: "All right, you got me. How do you know they're covering something up?"

"Because they both remembered the details of a heart attack twenty-four years ago. What he looked like lying on the floor. Gray long johns. The egg-and-rye thing . . ."

"I might have remembered that, the egg and rye. 'Cause it's unusual."

"Audrey's name . . ."

"They could have remembered that from reading the paper."

Lucas shook his head: "Why? She didn't change it until she married Mc-Donald, eight years after her father died. You think they were tracking her?"

Marcy nodded. "All right. They remembered too much. What do we do next?"

"We go over and jack up the doctor."

"You notice how I'm being the nice little housewife and sweetie pie? Get the coffee, girl-talk about hair, let it pass when you hint to the good sheriff that we're up here for a little whoopee?"

"It's making me nervous," Lucas said. "The pressure'll start to build. Sooner or later, you'll explode."

"That could happen," she said.

DR. STEPHEN LANDIS couldn't see them until the end of his patient day, at four o'clock.

"You can come right here to the clinic," the nurse said. "Four o'clock sharp. He has some patient visits to make out in town, starting at four-thirty, so you'll have about twenty minutes."

"You mean, he actually goes out and visits people?" Marcy asked.

"Of course."

"Amazing."

Back on the street, Lucas looked at his watch: an hour to kill. "Let's go see the undertaker," he said.

THE UNDERTAKER WAS a roly-poly young man in a plaid suit: he didn't remember the case because he was too young. "Dad might remember, though," he said. "He's out in the garage . . ."

The senior undertaker was a pleasant fellow, dressed in cotton slacks and a V-necked wool sweater. He was in the back of the mortuary's heated garage, hitting golf balls into a net off an Astroturf pad.

"Yep, I remember Mr. Lamb," he said, slipping his five-iron back into his golf bag. "Actually, I don't remember Mr. Lamb as well as I remember the daughter . . . the older one."

"Audrey," Sherrill said.

"Don't remember her name. Audrey could be right. I do remember that she handled all the arrangements. Her mother came along, of course, but it was Audrey who settled everything."

"Cremation, I understand," Lucas said.

"Yes, it was. Quite a bit cheaper, you know. I applaud that, by the way. The family didn't have a great deal of money, and with the breadwinner gone, they had to watch their nickels and dimes. The young woman marched right in the door, said we could forget about a big funeral, they didn't have the money, and she wanted the body cremated. Period. No argument allowed."

"Did she pick up the ashes?"

"Yup. In a cardboard box. She said they didn't need an urn, they were planning to scatter them over the family farm."

"Tough kid," Lucas said.

"That she was," said the senior undertaker. "Never saw a tear from her, except once when the sheriff happened to come by while they were making the arrangements, and then she couldn't stop bawling. That was the only time." He took another iron out of his bag. "What do you know about the two-iron?"

"If only God can hit a one-iron, then it'd probably take a prophet to hit the two," Sherrill said.

The senior undertaker looked at her with interest. "You're a golfer."

"A little," she said. "My husband was a two-handicap."

"Was?"

"He died."

"Ah. That *will* play hob with your handicap," he said cheerfully. Then, "Do you think that young lady—Audrey?—do you think she might have killed her father?"

Lucas looked at Sherrill and then back at the senior undertaker. "Why would you ask?"

"Well, because you're here, obviously. And because there was something very cold and unpleasant about that young girl. It crossed my mind when we were setting up the funeral arrangements that she cared less for her father than she might for a clod of dirt. When she came to pick up the ashes—and she drove herself, by the way, and she was too young to have a license, I'm sure—I watched her from the window when she went back to the car. She opened the car door and tossed the box in the backseat like you might toss an old rag. There was something in the way she did it. I thought at that very moment that the ashes might never make it to the family farm. That they might not make it further than the nearest ditch."

"But she was bawling about it, you said."

"Oh, and very conveniently, with the sheriff." The senior undertaker shook his head. "You see a lot of very strange things in this business, but that has stuck in my mind as one of the strangest. No. Not strange. Frightening. I locked the doors for the next few weeks. I would dream that the little girl was coming for me."

"HE DIED OF a heart attack," Dr. Stephen Landis said. Landis was a roughneck fifty-five, with sparkling gold-rimmed glasses and heavy boots under his jeans. A stuffed mallard, just taking wing, hung from the wall of the reception room, while a nine-pound walleye was mounted over his desk in his private office. "He'd been having some problems—cardiac insufficiency—and he wouldn't stop drinking or smoking. I told him if he didn't stop, he was gonna have a heart attack. And one day he keeled over. Drink and cigarette in hand."

"He was smoking when he went?" Sherrill said.

"Still had the cigarette between his fingers," Landis said.

"But you didn't do an autopsy?" Lucas asked.

Landis shrugged. "There didn't seem to be a reason to do one. He'd been sick, it seemed apparent that it was the onset of a heart problem. And then he had a heart attack."

"Aren't you required to do an autopsy when the person didn't die under a doctor's immediate care?" Sherrill asked.

"Not then. Back then, not everything was regulated by the legislature yet. You could use your judgment on occasion."

"Did you ever treat Mrs. Lamb?" Lucas asked, injecting a slight chill into his voice.

Landis's eyes drifted away from Lucas's. "I may have seen her a time or two, but the Lambs moved away, you know . . ."

"Did you ever treat her for injuries that might have been inflicted by her husband?"

"No, I didn't. Well—you probably heard this from somebody else, or you wouldn't be asking the question. There were rumors that George used to knock her around. And I had her in one time, and she had some bruises that looked like they might have come from a beating. She said she fell down the stairs. I doubted that, but the bruises were old and . . . I let it go. Maybe I shouldn't have, but she wasn't interested in talking about it."

They sat in silence for a moment; then Lucas said, "No sign of anything but the symptoms of a heart attack."

"Not that I could see."

"And you examined the body carefully."

"I examined it. Briefly."

"No tissue cultures."

"No."

"You never came to suspect that anything unusual might have led to George Lamb's sudden death."

"No. He had heart trouble. If anything, I was *expecting* a heart attack."

Outside, Sherrill said, "I see what you mean—another case of remarkable memory. Lamb had a cigarette between his fingers when he died."

"There's something here," Lucas said, turning to look back at the front of the clinic. "I have trouble thinking what it might be."

"Maybe she's some kind of town philanthropist and gives them money or something, so they protect her," Sherrill suggested.

"Have you seen her? She doesn't look like she'd give a nickel to a starving man. And if it has been that, somebody would have mentioned it."

"So what do you want to do?"

"Let's go check into this motel. Get some dinner."

LUCAS ALWAYS EXPECTED a certain amount of awkwardness when he and a new woman friend got around a bed, and the room at the Sugar Beet Inn was basically a queen-sized bed, a television set, and bathroom; along with the built-in scent of disinfectant. Sherrill wasn't quite as inhibited: she pulled off her jacket, tossed it on the chair, jumped on the bed, giving it a bounce, then hopped off to check the TV. "I wonder if they have dirty movies?"

"Give me a break," Lucas said. "Come on, let's find a restaurant."

"Too early. It's barely five o'clock. I wanna take a shower and get the road off me," she said. "You wanna take a shower?"

"If we take a shower, we'll probably wind up on the bed, dealing with sexual issues," he said, injecting a tone of disapproval into his voice. "We're here on business."

"Quit bustin' my balls, Davenport," she said. She pulled her sweatshirt over her head. "But if you want to sit out here and wait . . ."

"I suppose we'd save water if we both got in there."

"And water is precious out here on the prairie."

"Well, I mean, if it's for the environment . . ."

THE DESK CLERK at the Sugar Beet told them two restaurants would be open: Chuck's Wagon, a diner, and the Oxford Supper Club, which had a liquor license. They drove down to the supper club and were met at the entrance by a cheerful, overweight woman with hair the same tone of orange as the county clerk's, and a frilly apron. She took them to a red-vinyl booth and left them with glasses of water and menus.

"That hair color must be a fashion out here. She looks like a pumpkin," Sherrill whispered.

"Mmm. Open-face roast beef sandwich with brown gravy, choice of potato, string beans, cheese balls as an appetizer, and pumpkin or mince pie with whipped cream, choice of drink, seven ninety-five," Lucas said.

"You ever hear of cholesterol?"

"Off my case. I'm starving."

Lucas ordered a martini, to be followed by the roast beef sandwich; Sherrill got the Traditional Meatloaf with a Miller Lite up front. They ate in easy companionship, talking about the day, talking about cases they'd worked together and what happened to who, afterwards. Touched lightly on Weather's case. Lucas got a Leinenkugel's and Sherrill got a second Miller Lite, to go with the pie. They were just finishing the pie when Lucas felt the khaki pants legs stepping up to the table. He looked up at two sheriff's deputies, two men in their late twenties or thirties, one hard, lanky, the other thicker, like a high school tackle, with the beginning of a gut.

"Are you the Porsche outside?" asked the one with the gut.

"Yeah. That's us," Lucas said.

"So you're the guys from Minneapolis."

"Yeah. What can we do for you?"

"We were just wondering if you're done here," said the lanky one. His voice was curt: his cop voice.

"I don't know," Lucas said. He was just as curt. Across the table, Sherrill had swiveled slightly on her butt so that her back was to the wall, and her legs, still curled up, projected toward the deputies. Their attitude was wrong; and other patrons in the restaurant had noticed. "We didn't get very far today. We weren't getting a lot of cooperation."

"We were just talking over at the office about how everybody was cooperating, and you were being pretty damn impolite about it," said Gut.

"Not trying to be impolite," Lucas said. Swiveling a bit, as Sherrill had. "We're trying to conduct an investigation."

"Yeah. I bet you were investigating the hell out of this chick up to the Sugar Beet," Gut said.

Sherrill said, "Hey, you . . ." But Lucas held up a peremptory finger to silence her, and she stopped and looked at him; then Lucas said to Gut, "Fuck you, you fat hillbilly cocksucker."

Gut looked at the slender man, who stepped back a bit and said, "Let's cool this off," but Gut put his fists on the table and leaned toward Lucas and said, "If you said that outside, I'd drag your ass all over the goddamn parking lot."

"Let's go," Lucas said. "I'm tired of this rinky-dink bullshit."

LUCAS TOSSED A twenty on the table and followed Gut toward the entrance; the lanky man said, "Hey, whoa, whoa," and Sherrill said, "Lucas, this is a bad idea . . ."

But six feet outside the door, Gut took a slow, short step, feeling Lucas closing behind him, spun and threw a wild, looping right hand at Lucas's head.

Lucas stepped left and hit the heavy man in the nose, staggering him, bringing blood. As Gut turned, bringing his hands up to his face, Lucas hooked him in the left-side short ribs with another right; when Gut pulled his arms down, Lucas hit him in the eye with a left, the other eye with a right, then took the right-side short ribs with a left, then crossed a right to the face. Gut was trying to fall, staggering backward, got his back wedged against a pickup truck, and Lucas beat him like a punching bag, face, face, gut, face, ribs, face, face, like a heavy workout in the gym.

Lucas felt it all flowing out: the frustration with Weather, the attacks on Weather and Elle, the uncertainty, the depression. And heard Sherrill screaming, flicked somebody's arm off his shoulder, was hit from the left and turned, almost punched Sherrill in the forehead, felt another man moving behind him, spun, and saw the lanky man covering Gut, holding his hands in front of him, shouting something . . .

The world began to slow down, and Lucas backed up, hands up, Marcy pushing him, shouting. He could barely hear her. "Okay," he said finally, through the roaring in his head. "Okay, I'm done."

Marcy faded in. "You're done. Are you done?"

"I'm done . . ." He dropped his hands. They were dappled with blood, and blood from Gut's nose was sprayed across his shirt. He said, "This shirt's fucked."

Gut was stretched on the ground next to the pickup running board, groaning, the lanky man leaning over him, saying, "Breathe easy. Come on, you're okay."

But he wasn't okay. He said, "I can't, I can't, I can't . . ." Every time he tried to sit up, he moaned, holding his sides; he was blowing streams of blood from his nose. "We better get an ambulance," the lanky man said. "Get him over to the clinic."

"Can you call from your car?" Sherrill asked.

"Yeah, I can do that," he said, as if the concept were new to him. He hurried to the squad car, parked at the edge of the lot, pushing through a narrow ring of spectators. As he went, Marcy asked, quietly, "Are you okay?"

"Yeah, yeah, he never touched me," Lucas said.

"That's not what I meant."

He looked at her: "Yeah, I'm okay. I sorta let it all out, there."

"I'd say."

The lanky deputy was back, said, "The ambulance'll be here in a minute." Then to Lucas, "I ain't gonna try to take you in, 'cause we all got guns, but you're under arrest."

"Bullshit," Lucas said. "You two came here to try to push us out of a murder investigation and he took the first swing. If I don't get some answers, I'll get the goddamn BCA up here and we'll tear a new asshole for your department. You two are gonna be lucky to get out of this with your badges."

"We'll see," the lanky man said. "Why don't you go on down to the court-house. I'm gonna get the sheriff in. And you're not helping around here."

"Why don't you just come up to the Sugar Beet," Lucas said. "We've got a big room."

A siren started down in the town, the ambulance. The lanky man looked at Sherrill and then at Lucas. "All right. We'll see you up there."

"THIS IS JUST fuckin' awful," Sherrill said, on the way back to the motel.

"The fight?" That was odd; she'd always been one of the first to get in.

"Not the fight. The way the fight turns me on. You could bend me over the front fender right now, in front of all those people, I swear to God. Whoo. But you sorta hung me up there, dude. I don't think I coulda taken that skinny guy." She was vibrating, talking a hundred miles an hour. "Maybe I could have slowed him down. Didn't take you long with the fat guy, that's for sure. Man, if the skinny guy had gone for his gun, though, I'd've had to do something, and we coulda wound up with dead people out there. Whoa, what a rush. Man, the fuckin' adrenaline is coming on, now. It always comes about ten minutes too late."

Lucas grinned at her: "About once a year. It cleans out the system."

"What're you gonna tell the sheriff? I mean, we could be in some trouble."

Lucas shook his head. "There's something going on. We know it, and now they know we know. I think we might learn something."

"Jeez—I wish I hadn't used you up before dinner. I'm serious here, Lucas, I could really use some help."

"We might have a couple minutes."

"It won't take that long . . ."

THE SHERIFF SHOWED up a little more than an hour later. Lucas was walking back from the Coke machine with a Diet and a regular Coke, his hair still wet from another shower, when they arrived in two cars; the sheriff, the older deputy named Jimmy, the young, lanky man from the restaurant, all in the sheriff's squad car, and Dr. Stephen Landis in a two-year-old Buick.

Lucas continued to the room, pushed through the door, said, "They're here."

Sherrill tucked her shirt in: she'd been worried the room would smell too much like sex, which she thought would seem perverted so close to the fight—which Lucas told her *was* perverted—so she'd turned up the shower full blast, cold water only, and sprayed it against the back wall of the shower stall. Now the room smelled faintly of chlorine, with a hint of feminine underarm deodorant. "We're ready," she said, looking around. "Put your gun over on the nightstand. That'll look nice and grim. I'll keep mine, but I'll let them see it." She was wearing her .357 in the small of her back.

He nodded: "You could be good at this."

She came over and stood on her tiptoes and kissed him on the lips. "Remember that," she said.

The sheriff knocked a second later. Sherrill opened the door and let them in.

"DAMN NEAR KILLED him," the sheriff said. He was standing in front of the dresser, looking at Lucas, who was sitting on the bed, his back to the headboard. The other three men were standing near the door, while Sherrill stood at the head end of the bed, near Lucas. "He could still be in trouble."

"Bullshit. I cracked his short ribs and busted his nose. He won't be sneezing for a month or six weeks, that's all," Lucas said.

"That's a fairly clinical judgment," Landis said. "You must've done this before."

"I've had a few fights," Lucas agreed.

"In all my time as sheriff, I haven't had a man hurt that bad, except one who was in a car accident," the sheriff said. "We're talking to the county attorney to see if an arrest would be appropriate. We don't want you going anyplace."

"We're leaving tomorrow, I think," Lucas said. "But we'll be available down in Minneapolis. I'm gonna talk to a couple of friends over at the Bureau of Criminal Apprehension, maybe a guy in the attorney general's office. About coming up here and deposing you people on the murder of George Lamb: to ask you why you've been covering it up all these years. Why you'd send a couple of cops to roust us, in the middle of a murder investigation that you'd been reading about in the *Star-Trib*."

The sheriff shook his head: "We didn't send anybody to roust you. These idiots thought of it themselves." He tipped his head toward the lanky man, who shrugged and looked at the curtains covering the single window.

"The thing is, we can take care of Larry," the older deputy drawled. "Cops get beat up from time to time. The real question I got—not the sheriff, just me—is whether you can be talked to. Or if you're just some big-city asshole up here to kick the rubes."

"I've got a cabin outside a town half this size, in Wisconsin. The sheriff's a friend of mine, and he's been bullshitting me about moving up to run for the office when he quits, and I've thought about it. I've worked with a half-dozen sheriffs all over this state and Wisconsin, and this is the first time I've had trouble," Lucas said. "You want some references?"

"Already made some calls," the older man said. After a few seconds' silence, he said, "You want to talk, or do we do this all legal?"

"Talk," Lucas said.

The sheriff looked at the older deputy and said, "You think?"

"Yeah, I think."

The sheriff nodded and said, "The thing is, we don't know whether or not George Lamb was murdered. But he might have been."

"There were some problems at the time, with the way the death happened," the older man said. "Happened way too early in the morning. He got up early, for his job, but not in the middle of the night. It looked to us like he'd gotten sick the evening before, and they'd let him lay there until he died."

"He came to see me twice in the month before he died. He was feeling sicker and sicker, and at first I thought it was the flu. He'd had some diarrhea, he'd had some episodes of vomiting, dizzy spells, and so on. We'd had some flu going around at the time, and it fit," Landis said. He pulled a chair out from the dresser/desk and sat down. "I gave him some antibiotics for a lung infection he'd developed—nothing serious, he was coughing up some phlegm with pus in it. And we had an argument the second time he came in, and he never came back. Then he dropped dead. *Could* have been a heart attack."

"But you don't really think so," Lucas said.

Landis shook his head. "I think maybe it was rat poison. Arsenic. The thing is, when I went out and looked at this body, he had a rash, a particular kind of rash that flakes off the skin when you've been taking in arsenic for a while."

"You didn't take any tissue samples?"

"If we'd taken tissue samples, and sent them to a lab, then the fat would be in the fire," Landis said. "Other people would know about it . . ."

"You didn't want other people to know?" Sherrill asked.

The sheriff took off his hat, smoothed his hair back, and said, "My daughter went to high school with the Lamb girls. And the older Lamb girl had a reputation as knowing way too much about sex for a girl her age. Then, a couple of months before George died . . ."

Landis picked it up. "The mother brought in the older girl, Audrey, to the clinic. Said she'd been fooling around with one of the boys at school, wanted me to keep it quiet, but wanted her tested to see if she was pregnant. She wasn't. But I gave her a little standard lecture that I gave back then, about staying out of trouble, about saying no to boys, about using some protection . . . She sort of went along with the lecture until she got tired of it, then she got up and left," Landis said. "As she was going out the door, she turned and *looked* at me. The look was like ninety-five percent hate and fear. And she said, 'That's all fine and good, but not relevant in my case.' "

"Not relevant in my case," the sheriff quoted. "Hell of a line for a kid that age. The fact is, George had been f——" He glanced at Sherrill. "Having sex with her."

"When I told you that his wife had some bruises," Landis said, "I was telling you the truth. But not all of it. The woman had been beaten from head to foot."

"The whole goddamn house was a reign of terror," the sheriff said. "Steve told me what he thought was going on. I talked to the sheriff at the time, Johnny James, and he told me that there was nothing to do, unless somebody complained. So I caught up with George on his mail route one day and said if I ever heard of him screwing that little girl, I'd kill him."

"Did he believe you?"

"I don't know, but he should of, 'cause I would of," the sheriff said. "But it never came up, because he dropped dead."

"He was lying there on the floor, looking okay, except for this rash," Landis said. "We knew he'd been screwing at least the older girl, and maybe the younger one too; we knew he'd been beating the bejesus out of his wife. So the question was, do we do tissue samples? Didn't have to. No requirement."

"Steve came and talked to me, and we said screw it. Leave it alone. And we did. Shipped George off to the funeral home. And that was the end of it, until you showed up this morning."

They all thought about that for a moment; then Lucas rubbed his chin and changed the subject: "That fat kid I beat up," he said to the sheriff. "He's gonna be nothing but a pain in the ass for you. He's gonna be in trouble for the rest of his career."

"He's had a couple problems," the sheriff said.

"You oughta get rid of him before it's too late. And this guy," Lucas said, nodding at the lanky man. "He rode along a little too easily. He's gotta learn to stand up. He wanted to stop the whole thing, but he couldn't get the job done."

"I learned something," the lanky man said.

"I hope the hell you have," the sheriff said. To Lucas: "What do you think?"

"I think if you recast exactly what you told me here tonight, you'd have a perfectly good story if you ever had to go to court to testify. You know, that you thought it was a heart attack at the time—still think it was possible—but sometime later worked out that it might have been a poisoning. But by then it was too late, the body had been cremated. That kind of thing happens all the time. That's why we have exhumations."

"You think we might have to testify?"

Lucas stood up, yawned, stretched. "We're putting together a circumstantial case. So you might have to. But we've got a way to go, before we get anything together."

"But her husband . . . The papers say he was beating her, just like her father beat her mother. It seems to me there might be some justification."

"We're looking at eight murders and several ag assaults over the last ten years, including a couple of out-and-out executions of absolutely innocent people," Lucas said.

After a moment of stunned silence, the sheriff said, "Eight?"

Lucas nodded.

"God in heaven."

And Landis stood up and looked at the sheriff and said, "Old George did a lot more damage than we knew about. You shoulda killed him."

The older man pushed himself away from the wall. "So what're we going to do about tonight?"

Lucas shrugged. "Nothing happened to me. If you guys want to say nothing happened, nothing happened."

The sheriff took a quick eye-poll, then nodded to Lucas: "Nothing happened."

"If we need to talk to you again, an assistant county attorney'll be calling," Lucas said. "I'll give you a warning call ahead of time."

"I appreciate it," the sheriff said. "I'd also appreciate it if you'd get the hell out of my town."

"We're going tomorrow morning," Lucas said.

"And I surely wish you hadn't taken Larry out in the parking lot. I'm always shorthanded when the snow starts to fly."

"Sorry."

"But not too sorry," the sheriff said.

"Not too," Lucas agreed, and grinned at him.

The sheriff showed the faintest hint of a smile, and eased out the door. The older man was the last to leave, and at the threshold, he turned and looked at Sherrill, and then back at Lucas. "I once had a woman looked just about like that," he said to Lucas. "When I was just about your age."

"Oh yeah?"

"Yeah." He gave Sherrill a long look, and said, "She flat wore me out."

"Better to wear out than to rust," Sherrill said, from her corner.

"Yeah." And he laughed, a nasty laugh for an old codger, and closed the door.

27

THE SUN WAS only two or three fingers above the western horizon, the evening rush already starting, when Lucas and Sherrill dropped past the Dunwoody exit on I-394, zigged a couple of times, and rolled into downtown Minneapolis.

"Now *that* was a road trip," Sherrill said, enthusiastically. "Fightin', fuckin', and detectin.' So what's next?"

"I've got to work tomorrow," Lucas said. "You're working, right?"

"Yeah—but there's not much going on. I could probably get away to help, if you needed me . . ."

He shook his head: "Better not. I told you about the little talk with Rose Marie."

"I might have a little talk with Rose Marie myself," she said with a flash of anger. "Pisses me off."

"Probably wouldn't help."

"It'd make me feel better," Sherrill said.

"Do what you want," Lucas said. "And when you get a minute, send me a memo on the whole sequence up there in Oxford. All the details. Make a copy for yourself. Take both copies over to the government center, have them notarized for date, but don't let anybody read them."

"Just in case?"

"Can't tell what's gonna happen yet."

"When you say all the details, you want the part where I said, 'Oh my God, put it in, put it in'?"

"I don't remember that," Lucas said.

"I think you were looking at your watch. We're gonna have to talk about that, by the way."

Lucas shook his head: "Christ, I'm beginning to understand what that old guy meant."

"What old guy?"

"You know, the old deputy, who once had a woman like you. 'Flat wore me out,' he said."

She looked at him critically: "You still got a little good tread on you."

LUCAS KISSED HER goodbye outside City Hall—what the hell—and went down to his office, whistling, picked up the phone and got the brrnk-brrnk-brrnk message signal. The mechanical operator said there were six: all six were from Helen Bell, frantic, accusatory.

"Did you do this with Connie? Did you call Child Protection? Why? Why? Please, please call me . . ." and "Why aren't you calling? Did you do this? I'm getting a lawyer, goddamn you . . ."

He punched in her phone number and the phone at the other end was snatched up halfway through the first ring. "Hello?" Still frantic.

"This is Lucas Davenport. What happened with Connie?"

A moment of uncertain silence. "You didn't have anything to do with Connie?"

"Mrs. Bell, I haven't even thought of Connie since I last saw you. I was out of town all day yesterday and today, I just got back and got your messages."

"They came and got her," she wailed.

"Child Protection?"

"Child Protection, Child Welfare, whatever they call it. They say I gave her marijuana and beat her up and I never did any of that, she's my baby, I don't understand, they said some teacher called, but I can't find anybody at her school."

"Let me make a call," Lucas said. "I know a woman over there who might know something."

"Please, please get her back."

Lucas talked to her for another minute, then hung up, found Nancy Bunker's name in his address book, and punched her number in. She was just leaving.

"Yeah, I know about it. Doesn't look like much. The girl said her mother slapped her once during an argument, open hand, no injury, more like a girl fight. Said she's used some marijuana around school, but that was what the fight was about. Her mother was trying to stop her."

"So what're you doing with her?"

"Well, she's out at a foster home right now; we usually keep them a couple of nights, just to make sure. She'll be home tomorrow."

"Huh."

"What's your interest, Lucas?"

"Did you ever find the teacher who called in the information?"

"No, it was anonymous, but you know how it is—we don't take chances if there're reports of physical abuse. Especially drugs and physical abuse. And we want to get the kid off to a safe place, where she feels safe about talking about it . . . So, what's your interest?"

"I think you were deliberately set up to mess with the kid's mother. She's a source of mine in this Kresge murder case."

"Really? Set up?"

"I think so. I don't doubt that the kid smokes a little dope, but then so did you."

Bunker laughed. "Yeah, the good old days. So what do you want me to do?"

"How about releasing the kid to her mother? I'll pick her up, take her home."

"Damn it; I'd have to sit back down and turn the computer back on . . ."

"Another little tragedy in your life."

"You gotta be over here in ten minutes," Bunker said. "I'm trying to catch a bus."

"Taking a little undertime today?"

"Nine minutes, now."

"Be right there."

THE FOSTER HOME was in Edina, west of Minneapolis. Lucas picked up the papers for the foster parents, and on the way out, slowed by traffic, he called the medical examiner's office and got an investigator on the line. "I'm looking for a file on an Amelia Lamb. About twenty years old."

"Nothing here, Lucas. Are you sure of the name?"

"Last name I'm sure of; the first name, I don't know, there may be an alternative spelling."

After a few more seconds, the investigator said, "Lots of Lambs, but nothing like an Amelia."

"Can you get into the state death certificates from your computer?"

"I'd have to call, I could get back to you."

"Could you do that? This is kind of important."

The ME's investigator was back five minutes later. "You want Dakota County, and specifically, you want MercySouth. You want that phone number?"

"Give it to me." Lucas got the number, the date of Lamb's death, and the attending physician, and scribbled it all in his notebook. He called the hospital, spent five minutes working his way through the bureaucracy, and was finally told by an assistant director that he could see the records if he brought a subpoena with him.

"Even if the woman's dead?"

"It's our policy," she said.

"It's a pain," Lucas said. "But I'll get one for you. What's the name of your director out there?"

She gave him the name and he said, "Ask him to stick around the house tonight, we don't want to have to have a cop run him down. We can probably get the subpoena out there before midnight."

"Really? I think he and his wife are going to the chamber orchestra."

"Well—he should be home before we get the subpoena. If we do get it earlier, we'll just ask the orchestra people to page him during the concert."

"Hang on."

And *she* was back in five minutes: "The director tells me that I was misinformed. Since Mrs. Lamb is dead, and you're a police officer conducting an official investigation, we can show you the records." She sounded faintly amused.

"Gee. Thanks. That's really nice. Will somebody be in your records department, about seven o'clock?"

"There's always somebody there. Around the clock."

"Tell them I'm coming . . ."

CONNIE BELL STARTED crying when she saw Lucas. She had a small bag with her, and the foster mother patted her on the shoulder, and Connie said, "Did you do this?"

"No."

"Then who did?"

"I don't know," Lucas said, leading the way to the car. "But it was pretty mean."

"My mom is really upset, I thought she was going to fight those people last night, I've never seen her like that."

"Why don't you call her?" Lucas said. "There's a phone in the car."

Connie called, told Helen that she was on the way home, and that Lucas was bringing her. She handed Lucas the phone and said, "Thank you, thank, thank you . . ."

And when they arrived at Helen's home, Helen ran out and wrapped up her daughter, and they both started crying again, and after a moment, Lucas said, "Could you send Connie inside to get cleaned up? I'd like to talk to you for a minute."

Connie went, Helen watching her running up the steps.

"Do you have any feeling who might have done this?" Lucas asked.

"There was a literature teacher she had last year, who hated Connie—and several other kids too. If this was last year, I'd say her. But I can't believe that she'd wait a whole year. I've been racking my brain . . ."

"This is not the way they do things in the school system," Lucas said. "They've got a whole bureaucratic procedure they follow, and it's all very routine. This was strange, right from the start. I don't think it was a teacher at all. Could you think, really hard, about who it might be?"

"Okay, okay . . . but you're scaring me. Why?"

"Because it might be related to something else. Anyway, think about it. If you come up with anything, you've got my number."

"Okay." She stepped close and gave him a hug. "Thanks."

TRAFFIC WAS BEGINNING to ease as he headed south, down to Dakota County, finally to MercySouth. He went in through the emergency entrance, was directed by a nurse to Records, and found a dark-haired young woman sitting in a pool of light from a desk lamp, in an otherwise dark room full of file cabinets and computers. Her feet up next to a computer, she was engrossed in a Carl Hiaasen novel. A stack of what looked like thick textbooks sat on the floor.

"Good book?" he asked in the silence.

She jumped, turned, saw him, looked down at the book, and said, "Yes, as a matter of fact." She looked at the photo on the back cover. "And this Hiaasen is a yummy little piece of crumb cake, if I do say so myself . . . You'd be Officer Davenport, and you need some records."

"That's right."

"I'm supposed to Xerox your credential," she said. She went for the double entendre: "You'll hardly feel a thing."

"Young women these days," Lucas clucked. He gave her his ID, she xeroxed it, and said, "There's not much in the computer file—mostly just the bare bones. If you want to look at her actual file, we don't have the paper anymore, but it's on fiche."

"I'd like that, if I could."

"Sure." She found the right fiche, set him up with a reader, and went back to the novel.

THE FILE WAS short, and echoed the Oxford doctor's report of symptoms on George Lamb. Amelia Lamb suffered from flulike symptoms—gastric discomfort, sporadic vomiting. She saw the doctor twice, the visits two weeks apart. The discomfort had increased in the two weeks, and he ordered a number of tests. He noted that her blood pressure was high and that she had been asked to come in for a series of blood pressure tests, but there was no indication that any blood pressure medication had been prescribed. Four days after the second visit, she was brought to the hospital by ambulance, and was reported dead on arrival. The record noted that the daughter reported that she'd been suffering chest pains but had refused to come to the hospital because of cost, and she'd called only after her mother had collapsed.

"Relative reported that final collapse was accompanied by severe chest pains and rapid loss of consciousness. Myocardial infarction indicated." There was no mention of a rash.

Lucas looked at the woman with the book: "Is there a doctor around that I could talk to? Who'd have a little time?"

"I'm a fourth-year med student," the woman said. "What's the question?"

"Look at this blood pressure," Lucas said. "Should she have been on medication?"

The woman bent over the screen, read the report, and said, "She would now. That's definitely way high. But back then, the drugs weren't so good. You'd have to talk to somebody older, who'd remember. But back then, she might not have been."

"All right: then look at this. On her second visit, they do some tests. But the tests never show up in the records."

The woman bent over the screen again, skimming through the records: "You know what?" she said finally. "It looks like she died before the tests could get back. So when they got back, they probably just tossed them."

"Huh. And the body was sent directly out to a funeral home."

"Yup."

"Why wouldn't they do an autopsy?"

"Again, they didn't do them so often back then. Not for hospital deaths. And, uh, you'd have to keep this under your hat . . . or at least not say I told you. I've noticed this in other records . . ."

"Sure."

"You see this funeral home?" She tapped the screen. "The predecessor organization to this hospital, which was called Dakota Mothers of Mercy, had a deal with the funeral home. If the relatives didn't express a preference, they'd send the bodies out to this place, and the hospital would get a . . . consideration."

"A kickback."

"An emolument. If they sent them into Hennepin, for an autopsy, the body was up for grabs."

"So there would be a bias against autopsies," Lucas said.

"Unnecessary autopsies."

"You shoulda been a lawyer," Lucas said.

"Not enough money in it." The woman tapped the screen: "Here's something else for you. The insurance company called about it. That's the code for Prudential."

"They called?"

"Yup. That's what that is—the files were sent out in response to a request from Prudential."

"They send them out to Prudential, but they're gonna make me get a subpoena?"

"This was a long time ago," the woman said. "Things were really different."

The woman went back to the novel while Lucas made notes. When he was finished, he shut down the screen and gave her the fiche. "Thank you very much," he said.

She looked up from the desk. "Do you think if I, like, xeroxed my breasts and sent a copy to Hiaasen with my phone number, he'd call me up?"

"Certainly worth a try," Lucas said. "In fact, I'd recommend that you do it. How else will you know? If you don't, you could be like two ships passing in the dark."

"Cops are weird," she said. But as Lucas left, she was looking at the copying machine.

LUCAS DROVE TOWARD home, thinking it all over: he'd call Prudential in the morning, hoping that they'd still have a record of the call. In any case, they must have paid somebody some money, if they bothered to make the call. He'd bet that Audrey was the recipient.

As he crossed the Mendota Bridge, he noticed, for the second or third time, that there was no noise in the background of his brain: no chattering. He'd caught himself whistling again. In the last twenty-four hours, he'd gotten thoroughly laid, hugged by Helen Bell, and double entendred by a nice-looking medical student.

"Glacier's breaking up," he said aloud. "Ice is going out."

He wasn't sure what it meant, but it felt right.

28

SHERRILL SAW HIM walking in, came down to meet him, took his hand. "Can I take you to dinner tomorrow night?"

"Sure. But things are starting to cook with Audrey McDonald. Shouldn't mess us up, but if something comes up . . ." He was fumbling with his keys, opened the office door. She stepped in behind him.

"Tell me about it," she said. "About Audrey." He told her, and she said, "Goddamnit. If we weren't sleeping together, you could just come down and tell Frank that you need me to work on this, and I'd get another neat case to work on. Now, we'd sorta have to jump through our asses."

"Nothing happening yet, anyway," he said.

"Well, if you're going out to shoot somebody, call me," she said, as she went out the door.

"Do that."

THREE CALLS: TO Prudential, to the doctor who signed the death certificate, and to the funeral home that handled Amelia Lamb's body.

Prudential was cooperative, but the right guy would have to get back.

The doctor was cooperative, but had no memory of the event at all. "I was doing a surgical residency and working part-time as an emergency room doc," he said. "I worked emergency rooms for seven years and must've signed five hundred of those things. Maybe a thousand. I'm sorry, but I just don't remember."

The funeral home was confused, but a woman with a quavery, elderly voice finally found the record: Amelia Lamb had been cremated.

"Shit," Lucas said aloud.

"I beg your pardon?"

THE PRUDENTIAL GUY called back a half hour later, as Lucas was pulling together records on the murders proposed by Helen Bell, as well as the two proposed by Annette Ingall.

"We paid sixty-four hundred dollars on George Lamb, which was not an inconsiderable sum at the time; and then four and a half years later, we paid fifteen thousand on Amelia Lamb. That insurance policy had been in effect only three years, which was probably why we called the hospital on it," the Prudential man said.

"Who was beneficiary on the Amelia Lamb policy?"

"Uh, let's see . . . this is an older form . . . Um, an Audrey Lamb. Apparently her daughter."

"Not Audrey and Helen?"

"No, just an Audrey."

"How about on George Lamb?"

"That was . . . Amelia."

"Huh. Did Amelia Lamb have to take a physical?"

"Um . . . yup. Passed okay."

"Anything about high blood pressure?"

"Nope. But this form isn't specific—you'd have to see the original doctor's report, and that was so long ago . . ."

"Do you have the doc's name?"

"Yup."

But the doctor was dead. His son, a dentist, said his father's records had been transferred to other doctors when he gave up his practice, and records not transferred had been stored for ten years, then destroyed.

"Shit."

"I beg your pardon?"

LUCAS WENT BACK to the records for an hour, and finally came to a push-comes-to-shove point. If Audrey was guilty of all of this, then she must have killed O'Dell. But according to the investigative records, signed off by Franklin and Sloan, she left the building before O'Dell was killed. That was confirmed: she logged out of the building at 10:53. Two people visiting their son in the building, who had logged out after her, confirmed that they had left just as a *Roseanne* rerun was ending. *Nightline* ended a couple of minutes before eleven, and they were shown as logging out at eleven, while O'Dell was confirmed killed at 11:02.

It was possible, of course, that Audrey was a master burglar and that she had some way of getting into a building with a security desk in the lobby. Or that she had somehow obtained a key card for the elevator. But the first of those possibilities seemed laughable, while the second was only barely reasonable— she wouldn't have had much time to plan the killing of O'Dell, unless the killing was part of a long-range plan.

He thought about that for a moment. Maybe she did have a long-range plan. Maybe she had access to everybody she might ever need to kill. Then he shook his head. Couldn't think that way. If she was working off a long-range plan, which had somehow involved getting home keys for all her possible victims, then she was a perfect killer and they were out of luck.

He glanced at his watch, punched up his computer, and wrote a memo, with copies to Frank Lester, head of the investigative division, and Rose Marie Roux.

Halfway through, a sheriff's deputy called from Itasca County. "You called yesterday about the Baird case?"

"Yeah, thanks for calling back," Lucas said. "How well do you know the case?"

"I was lead investigator," the deputy said. "I pretty much know it all."

"I understand it was a firebombing," Lucas said. "A Molotov cocktail."

"Yeah, that's right. A mix of gas and oil in a gallon jug," the deputy said.

"Was there anything weird about the bottle?" Lucas asked.

After a moment of pregnant silence, the deputy said, "Like what?"

"Like scoring? Like with a glass cutter?"

Another beat. Then, "How'n the hell did you know about that? We never put it in the report . . ."

WHEN HE WAS done with the memos, Lucas printed them and walked them down to Roux's office and left them with the secretary. Homicide was just down the hall, so he stopped by.

Sherrill was at her desk: "Lunch?"

She was sitting next to Sloan, who was eating a corned beef sandwich. "If you don't think people'll think you're fucking me," she said, just loud enough for Sloan to hear.

Sloan never flinched. "Let's go," Lucas said. And to Sloan: "Have you got an hour, in an hour or so? To go over to O'Dell's place, and look around?"

"Sure."

LUCAS AND SHERRILL walked down the street to a cop hangout, got sandwiches, and Sherrill said, "I hope I can get past this wise-mouth stuff with you. I've been a wise-ass ever since we got together, and I'm having a hard time getting off that wavelength."

"I'll recite you a poem sometime," Lucas said. "It makes women feel all gushy and tender; they roll right over on their backs."

"You just did it to me."

"What?"

"Wise-assed me. I heard you read poetry. I always thought it was neat. Now you wise-assed it."

"Yeah." He looked up at her, serious now. "I'm sorry I wise-assed it. I do like poetry, and I do like reading some of it to women."

"Say a poem to me."

He thought, and then said, slowly, " 'It was Din, Din, Din you limpin' lump of—' "

"Get the fuck out of here," she said. "You did it again."

"We gotta do something about this," he said, grinning at her. "I really am serious. We've got to have at least one honest talk. Penalties for any wise-ass remarks."

"Tomorrow night. For dinner."

"Tomorrow," he agreed.

Sherrill's phone rang, and she took it out of her purse, listened, and handed it to him: "Rose Marie. Christ, she knew right where to call."

Lucas put the phone to his ear. "Yeah?"

"I didn't interrupt a tender moment, did I?"

"Yeah. I was about to bite into a cheeseburger."

"I called Towson about your memo. He wants to meet."

"It's too soon."

"No it's not. I'm sending a copy over for him to read. You should get over there at two o'clock. Frank is gonna go along. From the memo, I don't think we're likely to get her unless she kills somebody else. So you guys are gonna have to figure something out."

LUCAS DROPPED SHERRILL back at the office, picked up Sloan, and they walked together over to O'Dell's apartment building. The security guard recognized Sloan and sent them up.

"The basic problem is, if you go down in the elevator, you can't get back up without a key card," Sloan said. "Even if you have a key card, there's a monitor camera in the elevator, so a guard might recognize you . . . not that they spend a lot of time looking at the monitor," Sloan said, as they got in the elevator.

"So she gets off at another floor . . ."

"Nope. Can't get off at another floor. If you get in at the lobby, you can go to any one floor. If you get in at any other floor, you can only go down to the lobby. Unless you have a key card."

"How about the fire stairs?"

"The doors are locked in the lobby and the skyway. From those floors, you can't get in without a key, you can only get out. And you can't get out on any floor except the lobby or the skyway, even if you have a key."

"A key, not a key card," Lucas said.

"That's right—like a Schlage."

"How close do they track the cards?"

"They know how many each person is signed out for. O'Dell had three, two for herself, and one for her father, who lives way the hell out in South Dakota. We found her two cards, and her father still had his when he was here to pick up the body. So that was all of hers. But somebody else in the building? Who knows? There are almost three hundred cards out. I suppose we could try to find all of them . . . I'd guess a few are missing. The problem is figuring out how the McDonalds might have gotten one."

"Huh. If it was all arranged ahead of time, we're fucked anyway. What if she had to do it off the top of her head? Maybe a day's thought?"

Sloan shrugged. "You figure it out."

They got off on O'Dell's floor, and Lucas stood with his back to the door of her apartment. "She went down first, then she had to get back up to kill her."

"Right."

Lucas looked at the elevator: "Even if she's got a key card, there's a problem coming back up to kill O'Dell. She can't guarantee the guard won't look at the monitor out of sheer boredom, if he sees movement on the screen. If he does, she's dead meat. He's just seen her leave, and now she's going up to kill somebody. Therefore . . ."

"She doesn't use the elevator, she uses the stairwell," Sloan said. "She has a Schlage key for the door in the skyway. She signs out of the building, runs across the street to the skyway, goes up, walks across the skyway to the skyway fire door, uses her Schlage to get into the stairwell, walks up here. Where you have a problem: she can't get out of the stairwell. There's no key at all that'll get you out of the stairwell onto another floor. You can only get out in the skyway or the lobby."

Lucas worked on it for a moment. "Like this," he said finally. "She knows she doesn't have the votes to make a real deal with O'Dell: she claims she's got them, but Bone says she didn't, and she knows she doesn't. She's come here specifically to kill O'Dell—she knows that when she gets here. She can't just sneak up and do it, because she doesn't have any key. She doesn't have anything. So she calls O'Dell to talk about making a deal, and her only purpose is to get into the building. So she gets out of the elevator, and right when she arrives, before she talks to O'Dell, she walks over to the fire door, opens it, takes some duct tape out of her purse, tapes the lock, walks down the stairs to the skyway, opens that door, tapes it, and then comes back up here and rings the doorbell."

"O'Dell answers it, they talk, the deal falls through, and she leaves. O'Dell sees her into the elevator, and she goes down through the lobby and signs out," Sloan said.

"Then she runs across the street, comes up into the skyway, goes in through the taped door, runs up the stairs, knocks on the door, and boom. She has to do it then—even though she knows we'll look at her—because she can't count on the tape being left on the door for more than a short time."

"Which explains something," Sloan said. "O'Dell told Louise Compton that there was 'somebody at the door,' which meant that she didn't know who was at the door, which meant that she didn't know who'd be arriving. She wasn't expecting anyone, like a boyfriend. There was no easy explanation for that knock, at least not in her mind."

"So Audrey shoots her, checks her to make sure she's dead, runs back down the stairs, carefully pulling the tape off the locks . . . and goes home."

"Fuckin' cold, man," Sloan said.

"She *is* cold. I wonder if she was cold enough to wash the sticky stuff off the doors when she pulled off the tape? She'd need acetone, or something," Lucas said.

They were both staring at the fire door. Sloan reached out to the doorknob, pulled the door open, bent forward to look at the lock tongue, then knelt. Lucas squatted beside him.

"Looks like sticky stuff," Sloan said. He tapped his index finger next to what looked like gray tape residue.

"Wonder how many movers have gone in and out, using tape?"

"Up this high? None. That's why the elevator's so big. And I think this stuff would wear away, if the door was opened and closed on it enough. So it's probably fairly new."

"Let's get Crime Scene over here," Lucas said, standing up. "And let's get a search warrant ready, see if we can find some tape at her place that matches this sticky stuff—if the lab guys can make a match like that."

On the way back down in the elevator, Sloan said, "It's a reach."

"*She's* a reach. She looks like Old Mother Hubbard and she's really the Wicked Witch of the West."

THE HENNEPIN COUNTY attorney, Randall Towson; his chief deputy, Donald Dunn; and Richard Kirk, head of the criminal division, met with Lucas and Frank Lester, deputy chief and head of the investigative division.

"You're telling us she's a serial killer," Towson said.

"Everything points to it," Lucas said. "I'm not sure we could prove it to a jury."

"Make the argument."

"You've all seen the memo. The major point is this: We have too many unusual deaths. First, her parents. She benefited directly from the death of her mother—a fifteen-thousand-dollar life insurance policy that her sister apparently didn't share in. She probably got insurance from the death of her father—her mother was weak, and Audrey seemed to be running things, even then, as a kid. We also have four obvious and unquestioned murders: George Arris, shot in the back of the head in St. Paul; Daniel Kresge, who you all know was shot while deer hunting last week; Wilson McDonald, who she admits shooting to death; and Susan O'Dell, who was shot to death in her apartment. Audrey McDonald was the last person known to have been with O'Dell."

"I'd think that would almost be exculpatory, from what I get from your memo," Kirk said. "She could prove that she was out of the building before the killing happened."

"Things have changed in the last hour, since I wrote the memo," Lucas said. "Detective Sloan and I have worked out a way she might have done it. There might even be the possibility of some physical evidence . . ."

"How . . ."

He explained quickly about the duct tape, then said, "Let me finish this other thought. In addition to her parents and the four outright murders, we also have four mysterious deaths: Andy Ingall disappeared and has never been found after a supposed boating accident; eleven-year-old Tom McKinney was killed while riding his bicycle; and Mr. and Mrs. Sheldon Baird were burned to death in their cabin. We also have two aggravated assaults in the past two weeks. One was on my former fiancée, Weather Karkinnen; her house was firebombed, you've probably read about it. Normally, I wouldn't suggest that there was a tie, but I would here. You can read the full reasoning in the memo—Audrey has a history of attacking people to distract, as well as to eliminate, and I believe that's what she did here. We even have some evidence for this."

"And it is . . ."

"When Mr. and Mrs. Baird were burned to death, investigators found the remnants of a glass jug in their front room, and the glass had been scored to make sure the bottle broke on impact," Lucas said. "That feels like a pro job— but it happens that when my finacée was firebombed, remnants of the bottle used in that bombing showed the same kind of scoring."

"Jesus Christ," Towson said.

"Then, last week, another friend of mine was attacked, Sister Mary Joseph, from St. Anne's College. As it happens, Audrey McDonald knew her. And presumably knew where she lived, and attacked her for the same reason she attacked Weather. To get me off her back."

"And you can show that she benefited from all of these," Dunn said.

"She benefited financially from the killings of her father and mother—in addition to the money, she may have killed her father because he was sexually and probably physically abusing her, and she got rid of him. All the other deaths were done to push her husband's career: when you put them down in outline form, you'll find that he benefited from each of the other deaths . . . Look at page three of the memo, there's a chart."

"What about her husband?"

"I think her husband was killed because we were getting too close, and he was a rather notorious coward. If he knew about the killings, he might have ratted her out, if there was pressure. Also, she inherits, if she's found not guilty of murdering him. Running through his files after he was killed, we figured he could be worth about seven, eight million."

"I see one problem," Towson's deputy said, snapping the paper with his finger. "If I remember right, you guys had elected Wilson McDonald for the

Kresge killing. Looking at this, I ask myself, couldn't McDonald have done all of these? We know he was a brutal asshole. Look what he did to his own wife."

"It's worse than that," Lester said. "St. Paul's got a partial print, probably made by McDonald, on a shell from the gun that killed Arris."

"Not good," said Towson.

"No—but all that proves is that McDonald loaded the gun. I'll also say it seems that when O'Dell was shot in the head, the bullet might have come from the same gun. We can't prove the gun-slug connection, because the slug, a hollowpoint, came apart in her head, and there was nothing left but fragments. But a spectroscopic analysis of the metal from the slug in O'Dell's head and from the traces of a slug in the Arris killing suggests both came from the same batch of lead. We also have the gun—taken out of a car owned by McDonald but not driven by him since September—and the clip was full. But all the shells had his prints on them but the last two. The lead from those two came from a different batch, but the lead from the shells in the lower part of the magazine came from the same batch—*probably* the same batch—as the slugs that killed Arris and O'Dell."

"You'd drive a jury nuts with this stuff," said the criminal division guy.

"There's another point here. I think I can demonstrate by the recorded times of some cell phone calls that Wilson McDonald couldn't have killed O'Dell. And if he couldn't have killed her, then somebody else who knew where the gun was must have. Audrey McDonald. And like I said, I think we can show how it was done."

"But you can't definitively prove that was the gun that killed O'Dell."

"No."

"That's a problem," Towson said.

They all sat in silence for a minute; then Kirk said, "Pattern."

Everybody nodded. Dunn said, "Pattern, plenty of motive, we knock down any sympathy she might get with the killing of her mother . . ."

"Which is more than balanced off by the fact that her mother apparently stood by while her father was fucking her," Kirk said. "The defense puts a weeping woman on the stand who denies doing anything, but points out that if she did—which she didn't—it certainly would have been justified, a fourteen-year-old girl getting the ol' pork trombone from her own father. Matter of fact, if I was the defense attorney, I'd make the mother an accomplice. If Audrey's as smart as this stuff makes her, she wouldn't need too much of a hint to come up with something pretty lurid."

"Which, if we could drive a wedge between Audrey and her sister, we might get the sister to refute . . . Is the sister as wacko as Audrey?"

"No. But there was a complaint filed with Child Protection a couple of days ago that she beat her daughter and gave her dope," Lucas said.

"Aw, Jesus."

"But not justified," Lucas said. "In fact, I think Audrey filed it."

"Goddamn this woman."

"I'm sure he will," Lester said dryly. "But it'd be nice if we could get a few whacks in first."

Towson leaned over his desk, looking at his deputy and the head of his criminal division: "I'll tell you what, boys. We're faced here with the usual sloppy police work that virtually ties us hand and foot, even as we have to take our cases before drooling liberal judges who don't wish for anything finer than putting criminals back on the street where they can rape our Cub Scouts. However . . ."

"I wish I'd said that," Lester said.

"Part of a speech I'm writing," Towson said. "Seriously, Lucas, do you think she's gonna kill anyone else in the next few days?"

"I don't know who'd it be," Lucas said. "Me maybe—but I'm careful."

"You *be* careful," Towson said. "She apparently likes guns . . . Now listen. I'm looking through this memo, and I'm convinced. A trial is something else. Give me another few days' work on this thing. Nail down that stuff about O'Dell. Give me something harder. Work out a really tight timetable, and find a way we can put her there to pull the trigger. And anything else. Even people willing to suggest that she did it. We need more hard evidence: anything would help."

"What're you going to do?"

"I'm thinking that we might charge her with everything," Towson said. "All the murder counts, all the ag assaults. Put all the evidence together, argue the pattern. Then, probably, we'll lose most of them. But we'll have a chance of getting her for killing her husband, if we can make it part of the pattern. Because she's admitted it. The jury might let her go on the other ones, for lack of specific evidence, but we might get her on at least second degree, and maybe first, on her husband."

"She was pretty beat up," Lucas said. "They took pictures."

"We can handle that, if we can make the other things clear enough. If we get her on just second degree on her husband, and then whisper sweet nothings to the judge, he could blow off the guidelines, depart upward on the sentence, and put her away for twenty."

They all looked at each other; then Kirk said, "Right now, Lucas, I'd say it's sixty-forty against. It'd be nice if you could come up with something a little stronger. Give us another twenty percent, or so."

"It'd be nice," Towson said.

"I'll hit her tonight with a search warrant on the duct tape, maybe look for a glass cutter," Lucas said.

"Talk to us," Towson said. "We want to know every move from here on out."

29

AUDREY MCDONALD WAS packing Wilson's suits into cardboard boxes, after carefully noting labels, estimated cost—which she'd have to confirm with the tailor—and condition, all toward a tax deduction. The accountant had recommended a donation to Goodwill.

She didn't like the idea of Goodwill, but she did like the idea of the tax deduction. Still, she was muttering to herself as she did it. Shaking her head. Wilson had spent a fortune on clothing, and now she'd get only a fraction of it back. Nothing for the underwear. Perfectly good boxer shorts, and some bum was going to get them.

"So reckless," she muttered. "Just didn't care. Just didn't care what you spent on this. Look at this. Fourteen, fifteen, sixteen pairs of undershorts. Why would you need all those undershorts? You could have gotten by with three pairs, or five pairs. Sixteen pairs of undershorts. Look at this. This is silk. Silk undershorts?"

She was counting them again when the headlights swung into the driveway, glowing through the bedroom drapes. Helen? She hadn't called. She always called before she came. But who else? She went to the window and looked down.

LUCAS AND SHERRILL waited as Sloan pulled into the driveway with Del in the passenger seat; a squad car followed a few seconds behind Sloan, with two uniformed cops. Lights shone from several windows in the house, both upstairs and down, and Lucas handed the warrant papers to one of the uniformed cops, who walked up the stoop, rang the doorbell, and knocked.

"All glass cutters, all packages of tape, all one-gallon glass jugs, all guns, cartridges and/or cartridge parts, to include gunpowder, primers, brass, and bullets, all credit card records or billing statements involving gasoline purchases," he read, in the light coming through the window in the door. There was no answer, so he rang again, then opened the storm door and pounded. Still no answer.

"What do you want to do?" he asked.

"We're going in," Lucas said. "Let's not break anything yet. Let's check the garage doors."

The front door rattled and the cop at the door stepped back. A moment later, Audrey McDonald stuck her head out. "What?" she croaked. She looked worse than she'd looked in court: the bruises on her face were a sickly bluish yellow, with small reddish splotches. She still wore the bandages on her head, and her visible hair looked like broom straw.

"I'm sorry, ma'am," the cop said. "We have a search warrant for your house, for certain items."

He handed her the papers, and she took them, peered at them querulously. "A search warrant? Can you wait until I call my lawyer?"

"No ma'am. You're welcome to call your attorney, of course, but the warrant is served and we'll have to come in."

Her eyes drifted past the cop to Lucas, who'd begun to feel sorry for the woman: but when her eyes landed on him, they hardened into small black diamonds, like a cobra's, and he leaned back, though he was ten feet from her. "Okay," she muttered, breaking her eyes away. "But do I have to do anything? I feel awfully bad."

"You just go sit down, and we'll do all of it," the cop said.

She disappeared inside and the cop looked over his shoulder at Lucas. Lucas said quietly, "Keep an eye on her. She's not what she looks like."

THE MCDONALDS HAD a small cluttered workshop area in one corner of the basement, nothing more than an old chest of drawers with two two-by-eight-foot sheets of three-quarter-inch plywood screwed together to make the top of a small workbench, and a couple of steel shelving units with plastic boxes for storage.

Lucas had seen the workshop the first time in the house, after Wilson McDonald was shot. He went straight to it, checked all the tools. No glass cutter. He found a roll of black plastic electricians' tape, which he bagged, but that seemed unlikely to be the tape they wanted. He walked once around the basement, looking behind the water heater, the furnace, through racks of paint cans and a pile of hoses and miscellaneous gardening equipment: no gallon glass jugs.

Del was working the kitchen. When Lucas came back up the stairs, he said, "Got lots of tape. Duct, plastic mending, bunch of it."

"Good. Bag it up," Lucas said. "Check the wastebaskets and her car, see if you come across any small balls of tape that might be the right length. Two would be good." He went on through the living room, found that the carpet had been removed. Wilson McDonald's blood hadn't seeped through to the wooden floor, which looked freshly waxed.

Sloan had run quickly through the bedroom, not expecting to find much, and had moved on to a large, first-floor guest room which had a walk-in closet the McDonalds used for general storage. This was where Audrey McDonald had gotten the shotgun with which she'd killed her husband. The closet was jammed with motoring, golf, and boating equipment, all of it apparently belonging to

Wilson McDonald. The homicide cops investigating the shooting of Wilson McDonald had taken the gun and shells, but hadn't dug into the back of the closet. Sloan hauled everything out, found nothing of special interest, and then, as an afterthought, was patting down the weather gear, life jackets, golf and hunting jackets.

Just as Lucas walked in, he felt a heavy lump in the pocket of a golf jacket, and manipulated it out through the layers of cloth. Box of cartridges.

"Gimme a bag," he said to Lucas.

"What is it?"

"Boo-lets," he said.

Lucas held the transparent plastic bag and Sloan manipulated the box into it. Lucas turned the box on its side and read: ".38 Remington. Excellent."

Sloan stood up and said, "It'd be nice if her prints were on the box."

"Yeah, but I'm not holding my breath."

One of the uniformed cops stuck his head in the door: "Del says no glass cutter in the kitchen. No gallon jugs either."

"Okay . . . check the garage."

At the end of an hour, they still had no glass cutter or gallon jugs, but did have nine rolls of tape and the box of cartridges. Sherrill had been going through the house files again, and had pulled out a stack of Amoco credit card receipts; the McDonalds shared a single account, but the cards had separate numbers. "If they go back far enough, look for credit card charges in the Duluth area in the days before Ingall disappeared," Lucas said. "We found an Amex charge in Chicago, the day before, for Wilson . . ."

"They go back that far . . ." She started flipping through them.

A little more than an hour after the search started, McDonald's attorney showed up. "What's going on?"

Lucas said, "Search warrant. Mrs. McDonald has a copy. She's in the TV room." He pointed him through to the TV room, and Glass asked, "You really think there's something going on here?"

"I ain't doing it for the exercise," Lucas said. "You've got a problem, I think."

Glass wandered off to find McDonald, and the uniformed cop came back from the garage: "No jugs, no glass cutter."

"Gonna have to give up on the jugs," Lucas said. "The glass cutter could be anywhere, if she didn't throw it away. Anybody look in the silverware drawer?"

Del looked at the cop, and they both shook their heads.

"Watch this," Lucas said. He pulled open drawers nears the sink, until he found the silverware drawer, then pulled that out all the way and stirred through the contents. Nothing. Same with the cooking utensils drawer. Nothing.

"Fuck it," he said, pushing the drawers shut.

"The guy is a genius," the uniformed cop said to Del, who nodded.

Sherrill came out of the back, carrying an Amoco billing statement. "Got something," she said.

"Duluth?" Lucas asked hopefully.

"No. But Audrey filled up on successive mornings, the day before Ingall disappeared, and the day he disappeared. So sometime in that twenty-four hours, she drove off a tank of gas."

"Huh," Lucas said. "She could've been filling somebody else's car, or Wilson's car."

"Wilson filled up that night."

Lucas nodded: "All right. That's something. That's a straw, and we need straws."

"And that's about all we got," Del said. "I'd bet you anything that door in O'Dell's apartment was taped with duct tape, and we found duct tape, but I bet there's a roll of duct tape in every goddamn house in the city. A jury's gonna blow that off."

GLASS HAD BEEN walking back through the house, Audrey McDonald limping along a step behind him, and he heard Del's last comment: "Jury's gonna blow off what?" he asked.

"Just . . . nothing," Del muttered.

"Mrs. McDonald says she thinks you, specifically, Chief Davenport, have targeted her for a personal attack. We'd hate to think that was true."

"You know that's bullshit," Lucas said to Glass—and then his eyes skipped beyond Glass to Audrey McDonald, who was peering at him with her snake's eye.

"It *is* true, and I know why," she said. "Because if you can pin something on me, then Wilson's father will inherit, and his father and his father's friends run everything down there at City Hall."

Lucas was shaking his head: "I don't even know Wilson's father."

"Oh, bullshit," she snapped, picking up Lucas's word. But she looked so gray, so old-lady-like, that hearing the vulgarity tripping so easily from her tongue was almost shocking. "There's no way that he's going to let McDonald money get out of that goddamned family."

"Mrs. McDonald . . ." Glass cautioned, but Lucas was becoming interested. Audrey McDonald was not quite visibly shaking, but he could sense it in her: she was very close to the boil. But he didn't know what would happen if she did tip over the edge. So he pushed a little.

"Mrs. McDonald—can I call you Audrey?"

"No, you may not."

"Audrey, we know you killed your father, and we know why. We even know why you killed your mother, I'm sorry to say. For the money. It's not so clear that you killed all the others, but we think we've got a pretty good list, and stuff is beginning to turn up." He picked up a bag on the kitchen counter, with a roll of duct tape sealed inside. "You didn't use this duct tape on Susan O'Dell's doors, did you? Because if you did, our lab will be able to tell . . ."

"Lucas, Lucas . . ." Glass was sputtering, but Lucas wasn't looking at him. He was watching Audrey, the gray-faced, self-effacing little brown beetle, who was shuffling up to her attorney's elbow, then past him, and she said, "My parents, my parents . . ."

". . . and we know you went to Duluth the day before Andy Ingall disappeared, and that you fired that Contender pistol of Kresge's, the one that killed him, and——"

And Audrey launched herself at him, so quickly that Lucas was surprised, unable to quite fend her off without hurting her. Her right hand, hard and bony as a crow's foot, caught the skin at the side of his throat and when he wrenched away he felt her fingernails slicing through the skin; then Sherrill had Audrey around the waist and heaved her back, and Glass wrapped her up. "You fucking . . ." Audrey growled, still struggling to get at him, her black eyes fixed on Lucas. "You fucking . . . You talk to that fucking sister of mine . . ."

"Jesus, Lucas, you're bleeding," Sherrill said.

"Get me some toilet paper or something," Lucas said, watching Audrey McDonald as her struggles subsided.

"Gonna ruin your shirt," Sherrill said, coming back with a box of tissues. She pulled out a wad and pressed it against his neck.

"Worth it," he said, watching Glass wrestle Audrey McDonald back toward the TV room. He looked around. "Are we about done here?"

"Another hour, if we really think that glass cutter is here somewhere," Del said.

"Keep looking," Lucas said. "I'm gonna take off."

"I better come along," Sherrill said. "You're pretty cut up."

"All right," Lucas said. To Dell, "You and Sloan figure it out from here."

"You going home?" Del asked.

Lucas could feel the blood seeping through the tissue. "No. I'm gonna go talk to that fucking sister of hers."

HELEN AND CONNIE Bell were watching television when Lucas and Sherrill arrived. Helen opened the door, smiled at Lucas, nodded at Sherrill, then frowned and said, "Good God, what happened to you? Are you hurt?"

"Um . . . your sister scratched me. Sort of blew up."

"Why? Well . . . come in. Why were you talking to Audrey?"

Connie Bell turned backward on an easy chair to listen to the conversation: Lucas, Sherrill, and Helen were standing in the entryway, and Lucas said, "I've got some fairly bad news, I think. Uh, maybe you'd rather get it in a more formal way . . ."

"No-no-no, tell me."

Lucas nodded. "We think it's possible that, uh, your sister may have committed some of the murders you listed in your letter to me."

Helen took a step back, one hand going to her throat. "Audrey? Oh, no."

"Could we, uh, could we sit down, I just have a couple of things," Lucas said.

"The couch."

They stepped into the front room, and Lucas and Sherrill sat on the couch while Helen leaned against the chair where Connie was sitting. Lucas said, "If you want Connie to go do homework or something . . ."

"No way," Connie said. To her mother: "I'm old enough to stay."

Her mother looked at her for a moment, then nodded. "You can stay."

Lucas looked at Sherrill, and then asked, "When you were younger, was there ever anything . . . Did you think anything was odd about the way your father died? Or your mother?"

Helen looked at them in stunned silence, then said, "My father was an evil man. We don't talk about him."

"We know about, uh . . . we know about Audrey," Lucas said.

"What about Audrey?" Connie asked.

Lucas looked at Helen, who blinked rapidly, shook her head, then turned to Connie and said, "My father molested us when we were children. Audrey mostly, but I got some of it too. He never made me do anything with him, like he did with Audrey, but it was coming. He'd . . . handle me. But Audrey was four years older and that protected me."

"Jeez," Connie said.

"Do you remember the night your father died?" Lucas asked.

Again, Helen seemed stunned. Then she nodded, slowly. "I didn't know what was going on until the sheriff came—Mom wouldn't let me get out of bed. But I knew my father was sick, that's what they said up the stairs to me, Mom and Audrey."

"Was he sick for a while, or was it a sudden attack?" Lucas asked.

"He was sick for a long time, I think, more than a week . . . I don't know, exactly, I was only ten . . . but for a long time. Then the night that he died . . . God, it was cold, it was already snowing up there, that's one thing I remember about it. The wind used to whistle through that old farmhouse. It was a bad place. And I heard him having a terrible argument with Audrey, before I went to bed. We slept in the same bedroom, Audrey and I . . . Then, I don't think anybody went to bed. I heard him groaning, and in the bathroom, that's the last thing I remember about him—being in the bathroom. Then he was quiet, and then I think I went to sleep, and the next thing I knew, people were banging around and cars were coming, and he was dead."

"Had Audrey ever come up to bed?"

Helen looked down at her daughter, then at Lucas. "I don't think so. I don't think she ever came upstairs that night. She was downstairs, I think, taking care of him . . ."

"Huh. Okay. What about your mother?"

"Mother was . . . ruined . . . by my father. It was like there was no person left. I used to think, this is what a slave would be like, after they beat all the resistance out of him. 'Do this,' 'Yes, master,' 'Do that,' 'Yes, master.' She was like a rag."

"And she died . . . Was Audrey there when she died?"

"Yes. We both were. I think she had the flu, she was sick to her stomach, and sometimes she'd start vomiting, and Audrey would keep her in bed and spoon-feed her. And then one night she passed out, and Audrey called the hospital. She died on the way."

"Your mother and father were both cremated," Lucas said. "Was that Audrey's idea?"

"Yes."

"You didn't keep the ashes, by any chance."

"No . . . Mom used to walk over to a park that was a mile or so from our house, down here in Lakeville, and we didn't know any cemeteries, so Audrey just said it would be nice to sprinkle her around the trees in the park, she'd be there forever as part of the trees."

After a moment of silence, she said, "You think she killed them? Poisoned them, or something?"

Lucas nodded. "I think it's very possible. The insurance payments . . ."

Helen shook her head: "There wasn't any insurance, as far as I know."

Lucas said, "Huh." Then, "What happened after your mother died?"

"Well, we couldn't stay together. Audrey was barely eighteen, and so I went off to my aunt's home until I was of age. She got a scholarship and went to college. I worked my way through a tech school, a business course . . . and then she married Wilson and everything."

Lucas said, "I know this probably comes as a shock. But, if it would be possible . . . and I honest to God think you should do this . . . if I come over with a stenographer and an assistant county attorney, could we sit here some night this week and go over the whole thing? Your whole history? In a really detailed way."

Helen said, "I can't believe that Audrey . . ."

"Yes, you can," said Connie. "I told you, she's a mean old witch under all of that pretend stuff."

"Connie . . ." Her mother looked a warning at her.

But Connie said to Lucas, "Why'd you want to know about Grandma's ashes?"

"Well, just a thing," Lucas said.

"What thing?" Connie persisted.

"If your grandmother was poisoned, a lab analysis of ashes might turn something up."

Connie looked up at her mother, and Helen frowned at her and said, "What?"

"How about that lock of hair on her picture? You said you cut it off the day she died."

Helen put her fingertips to her mouth. "Oh, that's right. I'd forgotten; completely." To Lucas: "Would a lock of hair help?"

Lucas shrugged. "I don't know."

Sherrill, who'd been sitting quietly, finally chipped in. "The doc up in Oxford thought George Lamb was killed with arsenic. If Amelia was killed the same way, and it sounds pretty similar, then it would show up in hair." They all looked at her, and she said, "I read about it."

Lucas turned back to Helen.

"Could we have the hair?"

30

AT TEN MINUTES after midnight, Audrey was still packing. The cops had gone, taking a small box of miscellaneous junk with them. It wouldn't amount to anything, she thought. Tape? Everybody had tape—though she wished she'd taken a minute to clean those doors after killing O'Dell. But she'd never even thought of it.

On the bright side, she *had* thrown away the glass cutter. It was lying somewhere on the shoulder of I-94, gone forever. On the down side, she hadn't thrown it away after she bombed the Bairds. She'd thrown it away after she hit Karkinnen, but only because she hadn't thought she'd need it again. She hadn't *thought* about evidence.

She hadn't thought about it since the cremation of her mother. With all the other killings, if she'd been caught, she would've been caught, and that would have been that. There hadn't seemed any point in worrying about evidence, except in the most gross ways—don't leave any fingerprints, don't buy any guns.

She'd have to start thinking.

She'd gotten to Wilson's sweaters. He'd spent a fortune on sweaters, though they made him look the size of an oil tanker. He thought they made him look like a football lineman; in fact, they made him look even fatter than he was. "Three hundred dollars for a sweater. I remember when you told me that, I couldn't believe it. Three hundred dollars. And it's not just the three hundred dollars; if we'd saved it, if we'd put it in Vanguard, it would have tripled by now."

Lights in the driveway. She froze. Cops again? She drifted for a few seconds: She hated the police: that Davenport, he was the devil in this deal. A year from now, if she could find a gun, she'd take care of him, all right. Give it a year or a little more, and then one night, maybe in January, when people's doors were shut and windows were closed, she'd wait by his house. If she could find a gun like the one she'd used on Kresge: now that was a wonderful gun. Wonderful . . .

And snapped back. A car in the driveway. She hurried to the window, looked down, and saw Helen walking across the driveway toward the front door. Helen? She hadn't called.

A thought stuck her. Helen had been talking to Davenport again. She turned and hurried toward the stairway, as the doorbell rang downstairs.

HELEN LOOKED STRANGE: ordinarily neat, her hair was in disarray, her face pinched, her mouth tight. She didn't take off her coat, but simply stood in the entryway.

"I don't really know how to ask you this, Audrey. I'll just tell you what Chief Davenport told me. He thinks you killed Mom and Dad. Poisoned them. I told him I didn't think you did, and then I thought about it all evening and finally thought I better come over."

"Mom and Dad? Mom and Dad? Do you think I killed Mom and Dad?" Audrey was horrified, even as the small kernel in the back of her brain hardened around her secret knowledge.

"I . . . don't think so," Helen said, but her eyes drifted away. When they came back, she said, "Chief Davenport thinks that's why they were cremated. To cover up."

"That's ludicrous," Audrey snapped. "Davenport is all tied up with Wilson's father; they're trying to keep me from the money. Wilson's money will go to his father, you know, if they decide I've committed a crime. That's all it is: it's about money."

Helen looked at her for another moment, a little too coolly, Audrey thought, then said, "Okay. I just had to ask. Chief Davenport asked me not to talk to you, so please don't mention it—but I had to come over and ask you."

Audrey turned away, and started wandering back toward the kitchen, as though disoriented, as though saddened by this sisterly betrayal. "You must talk to him all the time," she said.

"Only three times," Helen said. "He doesn't seem like a bad man."

Audrey spun: "Oh, snap out of it, Helen," she snarled. "You never figured out how things work. You sit down there and sort your little auto parts and the world just goes by. You should ask yourself someday, 'What happens when I get old? What happens when I'm trying to live on Social Security, when nobody wants me anymore?' Helen, you just don't have any idea."

Helen turned to the door. "Don't worry about me; just worry about yourself, Audrey . . . By the way, after Mom died—did you know this? I think you did— I took a lock of her hair to put with her picture on the piano. Chief Davenport took it with him. He's going to have it analyzed by the laboratory."

"Well: I'm sorry to see you lose your precious lock, but at least it'll show she wasn't poisoned," Audrey snapped.

"I hope so," Helen said. "Audrey, when all this is done, we've got to sit down and talk. So much stuff happened when I was a kid, I never got it straight."

"I'll set you straight," Audrey said. "Come back when it's done."

Helen left, the heavy door wheezing shut behind her: Wilson had insisted on the special door, three inches thick, saying, "It's the first thing people will know about us." Two thousand dollars for a door . . .

"Fuck," she said aloud, wrenching her mind away from Wilson. A lock of hair! Could it really be analyzed, or was it a game that Davenport was playing with her? Was there any way to find out?

Maybe the Internet, though it seemed far-fetched. She went to the library, waited impatiently to get on-line, brought up the Alta Vista search engine, and typed in: "ARSENIC + HAIR."

Almost immediately, she got back a list of articles, and her heart sank. The first one was, improbably, on Napoleon. She opened it, and it referred to arsenic content in Napoleon's hair. Shit. She went to the next one, something to do with analysis, and it also mentioned arsenic in hair. Hair.

She punched the off button on the computer, and the computer's fan moaned as it closed down. The computer didn't like that, she thought. Didn't like to be up and running, and then cut off.

Fuck the computer.

Arsenic and hair. She had to do something, and do it quickly.

31

LUCAS WENT TO lunch with Del, who said, "I can't shake free of this opium thing. A couple of the old ladies have been calling every day, wanting to know what we're gonna do."

"That's your problem, thank God," Lucas said. "Go over and talk to Towson or one of his guys, see what they want to do."

"They want it to go away," Del said. "So does Rose Marie. Nobody wants to deal with it. *I* don't want to deal with it anymore. Hell, I'm going on vacation in two weeks. I'm finally getting my shot at Cancún. But now these old ladies, they want something done."

"Why? Tell them to keep their mouths shut, and everybody'll forget it," Lucas said.

"They're not thinking that way. They've all been getting together in these fuckin' . . . covens. They think they've got to pay their debt to society," Del said morosely.

"Jesus. Well, you asked for it," Lucas said brightly. "I feel for you, pal. But when that doc told you about it, you coulda walked away."

"Ah, man, you gotta find a way to help."

"Not me." Lucas laughed, and thought, *My God, I think I just chortled.* "I'm not Narcotics. Go talk to the guys down there."

"They treat me like I got the plague . . ."

"That's 'cause you *got* the plague," Lucas said. "I don't want to hear about it."

"Fuck me," Del said, moodily. "I wasn't cut out for this."

Lucas laughed again, said, "Nobody is. Sixty old ladies? Is that what it is? You poor fuck. You're dead meat."

Del looked at his watch. "That lab report is about due."

"Let's get back," Lucas said.

"You think you got her?"

"It's almost too much to hope for," Lucas said. "When Helen said she had a hair sample, my teeth almost fell out."

LUCAS HAD A message when he got back: "Call Davis." Davis Ericson worked in the state crime lab. He punched in the number, and Ericson picked up.

"What'd you get?"

"Lucas. Tell you what, I've never seen this before. Not in real life."

"What? You got arsenic?"

"The hair is stiff with it," Ericson said. "She must've been eating it for a month before she croaked."

"Goddamnit, Davis."

LUCAS PUNCHED IN the county attorney's number, waited for three minutes, and Kirk, the chief of the criminal division, picked up. Lucas explained about the lock of hair.

"If Helen can swear that it came from her mother, then that might do it," Kirk said.

"That's where Helen says it comes from."

"Give me her name and address. We'll set up an appointment for a deposition."

"What about Audrey?"

"Easiest way to do it is, we'll talk to the judge, and have bail revoked on the killing of her husband. And then before tomorrow's bail hearing, we'd get an arrest affidavit put together on her mother, and arrest her on that. Maybe boost the charge on her husband to first degree."

"So how long is that gonna take? The bail revocation?"

"Mmm . . . we'll have to get some stuff in writing. If you'll set out the circumstances of obtaining the hair sample, and describe the lab test—just in general terms—and walk it over here, I'll have a secretary put together an affidavit and we'll have the judge sign it this afternoon. If you can get your memo over here in an hour, we'll have it done by the end of the day."

"And then we pick her up."

"Yup. We could have her inside for supper."

"Excellent," Lucas said.

AUDREY HAD BEEN up most of the night, packing. She wanted to have it done in case she was rearrested, so that Wilson's clothing wouldn't still be hanging in the closets when she got back. She was eradicating the sight of him.

And she would probably be rearrested, she thought. If Davenport really had that hair, he would probably be coming for her in the next day or two. How long would a lab take? She had no idea. But she was certain it couldn't be done before nine o'clock in the morning.

By seven-thirty, with four hours out for sleep, she was done with the packing. After a last quick check around, she hauled the boxes down to the front entry, and stacked them. After a quick shower and a change of clothes, she went to the library, fired up the computer, brought up Word, and wrote for half an hour, editing and reediting as she worked. Satisfied, she dumped the document to a floppy disk, put it in her purse.

At nine o'clock, she was out of the house.

THE GOLD BUG was a custom jewelry boutique on the south side of Minneapolis. A half-dozen craftsmen worked out of a small common smelting area, with actual fabrication of jewelry done in separate shops on a wing off the smelting area. She'd been there once before, with a ladies' tour group from the country club, to look at gold jewelry and how it was made.

She hadn't bought any gold, but she'd found the tour interesting.

A tall, bony redheaded woman was working at the desk, looked up and said a cheery "Hello" as Audrey tentatively poked her nose through the door.

"Hello. Are the shops open?"

"Sure. Go on down. Do you know . . . ?"

"Yes. I've been here before."

Audrey scuttled away down the wing, walked past the open fire door that led to the smelting area, slowed, looked inside. A sign beside the door said, "Please come in and watch; but please be quiet."

One man was working at an exhaust hood; three other hoods were vacant. He looked up, focused on her.

"I'm sorry," she said. "Is it . . . okay?"

"Sure. Come on in. I'm just smelting a little gold, here."

She walked in with her purse clutched in front of her, an old lady. She'd have to work on this image, a little, she thought. If she got in the newspapers, perhaps she should look younger . . .

The goldsmith had gone back to his work, a small crucible that he worked with a torch; she couldn't see exactly what he was doing, but didn't particularly care. She wasn't interested in goldwork. With her eyes fixed on the torch, she drifted to another one of the exhaust hoods. The table beside it was empty. Goddamnit. She passed behind him, now looking around at the equipment, then turned so she could watch him from the other side. He was vaguely aware of her, she thought, but he was used to being watched, and paid no real attention.

She moved up to the next exhaust hood, and saw the bottle.

That was it. She stood next to the table, and when he momentarily turned away, his back more toward her, she reached carefully out, picked it up, and slipped it into her coat pocket. It was small, no bigger than a shotgun shell or an old iodine bottle. With the bottle in her hand, she moved closer to him.

"Very interesting," she said finally, as he finished a small pour into what looked like a lump of plaster.

"Simple enough, after you've done it awhile," he said.

She had no idea of what was going on, said, "Thank you," and still looking carefully around the smelting room, drifted out the door. She stopped at two of the shops, looking at their small display cases. Then, glancing at her watch—it was already past ten o'clock—she headed for the door.

"Have a nice day," the redhead said, as she left.

You betcha.

TWENTY MINUTES LATER, after a quick stop at a drugstore to buy a pack of razor blades, she fixed the pill in the parking lot of a Burger King. First, she took one of the Prozac capsules she'd gotten from Helen, carefully pulled the cap apart, spilled the drug into the palm of her hand and flicked it out the car window. Then she took out the bottle she'd stolen from the Gold Bug and looked at it. The simple label said, *CAUTION*, and below that, in small letters, *Sodium Cyanide.* And below that, *Poison: If ingested, get physician's help immediately. For industrial use only.*

When the club ladies had visited the gold workshop, one of the goldsmiths had joked about using the cyanide to purify recycled gold. The same stuff Hitler's boys had used to kill themselves, he'd said. She hadn't known exactly what he was talking about—purifying the gold—but she remembered what he'd said about Hitler's boys.

The cyanide was an off-white powder, innocent enough. She poured a little on the sandwich box, cut it up with the razor blade, then carefully refilled the Prozac cap with the cyanide. Then she slipped the top back on the cap: not bad. If you looked at it closely, it wasn't quite right. But who looked at pills that closely?

She wrapped the pill in a napkin and put it on the car seat; the sandwich box she carried to a trash can and pushed it inside. A pay phone hung on the wall just inside the Burger King door, and she went in and dialed Helen's number. Helen should be working, Connie should be at school. No answer. As a double check, she got the number of the auto parts place from directory assistance, called, and asked for Helen. Helen answered a second later, and Audrey clicked off as soon as she recognized her sister's voice.

Helen's house was no more than ten minutes away. If she tried to do something subtle, to sneak in, she'd probably draw more attention in the neighborhood than if she barged right in. She parked on the street, waited until she could see no one on the sidewalk, then hurried up the walk, through the outer porch, and rang the doorbell. No answer. She leaned on it the next time, ringing for a solid minute. Nothing.

Good.

She took her keys from her purse, found the key for Helen's house, opened the door and went inside. The house was deathly quiet. She went straight through to Helen's bedroom, to the corner where she kept her computer. Switched it on, took the floppy disk from her pocket, went to the *My Documents* folder. Helen had written a note to herself two months earlier, but the computer would update the time to show the last entry. Audrey slipped the floppy in the drive, brought up the text she'd written that morning, pasted it into the earlier note. Then she cut the text of the note itself, and checked her work.

If I die . . . the note began.

I'm sorry about everything! I killed those people, not Audrey! But Audrey was my only support, and I had to do something if Wilson was going to move up at the bank! If Wilson had lost his job all those years ago, what would have happened to Connie and me? Without the money from Audrey, we would have been on the street! My former "husband" is good for NOTHING!!! But I didn't kill Mr. Kresge! I think that must have been an accident! And Chief Davenport, if somebody shows this to you, yes, I called you. I could no longer stand the way Wilson was treating Audrey! I was afraid he would kill her! I thought you would do an investigation and his treatment of her would come out and nobody would ever know it was me that called you, and Audrey could keep helping me, because now, if they got divorced, she'd get all kinds of money! Connie—I love you. You go stay with your aunt Audrey, because she really loves you. I'm sorry for all of this!!

And at the bottom of the note, she'd left all the fragments of sentences that she'd pushed while editing: *I fearedilling heraaacidentkill treeting Wil;slonMister-KresgeWithout money I got from Audrey.*

It would, she hoped, look like a practice note; she was especially proud of all the exclamation points. Helen used them everywhere, as though they were periods.

She closed the file, shut down the machine, put the disk in her purse, and headed for the bedroom. Helen carried a pill case with a chiming clock to remind her to take the pills; she took one at noon every day. The Prozac bottle itself she kept in the bedroom, in her bureau drawer. Audrey found the bottle, unscrewed the top, looked inside. A dozen pills. Carefully unwrapping the cyanide pill in the napkin, she let it drop on top of the pills in the bottle, and replaced the bottle, shut the drawer.

Out of the house: she'd been inside no more than ten minutes, she thought. As she drove away, she moved in the car seat and felt the cyanide bottle in her pocket. She should ditch it somewhere, she thought. But she liked the idea of it. A bottle of death. She thought about it for a while, then stopped in a park, where a thin shell of woods surrounded a small drainage lake. She stepped just inside the tree line, picked out a good-sized oak, walked over to it and sat down. Probed the ground with her car key: Damn. Frozen.

She looked around, spotted a culvert protruding from the edge of an embankment. She walked over to it, pushed the bottle well under the culvert. The bottle should be safe for years, she thought. Did cold weather affect cyanide? She had no idea.

Now, she thought, standing up.

Where are you, Davenport?

32

T WO UNIFORMED COPS with a warrant stopped by the McDonald house at four o'clock, and found it empty. Audrey McDonald's car license-plate number was put on the air, along with a description. She was eating at Baker's Square Restaurant, having waited impatiently all afternoon. Two cops went by while she was inside, but she missed them all going back home. At seven, the uniformed cops swung by her house again, and saw lights. Audrey McDonald came to the door.

SHERRILL CALLED: "WE'RE supposed to go out to dinner tonight."

"Damn it, I'm sorry—but we're busting Audrey McDonald right now," Lucas said.

"All right. Tomorrow for sure."

"Tomorrow."

AUDREY WAS PROCESSED through the county jail, then taken to an interview room to wait for her attorney. J. B. Glass arrived a half hour later, a little white wine under his belt. He found Lucas waiting outside the interview room with Sloan, and said, "What the hell happened?"

"Your client's a serial killer," Sloan said laconically.

"What, Sugar Pops or shredded wheat?" Glass said.

"Her mother and father for starters," Lucas said.

"You're *really* telling me I've got a millionaire client who might be a serial killer?" Glass asked in a hushed voice. He rolled his eyes to the heavens, the view toward which extended twenty-eight inches to the basement ceiling. "I don't want to seem cynical, but . . . thank you, Jesus."

Then he was all business: "I want privacy with my client."

"She's in the room," Lucas said.

"Have you talked to her?"

"Nobody's talked to her," Lucas said. "She opened the door to her house and said, 'I want my attorney.' Nobody's said a word to her since, except 'Stand up, sit down, turn to the right.' "

"Good." Glass nodded. "I'll tell you, though, it's gonna be a while before you can see her."

"We can wait," Lucas said.

THEY WAITED. GLASS talked to her for a half hour, asked Lucas if he could get a couple of cans of Diet Pepsi for them. Lucas walked through the dark hallways to a Pepsi machine, got two cans, walked back, passed them through the door.

"Thanks," Glass said, as he shut the door.

Another twenty minutes passed, and then Glass opened the door and said, "Come in."

Sloan led the way, carrying a portable tape recorder. Lucas nodded at Audrey. She fixed him for a moment with her cobra eyes, then broke off and looked down at the table. When Sloan was ready, and had a cassette running, he said, "This is a preliminary interview with Mrs. Audrey McDonald, in the presence of her attorney, Jason Glass, conducted by Detectives Sloan and Davenport."

He ran the machine back to make sure it was working, replayed the statement, pushed record again, added the time and date, and turned to McDonald.

"Mrs. McDonald, you have been rearrested after the revocation of your bail granted after the killing of your husband, Wilson McDonald . . . The bail revocation, however, is based on what we believe was the murder of your mother, Amelia Lamb."

"I did no such thing. I loved my mother," she said, calmly.

"Mrs. McDonald, did you know that your sister saved a lock of your mother's hair after she died?"

"Yes, I knew that."

"We had the hair sample analyzed by the state crime laboratory, Mrs. McDonald, and the hair was found to contain amounts of arsenic which would be lethal to a human being."

"I don't know anything about that," she said.

"Um, do you know where she lived—Mrs. Lamb—at the time she died?" Glass asked Lucas.

"In Lakeville."

"Have the police inspected the house they lived in?"

"Not yet."

"It was a very old house—you find arsenic all over the place in those old houses. It's in the wallpaper, the paint, people used it all the time to spray for bugs. Mrs. Lamb may have had arsenic in her hair, but there's no reason to think that my client put it there. In fact, she did not."

"Did you get large insurance payments from both the death of your father and your mother, Mrs. McDonald?" Sloan asked.

"She won't answer that," Glass said. He looked down at Audrey. "That's something we've got to look into ourselves, before we start discussing it."

"Did you use the insurance payments to put yourself through St. Anne's, where you met Sister Mary Joseph?" Lucas asked.

Glass shook his head: "We'll refuse to answer that."

"We have gray duct tape from your house with only one set of fingerprints on it," said Sloan. "The adhesive on the duct tape matches exactly adhesive taken off the door locks outside Susan O'Dell's apartment. Did you put that tape there, Mrs. McDonald?"

"No, I did not."

The questioning went on for half an hour, Audrey growing more and more angry. Finally, she turned to Glass and said, "How much longer do we have to do this?"

"You want to stop now?"

"Yes."

"Then we're done," Glass said. To Sloan, "No more questions." Sloan looked at Lucas, reached out to the recorder. Before he could turn it off, Audrey hissed at Lucas. "You think you're so smart, but you just don't understand anything."

Sloan froze, then, as unobtrusively as possible, let his arm slide sideways and rest on the table next to the recorder. Sometimes you got the best stuff after the formal questioning was done.

"I think I do," Lucas said. "I've talked to your friends, I've talked to your sister. We don't have every piece, because you got rid of some of them. But there's enough left to hang you, Audrey."

"So dumb," she said. She stood up, and turned toward Glass. "Will there be another bond hearing?"

"Yes, tomorrow morning."

"Gonna cost you a little more, this time," Lucas said. "And when we finish all the paper on your mother, we'll just pick you up again. It'd be easier just to stay put. Mr. Glass could arrange for your sister to watch your house."

"My sister . . . my sister," she said. She pushed her hands up through her hair, as though she were about to tear it out. "My sister gave you a lock of Mother's hair?"

"Yes."

"That was good of her. And my sister told you about this whole murder idea in the first place, didn't she?"

Lucas looked at Sloan, then nodded. Glass opened his mouth to say something, then shut it.

"And did my sister tell you that all those years when I was supposedly killing these people, her sole support came from us? From Wilson and me? That we gave her cash to keep her head above water? That if Wilson didn't do well, if he lost his job or lost a promotion, she'd be hurt as much as we would? Did she tell you about our father feeling her up, about finding a box of rat poison in the machine shed and pouring it into Dad's whiskey? Did my sister tell you all of that? Did she tell you about fighting with Mom about screwing boys out by the cornfield in Lakeville? And more than that, screwing them for money? Did you look at everything you have, and ask, 'What if her sister did it?' And did you ask, if you send little Audrey McDonald off to prison, if she could tolerate it? I'll answer that for you: I'm claustrophobic. I wouldn't last a year in a prison. I'd find some way to hang myself. And then who gets my share of the money? My sister? That's what she thinks . . ."

Lucas was astonished: at that moment, he believed that Audrey believed. She was utterly convincing, a beetle-hard, scuttling young-old woman. "Jesus," he said.

"We gotta stop," Glass said convulsively. "We gotta stop this."

He put an arm around Audrey to stop her: and for a moment, the woman's dead cobra eyes gave something away, a spark, something almost like humor. Then the moment passed, and she was as sullen as ever.

Lucas looked after her as she left: What was this all about?

LUCAS AND SLOAN stopped at a greasy spoon on the way home, Lucas following Sloan out in separate cars. As they walked inside, Sloan said, "What if the sister did it?"

Lucas shook his head: "No way."

"Why not?"

"She was too young to kill her old man; I don't care if he was groping her. But the big thing is, why would she ever risk calling attention to that whole string of killings? Even if she blamed them on McDonald, there was always the possibility that McDonald would be able to prove that he didn't do it . . . and if he could prove he couldn't do any one of them, then all of them would be in question. Nope. Whoever killed these people—Audrey—is too smart to have called attention to them."

"But what . . . what if she saw Wilson McDonald going down, and shot Kresge specifically to pull McDonald down, so that Audrey would get his money? And then, when you get on top of Audrey, she decides to sacrifice Audrey? I mean, what if she's three layers back, waiting for Audrey to die in prison? Or even planning to poison her if she's acquitted?"

"No fuckin' way," Lucas said. "You gotta know the people."

They found a booth, ordered beer and fries: "She scared the shit out of me, man. And I'll tell you what, Glass was looking at that tape machine like it was solid gold," Sloan said. "Anybody who listens to that tape is gonna believe her too. Like a jury."

Lucas shook his head again: "Not if they listen to Helen at the same time. Helen is just . . . an innocent. She picked up on McDonald because the pattern became so clear to her over the years. She talked to them often enough that she knew when a promotion was up, and then she'd read about some guy from the bank being killed, and then it'd turn out to be a guy in McDonald's department. Nope. She even waited longer than she should have. And why in God's name would she offer her mother's hair? If she knew her mother had been poisoned . . ."

They ran over it for another hour, building the case against Audrey. In the end, Sloan said, "You'll have to admit, most of it could be built the other way."

"Naw: jury'd never go for it. And remember, she killed her old man."

Sloan shook his head. "Just wish there was some way to pry the sisters apart. Put one of them in Kansas while somebody's getting killed in Minnesota."

As Lucas put the beer bottle to his mouth, the light went off in his head: "Oh, shit," he said, the bottle frozen in front of his face.

"What?"

"In the Arris killing. We never looked at that tape for women."

"Huh. Where's the tape?"

"My place. St. Paul gave me a copy of it, and I left it at my place."

"Can I come along?"

THEY STUCK THE tape in Lucas's VCR, and the bad picture came up on the screen. They watched Arris go by, followed by several women, and then, a minute later, another woman, walking rigidly down the hill. "There she is," Lucas said.

"That's fuckin' Helen," Sloan said.

"No, no, that's fuckin' Audrey," said Lucas. He ran the tape back. "Look at the way she walks."

"Looks like fuckin' Helen to me."

"Remember, this is eight years ago. Audrey'd be thirty. Helen would only be in her mid-twenties . . . They look alike, but that woman is not twenty-six."

Sloan was on his hands and knees, peering at the screen. "Goddamn. Could be Audrey."

"Is Audrey," Lucas said.

"Selling it to a jury'll be hard," Sloan said. "You'll get one dumb shit on there who'll believe nothing but his own eyes, and his eyes'll say it's Helen."

"I wonder if we can get this enhanced somehow," Lucas said. "Maybe the Feebs?"

"I don't know . . . Tell you the truth, if there was a way to ditch the tape, I'd do it. It confuses things. But now that I keep looking at it, I think you're right. She moves like Audrey does. She *scuttles*."

THE PHONE RANG as they ran through the tape one last time. Sherrill. "Did you get her?"

"Yeah, I think—but it's gonna be a close call," Lucas said.

"You want me to come over and comfort you?"

He didn't, especially, but he said, "Come on over."

"Nah. You don't sound like you mean it," she said. "Tomorrow night, though."

And she was gone.

"Fuckin' cop-women," Lucas said.

"That's what you're doing," Sloan agreed.

"Fuckin' was an adjective, not a verb," Lucas said.

"Could've been a verb," Sloan said.

SLOAN LEFT, AND Lucas sat in his study for a while, doodling, running through the case in his mind, looking for loose ends. He didn't find many, except to note that they'd have to reinterview half the people who worked at the bank. They'd have to find witnesses who saw Audrey McDonald firing the Contender pistol; they'd have to find witnesses who would testify about promotions, and who was competitive for them . . .

He finally trundled off to bed, lay restlessly for a while, finally fell asleep.

IN THE MORNING, he moved sluggishly around, looked at the clock: already nine. He dressed, stopped at a fast-food place for French toast, then headed downtown. He called the county attorney's office and got Kirk.

"Had the bail hearing yet?"

"Yeah. The judge was a wee bit skeptical about the arsenic. J. B. did a pretty nice job. We got the bail up to a million, but she was ready for it."

"She's out?"

"Twenty minutes ago," Kirk said.

"How about the arrest warrant on her mother?"

"We're slowing down on that. J. B. brought up this stuff about the old house they used to live in, and we heard about this business with her sister, so we're gonna have the house checked and depose the sister. I mean, we've got her on a million, I don't think she'll run."

SHERRILL DROPPED BY at midmorning, carrying a doughnut and two cups of coffee. "She's out, I hear."

"Yeah," Lucas said in disgust. "I'll tell you what: if she was a black guy with a record, she'd be washing dishes in Stillwater by now."

"Sloan told me about that whole rap about her sister: that's pretty weird."

"Yeah, I don't understand that," Lucas said. "It's a fucked-up defense. You put Helen on the stand, the truth is gonna come out."

"You don't think there's any chance that Audrey's telling the truth? That it's Helen?"

"No, I don't."

"The one thing that's hard for me to get over is her appearance," Sherrill said. "She's only five years older than me . . ."

"Really? I thought you were sixteen . . ."

"Shut up. I'm being serious. The thing is, if you take the attack on Elle, where somebody beat her up with a ball bat, who do you think would be most likely to do that? Helen, who looks pretty active, pretty good shape, still young? Or Audrey, who looks old, slumped over?"

"Whatever she looks like, she's only thirty-eight," Lucas said. "She——"

He stopped, put a hand to his forehead. "What?" Sherrill asked. "A stroke?"

"Aw, man," Lucas said. He picked up the phone book, talking fast: "I think this might have gone through my head the night we were at St. Anne's, the night Elle got hit, but it went away; it's like it *was* a stroke . . ."

"What, what?"

"If Elle takes the phone call, and grabs her keys, and runs out the door and gets jumped . . . whoever called her must've been standing right there. Must've been calling from the bushes. Must've used a cell phone, not a pay phone. All the other tips we've had have come from pay phones, it must've blocked me off or something . . ."

Sherrill snapped her fingers: "Phone records."

"Absolutely."

The man who could get the records was away, but was expected back before lunch. In the meantime, the company would try to reach him, to hurry things up.

Lucas said to Sherrill, "If this pans out, she's dead meat."

"What if it's Helen's phone?"

"That'd be a problem," Lucas said.

"So we wait?"

"We wait." Lucas looked at his watch. "Shouldn't be more than an hour or so."

DEL STOPPED IN: "I'm being haunted by these old ladies," he said.

"Tell them if they insist on going to jail, they'll be raped by bull dykes," Sherrill suggested.

"I think some of them are gonna need to be rehabbed," Del said. "They're all getting different lawyers; there's gonna be fifty-eight lawyers to deal with."

"Too bad the pinking shears thing wasn't fatal," Lucas said nastily. "Think how much better off you'd be."

"That's the truth," Del said sincerely. "Jesus, what a mess."

"When're you going to Cancún?" Sherrill asked.

"In a week," he said. "Hope this is done by then. I'd hate to have it hanging over my head for the whole time I'm down there."

"THE THING IS," Sherrill said, after Del had gone, "what if Helen really loves Audrey—they've been through a lot together, and they're sisters—and decides to help her out? What if we go talk to Helen, and she starts taking the fifth? Audrey gets on the stand, blames everything on Helen, and Helen refuses to talk . . ."

"I don't think that would happen. Audrey killed their mother and . . ."

Lucas trailed off and Sherrill said, "What? Again? Something else?"

"Yeah. What if Helen wasn't here to defend herself?"

HELEN WAS WORKING at the auto parts place. Lucas found the name in the Yellow Pages, called her. "You've got to take time off, and meet us at your house," Lucas said. "I'm sorry, but this is critical for both you and Connie. I'll talk to your boss if you want."

Lucas took the Porsche. Sherrill, getting the go-ahead from Frank Lester, trailed in a city car. The bomb squad was ten minutes behind her, a crime scene crew a few minutes behind that.

Lucas thought of the lie that Audrey had told during the interrogation, how harsh, straightforward, how *honest* it seemed. But not unrehearsed. And there was a smugness about her when they came to take her away. She must have known that whatever case she could make against Helen would be denied by Helen, and that Helen's denials might even be provable in some cases. She may have understood that Helen was simply more believable than she was. She might even have understood that finding a hank of hair with arsenic in it didn't mean much unless Helen was there to swear that the hair had been taken from her mother . . .

She must have deduced that the police case rested squarely on Helen; and that if Helen was dead, Audrey had all kinds of defenses available.

And that little spark in her eyes, that smugness at the very end.

She thought Helen was out of it.

How would she do it? She'd used firebombs, guns, and poison. Guns were out, because she couldn't have known that she'd be free. Some kind of bomb was possible. Some kind of poison.

HELEN ARRIVED: RESISTED. "I know Audrey. She would never do anything like this. Never. We've been together since we were children."

"Mrs. Bell—we're pretty sure she killed your mother and father . . ."

"She says she didn't," Bell said stubbornly.

"We think she did. And if you don't think there's any chance, why did you give us that lock of hair?"

"I . . ."

"Believe what you want," Sherrill said gently. "But just let us look. If we're wrong, no harm has been done."

NO BOMB.

The bomb squad went in with sniffer equipment, found nothing. They checked the furnace and gas water heater for tampering or gas leaks. Nothing there either.

"Pills," Lucas said. "What kind of pills do you take? Aspirin? Something in capsules, I think . . ."

"Prozac," she said. "I take Prozac."

"Where do you keep it?" Sherrill asked.

"In my bedroom."

She got the bottle of Prozac and they poured the pills out on a clean garbage bag on the kitchen table. One of the crime scene techs had a hand glass, and Lucas used it to look at the capsules. After a minute, he shook his head. "I don't see anything."

"We do have aspirin," she said. "Not in capsules, though."

"We could take a look," Lucas said.

"And I've got some antibiotics left over from a cold last winter. And there're some of those timed cold pills; now those are capsules, I think."

"We'll take them all," Lucas said. "The problem is, we don't want anything Connie would take. How about food? Is there any food that is absolutely yours, that Connie wouldn't eat?"

"I've got some of that diet drink, but the cans are sealed . . ."

"We better take a look," Lucas said.

"Look: I've got to get back to work," she said. "Since it's not a bomb, maybe we could do it this evening?"

"I suppose," Lucas said. "Jesus: it's gotta be something."

"Unless you're wrong about her."

"I'm not wrong," Lucas said. "I've got . . ."

He heard the tinny music in the back of his head, but didn't react until he noticed Helen looking at her purse, a peculiar expression on her face. "What?" he asked.

"That's my pillbox," she said. "I keep a pillbox in my purse, it's got a little alarm clock so I always take my pill at the same time every day. I just filled it up this morning."

Lucas picked up the purse, clicked it open, found the pillbox. The box was playing "My Bonnie Lies Over the Ocean."

"Push the button to stop it," Helen said, as the two guys from the crime scene crew stepped up to Lucas to look at the box. Lucas carried it into the kitchen, dumped it on the garbage bag.

"Gimme the glass," he said.

He spotted the pill in a half-second: "Got it."

"No." Helen didn't believe it.

"That goddamn pill has been messed with," Lucas said. He handed the glass to the crime scene man. "What do you think?"

The crime scene man squinted through the glass: "And guess what? There's nothing better in the world than gelatin for picking up a fingerprint."

"There's a print?" Lucas asked.

"A piece of one, anyway," the crime scene man said. "Gimme a Ziploc, somebody."

"No," Helen said. "No."

They pulled the capsule apart with forks, avoiding what appeared to be a fingerprint smudge. White powder spilled out. Lucas pulled apart one of the Prozac capsules from the bottle. "It's different stuff," he said.

The lead crime scene tech got down close to the table, an inch from the white powder, barely inhaled, then straightened up, wiping his nose.

"What?" asked Lucas.

"Almonds," the tech said. "That stuff is cyanide."

33

LUCAS CALLED THE county attorney from Helen Bell's house, told him about the pill: "All right, that's it," Towson said. "Pick her up. We'll put her away this time. No bail. No nothing."

Lucas hung up and nodded to Sherrill: "We're gonna go get her. Want to follow me over?"

"I'll ride with you," she said. "You can always drop me back here to get the car."

"Let's go," he said. "We'll get a squad to meet us there."

Four miles out, Dispatch called and said a man from AT&T Wireless was on the phone.

"Patch him through," Lucas said.

"There're dozens of calls from that account in the past week," the AT&T man said. "What was the time and date?"

Lucas gave it to him and said, "Look for a 699 prefix."

After a moment's wait: "Here it is. Here it is, by gosh."

AUDREY WAS TALKING to a Fidelity account manager when the phone rang in her purse. "I better take that," she said, pleasantly. She was wearing her best, acting the banker's wife: she wanted to get the money out of Fidelity before some legalism held it up. If she could get the cash and stash it somewhere, she would be good for at least a few years, no matter what else happened.

"Let me get the rest of these numbers," the manager said. She was a young woman dressed in a nice Ann Taylor suit, with a pretty silk scarf, nothing flashy, nothing too expensive. Audrey approved; maybe Fidelity wasn't throwing her money away on exorbitant salaries.

Audrey answered the phone on the third ring and Helen said to her, "Did you do it?"

And Audrey could hear Connie in the background, saying, urgently, "Mom, hang up. Hang up."

"Do what?" Audrey said calmly, though she knew.

"You'd know, if you did it."

"That Davenport's been there again, hasn't he?" Audrey asked. "May I speak to him?"

"He's gone," Helen said. She choked on the words, and Audrey heard Connie say, "Mom, I'm gonna hang this up. You shouldn't—"

And the connection was gone. Audrey looked at the phone for a moment, then punched the power button and turned it off. Davenport had found the pill. She wouldn't need to talk to Helen again.

As she walked out through the Fidelity office, she met the young manager on her way back: "I'm sorry," Audrey said. "I've got something of a family emergency. I have to go home."

She drove back toward her house on remote control. She didn't have access to any serious money, so running was not a possibility. And with Helen alive, she didn't really have many options left. She could think of precisely one.

"I can die," she said to the car. She was overwhelmed with a feeling of sadness, not for herself, but for the world. She'd be gone. The world wouldn't have her anymore. "But they'll see then," she told the car. "That's when they'll see."

The car seemed to steer itself, but she knew where it was going: North Woods Arms, in Wayzata. The gun shop was a small place, a door beside a picture window, the window laced over with security bars disguised as wrought-iron curlicues. The area beside the door and around the window had weathered-wood siding, to simulate a North Woods cabin; small Christmas lights blinked in the window, around a festive display of nine-millimeter pistols.

A bell rang above the door as she walked in, and the owner looked up from a magazine. "Hello."

"Hello," Audrey said, glancing around at the rack of long guns. "I'm looking for a gun for my husband for Christmas."

"You've come to the right place," the owner said pleasantly. "Do you know what you're looking for, or—"

"Yes." Audrey unfolded a piece of yellow notebook paper. She'd thought that would be a nice touch. "A Remington 870 Wingmaster twelve-gauge shotgun."

"No problem," the owner said enthusiastically. "You know what he's going to use it for?"

"Ducks, I guess. He mostly hunts ducks. And geese."

"No problem . . ."

She took the 870 along with two boxes of No. 2 shells. The store owner took her check, carried the boxes out to the car, and said, "Tell your husband I said, 'Good hunting.' "

"When I see him," she said, and got in the car. The store owner thought that was an odd thing to say; he would mention it to his wife that night.

LUCAS AND SHERRILL had gotten to the McDonald house before Audrey, and a minute before two patrol cops in a squad car. Lucas knocked on the front door, got no response, and while the uniforms waited in front, they walked together once around the house. Nobody. Peering through the deck windows, they saw no sign of movement or light. Back in front, Sherrill rang the doorbell again. Lucas said, looking up at the bedroom windows, "Nobody's home. Feels too quiet. I hope she's not running."

They were standing in the "L" made by the front of the house, the living wing to the front, extending to the left, the three-car garage swinging off to the right. "Maybe put out a call on her. Or we could just wait," Sherrill said. The uniforms were leaning on the front fender of their squad car, chatting.

"I hope she's not looking for Helen," Lucas said. And thought about Elle Kruger, and his jaw tightened. "Or anybody else. By God, I'd like to be there to bust her; but maybe we'd better—Whoops. There she is."

AUDREY TURNED INTO the bottom of the driveway, saw the Porsche and the police car at the top. She reached up and pushed the garage door opener. The shotgun rode beside her, muzzle down, in the passenger foot-well, the butt resting against her hip. She'd loaded four shells, as many as it would take, and had two more loose on the seat for reloading.

And she was ready for it. On the way home from the gun store, her vision had seemed to narrow: on the highway, she could see only the road itself. On the driveway, she could see only the garage door, until she made the little left, then right loop that could take her into the garage. Then, she looked out the passenger-side window and saw Davenport walking toward the garage, and her vision narrowed to a small point: Davenport's face. A mean man, she thought. Harsh. A man like Daddy.

WHEN THE GARAGE door started up, the two uniformed cops pushed away from the fender of their squad car, and looked down the drive. Audrey rolled slowly up the drive, made a little jog that took her straight in toward the far door. Lucas and Sherrill started walking toward it from the front stoop, and the two uniformed cops started toward it from their parking spot at the edge of the driveway. The back of Audrey's car had just cleared the inside of the door when it started down again.

Lucas turned and said, "Side door." Sherrill followed him toward an access door at the near end of the three overhead doors, just ambling along without thinking about it. Lucas opened the access door and stepped into the semidark garage, which was getting darker as the end door dropped the last couple of feet. "Mrs. McDonald," he said.

AUDREY HEARD THAT, and looking left, saw Davenport step inside the garage. He was standing in a shaft of light from the open access door. She grabbed the shotgun with her right hand, took a second to make sure the safety was off, then opened the door with her left hand, pushed it out with her feet, and pivoted out of the car. The shotgun was long and awkward, and she had to maneuver it around the car's roof post. Still, once it was out, it came up smoothly, and she saw the surprise register on Davenport's face and heard him scream a word and saw a violent motion and then the muzzle was coming down . . .

THE DOME AND door lights came on in Audrey's car as she opened the door; and with that light, Lucas could see the shotgun barrel as it came up. Sherrill had come in behind him and he screamed, "Gun!" and battered her sideways as he went down behind a Lexus. At the same instant, the shotgun blew a foot-long finger of flame at him, and the wall behind exploded in a shower of drywall plaster.

BAAA-OOOM.

The sound came after the lightning flash—a long time after, it seemed, though he was suspended in air when he thought that. Then he was on the floor, groping for his pistol, dragging it out of the holster, rolling along beside the Lexus, and the shotgun lit up the garage again, blowing glass out over his head. He'd lost track of Sherrill, lost track of everything: the thunder of the shotgun was magnified in the enclosed space, and the lightning of the shots was now the only illumination, aside from the feeble dome light from McDonald's car.

AUDREY HAD BEEN blinded by the muzzle flash; she hadn't expected that, but she expected Davenport to be falling, so she dropped the muzzle of the weapon as she pumped it, and convulsively jerked the trigger again. Glass shattered and she registered a voice, screaming; and a surge of confidence ran through her. *Got him. Now to finish him.*

"LIGHT." LUCAS HEARD somebody screaming; his mind processed it as Sherrill, but he couldn't tell what she was saying. "Top."

BAAA-OOOM.

Three shots; and Audrey was getting closer, walking toward them. But some shotguns only held three shots. Was she reloading? Was this a four-shot chamber? And then suddenly, the overhead lights were on and he saw, from the corner of his eye, Sherrill scrambling away from a light switch, a gun in her hand. And at the same time, from his spot on the concrete floor, saw Audrey's ankle behind the back bumper of the sport-ute. He pushed his hand forward, couldn't see the front barrel of the pistol but squeezed off a shot. Twelve feet: and he missed to the right. Audrey did a little hop step, and he heard her pump, and a shotgun shell bounced off the floor and he adjusted a hair to the right and pulled the trigger again.

And this time, he hit her.

Audrey screamed and went down, and suddenly, her face was there, looking under the cars at him. And the barrel of the shotgun was pointing at him too and she was moving it toward his face. He rolled behind a tire as she fired, and the tire soaked up the blast; but he could feel the air torn apart beside him.

She'd be dealing with recoil; she might be reloading. He didn't think it, but knew it, and pushed himself just to the right and extended his arm again, still unable to find the front sight in the shadow under the car, but he was close, and her face was there, and he was tightening his grip on the trigger and she was moving the barrel back to him . . .

SHERRILL DROPPED ON her like a meteor. She'd crawled over the sport-ute, and dropped from the roof. She landed with her feet behind Audrey's neck, smacking Audrey's head facedown into the receiver on the shotgun. Lucas jumped up and ran around the end of the car and caught Sherrill's hand coming up with the pistol in it. "No, no . . ."

"What?" Sherrill looked confused.

"We got her."

Audrey wrenched her shoulders and neck around, looked up at them, dazed, blood running down her lips and across her teeth. "Who are you?" she asked.

One of the cops outside was screaming, "Davenport, Davenport, talk to me . . ."

"We got her, we got her, we got her . . ." With his foot, Lucas pushed the shotgun under the sport-ute, out of reach. "She's hit," he said to Sherrill. "Let's get her outside."

"I'll get the doors . . ."

Lucas got his arms under Audrey's back and knees, and picked her up as best he could; then the three garage doors started rising simultaneously, and light flooded into the garage.

The uniformed cops were there, pistols drawn. They reholstered as they saw Lucas carrying Audrey.

"Jesus Christ," one of them said. "What was that?"

"Shotgun," Lucas grunted. "She's hit. Get an ambulance out here."

"Put her down on the driveway, Lucas," Sherrill said. "Let's get her flat. One of you guys, you got a blanket in your car? She'll be going into shock . . ."

A cop got a blanket, spread it on the driveway, and Lucas put Audrey on it. She seemed only semiconscious, though her eyes were open. He stood up. "Damn," he said. "That was a little too close."

Audrey said something. Sherrill heard it, said, "What?"

She said something again. Sherrill said, "What?" and bent over the other woman.

And as she put her head close to the other woman's face, Audrey lifted her hand, and despite her awkward position, hit Sherrill in the eye with her fist, knocking Sherrill flat on her butt.

"Knock that shit off," one of the uniformed cops yelled at Audrey, stepping over her, and she unballed her fist and turned her head away, her eyes softly closing. Sherrill had crawled away, one hand to her eye. "Aw, man, that hurts."

Lucas looked at it: "You're gonna have a mouse. And a hell of a black eye."

Audrey mumbled again. They both turned to look at her, eight feet away, flat on her back, and her cobra eyes caught Lucas. And suddenly she smiled, a big, toothy smile with bloody teeth.

Lucas felt the hair rise on the back of his neck. He turned back to Sherrill, who looked up at him and shook her head once: "Fuckin' nuts," she said.

34

SHERRILL SAID, "SO Krause thinks maybe she *deliberately* let the lineman see her so we wouldn't suspect Wilson. And then *she* called to tell us about the lineman, because we were digging at Wilson."

"Smart woman," Lucas said.

"Nasty," said James T. Bone, who was just settling into Lucas's visitor's chair.

"I gotta go," Sherrill said. She stood on her tiptoes, black eye nearly gone, kissed Lucas on the lips, said, "See you tonight," and, "Bye, Mr. Bone."

When Sherrill closed the door, Bone looked sleepy-eyed at Lucas and said, "White fuzzy sweater and chrome revolver in a shoulder holster. My heart almost stopped."

"Wearing my ass out," Lucas said comfortably.

"I know how that goes," Bone said.

BONE SAID, "AUDREY . . . is she gonna fight it?"

"Her attorney's a friend of mine," Lucas said. "He says she's crazy as a loon. Maybe she is. She even denies buying or firing the shotgun, even though we had four witnesses, the receipt in the car, and the gun shop guy identifying her. He says she's having trouble remembering anything after the death of her husband. A shrink's looking at her now."

"Is she faking?"

Lucas shrugged. "I don't know. She's smart, that's pretty clear. But her whole life has been a nightmare. I think it's possible that she never did know the difference between right and wrong."

"And if the court decides she's nuts?"

"She'll go off to the state hospital."

"What if she's not nuts?"

"Then we have a trial, and we've got her."

"Huh." Bone looked out the window at the street. The weather had turned gray, and small flecks of snow bounced off the window. Although it was only three in the afternoon, most of the passing cars had their headlights on. A week after the fight in the garage, the world was beginning to settle down again. "I'd feel a lot better if I knew she was going away for a long time; like forever. I'd hate to see her get out of a hospital in a couple of years."

Lucas nodded: "So would I."

BONE HAD THE bank: of the top five Polaris executives in October, only two had made it to the end of November, Bone and Robles. "I've got my assistant winding up O'Dell's affairs here. I talked to her father—he's having trouble dealing with her death."

"Death of a child," Lucas said. "Just 'cause they're grown up, doesn't make it any easier."

"No, I don't expect it does," Bone said. Then, "Have you seen Damascus Isley lately?"

"Not since we had lunch together a while back."

"I saw him at the bank. We talked a little basketball . . . He's on a strange diet, a Big Mac every day with popcorn."

"He told me he was thinking about it," Lucas said. "I hope he can stick it out."

"I think he will. He was on the diet for one week, he told me, and lost eighteen pounds. He knows that won't keep up, but when he got on the scale after the first week, he said his wife went out to the bedroom and cried for fifteen minutes. Outa joy, I guess. He was freaked out. I don't see any way he'll relapse."

BONE SAID, "THIS Audrey McDonald thing has torn me up."

"Yeah?" Lucas had an archaic typewriter tray in his desk, just the right height for feet. He pulled it out and put his feet up.

"Yeah. I was gonna run a major bank someday. But it wouldn't have come this soon, if Audrey hadn't blown old Dan Kresge out of his tree stand."

"Won't you be out of a job, if the merger goes through?"

"Sure. But some problems are cropping up with the merger," Bone said, showing a thin smile. "The road might not be as smooth as it looked. Even if it happens, once you're running a place, you can usually go someplace else, and run that. It's the breakthrough to the top that counts."

"Sloan talked to you about your relationship with Marcia Kresge . . . I'd think that might have been a dangerous relationship for somebody trying to get to the top," Lucas said.

"Eh . . . it's easier in a private company. You don't have to deal with elections and all your insane bureaucratic rules. I doubt Dan would have cared; he probably would have been amused. Marcia wasn't any more of a potential problem for me than Miss Fuzzy Sweater is for you. Besides, that's all done."

"All done?"

"Yeah." Bone seemed mildly embarrassed and turned to look out at the street again. "You met my assistant, Kerin Baki."

"The glacial blonde."

"Yeah. When the whole scramble started, after Kresge was killed, she started working to get me the top job. She did everything right: pretty much managed the whole show. And when I asked her what she wanted out of it, she said she wanted a favor from me. But she wouldn't tell me what it was until after I got the job."

"And you got it."

"Yeah. So after things settled down a little, when Audrey McDonald was arrested, I got her in my office and asked, 'What's the favor?' "

Baki had been a little uncomfortable when he pressed her, Bone said, but finally sat down and outlined what she wanted. Basically, she was tired of living alone. She wanted to find a man who was as smart as she was, who worked as hard as she did, and had similar interests. That was difficult.

"What she wanted from me," Bone said, as Lucas started smiling, "is, she wanted me to take her around—just as a friend, as an associate—and introduce her to guys I knew in the banking and investment communities who might be candidates."

"Just as a friend," Lucas said.

"Yeah. 'Mr. Bone,' she said, 'I don't have a chance to meet many people like that, socially, because I'm always here. And I know this sounds a little cold and a little calculating, but I don't have many more years to go if I want to have children and a normal home life,' " Bone said, mimicking Baki's precise soprano. "And she pushed her glasses back up on her nose, which is about the only thing that's ever been wrong with her—her glasses slide down."

"Yeah," Lucas said. "She's, like, vulnerable."

"I said okay," Bone said. "I could understand that. So I took her around to a couple of places, a couple of outside meetings she wouldn't normally have gone to, and she made quite an impression on a couple of guys. I got some calls asking about her status . . . I told her about them, and she was pretty interested."

"You chump."

"You know how the story comes out?"

Lucas knitted his hands across his chest and said, "Let me guess. You decided to take her out for a dinner . . ."

"Dinner meeting."

"And then you have to take her home afterwards."

"I just went up for a minute; I'd never seen her place."

"And you didn't come out for a while."

"Quite a while."

"And the glacier melted."

"You might say that . . . And she's told me I've seen the last of Marcia Kresge," Bone said. "She also mentioned a couple of other women that I had no idea she knew about."

"What about the kid thing?"

Bone shrugged. "I always thought, maybe, you know, with the right woman . . ."

THE PHONE RANG, and Bone stood up. "I gotta go," he said, but Lucas held up a finger: "Hang on a second." He answered the phone, "Hello?"

"Lucas, this is Del." Del was on a cell phone; his voice sounded like he was shouting through a hollow log, with a roar in the background.

"Yeah. What's going on?"

"Aw, I'm calling from the plane . . ."

Engine roar. "That's right," Lucas said. "Cancún. I forgot. Have a good time."

"If anybody comes asking for me, tell 'em ten days, would you?" Del shouted.

"Sure."

"Nobody's come asking yet?"

"Not to me," Lucas said. "Should they?"

"Can't hear you too good. See you in ten days," Del shouted. And hung up.

LUCAS LOOKED AT the phone, puzzled, then hung up and said to Bone, "We play a little ball at the Y on Wednesday nights, bunch a cops, a few lawyers. Sort of a cross between basketball and hockey—you know, no harm, no foul. If Kerin'll let you, you're invited."

"Yeah, that'd be nice," Bone said. "Maybe Isley'll be around in a year or so." They shook hands, and Bone said, "See you."

HE WENT OUT the door, but ten seconds later was back: "Uh, there's some people here to see you," he said.

"What?"

"Some . . . people," Bone said.

Lucas, frowning, stepped out in the hallway. He wasn't sure until later of the exact number, which was twenty-four, but he knew at a glance that there were a lot of them.

Old ladies.

Gathered like a flock of curly-haired, white-fleeced sheep, each clutching a purse and what seemed to be a brand-new gym bag. One of them, a sweet-looking grandmotherly woman with a trembling chin, said, "We've come to turn ourselves in."

"In?" Lucas asked. And Bone said, "Gotta go." And left.

"We're the opium junkies," the grandmother said, and the other women nodded. "Del said our best chance for leniency was to come down and surrender to you."

"Sonofabitch," Lucas said. He looked in at his phone as the grandmother recoiled; Del was probably halfway to Mexico.

"I beg your pardon?" she said, clutching the gym bag more tightly.

"Nothing. Stay right here," Lucas said. "Don't move. I'll be right back."

He trotted down to the chief's office. "No, Rose Marie's gone," the secretary said. She seemed to be biting the insides of her cheeks.

"Where?"

The secretary had to struggle a bit to get it out: "Cancún."

Lucas looked at her, a hard look, and she put her hands to her face. He turned on his heel and headed down toward Violent Crimes. He imagined he heard explosive laughter coming from the chief's office just before the door closed behind him.

In Violent Crimes, Loring was sitting on an office chair, peeling a green apple with a penknife. "Seen Frank?" Frank Lester was the other deputy chief.

"Nope."

"How about Sherrill?"

"Nope. They left. Together."

"Together?"

"Yeah. They said they were going to Cancún."

"You sonofabitch," Lucas said hotly.

"What?" Loring asked, surprised. "What?"

"You know what."

"No, I don't know what." He really seemed confused. On the other hand, he lied well. "What?"

THE HEADS OF Intelligence and Narcotics were gone. Nobody knew when they'd be back. Sloan and Black were missing, Franklin was gone.

On one of his trips past the old ladies, the grandmother said bravely, "We brought our things."

"Your things?"

They held up their gym bags. "Toothpaste and pajamas and so on. For the slammer."

"Aw, Jesus Christ," Lucas said.

He finally went back to Loring, got him out in the hall, explained the situation. ". . . surrendering, and I want you to help with the processing . . ."

Loring was backing away. "Fuck that," he said. "They're yours."

"They're not mine," Lucas shouted. But Loring was running toward the exit. "Goddamnit, get your ass back here. Get back here . . ."

Loring was the last of them.

Lucas walked back toward his office, where the little flock gathered with their purses and the gym bags, awaiting justice. All up and down the hallways, the doors were closed.

Nobody home, except him.

"Is there a problem?" Grandma asked.